THE DEMON QUEEN TRIALS

C.N. CRAWFORD

CITY OF THORNS

❧ I ❧

2

I tried not to stare at the frat boy I'd punched last night, but three things were making this hard. One—the bruise around Jack's eye was a deep, shiny purple that caught the glare of the classroom's fluorescent lights. Two—he didn't even belong in this class. And three —he was sitting in the back making a grotesque gesture that involved waggling his tongue through V-shaped fingers.

Suffice to say, my presentation was not going well.

Jack Corwin had been harassing me since high school. I would have expected that by senior year of college, he'd have grown past finger-in-the-hole gestures and fake orgasm faces, but Jack liked to buck convention. Why give up that level of obnoxiousness when it was his defining trait?

I'd prepared so well for today, putting in hours of memorizing the names of the relevant psychological studies. I'd selected a knee-length black dress with a white collar—cute but professional, and only slightly goth. I'd copied down my notes and pulled my bright red curls into something like a neat ponytail. And yet, my preparation didn't matter when confronted by that waggling tongue.

Focus, Rowan. Forget him.

I squared my shoulders, surveying the rest of the class. My classmate Alison twirled a blonde curl around her finger, looking at me expectantly. She gave me an encouraging smile.

I glanced at my notecards and started to read again. "As I was saying, the concept of repressed memories is fraught with controversy." I raised my eyes. "Many psychologists dispute—"

Jack made a circular shape with his finger and thumb, then slid his other index finger in and out, opening his mouth wide in an orgasm face. The lights gleamed off the strange silver pin he always wore, which was shaped like a hammer.

"Sorry. Uh, dissociative fugue..." I started again. "Which is in the DSM—"

In the back of the classroom, where no one but me could see him, Jack was thrusting his crotch up and down in a pounding gesture.

Anger simmered. For a number of reasons, he was the last person I wanted around, and I finally pointed at him. "Is he supposed to be here?" I blurted. "He's not in this class. Why is he here?"

Unfortunately, no one else had seen what he was doing, so I just looked like a dick.

My professor, Dr. Omer, raised his dark eyebrows and stared at me. When he glanced at the back of the room, Jack looked like the picture of innocence. He held his pen in his hands as if he'd been taking notes the whole time, eyebrows raised. *Just a studious kid here, trying to learn.*

Dr. Omer steepled his fingers, then frowned at me. He didn't say anything because he was doing that psychologist thing where they looked at you in silence and waited for *you* to realized that you had done something inappropriate. I swallowed hard.

Here was the thing: Jack had followed me last night and cornered me outside my house. In fact, he'd been stalking me for years. There was a legitimate reason I'd given him a black eye.

But this wasn't a therapy session, and I wasn't trying to be professional. We were here to learn, or at least to get a passing grade on our transcript and move on.

"He's not in this class," I repeated more quietly. "I don't understand why he's here."

I could feel the class's eyes on me, and heat spread over my neck.

Considering I was pale as milk, it was hard to hide it when I was blushing.

"He's auditing the class for the rest of the semester," said Dr. Omer in a calm voice. "He has permission to be here." He pressed his fingers against his lips for a moment, frowning. The psychologist stare. Then, "Is there a problem with your presentation? You are usually prepared, Rowan."

Normally, I adored Dr. Omer's calm demeanor, but now it seemed off, like he was calmly ignoring the house that burned around him.

I took a deep, slow breath and tried to center myself by thinking about my feet, rooted firmly to the floor. *Just focus and get through this, Rowan.* Tonight, I'd have drinks with my best friend, Shai, for my twenty-second birthday. Beer, pizza, gossip about her amazing new life. All I had to do was get through this next twenty minutes.

"No problem at all." I smiled. "I was just confused for a moment. I'm actually very prepared." I cleared my throat. "Dissociative amnesia is theorized to be a state—"

Wait. Was he really going to be in this class for the rest of the semester? I had to take this class to graduate.

I glanced through the window at the City of Thorns—the magical city that loomed over Osborn, Massachusetts. I planned to get in there for graduate school, and I wanted to do so as soon as possible.

"Rowan?" Dr. Omer prompted, a hint of annoyance in his tone. "It might be better if you try this again on a day when you're more prepared. I don't think this is the best use of our class time."

Ouch. My hands were shaking, but I wasn't sure if that was the result of anxiety or anger.

"No, I've got it. Sorry. I was thrown off by the projector not working." I swallowed, ready to regain my composure. "What I'm talking about is an inability to access memories in the unconscious..." I flipped my notecards around, trying to weave my thoughts together into something coherent. "Particularly autobiographical memories, the things from your life..."

I looked up at Jack again to see him leaning back in his chair, massaging his nipples with his tongue lolling out of his mouth.

At that point, two ideas became tangled in my working memory.

One was the next phrase on my notecard, which was "If you could imagine..." The other was *I'd love to hit that fucker again*. With my brain tripping over the two thoughts, I stared right at Jack and blurted, "If you could love fucker again..."

Which made no sense but definitely sounded inappropriate.

Shocked, half-stifled laughter interrupted the silence.

The class turned back to Jack. He'd immediately adopted his innocent note-taking pose again, looking baffled at my pronouncement. His eyebrows rose, innocent.

My stomach plummeted.

Kill me. I'm praying that the floor could swallow me up now.

I felt the warmth creep over my cheeks as a terrible silence fell. The lights buzzed and flickered above me, and my mouth went dry. "I said the wrong thing." I gestured at Jack. "He was making faces..." I trailed off, realizing how lame this sounded.

Jack's obsession with me had started years ago when he asked me out as a freshman at Osborne High. I'd said no, and that had made him mad. So he'd started rumors that I'd banged the whole baseball team. Everyone had believed him. They'd called me Home Run Rowan for the next four years, and he'd even photoshopped my face onto nude models. That was what my high school experience had been like.

But no one needed to hear that. They wanted to get this over with and move on to Taco Tuesday in the dining hall.

"I just said the wrong thing," I added again.

Dr. Omer pressed his two palms together in front of his mouth. "Okay, I don't know exactly what's going on here, but I sense there is some interpersonal conflict, and I don't think this is a productive forum for discussion. If there's an issue between you two, we can explore that after class."

Jack looked sheepish and raised his hand for the first time. "I think I know what's happening. Rowan was upset when I turned her down for a date last night, and she didn't know how to handle it. She lashed out." He gestured at his eye. "But I swear, I'm ready to put the physical assault behind me. I'm ready to focus on Abnormal Psych. I'm a very good student. If you'll look at my transcript, I think you'll find that I'm one of the best students you've ever seen."

7

"Oh, my God!" Alison's eyes were open wide. "Did you really give him that black eye, though?" she asked me. "I'm not trying to be dramatic, but I'm literally physically scared right now."

Someone said something about calling the police. Others guffawed, half shocked and half thrilled. From their perspective, this was probably the best thing that had happened to them all semester. This was better than Taco Tuesday. This was *drama*.

I crumpled my notecards in my hands, and my heart slammed against my ribs. "Wait. I hit him, yes, but he deserved it. He's the problem here, not me."

Already, I could see the recommendation letter from Dr. Omer disappearing before my eyes. Goodbye to grad school in the City of Thorns; goodbye to my lifelong dream of closing an unsolved crime.

Unhinged. I seemed completely unhinged.

They had it all wrong, but nothing makes you seem crazier than trying to scream that you're the only sane one.

"Okay, you know what?" I tossed the notecards in the trash can. "I think my presentation is over."

My entire body buzzed with adrenaline as I rushed out of the room.

❧ 3 ❧

I sat on the bed in my basement apartment, sketching the gates of the City of Thorns.

After my shitty day, I'd gone for a long run. I'd pushed the pace hard, and my muscles still burned as I stretched them on the comforter. Running was the best way I had of dealing with stress, losing myself in physicality. It was also the one time I felt really good at something. The only problem was that sometimes, when my feet pounded the leaves in the woods, I'd have glimmers of flashbacks to the night Mom died. I'd hear her voice, telling me to run.

I shook my head, clearing my mind of the dark memory. Instead, I focused on trying to perfect the picture of the gate. This drawing served no purpose, but I'd become completely obsessed with the gate's contours—the wrought iron entrance to the demon city, decorated with a skull in the center, strangely beautiful and forbidding at the same time. Maybe it wasn't the healthiest obsession to draw the same thing repeatedly like a psycho, but at least I wasn't thinking about Jack Corwin.

I exhaled as I shaded in the skull. Living here was all part of my plan to save money for grad school in the demon city. Down here, I was saving every dime I could, living in a cellar with six other broke

9

students. Our rooms were divided by thin wooden walls, and we shared a bathroom and a kitchenette that was mostly a hot pot and kettle.

My phone buzzed—a call from Shai—and I swiped to answer. "Hey."

"Oh! You actually answered instead of pretending you were busy and then texting two minutes later."

I grinned. "Who talks on the phone anymore? It makes everyone nervous except you."

"So what are we doing for your birthday? Because there's this amazing Thai takeout place I want to try, and I could bring it to you with, like, a couple bottles of wine."

I smiled. "My new place is a shabby basement with spiders. And compared to your fancy Belial University dorms, it'll seem like a full-blown shithole."

"Is it really that bad?"

"Hang on." I snapped a few photos to get the point across, then emailed them to her. "Okay, check your mail. See, if we were texting like normal people, this would be going much more smoothly."

After a moment, I heard her say, "Oh, okay. Well, yeah, it's small. Nicely decorated, but small. I don't love the idea of spiders...I wish I could have you here, but I *think* you could be legally murdered by demons if I sneaked you in."

I nodded. "I'd like to avoid that. Maybe just a drink somewhere in Osborn?"

"Hang on...I'm zooming in on your photos to see if I can find anything embarrassing."

"I've drawn thirty-two pictures of the City of Thorns gates, and most are taped to the wall," I said, "so that's fairly embarrassing."

"Yeah, but I already knew you were a weirdo. I was hoping to find you were some kind of secret sex freak, too. For a second, I thought I saw giant red dildos by your bed, but now I can see they're fire extinguishers."

"What's the opposite of a sex freak?" I asked. "That's me."

"Okay, but why do you have two fire extinguishers next to your bed?"

I sat up straighter, getting anxious just thinking about it. "There's no way out of here, Shai. There's a tiny window over the bed, but it doesn't open. So if the house were on fire, I'd have to fight my way out from a far corner of a basement while the walls burned around me."

She inhaled sharply. "Oh, shit. Can you find another place? That doesn't sound safe even with the fire extinguishers. Is that even legal?"

"Probably not, but I installed fire alarms, too. And I stocked up with the stuff stuntmen used to get through flames."

"Wait, *what?*" she cried.

I mentally reviewed what was under my bed. "Fire-retardant clothing and gels to stop my skin from burning, Hollywood-style. I could walk through flames if I had to. Oh! And I bought a gas mask in case I need to get through billowing smoke. I'm pretty much set with the fire stuff."

"Of course. So you're still kind of a prepper, I'm guessing?"

"Yes, so in the event of a demon apocalypse, come here. I've got several large bags of beans and rice and some fish antibiotics."

"Nice," she said. "Are we going to kill the demons with burritos and penicillin?"

"In case the shops and doctors' offices close. And I've got a water purifier in case the reservoir is contaminated."

What I didn't mention was my weirdest prepper item: the fox urine, which was something hunters used to disguise their scent. If the demons rampaged around Osborne, hungry for blood, I'd drench myself in fox pee. They'd never find me. But Shai didn't need to know that. Even with my best friend, I had a line of weirdness I didn't cross.

"Okay," said Shai. "Well, since there's no apocalypse going on right now, let's figure out somewhere for margaritas, okay?"

"I'm happy with wherever. It'll just be fun to see you and get out of the basement. And I definitely need a drink. I gave an absolutely disastrous presentation today in my Abnormal Psych class."

"Shit. Okay. Just give me a chance to call around and see if I can get us reservations, huh? I'll text you in a few."

She hung up, and I leaned back against my pillows. A flicker of movement caught my eye, and I glanced at a spider skittering over the floor. The scent of mildew and mold hung heavily in the air.

I pulled my drawing pad and pencil into my lap, then finishing the filagree on another image of the gates to the City of Thorns.

There were only two kinds of mortals allowed in the city: the servants born into their roles, and the students like Shai who could afford it. Every year, Belial University in the City of Thorns accepted around three hundred mortal applicants. At Belial, the demon university, they learned to suffuse their careers with the magical arts. Graduates like Shai always landed plum positions in whatever field they wanted.

But in my case, education wasn't the *real* reason I wanted to get into the demon university.

I wanted revenge. I wanted to find the demon who killed my mom.

When the picture of the gate was finished, I flipped over the page and started jotting down some financial numbers. Right now, I owed seventy-five thousand in student loans, with seven percent interest. If I was going to pay that back, and also save up the hundred grand to get into Belial University on what would likely be poverty wages after graduating...

My stomach churned.

Whenever I started making these calculations, the weight of impossibility started pressing down on me. I'd done it a million times, but the numbers never added up. With my loan interest, I'd save up the hundred grand roughly...

Never.

I would never have a hundred thousand dollars to get in.

Increasingly, I was starting to think about plan B: break into the city, then find a way to blend in. There had to be a way. Even an ancient demon city would have a weakness.

As I started to mull over my more dangerous and unhinged plan, my phone buzzed with a message from Shai: *Cirque de la Mer. Two for one cocktails tonight. Meet me there at 8:30 xo*

Really, it was probably a good time for her to interrupt my breaking and entering schemes before I came up with something that could get me killed.

SITTING AT THE WHITE MARBLE COUNTERTOP AT CIRQUE DE LA MER, my red hair drenched by the September rain, I sipped a Guinness and licked the foam off my lip. I still wore my black dress and boots, but I'd accessorized a bit with black nail polish, eyeliner, and silver rings. This was my look: ginger Goth Puritan.

Behind the bar, enormous windows overlooked the Atlantic Ocean, and the sea twinkled under the starlight. Dubstep boomed around me. I liked it here, with the loud music to drown out my own thoughts and a gorgeous view of the sea. Of course, this was probably the most expensive bar on the north shore of Massachusetts, but for tonight, I wasn't going to worry about money. The loans were too ridiculous to worry about at this point, and I might as well owe a billion dollars.

When Shai sidled up next to me at the bar, she flashed me an enormous smile. Her dark hair fell in two long braids over a cream-colored dress. She wore vibrant red lipstick that perfectly complemented her tawny brown skin.

I'd really needed to see a friendly face.

She hugged me. "Hello, birthday girl. What are we drinking? Tequila shots?"

"I swore off them after the Harvard Square incident."

She grimaced. "Oh, right. Okay, well, let's eat and get cocktails so you don't get messy." She raised her hand, and the bartender immediately came over with a smile. Shai ordered us two mojitos and a butternut squash pizza.

With that accomplished, she turned back to me, eyebrows raised. "Okay, what was this about your nightmare of a day?"

I sighed. "Jack Corwin turned up in the middle of my class presentation and made orgasm faces when I was trying to focus, and then he claimed that I punched him in the eye. "

Her hand flew to her mouth for a moment. "First of all, fuck that guy. Second, has he lost his mind? Why would he think that people would believe that you punched him?"

I cleared my throat, cringing. "Well, about that part. I did actually punch him."

"*What?*"

"After he tried to ram his tongue down my throat," I said defensively.

"So he assaulted you first? You need to call the cops. He's escalating things. He's been stalking you for years now."

The bartender slid our mojitos across the bar, and I grabbed mine instantly. I took a sip, letting the mint and lime roll over my tongue. "I reported it at Osborn State and to the police, but they decided a long time ago that I'm overreacting. Apparently, being a douchebag isn't illegal, and I'm not sure they'd see what happened last night on my terms, either. His dad is a congressman or something, so..." I took another sip. "You know what? I'm sick of thinking about him. Please tell me about the City of Thorns. Let's leave Jack out of tonight. I want to hear about the demons."

"Where do I even begin?"

I raised my eyebrows. "Do you think demons can leave?"

She shook her head. "I think so, but not for long. As far as I know, there's some kind of magical spell from hundreds of years ago that keeps them mostly tied to one demon city or another. But occasionally, they can travel between them. Why do you ask?"

"That night my mom was murdered—"

My sentence trailed off. I could already feel the air cooling, the atmosphere growing thorny as I raised the painful subject. There was no easy way to say, *One night, a demon with a glowing star on his head hunted down my mom in the woods and burned her to death.* And since the horror of that night felt raw even now, it was hard to talk about it without feeling like I was drowning in loss again.

Sometimes, I thought the only thing keeping me afloat was the certainty that I'd avenge her death. That I would get into the City of Thorns and find her killer.

But this was too dark and weird, wasn't it? Worse than the fox pee beneath my bed.

❄ 4 ❅

We were sitting at the marble bar, with the night-dark sea glittering before us. I didn't want to ruin the evening, and so I waved a hand. "Never mind. I want to hear more about your daily life. What's it like?"

I could feel the tension leave the air again. "Fucking amazing," Shai said. "I might do another year. Any chance you can get the tuition for next year?"

"I'm working on a few ideas for getting in." Wildly illegal ideas at this point. "What's your dorm like?"

"There's a balcony and servants. Even the ocean is more beautiful there. It's not like the Atlantic—it's like this gorgeous tropical ocean made with magic. Okay, so the city has seven wards, each one associated with a demon. And the university buildings are organized the same way. I'm in Lucifer Hall, and it's this enormous stone castle-like place."

Even putting my vengeance plans aside, my jealousy was crippling. "How are your classes?"

"Amazing. They're held in lecture halls that must be four hundred years old, with seats curved all around a stage." She sighed. "I know, it's a huge expense. But I wanted to learn magical arts, and you can't exactly do that at Osborn State. Belial is the finest witchcraft institution for mortals. I'm desperate to stay another year."

"What are the demons like?"

She ran her fingertip over the rim of her mojito. "Well, my classes are mostly with aspiring mortal witches, but there are a few demons, and the professors, obviously. They're beautiful and intimidating as shit. Some of them have horns, but not all. I haven't met anyone who seems particularly evil. At least, no one worse than Jack." She turned and lifted her empty glass, motioning for the bartender to bring us another round, then swiveled back to me. "I've heard the king is evil—him and the Lord of Chaos. They're both terrifying, but I've only seen them from a distance."

My eyebrows shot up. "Okay, start with the king. What's his deal?"

She leaned in conspiratorially. "King Cambriel only recently became king. He slaughtered his father, King Nergal, who'd ruled for hundreds of years. Cambriel cut off his dad's head and stuck it on the gate to his palace."

I shuddered. "That's fucked up."

"The only way a demon king can die is if his heir slaughters him, and Cambriel did just that. Now he's apparently looking for a demon queen, and there's all kinds of gossip about which female he might choose."

As I finished my first mojito, the bartender brought over two more.

"And the women *want* to marry this guy with his dad's head over his front gate?" I asked. "Sounds like quite a catch."

"To the female demons, he is." She slid one of the mojitos over to me. "And the Lord of Chaos is the other eligible bachelor in the city. He's an outsider—a duke from the City of Serpents in England, so he was leader of a demon ward there. No one knows why he left, but obviously, it was a scandal. Dukes don't normally leave their cities. But the most important thing is that he seems to be filthy rich."

"If it was such a big scandal, how come no one knows the details?"

She stirred her drink with her little black straw. "There's no communication between demon cities. Demons can arrive in a new city, but they can never speak about the old one. It was one of the conditions of surrender in the great demon wars years ago, sealed by magic. The Puritans thought that if demons spoke to each other, they could grow strong and rise up against the mortals again, so he can't say a thing about the English demon city."

"Wow."

"So." She leaned closer. "No one really knows anything about him. But here's the scariest thing: on the rare occasion that a demon comes into a different city, they have to pass an initiation called the Infernal Trial. It's supposed to prove that the demon gods have blessed the new arrival. I don't want to say it's barbaric because that sounds judgmental, but it *is* barbaric. In the City of Thorns, the way the Trial goes is that the demons have to run through the forest and try to kill the newcomer. Only those who survive can remain. Most of them die before they can be initiated, but the Lord of Chaos slaughtered fifty other demons. Obviously, all the women want to fuck him because he's terrifying."

I stared at her. "This is all legal?"

She shrugged. "Their city, their laws. They can't kill humans without starting a war, but demons are fair game."

This was *fascinating*. "What does the Lord of Chaos look like?"

"I've only seen him from a distance, but he's shockingly beautiful. Like, fall-to-your-knees-before-him beautiful. He has silver hair, but not from age. It's sort of otherworldly. And he has these stunning blue eyes, devastating cheekbones. He's huge. I have a crush on him, and on a wrath demon named Legion. He has long black hair and these sexy-as-hell tattoos. Both of them are, like...stunning. Legion looked at me once—a smoldering look. Not even joking, I forgot to breathe."

I leaned closer. "What about a star? Have you seen a five-pointed star on anyone's head?"

A line formed between her brows. "What are you talking about?"

And there I was, back to my obsession—my mom's murder.

I shook my head. "Never mind. I just heard a rumor about marks on demons' foreheads. Might be bullshit."

As the pizza arrived, I pulled off a slice for myself and slid it onto a small plate. It looked surprisingly good, even though it was vegan.

Shai drummed her fingernails on the counter. "Why do I get the feeling you're always hiding things?"

"Some things are meant to be hidden." My mouth was watering for the squash and garlic. I took a bite, and while the vegan cheese burned my mouth, it still tasted glorious. I wasn't sure even the magically inspired food of the demon world could compete.

When I swallowed the hot bite, I asked, "Are you going to show me any of the healing magic you've been learning? If I have a headache, can you fix it?"

She wiped the corner of her mouth with a napkin. "I'm not ready yet. And anyway, I'm a veterinary student. I can't treat humans."

I pointed at her, feeling a bit tipsy now. "But if someone shot me in the shoulder, could you fix it with magic, or would you turn me into a cat or something?"

She shuddered. "Probably half-cat, half-human. It would be horrible."

We went quiet for a while as we ate the rest of the pizza.

When we finished, I turned to look behind me and found that the club was starting to fill up.

"Are we going to dance?" asked Shai.

I was now two mojitos and a Guinness into the evening, and so I shouted something about it being my birthday as I took to the dance floor.

They were playing my favorite, Apashe. As the beat boomed over the club, I found myself losing myself in the music. I forgot my college loans, my disastrous presentation, the spiders that crawled over me when I slept. I forgot about Jack and the five-pointed star. I let go of my lust for revenge.

At least, I did so until the music went quiet and tension thickened the air.

Sometimes, you can sense danger before you feel it, and this was one of those moments. Darkness rippled through the bar, floating on a hot, dry breeze. I went still, disturbed to find that everyone was staring in the same direction with an expression of horror. Goosebumps rose on my arms. The warmth felt unnatural, disturbing. I didn't want to turn around.

When I finally did, my stomach swooped. There, in the doorway, was a demon with otherworldly silver hair and eyes like flecks of ice.

The Lord of Chaos? His size and breathtaking beauty almost made me dizzy. He looked like a freaking god.

Maybe it was the mojitos, maybe it was his stunning physical perfection, but I felt magnetically drawn to him. I wanted to slide up closer to him and press myself against his muscular body. As I stared at him, my heart started to pound faster.

Divine. His silver hair hung down to heartbreakingly sharp cheekbones. He sported a high-collared black coat that hung open. Under his jacket, he wore a thin gray sweater that showed off a muscular body. It looked soft, but I could tell the abs beneath it were rock hard. I found my pulse racing as I thought of running my fingers over the material and feeling his muscles twitch.

I'd never enjoyed sex—not once in my life. But as I looked at him, I thought *there* was a man who could actually satisfy me.

I clamped my eyes shut. Wait, what the fuck was wrong with me? He wasn't even human. He was another species, one that used to eat humans.

But when I opened my eyes again, I felt like I was melting. In contrast to his pale blue eyes, his eyebrows were dark as night. The effect seemed shocking, mesmerizing.

But when he slid those pale eyes to me, an icy tendril of fear curled through me. His fingers tightened into fists, and he lowered his chin like he was about to charge at me.

I froze. My heart started beating faster now for an entirely different reason. I had his attention, but not in a good way.

This was a look of pure, unadulterated loathing, a look of palpable hatred that sent alarm bells ringing in my mind. He *hated* me.

Holy hell.

What did he think I'd done to him?

5

T ension thickened the air, and my knees felt weak.

The demon dominated the room. His eyes locked on me. Every cell in my body was telling me to turn and run, to save myself before it was too late. He might be beautiful, but this creature was pure death. He'd tear my throat out in an instant.

It felt like ages before the look of raw hatred disappeared, replaced by a cruel, mocking smile. He dragged his gaze away from me. Now, he looked at ease, like all of this was amusing to him. He shrugged. "Well, don't stop the fun, my mortal friends." He spoke with a posh English accent. "One might get the unpleasant idea that demons aren't welcome here."

With a slow, graceful gait, he crossed to the bar, his enormous body seemingly radiating lethal power.

Though I trembled and backed away from him, I found myself unable to stop staring. Shai tugged on my arm, pulling me away, and I nearly stumbled as she dragged me from the bar.

When we were no longer so close to him, she whispered, "What was that all about?"

My mouth had gone dry, and my head was spinning. "You saw that, too? The look he was giving me? I have no idea what that was about."

"Maybe you look like someone he knew." She glanced over my shoulder at him. "That's the one I was talking about. The Lord of Chaos. What's he doing here?"

When I turned to look at him again, he slid his glacial gaze toward me. He arched an eyebrow and lifted his whiskey glass like a toast.

Drawn to him like a moth to a flame, I found myself walking closer to him again.

As I did, a mocking smile curled his lips "Didn't think I'd be seeing you again after all these years."

I cleared my throat. "You must have me mistaken for someone else."

The cold smile he gave me dripped with venom. "Oh, I don't think so, love. I'd know your face anywhere. It's haunted my nightmares for a long time."

The ground seemed unsteady beneath my feet. "I've never seen you before in my life." I tried to steady my voice, but it came out shaky. "Pretty sure I would have remembered a six-foot-five, silver-haired demon."

"Don't stop dancing on my account." He glanced away from me again, dark magic coiling around him. "Why let your horrific past get in the way of your fun?"

For a moment, I wondered if this had something to do with Mom's murder. After all, a demon had wanted her dead. Had he confused me with her? But I quickly dismissed the thought. I didn't look enough like Mom for anyone to mistake us. We had the same pale skin, heart-shaped face, and arched eyebrows, but my eyes were deep brown, while hers had been blue. I had higher cheekbones, a wider smile. Mom's hair had been blonde, but mine was a shocking red with a few blonde strands.

And most importantly, I was sure Mom didn't have a horrific past.

My breath shallowed. The room felt too hot, stifling. I turned to Shai, desperate to leave. "I'm going to go out and get some fresh air. Maybe we can find another bar."

"I'll settle the tab," she said.

"Thank you."

Unnerved, I hurried to the door. When I pushed through to the street outside, my skin started to cool under a light rain. Cirque de la Mer was on a narrow, cobbled street in the old sailor district by the harbor. Across the street stood a brewery, which might make a better option for tonight. They served hot dogs, and for whatever reason, I didn't imagine demons went to places that served hot dogs.

I hugged myself as I shivered. Somehow, I'd made an enemy of a terrifying demon duke, and I had no idea how. One thing Mom taught me before she died was that everyone had a weakness. The Lord of Chaos's weakness—I'd guess—was the woman he'd mistaken me for. The woman who haunted his nightmares.

I took a deep, calming breath. Out here, the salty breeze skimmed over my skin, the scent of the Atlantic heavy in the air. I licked my lips, tasting salt.

Here was the thing: I used to think my mom was deeply paranoid with the way she talked about defending yourself and finding weaknesses. She was a social worker who helped people with traumatic histories. And I had to wonder if she'd had one of her own, because she relentlessly pushed me to take self-defense classes, to learn martial arts. She was obsessed with fighting, convinced that enemies were after us. She was sure that one day, a demon would come calling.

I did everything she wanted me to do. I took every martial arts class in Osborn, and I practiced with her on the weekends. She taught me to search out other people's weaknesses in a fight, to exploit them, to fight back. I always thought she was training me for a war that didn't exist, but the night she died, I learned the war was real. I just had no idea why she'd been killed.

As I stared at the glass doors of the brewery, three frat boys stumbled out, already drunk, wearing their Alpha Kappa shirts. I slunk back into the shadows, hoping to go unnoticed.

A slender blonde hurried out behind them, her shoulders tense. She was staggering, clearly drunk. But she looked freaked out, too. I had the sense she was trying to get away from someone.

When the door slammed open again and Jack prowled out after her, I had my answer. I wasn't the only one he terrorized.

His eyes were locked on the girl, and my heart sped up.

"Jen!" he slurred. "Where you going? Jen! Stop being a fucking bitch! You should feel lucky I paid attention to you. You should feel lucky...I'm the best quarterback Osborne State ever had. I have business plans you can't even imagine, Jen. I'm gonna be a billionaire. A trillionaire! I'm gonna be on TV."

I had no idea what he was talking about, but it was confirming the suspicions I already had about him. Narcissistic personality disorder: inflated sense of self-importance, preoccupation with power fantasies. A deeply insecure foundation badly covered up with pretenses of superiority and exaggerated achievements.

The blonde—Jen—stumbled over one of the cobblestones. That was when he lunged for her and grabbed her arm. She turned to face him, her eyes wide. "Let me go! You're being a dick, Jack."

"Jen!" he shouted in her face. "You were being a disgusting slut. You should be *grateful* I'm even talking to you." With that, he gripped her arm hard and started to drag her toward the alley beside the bar.

"Stop it!" she yelled.

He pulled her in close to his body and clamped his hand over her mouth.

Oh, fuck this. I'd seen enough. My fight-or-flight response had started to kick in, and adrenaline pumped hard through my veins.

6

I rushed after them and shouted, "Get your hands off her, Jack!"

He whirled around, and the surprise on his face quickly turned into a leer. He wasn't giving up his grip on the blonde.

He grinned widely, moving closer to me with Jen in his arms. "Rowan, baby, are you stalking me? Were you hoping to get another chance with me? I told you, I don't want you to suck my dick. I'd get a disease."

He jerked her along with him as he staggered over to me.

"Let go of her," I said coldly.

He kept moving closer until I could feel his rancid breath on my face. He reeked of vomit, which told me he had probably just been kicked out of the brewery for puking. Classy.

The silver hammer on his shirt glinted under the streetlights.

"Let go of Jen," I said. "I don't want to have to hit you again."

A lie. I definitely wanted to hit him again, but I didn't want to get in trouble for it. I was honestly surprised he hadn't pressed charges already.

Jack, sadly, was too stupid to heed my warning, and he didn't release his victim.

Now, my heart was starting to speed up, and anger coursed through my blood.

Male voices echoed from the left, and I turned to see that his friends had come back to find him. I hoped one of them would intervene so I wouldn't have to get my hands dirty. Instead, one of them whooped at him, delighted. "Jack! You got two. Can we join the party?"

"I asked you once, nicely," I told Jack. "If I have to ask again, I'll hurt you."

"You know what your problem is? You're too uptight. I swear to God," he slurred, "you should never have turned me down. I could have fucked the bitchiness out of you."

At last, he dropped his grip on Jen, and she started to sprint away. But then he lunged for me. He grabbed me by the throat and pulled me close against him. His grip on my neck was crushing.

Mom was right. The world was a dangerous place, and we had to find our enemies' weaknesses.

Fortunately, Jack's wasn't hard to find. I brought my knee up hard into his groin. His eyes went wide, and when he hunched forward, I slammed my elbow into one of his kidneys. He let out a quiet moan and fell back.

I was shaking with the realization that I might have done serious damage.

"Whoa," one of his frat brothers shouted. "What the fuck is happening?"

Jack, now incapacitated, was on the ground. But his three brothers were rushing over, surrounding me.

"Holy shit, Jack," one of them yelled. "Is this the chick who punched you last night, too? The one you turned down?"

Someone shouted that they were calling the cops.

Unfortunately for me, if anyone was going to get arrested here tonight, it would probably be me—the crazy woman who'd beaten the crap out of a congressman's son. The one who'd had an outburst in class. The one who already had a questionable file at the Osborne Police Department.

Where the hell was Shai?

I clutched my phone, hesitating, until one of the frat boys smacked it out of my hands. He grinned at me. "Oopsie!"

"Dude!" one of them shouted, though I wasn't sure who he was shouting at, or if he even knew.

All of them were wasted, which made them more dangerous. I wasn't scared, though. Just angry.

Jack pushed himself up on his elbows, grimacing. "You can't keep attacking me just because I won't let you suck my dick. It's kind of funny how pathetic it is, though."

Lying sack of shit.

One of his brothers wrapped his arm around my shoulders. "Come with us, Ginger. If you're that desperate, I can find something for your mouth to do."

I slammed my elbow into his ribs, but another guy was already grabbing for my arm. My panic surged as I realized how badly I was outnumbered. Frantic, I was ready to land another punch when something in the air seared my skin.

Time seemed to freeze. In slow motion, a hot, dry wind rushed over me, toying with my hair. Slowly, the frat boys around me staggered back, eyes wide, and then the world returned to normal speed.

I gaped as the nearest of the brothers fell to his knees, blood dripping from his nose.

What the hell?

Looking around, I found that the four other frat boys had fallen, too. They moaned, gripping their skulls. Jack whimpered, and blood gushed from his nostrils onto the cobblestones. My stomach swooped.

Just as the frat boys started screaming in agony, I turned...and there, just as I'd expected, was the Lord of Chaos. He loomed over the dark street, and my heart skipped a beat.

The air felt warm, electrified. A high-pitched scream rent the air, and I turned back to see Jack's face contorted in pain.

Holy shit.

As much as I hated these guys, I didn't want to stand there and watch their heads explode. This was sadism, and the agonized noises they were making turned my blood to ice.

I whispered, "Stop." Then, louder, "*Stop!*"

The Lord of Chaos flicked his wrist, and his pale eyes slid to me. "What was that?" he asked in a mocking tone. "Do you want me to believe that you feel mercy?" The wisps of dark magic snapped back into his body. "That's a fun idea. I like to see you trying new things, no matter how absurd."

I looked away from him at the frat boys, who moaned as they began to pick themselves up. At least two of them were sobbing, blood still pouring from their noses. They started to stumble away—slowly, at first, then trying to run.

My body shook with the horror of whatever *that* had been.

When I looked back at the demon, I caught an amused glint in his eyes. "I thought you'd enjoy that."

"Thanks for helping?" I said. "I guess?"

His smile faded, and he moved closer to me with preternatural speed. Peering down at me, his piercing eyes sent a shiver through my body. "Oh, I don't think you want to thank me," he murmured. "Do you? I think you must know what exquisite punishment is in store for you now, love."

I could hardly breathe.

What the *fuck*?

I *had* to get away from him, but it was a mistake to turn your back and run from a predator. It was a mistake to act like prey. Right now, I was fighting an overpowering instinct to lower my eyes in submission. "You're going to have to tell me what you mean, because I have no idea what you're talking about."

His hot power thrummed over my damp skin, raising the hair on the back of my arm. "You must know why I'm here." He leaned down and whispered, "I'm here for revenge."

His scorching magic snaked around me, a slow brush of hot power over my skin. He was freezing me in place, taking complete control over my body. All of my muscles froze.

"Stop it," I hissed.

But I could already feel his magic sliding inside my mind, and my vision began to dim. I was in his hands now.

❧ 7 ❧

I woke in total darkness to the sound of dripping water, my back pressed against a cold stone floor. My dress had ridden up around my hips, exposing my legs, and my right thigh lay in freezing cold water. My teeth chattered.

Down here, the air smelled stale and mildewy, though not wildly different from the basement where I lived.

Shivering, I sat up straight, my mind whirling.

From what I'd gathered, the Lord of Chaos had kidnapped me, and he'd locked me in a basement. I hadn't expected an amazing birthday, but this certainly fell far below my worst expectations.

My heart thundered in my chest. I shot to my feet, searching for my phone. Only then did I remember that one of the frat boys had smacked it out of my hands.

Swallowing hard, I wrapped my arms around myself. "Hello?"

My own voice echoed back to me. The only other noise was the sound of dripping water.

After a few minutes, I started feeling around in the darkness. My fingertips brushed over a slimy wall, moss, ivy, and then iron bars.

Okay, I wasn't in a basement. I was in a jail cell. Or a dungeon, perhaps.

"Hello?" I called again.

As I stared into the darkness, flames burst to life in the torches on a stone wall across from me, making me jump. But since no one was around, I could only imagine that magic had lit the torches. Now, warm light wavered over my cell, illuminating the iron bars that locked me in.

I surveyed the dim space. Vines grew over three of the walls around me, and across from my cell was a crude stone wall with the torches. That was about it.

As my heart raced, I crossed to the bars and gripped them, waiting. Down here, it was cold enough that my breath clouded before my face.

A few moments later, I heard the sound of footfalls.

Then the Lord of Chaos arrived before my cell, his perfect features gilded in the torchlight. It was too bad he was a demon and an unrelenting asshole because he was heartbreakingly beautiful. He stood with an eerie, demonic stillness that made goosebumps rise on my skin. The amygdala—the part of my brain that assessed a threat—instantly picked him out as *predator, not human*. My brain was telling me to get the fuck out of there, and it didn't seem to care that there were bars.

"There you are, love," he purred.

I stared at him, trying to remember how to form sentences. "Don't lock someone in a dungeon and then call them *love*."

He chuckled softly, taunting. "Sorry, is that bad manners?" His smile faded fast. "I guess I don't give a fuck, Mortana."

"Why am I here?"

"Because I loathe you more than any other living person, and I've always wanted to see you on the other side of these bars." His cruel gaze brushed slowly up and down my body. "It's fucking delicious. Especially seeing what a sad little life you've been living among the mortals. Oh, how the mighty have fallen."

I pointed at him. "You need to understand that everything you're saying is wrong."

He stepped closer, his eyes piercing in the gloom, and gripped the cell bars. "This night has been delightful. I never quite imagined it being this good." Despite the fact that he was threatening me at every

29

opportunity, his voice felt like a soft, seductive caress. It brushed over my bare skin, sending a hot shiver through my body—a deeply confusing sensation. "This might be the greatest thrill I've ever experienced. Don't you remember what it was like when you used to come see me?"

Panic was stealing my breath. "I'm not the person you think I am. How can I make you see that?"

An ice-cold smile. "Oh? Have you had a change of heart in the past few centuries? Are you *nice* now?" His voice dripped with sarcasm. "Shall we have a bake sale to fund sports for underprivileged mortal children?"

"I'm not two centuries old. I'm *mortal*. Can't you tell the difference? I'm from Osborn. I went to Osborn High School. I was Lady Macbeth in one of the plays junior year, and I fell off the stage. Jared Halverson asked me to the prom as a joke, and I got dressed up in a black gown, and he never showed up." I blurted these last few tidbits of information in a desperate attempt to explain how utterly nonthreatening I was.

His smile only deepened, his beauty making my chest ache. "Well, this *is* a rather sad display. You're really going to play it this way? The night before your execution, Mortana, and you're going to pretend to be a mortal who's pathetic even among the other humans? This is fascinating."

I ignored the degree to which he was insulting me and focused on one word: *Mortana*. There, I had a name. I pointed at him. "Okay. Let's start here. Mortana. That's not me. My name is Rowan Morgenstern. If you'll check my wallet, you'll see my ID. I'm twenty-two years old. It's my birthday tonight. I gave a presentation about repressed memories today, and I fucked it right up. I live in a basement with spiders." It seemed I was unable to stop spewing irrelevant information.

What were the chances an ancient terrifying demon would accept a Massachusetts license as proof of identity? Not great, I thought.

My heart was racing out of control. "There's got to be some way that I can prove I'm not Mortana." Never before had I felt so desperate to be back in that spidery basement.

He gave a bitter laugh. "Here I was, hoping for remorse. I thought you might want to unburden yourself before your death. But I see I won't get that particular pleasure."

My mouth went dry. "Before my death?"

"You must remember the prison gallows," he said quietly. "I certainly do."

I shook my head, my heart thundering. "No. I don't!" I shouted. "Because for the last fucking time, I'm not Mortana!"

Shadowy magic spilled around him, then shifted in the air. "You've been out of the city gates long enough that you will die quickly. You will die like a mortal if I kill you tomorrow morning before your magic returns. It's not really the death you deserve, but it's the one you'll get. You can thank me tomorrow, love, for your mercifully quick death. Assuming you're not ready to thank me now."

And with that, he turned and strolled away, shadows coiling around him.

As I watched him leave through the cell bars, the torches flickered out, and darkness filled the prison again.

Forcing myself to take a deep breath, I tried to corral my racing thoughts into a plan. Screaming and begging would do no good. In the darkness, I searched out a dry part of the cell and slid down into one corner. And as I sat in the silence, I realized my first mistake. Dr. Omer would have called me on it right away. You can't just *tell* someone they're wrong—they'll just argue back. You have to gently guide them to the conclusion themselves so it seems like their idea.

I dropped my face into my hands, my chest tight.

On the cold cell floor, a sense of loneliness hollowed me out. Was I really going to die in this place? Buried with all my secrets? There were so many things I'd never told anyone. Things that were too dark, too scary.

I hadn't told anyone that the night mom died, I'd been covered in ashes. My senior year of high school, the police had found Mom's charred body in the Osborne Forest. They'd found me by the side of the road half a mile away, shaking and covered in soot. When I talked about her murder, I could always sense the change in the air. I could feel muscles tensing, breath sucking in. No one wanted the absolute horror of having to hear more about a mother incinerated in a forest.

People looked at me differently after learning about what had happened, as if the tragedy had cursed me. And it had.

I didn't tell anyone how I'd been nearly catatonic, with confused memories of the night. I hadn't told Shai that when the police had interviewed me, I'd been incoherent, and that I'd been a suspect for a while. All I could remember was that Mom had injured her ankle. She'd told me to run, fast, to get help. I'd known we were in danger, and I'd started to take off in the dark woods. But then I'd heard it—the inhuman sound like a growl. The smell of flesh burning, and her screams. That's when my memories became muddled, but I remembered a five-pointed star burning bright in the darkness.

The only thing still clear to me from that point on was the bone-deep terror.

After the police interviewed me, they came to the conclusion that I was delusional, possibly on drugs. Demons hadn't killed mortals in centuries. It wasn't even possible, they were certain. *Have you lost your mind, Rowan?*

Eventually, they'd come up with a half-baked theory that the murder was probably drug-related. But that wasn't Mom. She never did drugs.

At school, the rumors had gone wild. People who didn't know a thing about Mom had said she was a prostitute, a drug addict. Some had said I'd killed her in a fit of rage—that I'd poured gasoline on her and lit a match.

When I found the real killer, I'd know what actually happened.

"Fuck," I muttered. Then, louder. "I am not Mortana!"

A sigh sounded from the next cell. Was someone there?

"Hello?" I tried again, this time more quietly. I felt oddly relieved to have company. "I didn't know anyone else was here."

The only response was another sigh. *Definitely* someone there.

Hugging myself, I swallowed hard. "I'm not supposed to be here. I know, right, everyone probably says that, but I'm mortal. I don't think demons are supposed to imprison mortals. Don't suppose you know how to get out of here?"

No response.

"I guess you wouldn't be here if you did. Have you ever heard of someone named Mortana?"

Water dripped into the puddle next to me.

I dropped my head into my hands, my body still buzzing with panic. "I'm not her. I'm not a demon, and I'm not two centuries old."

Somehow, my new prison friend's silence only made me want to tell him more. Because the Lord of Chaos was right. I *did* want to unburden myself, but not because of guilt. My secrets were weighing me down, stealing my breath, and I wanted to be free of them.

"Let me tell you something, prison mate," I started. "I'm twenty-two. And I can't die tomorrow. In fact, I *refuse* to die tomorrow. Do you want to know why? I've never even been in love. I had one boyfriend my freshman year of college. He was into comics and played the piano, and he was tall and cute. But he always told me I needed to exercise more, and I started to resent him, and when we finally had sex, it was...so boring. I remember reading the spines of the books on his shelves, waiting for it to end. I remember a mosquito biting my butt cheek. Then he broke up with me for a girl from his town, and that was that. That was my only relationship."

My mind was racing. I'd never actually told anyone this before, and it felt good to get it out. And I didn't actually give a fuck what this stranger thought, so he was the perfect person to unburden myself with.

This was *freeing*.

"I think we need to talk about Jack," I went on. "You're a good listener, you know that?"

I launched into a diatribe about Jack in high school, the "Home Run Rowan" nickname, how Jared Halverson had posted my confused texts on social media the night he stood me up. Then I rambled about every indiscretion, every embarrassing thing or terrible thing I'd ever done. The time I'd written a friend a bitchy email about my math teacher's sweat stains and accidentally sent it to him. My weird snack of microwaved tortillas with sugar and butter. The time I'd thrown up repeatedly in a trash can in Harvard Square Station after too much tequila. The cab driver with mutton chops I tried to hit on in

Cambridge. How I'd peed outside a Dunkin' Donuts because they wouldn't let me use the bathroom. How I'd never actually had an orgasm, and I wasn't convinced they were real—the idea seemed like an elaborate hoax. I explained how I'd given up on men and started wearing granny panties from Rite Aid because what difference did it make?

For at least an hour, I unleashed every embarrassing or selfish thing I'd ever thought or done.

"...and can you explain to me why the *one* guy who seemed like he would actually be able to sexually satisfy me is also a demon, and also he kidnapped me and threw me in a prison? That's how I know there's no God. It's too cruel. The sexiest person I've ever seen, the guy who'd make me want to wear lace underwear instead of the pharmacy stuff— he's the Hannibal fucking Lecter of the supernatural world. Are you *kidding* me?"

Silence filled the cells, and I realized my eyes were growing heavy.

A man's voice came from the next cell, hardly a whisper: "Are you done?"

I sighed, only now realizing that I'd pretty much run out of material. "Yeah, I think that covers my life pretty much," I said, and dropped my head into my hands, exhausted.

But there was only one thing I didn't cover—my mom's death at the hands of a demon with the mark of a star. Because I was still determined to find my way out of this. And I wasn't ruling anyone out. Not the Lord of Chaos, and not my quiet prison friend.

Any demon could be guilty.

As I sat on the cold floor, I was sure of three things.

One, I was going to find a way out of here.

Two, I'd find a way to stay in the City of Thorns.

And three, I would get revenge on the demon who killed my mom.

❧ 8 ❧

I usually couldn't sleep when I was anxious about something. And lying in a demon prison the night before I was supposed to be executed *should* have made me anxious

But strangely enough, I closed my eyes with a sense of peace.

Maybe it was the certainty that I could fix this. Or maybe it was the freedom I felt after finally unleashing my secrets on the demon next door. Whatever the case, I woke up with my head resting on my arms. I stank of sweat and mildew, and I desperately had to pee. But I'd slept.

A few flecks of light streamed in through cracks near the ceiling.

I sat up straight, hugging myself. "Are you still there?" I asked.

Silence greeted me.

Apart from the little sunlight, it was still dark as night in there. I hugged my knees close to my chest, teeth chattering. As I surveyed the dark cell around me, my eye fell on a point on one of the walls, just between the vines. A thin stream of light illuminated a carving in the stone, tucked behind the leaves.

I scooted over and started tugging at the ropes of plants, but it was still hard to read with the darkness. Instead, I traced the letters with my fingers, feeling their contours.

_L...U...C...I...F...E...R..._

Shuddering, I kept going. It took me a minute because the carvings seemed old and faded, but eventually, I had a phrase mapped out in my head.

Lucifer urbem spinarum libarab...

The rest of it had faded. But if my high school Latin translation was correct, it said something like _Lucifer will set the City of Thorns free._

Interesting. But not helpful for my release, was it?

I shifted away from the wall and hugged my knees again.

In the silence, I could concentrate on my game plan for getting out of this situation. It hinged on being able to convince the Lord of Chaos that I was not who he thought I was. All I had to do was sow doubt in his mind. Once I bought myself some time, if I could stall this execution, I'd work on making him realize I wasn't Mortana. Whatever his deal was, I was sure that he didn't want to start a war by killing a mortal. Our two species had managed to keep the peace for hundreds of years.

When I heard the footfalls echoing through the prison cells, my body became alert, and my pulse raced. I shot to my feet, ready to convince him. As the visitor moved closer, the torches sprang to life again, and warm light danced over the stone wall across from me.

The Lord of Chaos crossed slowly before my cell, eyes ice blue. He was wearing a white button-down shirt with the sleeves rolled up to his elbows, exposing a disturbing tattoo of a snake formed into a noose.

The warm power radiating off him made my breath quicken. I'd never before been this close to a demon, and everything about him was unnerving. He looked similar to a human, but too tall, too perfect, and too eerily still.

And now it was time for me to present my case.

"I don't suppose I get a trial?" I asked.

He shook his head slowly.

"You mentioned she hadn't aged in two hundred years," I began. "How long has it been since you've actually seen Mortana?"

Curiosity sparked in his eyes, "Is this your defense?"

Lead him to the conclusion. The problem was that this was hard to do when he was hardly saying anything. I needed to use _his_ own words.

"You're certain that you want revenge by killing Mortana? And that your memory couldn't be wrong after all that time?"

He just stared at me for a moment with that unnerving stillness. I wasn't sure this was going well.

Then he replied, "When I say you look like her, I mean you look *exactly* like her. My memory isn't faulty. I haven't forgotten a single contour of her face. I do not forget things," he said in a clipped tone.

My heart started pounding, but with hope. He was now referring to her as a separate person. "You haven't forgotten a contour of *her* face. Did you notice how you spoke about her in the third person?"

Without another word, he pulled a key from his pocket and unlocked my cell. Looming over me, with magic that brushed over my skin, he stepped inside.

I found myself moving away, cold dread skittering up my spine. In the days before mortals had weapons to fight back, we were simply the demons' prey. When they weren't seducing mortals, they'd drink our blood. Tens of thousands of years of evolution were telling me to get the fuck away from him.

A million terrible thoughts flitted through my mind, and I stood with my back pressed against the wall. "The Osborne police are very good," I lied. "If you killed me, they'd find out."

He cocked his head and spoke in a velvety murmur. "Oh, I doubt that very much."

9

My breath caught in my throat. "Do you still think I'm Mortana?"

He studied me so intensely that I felt he was seeing right into my very soul. "I listened to everything you said last night."

I stared at him. God, what had I said to him? "That was you in the next cell?"

"You've managed to plant a seed of doubt in my mind. Mortana had far too much dignity to engage in a charade like that. The prom situation. Crying alone in your basement apartment at night. The fear of ladybugs. Having a lucky pen that you hold to feel a sense of security."

"I'd like my pen back, please," I whispered.

"Practicing karaoke songs alone in your room even though no one has ever invited you out. I don't think I ever understood the desire some mortals have to end their lives until I listened to the details of yours last night."

I narrowed my eyes. "Look, I might be a bit of a weirdo, but I've never wanted to end my life."

"Not you. I mean me. I have seen darkness that you couldn't imagine, horrors that would twist your soul. And yet, never before in my several hundred years of existence have I been so ready to shuffle off this mortal coil as I was listening to your sad monologue." He pressed a finger to his lips. "I think it was the bit about the yogurt pouches you keep in your purse because you have no one to eat lunch with. Even though they're meant to be consumed by infants."

This was just insulting. "At least I don't kidnap people like some kind of Buffalo Bill psychopath. Call me crazy, but I'd say that's a worse flaw than purse yogurt. And by the way, they have probiotics, so my microbiome is fucking pristine."

He stared at me, shadows thickening around him.

"My point is, you're not perfect, either," I added. "And you're weirdly obsessed with Mortana."

A ruthless look slid through his eyes. "I never said I was perfect. Frankly, I'm an absolute arsehole with an unhealthy revenge obsession. I'm not *depressing*, though, and I have never made my shirt into a bowl for dry cereal to eat alone on a Saturday night."

Revenge. I'd managed to keep him talking, and he'd brought me back again to what he wanted. This was what I could use. And as it would happen, an unhealthy obsession with revenge was something I understood very well. It seemed this demon *arsehole* and I had something in common.

Dr. Omer's teaching played in my mind. *Build rapport by reflecting back your client's words to him.*

"Okay, so you have a seed of doubt," I started. What would Dr. Omer say? "Let's explore that."

He shook his head slowly. "I admit you *might* not be a demon. You do look exactly like her, though, which is perplexing."

"Maybe she's a distant ancestor."

He shook his head. "Demons rarely procreate. And when we do, we only sire other demons. You can't be a mortal and a descendant of Mortana."

I bit my lip. "Coincidence?"

He considered the notion. "Every now and then, a demon has a mortal doppelgänger. It's rare but possible."

I sighed, relief unclenching my chest. "Good. Yes. That must be it."

"But to prove it, I require two pieces of evidence."

A little spark of hope. "Whatever you need."

His gaze swept down my body. "To start, Mortana had a small scar on her upper thigh. I will need to see your legs."

"You want me to lift up my dress?"

"Yes."

"Fine."

But at that point, I remembered exactly what I'd told him last night—about how he was the only man I'd ever seen who'd make me want to wear lace underwear. How he was the only one I thought could ever give me an orgasm. Mortified, I felt heat creeping over my cheeks.

"Go on," he said softly.

My nostrils flared, and I glared at him as I lifted up the hem of my dress to a point just below my underwear.

The Lord of Chaos cocked his head, staring at my thighs as the cold dungeon air raised goosebumps on my skin. He looked riveted, his eyes growing brighter. Then he moved closer, and he reached down to lift my right leg from under the knee, pulling it up outside his thigh like we were engaged in some kind of dungeon tango. He was just inches from my hips now, examining my skin. With his free hand, he traced his fingertip over the very top of my thigh, and shivers of heat rippled through me.

Holy *hell*, that was distracting. The magical pulse coming off him was seductive, intoxicating. Warmth radiated over my skin from the point of contact. I'd never seen anyone so fascinated with a little bit of skin, nor had I ever realized that a single touch could be so powerful.

"See?" My voice came out in a whisper. "No scar."

He dropped my thigh. When he stepped back, I felt cold again.

He frowned. "Interesting."

I exhaled. "And what's the other thing?"

He curled his lips and bared two sharp, white fangs, then licked one.

I shivered. "What?"

"Mortal blood tastes different than demon blood."

Primal fear slid through my bones. "You want to drink my blood? Like the old days?"

"All I need is a little taste."

My heart pounded hard. "You realize this seems terrifying. Is there not a more clinical way to do this? A syringe, maybe?"

"I don't have a syringe. But you might find it's not as terrible as you imagine. Mortal women once flocked to offer their necks to demon males," he murmured. "They loved it."

"Sure, they did."

He gave a slow, infuriating shrug. "I have told you that I'm an arsehole, right? So I don't really care if I imprison an innocent person, and frankly, I don't think your life here would be much worse than your life in the Osborne basement. I'll feel no guilt about leaving you locked up here. So you can let me bite your neck, or you can stay here in the dungeon forever. Those are your options."

Maybe it was time to start bargaining. "Okay. I'll let you taste my blood. But when you're done, I'm not going back to Osborne. I want to stay in the City of Thorns."

He frowned. "You can't. If you *are* mortal, then you don't belong here. The only mortals who can stay are students and servants who inherited the role."

I folded my arms. "I'm sure someone called the Lord of *Chaos* can find a way to bend the rules."

He flashed me a crooked smile. "What is it, exactly, that makes you think you have leverage to make any sort of demands?"

I knew his weakness now—a lust for revenge. Something I understood implicitly. And the thing about a sense of vengeance as burning as his was that it could spread like wildfire. You didn't just want to end the life of one person—you wanted to kill anyone who helped them, anyone who let it happen. You wanted scorched earth.

"You want revenge, yes?" I asked. "You said Mortana haunts your nightmares. That's a pretty intense loathing. So is she the only one, or is there someone else you want dead?"

His eyes were glowing brighter, and I had the sense he understood where I was going with this. "She didn't work alone."

I took a step closer, tilting my head back to look up at him. "So I could pretend to be her. Get information from these other people you hate. I could be your spy."

His body had gone as still as the stones around us, sending a chill dancing up my nape. At last, he said, "Assuming this isn't all an act, I don't think you'd make a convincing succubus. You're not seductive."

I winced. *Ouch.* "Anything can be learned. Even how to be seductive like a succubus." Whatever that was.

He looked transfixed with me. "I will consider it once I've tasted your blood. I need to know for sure that you're mortal before we continue any further."

I opened up my arms. "Okay. Go ahead. *Bite me.*"

Instantly, his warm magic slid around me like a forbidden caress, heating my blood. He had me completely pinned with his piercing gaze, and I felt my nipples going hard under my dress. To my shock, I found that he was right. I *wanted* him to bite me. I wanted him to grab me, shove me against the wall, and clamp his teeth into my throat. In fact—bizarrely—I wanted him to do all kinds of filthy things to me.

He stared into my eyes, and dominance emanated from him. His seductive scent wrapped around me, earthy like burning cedar. There was something more powerful than fear snaking around my ribs: the instinct to submit. This instinct, forged by thousands of years of evolution, was telling me to give in to him if I wanted to live.

He reached for my waist and pulled me closer. The next thing I knew, I was pressed against his body, his muscles as unyielding as the stone walls around us. Then awe slid over me as I watched his pale eyes go dark. He moved so smoothly that I'd nearly missed that he was pressing me against the wall. I felt the cold stone against my spine, chilling my skin through my dress. His knee slid between my legs.

It was hard to ignore how dangerous he was, how otherworldly. How he could end my life in a single heartbeat and move on to his next victim.

"Arch your neck," he said in velvety voice.

I couldn't resist the urge to submit to his command. My eyes closed, and I tilted my head to give him access, making myself vulnerable to him. I felt his breath warming my throat, and a pounding heat swept through my body. My breath sped up, and my nipples felt exquisitely sensitive under my dress. I didn't want to feel turned on by my supremely arrogant demonic abductor, and yet, here we were. The heart wants what it wants.

When I felt the brush of his canines over my throat, my breath hitched. Liquid desire slid between my thighs. I didn't tell my arms to wrap around his neck, but they did anyway, welcoming him to my body. He felt as solid as the wall behind me. My pulse pounded, and I waited for the sharp sting of his teeth puncturing my skin. Instead, what I felt was a warm kiss.

Oh, *God*, that felt good.

A pulsing, sensual heat was spreading from the place where his mouth met my throat, and his tongue swirled over my neck. Then a sharp stab of pain curled my toes, made my heart slam against my ribs. His fingers tightened on my waist as his fangs sank into me, claiming me. Pleasure washed over the pain until all I could feel was the sexual ache building in me.

This was supremely fucked up.

I only tilted my head back more, giving him more access. I was tightly coiled with desire now, and I fought the urge to pull up the hem of my dress again. But I *needed* release, and he was the only one who could give it to me.

After a moment, he pulled his canines from my throat, and I started to fall against his chest, arms still wrapped around his neck. I'd never wanted someone so badly in my life. Clearly, my body had terrible taste in men. Really, just the *worst* possible taste. He was arrogant, insulting, a self-professed asshole who'd locked me in a literal dungeon. Oh, and he was a centuries-old blood-drinking demon.

"There," he whispered, brushing a hand down the back of my hair. "Mortal."

I leaned against the hard, muscled wall of his chest, and when I looked up at him, I saw that he looked nearly as dazed as I felt.

"That was horrible," I lied. "I hated it."

He leaned down and whispered, "I don't believe you. But I suppose I am sorry about the abduction."

I glanced down at the powerful arm wrapped around my waist, at the eerie snake tattoo. Then I pushed him away. "Okay. Let's discuss how I'll stay in the City of Thorns as your spy."

"Is that what we're doing? Because I detest mortals nearly as much as I hate Mortana." He tilted his head. "But you do taste fucking delicious, so that softens the hatred a bit."

I touched my neck, surprised to find that the two puncture wounds were already healing. There was hardly any blood at all.

"But you're tempted by my plan, aren't you?" I smiled at him. "Because you're the Lord of Chaos, and you know that a mortal twin of a succubus can turn this city upside down."

"And why do you want to stay here so desperately?"

I shrugged. "You summarized it yourself. My life is desperately sad. The yogurt pouches, the T-shirt cereal bowl. It fucking sucks, even for a mortal, and I can't go back."

"Here's what you have to understand. There is, in fact, one circumstance in which demons are allowed to kill mortals. In which we can drain your blood with impunity or throw you into a fire pit. And that is if you enter the City of Thorns without permission, or under false pretenses. If the king or his soldiers determine that you're actually mortal, then you will die, and probably in an excruciating way. So are you actually sure about this?"

Not at all. "Yes."

He arched an eyebrow. "And once I fill you in on the secrets of the City of Thorns, once I tell you what I want, there will be no going back. I'm not letting you leave this city freely with my secrets, to wander around telling people what you heard. I'd have to kill you first."

I bit my lip. "Are you saying I can never leave?"

"You can't leave until you've helped me achieve my mission."

"Which is?"

He shook his head slowly. "I can't tell you that yet, can I? You're either in or out. And you need to make your choice now. If I take you up to my apartment to divulge my plans, you will have crossed a threshold that you cannot return from until the mission is complete."

Fear skittered up the back of my neck. But I already knew it was too late, that there was no going back. Because I was so close to having answers now. I needed to know what happened to Mom, and I wasn't going to get another chance after this.

Now or never.

And the truth was, it wasn't just that I wanted vengeance. I also wanted to get rid of the cloud of suspicion that hung over me at all times, that maybe I'd been involved.

With a tight chest, I nodded. "I'm willing to take risks. But since what I'll be doing for you is dangerous, I'm going to need you to pay off my undergrad student loans. And I'd like to transfer to Belial University."

He shrugged. "I can easily pay your loans. I can buy you a mortal degree if you want. But you cannot be at the university because *Mortana* would not be at the university."

My eyebrows shot up. "You can't just *buy* a degree."

He looked at me like I was mad. "Of course you can. You can buy anything."

I nodded, realizing he was probably right. My stomach twisted in knots as I realized I was about to undertake something extremely dangerous. "Okay. Whatever the dangers are, I'm in. Let's do this." I clapped my hands together. "And now I'm going to need you to show me where the bathroom is before your opinion of my dignity falls even further."

☙ 10 ❧

Blindfolded, I walked through what I thought was a series of
tunnels. The Lord of Chaos held my hands to guide me, and it
kind of felt like we were on the most fucked-up date in
history.

After a minute of walking, I whispered, "What's your actual name?"

"Orion," he said quietly.

I found the sound of his name dark and intoxicating.

And as we walked in silence, I could only feel a wild exhilaration
that I was actually getting what I wanted. Forget saving money. Forget
breaking in.

Now, I would get to stay in the City of Thorns.

After a few minutes of walking in the cool air, we reached a set of
stairs. With his hand in mine, Orion led me up the stairs until I heard
the creaking of a door.

When he pulled the blindfold off, I found myself standing in what
looked like a heavily columned Mediterranean palace. Everything
seemed to be made of pale, golden marble. A splash of blood-red
poppies bloomed in an ivory vase by one of the open windows. When I
glanced at the ceiling, I found it painted blue and dotted with stars
that glowed with magical light. On two sides of the room, glass

windows overlooked a sea that glittered like blue topaz. This place looked nothing like the grim Atlantic. This place was *paradise*.

On a third side, the wall was open to the air, and a covered balcony overlooked the sea. There, an overhang shaded a bed with a white duvet. On the other side of the seaside balcony, a table had been set up with two chairs. A warm, salty breeze filtered into the room.

Holy shit, his life was amazing.

I managed to close my gaping mouth, and I turned to Orion to find that he was on his cell phone. "Morgan? Please bring breakfast and coffee for two." He hung up, then gestured to the balcony. "Let's discuss my proposal out here."

Before I followed him into the buttery morning light, I lingered for a moment to survey the rest of the room—the books lining the walls, the cream-colored sofas. Would I get to stay here?

A warm breeze rushed into the room, and I followed him onto the balcony. Out here, the sun dazzled over the sea.

As I took my seat at the table, the door opened, and a man with a salt-and-pepper beard and a crisp white shirt entered. He looked like he might be about fifty, in excellent shape, and sporting perfectly applied eyeliner.

Orion smiled. "Morgan."

"Orion, darling! You're up early, aren't you?" He spoke with a lilting Welsh accent.

I smiled at him as he slid a tray of fruit, yogurt, and coffee onto the balcony table. But before I could open my mouth, Orion introduced me. "I have Lady Mortana with me. Former advisor to King Nergal. She was living in the City of Serpents, and she has returned here after a long time away."

Morgan smiled at me. "Welcome, darling. I can see why you'd return to the most amazing city in the world. No mystery there." Morgan nudged a bowl of fruit in front of Orion. "You're not having the donuts today. You can't eat junk and look nice forever, even if you *are* an ancient and powerful demon."

Orion draped his arms over the back of his chair. "I like the donuts. They're the zenith of human civilization. Especially the ones with the raspberry jam in the center."

"That's not the bloody zenith of human civilization." Morgan looked at me, shaking his head. "Honestly, he can be so patronizing sometimes. There's plenty of other achievements to choose from. The Great Library of Alexandria comes to mind."

Orion plucked a strawberry. "And do you know what happened to the Great Library of Alexandria? A mortal mob burned it down, destroyed its contents, then flayed alive the scholar Hypatia because women who knew things were apparently witches. Yes, that's a great example of mortal civilization, I'd say."

If I spent enough time with Orion, I was worried I'd actually start hating mortals, too. He really did have a knack for making us sound terrible.

Morgan held up his digital watch. "Okay, forget the ancient world. We've grown better since then. We have Apple watches now. I know exactly how many steps I walked today, and that I've stood up twelve times so far."

Orion let the silence drag, just staring at Morgan. *There* was the Dr. Omer technique in action.

Morgan looked increasingly uncomfortable and adjusted his shirt sleeves. "Look, I'm going to have to come in prepared with a better answer after doing a bit of research. The zenith of human civilization isn't something you can just come up with off the top of your head. There's a lot to choose from. A *lot*."

"While you're mulling that over, I have another favor to ask of you." Orion turned to look at me. "I'm sure our new king will want to see Lady Mortana soon, but obviously, she can't meet him dressed like a peasant."

I was wearing the best outfit I owned.

Morgan nodded at me with concern. "Dolce e Malvagia opens at ten. Gorgeous clothes. Do you want me to pick out some things and send them up?"

He nodded. "Select a bunch of dresses for Mortana to try on, bathrobes, pajamas, everything she might need. You can put it on my account."

"Right." He looked me up and down. "Lovely hourglass figure. Favorite color?"

I had no idea what Mortana's favorite color was. But if she'd been out of the city several hundred years, what were the chances anyone else would know? "Black." Seemed a safe answer for a demon.

Orion steepled his fingers, and he looked between the two of us. "Morgan, there's something else important I should tell you about Mortana. She is a succubus. You may warn the others."

I watched the color drained from Morgan's face. "A succubus?"

By his reaction, I gathered that this was a big deal. I smiled at him and shrugged, deciding it was probably best to say as little as possible at this point—particularly since I had no idea what was going on.

"The last remaining succubus," Orion added. "She will be taking up residence in the Asmodean Ward after she meets the king."

Morgan's gaze flitted nervously between the two of us. "Can she kill me?"

"She won't kill you," Orion said in a soothing tone. "It's against the rules, isn't it?"

Morgan still looked horrified. "But the whole Asmodean Ward is abandoned. I thought the Lilu were extinct. I was told they're very dangerous."

Orion lifted the coffee pot and poured two steaming cups. A lock of his silver hair fell before his eyes. "*Nearly* extinct."

He nodded and backed away, then hurried out of the room like a ghost was on his heels. The door slammed shut behind him.

I stared after him. "A mortal servant, I take it?"

"Yes, and he is under the mistaken impression that I care about his views on nutrition. But I do value his help." Orion sipped his coffee. "I must fill you in on a few things."

"Agreed. What's this about being the *last* succubus? What happened to the rest?"

He poured a bit of cream in the coffee. "The Lilu were hunted into extinction hundreds of years ago."

I scooped some berries into a bowl of yogurt. "Why?"

Every time his eyes met mine, I felt an unnerving jolt, like an electric pulse in my chest. I hoped that he had no idea what effect he had on me—he was arrogant enough as it was.

"The Lilu were killed for two reasons," he said. "You know about the war between the demons and the Puritans, yes?"

I nodded. "In the 1680s, yeah." It was how demons had ended up locked up in this city in the first place.

"As part of their surrendering terms," said Orion, "King Nergal agreed to kill the Lilu. The Puritans hated all demons, but they *really* loathed the Lilu. They feared being turned on by a demon more than anything." He stared out over the glittering sea. "And Nergal agreed because other demons hated the Lilu, too. The Lilu had a power that threatened the rest—the ability to compel others of their kind, to control their minds, to seduce them to do what they wanted. They're also the only demons with wings. They were simply too powerful."

I squinted in the sunlight. "And how did Mortana manage to survive?"

"By being cunning, calculating, and evil as sin. King Nergal was a dull, tedious man, and Mortana was the opposite. She was witty and captivating, and nearly everyone fell in love with her. Including the king. She made a deal with him—she would help him round up and slaughter all the Lilu, and she would get to live. He kept her in a room in the Tower of Baal, and she became known as the Seneschal."

I wondered what she'd done to Orion. "The king was in love with her, then."

"Yes. Like many others." He stared at me over his coffee cup. "I confess, I marvel at the poor judgment of all those human males who rejected your beauty. Demons have better taste."

W as that a compliment? I could feel myself blushing now, but I had no idea how to respond.

"Mortana," he went on, "demanded that the king make a blood oath. She made him pledge that the crown would always keep her safe."

"What's a blood oath?" I asked.

"It's an oath sealed by mingling the blood of two people. If someone breaks a blood oath, it will result in an excruciating death based on the magic of a curse. The problem is, only the monarch made this oath. The rest of the demons in this city will probably still want to murder you for being a succubus."

I was losing my appetite for the berries and yogurt, and starting to feel like I was in slightly over my head. It seemed there were so many ways to die here in the City of Thorns. But I'd made my choice, and like Orion had said, there was no going back now. "How much danger will I be in?"

"It would be a lot more if you weren't with me. We will be spending a great deal of time together." A smile played over his sensual mouth, but it didn't reach his eyes. "I'll need to keep you closely guarded."

I swallowed hard. "Who is it that you want me to spy on?"

"King Cambriel."

Oh, good. I'd be spying on a murderous king. My stomach fluttered, but this had been, after all, my idea. "Cambriel cut off his dad's head and stuck it on a gate, right?" I paused with my spoon in midair. "You want me to get close to him?"

Steam from the coffee curled before Orion's face. "He will be looking for a wife. If the real Mortana were here, she'd be a strong candidate. She's the duchess of one of the wards. Some think she had a claim to the throne. I mean, she was mistress to his father. She's also widely rumored to have killed his mother, Queen Adele, centuries ago, but I'm not sure that he holds a grudge."

I stared at him. "Okay, slow down for a second. Mortana probably killed the king's mother, and I'm supposed to convince him to marry me?"

Orion shrugged. "It was never proven. Just rumors. They say Mortana hoped to take the queen's place, and one day, Queen Adele's body was found in a vat of wine with her heart cut out."

I frowned over my coffee. "Do you think Mortana did it?"

"Probably. That was her style. Queen Adele didn't drink alcohol, and that irritated Mortana, so the wine was a nice touch. Anyway, water under the bridge now, I'm sure. Charm the king, flirt, get him close to you. As long as I can teach you to act like Mortana, you'll have the chance to try to pry his secrets out of him."

My chest felt tight. "What, exactly, are you looking for?"

"I want you to find what makes him weak." Sunlight glinted in his pale eyes. "Because everyone has a weakness."

It was like he'd ripped the phrase from my own thoughts.

I raised my eyebrows. "Are you telling me you want to kill the king? I thought that only an heir can kill the king. So unless Cambriel has a child who wants him dead, he can't be killed, right?"

"Did your friend Shai tell you that?"

My throat tightened. I didn't want to get Shai involved in this. "What are you talking about?"

He looked out over the sparkling ocean. "I saw her with you in the bar, and I noted the Belial University insignia on her handbag. So while you were sleeping in the prison cell, I found her wandering around Osborn and interviewed her."

Oh, *shit*. I slammed a hand on the table and leaned forward. "You interrogated Shai?"

"Interviewed. I wanted her to tell me what she knew about you." He sipped his coffee. "And as for the king and his weakness—it's true that only an heir can kill the monarch, but the king can be imprisoned. There's more than one way to get revenge."

The coffee was starting to give me a little buzz. "Okay. You want to get rid of the king. And I take it this requires a high degree of secrecy so your head doesn't end up on his front gate alongside his dad's."

His icy gaze bored into me. "Precisely. A high degree of secrecy. You are the only one who knows what I plan to do." He leaned over the table. "And now you know why there is no going back. I cannot allow you to leave here until I've achieved my goal, and if this secret got out, it would be all over for me. Until I'm rid of the king, you are mine. And if you cross me and tell my plans to anyone else, I will murder your dear friend Shai."

Ice slid through my blood. Mentally, I tried to untangle the morality of this situation. I was going to help a demon imprison a king, but he wouldn't be able to *kill* him. And the king had murdered his own father...really, it could be argued that I was doing the right thing. My only deep regret at this point was that this situation put Shai's life in danger.

I finished my coffee. "I like to think of myself as being quite skilled at finding people's weaknesses."

"I believe that." He narrowed his eyes over his coffee, and I felt the air growing hotter around us. "You know, it's unnerving looking into the face of my worst enemy, even if you're only a doppelgänger. It's hard not to reach across the table, rip your heart out of your chest, and throw it into the sea."

Yikes. I'd definitely lost my appetite at this point. "Please try to resist the impulse."

"I'll do my best."

I bit my lip. "Are you going to tell me what she did to you?"

"I don't think that's necessary." For a moment, I caught a glimpse of vulnerability in his pale eyes. "But I'll do anything to get revenge. I will kill whoever I have to in order to make this happen. I have no moral code, only a burning lust for vengeance. Do you understand?" His words made my heart skip a beat, and the air burned hotter.

Got it loud and clear. No moral code. He was a psychopath.

He rested his arms on the table. "If this is going to work, you'll need to know about demons and the City of Thorns. You'll need to know a bit about what Mortana was like when she lived here, but not what she did in the past two hundred years. We're forbidden from sharing information between demon cities. And if this plan is going to work, your friend Shai is a loose end. She could identify you."

I took a deep breath. He wasn't going to suggest killing her, was he? "I'm sure she'll agree to keep the secret."

"Not good enough, I'm afraid. I'll need a blood oath from her."

I poured myself another cup of coffee from the carafe. "That doesn't really seem fair to her, does it? You get information out of this. I get to live in the City of Thorns and thereby have a less pathetic life. What does Shai get for the risk she's taking with a blood oath?"

He shrugged slowly. "Anything can be bought. I'm sure she has a price."

"Do you just have unlimited money?" I asked.

"Pretty much."

"Can I have a new cell phone, then? Mine was knocked out of my hands last night in the fight with the frat boys." I raised a finger. "Oh! And I'd like my lucky pen back."

A smile tugged at his lips. "I just told you I have unlimited money, and that's all you ask for?"

"I'd like my student loans paid off, like we talked about. And to get the undergrad degree. And while I'm at it, a hundred thousand dollars." Why not?

"Ah, that's more like it."

I stirred the cream into my coffee. "But will you need a blood oath from me?"

He shrugged. "I'll need a blood oath that you will keep my secret."

I blew out a long breath. "Okay."

"But just in case you don't value your own life sufficiently—and frankly, why would you? Given how sad your life—"

"Can you get to the point?"

He gave me a wicked half-smile. "Please consider Shai's life as well. I want you to do your best work for me."

I dropped my head into my hands, starting to get dizzy. "Do we really need to get Shai involved? I don't want to put her in danger."

He gave me that *you're an idiot* look again. "Then don't fuck anything up. It's really that simple."

I pulled my hands from my face. "And when this is over, Shai will be perfectly safe, right?"

"Yes, and you should try to learn the king's weakness as soon as possible. It's the best way for you to keep Shai safe, and to ensure that none of the demons slaughter you. If you stay here too long, you'll make a mistake, and then you'll be found out and killed."

My chest tightened. There went my hope of staying in an apartment like this. But more importantly, if I couldn't stay here long, I'd be kissing goodbye to my hope of finding my mom's killer. I wasn't going to do that overnight.

I sighed. I'd have to find out as much as I could, I supposed. "I'll do my best."

He scrubbed a hand over his jaw. "You know, you might not want to stay in Osborne after you leave. It's too close to the City of Thorns, and you could also be in danger at that point."

My mind was whirling. "Well, there isn't really much keeping me there."

"Yes, I did get that impression."

I gave him a sharp look. "But how do I know you'll keep your end of the bargain with paying off my loans and degree?"

"I wouldn't expect you to take my word. You can call the loan servicing company today to confirm."

Holy *shit*. Of all the things that were happening, the most thrilling aspect of it was the idea of seventy-five thousand dollars of debt cleared in one fell swoop. No more monthly payments. No more interest. No more lifetime of debt.

Wild euphoria rushed through me, and I grinned. "I want to be there when you pay the FedLoan Servicing people. I want to listen in. I want to *hear* it all."

I realized I was gripping his arm, and I must have looked a little maniacal because he was staring at me like I'd lost my mind. Obviously, Orion was deeply alienated from the mortal challenges of student loan interest, or he would have understood this elation immediately.

I released my grip on his arm, still unable to believe this was happening. "Before I get too excited, can I get an idea of what would happen if King Cambriel discovered I was a fraud?"

His eyebrows rose. "Well, let's just say it wouldn't be pleasant. It would be even worse than your life in Osborne, if you can imagine such a thing. Torture, a slow death in a fire, and your ashes thrown in the sea. Let's try to avoid that."

A shudder rippled up my spine. But after four years of dreaming of getting within these city gates, this was my chance to find out *something* about Mom's death.

Orion stood and pulled a dagger from a sheath. Eyes twinkling, he held out his hand for mine. I rose from the table and shoved my hand toward him, and as he gripped the knife, he looked into my eyes. "I need you to repeat after me. 'On pain of death, I swear a sacred blood oath to keep my mission a secret from other demons.'"

I inhaled deeply, then repeated the pledge verbatim. As soon as I finished the final word of the oath, Orion tightened his grip around my hand. He drew the blade across my palm, and the sharp sting of the cut made me wince. A line of red gleamed from my skin, and my blood dripped onto the table.

He then cut his own palm and pressed our hands together.

I wasn't sure if it was the sight of the blood or something about the magic of the oath, but as our hands clasped, my head swam. In my mind's eye, I saw a crystal-clear vision: stone walls, cracked to expose a bit of the stars. Then a shadow swinging over the stone—the bloodied, swaying feet of a hanged body. Wood creaked above, and a pain pierced my heart to the core.

Unnerved, I pulled my hand away again, and the vision cleared. I stared at Orion, my blood still dripping onto the table.

He frowned. "What?"

I shook my head. "Nothing. I just felt...pain."

He held out his hand again. "Let me heal you."

When I touched him again, I immediately felt his magic washing over my skin, a warm and pleasurable tingle.

But I hadn't been talking about the pain from the knife. I'd meant the absolutely heart-shattering sadness from the vision—the feet swinging over stone.

Had I somehow seen into Orion's mind? He had unfathomable darkness in him, I thought. But for now, he was my ally. And like Orion, I would do anything to get my revenge.

O rion's bathtub was on a second balcony, one floor up, set into a golden marble floor. The ceiling was held up by columns, and the sun slanted in over my naked body.

It felt completely weird to be nude out here in the light. I could say with some certainty that sun's rays had never hit my nipples before. But when I looked out across the sea, I couldn't see a single person out swimming or surfing. It was just me, the gently bubbling bathwater, and the sun.

I loved it out here, but I couldn't stay too long. I'd guess that succubi never got sunburns, and I had about ten minutes before the jig was up on that front.

The plan for today was that I would get new clothes, and then Orion would teach me about Mortana and the City of Thorns.

I grabbed the soap from the side of the bath and ran it over my legs, clearing off the grime from that horrible prison cell. In some ways, I couldn't believe my luck. What I thought was the worst night of my life was now turning out to be the answer to many of my problems—assuming I could do what Orion wanted and keep Shai alive. And myself.

Before I'd come upstairs to the bath, we'd called FedLoan Servicing together to pay off my loans. That had truly been one of the best moments of my life. I'd given my account information and PIN number, then handed the phone to Orion for him to provide his bank information. He'd passed the phone back to me so I could explain how much I was paying off—all of it. The guy on the other line had never taken a call like that, which had only delighted me more.

But now I could turn my full attention to the City of Thorns. So far, I hadn't seen what the city looked like, only the bright blue ocean. After so many years obsessing over this place, I would finally start to learn its secrets. As soon as we left the apartment, I was going to start collecting as much information as I could about every demon in the city, scouring the place for signs of someone with a five-pointed star on their forehead.

When I'd washed myself completely, I rose from the bath and grabbed a soft white towel off the rack. I dried myself off, then pulled on a black bathrobe. It was quite clearly not Orion's, as it was black silk with sheer lace sleeves and a slit up the thigh. In fact, the tag was still on it. It was *La Perla*—fifteen hundred dollars.

Holy *shit*. Morgan had expensive taste. I yanked the tag off as I adjusted the robe. The silk felt glorious against my bare skin, and I tied the belt around my waist.

I was so stunned by the luxury that I suddenly realized I hadn't seen the robe arrive. My skin prickled with heat as I wondered if Orion had seen me bathing, and I swept through his guest room into the marble stairwell. When I crossed back into his living room, I found Shai there, bandaging her palm. She looked so refreshingly normal in overalls and braids, and it was a relief to see her.

Orion was simply staring at his own hand, watching as it healed before my eyes.

I grinned. "Shai!"

She beamed at me. "Guess what?"

Wrapped in the silky bathrobe, I dropped down into a cream-colored armchair. "Please tell me bargained for something good, because he has nearly unlimited money."

"All my expenses at Belial are covered for as long as I want to learn, which might be for the rest of my life."

She *was* good at bargaining.

Orion met her gaze. "And you do understand that the blood oath means you will die a horrible death by magic if you talk to anyone about Rowan's real identity? I mean *anyone* besides us."

She wrinkled her nose. "Yeah. Got it. I won't let anyone know she's human or that I know her. And I honestly have no idea what all this is about, so I couldn't let any other secrets out, even if I wanted to."

"Best if you know as little as possible." His eyes gleamed. "For your own sake."

She gave me a tentative smile. "I have to run to my feline healing class. But text me if you can, okay? I want to know everything's fine with...whatever you're doing here."

"I'll be fine," I said with much more confidence than I felt.

As she hurried out the door, Orion leaned back on the sofa. He was a prick, but with the cut of his cashmere sweater, it was hard not to notice how gloriously strong his body looked.

"We have a week," he began, "to prepare you for your introduction to the king. Then you will take up residence in the Asmodean Ward."

I took a deep breath. "Just a week? Will I be ready?"

"The city is already abuzz with the news of the one remaining succubus. The king demanded an introduction this evening. I had to negotiate." He frowned. "But we'll have a lot of work to do if you plan to fool them."

When I crossed my legs, one bare thigh came into view from under my robe, and Orion's gaze slid to it. The feel of my thighs rubbing against each other was also my reminder that I still wasn't wearing underwear, which made me think about how Orion had perhaps seen me naked. And *that* reminded of the disturbingly pleasurable feel of Orion's mouth on my neck, and how my body had responded to him dominating me. With those thoughts roiling in my mind, my pulse raced. I tugged down the silky bathrobe over my thigh, hoping that he couldn't hear my pounding pulse.

He arched an eyebrow at me. "Why is your heart racing like you're about to die?"

Well, there went that hope.

I pulled the robe tight. "Did you see me naked in the bathtub?"

His body was so still that I could feel the hair raising on my nape. Beautiful as he was, these eerie differences in body language marked him out as a predator. "Your heart races when you think of me seeing you naked?"

His implication was bang on, but I rolled my eyes anyway. "You don't need to phrase it like that. I was just annoyed, that's all. Do you know that being annoyed can make your heart race? It's the raised cortisol levels. Anger."

A reminder to yourself, Rowan: he is a different species with fangs, lethal magic, and eyes that turn black. Do not forget.

"Well, you needn't be annoyed," he said quietly. "Morgan dropped the bathrobe off for you, plus several bags of clothes in the guest room. I'm deeply aware of how uptight mortals are with their bodies. I was alive during the Puritan days. But as Morgan is not interested in females, I thought it was fine for him to enter the bathroom."

I resisted the temptation to argue that I wasn't uptight because, truth be told, I *was*. And I was especially uptight around Orion because he made me want to open my robe in front of him.

I frowned and tried to change the subject. "You were alive during the Puritan days? I thought you weren't from this region."

A wry smile. "There were Puritans in England, too. I knew one named Praisegod Barebones who led their parliament. In fact, when I first met you, your outfit reminded me of his clothing."

"Goth-Puritan is my look," I said defensively, still clutching the robe closed.

"You're looking very flushed."

I cleared my throat. "It's hot in here."

"Morgan will return soon with the rest of your new clothes. Mortana always dressed beautifully."

I was still holding my bathrobe together as if I'd burst into flame if he saw an extra inch of my skin. "Okay. I guess I need to start learning as much as I can about Mortana and this world."

"You will need to learn to appear less uptight, or you'll end up thrown into a fire. She is a *succubus*."

I raised my chin. "I'll do fine." I mean, I had to. "Will I get to see the city itself today?"

"As soon as you're dressed. But for now, I'll start with the background of the City of Thorns. What do you know?"

I closed my eyes, trying to remember my history lessons. "The city gates were erected after the Infernal War in the 1680s, when the Puritans and the demons tried to murder each other in the Massachusetts woods. I always thought the point of the gates was to keep the demons in, but apparently, you can leave."

A hot breeze flowed into the room from the open balcony windows. "King Nergal negotiated the terms when he lost the war. Demons can briefly leave the city, but our magic fades after a few days. We become vulnerable if we live outside the city. Weak, slow-moving, and dull. No better than mortals, really." There it was—a sharp little barb delivered in a velvety tone.

My lip curled. "Do you have to keep putting in the digs? It might get in the way of our professional relationship."

"You need to understand how we think. We view ourselves as superior to mortals because—" He lifted a finger to his lips like he was thinking. "Oh, because we are. Demons are smarter, faster, and more graceful. For thousands of years, you worshipped us as gods. Sacrificed to us. Livestock, sometimes even your children. We're basically divine. Even the tedious American demons are superior to mortals."

I cocked my head. "And yet, here you all are, locked up behind city walls because you lost a war to us. Quite the conundrum."

The corner of his mouth twitched. "I'll admit that mortals have impressive military technology, which has made it harder to compete. They developed guns and learned magic they could use to bind us here. But mostly, there are simply more of you since you reproduce like mosquitos." He gave me a charming smile. "You infest the planet with your shrieking, yogurt-guzzling offspring, taking up more and more space every year and driving out all the other species like a plague of locusts."

I narrowed my eyes. "I'm fascinated that you all could lose a war to us so thoroughly, surrender so completely, and still convince yourselves of your superiority." I smiled back at him. "Have you heard the term 'cognitive dissonance'?"

"In a one-on-one fight without weapons, a demon would win every time. Do you have any idea how easy it would be for me to kill you?"

My smile faded. "Well, we have weapons now," I said sharply.

He arched an eyebrow, and he leaned closer. "Except you sense it, too. No mortal man has ever sexually satisfied you. Whenever I'm near you, you can feel my superiority to your men. You said I'm the only man you'd ever suspected was up to the task." His silky voice was like a sinful caress over my skin. Now, he'd moved close enough that his mouth was next to my ear. "And I do think you're right about that, Rowan."

A forbidden heat shivered through my body, and my thighs clenched under my bathrobe.

Oh, fuck.

As long as I was near Orion, I was in trouble.

CITY OF THORNS

❧ 13 ❧

I couldn't tell if he was hitting on me or trying to get a rise out of me. But if he was flirting, it was with the utmost condescension, so I wasn't going to reciprocate. The man's sense of superiority burned hot enough to suck the oxygen out of the room.

"Do you know the mortal expression 'beer goggles'? I had that when I first saw you, except with mojitos." I wondered if he could tell when I was lying. "You do nothing for me. Now that I'm sober, I view you as a kind of grotesque alien species. Freakish, really."

He leaned back, then went very still again, staring at me, and I felt like he was using one of Dr. Omer's tricks—waiting for me to admit that I'd said something stupid. His face was a mask of indifference.

Well, he could wait all day, because I could live with my obvious lies. I raised my eyebrows. "Were you going to teach me about something beyond the staggering dimensions of your ego?"

He spread out his arms over the back of the sofa, ignoring my jab. "Let's begin with the Lilu, the incubi and succubi. They are the lust demons, the seducers of our world. They feed off desire. Before demons were locked here in the City of Thorns, the Lilu would roam freely among the Puritan cities, seducing uptight mortals. They seduced demons, too. But for a mortal, sex with a Lilu means death. It was one of the major reasons for the war in the 1680s, the lusty Puritans dying of pleasure in their beds."

What a way to go. "So Mortana—wherever she is—would be trying to seduce mortals at any chance she got?"

He shook his head. "Mostly demons these days. We're no longer allowed to kill mortals without repercussions. She can draw power from demons just as easily without starting a war."

I still gripped my bathrobe like a chastity belt. "So I need to seem seductive."

"Flirtatious. Sensual. Seductive. Comfortable in your own body." He pinned me with his gaze. "Clearly, we will have to work on those things."

"When were the Lilu executed? After the war?"

He shook his head. "Not right away. For about ten years, they lived in the Asmodean Ward. Each ward worships a demonic god, and for the Lilu, it was Asmodeus, god of lust."

"Which ward are we in now?"

"Luciferian. He is the god of pride."

So Orion lived in the ward for the most arrogant demons. "Yeah, that checks out."

"In a densely populated city, it was harder for the other demons to tolerate the Lilu. They ruined marriages, manipulated people. Other demon females loathed the succubi, and demon males hated the incubi. Their mind control powers were forbidden, but they used them anyway. And that was a threat to King Nergal's rule over the populace. What if they controlled his mind? So in the 1690s, when Cotton Mather asked for sacrifices from the City of Thorns, King Nergal was happy to oblige. The other demons were happy to rid the city of the Lilu, and Nergal sacrificed them in the dungeons. They were hanged and their hearts cut out."

A shudder rippled over me. I'd just *been* in that dungeon, not realizing it was a place of unimaginable horror. "And Mortana was able to survive because of her blood oath."

"Exactly. She's always been impressively cunning. But she disappeared a few hundred years ago, and no one has seen her since."

I bit my lip. "Is it going to be a problem that I don't actually have any magic? I can't control anyone's mind."

He shook his head. "No, you'll just tell people you had a change of heart over the centuries. You won't do anything forbidden by King Cambriel. But the sexual magic...you'll need to make people think that you've been feeding off desire."

I closed my eyes and shook my head. "Sorry, exactly how do I do that?"

"That's simple, Rowan." His low, husky voice dripped with a seductive promise. "You and I will use our body language to make people think we're fucking." He quirked a smile. "Assuming you can feign attraction to a grotesque alien species."

I folded my arms in front of my chest. "I'll do my best to fake it, but if I'm supposed to be getting close to the king, won't it be a problem if he thinks I'm with you?"

He shook his head. "Not at all. Cambriel always wants what someone else has."

"I suppose that's why he killed his own father."

"He's from the Beelzebean Line. Envy. He already envies the attention I've received for killing so many in the Infernal Trial. And if you seem to want me, he'll use his position as king to take you. We'll just have to make it look real."

A hot electrical tension buzzed in the air. "So you'll be playing along with this charade, too. Pretending to want me."

He shrugged. "I'll do my best to fake it."

"Is there anyone here who knows Mortana well?"

A sly smile. "Everyone *hated* Mortana. They called her the king's whore. Her only ally was Nergal himself. I suspect she left here when he finally grew bored and refused to marry her, and she realized she no longer had a protector."

"Do you feel any empathy for her at all? Maybe she was just trying to survive while her kind was being slaughtered."

His brows knitted like I'd just said something insane. "No. I don't have empathy. And if I did, it certainly wouldn't be for Mortana."

"Right."

The door opened, and I turned to see Morgan striding into the room with bulging bags of clothes. He looked between the two of us nervously and dropped the loot. "Everything you need is in here. I have to run, I'm afraid." He backed away, staring at me. "Please be careful with her, sir, would you? No offense, darling," he added, glancing at me, "but I don't want you twisting his mind all up."

No one had ever been scared of me before. Was it...was it bad that I liked it? He saw me as fearsome.

I dropped the grip on my bathrobe and glared at him, then flashed a smug smile—the kind Orion had been giving me since I'd met him. "I'll try to be gentle with him, Morgan, but I make no promises." My voice sounded icy, cruel.

His face paled, and he pointed at me as if to say, *I'm watching you.* With that, he backed out the door, then let it slam behind him.

I turned to see Orion staring at me, his eyes a pale, heavenly blue. "That was disturbingly convincing. It was like I was watching the real Mortana come to life before me."

The thing was, it was easy to act in the ways that were expected of you. When people thought I was crazy during my presentation, I became flustered and desperate—I started to act crazy. When I was treated like an outcast at Osborn High, I couldn't help acting weird.

And if people thought I was terrifying—maybe I could rise to the occasion.

But instead of explaining all that, I just shrugged and said, "I contain multitudes."

His gaze pierced me, and he waited for me to give a better explanation.

I sighed, and my mind started turning academic, as it often did when I was unnerved. "In the world of social psychology, there's something called a self-fulfilling prophecy, or a behavioral confirmation. It means that people's behavior changes depending on what's expected of them. A person's expectations actually elicit certain behaviors."

"Right..." He ran his finger over his lower lip, studying me. "You're a bit of a nerd, you know that?"

I nodded. "Oh, believe me, I'm aware."

"Does this mean that if I treat you as if you're seductive, you'll suddenly be able to act like a succubus?"

I swallowed hard. "Well, we can certainly try."

I lay naked on the bed in Orion's guest room. While I was supposed to be practicing *not* being self-conscious, even alone, I felt deeply uncomfortable as the breeze rushed over my bare skin. The fact that it was dark outside and I was lying beneath a ceiling fixture that glowed like a spotlight wasn't helping my mood.

I'd be staying here for another week, in a guest room overlooking the sea. While the place was gorgeous, between a floor-to-ceiling window and the *missing* wall beside it—shielded from rain by a balcony, but still a nasty spot to trip—the room seemed to lack a certain degree of privacy. I didn't *see* anyone out in the ocean, but I still felt like I was naked in front of the world.

Plus, I couldn't help but wonder if Orion was thinking of me naked in here. We'd spent the day trying to work on my seduction skills—the walk, the flirt, the eyes that flicked down and up again, the dirty jokes.

I was shit at all of it. Problem was, Orion was hot as hell. If I let myself fall under his seductive spell, I'd burn up. When his fingers had brushed against mine at breakfast as we'd reached for the cream, I'd felt an indecent jolt of excitement. Unfortunately, I was a blusher, and as succubi did not *blush*, Orion had come to the conclusion that I was uptight and uncomfortable in my body. Hence, I was lying here, trying to get comfortable.

And it was true that I was uptight, but my unease was far worse around *him*. He was as dangerous as a forest fire.

When I closed my eyes, I could see his sensual, curved lips.

I glanced at the sea in the moonlight and pulled the blanket over myself, wondering if I could actually pose as a succubus.

With a deep breath, I surveyed the room, trying to ground myself. I needed to get out of my own head.

The decorations in here were simple—a white bed, a bare hardwood floor. The beauty of the place wasn't in the decor, but rather in the blue of the sea and sky, or the glittering of the stars. A warm, briny breeze rushed over the room. Feeling slightly less self-conscious with the beauty of nature all around me, I dropped the blanket and rose to my knees.

Except I could hear Orion's deep, seductive words playing in my mind. *You said I'm the only man you'd ever suspected was up to the task. And I do think you're right about that, Rowan.*

My eyes snapped open again, and I ran to the light switch. Darkness fell, and I crawled into bed and pulled the covers over myself.

Maybe I couldn't lie around in the nude, but I could sleep naked.

৩৫৩

"How did you sleep?" Orion asked me over coffee.

He had a book spread out before him, and his eyes were on the pages.

I cleared my throat. I didn't want to tell him about the filthy dream I'd had in which he'd kept me as his prisoner, tied to his bed. "Fine. I slept fine."

His gaze darted up to meet mine. "Why did you say it like that?"

"Like what?"

A smile tugged at the corner of his lips. "Like you wanted to climb over the table and throttle me."

Damn it. He could see right through me. I could feel myself blushing, and I shook my head. "There's nothing wrong. I slept fine, just had some weird dreams."

"About what?"

You, kissing me all over. "Just, um, monsters. What are you reading?" I took a sip of my coffee.

Orion's eyes gleamed, and he lifted the book so I could see the cover.

Fifty Shades of Grey.

I choked and spat out my coffee, then wiped the back of my hand across my mouth.

❦

HE SAT ACROSS FROM ME IN HIS LIVING ROOM, ARMS FOLDED. I WAS getting the impression that he was losing patience. "You meet the king tomorrow, and your body is still full of tension and nerves. Do you see how you grimace when you're nervous? How your neck muscles are tight and strained?"

I sighed, trying to focus on relaxing the muscles around my mouth. I took a deep breath. I couldn't help but wonder where Orion had spent the last two nights, and where he'd been at dinner.

"Let's see the Mortana walk you've been practicing," he said.

I rose from the chair.

It wasn't any of my business where he went when he wasn't here. But I'd been learning his patterns—a very early wakeup, as soon as dawn broke. Coffee, fruit in the mornings. Sometimes he dove off his balcony straight into the sea for a morning swim. He spent half the day trying to teach me how to act like Mortana—how she spoke, how she held herself, the kind of jokes she'd make. One afternoon, he'd told me to swim naked by myself, and I was supposed to think about how it felt to undulate under the water, how beautiful I was.

The other half of the time, he'd leave me by myself. I ate all my meals, delivered by Morgan, alone on his balcony. Once I'd eaten, I'd pull out Orion's smutty romance novels. The books that filled his shelves ranged from literary classics and Greek epic poems to full-blown modern fuck-fests with whips and spanking and lots of mind-shattering orgasms. Which, let's face it, couldn't be that good in real life. In the interest of learning, I chose the fuck-fest books to read over my dinners of scallops or salmon. And they were educational.

I did wonder, though—who was he eating with when he wasn't with me? And where was he sleeping?

Not that it was my business.

From the sofa, he arched an eyebrow. "You don't seem like you're focusing."

I straightened the way he'd taught me, then flicked my hair over my shoulder. I curled my lips in a smug smile.

He cocked his head. "Good. You've got the facial expression."

"I'm mimicking that smug 'I think I'm better than everyone' facial expression you always have."

He shrugged. "And now you need to believe it, too. You need to believe that you're the most beautiful person in the city, that others are privileged to be around you. That's what Mortana would think, that she blessed others with her presence. That she's a gift to the world."

I lifted my chin a little higher, just as Mortana would. *A gift to the world.*

"Let me see how you walk. This time, try keeping your footsteps in a single line, like a cat. Shoulders back, hips forward."

I straightened my back and lengthened my neck, and then I started to move the way he'd told me to, one foot directly in front of the other. I found that my hips swayed as I walked, and I strutted around the room in my new little black sundress. I could feel his eyes on me, watching the way I moved—or rather, the way Mortana moved.

"Shoulders back," he said quietly. "You need to look and act like you're thinking about sex at all times."

I pivoted, walking across the room again.

With his instructions, I found myself walking like a total sexpot—tits out, hips swaying from side to side. Maybe I was uncomfortable in my body, but Mortana was not. Mortana had done all the things I read about in those books—fucking men against walls, dragging her nails down their backs, biting the headboard while someone banged her from behind.

I twirled, thinking of how Mortana would feel swimming naked in the sea, or how she would feel with Orion watching her. Mortana would want his eyes all over her naked body. She'd get turned on, and she'd want him to know exactly how turned on she was. She'd want to torture him, tease him.

I spun again and decided that Mortana wanted to sit in Orion's lap. So I did that, wrapped my legs around his waist, my hem riding up to my hips. Instantly, his eyes turned dark as night. With a low, appreciative growl, his hand moved from my lower back all the way up to my hair. He threaded his fingers into my curls, pulling my head back a little. "Good girl," he said quietly. "Very good." His low voice rumbled over my skin.

But this was going too far, wasn't it?

I cleared my throat and jumped up from his lap, smoothing out my dress, tugging down the hem. "There." I exhaled slowly. "See? I can be Mortana. I don't have to do it all the time."

Orion's eyes were still pinned on me, filled with primal shadows. "Of course not."

Tomorrow night, I would meet the king, and that should be the scariest thing in my life right now. But truthfully, what scared me most was Orion.

❧ 15 ❧

T oday was D-Day.

I wasn't actually clear what the D stood for in the World War II version, but for me, it stood for *demon*, and possibly *disaster*. It was the day I'd be entering the demon world for real, leaving the safety of Orion's apartment. Most terrifying of all, it was the day I'd meet the demon king who'd severed his father's head and stuck it on a gate.

What kind of outfit did one wear for an introduction to a regicidal, patricidal demon king?

I frowned at my new underwear, which looked barely large enough to cover my nipples and ass. But I was, after all, a succubus now. Might as well get used to it. And with a little jolt of satisfaction, I realized I was actually quite comfortable standing stark naked in this glass-walled room.

Among the dresses, there were some more casual clothes, too. Black leather leggings, sleek pantsuits, little skirts and tops. But Orion had suggested that for my grand entrance back into the city today, I was supposed to dazzle people. Apparently, all eyes would be on me.

I plucked a camisole from the bed, one with sheer black lace and embroidered snakes. Its neckline plunged below the breasts at the center. Dark, sexy, demonic. I slid it on, and just as I'd expected, it barely covered my nipples.

I picked up the tiny matching panties and slipped into them.

Then I scanned the dresses. Lots of black, gray, gold. All of them were revealing in some way—tight bodices, slits all the way up to the hips, plunging backlines, short hemlines. First, I picked up a pale silver gown in a Grecian style, with a high waistline and delicate crisscrossing ropes around it. But the neckline went right down to the waist, and I wasn't sure I was ready for that.

Instead, I chose a short, silky red dress with a fitted top and long sleeves, and I wriggled it over my hips. It had a looser skirt, but the fact that the hem stopped just below my ass was definitely new to me. Then I slipped into a pair of thigh-high boots, which had small enough heels that I should be able to walk in them reasonably well.

When I turned to look at myself, I had to admit I looked hot as hell. With the boots on, I only had a small amount of skin showing— the tops of my thighs and my décolletage. And yet, somehow, this was a much sexier look than I was used to. My hair had dried, and it hung in waves over my shoulders, orange on red. It wasn't a *bad* look, I thought.

Fully dressed, I pulled open the door to the living room. Orion was still sitting on the sofa, leaning back with his arms unfolded over the sofa. And he was still as death, eyes burning like stars as he took me in.

Inhaling, I crossed closer to him. He slowly stood, his gaze boring into me. Dark magic whipped the air around him, and a low growl rumbled from his throat and skimmed over my body. I wondered if he was thinking of when I'd straddled him yesterday.

Then a wicked smile ghosted over his lips. "Good. You look like a succubus. Let's just see you move like Mortana one last time. I know you have confidence in your body in some ways. You can land a punch —I saw you take on those mortal fucks." His eyes had an otherworldly silver sheen. "That man who cornered you outside the brewery—was his name Jack Corwin?"

I'd forgotten how much he knew about me, as I'd spilled nearly all my secrets. "That was him."

"After everything he did to you, why would you tell me to stop hurting him? When I was twisting his mind with pain?"

He was doing that dominating demon stare that made me want to submissively drop my gaze. But I held his stare because Mortana would hold it. "I'm a normal person who doesn't want to watch someone's brain melt on the street. It's that thing called empathy. Even when you hate someone, you don't enjoy seeing them tortured."

"Empathy?" His eyes looked icy, cruel. "Sounds tedious. I'm glad I was never cursed with it."

"Exactly how many people have you killed in your life?"

He moved around to my side. "I'd love to tell you about each one just to see the horror cross your pretty face, but we have only a few hours left to work on your hunched posture."

I frowned. "Did you say *hunched?*"

"We'll try one last thing. I'm going to trace my finger up your spine, and as I do, I want you to straighten your back along with it. Lean into it, square your shoulders."

Already, I could feel the power of his magic tingling over my skin. When he touched my lower back, I nearly gasped at the pleasurable sensation. Just the feel of his fingertip on my back, through my dress, was like a hot, electric vibration through my body.

"Close your eyes. Let your shoulders relax and fall back. Imagine a thread pulling the top of your head toward the ceiling." With exquisite slowness, he stroked upward. My body responded to his touch, spine straightening, pulse speeding, and skin burning.

Holy moly, Rowan. Remember, this is just a job. And the bit about him being a demon. And also the bit about how he threatened to murder Shai.

As his finger brushed my nape, my neck lengthened. Then, with a touch light as a feather, his finger grazed back down again, and heat radiated from every point of contact. He let it rest between my shoulder blades. "Lift your chest. Raise your chin. You're proud of your beauty. It's part of your power."

My breath sped up, and I felt him move behind me, his hands going to my hips. I fought the insane impulse to lean back into his powerful body.

"Move your hips forward a little," he said quietly. "Open your eyes now."

I opened my eyes, already feeling different with my new posture.

"Perfect."

With graceful movements, he crossed in front of me. His beauty was deeply and unfortunately distracting. His gaze flicked to my mouth, and with a jolt of embarrassment, I realized I'd been licking my lips. A blush crept over my cheeks.

He cocked his head, his cheek dimpling with a sly smile.

I actually felt *sexy* for once. And now, I liked thinking of his eyes on me, on the naked tops of my thighs...in fact, I had the most inconvenient desire to show him my whole body.

I strutted across the room, swaying my hips like he'd showed me a million times, one foot in front of the other.

"Good," he murmured. "Now turn to face me."

I spun around, my curls bouncing. His stance was casual, hands in his pockets, shoulders relaxed. But something about the way his eyes burned, the way his jaw looked tight, told me that he wasn't actually calm at all. What was going on beneath that calm, easy exterior? Rage? Lust? Still trying to stop himself from ripping out my heart?

And where had he slept last night?

Whatever the case was, he was looking at me like he wanted to devour me.

"What next?" I asked.

"Now, when you walk back to me, try pretending a droplet of water is slowly moving from your neck down between your breasts. Trace it with your fingertip."

I started walking again, like a cat, and I moved my fingertip from my throat, down my chest. It was just like martial arts, wasn't it? Figuring out how to move my body in the right way.

I stopped when I could feel his hot magic skimming over me. Getting closer than I was now, looking into his eyes, felt like it would be too intense.

He raised his eyebrows. "Very good," he purred. "You need to always communicate through body language that you want to fuck someone. You make it clear through innuendo, eye contact, and touch."

I tossed my hair behind my shoulder.

"That was cute, but for starters, you have to stand closer than three feet. You know, like you did yesterday."

I swallowed hard, then walked closer to him. I stared up at him, imagining how it would feel to have his hands all over my body. *Just a job, Rowan. This is just a job.*

Amusement glinted in his eyes. "Now you'll need to lose the deer-in-the-headlights expression. Try a half-smile, an arched eyebrow."

I contorted my face on one side.

He grimaced. "Oh, no. Don't do that. Remember, you are a gift."

I let my face relax, then tried the smug expression.

His gaze brushed down my body. "Closer. Show vulnerability. Tilt your head back to show me your neck, like you're allowing me to bite you again, like you're inviting it."

This close to him, his sensual power was washing over me like a wave. I found myself staring into his endless eyes, my pulse racing. My nipples pebbled under the silky camisole. What I really wanted was for him to bend me over, pull down my panties, and stroke me—

Stop it, Rowan. He's not even human.

I knew what was happening. My id was taking over—the stupid, animalistic part of my brain that would fuck everything up for me if I let it. But maybe my id was what I needed here.

"Good," he said quietly. "You've got the eye contact down, now try using your sense of touch a little as you talk to me."

I reached out and touched his chest. I bit my lip as I traced my fingertips over the soft material, feeling the hard muscle beneath.

"You forgot to talk," he said quietly.

Ah. That was because my mind had gone totally blank.

He was *very* convincing at looking at me like he wanted to rip my dress off, but that was the job, wasn't it? He'd said that he'd try *acting* like I was sexy.

He reached for my arms and lifted them up, wrapping them around his neck so my body was pressed against his. As I reached up, my short hem rose behind me, and the warm breeze rushed over my upper thighs and the bottom of my ass.

Heat swept through my body. This was flirting? This felt positively indecent, and a hot pulse beat through my core. Looking into his eyes, I felt like I was going to plummet into a dangerous abyss.

My muscles clenched.

Demonic killer. Back away now, Rowan.

I pulled my arms from his throat, my jaw clenching, and looked away. My heart was pounding out of control, which was unfortunate, because now I knew he could hear it. "Okay, enough of that." I swallowed hard. "I think I've proven that I can put on the Mortana act." I plastered a smile on my face. "Why don't you show me around the city?"

"You'll need to stop blushing first."

I smoothed out my hair. "Fine."

"Have you memorized the map?"

I nodded. "I think so."

"Just remember that if you drop the Mortana act by accident," he cautioned, "you will end up in a pit of fire."

"Great way to help me relax."

But underneath the nerves and the fear, I was actually thrilled. Today, for the first time—after all these years—I was finally going to get a look inside the City of Thorns.

I was going to find my mom's killer.

O rion had led me into what I'd thought was a closet, but was actually an elevator. While we rode it down, I kept studying the map.

"You have to put that away when we get to the bottom."

"I know." I'd drawn the gates of the city so many times, but I'd never imagined what was inside it. This was forbidden information and deeply fascinating.

The map showed that the city was divided into seven sections— eight if you included the Elysian Wilderness, south of the Acheron River.

The Luciferian Ward—and the Leviathan Hotel, where Orion lived —were right on the eastern side overlooking the ocean. South of Luciferian was the royal Beelzebub Ward, and the great Tower of Baal where the king lived. Once I had the king's approval, I'd be staying in the Asmodean Ward—west of here, on the river. It was the smallest ward, and I suspected it had grown smaller over the years as the neighboring wards encroached on it.

Curiosity burned bright in me. I wanted to see everything—the old prison, the ancient demon temples, the demon bank. This place not only contained my mom's killer, but it was *magical*.

When we reached the ground floor, the elevator opened into a lobby, and I shoved the map into my new red handbag, next to my new phone.

I stepped into the bright sunlight of the lobby. From above, sunlight poured through a dome of windows like a Victorian greenhouse. The floors were ivory marble, designed with black tiles in an Art Deco style. Sweeping stairs led up to a mezzanine, with a black railing that somehow looked like sexy lace.

I'd never actually been in a place like this before, and I had to remember to keep my jaw closed and not look awed by the grandeur. Mortana would not be impressed by this place. She'd be bored by all of this. So I pulled my eyes away from the beauty of the building, and I focused on my catlike walk, on my swaying hips.

On the way to the door, we passed a handful of people, who gaped at me. Two gorgeous demon women with red eyes and curved ivory horns—one blonde, the other with raven hair—huddled together and whispered as I crossed to the door. I had the feeling that word had already gotten around, and I gave them a confident smile.

That's right, demons. The succubus bitch is back.

Orion pushed through the large glass door, then held it for me. With swaying hips, I found myself stepping outside into a city of golden stone. In the sun, the world gleamed around me, and my breath caught at its beauty.

With its narrow streets—clearly made in a time before cars—the city looked medieval. The hotel opened up onto a piazza of sorts, where cafés and shops lined a large stone courtyard. Arched passages jutted off from the square. In the center of the square, the stones formed a geometric shape sort of like an upside-down isosceles triangle, with lines curving off it and a *V* on the bottom.

Orion gestured at the symbol. "As you can see, Mortana, the Luciferian Ward is unchanged, and Lucifer's great symbol remains."

I sighed. "Delightful."

Now the real question was, did one of the squares contain a star symbol? And which of these fuckers burned my mom alive using fire magic?

When I surveyed the square, I realized all eyes were fixed in my direction. A shiver of dread rippled over me, but Mortana wouldn't look overwhelmed. Mortana would loop her arm around Orion's and smile smugly—the same kind of wry little curl of lips that Orion had been displaying since I'd met him. So I did just that.

With his body close to mine, his warm magic radiated over me, soothing and seductive at the same time.

Arm in arm, we crossed into one of the arched passages. In here, where it was empty, Orion leaned down and whispered. "I don't think people are thrilled about your return."

"Just the succubus issue?" I whispered back.

"That's part of it. And also, you're with me. The king and I are now the two wealthiest bachelors in the city, and the unmarried demon females have been competing for our attention. Infernal debutantes presented at court in a series of balls and soirées, each of them hoping to become a queen or duchess. Demon females wait years, centuries even, hoping to find the most advantageous match they can."

I looked up at him. "Why aren't you married?"

"I don't see any reason to marry."

"And the king?" I asked. "He's centuries old. Why marry now?"

Orion shrugged. "Before, he could fuck every woman in the city, and he probably has. No one had a claim to him. But a king is expected to marry, so he must choose a wife."

We walked through a series of narrow streets and stone stairwells, past shops and hotels. We swept past a round library belonging to Belial University.

Orion quietly explained to me that in the ancient days, Lucifer— the shining one—was the supreme demon god. Even now, Lucifer's power permeated the city. The temples were mostly abandoned, but some demons still left offerings to the old gods.

"Do you believe in them?" I whispered.

He glanced at me. "I don't know, but I don't really give a fuck if they're real or not."

Ah, of course. His arrogance knew no bounds—not even when it came to his gods.

In the Mammon Ward, we stopped for lunch at a restaurant by one of the river's tributaries, the Erebus Stream. It burbled past us, gleaming in the sun. We sat by a pedestrianized road of amber stone, and I watched the demons stride past in their designer clothes, some of them with metallic horns that sparkled in the afternoon sunlight.

Far across the square, the Bank of Thorns loomed over a square, with towering columns that made it look like an ancient temple. Black brambles grew over the stone.

A few mortals walked past, dressed casually in Belial University sweatshirts and leggings. They moved differently from demons, and their expressions were unguarded, in awe at the beautiful world around them. By contrast, every demon stood out to me as a predator, gliding along with lethal grace. The demons kept their features calm at all times.

None of them bore the star I was looking for.

I leaned back in my chair to sip the red wine Orion had ordered for us. I was no wine expert, but this was *amazing*. I let the dry flavor roll over my tongue, then swallowed. "Delicious."

He returned my smile. "Claret from grapes in the fields of Elysium. One of my favorites."

The waitress returned, staring almost exclusively at Orion. And who could blame her? The woman had functioning eyes, and he looked like a god. Her cheeks flushed as she took his order, and she flicked her long brown hair over her shoulder.

With a smirk, he said, "I'll have the duck breast."

I was pretty sure she actually *gasped* at the word breast. She bit her lip and cocked her head, as if he'd just suggested spanking her. "Yeah?" she said. "Is that all you want?"

Orion had said flirting was all about making it clear you wanted to fuck someone, and this chick was a goddamn expert. Frankly, she'd be much better than me at the succubus role.

I had to admit, I found it a bit irritating. For one thing, I was starving, and she still hadn't taken my order. For another, what if this were actually a real date? I mean it wasn't, obviously. I had no reason to be jealous, so I wasn't.

But *she* didn't know that.

The real question was how Mortana would handle this situation. Personally, I thought she'd be fucking pissed. Mortana liked being the center of attention, and she wasn't getting any right now. Nor did I think she would tolerate this kind of disrespect.

I cleared my throat. When the waitress finally turned to look at me, I narrowed my eyes at her and made my body go as still as possible. Having just experienced this a few times from Orion, I knew how unnerving it was. Plus, this was basically a bitchier version of Dr. Omer's *I'll sit in silence until you realize what you've done* technique.

I watched her rosy cheeks go pale, and then I slowly tapped my fingernails on the table. "Are you quite done with that little display?" My voice came out sounding cold and distant.

"Sorry," she stammered. "I was just taking his order."

"Oh, I don't think so, mortal." I chuckled. "But you know, your desire does give me strength." Never in my life had I sounded so imperious. To tell the truth, I wasn't entirely sure where this was coming from. "Your lust is making me positively ravenous."

I watched her throat bob as she swallowed. "Did you want lunch?"

Orion was picking up the tab, so I might as well get something expensive. "Lobster Fra Diavolo." An appropriate name when I thought about it. "I'm feeling a bit devilish." I bared my teeth. "And if that doesn't satisfy me, I'll need to feed on something fresher, so you'd best tell the chef to make sure it's good."

She stumbled back from me, then turned to hurry to the kitchen.

Shit. Was that what my id was like under all my repression? Did I have an evil side?

When I turned back to Orion, he was studying me closely. "Mortana, you really haven't changed at all."

I leaned closer to him and whispered in his ear, "I like being back."

He raised his wine to me in a toast. "To the most malignant, evil demon to ever grace this city."

Every time I looked around, I realized people were craning their necks, trying to listen in.

I sighed, looking out across the Acheron River to the south bank. "The Elysian Fields. I do remember them fondly. Is it true that during your Infernal Rite, you slaughtered fifty demons?"

He twirled the stem of his wineglass between his fingertips, and the crimson liquid glinted in the sunlight. "Well, I don't like to brag—"

"Liar."

Amusement curled his lips. "Fine. I love to brag. Yes, I killed fifty demons. And yes, I think the others find me terrifying."

Did the king find him terrifying, too?

I sighed, trying to get into my role. "It's been so long since I've seen King Nergal."

"Don't worry." He flashed me a dazzling smile. "You will see *his head* soon. But now you have unwavering loyalty to the new king, don't you? You know how it is here. *Vae Victis.*"

Woe to the vanquished. Expect brutal treatment at the hands of the victors. Another reminder that I couldn't fall into enemy hands here.

I lifted my wineglass, smiling, and repeated, "Vae Victis."

W hen we finished eating, the tour continued—one ward after another of honey-colored stone. The walls wrapped around the city's borders, punctuated by towers that looked out over Osborne.

I was thrilled I'd had the foresight to choose the most comfortable boots, because we walked for miles—through the Belphagor Ward with its Hall of Guilds, and the old Parliament by the river. We saw the haunted prisons in the Sathanas Ward, and the gallows outside where executions took place. A three-headed guard dog snarled at us outside its iron gates. It must have been the magic of the place, but the city was far more enormous than it appeared from the outside.

I noticed that the fashion looked slightly different in each ward. In the Luciferian Ward, there had been a lot of silk dresses and large belts with plunging necklines. In Sathanas, I saw bustiers and men in suits with thin ties.

But the Asmodean Ward was something altogether different. Here, canals flowed through the city instead of roads, and deserted boats floated in turquoise water. The streets were narrow and deserted, occasionally opening up onto squares with faded grandeur. Classical buildings were adorned with columns and tall windows, and the faded stone looked like it had once been painted bright colors. Many of the façades were crumbling, the windows boarded up. An empty fountain stood in the center, carved with statues whose faces had been smashed.

My heart clenched. Sadness permeated the air here like a dark miasma. I felt the loss of this place viscerally.

Across from us stood a palatial building with arched, mullioned windows. A canal flowed on one side of it. Workers were rushing in and out, carrying furniture inside and replacing broken windowpanes.

Orion pointed to it. "There. That's your home for now. No one has lived in the Asmodean Ward in centuries, but they're making sure it's fit for Mortana."

I turned to look behind me, unnerved to find that three female demons had followed us into the abandoned ward. There was nothing for them here—no restaurants, no shops. No one lived here. They were simply watching us, and they didn't seem to care about being subtle.

A tall, brunette demon with sapphire eyes and black horns was glaring at me, arms folded. The look in her eyes was pure wrath, sending shivers through my bones. In her leather shorts and corset, she looked as sexy as she was terrifying. Two blondes flanked the horned one, all of them statuesque. But the most interesting thing about this trio was that the horned one had tattoos of flames on her arms. Did she have fire magic?

I needed to know how common flames were among demons.

Moving closer to Orion, I wrapped my arms around his neck, and I shot a smug smile at the trio. In response, Orion wrapped his hands around my waist. His intense magic sizzled over my body, heating me.

I reached up and pulled his head down closer to my mouth. "Orion," I whispered, "I can see that people want to kill me already. I need to know what their powers are like."

"What do you want to know, love?"

"What about fire magic?" I whispered.

His arm brushed down my back, and he looked over my shoulder. He reached for my hand, then he led me toward a building that looked like an abandoned brick mansion, the windows boarded up with wood. He kicked through the ancient wooden doors into a room of faded marble and dusty tile floors.

I coughed in the stale air. I could see that at one point, this place had been truly stunning. Busts in alcoves lined the hall, carved with flowing hair and crowns. But their faces were smashed, too. A few of the statues had been pushed to the ground and lay shattered on the marble. An old, dusty diary had been forgotten on the floor, as had a moth-eaten cape. Two crystal glasses and a decanter stood on a table. A maroon stain darkened one part of the floor, disturbingly the color of dried blood.

It was hard not to be curious about an abandoned demon mansion, so I peered through one of the doorways to see something that looked like a ballroom, covered in dust and cobwebs. A harpsichord stood in one corner, and more crystal glasses and plates littered the tables. It was like the Lilu who'd once lived here didn't see it coming. Like they'd left mid-meal. It made my heart twist to see it.

"Why was this all left here?" I asked. "If the Lilu are gone, why did no one take over their palace?"

He turned to look at one of the smashed busts, and he traced his fingertips over its rough contours where the face used to be. "Demons are superstitious. When something terrible happens, a place is thought to be cursed. Haunted."

"Do you believe that?"

He shook his head. "No. Haunting requires a soul, and I don't believe we have them."

But for some reason, since we'd come in here, the shadows seemed to thicken as if this place spooked him. Hot magic warmed the air around him.

"Do you think mortals have souls?" I asked.

His eyes slid to mine, his expression distant. "I've never spent any time thinking about mortals. Maybe you have souls. It's honestly difficult to take interest in fragile little creatures that only live for a few years."

I'd *really* have to just get used to his condescension. "Right. Okay. I suppose none of that matters right now."

"You wanted to ask about fire magic." His gaze pinned me. "Why fire magic specifically?"

I shrugged. "There was a demon woman outside with fiery tattoos.

I'd heard a rumor that demons can light people on fire, and I happen to be more than a little terrified of it."

"That's Lydia—Duchess of the Luciferian Ward, House of Shalem. Fire magic is rare. Most of us possess only strength and speed relative to mortals. A few have ice magic. The ability to summon water, or to cause a storm—there are some examples of elemental magic. But fire— only the most powerful can summon fire. Those from a branch of royal lineage. Some say it means you've been touched by Lucifer himself."

Now *this* was the most important thing I'd learned since I'd arrived. "So who's on that exclusive list?"

"The king, Lydia, and Mortana."

And now I had three suspects.

Orion raised his hand, and flames burst from his fingertips like candles. The fire danced in his eyes. "And me."

I stepped back from him, my heart pounding, and the flames disappeared.

He looked at me with curiosity. "You really *are* afraid of fire."

I exhaled slowly. "Yeah. It's a thing I have."

He took a step closer. "You're here with me, working with me. I'll make sure that no one hurts you. Understood?"

Either he was telling the truth or he was a very convincing liar.

He turned, heading back for the door. "Let's go, love. I don't like it in here."

Add Orion to the suspect list, then.

Fuck.

18

We reached our endpoint in the Beelzebub Ward, where we stopped for dinner at a riverside restaurant called Valac's. The setting sun cast dazzling red and orange rays over the river just to our south.

Everything in the royal Beelzebub Ward, where envy ruled, looked as though it were gilded. Sandstone streets, trees that bloomed with yellow flowers, women in metallic dresses, cheekbones highlighted with gold dust. The setting sun washing it all in amber.

Orion had left me on my own to get dinner. He'd said something about wanting to speak to the king before my arrival. And with him still footing the bill, I ordered crab legs with butter and garlic mashed potatoes, along with the most expensive red wine on the menu. I wondered which kind of wine Mortana had used to drown the queen, and frankly, it seemed like a real waste.

The task that lay ahead of me tonight made my stomach churn: charm a king and convince him I was a succubus. Fail, and my best friend would be murdered. And I'd die in a literal fire.

I let out a long breath, scanning the scene around me. From here, I could see the bridge that crossed the Acheron River—the Bridge of Harrowing, according to the map. On the other side of the river, shadows pooled in the darkening woods. A warm breeze rushed from the south, carrying with it the mossy scent of the wild forests.

Nowhere had I seen the star I was looking for, and I desperately wanted to ask about it. I couldn't just bring it up cold, though. Not when Orion himself was a suspect.

In the City of Thorns, I was like an undercover cop.

I'd once watched an old Keanu Reeves movie called *Point Break* where he played a cop infiltrating a gang of surfer bank robbers. He blended in, got to know their culture, and waited for information to come to him. He didn't just start interrogating the other surfers. Only when he got them to trust him did they reveal their secrets.

As I sipped my wine, staring out at the Acheron, I mulled over the horrible but real possibility that Orion was the killer. What if he'd known exactly who I was when he found me in Cirque de la Mer? What if he'd dragged me here under false pretenses to spy on *me* after killing my mom four years ago?

But the theory didn't really hold up. Why would he spy on me? He had lethal magic at his fingertips and zero empathy. He could torture answers out of me if he felt like it.

My heart kicked up a notch as I realized that Lydia, the tattooed woman, was sitting at the table across from me. Her lip curled as she stared back at me, and my blood turned to ice.

I couldn't let her actually see that I looked nervous, though, so I kept my expression bland and gazed at the flowing river.

"Mortana?" Orion's deep voice pulled me from my musings, and I turned to see him. In the sunset, his beautiful face was bathed in rosy hues. "It's time to get ready for your meeting with the king. And I'm afraid tonight might be a more difficult than I'd imagined."

My stomach sank.

❈

ORION AND I APPROACHED THE OUTER GATES OF THE TOWER OF Baal, arm in arm. The palace looked ancient, the outer wall carved with arrow slits. A sandstone path led to an arched gateway. From here, I could just about see the former king's head impaled on the outer gates above the first entryway. My blood turned cold as my heels echoed off the stone.

In the past hour, we'd taken a cab back to Orion's house in the Luciferian Ward, and I'd readied myself. I'd picked out a gorgeous dress—long black lace with a slit up the thigh and a neckline so plunging that a bra wasn't an option. I never wore stuff like this, but Mortana did. And you know what? Mortana looked fucking hot.

While I'd been fixing my hair, Orion had dropped the bomb. There was so much controversy about the return of the succubus, I wouldn't be meeting the king alone. In fact, I'd be meeting a whole council of demons, and they would decide my fate. The whole Infernal Quorum would be in attendance—a duke or duchess from each of the city's wards.

Including Lydia.

And if any of them sensed I was an imposter, I'd be thrown into a pit of fire right there in the Tower of Baal.

As we drew closer to the outermost gate, I considered why the king would need the input of a quorum. He had the ultimate power here. But my guess? He wanted to be able to blame other people if Mortana turned out to be a royal disaster. After all, it was their decision, too, right?

Powerful people—even when they had total control—were great at blaming others.

My heels clacked over the stones, and I tried not to dwell on the flames. It was just that of all the methods of execution, *that* was the one that really scared the shit out of me. But I was doing this for Mom, and now for Shai, so no matter what happened, I had to get it right.

When we got closer, I could see that the old king's head looked remarkably well preserved, with a full head of black hair and his skin still smooth. But his eyes were closed, and his facial muscles looked slack. Torches fixed to the walls cast wavering light over the sandstone walls, and the dancing shadows almost made King Nergal's head look like it was moving, the dead lips gibbering. I let out a long, slow breath.

With my arm looped through Orion's, I leaned in to whisper, "Is this normal for demons? The severed head?"

He looked at me with confusion. "Of course not."

Thank God. So they weren't all sociopaths.

Then he added, "There would be no reason for other demons to keep a severed head above their gate. It's only because he was the former king. It's a reminder to the world that King Nergal was defeated by someone stronger, and that Cambriel is the rightful king. *Vae Victis*, remember?"

"The severed head doesn't bother people who live here?" I whispered. "It's a bit macabre."

He shrugged. "He wasn't very popular."

I found myself staring at Orion, trying to read him. His face showed absolutely nothing, and the head clearly didn't faze him. I wondered if all demons lacked empathy.

In mortal terms, someone with no empathy was called a psychopath. From what I understood, psychopaths had reduced activity in their amygdala, the part of the brain that created anxiety. So psychopaths didn't feel fear as deeply as the rest of us, or any emotions, really. That meant they sometimes went to disturbing lengths to feel things. If they grew up middle class, they could chase a high buying and selling stocks, or go into politics. If they grew up around violence, maybe they'd cut off their dad's head and stick it on a gate.

We crossed through into a stone courtyard, and I realized there was yet another gated wall before we got to the tower. The king had a *lot* of protection. "Orion," I whispered, "do you ever feel fear?"

He frowned. "What would I be afraid of? I could kill nearly anyone."

Oh, dear. "Do you ever feel bad for someone? I'm just trying to understand what kind of people think the decapitated head is a good idea."

His lips curled with a taunting smile. "If you want to understand what kind of people think it's a good idea, you can read your own history. It's where we borrowed the custom from. Mortals were doing the exact same thing when we closed the city gates in the 1600s. The heads of defeated enemies jutted out of Boston Common in the 1670s." He shrugged. "Demon culture simply moves more slowly."

Well, I'll be damned.

He had a good point. Demons and mortals alike were fairly terrible at times.

At the other side of the courtyard, two hulking, muscular demons stood guard before a door carved with a sigil. It almost looked like an insect with long legs, and it must be the symbol of Beelzebub.

The guards' ivory horns curled from their heads, the color matching their pale, waxy skin. They glared at us and clutched their spears. Silvery magic curled off their bodies, and a low growl rumbled over the stones beneath our feet. The sound rose to a sort of deep, morose song that filled the air.

A shudder crawled up my nape at how unfamiliar this was. But I managed to keep my sexy, catlike walk going. My hips swayed. It was the weirdest thing, as I'd never met Mortana. I hardly knew a thing about her. And yet, I felt like I had an intuitive sense of how she thought. Her confidence, her disdain for others, her ability to control a situation. She was like my ruthless shadow-self coming to the surface. My id. She was the primal part of the brain, unburdened by self-consciousness or anxiety. The id was all desire and aggression, and maybe it was kind of fun letting it come to the surface.

When we got to the door, the two guards shifted out of the way. Now, the gates opened into a field of wildflowers in gorgeous fiery hues —amber, pumpkin, cherry red. A stone path carved through the field, leading to a gilded tower of concentric circular floors, which narrowed at the top. Closer to the tower, a red carpet had been laid out for our arrival.

It was the most grandiose thing I'd ever seen, and clearly, it had been built to intimidate. Around the tower, demons milled about in gorgeous ballgowns and suits. It looked like a Met Gala, with outrageous gowns of crystals and metallic colors. There were red dresses with long trains that trailed over the grass, men in pinstripe suits or velvet with enormous sashes. I could have transposed the scene to New York but for the fact that half the attendants had horns.

Tonight was apparently quite the event. Everyone wanted to be here, possibly to watch a succubus roast in a fire.

I stole a glance at Orion, taking care to maintain my placid expression. His silver hair gleamed in the moonlight, and when he turned to look at me, I felt an unwelcome fluttering in my heart. The thing was, I was starting to feel safe with him, like he was my protector. And that was absolutely stupid, considering he was one of my suspects.

And as we drew nearer to the red carpet, I felt all the demons' eyes on me. The crowd started to close in. My heart was fluttering hard, my stomach twisting. I did my best to look bored, even if I was anything but.

In my black gown, I was wearing one of the simplest dresses here, but I thought it made sense. Mortana was a badass bitch with the confidence to show herself off. She wouldn't rely on the clothes to do it. Why give all the attention to the designer when it could be on *her?*

Did I feel her confidence? Fuck, no. But I'd be doing my best to fake it.

The demons stared at us as we climbed up the steps to the tower itself. Two more guards stood at the top of the stairs, and they pulled open the doors.

The first thing I noticed was the pit of fire, flames dancing above it like a portal to hell.

And that's where I'd find myself tonight if I wasn't able to master my fear.

19

The fire pit was set in the center of the hall. Nausea climbed up my throat, and my breath started to grow shallower.

Stay calm. Stay calm. Stay calm.

This would be a *great* time to have my fire-retardant clothing and blankets and gels, although even those things would only last for so long. That pit was eternal.

Panic started to dig its claws deeper into my heart. If I didn't master this worry soon, the jig would be up for sure.

I had to manage my breathing, to keep the breath deep and slow so my body didn't go into panic mode. I was in control of what happened —as long as I could fake it convincingly, I could get out of here with my skin still on my body. I could keep Shai alive, too.

Slowly marshaling a sense of calm, I took in the space around me.

When I'd heard *Tower of Baal* and *demon fire pit*, I hadn't expected the place to look so sleek and modern. It shone with burnished sandy marble. Above us, circular floors reached up to an oculus, through which I could see the moon. And there *was* a fire pit in the center, yes, but there was also a banquet laid out to my right, with civilized canapés and hors d'oeuvres. Behind the banquet, windows overlooked a garden bathed in moonlight. To the left, a pool curved to the side, with a swim-up cocktail bar. Mortal waitresses in short dresses glided around with trays of drinks. All perfectly civilized.

Five demons stood around the fire pit drinking champagne and cocktails—Lydia of the fire tattoos, and four males. Each one of them represented a ward, and the king led the sixth.

From Shai's description, I recognized Legion—long black hair, golden-brown skin, his sleeves rolled up to reveal vicious black tattoos. The leader of the Sathanas Ward, wrath. Shai was right. He was hot, but also terrifying.

Perhaps not quite as scary as Lydia, whose eyes burned with little flecks of fire as she glared at me. The firelight cast dancing shadows over her features, and a menacing smile curled her lips. A cat about to slaughter a mouse.

As a human woman slipped past me with a tray of bright red cocktails, I plucked one off and took a sip. The alcohol would help me calm down, and I could at least *look* like I was enjoying myself.

The king himself sat on a gilded throne on a dais, just on the other side of the fire pit. His long blond hair draped over broad shoulders. Silver horns jutted from his head, and his eyes were dark as night. He wore midnight blue clothes that clung to his enormous body. Firelight wavered over him, further enhancing his otherworldly appearance. His expression was unreadable, his body as still as the stone walls around us. Like Orion, he radiated pure power.

"Mortana, Lady of the House of Lilitu." His low voice rumbled over the hall. "The last succubus. You return to us."

Somehow, having Orion by my side was helping me. I'd been watching him so carefully throughout the day that I'd developed a good sense of how to mimic his overwhelming confidence.

I smiled, then gave one of the lazy shrugs that he would give, as if I were totally at ease. "The City of Serpents started to bore me." I took a sip of my red cocktail, which I think was pomegranate juice with vodka. "And then I thought of the City of Thorns. I did have such *fun* here." I projected my voice over the hall.

I lifted my chin like Orion had told me, and I drained half my pomegranate martini. *Not a care in the world.*

The king's dark eyes landed on Orion. "Do you know why she left the City of Serpents?" His rings glinted in the warm light.

"Now, now, King Cambriel," said Orion, his tone faintly mocking, "you know I can't say what happened there. Our cities are shrouded in secrecy."

He was really going to take that attitude with the demon king? I'd expected deference, but I supposed that was too much to expect from someone with his ego.

"Indeed," said the king in a cold tone. "Which is why we still know nothing of why you left your ward in the City of Serpents, though I'm sure it involved a scandal. And I do wonder if that particular scandal involved this succubus. But I suppose you're right. These things cannot be discussed." The king turned his dark gaze back to me. "My father was very fond of you, Lady Mortana."

The severed head outside was fond of me. I fluttered my eyelashes and took another long sip of my drink, trying to untangle the weirdness of all this. Somehow, this felt like a test. I sensed that if I showed loyalty to the dead king, I'd fail.

"As you saw on your way in," the king went on, "the former king has been vanquished. *Vae Victis*. Do you grieve his death, Mortana?"

This definitely was a test. How did I respond in a way that would flatter King Cambriel? Orion had said King Nergal was dull and tedious.

I widened my eyes, my hand flying to my chest with mock horror. "Is King Nergal dead? Honestly, given his personality, I'm amazed anyone could tell."

Unfortunately, King Cambriel didn't smile a bit, so that only made my stomach muscles clench tighter. I'd already emptied my cocktail, and the alcohol was starting to go to my head. I dropped my glass on the tray of a passing waitress.

A heavy silence still filled the room, and my pulse raced. After an endless few moments, titters broke out at last, and I relaxed just a little.

Had I gone too far?

The thing was, I had a feeling Mortana would go too far. It was part of what made her interesting. She wouldn't have made so many enemies without shocking and insulting people along the way. She knew how to get attention and keep it.

The king's lips curled just a little. He liked Mortana's cruelty. "You don't mourn his death, then? You must have been fond of him once."

"Well, I was very fond of *one* part of him, but that part seems to be gone now, since there's just the head left."

Holy shit. It was fun to be evil. Was I turning into Orion? *Empathy? Sounds tedious.*

When Orion's pale eyes slid to me, I could see the amusement in them.

One of the king's fingers tapped the armrest. The flames of the fire were gleaming off his golden crown. While Orion's beauty was sensual, the king had a sort of stark elegance. Refined, masculine features and straight black eyebrows.

"What do you intend to do here?" The king's voice boomed over the hall.

There was a question I didn't know how to answer. A bit of anxiety snapped through my nerve-endings, and I felt my fingers tightening on Orion's bicep. Maybe we should have prepared for this question.

In response, Orion slowly reached over and stroked his fingertips over my wrist. His warm magic pulsed into me, and instantly, I felt my muscles relax. *Wow.* He could just *do* that? Mortals spent years training in graduate school for counseling techniques to help people manage anxiety, and all Orion had to do was touch them. Boom. Anxiety gone.

I still had to figure out an answer, though. So far, it looked like demons mostly went to fancy restaurants and bought gowns. What would my id say? What did I want?

I fluttered my eyelashes as the flames danced between us. "Well, I do intend to use that pool bar of yours, if you'll let me. And perhaps Orion can join me." Drawing more from my id, I turned to Orion, stroking his large bicep. The look he gave me was deeply carnal, which was good, since I was supposed to be inspiring envy in the king. "Oh, do you know what else I'd like to do? I'd like Orion to fuck me hard against a stone wall, since we haven't done that yet."

Holy shit. *Too much id. Too much id.*

With a low growl, Orion's eyes darkened to shadows, and his heated expression seared me.

Was that a warning that I should shut my mouth, or something else?

At that moment, the flames in the fire pit rose higher, burning the air and scorching my skin. Was this Orion's fire magic at work, or the king's?

"You certainly have my attention, Mortana," said the king sharply. "And what, exactly, is your relationship to Orion?"

One thing I'd learned from Dr. Omer was that when you didn't want to answer a question about yourself, you deflected it back to the other person. You made it a question about them.

I jutted one hip and smiled coquettishly. "Your Majesty, I'm delighted by your interest in my love life. What is it, I wonder, that makes you so intrigued? Is this something we should explore, perhaps?"

Explore. That was a Dr. Omer's word, but he'd never used it quite so suggestively.

The king gave me a faint smile. "You are the last of your kind, Mortana. A curiosity. That's all." But now he was giving me the same look Orion had, like he wanted to lick me from head to toe. Considering gorgeous women in the City of Thorns were a dime a dozen, it was clear Orion was right about what attracted the king's attention. Jealousy was the key to his heart. He wanted me because Orion had me.

I turned to Orion, giving him a full view of my cleavage, and touched my finger to his lips, then traced it down his body. I felt his muscles twitch beneath my touch.

"The city could use a succubus again, I think," I said loudly. "Don't you?"

The look in Orion's midnight eyes sent my heart racing. It was hard not to think of how I'd felt with him pinning me to the wall, with his teeth in my throat.

I breathed in deeply, then turned back to the king. He was gripping the armrests hard, leaning forward on his throne. He almost looked like he wanted to leap over the fire pit and grab me.

For the first time, the king stood, and I saw exactly how tall he was

—just about the same size as Orion. The two men towered over the other demons. He opened his arms. "The dukes and duchess will advise me as to whether you may stay here in the City of Thorns. But of course, I will make the ultimate decision. And I do think you should stay."

I exhaled slowly. This seemed like a victory, right? It seemed like no matter what the Quorum said, the king would keep me here.

"Your Majesty." A husky, feminine voice turned my head.

Lydia, the Duchess of Shalem, had stepped forward. She was stunning in a gold dress that revealed her fiery tattoos. Her legs were long and athletic, and her dark hair curled in shiny waves over bare shoulders. For one moment, she shot me a withering look, then she schooled her expression and gazed at the king again. "Your Majesty, as the lone female leader in the City, you know that I do not share the petty and trivial concerns of the rest of the females."

Nice. She's really going to start her speech by explaining she's not like other girls?

She lifted her chin. "Many of our city's females may object to Mortana's presence here because they see her as a rival. They're only concerned with their marriage prospects, the desire to seek wealth, and other superficial matters. They see her as a threat to the attentions they could receive from Duke Orion or from you. Frankly, their preoccupations with celebrity and wealth speak of the decline of our society."

Orion rolled his eyes. "Are you going to get to a point at any time this evening?"

She curled her lips. "But as you know, I see beyond these frivolous feminine concerns, and I am not like other females. My concerns are deeper. May I point out that the Lilu were barred because of the danger they pose to other demons? Once, the City of Thorns chose to rid its streets of them because they used mind control to manipulate others, to satisfy their own depraved needs. They are an abomination among demons."

Well, the claws were certainly out, but the real question was how *Mortana* would feel about that remark.

I didn't think she'd like it one bit. She'd be ready to fight back.

20

I turned to Lydia and snarled, baring my teeth. The sound came from deep within my chest, and it rumbled over the hall.

Well, *hello*, Mortana's aggression. I'd just become familiar with my animalistic side, I guess.

Looking back at the king, I smiled again. "I think you'll find I don't need mind control to satisfy my *depraved* needs."

The king's sharp jaw clenched, and a dark smile curled his lips. His knuckles went white as he gripped the armrests.

A duke stepped forward—this one with dark hair, copper skin, and deep brown eyes. "We all know what the Lilu were like in the past. They cheated us out of our money using their seduction. Some of us are even old enough to remember." He glared at me. "Mortana lured my brother away centuries ago, and I haven't seen him since. Immediately after his disappearance, his gold disappeared along with him."

Okay, Mortana sucked. But I still had to stay in character because that's how I'd get out of here alive.

Another duke folded his arms. He was tall and thin, with dark curls that fell before his eyes. "If no one else is willing to say it, then I guess I will. Everyone knows *she* killed Queen Adele."

I raised a finger. "Everyone does *not* know that, because I never killed the queen." I could say this without worrying about looking like I was lying, because for once this evening, I actually wasn't. Maybe Mortana once killed a queen, but I hadn't. "Those were merely rumors. Nothing was ever proven."

Orion's face was a mask of calm. "Why let yourselves be swayed by gossip from four hundred years ago?" He shrugged. "I suppose it doesn't matter to me, but I've been enjoying fucking her, and I'd hate to lose my favorite plaything." He arched an eyebrow, his pale eyes gleaming with wickedness. "I'd heard the rumors about succubi, how they'd beg on their knees, but never before did I get to experience the wild desperation of the Lilu."

Shocked murmurs rippled through the room, and a hot tendril of anger coiled through me. Did he really have to put it *that* way? Absolute *prick*. I shouldn't care what the demons thought, and I was only playing a role. But still, I wasn't sure how much humiliation I could take in this place.

And yet...

I could already see it had worked, because now the king looked ravenous for me.

Lydia cocked a hip. "You filthy scoundrel. Lord of Chaos, you weren't here then. You don't know what she was like. And she had the most motive, desperate to be queen. Only Mortana would be cruel enough to leave the Queen Consort in a vat of wine. I don't care about the trivial issues of marriage, but how do we know Mortana won't slaughter the rest of us for power?"

I sighed. "You can't possibly believe I'm the only cruel demon in the City of Thorns. It could have been anyone."

A gaunt duke with luscious brown curls wrapped his bony fingers around his wineglass as he stared at me. The firelight gleamed off his ivory horns. "You may not remember me, Mortana. I wasn't a duke when you left, but I am now." He grimaced at me. "You hardly gave me the time of day back then. A succubus like you was too good for a gluttony demon."

I realized after a moment that his drink wasn't wine at all. It looked like *blood*. He was a glutton for human blood.

Disturbing...

I blinked at him. "Oh, I still think I'm too good for you. That hasn't changed."

I was trying to stay in character. The problem was, staying in character meant pissing people off. And how much did I need them to like me in order to get the approval of the Quorum?

With a furious expression, he knocked back the rest of his blood. "Let me just spell this out. If you become duchess of the Asmodean Ward, that means less tax revenue for the rest of us."

Duchess...*right*. As the last Lilu, I'd be the automatic leader. They'd be sharing power with me. Of course none of them wanted that.

But the king made the ultimate call, right? If he wanted something enough, I was sure he'd find a way to get it. My goal needed to be getting him on board as much as possible, and jealousy was the key to his heart.

I turned to Orion and brushed my fingertips over his abs. As I did, I felt his muscles clench, which was a strangely delicious feeling. My cheeks were growing hotter.

"Look, if you all decide you don't want me here, then I can leave, of course. I can live anywhere. And perhaps I can compel Orion to come with me. I think there's something about him—a very large thing, in fact—that I'm really quite attached to. I can't imagine any other male coming close."

Orion grabbed me off my feet. He moved swiftly but gracefully, and the next thing I knew, he was lifting me against a column. I stared into his hypnotizing blue eyes, and I wrapped my legs around his waist. With a wicked, seductive smile, he pinned me against the stone.

When the air hit the top of my thighs, I realized that he'd pulled my dress up nearly to my hips.

Whoa. Hello.

I stared into his eyes. At this point, I was glad for the wine *and* the cocktail I'd downed, because in normal life, I was never this uninhibited. As Orion had pointed out, I was a bit tightly wound. But it wasn't just the alcohol, was it? Orion had his own sort of intoxicating powers. His seductive, velvety magic stroked my body. As he held me against the stone, his eyes looked dark, dangerous. I stared into his perfect, masculine features, and the world around me seemed to dim. I wanted him to lower his mouth to mine, to kiss me deeply.

God*damn* it. Terrible taste in men, Rowan. Absolute worst.

A breeze rushed through the hall, skimming over my bare skin. The strap of my gown had fallen, nearly exposing my entire breast. In fact, half my nipple was showing, tightened to a sensitive point against the silky material.

In any normal situation, I'd gasp and rush to cover myself up. But in any normal situation, I wouldn't be thrown into a fire pit for being self-conscious, so I took a deep breath and let the strap fall even more.

I watched Orion's eyes as they brushed down my chest, and I heard his sharp intake of breath. He pressed in harder between my legs, and I bit my lip. From the feel of him, he wasn't just faking his desire. And what I'd said before about how I couldn't imagine any other male coming close to him? Holy moly, I wasn't wrong.

Orion started to lower his mouth to mine, eyes black as night—

"That's enough!" The king's voice boomed through the hall.

I was horrified at how disappointed I felt at the interruption.

Orion lowered me, and the hem of my gown fell to the floor once more.

I knew my cheeks were flushed and my chest heaving as I pulled my strap up again. It was hard for me to focus. Only the sight of the rising flames, now towering several feet above us, sharpened my senses again. When the flames died down, I could see the king on the other side of them, his jaw clenched and muscles tense.

We'd certainly gotten his attention. The firelight danced over his tan skin and blond hair, making him look like a gilded statue forged from the flames.

My adrenaline was pulsing hard through my body. Had we actually pulled off this act?

The king pulled his gaze from me, surveying the Quorum. Then a smile curled his lips. "I think the City of Thorns could use a succubus."

A silence fell over the room. Just as I thought, the king would be making the call, regardless of what the others thought. Their faces were grim, furious.

One of the dukes, with platinum blond hair and gold rings on his fingers, stepped forward. "We cannot, of course, disagree with your wisdom." He looked furious. And as I stared at him, a golden symbol started beaming from his head—something like a crescent moon.

My heart slammed on my chest. *That* was what I remembered from the night Mom was killed. It was a symbol just like that, shining from a demon's head. Only it had been a star instead of a moon.

My blood was pumping so hard now I *nearly* dropped character. I'd actually made progress.

But when I saw Lydia's eyes on me, the curl of her lip, I made sure my expression looked serene. Mortana wasn't surprised by anything here. This was all business as usual.

The king steepled his fingers as he stared at his quorum. "Don't you agree that the city could use a succubus?" His voice rumbled off the marble. "A duchess for the Asmodean Ward?"

He wanted them to agree with him. He *knew* they didn't—they'd just said so—but they wouldn't argue with a king. And as long as they agreed out loud, he would have someone to blame if the succubus turned out to be a complete disaster. *Why did you all advise me to allow her in?*

The five demons murmured, then nodded.

Only Lydia looked completely stone faced. "We could use a succubus. The king in his infinite wisdom can see this. But any demon who enters the city must be tested in the Infernal Trial, is that not correct? It's how we know that the gods bless someone's presence." Ferocity burned in her eyes as she turned to us. "Orion, you remember your Trial. You killed some good friends of mine, in fact. Now, it must be Mortana's turn."

"That's only for new demons," he replied. "Mortana lived here once before. She's returning to her former home." He was trying to seem casual, but I could tell by the way he'd answered—a little too quickly— that this was *bad*.

Lydia smiled pleasantly. "Yes, but she never passed the Trial because she lived in the city at its founding. There were no trials in the 1680s. The law says that any demon entering the city must pass the Infernal Trial unless they have passed it before. I think you'll find that there are no exemptions stated for those who lived here when the city was founded." Her smile deepened as she looked at me. "You haven't gone soft in the City of Serpents, have you, Mortana?"

Fear settled in my gut.

The king stood, and warm light danced over his sharp jawline. "It is agreed, then. Mortana will join the City of Thorns as long as she can pass our initiation. Then we will know if even the gods approve of her presence here." He turned to look at me, his crown gleaming. "Your Trial begins at midnight tonight. You have been formally summoned."

I couldn't exactly say no, could I? Mortana would say yes. She would be one hundred percent confident of her ability to get through this.

I could either break character or commit myself to a life-threatening trial.

So I found myself opening my mouth and saying, "I can easily pass an Infernal Trial. Of *course* the gods want me here." I chuckled softly. "I think we all know that."

Lydia was seething at me, her lip curled a little. "But what if Duke Orion tries to help her? Clearly, they have a relationship. We all know how skilled he is at killing. What if they *cheat?*"

The king cut a sharp glance to Orion. "Well, the duke will remain with me on the other side of the Acheron River, just outside my tower. We will be watching for you to cross over, or listening for the victory cry that would herald your death. We will have cocktails."

"And no flying," spat Lydia. "You can't use your wings."

Now there was one rule I'd have no problem sticking to. I didn't have wings, or magic, or really any hope to survive the rest of the night. Not unless I figured out a plan *real* fast. Maybe a quick, secretive exit from the city before anyone noticed.

Except the king wasn't dismissing us. No, he was drawing a dagger from his belt. Dread started to bloom in my chest as I realized what was happening now.

The king held out his palm and carved a slash in it. Crimson blood slid down his hand on to the marble dais beneath him. "Good. We will seal this sacred commitment with a blood oath."

Holy hell. Looks like I'd be working on a plan B.

🦋 2 1 🦋

I paced the floor in Orion's apartment, gripping the bandage around my hand.

We'd managed to rush out of the Tower of Baal before anyone realized that I didn't heal like a demon. Still clutching my hand, I pivoted, pacing across the room again.

By contrast, Orion barely moved an inch as he watched me. Then he leaned back and spread his arms out across the sofa. "I'm starting to think this was all a mistake."

That wasn't exactly what I'd wanted to hear.

"What I would do," he went on, "if you hadn't agreed to the blood oath, would be to rush you out of the city. Then I'd make sure you stayed hidden. But you agreed to the blood oath." He leaned forward, pinning me with his gaze. "Why, exactly, did you do that? You just signed your own death sentence."

"I was staying in character," I shot back, exasperated. "If I broke character, I'd be dead, right? In a fire. Mortana would never back down from a challenge. Mortana would do the Trial in a heartbeat. I have more of a chance in the Trial than I do in a fire pit. It was just a calculation of the odds."

"Mortana would do the Trial in a heartbeat," he repeated, and his eyes gleamed in the dim light, cold and ruthless. "Why are you talking about her as if you knew her?"

That was a good question. Why *did* I feel like I knew her?

I gripped my injured hand hard. "I don't know. She's like my id."

"Hmm. That sounds like a mortal thing I don't want to explore further because it'll annoy me." Orion's eyes narrowed. "The thing is, Rowan, Lydia will likely kill you with her fire magic. And I'm supposed to stay at the Tower. Even if you manage to survive the Trial by hiding, the other demons will quickly realize you don't have any powers. *Then* you'll die in a fire pit. And if you fail to show up, you'll die from the blood oath."

I stopped pacing to stare at him. "Are you trying to be helpful?"

He rose and grabbed my injured hand. "I'm going to heal you. I forgot quite how long it took for humans to heal. Ridiculous." He pulled me closer to him and sat again, and I plopped on the couch by his side. He unwrapped my bandaged palm, and our heads leaned close together as we peered at the deep gash. He brushed his fingertips just to the right of the red slash. As he did, warm, healing magic skimmed over my hand. I stared as my skin smoothed over before my eyes.

"Are you healing me because you feel empathy, Orion?" I asked.

"I don't want blood on my floor," he murmured.

When the skin looked good as new, I pulled my hand away. "What can you tell me about what the Trial will be like? I need to make a good plan."

Our faces were close now, and a line formed between his eyebrows. "A good plan," he repeated, his tone suggesting it was the most absurd thing he'd ever heard.

Orion probably never needed to plan things, did he? He could show up and kill people.

"Just tell me how you think the night will go," I prompted.

"It'll begin in an old oak grove in the Elysian Wilderness. The other demons will be in different locations throughout the wood. They won't know which way you're moving, but they'll try to hunt you down by scent. If you stay in one place or try to hide, they'll converge and kill you. If you try to run, they'll smell you and kill you. They are far, *far* faster than you.

And it's not just the five demons from the Quorum, mind you. It's anyone from the city who wants to participate. It could be a hundred demons. In order for the Trial to end, you'll need to survive for a full hour."

Despite the horror of what he was telling me, an idea was starting to form in my mind. "Lydia has fire magic. The others don't. So can fire hurt them?"

"Yes. Some only have strength and speed, and others have forms of elemental magic. You could be frozen to death, although Nama isn't great at hitting a moving target. It's more likely that she'd trap you in a wall of ice or something, then beat you to death and carve your heart out with her claws."

My throat went dry. "How thick is the ice?"

"It's not incredibly thick. I could probably punch my way through it. It's like glass."

My heart pattered in my chest. "Okay. I have a plan. Can we send Shai out to pick up a few things from my apartment?"

He frowned. "You can't use a gun, if that's what you're thinking."

I shook my head. "No. This is specialty equipment. Oh, and do you think Morgan will let me borrow his watch?"

"Yes. But what do you need?"

I closed my eyes, reviewing the items I had in mind. "My fire-retardant gels, clothing, a gas mask, and a fire blanket. Also, I have a knife that can shatter glass. Oh, and I'll need gasoline or another liquid accelerant, but she won't find that in my apartment. Obviously. I'm not insane."

He stared at me. "May I ask why you have these things?"

"Well, you have magic, and I have my own superpower. It's called anxiety. It's a pain in the ass, but I'm prepared for every fire scenario you can think of. And Facebook's algorithms identified me as anxious, so they started advertising things like a knife that can cut through glass if you drive your car off a bridge into a river." I frowned. "I don't even have a car, but I have the knife."

He looked transfixed. "Right."

"I'll also need bleach and ammonia. And a tool belt."

His body was completely still. "Is this just a random list of items?

Have you done that thing that mortals do when their minds break from too much stress?"

"Oh! And this is crucial: we need to tell her to get the fox urine from under my bed," I added. "And a Super Soaker."

"Ah." His features softened. "Your mind *has* broken."

I reached out to touch his arm. "It hasn't. Trust me. I have a plan."

"Does this plan involve attacking demons with fox urine?"

I shook my head. "No. I have a better plan."

He still hadn't moved an inch. "The contents of your bedroom concern me."

"I just want to be prepared for the apocalypse, Orion. That's all. And that apocalypse is here, even if it's just for me."

"That's not what *apocalypse* means."

I lifted a finger. "Let's stay focused. Fox urine, bleach—"

"This sounds insane," he said, cutting me off, and scrubbed a hand over his jaw. "I thrive in chaos. I like to watch things burn. But this situation is making me feel something different, unfamiliar. I don't like it," he said in a clipped tone. "This is making my heart beat faster, almost like a...like a *warning*. As if something bad is about to happen."

My eyes widened. "Yeah. That's anxiety. Are you feeling anxious for my safety, or are you worried you'll be caught out?"

His gaze shuttered. "Don't be ridiculous. I'm a lethal four-hundred-year-old demon of chaos, imbued with godlike powers. I fear nothing."

"Not sure I believe you anymore, Orion."

I may not know magic, but I know anxiety.

D arkness surrounded me in the oak grove. Beyond the stench of fox pee, the air smelled of moss and soil, and faintly of gasoline.

For years, I'd been waiting for the demon apocalypse, and now it was happening. At least for me.

My knees shook as I waited for the sound of the klaxon that would herald the beginning of the Trial.

There was only one rule: no flying. As the Lilu were the only type of demons with wings, if I could actually use them, I'd be simply flapping around above the trees the entire time.

I glanced up at the sky. Clouds covered the moon, which was both good and bad. The bad part was that I'd be reliant on the night vision goggles I'd bought last year off Amazon (in case of the apocalypse), and they weren't great. But the darkness was good, too. It gave me a little cover for the ridiculous suit I had on—a navy flame-retardant suit, with the safety stripes covered up. The demons might not notice the night vision goggles, the safety gloves, or the backpack I carried filled with supplies. They wouldn't see the sheen of the flame-retardant gel on my cheeks and chin.

And when this ended, I'd need to get this shit off quickly before anyone could see what I'd been up to.

Sweat ran down my body under the suit. Tonight, the forest air was hot and humid, and heavy with tension.

Demons never considered using tools or weapons. Honed by evolution, they didn't need technology. But me? I could only hope that my little arsenal would help me. And I prayed that the fox pee would disguise my scent, the way hunters used it in the woods.

My heart slammed against my ribs. Any moment now, the Trial would begin.

With my goggles on, I scanned the trees for signs of movement. My vision was black and white, and I could just see the trunks around me.

My plan for now was to get as close as possible to the river as quickly as I could. Before coming out here, I'd installed a compass app on Morgan's Apple Watch, so I knew exactly which way was north, and the river was about four miles. When I got there, I'd spend the rest of the time fending off attackers.

With a thundering heart, I checked my borrowed watch—two minutes until midnight.

In high school, I'd run track and cross country. I'd even made it to nationals. This felt a lot like the start of those meets, burning with adrenaline, waiting for the gun to go off...except in this race, I could end up battered to death by an angry mob of demons, so the stakes were just a *tad* higher than coming in second.

I watched the countdown on my watch for a few seconds, then pulled out my first weapon—the Super Soaker.

When the klaxon sounded, I started to run.

Unlike my high school track meets, I was carrying about ten pounds of weight, encased in a metallic suit, and wearing goggles. I was already sweating into the suit, so speed wasn't on my side tonight. As I ran, I breathed in the musky, acrid scent of fox pee, and my eyes watered.

With my night vision goggles, I scanned the trees for signs of movement. I ran for about ten minutes, sucking in breath sharply, without seeing a single demon. I thought I'd probably made it a mile and a half.

Only fifty minutes to go.

When my foot loudly snapped a twig, it occurred to me for the first time that speed might *not* be the most important thing. If they couldn't see me easily or smell me, they'd be relying on sound. That twig breaking the silence might as well have been a cannon going off.

I froze, scanning the woods around me and catching my breath.

My heart skipped a beat as I saw a demon moving toward me. Unlike me, he moved with shocking speed, his body like wind through the trees. But he was still some distance away.

Before he could get to me, I used the Super Soaker to spray gasoline on the ground between us. I created a wide arc, at least twelve feet, then dropped the gun and snatched the deodorant from my tool belt. I'd superglued a lighter to the can using a plastic binder clip, so it stuck out at just the right angle to form a blowtorch. The lighter itself had a rubber band around it to hold the flame when it was depressed.

My body shook as I flicked the lighter and the flame sprang to life. Then I pressed the top of the deodorant. Four feet of flames shot out into the air, and I lunged forward, angling the fire toward the gasoline. The reaction was instant—an enormous wall of fire surrounding me.

Now the demon was just on the other side of the flames—and by his luscious curls and ivory horns, I recognized him as a duke. The blood-guzzling gluttony demon bellowed in rage, and the sound slid through my bones. It wasn't just the sound itself that sparked my fear —he'd just alerted the entire demon army to my location.

I snatched the Super Soaker from the ground and sprayed through the flames toward the demon. The fire spread in his direction, and he backed away, staring at the flames and roaring.

I pivoted and broke into a run before more of them could find me. I had to put as much distance as possible between the bellowing demon and me.

I usually ran five days a week, often six to seven miles, maybe up to ten, and even with my backpack on, the adrenaline was giving me extra strength. I pumped my arms hard, running faster through the trees than I'd been moving before. But when I stole a glance behind me, I

saw movement in the distance. A demon was closing in on me. No—
not just a demon. With my goggles, I saw two...three...six?

Fuck. They were all over, and I still had a mile to get to the river.

New tactic.

My hands were shaking as I pulled off the night vision goggles, and
I felt blind without them. Vulnerable. But for what I needed to do
next, I couldn't have them on.

I unzipped my backpack and found the gas mask. When I slid it on
over my face, my sense of vulnerability only increased. I pulled the
hood over my head and tightened it as quickly as I could, and the
eyepieces fogged a little.

Just like I'd done when I was mixing chemicals earlier, I had to test
the filter first. I covered it, checking to make sure no air was escaping
into the mask from other gaps. With the filter covered, I couldn't
breathe at all, which was both terrifying and what I wanted.

Now I was ready.

I knelt down again and reached into the backpack for my glass jars.
I started hurling them at the tree trunks, one by one. Within
moments, the demons were coughing, then screaming.

I couldn't see very well through the darkness and the goggles, but I
didn't think they were moving any closer to me.

I had no idea if demons were rushing at me from the north, but I
hurled another jar in that direction, just in case, until I was surrounded
by a cloud of homemade mustard gas on all sides.

Right now, the bleach and ammonia mix would be searing their
lungs, stealing their breath, and burning and blistering their skin and
eyes.

Was this prohibited by the Geneva Convention? Okay, *technically*
yes, but those laws had been written for mortals. The demons would
recover, even if the next twenty minutes would be deeply unpleasant.

I grabbed my backpack and started moving again.

With the gas mask on, I couldn't run anymore. For one thing, I
could no longer see where I was going, and for another, it was incredibly hard to breathe in that thing. I could only hope the mustard gas
took out any demons around me.

I checked the watch, making sure I was still heading north.

Twenty-one minutes. I only had to survive twenty-one more minutes, and I'd be free. Holy shit, this was actually working.

When I thought I'd cleared enough distance from the mustard gas, I pulled off my gloves and took a little breath, testing the air. My skin wasn't burning, and my lungs felt fine. I pulled the gloves back on and tried loosening my gas mask. Lungs seemed okay...

I took a deep breath. My eyes stung a little, but that was it.

I pulled the gas mask all the way off and took a few breaths, then quickly slipped my night vision goggles back on. Backpack hoisted, I started to run. I was closing the distance now, only a half mile or so to the river.

As I zoomed between the trunks, a chill rushed through the air, and the trees became hazy through my night vision goggles. Before I could figure out what had happened, I slammed into a wall of ice. A jolt of pain shot through my skull as the force of the crash cracked my goggles. I ripped them off and stared around me at a large sphere of ice.

Nama had already trapped me in here, and I didn't know how far away she was. But just as Orion had said, the ice was thin as glass.

As quickly as I could, I sprayed the ground around me with gasoline, then reached for the glass-breaking knife in my pocket. It didn't look like much more than a bit of plastic, but hidden within the plastic was a blade that popped out on impact. I slammed it hard against the ice, and it shattered around me.

With a thundering heart, I grabbed my flamethrower. I flicked the lighter on, pressed the deodorant, and blasted flames at the ground. Fire erupted around me, and fear twisted my heart. I *hated* fire.

But Nama was still running for me, and I blasted flames in her direction using the Super Soaker and the homemade flamethrower. In the distance, I stared in a sickening sort of horror as her hair and clothes caught fire from the flames on the ground. She screamed, the sound curdling my blood.

My pulse raced out of control. *She's a demon*, I reminded myself. *She'll get better*.

I only had a half mile left to go, and I checked my watch.

Ten minutes.

I just had to survive ten minutes.

I started to run again, but this time, I couldn't see the trees. I flicked on a light on the Apple Watch—which wasn't ideal, since people might see it. But it was the only way I could see to avoid running into an unyielding trunk. I ran with the flamethrower in one hand, pumping my arms hard as I headed for the river. The backpack bounced behind me, and I bounded over roots and stones. I was sweating *hard* in my suit as my body overheated.

As I moved closer to the city, I could turn off the light on my watch, as the lights from the town square illuminated the forest.

Suddenly, I heard Lydia's husky voice cut through the forest. "Demons, hear me! I'm following her trail! She's by the river!"

So *that's* how they'd been finding me, even through the stench of fox piss. They were tracking me through the woods, looking for the broken branches I'd left behind. And broken demons, too.

And now, Lydia was trying to summon all the demons to attack me at once.

Four minutes left.

Through the forest, I heard the bellowing of demon war cries—a deep, malignant sound that slid through my bones and sent my heart racing out of control. The ancient part of my brain was telling me to panic, that predators were coming for me. And for once, that anxious part of my brain was fucking right.

Get to the river, Rowan. Get there now.

The demons were coming to her call, bellowing for my blood. They were all heading for the river, closing in. Their otherworldly cries turned my blood to ice, and panic scraped up my spine. But I could see the river now through the trunks, glimmering in the lights from the Tower of Baal.

Three minutes left.

And what's more, I could smell the scent of gasoline I'd poured out two hours ago.

It was time for the pièce de résistance—my real shock and awe.

When I reached the riverbank, I pulled out the flamethrower and flicked the lighter. As I touched the arc of flame to the ground, a wall of pure fire raced out from either side. I'd created a mouth to hell.

I leapt through the fire into the ice-cold Acheron River and swam down to the bottom, deep into the murk. Turning, I swam east for a moment and then I unzipped my fire suit. My lungs started to burn as I held my breath and stuffed the suit and tools into the backpack. I zipped it up and let it sink to the bottom, and then, my secret hidden, I swam to the northern bank.

And as I pulled myself out, I heard the sound of the klaxon blaring. There they were—the king standing by Orion's side, waiting for me. My little victory party. A small crowd stood behind them, staring at me.

Holy fucking shit.

Holy fucking *shit*. I'd made it.

Joy surged through me. I'd *survived*. Maybe everything was going to be okay after all. Had I really done this?

Soaking wet, I hoisted myself onto the bank, trying to hide exactly how exhausted I was.

I saw the king raise his cocktail glass in a toast to me, and Orion's pale eyes shone brightly in the darkness.

Under my fire suit, I'd been wearing a sleek black outfit—fitted black pants and a corset. If I weren't soaked in river water, I might *actually* look pretty good right now.

As I stepped into the stony esplanade before the Tower of Baal, I raised my arms in victory and surveyed the demons around me. No one was exactly cheering at my survival, which seemed a bit rude. In fact, they looked a little pissed off.

And as the klaxon continued to blare, I felt a sharp tug at my wet hair, dragging me back onto the stones. I slammed down hard on the ground. The next thing I knew, Lydia was on top of me. She wrapped her hands around my throat and squeezed, fangs bared and a maniacal look in her eyes. Then she raised one of her hands, and gleaming claws burst forth.

She was going to cut my heart out, wasn't she? That was how demons killed each other. They ripped each other's hearts out with their claws.

"There's only room for one queen," she hissed under her breath.

I couldn't breathe. Oh, holy fuck, I couldn't breathe...

❧ 23 ❧

Hypervigilance: a heightened state of anxiety and alertness, a tendency to scan the environment for threats.

In my everyday life, it was dysfunctional. In the world of demons, it didn't hurt to turn up the dial, because somehow, I'd missed that Lydia had been sneaking up behind me, and now she was crushing my throat.

As my vision started to go dark, enormous hands reached down and ripped Lydia off me.

The sound of the klaxon died out at last.

I sucked in air, trying to hide exactly how fragile I was. I wanted to gasp deeply and audibly, but I was worried that would make me look too mortal. All eyes were on me right now. Had they noticed how easily she'd taken me down? Did they know I was mortal?

Unwilling to look weak in front of the others, I forced myself up.

But as I steadied my breathing, a rush of movement caught my eye. I turned to see the blood-guzzling demon running for me from the bridge, the wind whipping at his luxurious curls. With a bellowing war cry, he was charging for me at an alarming speed. Moonlight glinted off his ivory horns, and long silver claws shot from his fingers. If I tried to run, they'd all see how slow I was.

"It's over!" called the king. "The Trial has ended."

But the duke wasn't listening, and he was almost upon me. Ten feet away...two feet away...

I froze in place, staring at him. The bloodthirsty duke reared back his arm, ready to strike at my chest—

Fast as lighting, Orion shifted in front of me, blocking the hit with his enormous body. I heard the sound of claws ripping into his flesh, and my stomach tightened.

Horrified, I wrapped my arm around his back to keep him upright and craned my neck to see the damage. The one way a demon could die was having his heart cut out.

The duke's eyes were wide as he ripped his blood-covered claws out of Orion's chest.

"What have you done?" someone shouted. "Did you kill the Lord of Chaos?"

My heart slammed against my ribs. Orion was clutching his chest, bleeding all over the stones.

The world had gone dreadfully silent, and panic tightened my throat. "Are you okay?" I whispered.

Before us, the duke's claws retracted, and his hand flew to his mouth. "Oh, Lucifer save me, I didn't mean to do that. I was aiming for the succubus. Why did you jump in the way, you idiot? You know what it means if she survives."

Orion raised a bloodied hand. "I'm fine," he said at last, and then he darted forward and grabbed the duke by his neck. The duke's eyes bulged, and Orion lifted him by the throat, choking him. Silver claws shot out from Orion's fingertips.

Oh, *God.* He wasn't going to—

Orion's claws sliced into the demon's chest, and one sharp, ruthless swipe carved out the heart. The glutton demon's bony corpse fell to the ground with a *thud*, his chest cavity gaping open and his body still twitching.

Holy *shit*.

My gorge rose, but I couldn't afford to throw up. I had to look like that was normal. All perfectly normal. Oh, *God*, the way it glistened...

Orion shrugged. "What? He attacked me. I was well within my rights to end his life, as I'm sure you all agree."

The crowd murmured. The shocked excitement in their eyes reminded me a little of the glee in my classmates' faces when I'd had my meltdown.

Orion turned to look at me, brow furrowed. Was that a flicker of worry in his pale eyes?

"You're okay?" I asked again. "I think we should get you home." And I had to get out of here before the bruises bloomed all over my throat.

But the king was prowling closer, dressed in a finely cut midnight suit. His dark eyes were locked on me, and a smile curled his lips. "Good. Everyone survived, then, it seems. Lady Mortana, house of Lilitu. Duchess of the Ward of Asmodeus. After tonight, the abandoned ward will no longer be abandoned." He raised his hands to the dark skies. "The council of seven is reunited!"

Instead of cheers, only silence greeted his pronouncement. Then, the sound of a throat clearing broke the silence. The king lowered his hands to look down at the twitching corpse on the ground.

"Or, nearly reunited. We will have to get a new one, I suppose." He raised his hands to the skies again. "Anyway, the celebratory party begins immediately in the Temple of Ishtar!"

Orion had just been nearly stabbed to death, another duke died, and they wanted to throw a party? I was so caught up on that thought, I nearly missed the other part—*Duchess*. That was me now. A demonic duchess.

A few people clapped, but it didn't sound enthusiastic. Orion was standing straighter now, and I let my arm drop from his back.

My gaze flicked to Lydia, who still seemed furious. Darkness coiled around her, curling into the night sky like smoke.

If I hadn't been nearly strangled, I'd probably make a big, cocky pronouncement right now, like Mortana would. But my voice box had been crushed, and I didn't think I'd sound normal when I spoke.

Clearly, I had to watch my back here. Lydia would rip my heart out the first chance she got.

I hadn't really thought about the implications until now, but as the only person in the Asmodean Ward, I would be its leader by default. Lydia was no longer the only female on the council, and she didn't like that one bit. I'd be part of the Quorum now. Close to the king. A rival for the role of queen.

She just had no idea I wouldn't be here that long.

I glanced back at the Bridge of Harrowing and saw that some of the other demons from the forest were starting to stumble out, looking like zombies—bodies scorched, clothing singed. Some had blistered skin and watering eyes.

This night had been brutal for lots of us, but I supposed only a single death was a victory.

Orion pulled me close to him, almost protectively. "My lady will want to dry off, and I'll need a change of clothes after that unfortunate incident. We will soon join you at the temple."

He grabbed me by the hand, leading me to the street on the far side of the esplanade. Within moments, a sleek black car pulled up, and Orion opened the door for me. I slid inside and buckled up while Orion told the mortal cab driver to take us back to his apartment in the Leviathan Hotel.

Now, for the first time tonight, I felt the full weight of my exhaustion. My muscles burned with fatigue, and my throat felt raw. Even without the other clothes, I still smelled faintly of fox pee.

Never in my life had I craved a bath so badly.

When the car started rolling, Orion turned to look at me. "Congratulations," he said softly. "Duchess Mortana of Lilitu."

THE FIRST THING I'D DONE UPON OUR RETURN TO ORION'S apartment was to run upstairs to the balcony bath. As I'd filled it with scalding water, I'd stripped off my clothes. Now, I was leaning back into the hot, bubbling bath as the steam curled around me. I let my muscles melt and scrubbed my body clean.

While I soaked in the heat, I gazed up at the stars. I could just about make out the North Star, I thought, at the end of the Little Dipper. Mom had taught me to find it, another survival technique. I looked for it at night sometimes, centering myself. It was just that the compass app was a lot easier and worked even when there were clouds.

I let out a long, shaky breath. My mind kept flicking back to the demon I'd hit with fire. Hair blazing, clothes flaming...*horrible*.

I shuddered, suddenly struck by the feeling that I didn't want to be alone.

Half of me wanted to call Orion in here while I bathed to keep me company. But like the primal keening of the demons' war cries in the wilderness, I sensed instinctively that it wouldn't end well.

I rose abruptly from the bath. Water dripped off my bare skin in the cool night air, and I started to towel off.

Sex with Orion absolutely could not happen. For one thing, he'd threatened to kill Shai, and I'd just seen exactly how efficient he could be with killing. In under a second, she could be dead. On top of that, he was a suspect. I was sure that the police had rules about not sleeping with anyone under a criminal investigation.

His attraction to me was probably fake, anyway.

I mean...it didn't *feel* fake. That encounter in the Tower of Baal, with my legs wrapped around him—it *really* felt like he hadn't been faking that desire. The heated look in his eyes, the exquisitely sensual stroke of his magic over me, the feel of his hardness between my thighs...

I started to towel-dry my hair, flipping it over my head. Anyway, he was bad news.

Once dry, I slipped into the clothes I'd laid out for myself—tiny, silky underwear in a deep blue, and a matching lace demicup bra. I stepped into the underwear, doing my best not to think about Orion, and then pulled on a soft black dress. It was kind of a cute 1960s look —short as hell, but with long sleeves and a turtleneck, and smoking hot when paired with thigh-high boots, succubus style.

When I came downstairs again, I found Orion sitting on his cream sofa with a glass of whiskey. He'd changed into a white button-down shirt with the sleeves rolled up to the elbows, exposing his creepy snake tattoo. He wore forest green pants that looked like raw silk and probably cost ten thousand dollars.

"The duchess returns," he said as I sat beside him. "You know, love, I didn't think a mortal could do what you did. It seems you're capable of great surprises." His voice was a velvety caress. "Your not-so-adoring crowd will be expecting you soon. Mortana doesn't tire, I'm afraid."

"How's your chest?"

"Same as it ever was." A sly smile. "Fine on the outside, dead on the inside. Fortunately, only metaphorically."

I crossed my legs, and his gaze flicked to my bare thighs for just a moment before he rose. "Stand up. Let me heal your bruises."

I pulled down the high neck of my dress. He frowned, then touched me lightly, just beneath my chin. I closed my eyes as the sensual feel of his magic washed over me. Simmering waves snaked around my throat, making my muscles relax.

He pulled his hand away. "There. good as new."

Sighing, I sat again. "Don't you want to know everything that happened?"

He took a seat across from me. "I saw the ragged remnants of your enemies. Did I mention that there's something kind of terrifying about you?"

"You killed fifty demons, didn't you? That means you ripped out fifty demon hearts in the forest. I think you're more terrifying."

He gave an easy shrug. "But I'm obviously dangerous. People can tell that as soon as they meet me. You disguise it. You're a lion dressed as a lamb." He frowned. "And then in a second lion disguise, since you're also supposed to be Mortana."

"I have layers." I raised my eyebrows. "And maybe a dark side."

"About that." He leaned forward, his blue eyes piercing me. "You told your secrets, Rowan, in that prison cell. But you didn't tell all of them, did you? There was something you kept hidden."

Even from myself. That thought rang out in my mind—a voice that wasn't quite my own.

Hidden from myself.

What the fuck?

I gave Orion a tired smile. "No, I don't spill my darkest secrets. They make people uncomfortable."

"I doubt you'd find that to be the case with me."

I doubted that, too. My darkness would be nothing to him. He held a world of shadows within himself.

But I wasn't about to spill my guts to one of my suspects, and I had a very important question to ask him. One that related to *my* investigation. "Orion, when we were in the Tower of Baal, one of the demon males had a symbol on his head. Like a crescent moon. What is that?"

He shifted into the cushion and spread his arms out across the sofa back. When human men took up space like that, it was a defensive posture. Was it the same for demons?

"Sometimes, we shift to a more bestial, darker form. Black eyes. Sometimes, scales emerge. And we'll have a demon mark. When we shift, it can appear."

"What makes a demon shift?"

"We feel emotions very, very intensely. And when that, happens, it can reveal our true selves."

Fascinating. "But you don't feel empathy."

"I don't. Some of us shut things down. It makes it easier to think logically in the haze of emotions."

"Okay." I bit my lip. "But back to the mark—"

His eyes were growing darker, weren't they? This topic was making him shift a little. Weird.

"Does every demon have their own unique mark?" I asked.

"Yes."

I drummed my fingertips on my knees. I needed to be an undercover cop about this and not push the point too much, but the desperation was building in me. "So do you know what everyone's mark is? Have you seen them all?"

"No, most demons keep them hidden. Sometimes, the marks betray things about people they'd rather keep secret. Powers, the truth about their lineage..."

"What about a star?" I asked, gripping the armrests.

As soon as the shadows slid through his eyes, it was clear I'd struck a nerve. He was shifting, wasn't he? And it wasn't just his eyes that changed. The room was going darker around us, and his mood swallowed up the light. "Why, exactly, are you asking about that?" His voice was a low, quiet warning.

What the hell... Maybe demon psychology was different than humans', but he was definitely defensive. I'd stumbled into some kind of dangerous territory.

I inhaled sharply. "No reason. I just thought if there was a moon, there must be a star."

He sucked in a deep breath. "A star identifies the Lightbringer, our destined leader. No one has seen that mark in a long time."

An ice-cold chill rippled through me. "Not on the king, then?"

"I've never seen his mark. No one has." The shadows around him seemed to sharpen into blades, growing darker.

And all of this was a *fantastic* reminder of why I couldn't be seduced by his beauty. Did he look perfect? Yes. Was he sketchy as fuck and possibly a murderer? Also yes.

"It seems like you killed that duke very easily," I said. "Was it really necessary?"

"He wanted to kill you so badly, he wasn't playing within the rules. He seemed like a liability."

I frowned. "So when you have a difficult interpersonal situation... do you often just kill the person to make things easier?"

His eyebrows rose. "'Difficult interpersonal situation'? Is that what you call it when someone tries to kill you?"

"Okay. Point taken." My head was spinning, and I wasn't quite sure I was keeping up with the level of danger in this world.

I glanced at the macabre tattoo on his arm—the noose made from a snake. "Since you're not going to tell me about your mark, how about this: why did you get that tattoo?"

A muscle tensed in his jaw, and he rose, towering above me. "We should go to your victory party."

Wow. Another off-limits conversation. "Give me a second to do my hair and makeup."

I could be allied with my worst enemy. But at least I'd learned something new. If I wanted to identify my mother's killer, I'd have to try to provoke strong reactions from every demon. I needed to see their marks.

Unfortunately, I'd have to anger a *lot* of demons in the process.

❦ 24 ❦

W hen our cab arrived at the Temple of Ishtar, another red carpet stretched out to greet us.

The temple was just north of the Tower of Baal and south of where Orion lived. Small crowds of demons flanked either side, snapping photos on their cell phones. It was after one a.m., and I was starting to get the impression that no one here slept. As I stepped out of the car, I felt underdressed for this crowd of onlookers. But Mortana wouldn't be self-conscious, so I just gave everyone that smug demon smirk. When Orion was by my side, I made sure to walk with a swing of my hips over the carpet.

A humid ocean breeze rustled through my hair, and I licked the salt off my lips. The Temple of Ishtar was actually a bar now, but it still looked like a temple, with Doric columns and carvings of a beautiful, winged woman jutting out from the roof.

With Orion, I ascended the steps and passed through the towering open doors. There, I found myself in an enormous hall of golden stone. Demons in gowns and suits stood on a floor of blue and gold tiles. On the walls to the right and left, mosaics formed images of golden lions. Directly across from us, the columns were open to the sea, and a balmy breeze rushed in. Sparkling phosphorescence made the waves glitter under the night sky.

I glanced at the golden-brick cocktail bar to my right, where row upon row of liquor bottles stood before the mirror. God, this place was amazing. It was unfortunate I wasn't actually a succubus.

When I glanced at Orion, a shiver of unease rippled through me. For a number of reasons, I didn't want him to be my enemy. But given how he'd reacted to the star question, I'd have to keep my eyes open to the possibility.

I watched as he crossed to the bar and chatted with the bartender. Was he avoiding me?

After today, my nerves were completely shot. But *Mortana*, my shadow-self, wanted a drink. So when a server brought over a tray of bubbly cocktails in champagne flutes, I plucked one off and took a sip, tasting gin and lemon.

When a hush fell over the room, I turned to see King Cambriel arrive, his golden hair falling over a gorgeous velvet suit. He walked arm-in-arm with Lydia, who wore a black leather jacket over a silky gown with slits in strategic places. The dress showed off little glimpses of her waist, her ribs, and part of her thigh. She looked cool as hell.

What was *not* as cool was the way she snarled at me when she met my gaze.

She didn't know this, but I was probably the one person in this bar who didn't actually care that she was on the king's arm. At least, not beyond the fact that I had a deal with Orion.

I had two goals here tonight. One was to get the king's attention so that I could start to learn about his weaknesses. But the other was my own. Could I sufficiently rile up this crowd that I saw some of their demon marks? Could I churn up emotions powerful enough to make some of them shift?

Orion had said that he, the king, Lydia, and Mortana all had fire magic. That meant three marks I needed to see in order to rule them out.

Right now, Lydia had the king's attention. I *thought* I had an idea of how to enrage her and provoke the king's emotions at the same time. I watched as Lydia grabbed a champagne flute, then leaned in, whispering to the king in a conspiratorial way.

Time to get his attention, and that meant getting Orion's attention. Jealousy would be my friend tonight.

But before I could find Orion, a female demon with a halo of white curls caught my eye. Her cheekbones shimmered with pale glitter. With a tight smile, she sauntered over to me. "Well, Mortana. Congratulations are in order." She touched her throat and swallowed with a grimace. "I've never met a demon with your powers of poison before. Quite intriguing. Miasma magic."

I gave her a fake smile and a shrug. "I don't often have a reason to poison people."

"I'm Nama."

Ah...the one with the ice powers.

When her glance darted over my shoulder, her expression changed. She licked her lips, and her pupils dilated. I stole a quick look behind me to see Orion.

So that's why she'd approached me. *Keep your enemies close...*

Her gray eyes locked on mine again, and the look she gave me sent a chill through my body. "It's interesting to see the duke getting close to someone new. Before you arrived, he and I were going to be quite good friends." She flicked her white hair over her shoulder. "I'll admit we haven't had the chance to become properly acquainted yet, but I think I'm considered one of the best marriage matches for him."

"Oh?" I took a sip of my cocktail, trying to get into the bitchy Mortana mindset. "Considered by whom?"

Her lips thinned. "By many. He and I both come from wealth. You know, we have a lot in common. We both love the sea."

My shadow-self found her irritating, so I lifted my cocktail glass and stared into it. I swirled my drink, looking disinterested in her. "Everyone loves the sea. Why would you possibly think that would make you well suited? It's akin to liking sunlight."

"He likes pastries, and I'm an excellent cook," she said sharply. "And when I injured my thigh in a sea cave, he healed me. Listen, Mortana, have you been spending a lot of time around mortals, by any chance? You seem as dull-witted and unsophisticated as they are. There's something really not right about you."

I gave her a patronizing smile. I was starting to find that it wasn't hard at all to come up with what Mortana would say. "Maybe I'm unsophisticated, but I'm going to guess that you hurt your thigh on purpose, then ran to Orion crying that you needed help. Don't you think he could smell the desperation?" I sipped my cocktail, watching as her cheeks went red. "Don't mistake pity for affection, my dear."

Wow. Mortana was a bitch. And maybe it was kind of fun.

Nama's eyes darkened to shadows, and her jaw went tight. She leaned in and whispered in my ear, "You're older than I am, Mortana. But I've been told why the king wisely rid the city of your kind. The succubi whores like you brought disrepute to our city, begging for cock like you did. Disgusting. Dirty. I heard what he said about you. How you beg for it on your hands and knees. And you might charm Orion for a week with whatever tricks your twat can manage, but he'll quickly see that you are *all* used up. No better than a mortal whore. He'll want someone younger. Cleaner. They always do. Tell me, harlot, do you know what happened to the succubus Jezebel in the ancient world?"

I kept that serene smile on my face, but I had no idea. "Of course."

"Maybe you'll find yourself thrown from a palace window, trampled by horses, then eaten by stray dogs," she hissed. "Just like Jezebel."

Ah. Learned something every day.

❧ 25 ❧

I kept my face calm and raised an eyebrow. "Is that a threat, Nama?"

"None of the demon males stepped in to protect your kind when you needed it. They fucked you, then left you to die. All it takes is one look at your harlot-red hair and the repulsive way you move to know you're not wife material. You're an easy, available hole." She backed away and fluttered her eyelashes at me. "Nice talking to you, Duchess." Then she spun on her heels to walk away.

Her words were directed at Mortana, but there was enough personal stuff included there to make my stomach tighten with anger anyway. No better than a mortal? *Harlot*-red hair?

Had to say I didn't like Nama very much.

And when I turned to see that she had sashayed over to Orion, that she was giggling up at him, I felt a tiny little ember of my own jealousy burning. But that was absurd. Orion and I didn't have a *real* relationship, obviously. He'd hired me to do a job, I was treating him as a suspect, and that was that. But I found myself staring as Nama looked up at him adoringly, lightly stroking his tattooed arm. My id—my shadow-self—was getting angry.

I glanced behind me and found that the king's attentions were occupied with Lydia.

It was time to turn all this annoying shit to my advantage, *now*.

I turned back to Orion and Nama. Now, Orion was looking at me, the corner of his mouth quirked in a half-smile. It was almost like he knew I'd felt jealous. But there was no way he could have sensed that, so that was probably me being paranoid.

I summoned my id. With a seductive smile worthy of Mortana, I beckoned Orion toward me.

If I said it wasn't satisfying to watch him brush Nama off and walk closer to me, I'd be lying. She was giving me the look of death, like she was going to rip my head off any second now. The unfortunate part was that she probably could.

Orion prowled closer with languid movements, eyes locked on me. When he was just inches away, I reached up and pulled him down closer, whispering, "Let's make the king jealous."

"Hello, love." His low whisper was a seductive stroke up my spine. My pulse started to race. "Are you ready to leave your inhibitions behind?"

Just being close to him and feeling his magic pulse over my body made my breath hitch, even if all this was just for show. "Yes." *Must... remember...he's my suspect...*

Taking me by the hand, Orion led me to a chair near the king. In the next heartbeat, he was pulling me into his lap. I could feel all eyes on us now, but my attention was on Orion. His exquisite beauty was still shocking to me. His lids looked heavy as his eyes darkened. I felt a blush creep over my cheeks.

"Your friend Nama seems to think I'm taking something that belongs to her," I said quietly.

His fingertips brushed up my leg just above my knee, and heat rushed through my body. "I belong to no one." With excruciating slowness, his hand moved further up my thigh, then slid under the hem of my dress, his touch scorching. He leaned in, lips lightly brushing over mine. The Lord of Chaos had an excruciating capacity for restraint. The graze of his lips against mine was making my nipples go hard in my silky bra. His hand moved higher, dragging my hem with it. His fingertips stroked slowly up and down my skin...

God, I wanted to take him somewhere alone.

This is just a job.

I wondered if he could hear how fast my heart was beating now. Did he realize that when I told him I didn't find him attractive, I was lying through my teeth?

For his part, his muscles seemed tightly coiled. Maybe this restraint wasn't so easy for him.

Unable to contain myself anymore, I pressed my lips against his. Under the hem of my dress, his fingers tightened on my flesh. He kissed me back slowly, deliciously, his tongue brushing against mine. When he pulled away from the kiss, my heart was racing out of control. I ached for him. And if all of this was happening in front of other people—that wasn't my fault. That was *Mortana's* fault.

I could feel everyone watching us now, but to my shock, I found that I actually didn't care.

He moved his mouth close to my ear. "Why do I get the feeling that you want more?" His deep purr made me melt into him.

I could feel my cheeks heating. "Just doing my job," I whispered back.

The brush of his fingertips was a slow, maddening touch that left a trail of heat in its wake, now near my panties. I felt as if there was something reverent in the way he was touching me, and my core pulsed, aching for him. Slowly, he moved his hands over my panties, brushing his fingertip down the front. I gasped at the sensation. I was sure that he could feel *exactly* how turned on I was through the silk, and I felt my cheeks going redder. From him, I heard a quiet growl that seemed to reverberate over my skin.

I should probably stop this now. Succubus or not, I wasn't going to fuck him right here in front of a crowd.

"I think that's enough," I whispered.

When he pulled his hand away from me, out of my dress, I rose from his lap. I felt my cheeks and chest flushed with heat as I looked around, seeing everyone's judgmental eyes on me. Nama looked like she was about to crush the glass she was holding.

But there was *her* demon mark—a byzantine golden symbol that beamed from her forehead.

Several females gaped at me, seething, their marks blazing. One had the mark of a serpent, the other a triangular shape. It seemed that Nama wasn't the only one who had designs on Orion.

But Lydia and the king? The ones I actually hoped to see? No demon marks on display.

I was still catching my breath when I caught the king's eye. That had gone a little far, hadn't it? But I'd gotten what I'd wanted—his attention.

He crossed over to me swiftly, his eyes dark as night, pale hair draped over his velvet suit. His jaw was set tight, and he boxed me in until my back was against a column. He pressed his hands on either side of my head, his crown gleaming in the lights of the bar.

My heart skipped a beat. I'd *definitely* gotten his attention.

His stance was possessive, dominating. And since I was supposed to be an ancient and powerful demon, I couldn't shrink from it. "I hope you will find your new accommodations in the Asmodean Ward to your liking. I had my mortal servants working day and night to get it in good condition. I had my best magicians working on it, too. I can give you *anything* you desire."

I smiled serenely. "I haven't had a chance to see it yet. I was at Orion's apartment earlier."

His muscles visibly tensed. "Why be with a duke when you could be with a king?" He sounded almost pleading. This was driving him mad. "I don't understand."

I looked into his chiseled features. "I could be with a king?"

"Don't you remember, in those days when you were with my father," he said through gritted teeth, "don't you remember how much I wanted you?"

Of *course*. Motivated by jealousy, the little prince wanted what his father had. The succubus mistress.

"Did you?" I asked with a smile. "It seems so long ago. It's just that I notice Orion more. He pays so much attention to me. He tells me things, all about himself. You haven't really told me about yourself. It's hard for me to desire someone unless I know what makes him vulnerable."

Over his shoulder, I could see Lydia fuming. Unfortunately, I couldn't see her mark.

"Tomorrow," he replied. "I'm having a party in my penthouse suite in the Tower of Baal. You must be there. I will *not* take no for an answer. Come by yourself. There's no reason to bring the duke."

But the duke, paradoxically, was the key to his affections. All my power over the king depended on his jealousy.

"I'd love to come, but Orion will be joining me. Once you tell me more about yourself, we can get to know each other better."

He nodded curtly, then dropped his hands. With the look he was giving me, I had the sense that he didn't hear "no" often. "Fine. Bring the duke," he muttered. "He isn't a threat to me."

Good news for Orion's spy mission: the king wasn't a very good liar.

❦ 26 ❦

It was nearly dawn by the time we reached my new home in the Asmodean Ward. Orion and I jumped in a cab, not saying a single word about our very public kiss. I only told him we had party plans for the next night, and he seemed pleased at my progress.

When we arrived at my house, a man in a black suit and hat opened the cab door for me. A second doorman opened the building's front doors into a hall with pale blue and gold tiled floors. High above, arches of a pale buttery stone swept over us. Sweeping staircases led up to a mezzanine floor.

In the center of the lobby, the ceiling was painted with an image of a nude woman, a snake wrapped around her legs and body. Lilith, I thought. While most of the hall was gleaming, restored through magic, the ceiling had faded and chipped over time.

To my surprise, Orion stared at the fresco for a long time, his body completely still. He normally seemed so bored with things, but either the naked woman or the snake had caught his attention. In fact, I sensed him shifting a little, the shadows bleeding into the air around him.

While he studied Lilith, I crossed to the far side of the hall, where arches opened onto a courtyard with an enormous pool. Beyond the pool, I could see the river through a set of columns, the dark water glinting with just a hint of morning light. And just on the other side of the river was the forbidding Elysian Wilderness. I shivered, not wanting to remember the hour I'd spent there, fighting for my life.

Orion said the Puritans thought the natural world was dangerous. Right now, I felt their fear. I understood why the devil scared the shit out of them. The primal power of these demons, their bestial side—it was terrifying.

"You need sleep." Orion's deep voice pulled me from my worries.

"No arguments here." My body was exhausted at this point, and I desperately wanted rest. I followed Orion up a flight of stairs, and we stopped at a door that had once been painted a deep maroon, the color now faded with time. He slid a skeleton key into the lock, then opened the door, handed me the key, and flicked on a light. I found myself staring at the key in my palm, then tracing its shape.

I owned a key like this. It was one of the few things that I'd always kept close to me until the night Orion had abducted me. My heart raced as I stared at it, and then I slid it into my pocket and followed him into the apartment.

The walls within were stone, like a medieval castle, except they were smooth and gleaming. Enormous windows overlooked the pool, the water of which had started to glitter a little with peach light as the first blush of sun began to tinge the sky with gold. Stairs led to a loft floor, which must be where the bed was. A chandelier hung from the ceiling, a circle of wood that looked as if it had once held candles, but now boasted electric lights.

"The king must have had this place wired today," said Orion. "He's desperately trying to impress you, I think."

"He told me that he used to lust after Mortana when she was with his dad." My lip curled. "He really has a lot of Oedipal stuff going on."

"Of course he wanted his father's lover." Orion crossed to an open archway and peered in. "He's made everything modern. *Ridiculously* so. He's put a cappuccino machine in the kitchen, and even I don't have one of those. I'm wondering if I need to seduce the king now."

I crossed to the stairs, then turned to look at him. "Will you stay? I mean, you said I might be in danger."

Amusement shone in his pale eyes, and he dropped down on one of the leather sofas. He stretched out his arms across its back, and I had a feeling that he was *well* aware of how hot he looked as his shirt clung to his magnificent body. "I'll be here."

Somehow, he'd made that one sentence sound like an indecent invitation.

"That kiss in the bar was just a job, of course." Why did I say that? I sounded desperately defensive.

"Of course. I'm glad we're in agreement." A smile played over his lips. "Go to sleep, Rowan. I'll be here."

❧

EVEN AS THE SUN POURED INTO THE ROOM THOUGH THE ARCHED windows, I continued to sleep on the softest bed I'd ever touched. By the time I woke, the afternoon sun was already high in the sky. I'd slept in my underwear, and the sheets felt silky against my bare skin.

I sat up and rubbed my eyes, taking in the sun-drenched space around me. The loft above the suite included a large bedroom with a railing on one side and a marble bathroom and bathtub on the other. I rose from the bed and crossed to the bathroom to splash water on my face. Mentally, I tried to reorient myself. Night and day seemed mixed up here.

I pulled off my underwear and turned on the shower. Steam started to billow around the tiles, and I grabbed the soap and washed.

My pulse raced whenever I thought about Orion's lips brushing over mine. When I thought of what he'd look like without his shirt on...

Insanely, I wanted him in here with me.

Everything about him distracted me. I turned down the temperature of the shower until a blast of cold water started to clear my head and sharpen my senses.

Tonight, I was supposed to go to a party in the king's penthouse. I was *pretty* pleased with how well I'd been able to get the king's attention. But what if I learned his weakness before I solved my mom's murder? I hadn't seen a single star, and I'd need to be here a while to hunt the killer down.

Could I just...lie to Orion until I got what I needed?

Shit. No. Not when he'd threatened Shai's life.

Goosebumps covered every inch of my body in the freezing shower, and my nipples were hard as rocks. With teeth chattering, I turned the shower off.

I grabbed a towel and began to dry off, only to recall that I had no clean clothes upstairs.

Chilly, I crossed to the balcony. When I peered over the edge, I saw that someone had delivered all my new clothes from Orion's apartment.

Gripping the towel around myself, I headed downstairs. A knocking sound echoed into the room, and I watched as Orion moved to open the door, his silver hair ruffled.

What I didn't expect to see—what I really didn't *want* to see—was Nama sauntering into the room with a basket of fresh-baked goods.

She'd come to prove herself to him with croissants.

27

Her white hair cascaded over a thin white dress. On the one hand, it looked like an innocent sundress. On the other, I didn't think it was an accident that when the afternoon sunlight hit the material, it became almost translucent. I could see the shape of her breasts through the fabric, the nipples standing at attention, and with the angle of the light hitting the doorway, she practically glowed.

She shot me a look of death, then smiled at Orion again. "I was bringing you some chocolate croissants at the Leviathan Hotel, but your doorman told me you were here. I must say, I found it a bit shocking. I wanted to make sure no harm had come to you, given what we know of her kind."

With my chin held high and proud like a demon's, I descended the stairs. "As you can see, he's fine."

Orion grabbed one of the croissants and dropped back into a chair. He met my gaze and gave me a wicked smile, eyes twinkling. "She didn't leave any marks that will last forever."

I bit my lip, watching Nama's reaction. Her demon mark beamed from her forehead. If all the demons were so easy to provoke, I'd find the murderer in no time.

Clutching my towel with one hand, I plucked a warm croissant from the basket. "Thanks for the breakfast. You can go now." Ahhh... my id was a fucking bitch, but definitely fun. "Feel free to pop by tomorrow morning, Nama. We might have worked up an appetite again."

The mark blazed from her skin. She pressed her lips into a thin line, and she turned to go. But before she left, she whipped around and grabbed me *hard* by the back of my neck. I dropped my towel as she yanked me close to her ear, and she whispered, "There's something not right about you. Something besides you being a whore. I saw you in the forest, dressed in that strange suit. I smelled that putrid scent. You smelled like animal piss. No one believes me because they think I'm mad, but I plan to find out what your game is."

"Get your hands off her, Nama," Orion snarled from behind.

She released my neck and hissed at me. An actual hiss, like a snake.

With a furious blush crawling over my cheeks, I scrambled to pick my towel off the floor. I wasn't sure what was more horrifying right now, being fully exposed in front of these two demons, or the fact that Nama might know I was mortal.

The door slammed behind her, and I hastily wrapped the towel around myself. When I turned to Orion, I could feel that my cheeks were burning red.

For his part, he looked fucking delighted. Infinitely amused.

"What?" I snapped.

He just shrugged. "That was a gorgeous view I wouldn't mind seeing again. That's all."

My jaw tightened. "We have a problem."

"We do," he agreed, his smile fading. "She's watching you too closely because she's threatened. But I don't think you need to worry about her. She doesn't have a lot of credibility here. Everyone knows she's unhinged. She's never learned to control her emotions." His eyes lingered over my bare shoulders. "I liked you better without the towel."

"Can you turn around so I can get dressed?" I asked.

With a sigh, he turned to face the other direction. "When we're at the king's penthouse tonight, he may want to see you alone, but I want to stay close to you. The king, as you might have gathered, can be dangerous."

With Orion's back to me, I dropped the towel to the floor. When it hit the tiles, I heard a quiet growl rise from his chest, nearly imperceptibly. He wanted me.

What would it take to make *his* demon mark come out? To see if he really belonged on my suspect list?

Stark naked, I crossed to the bags of clothing on the sofa, then glanced at him from behind. "What should I wear? Sheer black panties or the white ones with the ribbons and garter belts?"

A sharp intake of breath. "Sheer black." His voice sounded low, husky. His hand at his side was now clenched into a fist.

"You're sticking with me at the party tonight," I said, slipping into the sheer black underwear. "So you *are* my protector, then." I pulled them up over my hips, then grabbed the matching bra. "As long as I don't betray you or fuck anything up, in which case, you'll murder my best friend."

"That's a good summary."

I looked through the bags again until I found a silky red sundress. I slipped it on, and it hit my thighs just below my butt. "You can turn around now."

When he pivoted, his deep gray eyes shimmered like stars, but for the first time, I saw something like sadness in them. "You really look so much like her. It's disturbing."

"Well, I'm not her." Weirdly, that didn't feel entirely true. Last night, I'd inhabited her character so easily that she'd felt like a part of me. And worse, I liked being her. It was oddly freeing. "You haven't actually revealed anything about yourself, though. You haven't told me what Mortana did or why you're so desperate for revenge."

His eyes seemed to be searching mine, and silence spread out between us. At last, he said, "Mortana was involved in my mother's death. When she died, I made a blood oath that when I found Mortana again, I would slaughter her."

Something sharp pierced my heart. All this—the spying, the rage, it was all to avenge his mom. He and I had way more in common than I'd expected.

"And her close blood relatives," he added. "To stamp out her family line forever. Except I think everyone in her family is already dead, except her."

Panic twinged in my chest. "I look *exactly* like her. Are you sure I'm not her descendant?"

He sighed. "If you're mortal, you're not her descendant. We don't breed mortal offspring. Hardly breed at all, really, which is why it's unlikely there would be any family line to destroy. She killed all her own relatives when she helped King Nergal with the Lilu purges."

My chest unclenched a little. "I'm sorry about what happened to your mom."

His brow furrowed. "Well, it wasn't your fault. You're not actually Mortana."

"No, that's just something mortals say." I took a deep breath. "Someone killed my mom, too." As soon as the words were out of my mouth, I was surprised I'd actually uttered them.

"Ah." He cocked his head, going very still. "That's what you weren't telling me. Your mother was murdered."

"Someone burned her to death in the Osborne Woods. I was there..." My chest went tight, and it started to feel hard to breathe. "I was with her, but I don't remember most of it. Just the scent of burning flesh, mostly, and..." Emotion tightened my throat, and I trailed off. I shouldn't be sharing so much with one of my suspects. So much for being an undercover cop.

He reached up and brushed a tear off my cheek. "What?"

"Some thoughts that are a bit too dark for other people to hear," I said.

"Not for me." His eyes were an endless blue. "I think you'll find I don't have any limits in that regard."

The guilt was eating at me from the inside out. "Okay, well, here's a question for you. Why am I still alive when she burned to death? Why did I keep running?"

His eyes darkened to shadows. "We're compelled to keep ourselves alive. It's the law of nature. And as your mother, she was compelled to keep you alive. That's the law of nature, too."

"So you don't feel any guilt for surviving when your mom didn't?"

The air was growing hotter around us, nearly scorching. "I didn't say that." His voice was barely a whisper.

I nodded. "That's why you want revenge so desperately, too. Isn't it? To make it right."

"Or maybe my rage drives me because it's all I have. It defines me and burns away the guilt. There's nothing else left in me but wrath."

I felt like my chest was splitting open. In my hunger for revenge, would I become like him? "Do you feel guilty for anything?" I ventured. "Or have you found a way to turn that off?"

Shadows darkened around Orion. "I told you." A ragged edge under that seductive voice. "Beyond a hunger for revenge, I feel almost nothing at all."

My pulse sped up as I sensed something changing around me. When psychologists looked for signs of lying in mortals, they looked for indications of anxiety. In most people—those who aren't psychopaths—lying makes them nervous. It's why polygraphs show increased heart rates, or why a liar pulls eye contact. People lying might fidget, look away.

Demons didn't show emotions in the same way. They never fidgeted or lowered their eyes out of nerves. But they could shift, and their bodies seemed to change the air around them, making it hotter or colder.

I'd moved closer, just inches from him now. "I'm not sure I believe you. But I think you should know that there's something I would want revenge for. If you lay a finger on Shai, I'll find a way to kill you."

Demonic stillness, eyes dark as night.

Not my protector. Not really. Must remember that.

A dark chuckle. "Do you still think it's wise to threaten me? As fragile as you are?"

"You forget, Orion, I passed the Trial all on my own. I don't break that easily." I delivered these lines with a lot more bravado than I actually felt.

His lips were curled with a dark smile. "No, I don't suppose you do. I suppose I can feel something besides a lust for revenge, and that's a surprise."

Was that nearly a compliment from Orion?

But his eyes were still dark as night as he was starting to shift. A demon's black eyes conveyed a message to mortals: *If you were smart, you'd probably run.*

And maybe that was something I should keep in mind around this predator. "Can I have a few hours to myself? I need to clear my head."

And you make that very difficult.

❧ 28 ❧

With a margarita in one hand, I dipped my legs into the pool outside my room. Since I'd slept through most of the day, twilight was already spreading its coral mantle over the sky, and the shadows were growing longer. The setting sun bathed the golden stones in blood-red light, and it dazzled orange off the flowing Acheron River. On the far bank, shadows pooled in the wilderness.

As requested, Orion had left me alone—with his number programmed into my new cell phone. If Nama or Lydia, or anyone else, cropped up looking for trouble, I was supposed to hit *star seven*, and my protector would appear in a whorl of shadows.

I also had the doorman and mortal servants looking out for me, one of whom brought me a pitcher of margaritas and vegan tacos. And most importantly, Shai was on her way over for a dip in the pool with me.

This would continue to be *my* pool, if I had my choice—if I didn't have to leave here, and if Shai's life weren't at risk. This place was intoxicating in a way that started to make me wonder if I'd lose my mind here. I wanted to sink my claws into this city. I wanted to take it over like an invasive species. When I thought of Nama, a sense of competitiveness started to rise in me.

I had an insane impulse to stake my claim on this city—permanently. I wanted to *actually* be the demon duchess, to bring the Asmodean Ward alive again. The incubi and succubi didn't deserve their fate. Whoever Jezebel was, the woman probably hadn't deserved to be thrown from her palace window and eaten by dogs. I wanted to plant my roots here as a succubus just to spite the rest of these judgmental fuckers.

So clearly, the intoxicating powers of this city were making me go mad, because none of that could happen. I had very limited time here.

And why was I starting to care about the fate of the Lilu? I sipped my tart cocktail, letting the taste of lime roll over my tongue.

I suppose, for one thing, people thought I was a Lilu, so I was starting to feel like one. Behavioral confirmation. For another, it was just the injustice of it all. It seemed like the Lilu had been murdered because of others' raging jealousy and insecurity.

"Mortana!" Shai waved at me as she crossed through one of the arches. She wore a yellow sundress, and her hair in a halo of curls. "Nice place."

I grinned at her. "Come in the pool with me."

"As long as I can eat tacos in the pool."

"Of course." I pointed at her margarita waiting by the side of the pool. "And you have a drink."

Shai pulled off her dress, revealing a bright red bathing suit, and slipped into the water.

In the City of Thorns, it seemed like the weather was permanently tropical. Another reason it would be great to sink my roots into this place.

I let out a long sigh.

"What? Why do you sound like you're not enjoying this paradise?" Shai took a bite of her tacos.

"I'm feeling guilty that I got you dragged into all this."

"Dragged me into all what? Tacos and margaritas in a pool? It's not your fault you look exactly like some succubus."

"I know," I whispered. "But if I fuck anything up, Orion says he'll kill you. Your life is in danger, Shai."

She snorted. "Do you think I'm an idiot? I made him swear a blood oath to keep me safe."

I stared at her. I'd never considered just extracting promises from him like that. "Wait, *what?*"

She took a sip of her margarita. "It's all about leverage, darling. My mom taught me that during the divorce. You figure out what they want, and you threaten to destroy it if they don't meet your terms."

My jaw dropped open. So her life wasn't at risk... "Sorry, what did you threaten to destroy?"

She squinted in the sun. "Well, don't take this the wrong way, but I knew he needed you for whatever his plan was. So I threatened to get rid of you if he didn't agree." Another bite of tacos.

"*What?*" Shai once got mad at me for killing an ant. "You threatened to kill me? You're a vegan!"

"Well, he doesn't know that," she whispered. "And you always go on about psychopaths. I feel like I learned a few things from you. I know you said psychopaths don't get nervous, but I don't think he realizes that, either. Because my palms were sweating and my heart was beating out of control. But I kept my voice totally calm, and it worked." She smiled at me. "I sounded really scary, I think."

"What did you say?"

She shrugged. "I watched a true crime show once about a psychopath who murdered his mom by cutting off her head. So I just said that if he didn't do what I wanted, I'd cut your head off."

"How does he know you're not going to murder me now?"

She waved a hand. "It was a whole thing. He made me swear a blood oath in return—not to hurt you or tell anyone what you really are. He felt like he was actually getting a good deal out of that. Since I have no intention of actually murdering anyone, I've really never made an easier deal in my life. I've got my tuition paid, plus I got a much better apartment than the one I had before. And he has to keep me safe. And I got a really great cappuccino machine. This has all worked out nicely for me. You have literally nothing to feel bad about."

"Holy shit, Shai. He never told me any of that."

She shrugged. "Of course he didn't. I'm his leverage. He can get you to do what he wants as long as you think my life is at risk. He should have asked me to keep quiet during the blood oath, but you came down and interrupted, and then I think he got distracted."

I bit my lip. "Well, this is a very interesting development. So I can...stay as long as I want here."

She frowned at me. "I'm not sure I like the look on your face. What are you scheming now?"

"I don't want to leave."

She shook her head. "But you can't keep this lie up forever, can you? What would happen if the king found out you were lying?"

I cleared my throat. "Well, that *is* a little hitch in my plan."

"No, really—what does happen if the king learns you're lying? Demon dungeon?"

"Fire pit."

Her eyes widened. "Fucking hell, Rowan. Obviously, you can't stay."

I lifted my finger to my lips. She couldn't say my real name that loudly.

She had a point, except I think I was so scared of the fire pit, my brain refused to consider it was a possibility. I was in some kind of advanced state of denial. "But what if I can keep the deception going? Orion will keep me safe until I can find the information he wants."

She rested her elbows on the side of the pool. "I mean, I can see why you'd want to stay here. You're living like a queen, and this is heaven. But is it really worth the risk of a fire pit?"

"It's not just the pool and the luxury. Shai—I'm almost positive a demon killed my mom. One with fire magic. And I want to find out who it was." I left out the bit about avenging the Lilu, and the feeling that my shadow-self was growing more powerful, because she'd think I'd lost my mind.

She frowned, her dark eyes piercing me. "I can understand the temptation. But then what? What does it get you?"

"I want to know the truth." And I wanted to murder the fucker, maybe.

"Have you found anything out so far?"

I let out a long breath. "I have a short list of suspects. Orion is one of them."

Her eyes widened. "Fuck. Why would he have killed your mom?"

I shook my head. "I don't know why *anyone* would. I only know two things—I think it was someone with fire magic, and I think it was someone with a demon mark shaped like a star. You know, the shiny forehead things?"

"I've seen one once. Not a star."

"I haven't seen that particular mark yet, either, but I keep looking. That's all I remember from that night. And Orion is one of just a handful of demons with fire magic—along with Lydia, the king, and Mortana herself. Orion says the star mark means that you're destined to be the demon leader, blessed by Lucifer. So my guess is that the king is the top suspect. But no one knows what the king's mark looks like, so I'm not sure."

Shai stirred her drink with her straw. "Maybe if you want to find the killer, you need to learn more about your mom instead of learning more about demons. What was her connection to this world?"

"I searched all her things after she died, looking for clues. I couldn't find anything." I closed my eyes, running through my memories until something sparked in my mind—something I'd seen recently. "Except a key." My eyes snapped open. "It was a skeleton key like the ones they use here. Like the one Orion used to unlock my apartment door. I found it hidden in a drawer, but I never knew what the key went to."

"Do you still have it?" she asked.

I nodded. "She didn't leave much behind. Just the key, some clothes, old books, and enough money for a few months' rent. So I kept the key." In the gathering shadows, as darkness fell, it was hard not to feel a pang of sadness. Mom had a whole life she'd never told me about.

"I can go in and out of the city," said Shai. "I can grab the key. If you can find what it goes to, maybe that'd be a clue."

I smiled at her. "Thanks, Shai."

She grabbed her cocktail off the side of the pool. "What do you have planned for tonight?"

I took a deep breath. "Spying for Orion, of course. In the king's penthouse."

Her eyebrows rose. "But you'll be careful with all this, right? Because everything you're telling me sounds dangerous as hell. Particularly the fire pit situation, considering the king is one of your suspects."

"Yep. And Orion, too. I don't trust him at all."

"Is that right?" Orion stepped from the shadows, his pale eyes burning like stars. He wore an expensive-looking charcoal-gray suit. "And here I was imagining we might be friends."

My stomach flipped.

He cocked his head. "We have a party to get ready for, don't we?"

❧ 29 ❧

In the Tower of Baal, we stepped into the elevator to ride up to the penthouse floor. I wore a dress made of a sheer material that showed off my legs, but with strategically placed blue filigrees to allow a bit of modesty.

As soon as the elevator started, Orion turned his piercing blue eyes to me. "I'm curious what you and Shai were talking about. You said you don't trust me, which makes sense, because I'm a dick. But there's more to it than that, isn't there? There's something specific."

I crossed my arms. "Fine. You want revenge, and I do, too. I want to find my mom's killer. Someone killed her with fire magic in the Osborne Woods, and I want to know who it was."

His eyes went wide. "Ah." He turned and pressed the emergency button, stopping the elevator. "There we are. You think I could have killed your mother."

I shot an irritated glance at the door. "Do we have to have this conversation trapped in an elevator?"

"I'm afraid so."

I crossed my arms, looking impatiently at the door. "You have fire magic, so yes, you're on my short list of suspects."

He slid his hands into his pockets and shrugged, looking up at the ceiling. "I'm ruthless, lethal, lacking in empathy. I don't hide my flaws or lie about what I am, so that's no secret. I'd murder a mortal woman if it got me what I wanted." He met my gaze. "But I didn't burn a mortal woman to death in the Osborne Woods. I'm not morally against the concept, it's just that it wasn't me."

Either he was really good at lying, or that was the truth. As I stared at him, I felt my chest unclench. "Okay."

His eyebrows rose. "I take it Shai told you that I can't kill her."

"It did come up. She's not actually a psychopath, by the way. She just used that to get you to agree to the blood oath."

He narrowed his eyes. "Hmm. Finding another person you care about that I could kill would be the easiest way to bargain..."

"That's not really what a bargain is. That's a threat, Orion."

He shrugged, his expression cold. "Well, clearly, it would be the easiest option, but it won't work. From what I understand, you don't actually care about anyone else. Shai is your only friend, and your family is dead."

I swallowed hard. "That's a depressing summary."

"How about a new bargain, then? You get me what I want, the truth about what makes the king weak, and I'll help you find your mother's killer. Once I get what I need, you'll get what you need."

I bit my lip, staring at him. This all came down to a single question—did I actually believe him? It was hard to say. But since I didn't have many offers of help here in the City of Thorns, I'd accept for now. "Fine. I'll take this deal before you come up with something worse."

"And then you'll need to leave the City of Thorns as soon as we are finished. Every hour that you're here is another hour that you risk ending up in the fire pit."

He turned and pushed a button to make the elevator move again. We started rising, and within moments, the elevator doors opened into the penthouse apartment.

Holy moly... It was like nothing I'd ever seen—a pool inset into a marble floor and towering glass windows that opened onto a balcony. Beyond the balcony, the sea glittered under the stars. A balmy breeze rushed into the apartment, toying with the demons' long, silky gowns.

The king stood on the other side of the pool, martini in hand. Subtly, people swarmed around him like moths to a flame, eyes flitting to him, fingers reaching out to touch his arm. But his attention was locked on Lydia and one of the dukes.

When my eyes met Nama's, my pulse started to race. She wore a long white gown that matched her wavy hair, plus earrings that looked like dripping icicles. But despite the delicate beauty of her outfit, her lip was curled, exposing her teeth like an animal about to attack. She pulled her gaze from mine, then smiled at Orion. When he didn't seem to notice her, she stalked over to him. "Hello, my duke." Her voice sounded shaky, angry.

Orion seemed to be looking right past her. "You again, is it?"

When a server crossed to us with a tray of cloudy purple cocktails, I plucked one off for myself and took a sip. This one was gin, lemon, and the faint hint of violets.

And as I surveyed the room again, trying to catch anyone's eye, I was starting to get the impression that people were ignoring me on purpose. This was a demonic cold shoulder.

No one wanted a succubus duchess here. The demons had tried killing me in the woods, and when that didn't work, they'd try a social freeze.

I pretended I wasn't listening as Nama started talking to Orion again, but I absolutely was.

"Your new succubus friend reminds me of a mortal sometimes," she said, as though I weren't standing right there. "The way she moves. Her slowness." Her jaw tightened. "You know the fear that mortals have, since they were our prey for so long? I sense that in her. She was wearing something strange in the woods, and she smelled like animal piss. What's she so afraid of?"

Nama was a twat, but she was a perceptive twat.

Orion flashed her a taunting smile. "She's afraid of me, I should think. And you should be, too."

Nama pouted at him, then lifted her chin. "But we're going to be great friends, you and I. We are alike. Do you believe in a soul bond?"

"I'm afraid I don't have a soul, Nama," said Orion. "I'm divine on the outside, I know. But I'm absolutely empty inside."

I was starting to think this was the mask he wore—cold and uncaring, devoid of emotions. Underneath his sarcasm, under the sensual smile, was a well of buried pain.

Nama's smile looked twisted and strained at his comments. "I don't believe that for a moment. We're fated to marry. You can pretend to deny it all you want, but I've foreseen it." Only now did she shoot me a withering look to acknowledge my presence. "And if you're not going to look into the truth about this one, then I will. She looks...fidgety. Anxious. *Mortal*."

My stomach clenched. What if she started asking around about me in Osborne?

I couldn't worry about that now while Nama was scrutinizing me for signs of anxiety, so I tried to summon my dark side—which, as it turned out, involved finishing the cocktail fast.

I closed my eyes as I drank it down.

I'm not Rowan. I am Mortana, succubus, seductress, devourer of souls. I will eat the weak for breakfast.

When I'd finished the drink, I had a nice little buzz. Despite my new anxieties, I had to keep up the seductive charade while I was here in front of the demon crowd. With a little smile on my face, I started walking toward the king, crossing alongside the pool. I imagined the trickles of water running down my body as I walked, my eyes locked on him. The warm lights of the room cast a flattering light over his masculine features and sharp jaw.

He slid me a curious look as I approached, and I could see Lydia tensing, her eyes going dark.

I wanted him alone. If I were going to learn his weakness, it would have to be away from the others.

When I was standing next to him, I leaned in to whisper, "There's only one thing you could do to turn my attention from Orion to you."

Then, with that catlike walk. I headed onto the balcony. Out there, the briny sea air rushed over me, and I stared out at the sparkling sea. I'd feel fairly stupid if I did all that and the king failed to join me, but I supposed I had to stand there with the confidence of my shadow-self.

And when I turned to look back, I found that the king *was* stalking outside to join me, a cocktail in hand. The salty air toyed with his blond hair. "As always," he said quietly, "you intrigue me, Mortana."

I leaned back with my elbows over the railing and smiled at him. I was tempted to look inside to see what Orion was doing, but that wasn't my job here. Jealousy was a game I was playing with the king; it wasn't for me to indulge in.

I sipped my drink. "You know, this city is even more beautiful than I remember. They say a king is tied to his land, so I'm sure you've only enhanced its appeal."

"I think the City of Thorns has been missing its last Lilu. We can't be whole without your kind. We're a city of seven wards, seven gods. We made a promise to the mortals, and you are the single living exception." He raised his glass. "Exactly how did you extract such a deal from my father?"

I shrugged and let the strap of my gown fall just a little. "I made him happy. You know, I always thought I should be queen."

"So did I." There was something fierce in his voice, a desperate edge to it. "Maybe I still do."

"Well, it's not too late." I sipped my drink. "But if our relationship is going to progress, I need to know the real you."

He put his drink down on the railing, then moved closer and planted his hands on either side of me. The wind whipped at his pale hair. "In what way do you want to know me?"

I reached out to stroke his jawline. "The thing is, Your Majesty, everyone has a weakness. Even a king like you."

"I'm not sure that's actually the case, Mortana."

"*Everyone*," I repeated. "If we're going to be equals, then I need to know what makes you vulnerable. If you only know someone's strong side, you don't really know them at all."

"And what makes you vulnerable, Duchess? Is there anything that you fear?"

Dammit. A deflection. It's like he'd been studying with Dr. Omer.

Maybe I could answer. What made my shadow-self feel vulnerable? I closed my eyes, trying to tune in to what Mortana would feel. If I were answering the question for myself, there'd be a wide array of fears to choose from, spanning the gamut of likely to nearly impossible: fire, dying alone, childbirth, imprisonment in North Korea, choking on a stray zipper that got into my cereal, bug infestations, making selfish choices, getting trampled by a moose...the list was pretty much endless. But Mortana? She was different. She was a survivor. She didn't agonize about being selfish or flawed—she just survived.

"Being hunted and trapped." I opened my eyes. "For obvious reasons. I'm the only one left. And you?"

"I fear nothing, because I have been blessed by Lucifer as his true leader." His tone was silky, deep.

Alarm bells rang in my mind. Did *he* have the five-pointed star, then?

He stepped back from me and pulled a knife from his pocket. The blade glinted in the moonlight, and he drew it across his palm. For just a moment, his skin flashed with bright red—but then the cut was gone again in an instant. Demons healed quickly, but this was different, almost immediate. Like an arrow bouncing off a dragon's hide.

He held up his palm. "I'm afraid to disappoint you, Mortana, but nothing about me is vulnerable. That is what it means to be blessed by Lucifer."

Shit. Was that actually true? If so, why was Orion so convinced otherwise?

"Well, that's disappointing," I said. "I like to leave my mark on a man. Drag my claws down his back." I bared my teeth. "Or mark him as mine with my fangs. I like to deliver pain with pleasure. If you can't be hurt, I'm not sure we'd be well suited."

He moved in again, pressing his hands on either side of my hips. "Maybe we could find a way to work past that."

I arched an eyebrow. "But how?"

The sea wind whipped over us, and my red hair tangled with his. Over his shoulder, I saw Orion standing in the doorway. His eyes looked dark, and darkness seemed to stain the air around him. That was how he looked when he was pissed off.

Why was he annoyed now? I was doing exactly what he wanted. In fact, I think the king was actually about to tell me something.

I turned my attention back to the king and licked my lips. "How could we arrange that? If Lucifer protects you all the time, how can I leave my claw marks on you like I did on the duke?"

The king's eyes raked down my body. "No. You won't see him anymore." His voice had a desperate edge. "I've watched you for too long to let you go to another man again. When you were with my father, the jealousy ate at me, like it did at my mother. You were the goddess of envy, inspiring it like no one else before. I vowed to have you as my own." He dragged his eyes up to mine again. "But I don't trust you."

Damn. I'd have to play on his desperation to override the sensible side. I shrugged. "Well, perhaps we're not suited to each other. I'm sure there's another demon female who would make a wonderful queen for you. And as for me? Orion can satisfy me like no other male ever has. You can see how all the females look at him, can't you? Everyone wants him."

He reached up and grabbed me by the neck. "No." Ice-cold rage laced his tone, and his fury tightened his jaw. "I *will* have what he has. I'm the king, and I deserve what I want."

Fear was starting to climb up my throat now. Panic clanged in the hollows of my mind, sharpened by my species' thousands of years as prey. My amygdala was telling me to get the fuck out right now—that was a very, *very* powerful demon was about to rip my throat out or take what he wanted from me. But I could also tell I was close to getting the information I needed. He seemed out of control, ready to do anything to have me.

"You know what I want," I whispered. "I want to know all of you. Not just the powerful side."

"I want you now." His eyes gleamed, midnight dark, and he gripped my waist like he was about to rip the fabric. "There is one way—"

"King Cambriel." Orion's voice cut through the tension like a knife. "Do not touch what's mine."

To my surprise, the king simply dropped his grip on me. His eyes glinted with darkness as he slowly stepped away.

I looked beyond the king to see Lydia stepping outside next to Orion. The king pivoted to find the two of them standing behind him.

Lydia was seething, and fury burned in her eyes. Was the king attracted to the jealousy of others, too? If so, he had a feast right here.

I exhaled, trying to hide my frustration. I'd been so close to learning what Orion wanted. But the king had been out of control. And maybe—just maybe—Orion actually cared for me.

My one burning question was why the fuck the king was so scared of Orion.

❧ 30 ❧

I met Orion's gaze as he prowled over to join me. His shoulders looked relaxed, but his eyes were dark as night. The king's frenzy had disturbed him.

Lydia shot me a sharp look, and her lip curled in a snarl. "She is not to be trusted," she hissed. "Can't you see that? Nama thinks she's lying about her identity."

King Cambriel glanced at me, his jaw tight, and then he locked his gaze on Lydia again. "Do you think I'm an idiot?" His voice boomed over the party, and the guests inside went quiet as they turned to look. "Do you think I can't detect a threat? Or that I can't look after myself? I am Cambriel, heir of the fallen Seraphim Beelzebub. As the rightful heir to the throne, I am protected by the gods themselves. Obviously, I don't need rumors spread by lunatics like Nama to keep me safe. I thought you were above gossip, Lydia. Not like the other females?"

He stalked inside once more, smoothing out his suit jacket.

Wow, that was harsh. Lydia stared after him for a moment, then turned to look at me. She gripped her cocktail glass, and the wind raked at her dark hair. The king had just humiliated her, and she looked like she was about to take out all that rage on me. Her eyes went dark as night, and fire blazed from her fingertips, melting her glass. Molten glass pooled at her feet, and my stomach dropped.

"You're ruining everything," she rasped. "I am meant to be queen in the City of Thorns, and you're burning down my plans. Did you hear how he just spoke to me?"

From across the balcony, she lunged for me, and my heart leapt. But before she could reach me, Orion shot out of the shadows and grabbed Lydia by the arm, halting her attack.

Fury contorted her features, and she pivoted to face him. "And where the fuck did you come from, Orion? Who are you, really? You've never managed to explain to anyone why you're here."

A muscle clenched in his jaw. "I don't need to explain why I'm here. In fact, I'm not allowed to. That's what the Trial is for. I passed, and that means the gods want me here. You wouldn't doubt their judgment, would you?"

"Of course not," she conceded.

"Just like Mortana survived the Trial. You know the king doesn't allow blasphemy. I'm sure you wouldn't want to make him angrier."

She shot me one last furious look, then turned and hurried back into the penthouse.

I exhaled slowly. It had felt like the king was about to confess his weakness to me, and I wondered if I'd get another opportunity. After this point, Lydia and Nama would make it their mission to uncover the truth about me.

How long until they simply figured it out?

Orion stepped closer to me, his eyes still black as jet. He leaned down to my ear, and heat from his body warmed me. Whenever he was near, I could feel his power rushing over my skin, a wave of sensual magic. He brushed my hair back from my ear, then whispered, "I had to stop him. He looked like he could have hurt you."

I'm not sure where the impulse came from—if it was from me or all part of the act—but I found myself reaching up and touching his chest. As I did, I heard a sharp intake of breath.

"He nearly confessed the truth," I whispered. "First, he said Lucifer protects him as the king..."

"That's a lie," he whispered. "He uses some form of magic to make himself invulnerable."

I stepped back a little to look into Orion's eyes, wanting to know more. Why was he so obsessed with this? And what did it have to do with Mortana?

But even if the king was easy to manipulate, Orion was not. He wouldn't tell me easily. I pressed myself against him and whispered, "I was close. He's incredibly jealous of you, and I think he was on the verge of telling me how I could leave claw marks on him—"

Orion let out a low growl, then shifted until our foreheads touched. He cupped his hand around the back of my neck. "Did you tell him the truth? That I was the first man you'd ever seen who could truly satisfy you in the way you need?"

My heart was racing faster, my chest flushing. "Did I say that?"

His hooded expression made my breath catch. "Let's make him more jealous, shall we?" He lightly traced a finger over my jaw. "You were close to finding the truth. Maybe we can push him over the edge. I aim to show the king exactly how much you want me."

Was this really just about getting information from the king, or was Orion trying to prove something?

He took me by the hand and led me back into the party. The lights were dimmer inside now, flickering like candles and reflecting off the pool. All eyes were on me as we walked inside—the succubus harlot. I tried to ignore the feeling of being self-conscious as everyone gaped.

Near one of the walls, Orion took a seat in a leather chair, then pulled me into his lap. Only his shocking beauty was able to make me forget the uncomfortable feeling of being stared at. Orion's gaze slid over the room—probably making sure the king was watching—and he stroked his hand down my spine. Hot, sensual magic followed the trail of his touch.

When his eyes met mine again, his hand moved upward, cupping my neck. I leaned in, and my lips met his. My mouth opened against his, and heat swept through my body as his tongue flicked in. I stroked my hand down his chest, feeling his abs tighten under my touch. Every thought I'd had about the crowd around us seemed to melt away, and there was nothing but the deep, sensual pleasure of his kiss. I felt my nipples going hard under my silky gown, and molten heat pooled in my core. His tongue entwined with mine.

As he finished the kiss with a nip to my lower lip, he pulled back. The look he was giving me was molten, hungry. His expression was positively primal, like he was about to rip my dress off, throw me up against the wall, and fuck me right here.

Was that the look he was giving me, or was that what I wanted to happen?

His breath sped up as he pulled down the strap of my dress, just enough that he had a good view of my hard nipples. A growl rose from his throat, and I saw his fangs lengthen like he wanted to devour me.

This was all very out of character for me, but I wasn't exactly stopping him as he reached down for the hem of my dress and slid his hand beneath. My gown was dragged upward as he traced his hand higher, exposing more of my skin. "Are you going to get cocky, love, with the two most powerful men in the city fighting over you?"

"*Get* cocky?" I said, because I was Mortana. "I know my worth."

He tilted me into him, my hips shifting in his lap. One of his hands stroked slowly up and down over my ribs. I could feel his magic, his heat, through the thin material. My breath was hitching, my pulse racing as his other hand slid around my upper thigh. He was touching me like I belonged to him, but his expression held a certain reverence that I hadn't seen before. The seductive scent of burning cedar curled all around us, and desire coiled tight within me.

His eyes darkened to black, and I sensed he knew how much I wanted this. He was responding to me as much as I was to him. He brushed his knuckles over my thigh, the sensation so maddening I could no longer think straight.

I should probably stop this now.

I mean, we were in a room with other people, for crying out loud... but my breasts ached for his touch.

From behind me, I heard the sound of a throat clearing, and Orion's hand tightened on my ass like he was claiming me. He whispered into my ear, "We got the king's attention."

A cold tendril of disappointment coiled through me. Right. Had this been about the information?

With my cheeks flushing a bright red, I turned my face a little to see King Cambriel looming over us. "Mortana and I were not finished with our discussion."

"The thing is, Your Majesty," said Orion sharply, "I don't really give a fuck."

I gasped. Was the king going to kill him for that impudence?

With me in his arms like an indecent bride, Orion rose. I felt as if the rest of the room had fallen away. It was just me and Orion now, his dark eyes shining with desire.

Without another word, he carried me outside. The sea wind chilled my skin, rustling my hair as Orion walked with me over to the balcony. Clouds had slid over the moon, and shadows swallowed up the night sky around us. The only light out there was from the party and the glittering phosphorescence of the sea.

My emotions were drowning out rational thought completely. My breath hitched, and I simply repeated, "Where are we going?"

"I thought I should take you out of there."

"On the balcony?"

"I don't want to give you over to the king. I want you in my bed, naked and moaning my name."

"Okay," I breathed. "Let's do that." I frowned at him, my heart still racing as I clung to his neck. "Why are we on the balcony? How do we get down from here?"

"You'll see, love." With me in his arms, he climbed atop the railing, and my heart stuttered in my chest.

Now, the sea breeze outside was whipping at us, and panic made my heart race. "Are you crazy?"

His dark eyes locked on mine, and he held me close against his powerful chest. "Do you trust me, love?"

"No."

His beautiful mouth curved in a dark smile. "You're very wise in that regard. But do you trust me at least not to kill you until I can bring you somewhere where I can make you come?"

"I guess?"

I tore my gaze away from him and glanced down at the ocean glittering far below us. Didn't he say only the Lilu could fly? He wasn't Lilu. "Wait—"

Before I could get the rest of my sentence out, he leapt from the balcony, and we started to plunge through the air.

❧ 31 ❧

The sea wind whipped over us as we fell into the darkness. Orion was still holding me tightly against his powerful chest, but we were falling toward the sea.

What the fuck, Orion?

Then, with a sound like a snapping bone, our fall stopped sharply. With a slamming heart, I gripped Orion's neck, catching my breath as I stared at the dark wings that spread out behind him. His feathers were tinged a deep silver at the tips, and they seemed to glow like moonlight. "What are you?" I breathed.

"Magnificent," he murmured.

Stunned, I stared at him. "No, really. I thought all the Lilu were dead besides Mortana. And that only the Lilu have wings." I just stared, trying to come to grips with what had just happened. "The female Lilu were succubi. So you're—what, an incubus? You're an incubus. Can you fuck me to death?"

Wickedness gleamed in his eyes. "Is that a request?"

"No, it was a concern."

"I promise to keep you alive." He flashed me a heartbreakingly beautiful smile. "Now you've seen the real me. And you're just about the only one."

"A bit more warning would have helped," I panted.

His muscled arms were wrapped tightly around me, one around my waist, and one under my ass.

"I couldn't risk anyone overhearing me," he said. "They need to think that you are the one flying, not me. You're supposed to be the Lilu."

In the darkness, his pale blue eyes seemed to glow.

I sucked in a sharp breath. "So...hang on, you're secretly a Lilu? And no one else knows?"

"No one except you knows that I am an incubus. And if the other demons realized that, they'd try to kill me." A faint smile. "They'd fail, but they'd try, and it would be messy and disrupt my plans."

My mind could hardly keep up with this new information. "So I'm the only person who knows what you really are?"

The corner of his lips twitched. "Either I trust you, or I'm just making stupid decisions because you robbed me of the ability to think clearly when you were sitting in my lap. When I could hear your heart beating faster and your breath speeding up, it was difficult to think straight."

With a jolt of surprise, I realized he was letting me know what made him vulnerable. "If you're an incubus, then how are you still alive?"

His wings pounded the air, and he held my gaze, his eyes searching mine. I'd never seen him look uncertain before, but he did now. "I've been in the City of Thorns the whole time," he said at last. "I've lived here for centuries. I was locked in the prison underground. The same prison where I locked you up that night. That's where I lived for hundreds of years, and for most of that time, I saw no one except Mortana. Until she disappeared."

"What?" My heart squeezed. "Didn't she leave two hundred years ago?"

He looked out over the sea as he flew, his face a mask of indifference now. "Yes."

"So you were in a dungeon by yourself for centuries." I had so many questions I wanted to ask that I didn't even know where to begin.

"Why does everyone think you're a duke? If you were a prisoner that long, how are you so stupidly rich?"

His expression had grown cold. "It's not mine. I demand money from the king."

Every response just invited more questions. "And why does he give it to you? Why is he scared of you?"

A bitter chuckle. "He has good reason to fear me."

Vague. Okay. "And does the king know you were in prison? Does he know that you're an incubus?"

"No. He only knows that I've learned one of his secrets, and he'll do anything to keep it hidden from the rest of the city."

It was hard for me to picture this powerful, dark force of nature in a prison cell for his whole life. Really, it was dreadfully sad. As we flew, the wind swept over us, whipping at my hair. "Was your mother with you when you were a kid? In the prisons?"

"Yes. But it wasn't long before she was executed. Mortana helped make all that happen. She helped round up every Lilu in exchange for her own protection."

"But how did you survive?"

I felt his fingers tighten on me, nearly imperceptibly. "Mortana liked to toy with me. And when she left, I was simply forgotten. No one knew I was there. Demons don't need to eat. We feel hunger, but we don't require sustenance to live. So I just stayed there." His eyes had darkened, and his expression seemed haunted. "Until at last, I found a way to escape."

I breathed in deeply, watching his wings as they pounded slowly under the dark night sky. "What do you mean, she toyed with you?"

Darkness slid through his eyes, and the wind seemed to grow more bitter. "I mean she amused herself by torturing me in her own way."

Holy shit. No wonder he was desperate for revenge. "And you have no idea what happened to her?"

"No," he said quietly. "I don't even know if *she* remembers what happened to her. I don't know that she has any idea who she is."

"What do you mean?"

He took a deep breath. "She once told me about a spell. It's one we use to forget what we've done, to rid ourselves of guilt. A spell for forgetting. She offered it to me, and I said no." The wind tugged at his silver hair, and his eyes gleamed in the night. "That was why, when I met you, I was so convinced you were Mortana. I thought she'd used the spell on herself. You seemed nothing like her, but I thought there was a chance she'd forgotten everything. I was sure of it until I tasted your blood."

I was pressed right against his chest, like he was clinging to me for salvation. This close to him, I could feel his chest muscles moving slightly as his wings shifted. "Must we talk about her right now?" he murmured. "I'm afraid the mood will be ruined."

But it was hard to let it go when he was a mystery I wanted to solve. "Why did she offer you a spell to forget your past? What was it you wanted to forget?"

"Because at the heart of me, Rowan, I'm evil." His gaze pierced me, the blue in his eyes shot through with shadows. "And sometimes, I'd like to forget that."

It was hard not to hear the ragged edge of pain in his voice. I almost wanted to touch the side of his face, to tell him that he wasn't all that bad. But what did I know? He hadn't told me his history.

The bitter wind was sharpening my senses as we flew. Now, the most pressing question was why I was going somewhere to be alone with an *incubus*, a creature that killed mortals with sex.

"Orion," I began, "we had a deal that if I helped you find out what made the king weak, you would help me find my mother's killer. But I didn't learn anything from the king—"

"I'll still help you"

I stared at the faint glow of silver in his wings. "Okay, and this still seems like a bad idea. As an incubus, won't you kill me? That's what incubi do. They seduce mortal women and kill them."

A sly smile played about his lips. "I may be evil, but I'm compelled to keep you safe, and I will. I won't do anything that hurts you."

"Why are you compelled to keep me safe?"

He swept down lower until I could feel the spray of the ocean against my skin. "I don't know, but it's deeply inconvenient. You're supposed to be my spy. That means putting your life at risk. How can you work for me if I can't tolerate risks to your safety?"

"If you were in prison all that time," I asked, "have you ever actually killed any mortals?"

"Not yet, I'm afraid," he said darkly. "I just obsessed over it for a few centuries."

"Wait, *what?*"

He took a deep breath. "Not the death, but the sex. It's how we feed and grow strong—from lust. So I dreamt of it day after day and night after night—feeding on mortals, drinking from their desire. Demons, too." His wings pounded the air. "I do want to kill that frat boy who attacked you, but I won't be killing him in a way that he enjoys."

I turned my head to see that we were approaching the yawning opening of a sea cave. Angling his wings, Orion swooped inside, and darkness swallowed us.

e touched down in the shadows and lowered me to the floor. When he spoke a word in a demonic language, lights sprang to life in a chandelier above us. The flames cast a warm glow on amber stone walls, and licks of fire rose in lanterns in alcoves.

I turned to look at Orion, whose wings were still spread out wide behind him. In the light, I could see how absolutely exquisite they looked, flecked with pearly white constellations that glowed like stars, blending to silver.

"Nice wings."

With a swirl of smoky, dark magic, his wings disappeared again. "They're all right." A seductive smile played over his lips. "You're the first person I've brought to my grotto."

When I turned to look at it, I realized it wasn't simply a cave. The walls were built with golden stones, and cool, blue water flowed into a pool inset into a tile floor. By the side of the fresh pool stood a bed of flat rock, covered with a mattress and turquoise pillows.

"What is this place?" I asked.

"When I got out of the dungeons, I needed to find a quieter hide-away. In my cell, I craved other people. But now that I'm around them, I'm not used to the noise of the city." The look in his eyes was endlessly sad, and his throat bobbed. "So this is where I go to escape. Except right now, it's where I want to be with you." He took a few steps closer to me.

I reached out to touch his chest, the steel beneath a soft shirt, and he shuddered. "But it must be hard to look at me when I look so much like her."

His eyes sparkled in the warm light. "It's confusing for me, too. But you aren't her. Apart from how you look, you're nothing like her."

"Because I'm not sexy?"

His expression turned fierce. "Because you're willing to risk your own life. Because you put avenging your mother's memory above your own safety. And because you're not afraid to admit your flaws. I guess we're alike in these ways."

"And we've both spent a lot of time alone." My pulse was racing as I looked up at him, still stunned by his shocking beauty. The candlelight wavered over his high cheekbones, sculpting the divine planes of his face. A dangerous pulse beat through my body, making it hard for me to think straight.

I reached down for the bottom of his shirt, and I slid my hands underneath the soft fabric. When I pulled it off him, my eyes went wide. Holy hell, he looked like a god. His body was thickly corded with muscle, his abs chiseled. He was a warrior dipped in gold.

A thrill lit up my body just looking at him, and I wanted to taste him. When I met his eyes again, I saw them searching mine. I reached for the straps of my gown, and I let it fall to the floor. I heard his sharp intake of breath, and his expression was reverent as his gaze roamed over my sheer blue underwear. With his eyes on me like that, need built within me.

Then he simply looked ravenous. He moved for me and lifted me up against the wall, his hands under my ass. I heard him moan quietly as his mouth met my throat. A hint of his fangs grazed over my skin again. Was he going to bite me? I didn't hate the thought, and I found myself arching my neck, giving him more access.

But instead of the sharp sting of teeth, I felt the warmth of his tongue swirling over my skin. My fingers threaded into his hair, and I closed my eyes. His sensual magic was stroking over my body now, a hot and dangerous caress. With my legs wrapped around him, I felt my hips rocking against his body.

As I gripped his hair, my breath sped up. "But how is it that you won't kill me? Isn't that the whole problem with incubi?"

A dark laugh. "It is a flaw, yes. But I can make you scream with pleasure even if I don't fuck you. It'll take an extreme amount of restraint on my part, but you'll be fine."

My core clenched at his words, and I was already slick with desire for him. "You're quite confident in your abilities." Truth was, I was, too.

He looked up at me with a seductive smile. "I'm an incubus. Along with killing, it's the one thing I know I'm good at."

The cool sea air rushed over my bare skin, and my nipples hardened. The look in his eyes was positively primal now, sliding into darkness.

I arched an eyebrow. "Did I mention that I've never actually had an orgasm?"

"You did." He stroked his hands up my ribs, his thumbs sliding under my bra. "That's about to change."

He caressed me just below my nipples, and my body went tight, heat flooding me. With hooded eyes, his gaze brushed down my body. "You are perfection, Rowan." He leaned down to kiss me, claiming me with his mouth.

As his powerful body pressed against mine, my lips opened for him. The kiss deepened as his tongue caressed mine. His thumbs slid up higher now, sweeping over my breasts—his touch so light that I shuddered against him. Incubi drank from lust, and I was giving him a feast right now. I felt myself melting into him, my knees already going weak. Another brush of his fingers over my breasts, and I clenched with desire.

With a nip to my lower lip, he pulled away from the kiss. I felt dazed as I stared at him.

"I want to see all of you, Rowan," he said, and it came out like a guttural plea. "I want you naked and spread out on my bed."

His gaze slid down to the apex of my thighs, where my sheer panties hid almost nothing. Dark shadows snaked out from his body like smoke, and he bit out a curse in another language. I sensed his restraint was slipping. I could feel the glorious, hard length of him straining against his pants—something else that set demons apart from human men.

He kissed me deeply again, tasting me. As my tongue brushed against his, my mind swarmed with images of the glittering sea. I felt like I was floating above it, still flying.

When he pulled away, his midnight eyes slid down my body, over my aching breasts, and then landed on the little scrap of material between my thighs. Lifting me from the wall, he carried me over to his bed and laid me down on the soft pillows. I was liquid, aching for him.

I thought he was going to lean down and kiss me, but instead, he knelt over me. Demonic magic snaked in the air around him, and his eyes were endless darkness. "Take everything off. I want you to show yourself to me."

My heart raced as my face flushed. I knew how stupid it was to come here with him in the first place, and yet, I needed him so badly that I wanted to do whatever he'd asked. I'd do anything for the pleasure he promised.

A seductive smile ghosted over his lips. "Take it all off. Now."

I reached behind my back and unhooked my bra. When I pulled it off, the ocean breeze rushed over my pebbled nipples.

A low, hungry growl rose from his chest. "Now take off the rest."

I slid my fingertips into the side of my panties. He seemed entranced with my body, which weirdly made me excited by the power I had over him. Because Orion was a powerful, ancient demon, feared even by the king. And the way he was looking at my body, it was almost with a sense of worship.

Basking in the attention, I was moving *very* slowly as I started to pull my panties down one millimeter at a time. Part of me ached to rip them off and spread my legs for him, but I was enjoying this too much.

When my panties were finally low enough to show him everything, I watched every one of his muscles go tense, his fingers clutching the pillows. His dark, intense gaze on my body was a thrill I'd never experienced before, and I wanted him to see exactly how turned on I was. But I still kept my panties moving at a glacial pace down over my hips.

His breath had shallowed, and he moved forward, planting his hands on either side of my head. "Why are you going so slowly, Rowan?"

"No reason." With a sly smile, I slid them down a little more around my thighs. "I just like the way you're looking at me."

He shifted back, then reached for my waist and lifted me. He turned me around until I was on my hands and knees, his body folded over mine. He covered my hands with his, and he whispered in my ear, "How about we go at my pace, love?"

When he'd first called me *love*, I'd hated it. But right now, it made me even wetter.

He moved away from me, but he stroked his hand slowly down my spine. As he touched me, my back arched, my ass rising to meet his touch. He kept tracing his hand down lower, over my ass, then between my thighs. An excruciatingly light touch, making me shiver. I wanted to force my hips back against him...

I gasped and raised my hips up even more. Shameless. I was throbbing with need for him. What I really wanted was for him to pull my panties aside, for him to fill me where I was wet. Aching for him, I let out a moan.

And that was when he pulled his hand away from me.

"Now," he said in a low voice. "Take those the rest of the way off for me, and I'll give you what you need."

✳ 33 ✳

I wriggled out of them quickly, and I heard his sharp intake of breath, then a low snarl.

From behind, he leaned over me again, hands covering mine for a moment. Then one of his hands moved slowly down, tracing over my breast, my nipple, making me gasp. Lazily, he moved his hand down to my abdomen.

Oh, God, he hadn't even touched me yet between my legs, and I was already insanely turned on. "Tell me," he whispered in my ear, "that you want me to give you what you need."

I turned my head, my mouth now only inches from his perfect lips. "I want you to give me what I need," I whispered.

Then, *finally*, he moved his hand lower. All it took was one light touch between my thighs to make me moan.

And because he needed his ego stroked, he pulled his hand away again.

"Come on, Orion." I'd never wanted anyone like this before.

"I just like hearing you ask," he said, his voice husky.

Slowly, lightly, he moved his middle finger in a circle just where I needed him. I groaned again, and I found my legs spreading wider, my ass moving against his length. My body was tightly coiled with desire, my toes curling. I wanted more of him—I needed him to take off his pants and fill me. My hips moved of their own accord, my body begging for more pressure. I wanted his hands all over me, and I'd become nothing now but animal desire. "Orion, I need more," I whispered.

At last, he slid one finger into me, then another, and I heard him groan my name. Pleasure was rising in me as he stroked in and out, my body clenching around him. I was moving against him, fucking his hand. Finally, for the first time, I was about to come.

"Rowan." That reverence in his tone, like a desperate prayer offered up to the heavens, started to send me over the edge. I was *writhing* beneath him, surrendering to the pleasure he was giving me.

Was this *actually* going to happen? For the first time, was I going to feel that release?

My hips moved against him as he plunged in and out of me, and my vision started to go hazy, filled with images of a midnight sea outside. My body shuddered.

My mind was going dark, shattering as spasms gripped my body.

At last, I climaxed, calling his name.

☙❧

My muscles had gone completely limp, and I pulled the sheet around myself, catching my breath.

When Orion lay down behind me, I felt that his body was still rigid, his muscles tense. I turned, kissing him deeply. Somehow, I still wanted more, but that couldn't happen. He twined his fingers into my hair, kissing me hard, desperately.

Then he pulled away with a groan. "This was more difficult than I'd imagined." His eyes were dark as night. "Rowan, we need to stop now. There's only so much torture I can take in a night."

I touched his cheek, my heart aching at his beauty. "Okay. You did it, by the way."

An amused smile. "I know."

When I turned away from him, tugging the sheets around me,

my heart was still pounding hard. Orion's powerful arms were wrapped around me, and I gripped one of them. "No wonder everyone makes a big deal out of orgasms. I had no idea. And no wonder mortals let themselves die at the hands of incubi. It was worth it."

A dark laugh from behind me. "Maybe for most mortals, it was worth it, since their lives were worthless anyway. But not for you, it wouldn't be."

The sound of water lapped gently against the rocks. "That's...sweet. I guess."

"Rowan?" he said quietly. "I don't think you should stay in the City of Thorns any longer."

Disappointment coiled through me. "You're kicking me out now? I thought you were going to help me."

He brushed my hair off my face. "I'm not kicking you out, but I don't want you to die in the king's fire pit. And I can't keep you safe until I know how to kill him."

I took a deep breath. "So you do plan to kill him. Even though he's the king and you're not his heir."

"Well, yes. I'm also considering killing Lydia and Nama, who are the two people most likely to report you for being a mortal. And I could kill anyone who—"

"Can we save the trail of death discussion for later?" I sighed. "I was enjoying the afterglow."

He pulled up a second silky blanket around me, and I curled into it.

"How often do you sleep in here?" I asked quietly.

"Often. It's where I feel the most comfortable."

My eyelids were growing heavy now, and the candles burning in the chandelier were starting to flicker and gutter out. I let my eyes close. "Orion? How did you escape the prison?"

He brushed my hair off my face, then kissed my forehead. "I dug an escape route. It took a very, very long time."

With his arm wrapped around me, I traced my fingers over his strange tattoo—the snake, formed into a noose. "And no one remembered you were down there?"

"One person did." His voice sounded distant. "But he's dead now."

The candles were growing dimmer, and Orion's chest moved slowly in and out behind me, lulling me to sleep.

"The king?" I asked. "Was he the only one?"

"You should go to sleep, Rowan."

Already, I felt myself drifting off to the gentle sound of the lapping waves. Man, it would be painful to leave. This place was *magic*.

But sleep started to claim my mind, and I dreamt of sweeping over a sparkling ocean, and lemon trees by a shoreline. Until the dreams started to grow darker—a dark mountain that spewed hellfire. A pit of writhing snakes.

Snakes that coiled themselves into nooses.

I WOKE WITH A GASP AND BLINKED IN THE DIM LIGHT. NOW, ONLY A single candle flickered over the grotto. I turned to see Orion sleeping next to me, his chest rising and falling softly. Dark sweeps of eyelashes contrasted with his pale hair.

As he slumbered, the Lord of Chaos looked strangely vulnerable. My throat went tight with emotion when I thought of him in the prison. All that time by himself after his mother was killed. He'd only been a little boy, hadn't he, when they were arrested?

Unable to sleep again, my mind started to turn over the enigma of Mortana.

From what Orion told me, she sacrificed other people to save herself. That was how she operated. I no longer thought Orion was a psychopath. He pretended to be one, but I suspected that underneath it all, his revenge mission was driven by love for his mom.

But Mortana? She sounded like a real psychopath. Someone with one guiding principle—making sure she got what she wanted. Maybe even a sadist? He'd said she tortured him in the prisons.

Why was I suddenly getting so angry about this?

I found my fists tightening so hard that my nails were piercing my palms. Red-hot anger flowed through me at the thought of Mortana, this evil woman who'd stolen my face.

My body felt electrified with rage. Oddly powerful, even. I wanted to rip Mortana's head off her doppelgänger body, but the *weirdest* part was that I felt like I could actually do it.

Wait...what was happening to me?

A flash of searing heat burned my wrist, and I looked down to see something like a tattoo flickering on my skin, black and red—burning like embers in a fire. I stared in fascination as something started to take shape before my eyes. A skeleton key smoldered on my wrist.

What in the world...

A golden light beamed over it. With a pounding heart, I started to realize where the light was coming from.

I touched my forehead, casting my wrist in shadow again.

Oh, fuck. Oh, *fuck.*

Powerful emotions could reveal a demon's true nature...

But I couldn't possibly be a demon. He'd tasted my blood, hadn't he? He'd been sure I was mortal. This had to be a nightmare.

At last, the smoldering skeleton key faded away on my wrist. Only then was I able to breathe, and I gasped, staring at the pale skin on my arm where the key had been. "Holy shit."

Orion's eyes opened, and he frowned at me. "What's wrong?"

I touched my forehead again, but the light seemed to be gone now. Only Orion's eyes glowed pale blue in the dark.

"I, um...I think I was just imagining things," I said.

He reached for me again, pulling me close to him, surrounding me with his arms. "You've had a lot to adjust to in the City of Thorns."

My muscles started to relax again in his arms, and I stared out into the dark grotto.

Diagnostic theories: temporary psychotic break with visual hallucinations, or night terrors from sleep paralysis.

At least, I hoped one of those theories was right.

I lay down again, nestling into his strong arms. I tried to force myself to relax, to let go of that horrible vision. A nightmare. That was all it was.

I turned back to Orion once more, and I caught him looking at me, his eyes half-closed.

"Orion," I whispered, "tomorrow, will you help me find out information about my mom?"

He nodded and murmured, half-asleep, "Yes. Then we need to get you out of here."

"What about the king's weakness?" I asked.

"I'll figure it out."

A nightmare. That was literally what Orion was, wasn't he?

Nightmare: from the Old English maere—an incubus. A creature that robbed you of breath in the night, that fed off you. The monsters that crawled from the shadows to drag you into the afterworld. But despite what he kept telling me, I didn't think he was really a monster. As much as it annoyed and inconvenienced him, he was putting my safety above his own goals. He cared about what happened to me.

When I closed my eyes again, my mind flashed with the image of the burning skeleton key. Why had it been so easy for me to summon my shadow-self here in the City of Thorns?

Dread slid through my blood.

Why did it feel like I knew Mortana?

A horrible thought struck me like a lightning bolt—the secret I'd been keeping myself from turning over in my mind. The thing I'd been running from.

What if it was me?

What if I was the one who'd killed Mom? What if I had a dark side I wouldn't admit to myself? That night was so chaotic, and I remembered being angry at her for making me run, for not explaining what was going on. I remembered thinking she was crazy.

Squeezing my eyes shut, I could feel myself shaking.

What if I was the real nightmare?

"Rowan," Orion whispered, "I can feel that you're panicking over something. What's happening?"

My stomach tightened. "Just what you mentioned. The danger in the City of Thorns."

"I can help you sleep, if you want," he said quietly. "It's an incubus thing."

I wanted to get away from my own terrible thoughts more than anything. "Yes, please."

And with that, a soothing magic rippled over me, coaxing my muscles to relax. My breathing and my heartbeat started to slow.

Confused thoughts whirled in my mind—an image of glowing star, the skeleton key tattooed on my arm, the writhing snakes. But none of it seemed as horrifying now.

In a world of demons and magic, it was starting to become difficult to know what was real and what wasn't.

☙ 34 ❧

The demon city was an inverted world, one where I seemed to sleep all day and rose as the sun was setting.

Maybe it was having an orgasm for the first time in my life, or maybe it was Orion's incubus sleep magic, but I slept long and hard. By the time I woke in his grotto, the late afternoon sun was slanting over the ocean, streaming into the cave in horizontal rays of coral.

It was the sunlight that reminded me of a painful reality: sexy as Orion was, he was still *technically* one of my suspects.

I rubbed my eyes, and the smell of coffee greeted me. When I felt the breeze rippling over me, I remembered I was still naked, and I pulled up the sheets around myself.

I smiled when I saw Orion sitting at a table by the side of the pool, coffee in one hand. "I've been waiting all day for you to wake. I even returned to your apartment and picked up some clothes for you."

"Thank you. I don't suppose the grotto has a shower?"

He nodded at the pool. "I have a natural bath. It's warmer than you'd think."

Of course. This was magic demon water, which frankly, was much nicer than Massachusetts water. It was a damn shame the demons had spent so long trying to eat us or fuck us to death, or we could have worked together.

Orion had already seen *all* of me, but for some reason, I still kept a sheet wrapped around me as I crossed to the pool. I dropped it only before I jumped in.

As I sank beneath the surface, the heated pool enveloped me. When I came up again for air, I folded my arms over the side and looked up at Orion.

He gave me an amused smile. "Still shy in front of me?"

"Maybe a little." I sighed. "I love it here. Is the grotto a secret from everyone else?"

"You're the only person in existence who knows it's here, besides me."

The warm water was lapping at my back and my breasts. What I was thinking was that it wouldn't be the *worst* thing in the world to stay here secretly for a while, assuming I cleared Orion off my list of suspects. But maybe hiding in a demon's sea cave wasn't a realistic life plan. And *maybe* trying to move in with someone after a single night was a bit much. "So should we investigate a murder?"

Orion reached for something on the table, then lifted an envelope. "While I was picking up your clothes, I ran into Shai. She gave me this to pass on to you. And as luck would have it, it's got the skeleton key you were looking for."

I rested my chin on my arms as I looked at him. "She just *gave* you that?" She didn't know he was going to help me. Why would she hand it over to him?

"Well, not willingly. She was standing outside your flat looking for you." He gave a lazy shrug. "So I forced her to tell me what she was doing there."

My fingers tightened into fists. "What do you mean, you forced her? Like, you threatened her?"

His eyebrows rose. "No, of course not. I can't threaten her when she knows I can't hurt her." He dropped the envelope on the table. "So I just controlled her mind with magic."

I stared at him. "You can't just mind-control people, Orion."

A line formed between his brows. "Yes, I can. That's how I got the key. I just told you."

I shook my head, starting to lose patience. "I know you're physically able to. I mean, it's...immoral."

"I am a demon," he said slowly, like I was an idiot.

I dropped my head into my hands. "Okay. But you feel guilt for something in the past." I looked up at him again. How did I explain this? "Guilt is about the realization that you've done something wrong. Like, you've done something to another person that you wouldn't want done to yourself, right? And it makes you feel bad. That's guilt."

He was staring at me like I was speaking a foreign language. "But I don't feel guilty for using mind control on Shai. You asked me to help you find your mother's killer. This key seemed to be one of your only clues, and I got it for you." He opened the envelope and pulled out the skeleton key on a long, black ribbon. "See?"

Maybe it was too much to ask a demon to understand the moral issues with mind control. One step at a time.

But more importantly, the key had my attention right now, because for whatever reason, my mom had a key to a room in the City of Thorns. And it reminded me a lot of the one I'd seen on my arm. "Do you think it could go to a room in the Asmodean Ward?"

"It looks like the keys in the Asmodean buildings. The locks haven't been updated in hundreds of years." He brushed his fingertip over it. "And this one has a faint carving of a skull. It's one of the few things I remember from before I was imprisoned. The keys like this..." He stared at it, lost in his memories. "I think I was scared of them, if you can imagine such a thing."

My mind shimmered with the memory of the key I'd seen flickering in and out on my arm. Had there been a skull there, too?

I hoisted myself out of the pool, my heart slamming hard. As my mind churned, I wrapped his sheet around me like a towel.

His gaze flicked down to the sheet. "You know how you were talking about guilt? Do you feel guilt for soaking my sheet in seawater?"

I looked down. "Sorry, I was distracted. Orion, what the fuck was my mortal mom doing with a key to a building in the abandoned Asmodean Ward?"

He turned it over in his hands. "If we locate the right building, I think we'll find out."

�֍ 35 ✥

We didn't start looking around until night had fallen and moonlight bathed the Asmodean Ward in haunting silver. For once, I wasn't wearing some sexy gown—just black leather leggings and a dark sweater. We weren't planning to be around anyone else, and it was the best way to blend into the night.

Tonight, the air in the City of Thorns was a little cooler than it had been, a nip along with the ocean breeze. The wind rushed through my red curls as we walked the empty streets.

Side by side, we followed the dark canals. Silent buildings loomed around us, the paint faded and chipped. Inside the once-grand houses and halls, we found portraits with their eyes crossed out, statues defaced. We tried the key in every lock we could find—the front doors, the bedrooms, the closets and drawers.

A sense of tragedy pressed down on every house, the sadness heavy in the air. And when we crossed into the building we'd been in before —the one with smashed busts and abandoned crystal decanters— Orion went very still. He stopped to look up at the ceiling, at the image of the nude woman with the snake wrapped around her. Only a thin sliver of moonlight cast a ghostly light over the place. I hadn't noticed it before, but the curtains and furniture looked scorched in many places, and the glass of a mirror had been blackened.

Lost in thought, Orion was as still as the broken statues. The air seemed to grow darker around him, the room hotter. The weight of an oppressive sadness thickened the atmosphere.

"Do you remember this place?" I asked quietly.

He let out a long sigh. "I used to stare at her. I remember lying on the sofa and thinking I would marry her someday, and that I would save her from the serpent wrapped around her body. I can see now she doesn't actually mind the serpent. I didn't know she was the mother of our gods. I thought she belonged to us and that she needed me." He turned, looking around the abandoned hall. "I remember the day the soldiers arrived."

"The king's soldiers?"

"I wasn't scared of our king's soldiers. I was scared of the mortals. They brought guns with them. But the part that scared me was the looks on their faces. I'd never seen such pure loathing like that before."

I stared at him. "There were mortals here?"

"The king surrendered to them and agreed to let them round up the Lilu like they wanted. It was the last time he allowed mortal soldiers into the city." He breathed in deeply. "I can't say they had any signs of the morality you keep talking about. I think they thought we were like animals."

"I'm sorry." My heart broke for him.

"It's not your fault," he muttered.

"But this must be so painful for you."

"I've thought about that day every day for hundreds of years." He crossed the living room to a patch of wooden floor that had been stained darker than the rest. "This was where they cut out my brother's heart. He fought back because he was trying to save our mother." He traced his fingers over the stained floor. "He was the one..." His sentence trailed off, and he stood again and turned, pointing to the hall. "And that was where they cut out my father's heart."

I could hardly breathe. "I guess this answers my questions about why you have such disdain for mortals."

His eyes gleamed. "It's confusing to me that I have such a high regard for you, but you're not what I expected."

The floor creaked as I crossed the room to the mirror, and I stared into its blackened surface. "What's with all the scorch marks? Did they start to burn this place?"

"That was from me. I couldn't control my fire then, but if I could have, I'd have burned the entire army down. And most of the demons with it for turning on us."

"How old were you?" I asked.

"Five."

The breath left my lungs. "They put you in prison when you were *five?*" I asked, a little louder than I'd intended.

I crossed the room and looked into another of the scorched mirrors, half my face obscured by the smoke. But I could see my eyes, my cheekbones. Moonlight streamed in through the old, warped windows, tinging my face in ghostly light as I looked at myself. "What happened to the other Lilu? Were they killed right away, or were there others in prison with you?"

"That would be a good question for Mortana."

I felt it again—that rising anger. He'd only been a little boy, and he'd watched mortals cut out his brother's heart right on his living room floor. I felt like my chest was splitting in two when I thought of it.

My anger was rising again, like magma buried in a volcano.

When I thought of little Orion screaming for his father, I wanted to find those very mortals and rip their hearts from their chests. Power flooded me, and I felt like I could pull those Puritan fucks from their graves and kill them a second time.

A dark power imbued my body. I was clutching the side of the table so hard, I was breaking some of the wood. I glanced at my arm, where the image of the skeleton key was flickering—one with a skull shape burning like embers.

It was happening again.

When a demon feels a strong emotion...

When I looked up in the mirror, I saw the faint hint of golden light beaming from my forehead, but the shape was obscured by the scorch marks. I slapped my hand over it, my heart slamming.

Fuck. *Fuck.*

"Rowan?" Orion asked. "Why can I hear your heart beating like you're about to be devoured? You'll wake half the city."

Orion had said a demon could erase her past, could wipe all her memories. She could get rid of the guilt...

What if I'd erased my own memories?

But I couldn't just stand here permanently with my hand on my forehead, could I? What was I so scared of—that I *was* Mortana? He'd said I was human.

I slowed my heartbeat until my muscles started to relax again.

I was, quite simply, seeing things.

Shaking, I pulled my hand away and shifted so I could see my forehead. Nothing was there. No demon mark, no golden light.

"Orion? I think I've been hallucinating things."

"Ah," he said. "That's because you're here. I'm seeing them, too, the ghosts of my past. In here, they feel more vivid than ever."

I let out a shaky breath and turned to him. "For a second, I thought I was turning into a demon."

He gave me a sad smile. "You can't turn into a demon. You're mortal."

Maybe the tragedy of this place was just getting to me. I reached into my pocket for the key and held it up. "Should we keep looking?"

⚜

WE APPROACHED A STONE MANSION IN A SECTION OF THE WARD I'D never seen before. Canals flowed on either side of the building, gently moving south toward the Acheron River. An overgrown garden rambled out front, and stone paths curved through uncontrolled shrubs and tangles of vines.

Three stories high, the mansion boasted grandiose columns and ornate carvings of gargoyles. Balconies on the second and third floors overlooked the canals and the garden.

"What is this place?" I asked.

"This was once the home of the duke of the Asmodean Ward."

I shivered as I looked up at it. "Why didn't they put me here, if I'm supposed to be the duchess?"

"When Mortana was the only one left, she stayed in the building where you are now. It became the new residence of the Lilu's representative." He glanced at me, his eyes bright in the darkness. "And she probably didn't want to be haunted by the memories of being instrumental in the death of her own father."

I stared at the mansion, my blood growing colder. If tragedy could cling to a place, this palace was dripping in it. It felt tangible in the air. "The duke who lived here was Mortana's father? What was his name?"

"Moloch."

Orion started leading me through the rambling garden to the front door. Above us, a wooden shutter slammed forlornly against the stone window frame.

He slid his pale eyes to me as we approached the mansion. "The City of Thorns isn't like your world. Here, magic imbues the air. Memories linger. Tragedy can wrap itself around the walls, the floors, the stone and wood. It stays there like a living and breathing thing. So if you are seeing things, I'm not surprised. This world was never meant for mortals, and even demons see things here sometimes."

When we reached the door, I slid the key into the lock. And as my heart skipped a beat, I found that the lock *turned*.

I held my breath as the door swung open, revealing the inside of a palace, one covered in cobwebs. A cold shiver rippled through me as I took in the haunted beauty. Thin rays of moonlight streamed into a hall with towering ceilings. A white marble fireplace was inset into a wall, with a faded mural depicting lions and owls. Statues on columns stood around the hall, their faces smashed. The floor was a mosaic of deep blue and gold, with patterns of delicate rosettes, cracked in many places.

Once, this place would have gleamed with wealth and elegance, but even now, it had its own sort of beauty.

My pulse raced. "Orion?" I asked quietly. "Why would my mom have a key to this place? My mortal mom? Do you think she could have been a servant here at one point?"

"It hasn't been inhabited in hundreds of years."

I shook my head, trying to clear the fog from my mind. "Right. Of course."

"Everyone always thought the duke disappeared during the purges." His quiet voice echoed off the tile as he walked around the hall.

"And that was the last anyone has heard of him?" I asked.

"Maybe. About twenty years ago, a body was found in the gardens outside. The heart had been cut out, and the corpse had been burned beyond recognition. The rumors were that it was Duke Moloch himself, but no one knew how he ended up here, or where he'd come from. There could be Lilu who escaped, who live outside of the City of Thorns without their powers."

A cool wind rushed into the room, rippling over my skin. Goosebumps rose on my arms. "Maybe my mom knew him."

A disturbing thought crossed my mind. I'd never known who my dad was.

"And if he were alive," said Orion, "Cambriel might have seen him as a rival for the throne."

I thought I heard a creaking sound above me. When I looked up, I could just about make out the faded paint, a ceiling decorated with vines and ripe fruit. "Why would Moloch be a rival?"

"Long ago, the demons were ruled by a mad king named Azriel. He was obsessed with the idea of returning to the heavens, of reversing the loss in the heavenly wars. He called himself a god. He started killing his own subjects, burning them to death in the forests, ripping their hearts out. If he'd remained king, he could have slaughtered all of his own. He'd have done the mortals' work for them."

"He sounds terrifying."

"It was Cambriel's father, King Nergal, who challenged him to a trial by combat. By his family's lineage, Nergal didn't have much of a claim to the throne. But only the rightful heir can slaughter a king, and Nergal managed to do it. If our gods exist, they didn't want the mad king to stay on the throne."

I turned to look at Orion, frowning. "And the duke who owned this place—was he related to the mad king?"

Orion nodded. "Moloch was his bastard son."

I closed my eyes, then rubbed them. "I'm just trying to process this. My mom—the normal, mortal mom I knew who made me macaroni and cheese and ate too many pizza rolls—she might have known the bastard son of a mad demon king."

"That seems like a good summary."

What. The. Hell? Why had she never told me about any of this? I'd spent my teenage years thinking my mom was sweet but boring.

How wrong had I been?

✁ 36 ✁

I kept walking, exploring, hungry to know more. A breeze rushed in, and I crossed to look at a set of old wooden doors, which opened to a courtyard. Out there, arches surrounded a wild garden, and thorny plants climbed over columns and crumbling statues.

Had Mom ever been here?

As I looked out at the garden, puzzle pieces started sliding together in my mind.

I turned to look at Orion, my heart beating faster. "Mortana was born here, right? She was the granddaughter of the mad king. *She* had a claim to the throne. Maybe this explains some of Cambriel's interest in her. There are two ways to conquer a rival for the throne, aren't there? You can either kill them or marry them."

Orion nodded. "That, and he desperately wants to fuck her. But yes, you're right. Mortana has a claim."

Orion had gone very still again. And when he did that, it always made me nervous. The air seemed to be growing hotter in here, the shadows thickening around him. His pale eyes bored into me.

"What?" I asked. "I can see you're worked up about something."

"What I'm having a hard time with," he said quietly, "is the number of coincidences. Like I said when we first met, demons sometimes have mortal doppelgängers. But what, exactly, are the chances that a mortal doppelgänger also possessed the key to that demon's house?"

Ice slid through my bones. He'd brought up a very good point. And yet, I had no idea.

I cleared my throat. "I don't know. But you said I was definitely mortal." I was clinging to this desperately now. "You said demons can't breed mortals. And clearly, I don't have any magic. Not even in the City of Thorns."

He held my gaze for longer than was comfortable, then pulled it away again at last. "You did taste mortal, yes."

I sucked in a deep breath. "I'm going to look around and see what I can find, okay?" A sense of dread was starting to rise in me, dark and unnamed fears I didn't want to confront.

And for whatever reason, I was starting to feel uneasy around Orion. If I learned anything about my mom in this place, I wasn't sure I wanted him to be there.

I crossed through the hall, suddenly eager to get away from him, and I found my way to a wide, wooden stairwell that swept to the upper floors. I hurried up the stairs, eager to learn more about this place. With the help of the moonlight, I surveyed the defaced portraits, the scattered clothes and ransacked rooms. I moved quickly and with a rising sense of desperation, feeling like I was on the precipice of a discovery.

I crossed out onto the balcony that overlooked the tangled garden, and a flock of crows burst from one of the gnarled trees below, startling me. My heart fluttered as I watched them take to the dark sky.

When I breathed in, my heart squeezed. I could smell Mom here. A faint, floral smell, velvety and tinged with jasmine. I missed her more right now that I ever had.

When I closed my eyes, I could almost feel her here, and my heart ached. I could see her vividly now, dozing in the chair before the TV, exhausted after work. She always had a hard time sleeping, and every little noise woke her. But it was a different Mom that I felt here—not the mortal one I knew, who watched nature documentaries and drank wine spritzers. *This* Mom wore her hair piled on her head and had servants bring her fruit. *This* one was full of confidence, radiant.

This one scared people.

My throat tightened. I didn't want Orion here as I explored. What if I found something that turned him against me?

My hands were shaking as I started moving again, searching one room after another. I kept going until, at last, I reached the master bedroom, one with a four-poster bed made of dark wood and a high ceiling painted with a constellation. But what stopped my heart was the portrait on the wall—a bust, and a woman with her dark hair piled atop her head. It was just as I'd been envisioning her. The portrait's eyes had been painted over, but I would have recognized the rest of her face anywhere. Her straight nose, high cheekbones, dark eyebrows...

I felt like the world was tilting beneath me as I stared up at Mom's portrait. What the *fuck?*

I couldn't breathe as the possibilities whirled in my mind. Did Mom have a doppelgänger, or...

I had to figure this out before Orion came up here.

I turned around, scanning the room, my heart slamming against my ribs. An ancient-looking wooden desk stood in one corner of the room, and I rushed over to it. I pulled open the drawers until I found a book, its black cover embossed with golden thorns, and a skull key like the one I'd seen on my arm. I don't think I was breathing as I turned the pages and read the ancient hand-written text.

On the first page, written in black ink, was a sort of nursery rhyme.

The Maere of Night
Gave girls a fright,
But one queen loved him well.
He lost his throne
But seeds were sown
In the garden of Adele.
A swindler king,
A golden ring
To keep his heart alive.
Take the ring,

Fell the king,
The city yet will thrive.

What was this? A nursery rhyme? A prophecy?

I glanced over my shoulder, making sure I was still alone. I wasn't sure if the text meant anything or if it was just a rhyme, but I pulled out my cell phone to snap a picture anyway.

When I turned the page, I found an index. This was a book of spells. And in the index, one of the spells had the image of a skeleton key next to it.

Locking Spell

My hands were shaking as I turned to its page. There, at the top, was a key that looked like the one on my arm...and along with it, the explanation I'd been dreading.

Spell to Lock Demon Magic

Used to lock demon powers during purges by mortals. This spell temporarily converts a demon into a mortal.

Holy *shit*. My hands were shaking so badly that I could hardly hold the book.

But I couldn't be Mortana, could I? I know Orion had said something about a spell for forgetting, but...

I'd know. If I were evil, I'd know. I didn't feel evil. Did anyone feel evil?

"Rowan?" Orion's voice had me nearly jumping out of my skin, and I might have yelped.

If he saw what I'd just found—if he knew that was a portrait of my mom—he'd kill me. That execution he'd originally planned for me? It could actually happen. Either I was Mortana, or I was a close relation. He'd vowed to kill her *and* her family. Not just a vow, a fucking blood oath.

I turned around and slid the book back into the drawer. "I didn't find anything," I said, trying to make my voice sound natural.

"What's wrong?" He moved toward the desk, his eyes glowing brightly in the dark.

He could always just tell, couldn't he? He could hear my damn heart beating.

Sucking in a deep breath, I hurried past him and made my way to the hallway. "I was just seeing things again. Like you said, this place seems haunted. Let's go."

"You're no longer interested in what happened to your mother?" he called after me.

"Just spooked, Orion." I took the stairs quickly, no longer sure what I was doing. I hoped he'd come out with me, that he'd leave this ghostly place behind—and the spell book along with it.

When I got outside, I hurried into the garden. Adrenaline flooded me when I thought of what he'd told me—the body found out here, burned beyond recognition. Someone I thought my mother knew...

As I surveyed the savage garden around me, I suddenly felt desperate to get out of the City of Thorns. Yes, I liked the pools and the luxury. I liked Orion a *lot*. But tragedy haunted every inch of this place, and it was starting to become clear that some of it might be mine.

Did Orion keep looking around up there? If he found that locking spell...

I kept walking through the rambling garden, my nerves electrified. As I ambled through the untamed thorns around me, I shivered. The sound of footfalls made my heart pick up, but as I started to turn around, a hand clamped *hard* around my nose and mouth. A powerful grip was smothering me.

Orion? I thrashed against the hand, trying to pull it off, but he was far too strong for me.

My lungs burned as the air left my lungs. And as I tried to kick at his shins, my vision started to go dark.

❧ 37 ❧

I woke in the darkness, tied to a chair. Pain split my head open, and my mouth was dry as a bone.

I smelled faintly of pee, but I didn't want to dwell on that. I needed to think about how I was going to get the fuck out of this situation. Besides the pee, the air smelled like smoke—burnt cedar and maybe iron.

Wait—the burnt cedar was Orion's scent.

"Orion?" I rasped. "I can explain." I really fucking couldn't, but it seemed like a good start.

Ropes chafed at my wrists as I tried to pull against them.

Footfalls echoed off stone, and when I turned my head, I saw a light shining from a tunnel. As it grew brighter, I could just about make out the contours of a small, arched space, like stone vaults underground.

"Rowan." The rasping voice came from the opposite corner, and I turned to see Orion in the shadows. Apparently, he wasn't the one who'd tied me up, because he was wrapped in chains. Blood poured from his shoulders and chest, and a pile of ash lay around him.

"Orion!" I shouted. "What happened to you?"

His eyes were drifting closed, like he was having trouble staying conscious. "Some fucking idiot mortal gave Nama a gun."

"*What?*"

"She shot me and chained me up. I tried burning my way through the chains, but...I just burned the chair. I can't summon any more magic right now, not when I'm riddled with bullets. I'm having a hard time..."

His bright blue eyes closed, and panic started to crawl up my throat.

The sound of footsteps grew louder, and Nama crossed into the room holding a lantern in one hand and a gun in another. Her white hair fell in perfect waves over a scarlet gown. "Hello, friends." She lifted the gun. "This is fun."

I glanced at Orion, but his eyes had closed again. He couldn't actually die unless someone cut out his heart, but it hurt to see him covered in blood.

With all the shit going on, I nearly forgot that I was supposed to be Mortana. Time to summon the imperious attitude.

I tossed my hair over my shoulder. "What are you doing, you fool? Untie me at once."

Nama's eyes widened, and her hand flew to her mouth. "Or what? What will you do if I don't untie you?"

Was she calling my bluff?

She lifted the lantern. "Andras! Gamigan! Lydia!" she bellowed. "She's awake. Bring the mortal with you."

"What are you doing?" I snapped. "You're insane."

"Oh, my slutty little friend," she cooed. "Madness runs in your blood, not mine. There was a reason we had to kill your grandfather. The Lilu are abominations."

Two of the dukes crossed into the room—the platinum-haired greed demon who led the Mammon ward, and a sloth demon with heavy-lidded green eyes from Abadon. And behind them, Lydia sauntered in—right next to Jack Corwin.

Jack? Jack was the idiot mortal who'd given Nama the gun. With his Alpha Kappa sweatshirt and old baseball cap, he looked completely out of place here.

My blood turned to ice, my thoughts whirling out of control. My two worlds were colliding now in the most terrible way possible.

Of course Jack was the idiot mortal in question. Right now, he looked fairly terrified, his eyes shifting from one demon to another. And when I looked closely, I could see that new bruises marred his face. His lip had been split, and purple bloomed over his cheekbones and jaw.

Nama handed the lantern to Lydia.

"What's going on?" I demanded through gritted teeth. I could no longer keep up the pretense of being calm and collected. Right now, my shadow-self was nowhere to be found.

With a smug smile, Nama folded her arms. As she did, the gun went off, and she screamed. Bits of rock and sand sprayed over the room.

Jack held up his hands. "Careful with that!"

Nama frowned at the gun. "These things are confusing." She shook her head. "Anyway, I had a hunch that you spent a lot of time around mortals, Mortana. You just seemed kind of grotesque like they are. You know, like an animal. A filthy, rutting animal."

I curled my lips in a snarl. "Have you lost your mind?"

She shrugged. "So I did a little digging. I spent today hunting around Osborne until I saw a picture of your face in a trophy closet. A track team." She wrinkled her nose and turned to the dukes. "Humans compete against each other in running races, even though they're slow as fuck. But do you really think it's fair for a demon to be on a mortal track team?"

My stomach plummeted, and I watched as she crossed to Jack. She gripped him by the hair, pulling his head back, then pointed the gun at his chin. "Then things got a little more interesting. This little fucker tried to shoot me. Apparently, he fancies himself something of a demon hunter."

Jack was shaking violently. *Holy hell.* Was I on the same side as Jack right now? I didn't like that at all.

Nama slapped him across the face with her free hand. "I beat him until he told me about the picture of Mortana. Except he said her name wasn't Mortana. He said her name was Rowan Morgenstern. And he is quite sure that you're mortal." She let go of him and whirled to face me. "*Apparently*, he can smell demons."

I shook my head, genuinely confused. "What?"

Nama pointed the gun at his pendant—the silver one with the hammer. "The Corwins are witch finders and demon hunters."

Jack nodded, a frantic look in his eyes. "I can smell demons. I could hunt them, if I felt like it." He held up his hands, his face pale. "But I don't! I never have. I just carry the gun for protection. I thought Nama was a threat. I knew your kind are all around, and I knew you might come after me because of what my family did. That was why I tried to shoot Nama. It was just self-defense. I swear—"

"Be quiet, you fuckwit mortal!" bellowed one of the dukes, a man with long black hair. "We did not come here for your trial. We came here to try the succubus. Nama claims that she's not actually a succubus. You're here as a witness. That is your role."

I flexed my wrists in the ropes. "And you all are the judges?"

Nama gestured at me with the gun. "The king seems taken with you, and he won't listen to me unless I have witnesses." She pointed the gun at the other demons. "These are my witnesses. What I really, *really* want is to attend a barbecue in the Tower of Baal, with a mortal whore as the main course. I haven't eaten roasted mortal in a long time."

Oh, *God*.

"Watch it with the gun!" said Jack, his hands up. "Since I've done what you asked, can I leave now? We had a deal. I told you she's mortal. She smells like a mortal, I swear to God. Burn her, have your fun, just let me go."

"Fine!" Nama barked. "I can't kill you since I might need you later. But if I ever catch you hunting demons, I'll rip your guts out through your mouth."

Jack turned and sprinted out through the tunnel.

I kept squirming, trying to pull at the ropes, but there was no point. Since I didn't actually have demonic strength, all I was doing was scraping my skin off. With a thundering heart, I turned to look at Orion. His eyes were starting to open again, and he met my gaze.

"Why is he here, Nama?" I asked.

She grimaced. "I want him to see that you've been lying to him. You're nothing but a filthy little doppelgänger, aren't you? I want him to realize that I was right all along. I'm the right person for him. And if you were *actually* a demon, you wouldn't have such a hard time getting out of rope bonds, would you? It's just *rope*. Any demon can break it."

"Maybe I don't care to prove myself to you," I said breezily. "Maybe I don't want to be part of your stupid little game."

This was the very definition of being caught between a rock and a hard place. If I told them about the locking spell, I'd die at Orion's hands. If I were a mortal, I'd die at theirs.

My body shook. "You think that he'll love you after you shot him?" I asked. "You're insane."

She crossed to me, her eyes wild and fanatical. "He'll see that I did it because I love him. All of this, everything that I'm doing, is for him. For us. We're meant to be."

Lydia crossed her arms. "Can we get on with it, Nama? Your obsession with him is frankly depressing, and it's making me regret sharing a gender with you. I should have listened to Legion. The duke of the Sathanas Ward said you were a lunatic."

"What, exactly, are we getting on with?" My voice was shaking so hard they had to know by now that I wasn't Mortana. I sounded *terrified*. "I told you that I'm not participating."

Orion's eyes opened just a little wider, pure black now. I could feel the room growing hotter.

"Maybe you need a little motivation." Nama pointed her gun at Orion. "Here's how the trial will work. I'm going to keep shooting Orion. His knees, his hand. Maybe his pretty face."

"You just said you loved him!" I shouted, sounding frantic. I couldn't keep up the act anymore.

Her face beamed. "Yes, Mortana. And if I can't have him, no one else will. That's how much I love him."

Lydia pinched her nose. "Oh, my God, Nama."

"So here's how the first trial works," Nama went on. "You prove that you're a demon and save him. Or you can stay tied to your chair like a weak little mortal and show him that you're an animal."

I gritted my teeth, my entire body shaking. "What if I don't care what happens to him?"

Nama grinned, her eyes maniacal now. She turned to Orion. "Then you prove that you don't deserve him! You don't even care enough to get up to help him. And I care enough about him to do all this."

"Excuse me," the Duke of Mammon interrupted, his golden rings gleaming. "We're not putting her on trial to see if she cares about Orion. I just want to ensure we're not giving our hard-earned tax revenue to a mortal. If she's a demon, I don't give a fuck if she cares about Orion."

"*I do!*" Nama bellowed, then whirled, aimed the gun at me, and pulled the trigger.

Pain exploded through my leg, the agony so shocking I could no longer think straight. My mind went dark for a second, and when my vision cleared again, I saw that she'd turned the gun back on Orion.

Nama's laughter echoed off the stone walls. "Now let's try Orion, my beloved. Show us how strong you are, Mortana. Show us you can use that fire magic of yours."

She pulled the trigger and shot Orion in his kneecap. I watched as his eyes went dark, and a blast of heat pulsed through the room.

I could feel it again—that rising anger. The rage. Pure strength coursed through my body, and an ancient fury that could melt rock to stone. Darkness spilled through my blood like ink. My shadow-self was rising to the surface like molten lava, and I could no longer feel the pain of the bullet in my leg.

Mortals and ruthless demons had murdered Orion's family in front of him when he was just a boy. They'd locked him in a room alone with his haunting memories. Most people would be broken by that. And now they'd dragged him here to a tunnel to torture him some more.

Fury ignited in my blood, and I could feel the ropes straining at my wrists. A light was beaming from my forehead, my chest growing hotter. Brighter. Deep down, the buried truth—the one I'd hidden from myself—was that I was stronger than all these fuckers.

And I'd kill to protect those I loved. I'd make them regret that they'd been born.

Nama aimed the gun at Orion's face. "It's so pretty, Orion. You know, I think that's your problem. Your face is too pretty, and I need to make you feel—"

I would bathe my enemies in flames. I'd stop when they lay as piles of ash.

The rope shredded behind me, and hot wrath erupted.

I didn't know the fire was streaming from my body until I smelled the burning flesh. Only then did I see the flames that filled the vault, a pure inferno of death. A vortex of molten heat.

They wanted to put me on trial?

I was Hell itself. I would burn the wicked from this earth. I was born to rule.

The flames snapped back into my body, and I gasped, looking down at myself. Pure power imbued my body, and my legs started to shake.

Magic. Powerful, terrifying magic.

The locking spell had been unlocked. I felt unsteady on my feet, in shock from what had just happened.

I was in a nightmare.

My clothes were singed, partly burned off, and my legs bare from the thighs down. Enormous piles of ash lay on the floor where three of the demons had been standing. To my right, soot covered Lydia and her seared clothes. Ashes filled the air.

Lydia gaped at where the other demons had been standing. "I guess Nama was wrong," she said in a daze.

With a slamming heart, I stared as she ran out of the tunnel. I looked down at my hands, at my glowing fingers. Flames flickered from them like candles. I felt a jolt of magic sizzle through my arms, electrifying me down to my fingertips.

When I turned to look at Orion, a new horror coursed through my bones. The chains had melted off him, and he rose to his feet, his eyes black as night. Seems he had strength in him, after all. His clothes had been burned off in places, exposing arms and thighs thickly corded with muscle.

The pure hatred in his features made my heart stop. Time seemed to slow down, and a phantom breeze toyed with his silver hair.

But it was the mark on his forehead that made me want to murder him.

A five-pointed star.

There he was—the fucking Lightbringer. The ruler of demons.

Battle fury rippled through my body, and I could feel the air heating up around us, but I had no idea if the source was Orion or me. I only knew the stones were starting to glow beneath us, red hot. The silence pressed on us, heavy as soil in a grave.

My shoulder blades tingled with some ancient instinct to unleash my wings.

Orion's lip curled, and shadows coiled around him like smoke. "Mortana," he snarled, his voice a frigid blade that cut me to the core. "There you are."

"There's the Lightbringer," I hissed. "You've made a remarkable recovery."

"I wasn't that hurt. I wanted to learn the truth about you as much as they did. And now I know. You managed to disguise yourself as a mortal."

I pointed at him, feeling like the betrayal was eating me alive. "I know what happened now. You killed my mom. You made a blood oath to murder everyone in Mortana's family, and that included my mother. This whole time, you were pretending to help me find her killer, and you knew it was you."

He shook his head slowly, and I wasn't sure what that meant. I only knew he looked like he was going to rip my head from my body.

I wasn't sure which of us moved first, but in the next moment, he was pinning me up against the wall, and my feet were off the ground. His hand clamped around my throat, and he pressed me hard against the stone. Endless darkness burned in his eyes. "Mortana," he snarled. "It is deeply unfortunate that the most beautiful person I've ever seen is also my worst enemy."

But I wasn't a weak mortal anymore, and I could fight back. My self-defense classes came roaring into my mind, except now with the strength of a god. I raised my arms, slamming my hands against his wrists. At the same time, I brought my knee up hard into his groin.

He dropped his grip on me, and I lunged forward, aiming for his face with my fist. But he grabbed my hand and twisted it behind my back, and when he shoved me against the wall with bone-breaking force, the air left my lungs.

"Did you know?" His quiet voice was like an ancient curse. "Did you know how I would feel when I learned the truth? Is that why you did it?"

"I don't know anything." I kicked back into his shin, hard enough that I heard a crack. "I have no fucking idea what's happening, Orion."

I whirled to try to punch him, but he was lifting me in the air. He threw me hard across the room, and I slammed onto the floor. The blow winded me. As a mortal, I'd be dead. As a demon, it was just a setback.

No wonder demons thought mortals were weak, I felt invincible.

From above, Orion looked down at me like a conquering god waiting for a sacrifice. "I know exactly who you are. You're my worst enemy, and you always have been."

I thrust my hips up and slammed the back of my heel into his knee where Nama had shot him—once, twice. With a growl, he stumbled back. From the ground, I kicked at his calves, sweeping his legs out from under him. When he fell backward, I leapt atop him. I clamped my hands around his neck, my thighs around his waist. I wasn't squeezing yet, but I was threatening it. I felt my claws emerge, ready to rip his heart out, and I pressed them against his chest.

"I don't know if I'm Mortana!" I shouted at him. "If I was once Mortana, she's as foreign to me as a stranger. I'm not what you think I am. You said Mortana only cares for herself, that she's driven by self-preservation. And you said emotions make a demon reveal her true self. But it wasn't self-preservation that unveiled my demon side. Every time I started to feel it rising, it was from wanting to protect you. It was thinking of you as a little boy in that prison." My chest ached from the hurt of all this. "My demon side came out because I wanted to protect you. I burned through the locking spell because I wanted to keep you safe. So I don't know who I am, but I do know that I'm not the monster you're looking for. But you? You're the one who betrayed *me*, Orion. You were pretending to help me find my mom's killer, when all this time, it was you," I snarled.

He stared up at me, transfixed. "What makes you think it was me?"

"I remember you from that night."

"No, you don't." His lip curled. "I never lied to you about what I am. I don't hide my faults or what I've done. If I'd killed your mother, I would have told you as soon as I met you. Except now I have a new flaw, and it's my worst one."

"What?"

"I could have killed you five times over in the last two minutes. I could kill you now. And something fucking idiotic is stopping me." His jaw tightened. "I have never loathed myself more than I do right now, and believe me, that's saying something, because I have plumbed some *amazing* depths of self-loathing."

"Stop changing the subject." Tears streamed down my face. "You have the five-pointed star. I remember it from the night my mom was murdered in the woods with *fire* magic just like yours. It was you."

"You might want to look in the mirror, Mortana," he spat. "I'm not the only one with fire, and it seems Lucifer has blessed us both. You and I are both marked as the Lightbringer. But if you think you'll take the throne from me, you're mistaken."

Dread bloomed in my chest. Horrified, I rose and stumbled away from Orion. With tears streaking my face, I reached into my jeans pocket for my phone. It was half-melted, no longer working, but in the black gleam, I could make out a reflection—one shining from my forehead.

A five-pointed star. The image hit me like a fist to my throat.

Without another word to Orion, I started running through the tunnels at full speed.

But I wasn't running from Orion now. I was sprinting from the memory I'd been running from all this time. The reason I was so obsessed with finding my mom's killer. This had been my worst fear— the darkest truth buried in the depths of my mind, the thing I so desperately wanted to prove wasn't true.

What if I killed Mom?

We'd had a fight that night. She'd kept wanting me to move from one apartment to another. She'd seemed paranoid, delusional. She'd thought someone was after us but wouldn't tell me who, and I only remembered that I hadn't wanted to go with her.

Orion had said he couldn't control his fire when he was younger...

I thought she'd lost her mind. I remember yelling at her, and I was so angry—

Sickness rose in my gut, and I hardly knew where I was running. I felt like the walls were collapsing around me.

Was I Mortana—and I'd forgotten?

Deep down at my core, under the lies I told myself, what if I was truly evil?

I ran and ran until I saw the moonlight in Osborne. I slipped into the shadows, my feet pounding along the waterfront. I sprinted past the brewery, the Cirque de la Mer. I didn't know where I was going, just that I needed to move.

But I could never outrun what I was really fleeing.

❧ 39 ❧

I leaned back on my bed in my basement apartment, staring at the wall. I poured myself another paper cup of cheap red wine, no longer caring that the spiders were crawling all over my bedspread.

Let them crawl.

I'd been down here for nearly a day, and I was on my second bottle.

If Orion wanted to come find me and throw me in prison again, it wouldn't be hard. I hadn't bothered to hide. I'd just come back to where I'd started—the mildewed basement I shared with six other people. Now, I had less fear but a lot more self-loathing. If Orion dragged me back, I'd go dressed in old leggings and a David Bowie T-shirt covered in wine stains. And I'm not sure I'd put up that much of a fight.

My gaze wandered around the room, then landed on the fire extinguisher. I broke out into a sort of hysterical dark laughter and spilled some of my wine on the duvet.

Guess I could get rid of all the fire safety equipment now.

My phone buzzed—another text from Shai, desperate to know what was going on. I hadn't been answering, because frankly, I had no idea what to say.

I was a demon, yes. But I wasn't going to deliver that news over text. Still, I should let her know I was alive.

I flicked open my new, extremely cheap phone. Unable to come up with anything better, I texted her a smiley face and a bottle of wine emoji.

That should cover it.

My head was swimming, and I was starting to feel faintly nauseated. When had I last eaten?

The room seemed to be wavering. Apparently, being a demon made you faster and stronger, but it didn't raise your alcohol tolerance.

And yet, I didn't want my head to clear. I couldn't face the possibility that my own fire magic had killed Mom.

When my phone buzzed again, I found a frantic all-caps message from Shai:

ARE YOU OKAY??! WTF IS HAPPENING? TWO MORE DUKES ARE DEAD?? I saw Legion in the Sathanas Ward. I got up the courage to ask him where Mortana was. He said no one had seen you, and rumor was that you'd burned two dukes. ARE YOU OKAY?

I dropped my cup of wine on the bedside table and started typing back to her.

I'm fine!

You know what? Fuck it. I was always so worried about what people would think or that I'd make them uncomfortable with the darkness I carried with me. I never wanted to burden anyone with my most disturbing thoughts. Maybe I could actually learn a thing or two from Orion. Maybe I could try...just coming out and saying things.

With a strange feeling of giddiness, I typed:

Turns out I'm a demon. I have fire magic. And a star mark. What if I'm the one who killed Mom? What if I'm evil?

I watched as the dots moved on the screen while she wrote back to me, and my heart pounded as if the judgment of St. Peter awaited me.

Evil people don't worry that they're evil, Rowan. They don't care.

My chest unclenched, and I dropped the phone. Holy shit. Of course she was right.

Why hadn't I been able to think clearly enough to consider that? A psychopath doesn't worry that she's evil. She doesn't feel anxiety. And me? Even as a demon, I had plenty of that.

I rose from my bed and yanked open my basement door. Orion described someone who at her core did not care for other people. And what I'd said to him was true—my emotions rose to the surface when I felt like I desperately wanted to protect him.

And I couldn't be Mortana.

I mean, I remembered being a kid. Crying in the ball pit at Chuck E. Cheese and peeing my pants in the second grade. Mom sending me to school with waffles for a year because I refused to eat anything else, and other kids laughing at my bony knees. The nights Mom spent petting my head because I had nightmares and kept asking for water.

I remembered being the fastest kid in my gym class but never being able to climb the ropes, and having a crush on Matt Logan even after he told me I was annoying. I remembered watching *The Price is Right* with my mom over early lunches and getting excited at the prizes.

I remembered getting Communion when I went to church with my friend Amy, even though I wasn't Catholic. I'd immediately puked over a statue of Santa Lucia.

And...now I understood why I'd puked, I guess.

Maybe magic could suppress memories, but could it really fake a childhood? With that level of specificity? I wasn't a five-hundred-year-old demon. I was Rowan Morgenstern, and that was all there was to it.

And most of all, I remembered how much I loved my mom because I'd felt safe near her. No matter how mad I'd been at her, there was no way I'd killed her. At least not on purpose.

When I went outside, I was surprised to find that it was night—I'd completely lost track of time. I blinked at the moon over Osborne, feeling oddly at home under its light.

Holy shit.

I was Rowan Morgenstern, but I was also a succubus, wasn't I?

A creature of the night. I belonged out here.

I glanced at the key tattoo again on my arm—now permanent. I still didn't know what had happened, but I could only guess that Mom had given me the spell to make sure I was always safe. That my blood tasted mortal, just in case.

I started walking toward the waterfront. It was colder here than in the City of Thorns, and goosebumps rose over my skin. The air tasted of salt and smelled of seaweed. By the cold sea, I let the shadows swallow me. I didn't actually have to be scared of being outside at night anymore. The mortals couldn't hurt me. The demons wouldn't dare.

The thing was, if I was a demon, I didn't really belong out here in Osborne, did I? If I didn't get within the city walls again, I only had about another day or two before my magic faded.

I wasn't mortal. Neither was Mom. She was Lilu—one of the exiled. She'd been living out here in hiding, always looking over her shoulder. Banished just because she was a succubus.

And my dad? If he was, in fact, Duke Moloch, he'd been killed just after I was born. About twenty years ago. Maybe he'd gone back to try to save me.

My mind snagged on the nursery rhyme I'd found, the one in the book. Had that meant anything?

The Maere of Night
Gave girls a fright,
But one queen loved him well.
He lost his throne
But seeds were sown
In the garden of Adele.
A swindler king,
A golden ring
To keep his heart alive.
Take the ring,
Fell the king,
The city yet will thrive.

It sounded like a nursery rhyme, but I was sure something important had been written into that poem. A secret I needed to unlock.

From deep within my brain, an ancient instinct was rising to the surface, and magic tingled down my shoulder blades.

I needed to take to the skies. I needed to be free.

My back arched, then wings burst from my skin. When I glanced over my shoulder, I saw them, black and feathered, flecked with gold. Beautiful.

This was a release—the unveiling of my true self. My wings started to pound the air, instinct carrying me higher and higher into the briny wind.

Orion hated me now. He was convinced down to his marrow that I was Mortana.

But I was going to find out the truth. I was going to learn exactly what happened to Mom, and who I was.

What makes a person who they are, their essence? Was it a soul or their memories? I didn't know. I only knew I wasn't the monster Orion imagined me to be.

I breathed in deeply and stared at the locked gates of the City of Thorns.

Deep within my bones, I knew that was where I belonged. I'd always known.

I was a Lightbringer—blessed by Lucifer. And whether he liked it or not, I would fight him for my place in the city I was destined to lead.

❦

Thank you for reading City of Thorns.

You can order the sequel, Lord of Embers, on Amazon.

If you would like to read a short deleted chapter from Orion's perspective—giving a glimpse into his last meeting with Mortana in the 1820s, check out our website.

On the following pages, I've included the opening chapters of another one of our novels, The Fallen.

LORD OF EMBERS

❧ I ❧

CHAPTER 1—ROWAN

I gripped a plastic bag to my chest, trying to keep it dry. A slate-gray sky spread out overhead. As I stepped in a cold puddle, rain drenched my socks through the hole in my shoe.

This was my life now—kicked out of the City of Thorns, back in my old neighborhood. As soon as Orion had discovered the mark of Lucifer glowing on my head, he'd decided I was his worst enemy. The oath he'd sworn kept me out of the demon city where I belonged. If he saw me again, he'd be compelled to kill me.

Shivering, I glanced across the street at the powder-blue house where I'd grown up and the crooked statues of the Virgin Mary the owner kept on the little patch of grass out front.

Behind it, the dark Osborne Woods Reservation stretched for thousands of acres. For a moment, a memory flashed in my mind—sprinting through those woods years ago in rain like this. I shuddered, sliding my hand in my pockets to run my fingers over my keys.

Not far ahead, a woman with a stroller hurried down the sidewalk with her baby to get out of the rain. My throat tightened. Mom used to send me out for Dunkin' Donuts across the street on weekend mornings. God, I missed her. Being in this neighborhood wasn't helping.

Witchcraft Point *sounded* like a magical neighborhood of curiosity shops and cobblestones. In reality, it was the old industrial part of town, a cluster of half-abandoned, boarded-up tanneries, broken windows, and shabby rentals. Fast food joints completed the bleak suburban sprawl.

I turned to look behind me at the demon city—towering walls of golden stone and gleaming turrets on Osborne's tallest hill to the east. It was warmer inside the gates, where the amber walls glowed with an unearthly light like an ancient Mediterranean paradise. Beyond the gates, the Acheron River sprang from the ground and flowed out to the candy-blue sea.

I had to get back in there somehow. Not only was it much nicer there, but I hadn't found the person who'd burned Mom to death in Osborne Woods.

Yet.

I turned away from the city again.

After a few days outside the City of Thorns, I could feel my magic and strength seeping out of my body. It was a deeply uncomfortable feeling, like growing sicker.

I glanced to my left. On a craggy hill behind the Dunkin' parking lot, the Osborne Gallows had once stood. Hard to imagine now, but bodies had once swung on the slope behind the dumpster.

I pulled the plastic bag of sweatpants closer, hoping they wouldn't be wet by the time I arrived at the home of Mr. Esposito, my mom's nonagenarian friend. Earlier today, I'd peered out my dingy basement windows and seen him walking to the bus stop in the pouring rain. His pants had sagged to his knees on his skinny frame, and he'd shuffled along, trying to get to a bench so he could pull them up.

I'd stood at the window, frozen in indecision. Should I run out to help him, or would that embarrass him? Was it better to pretend I never saw it? While I'd dithered over the decision, he'd reached the bench and restored his dignity himself. But it was clear to me what he'd needed—elasticated sweatpants that would stay on.

At Family Dollar, I'd spent twelve dollars on three pairs of sweatpants, discounted to four dollars each. Two for Mr. Esposito, one for myself.

I pulled out my phone, hoping to see a text from Shai, but my battery had run out. Raindrops slid down the dark phone screen, and I shoved it back into my pocket. These cheap sweatpants were comfortable enough, and they had pockets. I was starting to think I wouldn't wear anything else.

Mortana liked glamour. I wanted to wear pajamas all day. Not much of a life plan, maybe, but right now, I didn't have a better one.

After I dropped off these sweatpants, I'd get a bus to my favorite part of town, the historic district around Osborne Common, and splurge on a hot chocolate in Ye Olde Osborne Coffee Shoppe. Situated northeast of here, that part of the city boasted Georgian houses, quaint brick sidewalks, cobbled roads, and signs with pristine gold lettering. And while I was lifting my spirits there, I'd dry off, pull out my little notepad, and come up with my master plan.

When you had only a few dollars and half a box of cereal left, you really needed a plan.

I turned onto Gallows Hill Road, walking quickly. Colored flags fluttered in the wind, adorning an overgrown parking lot that had once been a used car dealership. The sky was growing darker now. Across the street, the broken windows of a mint-green concrete building had been boarded up with plywood. Just beyond that sat Mr. Esposito's ramshackle house—chipped white paint, a garden of weeds and tall grass, and a curtain hanging halfway down the front window. I really needed to come back here and help with the house a bit. No one else lived around here or kept an eye on him, and he didn't have any family.

The gate in the chain link fence was open, and I crossed through. I climbed the steps onto the front porch, where Mr. Esposito stored his cans and newspapers. On the porch, water dripped through the overhang onto rotting wood.

As I waited, shivering, I listened to the shuffling behind the door, accompanied by the sound of a walker hitting the wooden floor.

Even if my magic was fading in the mortal world, I could still hear like a demon. Was this why my mom had always seemed to know everything I was up to? I couldn't get up in the night to check my phone without her overhearing it.

After a few moments, Mr. Esposito opened the door. His thick white eyebrows crept up his forehead, questioning, and he peered at me through his glasses. "Rowan!"

I held up the bag of sweatpants. "I brought you something, Mr. Esposito. I accidentally ordered a bunch of men's sweatpants, and they don't fit. I thought they might fit you. I'm too lazy to mail them back, you know?"

"Oh." He smiled. "That's nice of you to think of me."

Mr. Esposito and I were alike. Neither of us had any other friends in Osborne, and we could barely manage getting through normal life without a series of disasters befalling us. When we had nothing to do, we sometimes ended up at a coffee shop for chess. He played slowly and deliberately and was a million times better than me.

With a shaking hand, he took the bag from me and gave me a feeble smile. "Do you want to come in for tea?"

The warmth sounded nice, but he looked exhausted. "I've got to run, but thanks. Chess soon?"

He nodded. "That would be lovely, Rowan."

I watched as he tied the plastic bag around the top of his walker. "You should get out of the rain. Night is falling fast." He frowned. "I don't think it's a good night for you to be out." His eyes became unfocused, his forehead furrowed. "Rowan, I think...there's something... something's not right."

Maybe he could tell I was a demon now. "Yeah. It's grim weather, isn't it? I'll see you soon, Mr. Esposito."

I waved goodbye as he scooted back to shut the door.

As he did, I felt the hair rising on my nape. My demon instincts screamed that I was being watched by a malign presence.

Orion?

✿ 2 ✿
CHAPTER 2—ROWAN

F or one moment, I thought hoped?—that it was my former incubus friend. Maybe he'd realized his mistake. Maybe, any minute now, I'd be back in the City of Thorns, looking out at the Atlantic.

But when I turned around, I found something much worse than Orion hurtling down the sidewalk. Five demon hunters were headed toward me, each one wearing the little hammer insignia of the Malleus Daemoniorum—Hammer of the Demons.

They stopped at the fence's opening, blocking me in. Jack was among them, along with his dad—an older, white-haired version of him who I'd seen in political ads. I was pretty sure I recognized two of the other guys from Jack's fraternity—large, red-cheeked men in white baseball caps, Patriots sweatshirts, and beaded necklaces. Basically interchangeable, except that one of them was drinking a beer. They didn't look threatening, and yet—

"Is this her?" Jack's dad asked quietly, his voice sending a shudder up my spine. He took a step closer onto the crumbling footpath. "Is this the one you saw in the City of Thorns?"

"Congressman Corwin." I cleared my throat. "Nice to meet you." I glanced to the right, wondering if I should run that way to leap the fence. Right now, they had me blocked in.

The fastest way, I thought, might be to the left—over the fence and into the driveway.

The congressman wore a navy blazer with a bright red tie. His hair was slicked back. He didn't seem to notice the rain picking up, drenching his neat hair. Over his shoulder, he carried a leather satchel.

Behind him, Jack nodded. "That's her. She seemed to know the other demons. They thought she was one of them. I said she wasn't."

The congressman took another step closer. I considered calling for help, but the only help available to me would be Mr. Esposito and his walker. If I knocked on the door and tried to get inside, there was a good chance these guys would follow me in.

Right now, my phone was dead in my pocket, so there weren't many options.

The congressman's nostrils flared as he sniffed the air. With a cock of his head, his jaw tightened.

Lightning cracked the dark sky, and my stomach clenched.

"Nice to meet you, but I need to go, so..." I trailed off.

I bounded down the stairs and ran for the fence. The jagged metal top cut into my palms as I leapt over it. I landed hard on the driveway, stumbling. But as I tried to break into a run, one of the frat boys blocked my path. Towering above me, he shoved me *hard*, slamming me onto the wet pavement. As I scrambled back to my feet, the rest of the guys surrounded me.

The younger ones parted, and the congressman crossed over to me. Lips curling, he gripped me by the shoulder, his fingers clutching me tightly. He sniffed the air again, eyes gleaming with anger. "*Jack?* I thought you said she was mortal."

Adrenaline started to pump. *Shit.* I wondered how much magic I had in my system right now. Three days outside the City of Thorns— was I still stronger than a mortal at all?

I smiled blandly. "I *am* mortal, of course." I blinked innocently. "It's not my fault the demons kidnapped me. Ask your son. He was there. He told them all I'm mortal, and that's how I ended up here in Osborne again, where I belong."

Narrowing his eyes, Jack moved closer. He inhaled deeply, his face growing red. "She smells different now, Dad. She was mortal before, but she's changed. How was I supposed to know they could change?"

I swallowed hard. "Can you both stop sniffing me? Also, can you..." I paused, trying to think of a polite way to say *fuck off*. "Fuck off," I blurted. "Please."

The congressman let go of me and opened his little leather satchel. "Are you sure she was mortal before, Jack?"

"I'm sure," he replied.

"The problem is, son, you're usually dead fucking wrong about things," his dad shot back, shocking me. We agreed on that, at least. "I want to take her alive for an interrogation."

My heart thundered. I didn't know precisely how demon hunters interrogated demons, but I had a strong suspicion it involved a whole lot of torture. "I'm going to have to decline that invitation, Congressman Corwin. I'm trying to cut down on the amount of time I spend being kidnapped and prodded with knives."

"I'm not asking." He reached into his bag and pulled out a metallic hook. It took a moment for me to register exactly what it was. Mortals didn't have claws like demons to carve out hearts, so they used implements instead. The sight of the instrument—like a small metallic scythe—sent a shiver of ice through my bones.

I hadn't actually tried to control my claws yet. Right now, I wished I'd been practicing that for the past few days instead of drinking boxed wine in a basement.

I moved to the left, trying to get around the hunters, but the congressman knocked me back again, and my head smacked against the pavement. Pain shot through my skull, and along with it, fury. I gripped my head, anger simmering. These could be the very people who'd murdered Mom.

Now my demon side was starting to rise.

Blocking out the pain in my head, I leapt to my feet and lunged forward. I landed my punch, but it didn't do much damage. The congressman slammed his fist into the side of my head again, sending me staggering back, and I hunched over, dizzy.

The blows were clouding my thoughts. I had nowhere to go. Orion thought I was Mortana and wanted me dead. The demon hunters wanted me dead.

Even a life of quiet desperation wasn't in the cards right now, playing chess with Mr. Esposito in Ye Olde Osborne Coffee Shoppe.

A wild, furious sort of panic gripped me, and I rushed forward, shoving Jack's father hard into the guys behind him. He fell back. I tried to make a run for it again, but Jack struck from the side, punching me in the head. I staggered as he moved behind me and threw my elbow into his ribs, and he grunted in surprise.

Right now, I might still have some demon strength and magic, but not a lot. If I'd been at full capacity, this fight would have been over.

One of the hunters lunged for me, swinging a glass beer bottle at my head. My hands shot out and blocked his arm, redirecting the strike of the bottle against his own forehead. Fragments of glass littered the rickety stairs.

He was down for now, but they were all around, one after another coming for me.

Jack was up again. He reached for my throat, and I dodged him, jumping to the side. He lost his balance and fell forward. I grabbed him from behind and slammed his head down on the jagged top of the chain link fence.

"Demon!" Jack's father hissed. "We will rid the earth of your kind!"

I spied an opening between the congressman and one of the others. *Now's my chance.*

But as I started to rush past him, the hook caught me in the side, ripping open my skin. Pain carved through me, and panic sunk its claws into my heart.

Oh, fuck, oh, *fuck.*

I gripped my side, freeing myself from the hook with a sharp tug. Grimacing, I fought to keep my thoughts clear. I couldn't die here...

A voice sounded in my mind, echoing as if it were coming from somewhere in the distance. *You must have a chance at the crown. Chaos. Chaos. Chaos.*

Was I hallucinating?

I stumbled into plastic bins, blood rushing from me.

I was going to die surrounded by enemies, bleeding all over Mr. Esposito's trash cans.

CHAPTER 3—ROWAN

S taggering, I fought through the pain. They could have killed Mom, and I couldn't die before I found out.

It was like a part of me had never left the woods. A part of me was still there, running through the trees, senseless with fear. A double version of myself, permanently trapped in the past. And only that part of me could remember exactly what happened. I had no idea who it was.

That night, I'd split in two. One part of myself would always be hearing her scream.

"Was it you?" I shouted.

No answer. The congressman took a step closer and gripped me hard by the throat, lifting me into the air and crushing my windpipe.

"What do you think, boys?" He grinned. "Should we still take her alive?"

I tried summoning my power, but I felt it sputtering within me, struggling to ignite. Snuffed out again like charcoal doused with water.

"Alive, yeah," said one of the frat boys.

The congressman dropped me hard, and I gasped for air. "Did you kill my mom?" I rasped.

He brandished the hook. "I might have."

A bit of lingering demon magic crackled between my ribs, then started to heat, surging along my arm. With an electrifying burst of energy, I whirled and landed a hard punch in his face.

His head snapped back, but he recovered fast and swung for me again with the hook. This time, I managed to block it, gripping his wrist before he could rip me open.

I snarled at him, growing feral.

He bared his teeth. "Your kind have been a plague on our great nation for centuries."

Blood was pouring from my side, and my brain swam with dizziness, my mind dancing with the memory of what Orion had told me. He'd loathed the mortals more than anyone, believed they had no mercy when it came to demons.

Strength was seeping out of me, and my mind grew dark. As I faltered, the congressman kicked me hard in the stomach. The blow ripped my side open a little more, and I stumbled back, shocked by the pain.

"What do you want from me?" I muttered.

His lip curled. "Demons like you are wild animals. Predators. And do you know what we do to dangerous animals? We lock them up so they can't hurt anyone. Sometimes, we hang trophies of your heads on our walls. A message to the others." He cocked his head. "I'm not sure you'll make it that long, though. A dying animal will find a dark corner to die in. You feeling that right now, demon?"

I *did*. My strongest instinct right now was to curl up behind Mr. Esposito's trash cans like a sick cat crawling off to die alone. With rising terror, I gripped my waist and stared at the blood pouring from me onto the driveway.

My mind flickered with memories of Mom's face, and I wanted to see her now more than ever. I stepped back, and my attacker slashed at me again, ripping the skin on the other side open. The screaming in my mind went quieter. I looked up at the congressman, taking in the smug curl of his lips. He was *enjoying* this. Blood dripped from his hook onto the pavement, a glistening pool of crimson.

Something snapped in me, and a burst of fiery magic sizzled between my ribs.

"You're right, Mr. Corwin," I snarled. "I *am* a predator."

Volcanic heat pooled in my chest and blazed down my arm and along my fingertips. I gripped the hunter's wrist as he swung at me again, the last vestige of my magic igniting in a burst of hot blue flame on his arm.

He screamed as his navy jacket caught fire. The flames licked at his face, and he dropped his metal hook, which clanged on the sidewalk. The smell of burning skin and hair nauseated me, but as much as I'd wanted to fight back, I wasn't going to watch someone burn to death.

I snatched the hook from the pavement and, with the last of my energy, slashed the congressman's throat. One quick swipe to his jugular, and his agony was over, his screams silenced. He fell to the ground, his body burning as the flames blazed higher. The other demon hunters screamed, stumbling over themselves to get away from me. They took off at a sprint down Gallows Hill Road.

The last of my magic drained from my body, and my legs felt weak. As bile climbed up my throat, I stepped past the burning body. I hoped the rain would put out the fire soon.

Mouth dry and body cold, a horrible thought struck me. I'd just killed a congressman. Lit him on fire and slit his throat. Right here, in Mr. Esposito's driveway.

Holy *fuck*. I wanted to lie down on the ground, but if I stuck around, I'd be arrested. What's more, if I went to the hospital or called an ambulance for myself, I'd be arrested.

Dizzy, I found myself shambling toward the road. I couldn't survive without medical help.

A voice called out from behind me, and I turned to see Mr. Esposito standing in his doorway, his figure hazy through the black smoke curling off the congressman's body.

"I'm sorry!" I blurted, unable to manage a full explanation.

Coughs racked his body for a moment, and then he shouted, "Rowan! Get to the City of Thorns!"

Another spasm of coughing shook his frail frame.

"Wait a minute. What?" He was right, of course, though I had no idea how he knew. As soon as I got within the city gates, my body would start to heal.

"Get to safety, Rowan," he said, and closed the door.

I could feel it now, too—an instinct, a tug between my ribs that pulled me east, toward the hill. My body had gone into survival mode, dragging itself toward the city, while I barely retained consciousness. That's where my body had been urging me to go, the City of Thorns, not behind the trash cans to die.

I moved faster, my legs carrying me through the shadowy streets. But mentally, I was starting to become delirious. Despite my injuries, my mind heated with memories of Orion's beauty—his pale eyes, high cheekbones, and sensual lips. His thickly corded muscles—

Why in the name of all that was holy was I thinking of that right now?

I was dying, and all I could think about was how much I wanted to sit in his lap. How it felt to have his lips graze over mine, his thumbs brush over my breasts. Heaven help me, I wanted to rip his clothes off and run my tongue over his chest. It felt like he was here right now, like I could reach out and touch him.

What the hell?

Take it off. Now. The memory of those words from him made an ache build inside me, a bittersweet pang that had nothing to do with my wounds.

I wanted it to happen again.

That's what you think about at a time like this?

What was this, some last desperate craving for life as I was about to expire?

I looked down at the trail of blood on the sidewalk, and realization dawned. Of *course.*

I was a succubus now. Sex wasn't just sex to a Lilu. Sex was *life.* It was healing and strength.

Sex would save my life.

I turned onto Walcott Street. I had two options now—find some random guy and make him kiss me, or make it the rest of the way up this hill.

Knowing what the men were like around here, I decided to take my chances with the hill.

But once I got into the city, what then? Orion still believed me to be Mortana, his worst enemy, and that was a serious problem. If I got anywhere near him, I had a horrible feeling he might try to kill me. True, something had stopped him before, but he'd literally made a blood oath to kill me, an oath he was compelled to keep.

And not just me. Orion was obligated to kill everyone in Mortana's family.

I didn't think I was Mortana, but whoever I was, I was probably related to her. After all, she looked exactly like me.

As my head swam with these thoughts, I realized I'd made it almost halfway up the slope, my blood mingling with the rainwater flowing downhill. Orange light from the streetlamps glittered off the dark puddles.

My thoughts were going dark, and I considered resting in the grass by the sidewalk, but as sirens wailed in the distance, I made my feet continue. I gripped my stomach, trying to stanch the bleeding. Blood seeped between my fingers. Across a wide street, the gates of the demon city emitted a pale, golden light, drawing me closer. The towering gates were wrought iron, twisted in the shape of thorns and vines, with a golden skull in the center.

Behind me, the sirens blazed louder, and red and blue lights flashed.

Moving faster, I dragged myself across the street. Police lights strobed, and I slumped against the gate.

Fuck. How did I open it?

The police bellowed behind me, screaming at me to freeze.

With tears stinging my eyes, I pressed a single bloodied hand against the golden skull.

A gunshot rang out, and a bullet seared my thigh. At that moment, the key symbol on my arm began to burn. Rays of golden light beamed from it, mingling with the gate's light. The pain ebbed, and the gate unlocked. I tumbled inside, and the gate swung closed behind me.

Weeks ago, I never would have imagined it, but now this place felt like home.

❧ 4 ❧

CHAPTER 4—ROWAN

I t was like I'd been drowning and had finally come up for air. As soon as I crossed the threshold into the City of Thorns, I felt the healing shimmer over my limbs.

I lay on the brick, the magic already starting to replenish in my body. The wounds in my side were knitting, and the bullet was working itself out of my thigh muscle, but I didn't want to lie here forever. It seemed mostly empty here, but I could hear a few demons talking nearby. If I were seen, word would quickly get back to Orion.

I stood, trying to get my bearings. I hadn't come through the main gate before. When I'd entered the city before, I'd been unconscious, and I'd left half-delirious through a tunnel system.

For the first time, I surveyed the city's entrance, a little stone courtyard I'd wondered about for many years. The entire place—the streets, the alcoves, the ornate turrets—was built of the same beautiful honey-colored stone as the exterior walls. Across the courtyard, a castle loomed. A carved lion overlooked enormous wooden doors, crisscrossed with iron and studs.

In the other buildings around me, arched windows overlooked the courtyard. Narrow alleys jutted off from the square—some with stairs that continued farther up the hill, some with stone walkways overhead.

Luckily for me, it was raining heavily, and almost no one was out tonight.

I stumbled toward the narrowest alleyway, finding it dark and abandoned. Rain pattered down, and thunder boomed.

As I walked, I ran my finger over the deep, fresh scar in my side. The wound didn't hurt at all, but it hadn't healed as much as I'd expected.

I kept moving until I found a small, dark garden with a fountain, like a tiny public park. Water flowed from stone serpent mouths, and ancient-looking runes had been engraved along the side of the fountain. Pale pink roses grew around it, scenting the air with their sweet perfume.

Looking for the driest patch, I curled up in the grass under a bench. I hugged myself, imagining a warm bed, and listened to the gentle sound of running water.

My eyelids grew heavy. Back in my true home once more, a blanket of sleep swept over me.

⟐

I AWOKE IN THE LITTLE ROSE GARDEN WITH MY CLOTHES DRENCHED. Best I could figure, I'd slept for an hour or two, and the rest had done me good. I felt better than ever, completely energized, and ready to take on the world. Did I like having demon magic? Hell, yes. I never wanted to leave this place again.

I exited the courtyard and found my way out of the network of alleys, reaching the river. As always, the air in the city was warm and humid, but the rain had kept the streets mostly clear. Nevertheless, I lurked in the shadows as I walked, not wanting anyone to notice me as I made my way back to my parents' house.

I followed the river east through the Sathanas Ward, filled with buildings adorned with carvings of monstrous heads and empty temples to the demon of wrath. Passing a windowless jail with an enormous iron door and a scaffold for executions, I soon reached the Asmodean Ward, the quarter once inhabited by the Lilu. At the easternmost edge of this section, the buildings thinned, and the river branched off into tributaries. There, I found my parents' dark mansion. It stood on flat ground against the river. Gothic gardens spread all about the property. Mist twined around a crumbling stone wall that surrounded part of their land and billowed around the mansion itself.

I swallowed hard as I entered the outermost edge of the gardens and made my way down a gravel walk, meandering between broken statues and thorny plants.

Wind howled through gnarled tree branches on either side of the path, and the scent of the nearby sea hung heavy in the warm air.

My feet crunched over the wet pebbles. I glanced up at the gargoyles, visible now through the fog. All I really knew about this place was that Mom had lived here, and Mortana, too, long ago.

And that Mom's husband might have burned to death right where I was walking now. He was my dad, or so I assumed.

A tragic presence clung to the façade, and I shivered, looking back at the place where a burned body had been found. Another indication, I mused, that it wasn't me who'd killed Mom. Maybe not the Hunters, either, since they couldn't enter the city.

A buried, molten anger rose to the surface, a searing heat that burned my forehead. Before me, rays of light tinged the mist with gold. A gust of wind blew the fog away, and when I looked down, I saw it— the symbol that had haunted my nightmares for years—the five-pointed star reflected in a puddle.

My heart beat faster. A memory buried in the recesses of my mind stirred, but I didn't want to see it.

An eerie, forlorn wind rushed over me as I climbed the steps. Crossing between the columns, I paused with my hand on the front door.

When we'd come here a few days ago, Orion had said that the City of Thorns wasn't like the mortal world. Here, the air was imbued with magic, and memories lingered tangibly. Tragedy wrapped itself around the wood and marble, hanging like a bitter, heavy miasma. The hair stood up on my nape.

The door was still open a crack from the last time we'd run out of here—when I'd fled the building. I pushed it open wider and stepped inside, standing once more among the cobwebs and smashed busts of my relatives. Sighing, I glanced up at the high ceiling adorned with faded paintings of vines and ripe fruit.

Eerie, yes, but I was glad to be here alone. This time, I could explore without Orion looking over me.

Loneliness cloaked the mosaic floor of blue and gold and the murals on the walls. Sadness tightened my chest, and I found myself hurrying up the creaking stairs.

When I reached the third floor, I walked slowly through the halls, stopping to peer into a bedroom with deep green paint, chipped by the passage of years, and a canopy bed of faded red material that smelled musty and stale. Moonlight streamed through an enormous pair of balcony doors.

My eye caught something I hadn't seen before—a portrait hanging on the wall. I'd never seen the face in the painting, but recognition hit me like a fist. I hurried inside, transfixed by the image, the likeness of a man with high cheekbones, dark eyes, and shocking red hair, nearly unnatural in its color. Red hair the same shade as mine, blending to blond at the tips, curling down around his chin. The image in the frame filled in all the missing pieces, the differences between mom and me. There was no doubt in my mind that he was my father. I felt a lump in my throat as I read the name below the portrait: Duke Moloch.

Orion thought Moloch had been burned just outside.

I ran my fingertips over the name engraved on the gold frame, wishing I could have met him just once.

And as I touched his name, my mind ticked over the words in the nursery rhyme that I'd found here last week.

The Maere of Night
gave girls a fright,
but one queen loved him well.
He lost the throne,
but seeds were sown
in the garden of Adele.

Was this about Orion?

Whoever had written that poem had intentionally cloaked the real meaning. Why had this poem popped into my mind just now? I stared up at my father. As the words played in my mind again and again, a thought took root.

This was a poem about a Lilu male—a Maere of Night. My father had been one, of course.

My gaze lingered over his fiery hair, and I wondered if I'd gotten my fire magic from him.

He lost the throne...

My father was the true son of the mad king Azriel from the old days. He could have been the heir, but he lost out to Nergal.

Seeds were sown in the garden of Adele...

Adele was King Cambriel's mother—Nergal's wife. And the seeds? Okay, I did *not* want to think about my newly discovered father's semen, but I'm guessing those were the seeds.

I shuddered, thinking of King Cambriel's cold beauty, his long, pale hair, his high cheekbones...

Like my dad's.

Dark eyes like ours. If you took Duke Moloch here, gave him blond hair...

Yeah, he'd look a lot like King Cambriel.

Had my dad knocked up Cambriel's mom?

I started pacing the room, and the old floorboards creaked beneath my feet.

If all that was correct, then Cambriel wasn't the true king at all. He was my half brother. My lip curled. Had he realized that when he'd leered at me?

He was someone with a rare fire power, like mine. Someone who could have lit Moloch on fire. Someone who could have burned Mom to death for knowing his secret.

I swallowed hard, my heart rate speeding up. Orion also had fire power. *Please tell me he's not also a relation.*

I sucked in a deep breath. Turning, I began to pace again, my hands shoved deep into the pockets of my damp sweatpants.

Orion had the mark of Lucifer. Unlike Cambriel, he was destined to rule—and only someone like that could murder a king.

The wind howled through the cracks in the old windows, and I pivoted again. The pieces of the puzzle were starting to slide together in my mind.

Orion had wanted me to identify Cambriel's magical protection, the thing keeping him alive. But a true king wouldn't need that. A true, destined king could only be killed by an heir.

That was Orion's plan, wasn't it? Orion had said he'd been blackmailing Cambriel. Now I knew why. He knew the king was no king at all.

Orion knew that *he* possessed the mark of Lucifer.

And as soon as he figured out what kept the king alive, he would kill him and take the throne for himself.

I crossed my arms as I paced and tried to remember the rest of the nursery rhyme. I had a photo of it in my phone, but the battery was still dead, so I closed my eyes, seeing the words in my mind's eye.

A Swindler king,
a golden ring
to keep his heart alive.
Take the ring,
fell the king.
The city yet will thrive.

My eyes snapped open. That was pretty clear, wasn't it? A golden ring.

I ran the words over and over in my head, certain that my parents had given me the secret to killing the king.

If the king took his rings off, he could be killed.

I bit my lip, wondering if this was why my parents had died.

They'd known how to end Cambriel.

❧ 5 ❧

CHAPTER 5—ROWAN

I left the green chamber and went into the room with the portrait of my mom. Moonlight spilled through tall windows, bathing everything in a ghostly silver. I was still wearing damp, blood-stained clothes. Going to an enormous wardrobe on one side of her bed, I opened the doors and stared at her dresses. They were a little threadbare but mostly preserved by time, silk dresses with puffed sleeves, some with beautiful lace, others with ruffled collars. None of them looked comfortable. My gaze went to a short white gown with full sleeves and a rounded collar. It must be a slip, or maybe a smock, with delicately embroidered trim.

In any case, I'd be borrowing it from Mom. I pulled off my wet clothes, standing cold and naked, and slipped into the white dress. I stared down at the shift, trying to imagine Mom in this garment. For a moment, I thought I smelled her floral scent.

A lump had formed in my throat, and I swallowed hard. I closed the wardrobe and turned to look at the room. Maybe I could stay here for a little while until I figured out a better plan. I'd avoid Mortana's old place, where Orion might look for me.

My curiosity sparked, I looked around the room, my eyes roaming over the dark wood and time-faded painted walls. It was so calm here, like a tomb. So different from the chaos I'd fled in Osborne.

I crossed back into the hall and wandered into an old bathroom with a copper clawfoot tub and cracked mosaic floors flecked with gold.

In here, I could definitely smell Mom's sweet, velvety jasmine scent. The ache of her loss bloomed in my chest. Her presence was so strong in this place that I could almost imagine her moving from room to room...

Mom used to hide things.

Important things. Her cash, a diamond ring, the checkbook. She had a drawer in the kitchen with a false bottom, where she tucked valuables.

I crossed over to a candle in a sconce on the wall and summoned a bit of fire magic, except I couldn't get it to rise. Staring at my hands, I bit my lip and tried to envision the flames. How did you make magic appear, I wondered.

I gritted my teeth, trying to force the fire up.

How did it happen last time? I envisioned my desperation...

My chest heated, and the warmth flowed down my arm and wrist and into my fingertips—exhilarating. But it was only the tiniest of sparks, like the lick of a match on my fingertip. I lit one of the candles, and the flame on my fingertip flickered out.

Warm orange light spread over the room, making me feel more at home.

Where would Mom hide something important here?

A desk stood beneath a window—the same one where I'd found the nursery rhyme. I crossed over to it and pulled open the drawer. With a hammering heart, I ran my fingers around its bottom, then slid my fingernails into it. I pulled up the panel—a false bottom—and stared down at a single piece of paper.

Written on the page, over and over, was one declarative sentence.

Long live King Nergal.

I pulled out the paper.

But why would anyone hide *that*—a simple statement of loyalty to the former king?

Disappointment twisted my heart. I ran my fingers over the handwriting. It wasn't my mother's elegant cursive, but rather a blocky, masculine text. Was this my dad's writing? Duke Moloch—the strange and unfamiliar name of a man who looked just like me.

Mr. Esposito sometimes said, "If you don't have a family, you don't have a life," which was a bit annoying, considering that neither of us had families.

I wanted something that belonged to my father. Since I had nothing else, I folded up the note and tucked it into my bra.

I turned back to the desk and slid open another drawer. A hot, dry breeze rippled over me, scented with burnt cedar.

Oh, *fuck*. He was here.

Shock rattled through my bones as I felt his molten magic thrumming up my spine.

I whirled to see the Lord of Chaos standing in the doorway.

The other one with the mark of Lucifer. My beautiful nemesis. Maybe I shouldn't have lit the damn candle.

Amber candlelight danced back and forth over his golden skin, sculpting his cheekbones. He pinned me with his stare, a faint smile on his lips, like he was about to catch his prey.

The shock of his masculine beauty stole my breath. A lock of his silver hair hung before his pale eyes, and my heart clenched. Why was he so fucking pretty? It was an unfortunate distraction from the fact that he was my enemy.

"Mortana," he said, taking a step closer. The raw hatred in his tone sent ice through my veins. "I'd hoped never to see you again. Why would you come back here, knowing that I wanted you dead?"

I crossed my arms. "What can I do to convince you I'm not Mortana?"

He shook his head slowly. "It won't work this time. I've seen your demon mark."

I took a step back into the wall. "Have you been waiting outside this house, or what?"

Moonlight washed over his enormous body and the black T-shirt that clung to his muscled chest. My gaze roamed his thickly corded arms and his tattoo—the snake tied into a noose. He *loved* to intimidate, didn't he? That was his thing.

The sardonic smile on his lips quickly disappeared, and malice shone from his eyes. "I haven't been waiting outside. I woke up with a hammering heart and a suffocating sense of dread. For a moment, I wondered if I was in Hell, then I knew what had shaken me from sleep and filled me with this overwhelming sense of repulsion. *Your* rotten presence, drawing me closer. It was you—back in the City of Thorns, against all reason. You could have bought yourself a few more days, Mortana, if you'd stayed away. You probably could have run. But your arrogance knows no bounds. Don't you realize I swore a sacred oath to kill you?"

I glared at him, my body rigid with anger. "*My* arrogance? And yet, here you are, so certain you're correct when you are dead wrong."

A thorny silence stretched out between us. "If you truly believe you are not Mortana, it is because you have erased your own memory. You once told me about the very spell that could make it happen. You offered it to me."

Fuck. Frustration ignited. "No. I remember my life as a child. I remember sitting in my mom's lap and having a stuffed lion named Leroy."

"How adorable. Too bad those memories are not real."

The world tilted beneath my feet. "No. That's not possible." The idea that my whole life had been false was too disturbing for me to dwell on for longer than a moment. "Look, I don't know who exactly I am, but that's why I'm here in this house. I'm looking for answers. Maybe I'm Mortana's sister, but several hundred years younger."

"Hmm." He was as still as stone, and dark heat radiated from his body. He pressed his finger against his lips, his eyebrows knitted. "I suppose you also think you are both Lightbringers with the same mark from Lucifer, both with fire magic. Identical. Interesting theory. Except that's not how sisters work, is it?"

"I'm not her!" My voice rose.

"And if you were an identical twin," he went on, ignoring me, "you'd also be four hundred years old. But you say that you're not. Nor are you a mortal doppelgänger, clearly." He stepped closer, and I felt his sinister power thrum over my skin. "Sorry, love. I don't believe you, and I'm afraid the oath compels me to end your life."

My mind spun. I was back to square one with Orion. Now he was sure I was the one who'd tortured him and killed his family.

And—okay. He was right. Sisters didn't look identical. But my memories were so real, so specific. The nights I needed Mom to lie in bed and rub my back when I had nightmares. The time I'd pissed myself at Nina McCarthy's birthday and had to go home early. The time I'd chewed on the back of a pen in class, and it had exploded in my mouth. A messy kiss sophomore year with a boy named Jeff who played the bassoon.

It couldn't be magic—what the fuck kind of magical spell would make all that up?

I swallowed hard, my emotions churning like waves in a hurricane.

"There are two of us with Lucifer's mark," I said desperately. "Why couldn't there be three? Something strange has happened, hasn't it? There should only be one destined monarch at a time. Otherwise, it makes no sense."

No reaction to that line of reasoning, just a step closer from the Lord of Chaos.

Darkness slid through my bones, and I could hear my own heartbeat. I was going to have to fight back against this pure wall of muscle, or I'd be dead. I had to tap into that predatory side, like I had before with the demon hunters.

Apart from my slow and steady breath, my body went completely still. A breeze rushed through the cracks in the window, toying with my hair. "I can see that there's nothing I can say to convince you."

My gaze swept over his brutal snake tattoo, the tail formed into a noose. Its dark, sinuous lines curved over his muscles. Shadows seemed to billow from him as he loomed over me. Intimidation was his kink.

"Why don't you confess?" he purred. "Let it all out, Mortana."

My heart was pounding so hard I felt like it was making the walls vibrate. His intense gaze penetrated me like he was trying to memorize each curve of my features.

"Well, well, well," he said, his voice silky, "I see it in your eyes. Even you are not convinced. I can read the doubt there. You wonder if you're evil. You wonder if you're Mortana, and you simply cannot remember."

My fingers tightened into fists. "You're really starting to annoy me, do you know that? Always so confident that you're right."

Another slow step closer. "But do you know what I love?" he murmured.

"Let me guess," I shot back. "Yourself? Reading smut. Being a big scary incubus with snake tattoos?"

He was at my throat before I could finish the next sentence, and he swiveled me around, pressing my back against the wall. Somehow, he'd done all this without hurting me. His fingers laced around my throat, but they didn't squeeze.

His knee slid between my thighs, pinning me in place. His body was as heavy and solid as the wall behind me.

"Snake tattoos..." He let out a low chuckle, but I saw no amusement in his eyes. "Ah, lovely Mortana. You are easier to pin down than you once would have been. Fragile, almost. Breakable, slow, and weak. You've lost that fighting spirit. But it seems you remember something from the past. Let's go over why I got that snake tattoo, shall we?"

What the fuck was he talking about? Remember *what*?

I pulled at his wrist, trying to move his hand away from my throat. "I don't know what you're talking about. I can see the tattoo for myself —that's why I mentioned it. You like to intimidate, don't you? Big, scary demon boy."

His knee slid further between my thighs, and he stroked his thumb over the pulse in my throat, a languid, sultry movement that sent a strange, forbidden shiver through my body. What the hell?

His pale eyes were half-lidded, and he looked like he was in a trance as he gazed down at me.

Lowering his mouth to my ear, he whispered, "Confess, love. Let it all out. Have you been faking your memory loss? Do you remember everything? Do you remember the snakes?" He pulled back again to study my face, intently trying to read my expression. His eyes flickered, dark and heated.

I held his gaze. "No."

Slowly, his hand brushed down my throat to my chest. Heat radiated off his body, warming my skin. His face was close to mine, his breath ghosting over my lips. I could feel my cheeks flushing.

Long silver claws shot from his fingertips, and my heart skipped a beat. The tips of his claws were already piercing the thin fabric of the little white dress. All his muscles were rigid.

I couldn't tell if he was using all his strength to stop himself from killing me or to convince himself that he needed to.

Holy shit. The threat of imminent death sharpened my senses.

And I wasn't just Rowan the mortal anymore. I wasn't Mortana, either—but I was a fucking succubus. I had power now.

I reached up and touched the side of his face. "Orion," I murmured. "Why are you pretending to hate me?"

Nearly imperceptibly, his features softened. His eyes grew dark all at once, and his lips parted. His claws began to retreat, but his knee remained firmly between my thighs.

I brushed my thumb over his lower lip. His sharp intake of breath did something to me, made my muscles go taut and my thighs clench around his knee. His midnight eyes swept down my body to linger on my breasts. I was sure he was remembering what I looked like naked, and for a moment, I felt like I was completely bare before him. I moved my hips forward a little.

Around us, the air grew humid, sultry, and I let my head fall back against the wall.

Entranced, Orion slid his hand higher again to cup my throat—gently this time, just below my jaw. Now, his touch was reverent. His thumb brushed over my lips like I'd done to him, and I took it in my mouth, sucking on it for a moment. Another sharp intake of breath from him.

That ice-cold expression had left his eyes, leaving behind a smoldering possessiveness.

This was the moment to act.

I slammed my forehead into his nose, and he dropped his grip on me, staggering back. I brought my heel down hard into his kneecap, buying myself some time.

Run, Rowan. That's what you do best.

Just when I reached the door, I felt his powerful arms wrap around me—one hand around my throat, the other clamping my arms to my sides. *Fuck*.

His claws were gone, but his iron body had me locked in a vise-like grip. Dread shivered through me. Something I'd said had flipped a switch in him earlier—the thing about the tattoo. Or something about snakes. Whatever it was, it had been exactly the wrong thing to say.

"You could be powerful, Mortana," he said quietly. "But I think you've forgotten how to fight like a demon. And in case your question was real, I don't know that I hate you anymore. I don't think I feel anything for you at all. It's hard to hate someone you no longer respect."

For a moment, his words hit me so sharply, I felt like I could hardly breathe. I don't think I'd realized until now how absolutely desperately I wanted things to be right between us. Because the sad truth was, I hardly had anyone else left.

"Is that so?" I tried to keep my voice steady.

"This new version of you has been nothing more than a tedious inconvenience. You are neurotic, dull, and unskilled at everything."

Rage erupted. I jammed my heel hard into his calf—once, twice. But this time, I had no effect on him. It was like slamming my foot into a stone wall.

Shit. That move killed in my self-defense classes.

I might be strong as a demon, but Orion was a force of nature, a demonic god hewn from stone and fury.

My heart slammed against my ribs. I shifted my body, trying to break free of his grip, but his arm only tightened around me.

The side of his cheek brushed against mine. "Mortana," he whispered. "It's not just the oath, or the fact that you murdered my family. It's not just your sadism. No, on top of all that, you are my rival for the throne. You are the other demon with the mark of the Lightbringer. You always knew I bore the same, didn't you? And that's precisely why you delighted in tormenting me in the dungeons."

I kept struggling against his grip, but I wasn't getting anywhere.

"You were the one who killed King Nergal, weren't you?" I said. "Only an heir could do it. I know it wasn't me. And that's how you blackmailed Cambriel."

"Good summary." His deep, languid voice betrayed not a hint of exertion. "And once I figure out what is keeping Cambriel alive, everyone will know that I'm meant to be on the throne. That I'm meant to be king."

If I could keep him talking, maybe I'd figure out a way to stay alive.

I turned my head, my cheek brushing against his. "But *are* you destined to rule? Or am I? It must make you wonder, since there are two of us."

His body was growing hotter. "You were born before me. I always assumed I was a correction of a terrible abomination."

When someone was delusional or psychotic, you couldn't argue with them outright. They'd just think you didn't understand them. You had to work within the boundaries of their belief system. "Fine. I was born first." I reached behind, sliding my hand under the hem of his black T-shirt, and stroked his abs, just above his belt. By the sigh he let out, I thought it was working. "The thing is, Orion, when I saw you in that bar in Osborne, you were desperate for one thing." I moved my hips against him gently and heard his intake of breath. "You wanted to know how to kill the king, because it's the only way the city will accept you as a ruler. Out of curiosity, have you tried to kill him before?"

"He comes back." His voice sounded husky, rasping. "That's how I know he's protected."

I rocked my hips again. "I know how to kill him now. If you kill me, you'll never know how to get him out of your way. You'll never convince the City of Thorns that you're the true king. Whether or not he was supposed to be crowned, he was, and you can't undo that unless he's dead. No one will accept you as king so long as he's alive. No one knows you're the heir. You need me."

There was a quiet chuckle from the wall of pure muscle behind me. "Oh, you know his weakness suddenly, do you? Why would I believe you?"

I stroked my fingertips under his shirt. My breath was shallow, heart racing. His magic curled around me, stroking my skin. "I'll make a blood oath. I'll tell you how to kill the king if you let me live. Everyone in the City of Thorns will know you're the true and rightful heir once you slaughter him. We both win."

"You forget something," he purred, stroking one of his fingertips over the pulse in my throat. Strangely, it made me shiver—but not from fear. "For one thing, I don't believe you'd willingly give up the throne. And for another, there is the oath. If I don't fulfill my promise, I will die."

❧ 6 ❧

CHAPTER 6—ROWAN

"I know there's a tiny spark inside your soul that tells you I might not be her."

The silence that followed told me that yes, I'd hit a mark. And maybe that was the only reason I wasn't dead yet.

"You certainly don't have the killer instinct she had," he said at last. "The thing is, love, I made this little promise to kill her whole family. I know you are related to her. So whatever way you slice it, I am bound to kill you. I can feel my heart constricting just standing here, touching you. Every moment I let you live makes me feel closer to death."

Desperation erupted in my chest. "There's got to be a way to undo the oath."

Another long silence spread out between us.

"There *is* a way," I said, and my fingers tightened on him. "I know there is. Sever the oath, and then I'll tell you what you need to know."

"The simplest thing would be to end your life." His eyes blazed with dark intensity.

But the question was, if he was so hellbent on killing me, why hadn't he done it already?

"It sounds like you're trying to convince yourself. You don't *want* to kill me." A mixture of fear and hope twisted inside me. "Something is stopping you. Why don't you start by admitting the truth to yourself? Some part of you actually *likes* me."

He lowered his hands, releasing me. "Every part of me loathes what you were. But no. You don't seem the same."

As I turned to face him, I tried to catch my breath. "I have information that you need. If I'm dead, you'd have to accept that Cambriel could be sitting on that throne for generations. If you kill me, you'll be murdering the one person who has the information you need. My parents were killed for a reason, and that was because they knew how to kill Cambriel."

Shadows stained the air around him like ink, and a warm breeze skimmed over my skin. My argument was a bit flimsy. Would it actually work?

He cocked his head. "Why don't you tell me how to kill the king, and then we will figure out how to break the sacred oath."

I crossed my arms "What is it about the past ten minutes of you threatening to kill me that makes you think I would trust you right now?"

Darkness spilled through his eyes, and he slid his hands into his pockets. His body language looked relaxed and casual, but there was real intensity in that midnight stare. "I need you to cut your palm and make an oath."

I looked down at my hand. "What, exactly, am I going to promise?"

"Two things," he said. "One, I need you to swear that you actually know how to kill Cambriel. If you're lying, you will die. Two, swear that you will tell me this secret as soon as I sever the oath. Agree to these conditions or forfeit your life."

I inhaled deeply. "I can't promise I can tell you how to kill the king because nothing in life is certain," I said. "I *can* promise you that I have a solid theory, one I believe is true and will share with you after you break *your* oath."

"Good. Slash your palm."

Holy shit, he was going for it. Maybe, deep down, he didn't want to kill me for some reason. I held out my hand. "Do you have a knife?"

His brow furrowed, and his claws shot out. "Just use yours." He raked a long silver claw against his palm, and crimson blood dripped onto the floor.

I looked down at my hands, willing my own claws to appear. I tried to imagine them gleaming from my fingertips.

After a few awkward moments, I looked up, meeting Orion's gaze. "How do I bring the claws out?"

He took a step closer, peering down at me. "You really remember nothing."

"Literally nothing of being a demon." I shook my head. "My claws and fire came out recently, but it sort of happened of its own accord."

"Was your life at risk at the time?"

My brain flickered with disturbing memories from earlier that night. Me, surrounded by enemies and bleeding by the trash cans. "Oh, yes. A group of mortals was trying to kill me."

The corner of his lips twitched. "Did you end their lives?"

"One of them."

"When your life is in danger, it provides a shortcut to your primal side. As a demon," he said, "you are part beast. A killer among prey. You need to remember how to connect to that side of yourself, to everything you've buried. To your pure, animal instinct."

The *id*.

I closed my eyes, trying to tap into the animalistic side of myself. I saw the congressman burning to death in the driveway and heard his screams. I smelled the smoke in my nostrils, and I wanted to be sick.

My eyes snapped open again. "It's not working."

"Try again, Mortana."

I narrowed my eyes. "Rowan. The name is Rowan."

A half smile. "Try again. I don't want your blood on my claws unless I'm ending your life."

With a deep breath, I closed my eyes once more and tried to summon my predatory side. Flames danced in the dark recesses of my mind, screams that pierced the silence.

I let out a long, slow breath. "I'll get a knife," I said quietly. "I'm getting sick of your mind games."

But before I could take a step away from Orion, he spun me around and pressed me against the wall, dominating me with his powerful body. I was no match for his strength, and he was letting me know it.

"You know, Orion," I said through labored breaths. "I think I actually hate you more now than ever."

Instead of responding, he lowered his head and pressed his sharpened fangs to my throat in a pure, primal display of dominance—trapping me here, even as I tried to free myself.

"You're a big boy. Use your words!" I shouted. "For fuck—"

I broke off in shock as his fangs pierced my skin, drawing blood. The pain of it robbed me of my thoughts for a moment, drowning out my ability to speak. I snarled and shoved my elbow back into his ribs as hard as I could. Anger seared me, rushing through my nerve endings, incinerating my worries.

He released his grip on me, his eyes dark as ink.

"When you're shifting," he said, "you don't think in words."

I looked down, pleased to see my claws glinting in the moonlight, the golden light of my demon mark aglow.

Catching my breath, I drew one of my claws across my palm. Blood streaked across my pale skin and dripped to the floor.

Orion grabbed my bleeding hand and stared into my eyes. "Good. Now, repeat after me. On pain of death, I swear a sacred oath that I believe I have a strong theory of how to kill King Cambriel."

I repeated him, word for word, stating that I would divulge the king's weakness as promised. I felt the magic of the oath skitter up my spine, and when the oath was done, I pressed my bleeding palm against his. He gripped my hand tightly, holding on with a firm grip. As our blood mingled, a vision started to burn in my mind.

I wasn't in my parents' house anymore, but in a dungeon with five large serpents...

Fear knocked the wind out of me.

The vision changed, and a body swung soundlessly from a gallows above me, her shadow moving back and forth over a silent pit. Her neck was bent, broken, and I could see that her eyes were still open— blue eyes, pleading. She was still alive. Terror choked me fiercely, like my soul was splitting in two.

Gasping, I pulled my hand away from his. I was shaking. "What the fuck?" I whispered, staring at Orion.

I was no longer in the prison but back in the mansion. I let out a slow, trembling breath.

He frowned at me. "What?"

I shook my head, trying to clear my head of the horrible vision. I wasn't scared of snakes, but those serpents had scared me half to death.

His eyes glinted. "You're mine for the next few days. That's about all the time I have before the oath kills me."

"There's something you should probably know. The entire Osborne police force is looking for me, and they might report me to the king. I broke the contract between mortals and demons when I killed someone."

"The king will probably find a way to sweep it under the rug. And if he doesn't, let's burn that bridge when we come to it. Tomorrow, we leave to find the Dying God."

"Sorry, what?"

He arched an eyebrow. "We're going to Hell."

I stared at him. "Hell."

"Until we leave, I'm not going to let you out of my sight. As soon as I do, I know you'll run, so you will be with me every moment of every day until I get the secret from you. And as soon as I get that secret, you will leave the City of Thorns for good. You will no longer be allowed within my kingdom."

I glared at him. *We'll see about that, dick.*

Maybe I didn't want to live my life on ramen noodles in a basement anymore. Not to mention that I was a wanted woman in the mortal realm. *This* was my home.

I looked down at my palm, watching it heal. When I met Orion's gaze again, I straightened.

He was right about one thing. I *did* need to learn to be a demon. And everything he'd said to me tonight filled me with anger.

It's just hard to hate someone you no longer respect at all.

Screw you, Orion.

"Where are we sleeping, then?" I asked with a sharp edge in my voice. "Your place or mine?"

His expression was cold, almost bored. "Yours. I'd rather not be seen with you again. It was embarrassing enough the first time."

I wanted to scream. "Guess what, Orion? You're not the only one with a dead family, but you're the only one using it as a license to be an absolute twat."

He let out a short laugh. "The thing is," he said blandly, "I don't really give a fuck what you think. Apart from our one little tryst, I find you tedious and pathetic. And the truth is, I was only drinking from your raging lust because that's how I feed. That's all. I want you out of my life."

I was so furious now, my entire body was shaking with adrenaline. "And that lust? That was inspired by your incubus magic. Because there's absolutely nothing appealing about a miserable twat with interpersonal problems. You know what I think?" I continued. "The world would have been better off if you'd never left the dungeon."

Stony-faced, he walked past me. The pure vitriol of his words made me feel like my chest was cracking open. I could hardly breathe.

✤ 7 ✤

CHAPTER 7—ROWAN

What. An. Asshole.

So, I was only interesting as long as I fulfilled his incubus lust for sex? Clearly, there was no need to bore him by ever speaking to him again. The miserable fucker could have silence.

I clenched my jaw, trying to master my anger as we walked through the dark city streets slightly west of my parents' place.

When we finally crossed into Mortana's old apartment building, the human male who opened the door for me was a welcome sight. He grinned at me. His hair was as red as mine, and a smattering of freckles flecked his nose.

I crossed into the hall, my gaze roaming over the grandeur of the lobby. It was like an ancient, luxurious hotel, the floors tiled with blue and amber. Golden stone arches stretched high above us, and a staircase curved up to the mezzanine, where I'd find my apartment. My gaze drifting upward, I stared at the seductive image of Lilith and the snake curled around her body painted on the ceiling.

I sighed and turned back to the human. "Good to be home."

He beamed at me. "Lady Mortana. I wasn't sure you'd return, but I did hope I could tell my girlfriend I'd met you." He cleared his throat.

"I've just started my internship here." He glanced down at the ground. "Sorry, I'm not supposed to speak to you."

Internship. In other words, the demons had convinced him to work for free. Orion would probably point out again that the demons learned their most evil shit from the mortals.

I flicked my hair over my shoulder, like Mortana would. "I suppose you can speak, mortal, since this weird stalker looming behind me isn't worth talking to."

His eyes darted between us, and he choked out a nervous laugh. "Okay, well..."

It was probably occurring to him that he, as doorman, should reject the stalker, except the stalker was six-feet-plus of pure muscle and ferocity.

"Doorman," I said imperiously, like Mortana, "don't worry about that idiot. I'll have coffee in the morning." I gazed over his shoulder at a fire extinguisher on the wall. "Did you bring that here?"

The mortal glanced back at it. "Just looking out for this beautiful old building. Since, you know..." He gestured to me, probably referencing my fire power. I could send this whole place up in flames at any moment.

"Right." I arched an eyebrow. "Nervous about fires, are you?"

He nodded vigorously. "Mortals can actually die from it. There are no fire alarms, and the building is definitely not up to code." His voice cracked as he spoke, and he looked at the ground again. "Is there anything else you need, Lady Mortana?"

I cocked my head, studying him. His suit looked expensive, but he hadn't gotten the hang of ironing his clothes properly because his white shirt was wrinkled. Obviously, he wasn't used to dressing up. Had I seemed such a mess when I'd been mortal? Shit. I had, hadn't I?

And that was only a few days ago.

I had a sudden overpowering urge to take him under my wing, to make sure he got paid for the work he was doing. To make sure no one took advantage of him.

"What's your name, mortal?"

His cheeks went red. "Carl."

Orion stepped forward, towering over both of us. "Well, this has been tedious as Hell, so we're leaving now."

My eyebrow rose again. "You really like that word *tedious*, don't you? Did you just learn it?" He definitely seemed annoyed right now. And considering how I now felt about him, of course I wanted to run with that.

I moved closer to Carl and leaned back against the desk. "I was actually getting to know Carl here. I think we'll be friends. He's *interesting*. You know, in our world, it's a novelty when someone isn't a terrible person. Have you ever considered that?"

A muscle twitched in Orion's jaw.

"So, Carl," I drawled, "sorry my stalker here is in such a hurry. He really doesn't understand fun at all. Not like us. Tell me, Carl, what are your interests besides smoke alarms and fire extinguishers?"

He swallowed hard. "Are you really interested?"

I shrugged. "Believe it or not, I happen to find fire safety fascinating, so you're off to a good start. It's been a while since I've met anyone I had anything in common with."

The growl that rumbled from Orion's chest was so quiet, I didn't think Carl's mortal ears could hear it. Maybe he was just impatient, but I could tell he hated that I was paying attention to the doorman.

Carl shifted from one foot to the other. "My hobbies. Okay. I like making tacos. And I'm an artist, mostly drawing with ink on paper. And I like history, like the witch trials, and beautiful old buildings like this."

Holy moly, he was like a male version of me.

"I've always been interested in the history of the Great Demon War—"

"The Great Mortal War," said Orion. "Mortals were the enemy."

Carl's eyes darted nervously between us. "But that was a long time ago. It's good that we're at peace now. We have so much to learn from each other, demons and mortals."

Orion shoved his hands into his pockets, narrowing his eyes. "Oh, I very much doubt that, Carl."

Carl didn't seem to hear him because he was staring only at me now. "You're the last one, Duchess. The last of the Lilu. I read about what happened to your kind." His throat bobbed. "That must have been terrible for you."

I could feel the air heating, and the electric lights flickered. Was that Orion's magic?

"If you don't stop talking to this moron," said Orion breezily, "I will rip out his ribs."

Now Carl was paying attention to Orion. He let out a whimper and stepped back behind the desk, visibly trembling. He glanced at me, his lips pressed tightly together, and shook his head. I understood what he meant—he wasn't going to open his mouth anymore.

"Orion." I sighed. "You really should be locked up for the benefit of the rest of the city."

Schooling my expression, I waved my hand and said goodbye to Carl.

I let out a long, slow breath and crossed to the stairs, still not making eye contact with Orion. He was a much worse person than I'd thought—which was saying something, as we'd met when he kidnapped me and threw me in a dungeon.

My heels clacked over the mosaic floor as I walked toward the sweeping staircase.

I once thought Orion and I were alike because we both wanted revenge. But I only wanted to kill *one* person.

Orion? I had a feeling he wanted to burn the whole world down.

❋ 8 ❋

CHAPTER 8—ORION

I lay on Mortana's sofa, staring up at her ceiling. I didn't have a blanket because you couldn't exactly ask someone for a comfy blanket after you'd told them you hated them and wanted them dead.

I turned on my side, staring out the tall windows. The canopy of night spread above the pool outside. The window was open a crack, and I heard a barred owl crooning in the distance. On the other side of the pool, the Acheron River rushed past.

Even on the best of nights, I found it hard to sleep. Tonight, there was no way I could drift off.

When I thought of Mortana, it was like inhaling death, exhaling ash.

Rowan was different. Even if I *knew* they were the same person, it was hard to think of them as the same. When she was around, embers smoldered to life in my chest for the first time in centuries, and I felt alive.

I hadn't woken with a feeling of dread and known she was here. I'd had a feeling of warmth in my chest, dead charcoal sparking. Without Rowan, my world was cold, silent.

Unfortunately for me, everything about her was a lie. And that was because everything about Mortana had always been a lie, a deception designed to crush my soul.

When I'd seen the star of Lucifer blazing from her head, I'd known. It had all been a lie—another one of Mortana's sadistic tricks.

A humid wind whistled through the crack in the window. But that wasn't what was keeping me awake.

I didn't trust her, not enough to think she'd *actually* tell me Cambriel's secret, even with the blood oath. Deep down, she was Mortana, and Mortana always found a way out. I'd let her live, but only because I was too bloody weak to kill her.

It was hard not to think of the way Rowan moved, the way she'd touched my skin.

Who was she, really?

She was identical—*identical*—to Mortana.

And yet, she'd tried to save me from the bullets in that underground tunnel. Mortana would never have done that.

For a moment, there in the abandoned mansion, I'd been certain it had all been another one of her tricks. I was sure she remembered everything when she'd mentioned the snake, as if taunting me for what I'd done. Exactly like Mortana had, and how could she have known if she wasn't there?

I rolled onto my back, staring at the ceiling.

She was taking over every one of my thoughts. She was a wildfire burning through my skull until I could hardly think with my own words anymore.

Now, I could only hear the things she'd said. *Why don't you start by admitting the truth to yourself? Some part of you actually likes me...*

Letting her live was a betrayal to all the Lilu she had killed. One by one, they'd been led to their deaths in silence under the ground because of her.

Isn't there any tiny spark inside your soul that tells you I might not be her?

Fuck.

All I had to do was end her life. Instead, I was letting her sleep in the same apartment as me. Despite my oath to the dead, I was going along with her plan. She'd incinerated my own thoughts the first time I'd kissed her—back when we were supposed to be pretending, in the

Temple of Ishtar. And now my mind wasn't my own anymore. She'd become my obsession.

Since I could not bring myself to kill her, the next best thing was to destroy whatever we'd had between us.

With several brutal insults, I'd burned it all. There you have it—a sacrifice on the altar of the dead. Maybe that offering would appease them for what I was doing now, failing in the mission they'd given me. I'd promised them I would kill her. I'd promised Ashur.

I find you tedious and pathetic.

I stretched my arms above my head and listened to the sound of Mortana rolling over in the bed upstairs. Was she having a hard time sleeping, too?

I kept thinking about the perfect curve of her ass in that sheer white dress, the way her hips swayed when she walked.

As a demon, she moved differently than she had before, smoother and more elegantly now.

Gods, I wanted her naked in my bed, but these thoughts were a betrayal to the dead, and I would no longer allow myself to indulge.

I clenched my fist, letting my claws pierce my palm to distract myself with the pain. I would think of the throne, the crown, nothing but the vengeance that had been my lifeblood. I absolutely would *not* think of her, or how it would feel to have her full red lips wrapped around my cock.

I closed my eyes.

Remember the past. Remember why you are alive.

Every morning, when I'd woken in the dungeon, I'd looked around at the four small walls of my cell. Before the mortals had come to arrest all of us, my father had given me a knife, and he'd taught me to whittle. I was little, but he'd trusted me with a tiny pocketknife. I'd been careful, so careful with it, my prized possession, and I'd used it to make sharpened sticks, which was about all I could do.

I'd had my pocketknife with me when we were arrested, and I'd thought I was getting away with something. I thought the guards had missed my little whittling knife when they'd searched me. It had taken me a while to realize the truth—they simply did not see me or my mother as a threat, not without our magic.

Before my mother was murdered, I'd made a birthday gift for her, whittled from a twig, a likeness of a queen with a lump for a head and ridges for a crown. I'd been thrilled with the idea that she would have a birthday celebration, even if it were in a cell. Each day, I'd ask her if her birthday was coming up, and she would say no. I suspect she'd seen me making the gift and knew I was excited about it. By delaying her birthday, she gave me something to look forward to.

"Soon, little one," she'd say. "Soon."

They'd killed her before I'd gotten the chance to give it to her. When I was twelve, they took the knife away.

After centuries down there, I could hardly remember my real name anymore. No matter. I only needed to remember vengeance, and so I focused on that one moment, the soul-shattering nightmare that had destroyed what I used to be and made me into a creature of revenge.

I became a new person—Orion, born in the dungeons. I'd named myself after the stars I could see through a crack in the stone—a constellation my mother had once pointed out to me. The old me had died.

And this, all of this, was the legacy of Mortana.

In the early days, there had been more of us. I was only a boy then, and I'd listen to them talk. Balthazar, Malphas, Saleos, Azazel, Marduk...each one of their names etched into my heart like a tattoo. Ashur lived in the cell next to me, and he would sing the old Lilu songs. I couldn't see him from my cell, but I remembered him from the City of Thorns, a towering, muscular figure with golden horns and long black hair. He'd worn golden cloaks, and his fingers glittered with jewels.

He'd always say we would avenge the Lilu, that one day, we would learn to fight back. We kept our families' memories alive by talking about each one of them. And some day, we would make our enemies pay, memorializing the dead in their blood. We would rip Mortana's heart out and stick her head on the gates. We would build statues to the dead.

We spoke of flames that would burn the city to the ground.

We didn't worship the gods down there, but rather at the altar of delusion.

And one by one, we'd hear the others led away, never to return. One by one, they left, their voices going silent, until it was Ashur and me, the last two.

Over time, Ashur's bravado grew quieter. His defiance started to bleed out of him.

For decades, we were completely forgotten. No one brought us food. At night, dreams of banquets tormented us. Food we could never eat, not even in our dreams. Then we'd wake, still starving, and remember where we were. I thought the hunger would last forever.

We turned into living skeletons, our intestines decaying inside us. I'd have eaten Ashur if I'd had the strength to break into his cell.

Ashur slowly lost his mind.

He forgot words to the songs. He asked me sometimes, plaintively from the other cell, to remind him of his name. He forgot his wife and children, and every one of the relatives he'd planned to avenge. Even when the guards remembered our existence and the food returned, his mind was gone.

Ashur was no longer. The man left behind spoke only in shrieks, refused to eat, even when he had food. The king saw no reason to keep a madman alive. At that point, death would be a mercy.

And that is how you kill someone with a clean conscience. You break them first, until they are no longer worth keeping alive.

When they took him away, I stuck my head through the bars to watch him escorted to the gallows. Ashur looked like a phantom from another world, bones and gray skin, and teeth that seemed strangely long in his emaciated face.

Our gazes met, and for a moment as they dragged him off, somewhere behind the madness, I saw a command to avenge him. And then he was just another name among the dead, one only I would remember.

It was my job to make this right.

Only I remained—the true heir.

But why was it always the least deserving who survived? Why did Ashur go, and my mother, and the beautiful succubus who used to give me apples—why were they all gone, and I was still here?

I knew why. I'd been blessed with a natural ability to kill quickly and easily. I was the one who would feed the Lilu graves with the blood of their murderers.

Outside, a flock of crows soared over the pool.

Mortana—Rowan—whoever—seemed to hate me now. *Good.*

But I still felt like her prisoner, thanks to that one tiny ember of doubt. That one spark of red light in the darkness—that question.

Was it really her?

❈ 9 ❈

CHAPTER 9—ROWAN

I listened as Orion climbed the steps, and my pulse started to race. Shirtless, he stood at the top of the loft stairs.

"What are you doing here?"

He crawled onto the bed, hovering over me. "I couldn't stop thinking about you."

Orion's hard, demanding body pinned me to the mattress.

I stared up at his beautifully sculpted face with what I hoped was an expression of pure hatred. He was, as he'd always told me, the worst person in the world. It was impossible to believe in a benevolent God when someone this hot was also this terrible, so that left only the demon gods who'd made him.

My gaze drifted to his sensual lips, and my cheeks flushed. He chuckled quietly, a dark purr that made my skin heat. Right now, it seemed nothing in the world existed but us, and I had his complete attention. He didn't find me boring at all now.

His smoldering gaze raked down my body, and his magic stroked my skin. "You're mine now," he said, his voice husky. His lips brushed over my neck, sending a forbidden thrill through my body. "Do you know how many times I've imagined claiming you?" he murmured against my throat.

Molten heat slid through my body. Each place where his body touched mine was sending forbidden shivers of pleasure racing through my blood.

"I don't care." I hissed. "I think you should know. I find you tedious and pathetic."

His thigh slid between mine, parting my legs—

An alarm sounded in my head.

No, not in my head. My phone was ringing. Well, that was good. I wasn't sure if the phone charger I'd found last night would actually work.

But who called on a *phone?* Who even had my number?

Orion wasn't here. I was lying tangled in the sheets of Mortana's loft apartment. Alone—which was good. The first coral rays of sunlight pierced the dawn sky, streaming into the room. What sort of sociopath would call this early?

I brushed my fingertips over the scar on my stomach, disappointed to find it still there. It definitely hadn't healed properly.

I picked up the phone and saw a missed call from Shai. She knew I hated talking on the phone.

I flopped back against the pillow. I needed coffee. Carl had promised coffee, hadn't he? I wondered if he'd bring it this early.

I rubbed my eyes. Orion was the worst, but even he wouldn't wake me with a phone call at dawn.

"Mortana!" Orion's voice rose from below.

"I won't respond to that name," I shouted back. "I mean, not after that."

"*Rowan.* I couldn't sleep. And while I was awake, wondering if I was making a terrible mistake, I noticed one of the king's spies prowling around outside. He was trying to hide behind a cypress tree on the other side of the pool. Does anyone know we're here?"

He was standing at the top of the loft stairs, shirt open and hair ruffled, not unlike the dream I'd just woken from, except this was much less fun.

"Does anyone know we're here?" I repeated. Finally, the fog of sleep cleared from my mind. "Only Carl. Why?"

"I'm just wondering why the king might be spying on you, and if someone has already alerted Cambriel." His eyebrows rose. "Hang on a minute. Who did you kill?"

"A congressman."

He frowned. "I don't think the king cares about mortal politics."

"He's also the head of the demon hunters. The Malleus Daemoniorum."

"Ah." His eyes glinted in the morning light. "They're the reason we are locked in this city. They continue to have power over this realm. Rowan, you chose the most inconvenient mortal to kill."

I pulled the sheet up over my tank top. "I didn't choose him. He came for me." I looked toward the window. "Why didn't the king come here first?"

"He'll be on his way from the Tower of Baal. We only have a few minutes to get out of here." He turned, bounding down the stairs. "I've got to take care of something before we go to Hell."

"What?"

The door slammed behind him.

My heart pounded. With my phone in my hand, I leapt out of bed and hurried down the stairs to change into fresh clothes.

At the wardrobe, I pulled on a long-sleeved black dress and a pair of boots. After zipping them up, I crossed to the window, shielding my body from view as I peered outside. Were there really spies outside? Cypress trees lined the riverbank, but beyond their trunks, I thought I saw figures moving...

What was Orion doing? Adrenaline lit up my veins.

I rushed over to the dresser and quickly packed a small leather backpack. What did one bring on a trip to Hell? I hoped my inability to burn would serve me well there.

Had Orion said something about a *dying god?*

I shoved a toothbrush and clean clothes into the bag. What if my magic powers didn't work in Hell? What if I *could* burn in the hellfire?

My pulse was racing out of control.

I grabbed my fire blanket, a small fire extinguisher, and my gas mask, and shoved them into the leather bag. I'd left the note from my dad on the kitchen counter, and I carefully slid that into one of the backpack's interior pockets for good luck.

Now *I* was ready to go, except I didn't know how to leave here without Orion.

My phone buzzed, and I flicked it on to find several texts from Shai. But it was the final text that made my heart skip a beat.

Any idea why I just got a summons to see the king?

Ah. So that's why she was calling. My heart thundered, mind whirling through the possibilities.

Of course. Jack knew I was friends with Shai. Jack would have told the king to go after my friend.

The Corwins had probably asked the king for my head on a platter.

Frantically, I typed back to her.

Shai. I need you to leave the City of Thorns.

I watched the three dots move across the screen with a growing sense of dread.

Are you kidding? I can't leave when I've been summoned by the king. Someone is coming to escort me.

My hands were shaking. If the king captured Shai, he'd use her to keep me here. As Orion pointed out, she was the only person I cared about. She was my leverage.

Hide, I wrote back. *Until I can tell you where to meet me. Orion will get us both out of here.*

Orion slammed open the door, blood spatter on his golden skin. I stared at him. "Who did you kill?"

Without a word, he strode up to me and took the leather backpack from my hands. Opening the bag, he removed the fire extinguisher and the other fire safety equipment.

"What are you doing?" I asked.

"We will have more pressing matters than fire where we are going."

He hurried over to the kitchen and pulled the fridge door open, then loaded my bag with snacks—cheese, fruit, and some bread from the counter.

"Grapes and Swiss cheese? That's more pressing than avoiding a fiery death in Hell?" I demanded.

"Swiss? Honestly. Comté is actually French, but it's a common mistake among the unsophisticated." He pinned me with his gaze, arching an eyebrow. "And you will find out why we need it soon enough."

I stared at the blood spatter on his neck again. "Are you going to tell me who you killed?"

"No one interesting." He dropped a bottle of water into the bag. "Just Carl."

My jaw dropped. "Of all the people to kill in this situation, you chose the harmless mortal nerd? The only nonthreatening person in the scenario?"

"Carl wasn't just an intern. He was spying for the king. When I took his phone, I found a text message to the king's spy agency letting them know you were here. But consider it an accident if it makes you feel better. My hands slipped, and I accidentally ripped off Carl's head and shoved his remains under the desk." He raised his eyebrows with mock seriousness. "Don't be so judgmental. It could happen to anyone."

"You ripped his head off," I repeated.

"On the plus side, he didn't tell anyone I was here, and now he won't be able to. Did any other demons see you last night?"

I was struggling to keep up. "I don't think so. No one was out in the rain. But the mortal police saw me enter the city."

"Shit. Okay. I can hear the army marching closer. We need to go before you meet the same fate as Carl."

My body buzzed with nerves as I slid my backpack on over my shoulders. "What's the best way out?"

"How well can you fly?"

I could fly...sort of, but Shai couldn't. I needed a path she could take, and I needed to make sure she could catch up to us. "Not really. Is there any other way?"

"I'll fly with you in my arms."

"You won't touch me," I said with venom.

A banging sounded at the door, and Orion went still.

I felt the air heating around me like a dry wind. Orion crossed to the window and slid it all the way open. He crawled onto the sill, his enormous body filling the frame—half out and half in. Outside, the rising sunlight gleamed on the swimming pool, so bright it was almost blinding.

I stared as he climbed through it, then perched on the sill. And then he seemed to fall.

✣ 10 ✣

CHAPTER 10—ORION

I touched down, then turned to look up at her, my beautiful nemesis.

Did she have any control over her wings whatsoever? She seemed to have forgotten everything about being a demon—how to shift, how to fight, how to instill fear into another person. In fact, she almost seemed afraid of herself.

Her red hair caught in the wind and the morning sunlight, like flames dancing around her. Was she going to jump, or was I going to have fly up there and get her?

Cypress trees surrounded the pool on three sides, giving us some privacy, but if anyone stopped to peer through the trunks and branches, they'd see us here. And the guards would break down that door at any moment.

At last, she leapt from the windowsill...and dropped like a rock, red hair streaming toward the heavens. She hadn't unfolded her wings and dropped right into my arms.

Instinctively, I held her tight, her heartbeat thudding against me. For a moment, I stared at her perfect mouth, and my mind brought up the memory of her lips parting against mine. She smelled like ripe cherries and the rich earth after rain. Heat sparked in my chest, embers of smoldering red. She was sexy as hell, no matter what she did or how much I hated her. And for an incubus like me, a woman like her was our lifeblood.

She glowered at me. "You can put me down now, dickhead."

Ah, good. She still hated me.

I let her down and started for the river. "Follow me."

Other demons in the City of Thorns hadn't spent over a century tunneling beneath the city. They had no idea what lay under our feet. It had taken me a long time to get from the dungeon to the old buried vaults, but once I had, I'd found a whole world underground—stone tunnels that had once been used for storing wine and food in the days before refrigerators.

I glanced back to see Rowan looking at her phone, seemingly unconcerned that the king might be handing her over to her executioners. She glared at me and shoved the phone into her pocket.

At the tree line, I looked in both directions, making sure no one was nearby. The sun slanted over the river, and the dark Acheron forest loomed on the opposite side. Cambriel's army had already passed by here. On the pavement beneath me, I could feel the vibrations of the king's army marching in the other direction. But soon, the soldiers would fan out across the city, searching every alley and alcove.

I found the vault covering, a round carving in the pavement marked with serpents, and lifted it. I climbed down into the darkness —not much of a jump down to the stone floor beneath—then looked through the opening, waiting for Rowan. She lowered herself, and I reached up to grab her by her waist, letting her down next to me. Then I slid the cover over the vault once more.

"This will get us out," I whispered. "Almost none of the other demons know the way around the vaults."

She still wasn't speaking to me. In the cold and wet down here, it smelled of the dungeons. In the dark, my mind slipped back again to the past.

King Nergal had capitulated to the mortals, and he'd learned his worst cruelties from them, the Puritans in particular. They taught him to terrify people. Break them, and they don't fight back.

When they'd marched us to the dungeons—the women, the children, the injured—they'd taken us past the severed heads of those slain. I saw my brother's head bleeding on top of a pike, and my father's. The mortals had done that.

That was the first time I'd felt something crack. When I saw their heads, I no longer knew exactly who I was because nothing was real anymore. The world had become a nightmare.

The thing was, for most people—even demons—it wasn't always easy to kill someone. If you recognized yourself in them, if you could see them as being like you, it was hard to end a person's life. This spark of similarity was protection, and Nergal didn't really *want* to kill all the women and children, the prisoners of war. That would be immoral.

That's why the king's soldiers had to change us first. Nergal had learned this from the mortals, too.

In Salem, they locked people in prisons. Most who went behind bars simply died there. Bodies full of lice, skin covered in lesions, gnawed on by rats. Those who survived were half-mad. And when it came time to kill them—I mean, they hardly seemed human anymore.

The Puritans, with their filthy prisons, had taught us how to control people. *They* taught us how to turn off empathy and get the results we wanted. Rowan liked to think empathy was a particularly human trait, but she was wrong. They could turn it off better than anyone. And when they wondered why they'd made me a monster, it was because they'd taught me to be strong.

The Puritans made people turn on one another, made them accuse their own family members. Mortana had learned that from them, and she'd suggested all this to the king—the dungeons, the mind games. And nothing breaks a person more than forcing them to kill their own family.

In the witch trials, the Puritans accused a little girl of witchcraft, terrifying her until she accused her own mother. The mother was hanged on Gallows Hill, and the little girl went mad.

To kill without guilt, turn your victim into a gibbering wretch. Strip a woman to her waist, tie her to the back of a cart, and drive her through the streets to be flogged. Lock her up with mud and typhoid, and a child she can't feed. When the light is extinguished in her eyes, put out the rest, the sack of flesh and bones and self-loathing that remains.

This was *civilization*—a mortal invention.

But I was still here. I'd been marked as the Lightbringer, and even though I'd nearly drowned in darkness, my soul smoldered inside me— red embers in a sea of darkness.

I would make things right again.

❧ 11 ❧

CHAPTER 11—ROWAN

I followed Orion through the tunnels beneath the city, memorizing every turn. Water dripped down the vaulted stones onto my head and backpack.

While Orion walked ahead, I pulled out my phone and started frantically texting Shai. With just barely a single bar of reception, I wanted to make the most of it before it disappeared completely. So, I quickly told her how to find the vault, which turns to take underground, and to run as fast as she possibly could.

Shai was all I had left. She was my family now, and I'd protect her until my dying breath. And unlike Orion, Shai wasn't going to turn on me because I happened to be a demon.

Ahead of me, Orion opened the door into a larger tunnel, one with light streaming inside. I recognized this one. This was where I'd run, half in a daze, after I'd learned what I was. After the fire had spilled out of me for the first time.

I hammered out another quick text to Shai.

The tunnel opened beneath a stone underpass that looked abandoned, strewn with newspapers, old cans, and a broken refrigerator. An enormous dumpster hid the narrow opening into the demon world. The grimy setting would put anyone off investigating.

When we stepped out from under the old train bridge, New England's beauty was on full display around us. Leaves swirled around us, wine-red and pumpkin orange, the first signs of fall. Victorian brick buildings stood on either side of a curving road, lined by cars on the right side.

Orion looked in both directions, then crossed to a sleek, steel-blue BMW sedan parked at the bottom of a gently rolling hill.

Out of nowhere, a strange fear sparked in my mind.

What if he'd left his keys behind?

We left the keys behind, and it was my fault for distracting him—

I felt my blood go cold, then shook the fear from my thoughts as he pulled the keys from his pocket.

I walked over to the car, glancing back at the dumpster. I needed Shai to appear *now*. I flicked open my phone to find two letters—*ok*.

Orion hit the button to unlock the car and got behind the wheel. "Get in."

We were taking a hundred-thousand-dollar car to Hell. Clearly, blackmailing the king was a lucrative line of work.

But Shai wasn't with us yet.

I opened the back door for Shai, mentally willing her to move faster.

Orion shot me a sharp look. "Rowan. Get in."

I slid into the front seat, and the hem of my dress rose to the top of my thighs. Orion's gaze locked on my legs, his eyes growing darker. The air around us heated. "Shut the doors." His low, masculine voice thrummed over my skin like a caress.

With a flare of warmth in my cheeks, I tugged down the hem of my dress.

He dragged his gaze to mine, then his focus moved to something over my shoulder.

I turned to see Shai burst from behind the dumpster. She sprinted over to the car and yanked open the back door. She caught her breath, her rich brown skin beaded with droplets of sweat. Jumping inside, she closed the door and started to buckle her seatbelt.

Orion stared at her. "Absolutely not."

I closed my door. "She knows I was in the city. Don't you want to cover our tracks? You can't murder her, too. Even if you wanted to."

She leaned forward. "Where are we going?"

"To Hell," he said quickly. "You might not like it."

She shrugged. "Can't be worse than Albany, and I nearly went there for college." She pulled an apple out of her bag and bit into it. "Speaking of which, can we discuss how I can get back into Belial University after this? Because it seems like I'm going to be kicked out."

I belted myself in, my mind whirling. Was Hell *actually* real, or was this a metaphor?

But we hadn't started moving yet, and Orion's eyes darted behind me again. He cursed under his breath and leapt out the door. I turned to see three demon soldiers running for us, their bodies flickering with blue and silver magic.

But they didn't get far. A great arc of fire burst from Orion's hand. Flames engulfed the soldiers, and they staggered around, screaming, smoke billowing from their bodies.

"Rowan." Shai's voice seemed to come from a distance.

I couldn't tear my eyes away. Shai was talking to me, but I could hardly hear her words. Bile rose in my throat.

"Rowan!" she shouted, shoving the back of my seat. "Don't look. Close your eyes and cover your ears."

She was right, of course. I leaned down, hands over my ears. I stayed there, hunched over, until Orion got back in the car and I felt the vehicle lurch into gear.

Slowly, I opened my eyes and sat up. Orion was speeding through the streets of Osborne.

"Okay, *what* is happening?" Shai shouted. "Why did Orion light those people on fire?"

Orion gripped the wheel hard as he took a sharp turn. "Is she why you said you couldn't fly? You wanted her to follow us?"

Well, he'd worked that one out quickly. "You wouldn't have agreed to save her. You can't kill her, but you're not required to go out of your way to help her."

"Ah," he said quietly. "Of course. Everything about you is a deception."

I heaved an exasperated sigh. "Can we *please* just go to Hell in peace?"

Shai leaned forward again. "Does anyone care to fill me in? Why are we running from the king?"

I inhaled deeply before turning to look over my shoulder at my best friend. "The mortal demon hunters tried to kill me. And Jack was there. I killed his dad in self-defense, and now the king wants to hand me over because the mortals have some kind of control over our city."

"Shit."

Orion veered wildly onto Walcott Road, my old street, and I faced forward again.

He glanced at me. "Why do you look like you're about to vomit all over my beautiful car?" He sped through a red light at an intersection, and I gripped the car handle.

My mouth was full of saliva, and I swallowed. "I guess I have a thing about watching people burn to death. You know, the whole empathy thing. And your driving isn't helping the situation."

"Hmm, I'm not sure I believe you actually have empathy." He shot me an irritated look. "And I burned them because it was the fastest way to kill them. Now they won't report anything to Cambriel or the mortals. You're welcome." He careened left at an intersection. "Remind me again why I didn't kill you."

"Because even if you hate me, I'm the closest thing you have to a friend?"

Shai leaned forward. "Can someone please erase the memory of those people burning? I'd like that part of my brain fully removed."

"Ask Mortana," said Orion darkly. "She's the expert at erasing memories."

"She's not Montana," said Shai. "*Mortana.* Whatever. I've known her since we were seventeen."

"You don't know she was actually seventeen," said Orion. "Do you?"

I was still fighting the nausea. "Well, Orion, if I erased my own memories, I wouldn't remember the spell, would I?" I hoped he felt the sting of that comeback.

Curving sharply, Orion sped onto the highway and headed north. And as he drove, he started connecting his phone to the radio.

"Do you want to let me handle the music so you don't crash?" I asked.

"No." He pushed play, and energetic yodeling blared from the speakers over a deep horn.

Yodelieyoidieohwapidilieayeooo—

I let out a long, slow breath. "Is this it?" I asked. "Is this what Hell is, right now?"

Orion stared straight ahead. "Of *course* you can't appreciate a skilled alphorn solo when you hear one. Philistine."

"Where are we *actually* going?" asked Shai. "Because it looks like we're going to Lawrence. Are we going to be eternally tormented in Lawrence?"

"Hell is not full of torments like you'd imagine," he said. "It's more boring than you'd expect. It's like...Vermont."

My eyebrows rose. "What's hellish about Vermont?"

"Have you ever been to Vermont?" he asked, his voice dripping with disdain.

"Yeah. It's really nice. I visited a maple syrup factory," I said. "Have you?"

"No."

"Okay, it's not hellish. It's beautiful. The leaves are gorgeous. There's amazing cheese and ice cream. Lots of trees. Maple syrup. Like, tons of cows. It's pretty idyllic, honestly. In what way is it supposed to be hellish?"

"There's nothing there," said Shai from the back seat. "The entire state is empty. I mean, apart from the cheese."

"Exactly," said Orion. "I read a history book once outlining everything that happened in the state of Vermont. Do you know what was in it? There were two chapters devoted to a Victorian prize sheep named Gold Drop. One chapter about farmers walking their turkeys to Boston in the eighteenth century. And then there was the greatest event to ever happen in the history of Vermont, which incidentally did not happen in Vermont. Ethan Allen—the great hero of Vermont, conquered Fort Ticonderoga, which is not in Vermont. And when he got there, it was basically empty, apart from two drunk Redcoats."

My brain was scrambling to keep up. "Okay. It sounds peaceful. How is that hell?"

"How is that *not* hell?" he asked, baffled. "Alone, with nothing but your own memories. Having to live with yourself and everything you've done, with no distractions. That is actual torture, love. You can trust that I would know."

I stared at him, trying to understand. "So that's where we're going? Vermont?"

He shook his head. "No. Not Vermont."

Shai threw her apple core out the window. "Right now, I'm aiding and abetting two criminals. The police could be after me. I'm starting to freak the fuck out. Rowan, you're without a doubt the most anxious person I've ever met. Can you explain why I'm freaking out more than you?"

"Because anxiety is spending all your time imagining terrible situations that might occur," I replied. "Whatever is happening right now isn't a million times different than the apocalyptic scenarios I usually envision. Every night, I go to sleep thinking of the sun exploding tomorrow because the scientists have got the calculations wrong. So this isn't as bad as that."

"I see. And will I be arrested by the mortal police or by the demons?"

"Don't worry about the mortal police," said Orion darkly. "Anyway, I'll need to drop you off soon, Shai. You won't be able to come where we are going. We have to go through the turnpike."

"The Mass Turnpike?" I asked, baffled.

"No. The Veil Turnpike. We're going into the underworld now. It's beyond the veil."

CHAPTER 12—ROWAN

"**W**hat does that mean?" I asked. We were zooming along the highway. "The Veil Turnpike?"

"Well, since you don't remember," he muttered. "Before the Great Mortal War, before I was born, the demons lived in the wilderness. Sometimes mortals sought them out, and demons fucked them or got drunk with them. Sometimes demons drank their blood. But really, it was a chance worth taking, given how boring the mortals' lives were."

Overhead, the sky darkened, and a chill rippled through the car. "But some of the Puritans got nervous about it. So they set up rows of sharpened pikes, which had two purposes in those days. One, to create boundaries, and two, to display the severed heads of demons and other enemies. They liked to give warnings that way. Sometimes, at a turn-pike, you could pay a toll to get through. They'd open the gate once you paid a price. And where we are going, love, we *will* be paying a price."

An eerie chill rippled over me, and I glanced up at the sky. It was darkening fast, the clouds starting to roil. A storm was rolling in, and it looked strangely unnatural.

Orion glanced over at me. "Open the glove compartment. I have gold and silver coins in there. We'll need them where we're going."

When I did as he asked, the coins practically spilled out onto the floor. I started scooping them up, dropping them into my leather bag. "Gold coins are for paying the toll, I guess?"

"Oh, no. It's not that sort of toll, love."

"What?" I asked. "How is it you can talk so much and clarify so little? It's like the world's shittiest superpower."

Lightning cracked the darkening skies, and Orion cursed under his breath.

"Lord of Chaos," said Shai from the back seat.

"Yes?"

"Weren't you going to let me out first?" she asked. "It feels like something magical is happening now."

Orion shook his head. "They've changed the location."

"So what's going to happen to me?" Shai's voice sounded far way, like she was shouting from a distance.

I turned to look at her. She looked fuzzy, like she was covered in Vaseline.

Fear snaked up my spine. The car seemed to be moving at a terrifying speed, the world outside flitting past in a blur. I was in a car going ninety miles an hour, driven by a complete maniac. I couldn't die in a car crash, but Shai still could.

I turned to look through the windshield again. Rain hammered against the glass. Green blurs rushed around us, and I think we'd veered off the road onto the grass.

"Can you slow down?" I asked.

"No."

Phantoms seemed to rush past the window, mouths agape and eyes wide. A disembodied voice whispered in my ears, "Do you travel with the dark one? Do you come to see the devil himself?"

Inhuman screaming rose around me, sliding through my bones.

Thou wicked creature. Thou wretch! Thou hast undone us body and soul. We shall not suffer a demon to live!

The voice grew louder, a chorus of voices around me.

Dark tree branches grew around the car, surrounding us like clawing fingers. Behind me, Shai was screaming.

Thou hast sacrificed thy kin! Woe unto thee with wickedness in thy veins!

"I did not sacrifice my kin!" I shouted.

The seatbelt tightened around me, choking me. I looked down. It had turned into a rope, one that snaked around my neck. My heart stuttered.

Dizzy, I closed my eyes, trying to master my control of myself. I pulled the leather bag closer, gripping it like it could keep me safe.

In my mind's eye, the image of a beautiful man with bronze skin flickered before me. Black hair, cheekbones sharp as blades, eyes like pale gold...

My heart fluttered at the sight of him.

If thou wilt confess the truth, thou shalt be free. We desire nothing more. Thou shalt not hide thy guilt. Dost thou desire to be Queen of Hell? Confess! A crown just for thee, a wicked star upon thy head...only confession may save thee from eternal flames...

My skin was growing hotter, my pulse racing.

Confess. Confess. Confess!

I opened my eyes again. I could still feel the sensation of a speeding car, but before me was a room made of crude wood and men behind a bench, dressed in black clothes and steep-peaked caps.

The image shimmered away again, but a primal fear shuddered up my nape. Through the blur of the windshield, I saw that Orion was trying to steer the BMW between the trees off the side of the highway. He no longer seemed in control of the car.

Confess!

"I don't know if I'm Mortana!" The confession surprised even me. "I don't remember what happened to Mom. Part of me liked killing the demon hunter. He deserved it. I didn't have any control over this." The confessions were flowing out. "Once, I forgot to pay for a coffee at Starbucks, and I didn't go back. It was a latte. When I'm alone, I say random words like 'corn muffin' and 'oyster crackers' in ridiculous accents. I have a priest fantasy. When I was depressed in high school, I spent a month doing nothing but watching *Love Island*, and I started to speak in an English accent. I had a sex dream about Orion two days ago, but then he turned into a spider, and it was still kind of hot? I pulled the fire alarm once in high school when I had a test—"

My stomach dropped, and I felt suspended in air for a moment before falling.

I slammed onto soft grass, landing hard with an exhale of breath. I stared up, my body buzzing. Overhead, clouds slid past, the lifeless gray of Earth in winter. I stared up at them, dazed and winded. Crows flocked overhead, squawking. I still gripped the leather backpack, clinging to it like a lifeline.

Slowly, I rolled over and looked around to get my bearings. Where was Shai?

The air had the sharp bite of winter, even in early September. An icy gust swept through the trees, strewing fallen leaves in a whirl of bright colors.

I surveyed the world around me. I was lying halfway down a steep, rocky hill that overlooked a valley. To one side, the terrain sloped downward to a dark forest with towering oak trees. On the other side, a hill led up to ancient walls with turrets and towers. Moss grew over stones worn with age. At the bottom of the fortress was a series of dark, misshapen caves. Orion stood near one of them, dusting himself off.

Faintly, I heard screams coming from the caves. Fear prickled over my skin.

Shivering, I got to my feet and slid the backpack over my shoulders. It was about twenty degrees colder here, and my teeth were chattering.

It was then that I realized my clothing had completely changed. I wore a long black dress with an extravagant lace collar and long sleeves. My hair was tucked in a bonnet of some kind. As far as I could tell by the freezing gust of wind rushing over my legs and ass, I was still in the same little underwear I'd been wearing before. But everything else had changed.

This was my goth Puritan look taken to an extreme.

I pulled the backpack off again and searched through it. Everything seemed intact—the money, the water bottles, and the snacks.

Orion ambled closer to me, and I realized his clothing had

changed, too. He wore a long, black cloak, and he stalked over with a wicked smile on his lips. "I turned into a spider? I'd love to know what happened in your sex dream before that. Care to elaborate?"

"Oh, good. You heard all that."

He adjusted the front of his dark cloak. "Tell me. Do I look like a priest in this?" A low, velvety laugh. "That's what you like, isn't it? Priests and me?"

"Oh, my God."

"Those were really your worst confessions?" He stepped closer, looking down at me. "You forgot to pay for a *latte*?"

"Am I supposed to feel bad about not being a serial killer?" I looked down the craggy slope. "Where's Shai?"

"She's mortal. She can't cross over. She's in a far safer place than we are. She's still in Massachusetts."

I stroked my fingers over my rough clothes. "So, this is Hell."

"Not quite yet." He nodded at the caves up the hill. "We will enter the underworld through there. And first, we go through Purgatory."

An agonized scream echoed out of the caves.

"Cool," I said. "Can you give me an idea of what to expect from the torture caves?"

"You can expect demons tormenting you, obviously. But you don't need to worry. It's only mental torture. It's just Belphegor demons fucking with your head. They call it the purification, but don't ask me why. You'll come out physically intact. And as an added silver lining, I can no longer feel the power of the oath here, so I'm not going to murder you. Probably."

Physically intact, but maybe not emotionally. "How long will it take?"

"Oh, four or five days."

"Seriously?"

"Time can pass differently here. But when you are done, you will feel blinding hunger and thirst."

I touched my backpack. "That explains the snacks. And can you tell me what's beyond? What is Hell, exactly?"

"There are many hells. They are places frozen in time, where people play out their same tedious and tragic life events, over and over.

We will be like the other mortals there. Once we get out of the caves, our magic won't work. And even if it did, we probably wouldn't want to use it."

"Why?"

"Because this underworld was made from Salem in 1692. They're not fond of magic."

I stared at him, my pulse starting to speed up. Osborne, like its neighbor, Salem, had been caught up in the witch-trials hysteria. In Osborne, thirty-two men and women had hanged, but many more died in the dungeons. "They're stuck in the past," I said, with a dawning sense of horror.

"Demons are drawn to emotions and sin. And that was how the devil came to Salem. The misery in Salem was powerful enough to draw some of the Belphegor demons to Salem, all because of the nonsensical ravings of a bunch of attention-seeking teenagers. The demons drank from tragedy, sadness. They came for the crushing emotional pain, and the Puritans served it up. The demons crawled here, slowly underground. They fed off the misery of typhoid and starvation, and skin lesions in the prisons, from all the lice—"

"That seems very specific."

"Believe it or not, love, I wasn't always the godlike beauty you see before you. Anyway, the Belphegor delighted in the sound of Giles Corey's rasping breaths, the frantic kicking of legs as mortals hanged. And that is how this underworld was created."

I swallowed hard. "Are the people from that time condemned to a miserable afterlife? Some of them were victims."

"Not as many as you might think, love. They were more than happy to watch one another hang."

"Of course. And demons? They're fine. Demons get *off* on evil in a totally normal and morally superior way."

"Right." He cocked his head. "I'll see you in Hell, love."

❧ 13 ❧

CHAPTER 13—ROWAN

He turned away, but I grabbed his arm, stopping him. I wanted to delay the next leg of our journey as long as possible because of the whole screaming and torture thing.

"Wait. The Dying God?" I asked quietly. "Who is he?"

"His name is Tammuz, a primordial demon of unparalleled power. He knew my mother."

A shudder danced up my spine. "Have you ever met him?"

"I visited him once. After I escaped. Stop stalling. There is no avoiding Purgatory if we want to break the oath." He turned and started walking, and I reluctantly followed him toward the towering stone walls. "I don't know for certain that he will break the oath," Orion said, "but I do know he's the only one who can." He ran his fingers through his silvery hair. "Tammuz might be one of the oldest demons among us. Maybe that makes him a god. Some say he is Lucifer's dark twin, a god of darkness. For part of every year, he dwells in the underworld. For the rest of the year, he rises from the dead. That's why he's the Dying God."

The wind carried the scent of death, and the sound of screaming rose louder.

The frozen ground was hard beneath my thin leather boots, and my teeth chattered. The wind stung my fingers and cheeks, and a dusting of snow was starting to fall from the heavens.

"Do the people in the underworld know they're dead?" I asked.

"No."

"You said that people there are trapped in their tragedies." My mind flashed with a fragment of a memory from the night Mom was killed, but it was gone again in a moment. One part of me remembered that night. One part of me was still there. "Is that how you feel about your time in the dungeon? Even if you're free, you are always reliving it?"

He turned to look back at me. For a moment, his mask of confidence dropped, and I saw what lay beneath the beautiful surface. Pain, exquisite pain. Then his gaze shuttered again, and he turned away. "Are you trying to be my therapist, Rowan? Because that is a *very* mortal concept, and you're not even qualified."

"No. I'm trying to figure out what made you such a dick."

As we approached the caves, he gave me a half smile. "I tried being nice once. It was boring and overrated."

He'd been saying all along what he was: ruthless, lethal, lacking in empathy. *I don't hide my flaws or lie about what I am.*

But was that the whole story, or had love twisted him? He'd loved his family, and they were taken from him. Maybe nothing terrified him more than feeling that pain again.

Or maybe, like he'd implied, I was hopelessly naive.

A ray of sunlight escaped the clouds, lighting up the frosted stones around us like a frozen diamond sea. My breath misted around my head. A dusting of snow covered the gray earth before the caves. Near the mouth of a cave, I slipped backward on an icy rock, but with an ungraceful wheel of my arms, I managed to steady myself again.

Orion gave me one last look before he crossed into one of the caves, and I followed after him. Inside, the darkness had a weight, and the silence coiled around us. Wrapped in shadows, I traced my hand against a rocky wall to guide my way until Orion sparked fire in the palm of his hand. Light and shadow writhed over the sand-colored walls, flickering over floor-to-ceiling stalactites and twisted columns of rocks.

Brittle ice cracked beneath my feet. I felt on edge, a sense of unease that increased when an icy wind snuffed out the light in Orion's hand.

Around me, lines of red light carved through the darkness, forming letters from a strange alphabet.

"This is how it begins," said Orion. "You've heard the expression 'the writing on the wall'? Divine judgement, supposedly. *You have been weighed on the scales and found wanting.* Here, in Purgatory, we will be forced to face what we've done. And for a little while, it will be hard to tell what is real from what is a vision."

I took a long breath. "So how will I know when it's over?"

"The writing will disappear." His voice was starting to sound more distant now, echoing from afar. "I will see you on the other side."

I tried to summon fire of my own. After a few moments, though I could feel the rush and spark of magic, the warmth in my palm, I still couldn't see a thing.

Whispers echoed around me, some saying my name, others the name Mortana, drawing the name out in a mocking tone. *Mortaaaaaana*—a chorus of singsong whispers.

"Orion?" My voice sounded muffled, drowned in the sea of whispers. How could whispers be so loud?

Symbols appeared around me, blood-red slashes in the darkness—a language I couldn't read.

From behind me, an agonized scream filled the cavern.

I whirled to see a pale light illuminating a figure on the ground—someone crawling, but there was something very wrong with her. Her arms and legs were bent at strange angles, her head tucked into her chest. I hated the sight of her mangled limbs.

A demon, perhaps? Her skin looked charred, cracked—

I took a step back. "Do you need help?"

But this wasn't real, was it? Orion had warned me—all the demons did was fuck with your head. I closed my eyes, hoping the horrific image would be gone when I opened them again. The creature was still there, crawling closer to me on twisted limbs.

Warm light wavered over the cave walls once more, and a creaking noise filled the cavern.

Do you want to know how you would die? a voice boomed.

"Fuck, no. Do I have a choice?"

I stared at one of the walls, where a hypnotic swaying of shadows moved back and forth, back and forth—until finally, its contours became clear. A woman hung from a noose, her neck crooked at an angle, her hair hanging down, swaying under a bough.

Bright red hair, pale skin. The black dress I wore now.

Sharp terror spread through my gut.

I wasn't in the cave anymore. I was at the bottom of Gallows Hill. A towering elm grew from a rocky ledge halfway up the hill, and I was staring up at my double dangling at the end of a rope. The tree's gnarled boughs were outspread, jagged black lines against a gray sky.

From the foot of the hill, I watched my double's legs twitch and jerk, feet dancing over rocks. The body swayed for hours, the branch creaking under the body's weight. Behind my double, four more bodies hung from nooses—women with purple skin, stiff limbs.

I couldn't move.

They were screaming that I'd sacrificed "my kin," and I wanted to scream, too. How long would this last?

Cold winter air stung my cheeks, smelling of cedar smoke and death. A jeering crowd stood around, screaming curses.

The bough groaned under the weight of my doppelgänger, and her body turned toward me. I caught a glimpse of her eyes—*my* eyes— bulging wide. Her fingers stopped twitching, but her body swayed soundlessly, casting a dark shadow upon the wintry earth.

Dread carved me out.

Why did I feel like this had happened before? It *had* happened before. I'd been here two days, replaying it all.

My breath shallowed. Those bright red letters still gleamed around me. I knew it wasn't real. This was a vision, except...

This *was* going to happen. This was my future.

It had happened before, and it would happen again. We were all trapped, repeating our own tragedies.

The air left my lungs, and I desperately wanted to get out of here.

A curtain of darkness came down over me, sparing me from the horrific vision at last. It was just me in the cave, shaking. But it wasn't over yet. Red slashes still gleamed from the cave walls. The burned woman was still here, shuffling across the cave floor.

I didn't want to see her eyes.

But when she looked up at me, the deep blue pierced me to the core. I felt something in my hand, cold and metallic.

"I'm so sorry," I muttered, looking down at the set of keys in my palm, so heavy I could hardly hold them.

Guilt ripped me open. I'd done something terrible, and the keys were the evidence. The keys were like a letter branded into my cheek —M for Murderer. I didn't want them anywhere near me.

Flames rose from the woman's body, and she screamed.

The keys filled me with a crushing sense of guilt for sins I could no longer remember. A horror. If I could get these keys away from me, maybe I'd feel better. Maybe I'd be free of the weight of guilt. My tattoo glowed, a golden skeleton key on my arm. Flames rose higher on the woman's body.

I threw the keys into the darkness, and they clattered against stone. I felt a moment's relief, my chest filling with air. The next moment, another set was in my hand, cold and heavy. My hands shook, and I felt as if rocks were pressing on my chest. When I held the keys, I couldn't breathe.

I threw them again, harder this time. The keys returned. I'd never rid myself of their crushing weight—

Again and again, I tried to free myself of them. I kept muttering that I was sorry, that I didn't mean it. I had no idea what I was apologizing for, and I could hardly hear my own voice. Days passed in the same way until at last, the woman disappeared, and the keys along with her.

I breathed in, slowly. Now, the only light in the space was from the vicious writing.

You have been weighed and found wanting.

At last, the letters started to fade into the dark. I let out a long, slow breath as a sense of relief washed over me. I was shaking, and tears rolled down my cheeks.

It was all over now. Fucking hell, that was brutal. And I didn't even understand it.

"Orion?" I whispered. I wiped the tears from my cheeks. I didn't want him to see me cry, but I didn't want to be alone.

That was when the hunger and thirst set in.

I tried to swallow, and my throat burned. Wild hunger ripped through my stomach. My muscles ached, and I thought of an ice-cold chocolate milkshake. I slumped against the wall, delirious.

I'd been standing the whole time, and my legs ached to the bone. Frantic, I slid the backpack into my lap and tore it open. With eager hands, I pulled out one of the bottles of water, thinking as I did that this wouldn't be enough. I'd have to drink Orion's too. But once I'd drained the water, a little more restraint returned.

He'd packed apples, and I ate two of them. These weren't ordinary apples. These apples had grown in the garden of the gods, handpicked by a divine being. Never in the history of food had anything tasted so sweet and succulent, a hint of tart flavor that exploded over my tastebuds.

"Orion?" I asked quietly. I can't say I was eager to have him wake up because I wanted to eat in peace. I mean, I was saving it for him, but it was nice to enjoy this in solitude.

I pulled out a challah roll. It could be moldy by now, but I didn't care. It was still soft and sweet, buttery. The cheese was Comté, the flavor rich and nutty. When I left here, I vowed to eat fondue every day. I would find a French person, thank them for their contribution to the world, and invite them to fondue.

My stomach started to cramp, and I realized I'd eaten too much too quickly. I'd probably started digesting my own organs. I doubled over, clutching my gut. Shoving the rest of the food into the bag, I slung it over my shoulder and started crawling along the cave floor.

"Orion?"

I crawled along on all fours, not unlike the demon I'd seen. After a few minutes, the nausea passed. The water and calories started to hit me, strengthening me a little.

"Orion?"

I forced myself to my feet, steadying myself against the wall.

Once I was upright, I held out my palm and summoned my magic.

Warmth tingled down my arm, and fire burst to life in my hand. Light —glorious light.

Never had I been so comforted by fire, but there it was, bathing the caverns in warmth.

But I didn't see anyone else. Maybe he'd already left the caves.

"Orion?" I moved faster through the cavern until at last, pale sunlight pierced the darkness from the mouth of the cave.

Then I saw him at last, slouched against the wall.

Sunlight bathed his enormous body. He was slumped over, a knife in his chest. What the *fuck?* I thought he'd said that the Belphegor demons wouldn't actually hurt us.

Horrified, I rushed forward.

✖ 14 ✖

CHAPTER 14—ROWAN

I hurried over to him and knelt. His silver hair hung in front of his eyes, and his coat was open. A knife hilt jutted from his black shirt. I touched his cheek, and his skin felt disturbingly cold.

A tendril of fear coiled through me. He wasn't bleeding. While his eyes were open, they looked lifeless.

For a moment, I was certain he was dead. I pushed his hair back, and fear hollowed me out.

Then the smallest spark flickered in his eyes.

"Orion," I whispered. "I'm going to pull this knife out, okay?"

What the fuck had happened?

On my knees, I grabbed the hilt. If I fucked this up, I could carve out part of his heart—the only way for a demon to die. I didn't know how much leeway I had with this. I wasn't exactly an expert in demon physiology and healthcare.

With one hand on the hilt, I pressed the other on his chest, next to the blade.

Slowly, carefully, I withdrew the blade from his chest. When I pulled out the last bit of the tip, his eyes fluttered. He inhaled, but he still wasn't bleeding. I stared at his heartbreakingly beautiful face, willing him to come alive again.

"Orion!" The panic in my voice echoed off the rocks. His skin felt ice cold, muscles slack. "Orion, wake up."

If he didn't come alive again, then the last thing anyone said to him would be, "I'm trying to figure out what made you such a dick."

His heart had been damaged, so much that it was no longer pumping.

Cold panic crawled over my skin. How did I fix this? I didn't have healing magic.

I froze. That wasn't true, though, was it?

An incubus healed through sex. I'd felt it when I'd nearly died on the way to the City of Thorns, when all I could think about was sex, even if I'd been bleeding all over the place.

I lifted his chin to look him in the eyes. Still alive—just barely. "I'm going to heal you."

His pupils dilated, mouth parting. Already, I could feel the silky warmth of Lilu lust magic caressing us, growing hotter. His eyes darkened, and the look in them was ravenous. I didn't even have to kiss him yet for the magic to start working, to feel electricity crackling between us. All I had to do was want him, which wasn't difficult. And that was good, because he looked very alert now, so I felt less creepy about kissing him.

My heart beating faster now, I slid into his lap. His shadowy eyes searched mine.

I leaned in, pressing my lips against his. Immediately, he seemed to draw strength from me, fingers tightening on my waist. His lips opened, and he kissed me deeply, desperately. Warmth spread through my body, making my pulse race.

As Orion healed, one of his hands moved up my spine, and he threaded his fingers into my hair. I could feel his pulse, his heart coming alive again, beating. He broke away from the kiss and pulled my head back.

His breath had gone shallow, and his hot magic slid over my skin. With a languid swirl of his tongue, he kissed my neck. I laced my fingers in his hair, pulse racing.

"I can't stand you," I said through labored breaths. My pride made me say it, since I knew how he felt about me.

"The feeling is mutual," he whispered against my neck, "but I will die if I don't kiss you."

For one bright moment, it sounded desperately romantic—until I realized he meant it quite literally. He would *actually* die if he didn't kiss me.

Still, I forgot that when he gazed into my eyes again and brushed his thumb over my lower lip. He was looking at me like I was the most exquisite thing he'd ever seen, and I felt my cheeks go warm. He kissed me again, hungrily, his tongue sweeping in. The way he was kissing me, it really didn't *feel* like he found me boring.

With one hand, he unbuttoned a few of the buttons on the front of my dress, then pulled away from the kiss, nipping my lower lip in a way that made heat rush to my core. Molten lust pulsed through me, making my thighs clench.

But I wasn't going to let this keep going on—not after what he'd been saying to me. I only needed to heal him, and that was it.

With an iron will, I stopped him from leaning in to kiss me again. He looked at me, his eyes an abyss of midnight.

With my mouth inches from his, I said, "I think we're done. You seem to be feeling better. And as we both confessed earlier, neither of us actually likes each other."

He closed his mouth, jaw clenching. His finger tightened on me. "I could die at any moment. And why deny yourself this pleasure?"

Never in a million years would I admit how much I wanted him. I brushed my hand over the center of his chest, feeling the smooth, completely healed skin beneath his shirt. "What pleasure? I was going through the motions so you didn't die. I was bored."

"Going through the motions? With me? I find that hard to believe."

"Looks like Purgatory left your ego intact." With a supreme act of will, I shifted out of his lap onto the rocky ground. "How did you end up with a knife in your chest?"

For the first time since I'd met Orion, I saw his ever-present self-assurance falter. He was catching his breath. "A snake."

I stood, buttoning my dress again. "A snake stabbed you?"

"No, a snake crawled up my coat, and I stabbed it. Except it was a hallucination." He reached for my backpack and pulled out a bottle of water.

"Orion...are you scared of snakes?"

He unscrewed the top. "The Belphegor demons fuck with your head. That's all."

I supposed I wasn't normally scared of keys. Maybe our tattoos came out to haunt us.

He downed his water quickly, then leaned back against the wall. His eyes had gone pale again. "And what did they show you?" He reached into a bag for his apple. "Did they bring back any memories of condemning all of your kin to death long ago?"

You sacrificed your kin... "It's very thoughtful of you to remind me exactly why I had to stop kissing you."

"Oh? I thought it was because you were bored and going through the motions."

I reached into the bag and pulled out an apple for him. "Have a snack. Maybe you'll become less annoying."

He bit into it, waiting for me to fill him in on what I'd seen.

I sighed. "I saw a demon crawling toward me, and I saw my own death, apparently. Hanging." I stared out of the cave at a forest before us. "It looked like it happened in the clothes I'm wearing now. Can we die here in the underworld?"

"Yes. But I won't let that happen. The demons were just fucking with your head, that's all."

"You won't let it happen?" I slid the backpack on. "Sounds very protective."

He gave me a faint smile. "Long enough to get that secret out of you."

He stood and smoothed the front of his shirt. Buttoning his coat, he walked out of the cave into the blinding winter sun.

I followed him, shielding my eyes from the bright light that glared off the icy earth.

When my eyes adjusted from days of darkness, I took in the scene before me. In the distance, a series of pikes jutted from the earth like bony fingers. On two of the pikes, human heads had been mummified.

And beyond that, a dark forest loomed for miles, the boughs and leaves glittering with ice like diamonds.

The ground felt hard beneath me, frozen.

Orion finished the apple and threw the core aside. "Rowan, why did you heal me? You could have solved all your problems if you'd simply twisted the knife. I'd be dead. There would be no oath to worry about. You could claim the throne for yourself."

"I have empathy, Orion. We've been over this concept before."

He turned to look at me, his expression already bored. "Ah. That died with me long ago in the dungeon." He arched an eyebrow. "But I do suppose I owe you thanks, don't I?"

"You're welcome."

"Did you see anything from your past, Rowan?"

I sucked in a sharp breath, my mind flashing to the horrible memory of those keys. "I saw a set of keys in my vision, and I couldn't get rid of them. It felt like some kind of condemnation." I lifted my arm and pulled up the sleeve. "Do you think it had something to do with this? Something to do with being a demon?"

We passed the gruesome pikes, and the wind toyed with his silver hair. "I'm sure you have things to feel guilty for, Rowan, but being a demon isn't one of them. We are strong, fast, beautiful. We are like gods. And most importantly, we shouldn't feel bad about something we can't control."

"The keys had something to do with Mom." As we moved into the forest, the branches shivered, dusting my black dress with a light fall of snow. "I didn't know my mom as a demon, even if she was one. I knew her as a mortal. She wasn't perfect or godlike or powerful. And she got frustrated and swore and took forever to wake up. But she was the person who used to make me feel better when I was upset. You know how sometimes I get anxious?"

"Oh? I hadn't noticed," he said dryly.

I ignored his sarcasm and went on. "Well, when I was anxious at night and couldn't sleep, she would bring me caramel tea. We would listen to this meditation story on her iPod about a nervous raven, and we would all relax together, me, mom, and the raven named Lenore.

Not a goddess, the person who always made me feel better. And I can't help feeling like I did something to put her in danger."

I thought he was going to make another sarcastic comment or tell me I was rambling, but instead, he fell quiet as we went deeper into the woods. A vault of icy branches arched above us. After a minute, Orion, speaking so quietly that I could hardly hear him, murmured, "My mother used to sing me a lullaby when I had nightmares."

He turned to look at me, and for a moment I, read the acute pain in his eyes.

"Anyway." His expression cleared. "That was a long time ago."

"What do you do when you have nightmares now?"

"Now, love, I *am* the nightmare."

I rolled my eyes, but it wasn't untrue.

CHAPTER 15 — ROWAN

CHAPTER 15—ROWAN

We left the forest, and a town common spread out before us, surrounded by zigzagging fences. Cows and goats milled around, languidly chewing on grass. Hills enclosed the common, dotted by timber-frame buildings.

As I took in the shape of the roads wending around the common, I started to recognize its contours.

"I think this is Salem Village. It's now called Danvers." I scanned the horizon, and I pointed to a gently rolling hill. "That's Hathorne Hill, named after one of the witch judges. Later, Danvers State Hospital was built there—a psychiatric institution rife with abuse. It's apartments now. But I always imagined Hathorne's evil spirit haunted the place."

His eyebrows rose. "How did you know all this?"

"Not much else to do in Osborne except learn the sinister history." I glanced at a large black house that overlooked the village—a forlorn-looking building with a gabled roof and a gnarled tree behind it. "This place is creepy as fuck."

"Rowan," whispered Orion, "don't speak too much here. Your accent will stand out."

Fine with me. I'd keep my fun facts to myself, then.

As we approached a dirt road, a man on horseback rode past. He wore a tall, tapered hat and a wide-brimmed white collar. He slowed, staring at us. Suspicious. My heart fluttered a little.

A man was staring at me from several hundred years ago.

It didn't look like Hell, but I knew what kind of dark impulses lurked in the shadows here. Like Orion had so vividly described, neighbors turned on one another. They threw each other in prisons, condemned each other to death.

A cold wind whispered over me as we followed the road past a tall white meetinghouse with mullioned windows and crooked homes. I looked longingly at the warm light, wishing I could be inside somewhere.

A few women passed us, dressed in warm shawls and bonnets and carrying baskets. They eyed us warily.

A river curved to our right, leading to the south.

When we were alone, I whispered, "Where do we find him?"

"In the old Osborne woods," he said quietly.

I swallowed hard. That was where Mom had died.

As we walked, the cold bit into my toes, and my teeth chattered loudly. "We have coins. We might need some warm soup or something on the way."

"I know a place. Keep your voice down."

I was already starving again, and my stomach rumbled.

We walked for what seemed like ages in the cold—past farms, a church, a cemetery with mossy stones and hollow-eyed skulls glaring at us, past horse-drawn carts. A few people nodded and said, "Good morrow."

When we reached a rocky hill, I knew we'd reached Salem Town. There was Gallows Hill, where they'd hanged nineteen people on a rocky ledge. Now, in modern Salem, it overlooked a parking lot behind a pharmacy.

But I was in the grim Salem, where one of the bodies still hung at the end of a rope, a macabre warning to others.

The woman's long gray hair hung down in front of her face, and her feet swayed over the earth. Her body looked stiff and gray, her fingers bony. Lesions covered her skin, probably from her time spent in jail.

My throat tightened at the sight of her, and a miasma of sorrow rose, choking me. Her family must have watched her die.

Never had I wanted to get away from a place so badly.

Orion kept walking along, the wind whipping his silver hair and long cloak. I wasn't sure if he was hurrying away from the corpse or if he simply wasn't interested.

I rubbed my hands together, blowing on them to try to warm them. My breath clouded around me, and I walked faster to keep pace with Orion. The frozen earth chilled my feet through the soles of my thin leather boots.

By the time we reached the famous House of Seven Gables, right on the water, my body was half numb. A stark, gothic mansion loomed over the Atlantic, a deep brown building that was nearly black. The multipaned windows and sharp peaks gave it a witchy appearance, and the iron-gray ocean glittered on the other side of it. Smaller houses surrounded a town square. Here, vendors stood by market stalls, selling vegetables and baked goods.

Just in front of the mansion, a man and a woman hung in the stocks, their heads and arms trapped in wooden openings. It must be an uncomfortable position for them to hold—bent over, necks crooked. A sign at the base of the stocks marked them as *fornicators*.

Mud clumped their hair and coated their hands.

"Whore!" someone shouted from a window.

The woman winced like she'd been hit with a rock.

Of course, the Jack Corwins of this world had always existed, hadn't they?

I tried not to stare at them, but the woman glanced at me from under a curtain of filthy hair, her face etched with misery.

Could fornication be worth this punishment? Depended on the guy, I supposed.

As we crossed behind them, I grimaced at the sight of their bare backs, covered in dried and frozen blood where they'd been whipped. They were naked from the waist down, blood dried in stripes on their skin.

Orion turned to me, looking bored. "We can eat there."

"What?" The comment was jarring, given the gruesome scene before us. "Orion," I whispered, "does this stuff not bother you?"

He glanced at the flogged couple like he'd just realized they were there. "I thought you were hungry. Follow me."

He led me to a wooden building. A gray sign above the door was marked with a picture of a cauldron. As soon as we entered, the smell of food made my mouth water. I surveyed a hall of dark wood, with wooden beams that crossed the ceiling. A large iron pot bubbled on the hearth, and a few people sat at wooden tables sipping beer. Others gathered at a wooden bar in the center of the room. The warmth was *glorious*.

Silence fell over the tavern, and everyone turned to look at us— men, women, children. I think even the cat on the bar turned to stare. But the cozy atmosphere drew me in, with firelight that danced back and forth over the room and steam rising from the hearth. After a few breaths, everyone turned back to their food and drinks.

Orion crossed to a table by the window. Steam clouded the glass, and I wiped my hand across it to peer outside. From here, we had a view of the town square. It was hard not to stare at the misery of two people in the stocks, but that was the point, wasn't it? Control people by making the punishments public. Extra humiliating, and it also kept everyone else in line. No one wanted to be in their situation.

It took me a moment to realize that Orion was speaking to someone else, and I snapped out of my dark daydream to see a young woman standing at our table. Her hair was covered with a white cap, and she stared at Orion with wide blue eyes. "And why would you be going to Osborne, Goodman Ashur? I never set foot in the place." She fluttered her eyelashes. "Osborne is full of evil magic and fornicators. The demon city is there, and I pray that they stay inside. But they say a devil lurks in those woods. They say he escaped in the Great War, that the binding spells do not touch him. You should not go near that place, I pray you, lest you die."

Goodman Ashur?

"It sounds terrible," said Orion with only the *slightest* hint of sarcasm. I could only hope this woman wouldn't notice. "*Fornicators?* So vile a thing."

She leaned in, whispering. "Detestable beasts. When you arrive in Osborne, tell them Goody Putnam herself said the devil has made his home in their woods because of their wickedness. Tell them I said their dark forest turns people into animals. Naked, dripping with blood. The women rut with the Shadow Man in the woods like foul beasts, on their hands and knees, shrieking in bestial pleasure." She looked absolutely delighted, her eyes dancing, cheeks pink. "They have made a diabolical covenant with him. I have seen it with my own eyes."

I wanted to say, "I thought you never went to Osborne," but I'd been told to keep my mouth shut.

If what she said was true and women were running around naked, rutting in the woods with a demon, maybe that explained why the Dying God hung around here half the year. Whoever he was, he was probably more fun than the dour-looking mortal men slurping soup in this tavern. No wonder he had a following. And no wonder Goody Putnam had gone out looking for him.

Orion straightened, and his pale eyes glinted in the warm candle-light. "Woe to him that coveteth an evil man. We seek to *expel* the devil from these good towns. It is our sacred mission, dangerous as it may be. It is my most fervent wish to drive this beast into hellfire and burn his devil's book so that no more innocent women may be corrupted by his malevolence."

"Of course." Her cheeks reddened, and she smiled at him. "You are a goodly demon hunter." She continued to stare at him, enraptured. "Aye, the Malleus Daemoniorum. We have heard that you would come to purify these shores. We have been waiting for you." She leaned in closer. "We are honored to have a man like yourself here to protect us, courageous and strong as you are."

You've *got* to be kidding me. Even here, women flirt with him?

Orion steepled his fingers. "And this devil. You think he's still in the Osborne woods?"

"Oh, aye. 'Tis a cursed forest. I seen him there a few times by myself, surrounded by naked women writhing in a shameful dance. Wild with lust of the flesh. The forest makes them feel evil things. Do you know, the devil looked at me for one moment, and he could sense the goodliness within me? It angered him. He did howl like a wild beast to drive me away into the night." Her hand strayed down her chest, her face glowing with the memory.

It *kind* of sounded like Goody Putnam had been wandering around the sex forest, hoping for a rut with the devil, but she was too weird, even for him.

"Most impressive, Goody Putnam," said Orion, his face deadly serious. "You are a blessed woman."

She giggled. "How tall are you? I have never seen a man so tall. You are taller than a stallion."

I opened my mouth to ask about food, but Orion touched my arm. "My wife has taken a vow of silence to repent for her sins."

I suppose I had to be his wife here, or I could end up clapped in the stocks like the unfortunate couple outside.

Wait a minute—*sins?*

The woman turned to me for the first time. "Oh, sins?" She frowned. "There is something familiar about her wanton face. Perhaps a terrible dream. But what sins? She must confess in public."

I could only shrug

The faintest of smiles curled the corner of Orion's lips. "To atone for her wicked temptations, her corrupted lust of the flesh that can never be satisfied. But she is repenting now."

"Oh." A look of disgust crossed the woman's face. "Aye, I can see it in her eyes." She shuddered dramatically. "Keep her away from that forest."

I kicked Orion under the table.

"And this devil," Orion went on. "Where in the forest did you see him, when you were out at night so carefully avoiding temptation?"

"Up on the rocky hilltop, under the moonlight." I could see the delight in her eyes. "I'll bring you the lobster, then, so you have sustenance for your fight against darkness." She shot me a sharp look, judgment burning in her eyes.

Don't look at me like that, Goody Putnam. I know what you were doing in those woods.

❦ 16 ❦

CHAPTER 16—ROWAN

Because Goody Putnam clearly had the hots for Orion, she'd let us take two pewter flagons of fruity, hot beer with us, which she called "chowder," fresh from the cauldron. Her jealousy had been palpable. I wouldn't be surprised if she found herself wandering into the evil woods later to help *Goodman Ashur*.

She might have been annoying, but the chowder was starting to make me appreciate her. Steam from the beer warmed my cheeks as we walked toward Osborne, and the hot metal kept my fingers warm.

A winding road led past tottering buildings from Salem to Osborne as we walked west, away from the sea. We passed gently rolling farmland. Cows stood in the cold fields, chewing grass, and wisps of steam rose from their bodies into the frigid air. Farmhouses were painted in subdued colors—pale yellow, cream, and deep brown. A dirt road threaded between them. Leaves trembled from boughs, bright orange like flickering flames.

"Orion, what's next for you?" I asked quietly when no one was around. "After you kill Cambriel and take over the city, what do you plan to do with your power? You haven't told me."

"I think I'll start with reclaiming everything they took from us."

I raised my eyebrows. "When you're done, will there be anyone left in the City of Thorns to rule over?"

"Let's assume some of them are smart enough not to get in my way."

As we walked further into town, the buildings became more crowded. Dark-wood houses leaned over the road, and I could no longer see the shore. By now, the sky was darkening over the sea, streaked with periwinkle and crimson.

From here, we could see the City of Thorns in the distance. I'd nearly forgotten it would be here, too, but there it was, crowning Osborne's tallest hill, its golden walls shrouded in mist.

I stared at it. Was a little Orion in there, imprisoned in their dungeons? Could he be stopped from becoming the damaged person he was now?

I grabbed his arm and nodded to the east. "What happens if you go in there?"

He leaned in close, his lips near my ear. "I tried it. It doesn't work. You can't get past the walls. And the Dying God tells me all tragedies are replayed here. They cannot be stopped."

I nodded, and we started walking again, closing in on the dark forest.

On the street where I'd lived—now Walcott Street, with the Dollar Store and Dunkin'— the buildings had grown more sparse. This was Witchcraft Point.

Gallows Hill, that craggy slope, rose up to our left. There on the ledge, beneath the jagged bough of an elm, dangled the bodies of four women.

The bough creaked and groaned beneath their weight, the sound carrying on the wind like a phantom,

That was where I'd been hanged in the vision. A little tendril of horror wound through me. From here, I couldn't see their faces, but I could see that their hair hadn't turned gray. They were young, like me. In a man's world like this, you could get in trouble for being old and ugly and past your prime. Or you could get in trouble for being young and tempting. Women like that made a man sin. And that, of course, was your fault, too.

I glanced at the four corpses as we went by, their bodies stiff and gray.

I stole a quick glance at Orion. When power was in the wrong hands, it was dangerous as hell. No way should Orion have absolute power over a kingdom. He was damaged, broken, obsessed with revenge. He would be an absolute nightmare. Executions, purges, torture—probably a slow and painful death for me, if he still thought I was Mortana.

"Why do I feel like you're scheming something?" Orion purred in a velvety tone.

I blinked innocently. "Because you're delusional and deeply paranoid?"

A quiet, joyless laugh escaped him, and his pale eyes were luminous in the dusk. "Scheming and evading. How very Mortana of you."

The wind toyed with my red hair. Was it possible that Mortana was just looking out for herself when she'd sold everyone out, because she had to?

We headed north into the forest. I thought my old house was right around here, and I wished I could travel to a different time.

The wind howled through the trees ahead, rustling the leaves as we approached the edge of the woods. In here, snow and ice encrusted many of the trees, and waxy orange mushrooms ringed some of the trunks.

Take the ring,
fell the king.
The city yet will thrive.

It was starting to feel like an instruction—one that my parents had left behind for *me*. Not for someone like Orion.

The question was, how could I possibly defeat him?

Clearly, he was more adept at killing than I was, and I'd made an oath to tell him about Cambriel's ring.

As we moved through the trees, the sun dipped lower, staining the treetops blood-red. Under the forest's canopy, shadows spread out, and a crow screeched, piercing the air.

In the forest, the air smelled of moss and soil. Snow fell heavier than before.

I felt the cold caress of something powerful, electrifying in these woods. A magic that drew me inexorably closer, beckoning me. I wanted to go deeper into the forest, to taste danger.

The distant howling of a wolf raised goosebumps on my skin.

We moved on through the trees, our footfalls crunching over frosty leaves. Maples and hickories grew tall around us.

Orion's eyes beamed from the shadows, luminous and demonic. "Rowan, do I sense fear? Are you afraid of the woods?"

"Maybe not fear. Sadness." I blew out a cloud of breath, my mind flashing with the worst night of my life, racing through the trees to get away from my mom's killer. With most people, this is where I would lie to them. No one *really* wanted to hear about something that terrible. But with Orion? The darkness didn't scare him. "My mom burned to death in these woods."

He stopped walking, his gaze locked on mine. "And what is it that makes you scared?"

I blew out another cloud of breath, thinking about his question. "Memories. I'm afraid I'll remember what happened that night."

A line formed between his eyebrows. "Are you worried it was you?"

I felt the breath leave my lungs. "No. But there are still things I can't remember."

"You feel guilty for something."

It was a statement of fact, and it was a hundred percent correct. I wasn't sure I wanted to admit it. "I have no idea what for."

"Maybe because you lived, and she didn't. And all you will see are reasons why you didn't deserve to live."

'Thanks," I said sharply.

"Not because they're the truth, because that's what happens when you're the one to survive. It feels like the gods made the wrong choice. When someone is hunting you down, like they did you and your mother—when someone more powerful than you tries to kill you—you make split-second decisions. And sometimes, those decisions are at the expense of someone else. If someone is starving to death, maybe they don't share all their food. When people are freezing, maybe they take a coat from a dying person. And when you were running from a killer in the woods, maybe you made the right decision, and your mom didn't.

Maybe you just kept going, and that's how you survived. Maybe that's why you don't feel you deserve it."

A stream of moonlight pierced the canopy. When Orion looked at me, I could read a deep, lacerating sorrow in his eyes. "Demons and mortals alike have a very strong instinct of self-preservation. It's how we are made. People are selfish when death is staring us in the face. There's no point pretending otherwise, and there's no point feeling bad about it."

Maybe he was right. "Okay."

"Trust me, love," he said quietly. "If you try to fight your true nature, you will lose, and you will break in the struggle. Accept what you are, and it will be less painful."

A frozen wind rushed over me. What, exactly, *was* my true nature? Maybe our natures changed over time, because I wasn't the same girl I'd been a few months ago.

The forest air kissing my skin felt warmer now. I felt lighter, too. Maybe what Orion had said resonated with me.

Mist twined between the trees, then seemed to snake and writhe around Orion. Moonlight tinged the fog with silver. I had no idea why it would get warmer at night, but I didn't hate it.

The air smelled thick with moss and salt, earthy and luxurious. I inhaled, my muscles relaxing.

I glanced at Orion. As always, he moved with languid, catlike ease. When he caught me looking at him, he gave me a faint smile. It was the first time I noticed he had a little dimple in his cheek, and I felt a strange flush of heat. Masculine power rolled off him, stroking my skin and making my heart race.

Catching my breath, I pulled my gaze away from him, walking faster. He was an incubus, and I was falling under his spell again. That was all that was. I gripped the straps of my backpack as I hurried along.

Remember, Rowan, he wants to get away from you. He can't stand you.

With that unpleasant thought, I sped up to get out of range of his incubus magic. We needed to get this journey over with and get out of each other's lives.

We couldn't be too far from Tammuz because I could hear the sound of the ocean rhythmically crashing against the shores. My body moved to the sound, swaying. Distantly, I heard the beating of a drum, and my heart pounded to its seductive rhythm.

It wasn't just Orion's words. Something was happening to me.

❦ 17 ❦

CHAPTER 17—ORION

G oody Putnam was bloody right about one thing: these woods did inspire a wicked lust. And because I was with Rowan, the music of the forest came alive—the rustling of leaves, the songs of owls and mockingbirds. Icicles shone with unearthly light.

And all I could think about was fucking her up against a tree.

She looked at me, and I recognized a flicker of sadness in her dark eyes. My heart clenched.

Part of me wanted to kiss her right here. She might *not* be the evil Mortana I'd come to know. She couldn't be.

But nothing was more dangerous than hope. Mortana had taught me that a long time ago. It was her greatest lesson to me.

Sometimes, she would tell Ashur and me that in a few weeks, we'd be set free. I remember the indescribable joy, thinking of what we'd do, of the sunlight on our faces. We'd count the days, looking through the cracks in the wall to see when the sun rose.

And when the few weeks were up, she'd pout and say, "Sorry, darling. I can't bear to lose you."

It happened again and again before I'd finally learned. I was her rival for the throne, and she delighted in seeing me crushed completely.

I think that was what killed Ashur at last, the disappointment of feeling so close to freedom, then having it destroyed. After one of Mortana's visits, he'd stopped eating.

When I looked at Rowan, I felt those embers heating again. *Maybe she was different...*

But I'd learned my lesson already. At the last moment, she'd probably find some way to deceive me, to leave me without the secret I craved. I must remember that. More likely than not, she would extinguish any flame of hope I had left.

"Do you feel that?" Rowan asked. "The magic of the Dying God is all around us."

She was right. Here, Tammuz's magic flowed strong. Whatever it was, a primal magic enchanted every bough, every rock, and the mossy carpet beneath our feet.

Rowan walked ahead of me, shivering, which against all reason made me want to pull her close. I had a coat on, and she did not. But I never felt the cold anymore. The dungeons hadn't been heated, and in January and February, ice had slicked the walls and the cold stone floor. For a hundred and fifty years, I didn't have a blanket. I'd learned to sleep on the ice.

For a moment, I considered giving her my coat, but that would be insane. If she *was* Mortana, I would have to kill her. And how was I supposed to do that if I could hardly manage watching her teeth chatter?

In the distance, I glimpsed a little stone cottage between the trees, and I felt an overwhelming urge to take her there and warm her up by a fire.

I had one purpose in this world, and it was not to make my worst enemy comfortable. What she'd done to my mother and Ashur and all the rest—that should have been enough to extinguish the smoldering fire of my lust.

Her hips swayed as she walked, inviting me closer. Even in her ridiculous woolen dress, she was making me hard. It was her succubus scent, like deliciously ripe fruit, and the fact that I knew exactly how glorious she looked naked. Alabaster skin, pink nipples—

Bloody hell. This would be a lot easier without *that* memory burned into my mind—Rowan's hips in the air and her body aching for mine.

I tightened my fingers into fists. I could tell myself she was my enemy, my rival, but my body had other designs. My body had decided she was mine, and that we belonged together.

Since I lacked self-restraint, I would have to rely on the groundwork I'd laid earlier: brutally insulting her. If I couldn't keep myself from her, I hoped that would keep *her* from *me*.

I can finally rid myself of your irritating presence.

It was the one sensible thing I'd done since she'd come back.

My gaze slowly raked down her back to her narrow waist. My hunger for her was unbearable, my incubus side starved for her touch, for the warmth she inspired in me.

She looked back at me, a question in her eyes. From all appearances, she didn't understand this world anymore, which made it harder to remind myself who she was.

As the sea wind toyed with her red hair, she seemed entranced with me. The magic of the forest was affecting both of us.

My gaze lingered over her heartbreakingly beautiful face, her full lips.

"These woods are enchanted," she murmured. "I'm starting to feel...a bit more like a demon."

A bit more like a succubus.

I wanted to maintain my mask of boredom and say something insulting, but instead, I moved closer. She pressed her hand against my chest. To keep me at a distance, perhaps, but her touch made my heart pound.

I could hear her heart beating in time with mine, hear the shallowing of her breath.

"There's a cottage." I nodded up ahead. "You could get warm there before we move on."

Mortana. She was Mortana.

She held my gaze steadily, breath clouding around her face. Something mischievous glinted in her eyes. "Do you actually find me tedious? When we first met, you told me that you didn't lie about what you were, and that's what made humans different from demons, but I'm not convinced you were telling the truth." Her eyebrows drew together, and a pink flush rose over her cheeks. "Why did you really let me live?"

Of course, she was absolutely fucking right, and she fascinated me more than anyone. I wasn't about to admit it, though, since it was the only thing saving me from complete self-destruction.

"If you think I like you, it's my incubus charm." I slid my hands into the pockets of my coat. "Everything I said stands. You're nothing but a beautiful irritant." I forced the words out, though it felt like I was hearing them from a distance, ridiculous words that had no meaning.

She cocked her head. "You did say beautiful, though."

Had I?

"But that's not really good enough. If you genuinely think I'm nothing more than an irritant and have no respect for me at all, then you have terrible taste. That makes you not good enough, I'm afraid. You've been weighed on the scales and found wanting. You know, Orion? Maybe a mortal man could truly appreciate me."

She turned away, and I felt it like a physical pain, claws plunging into my chest. Insane, irrational jealousy surged through my veins, even though I wasn't even sure who I was jealous of. A mortal?

My demon side took hold, darkness spilling out around me. My body was taking over my mind.

I prowled after her. I *had* to have her because she was mine.

Blood pumping hot in my veins, I grabbed her arm and spun her around to face me. Her eyes darkened, and her lip curled back, exposing her fangs. *There* was the beautiful demonic side of her, the ferocious succubus. She let out a hiss.

What was I doing?

"I don't find you boring at all," I admitted. "I hate you for what you did. But because I'm certain that I am cursed, I can't stop thinking about what it would feel like to have your legs wrapped around me and your mouth pressed to mine. And I can never, *ever* stop thinking about you."

With a wicked smile, she stroked her hand down my chest. "It's too bad you hate me, then, isn't it?" A little shrug of her shoulders. "I can easily find someone who doesn't. Didn't Goody Putnam imply the Dying God was beautiful?"

Aggression unfurled inside me, and I pressed her against an oak tree, boxing her in with my palms on the rough bark. I wanted to fuck her until she forgot he existed.

She stared up at me, her eyes wide. "Oh, dear. Are you jealous?"

She was toying with me, of course.

"I'm going inside. You'll freeze if you stay out here." I started walking, and I heard her follow me. We were close to the cottage now, a crooked little place made of stone and covered in snowy ivy.

"Why do you care if I'm freezing?" she asked. "Since you hate me."

She could see right through me, which was annoying. "I need to make sure you don't freeze to death before you tell me how to kill Cambriel."

This was a bad idea, but I was already pushing through the door into the little cabin. It didn't look like anyone had been here in a while, but it had the potential to be cozy. A fireplace in the hearth stood empty, and I crossed over to it. A pile of logs stood next to the fireplace, and I started sliding them in, one by one, arranging kindling on the bottom. A curled metal fire-striker lay on the floor, along with paper and flint. Vaguely, I remembered these little tools from my childhood, and I struck the metal against the flint until it sparked, igniting the paper. I dropped the flaming paper onto the logs and watched the flames spread.

It gave me a chance to clear my head and remind myself not to let this woman give me hope again. I pushed one of the logs with an iron poker, watching the flames rise. There was something deeply satisfying about lighting a fire in the dead of winter.

With the fire burning, I surveyed the rest of the cottage, a single room with a little wooden stairwell leading to a loft. A low bench sat across from the fireplace, and a black bearskin rug covered the floor. Mentally, I'd stabilized myself once more.

But when I looked up at Rowan, washed in the golden light of the flames, I could hardly think straight.

The magic of the forest had muddled my thoughts, I told myself, reviewing all the reasons I shouldn't touch her.

I rose from a crouch, trying to read something in her eyes. Was she going to attempt to break my spirit again?

I looked down at her, fighting the urge to kiss her.

Her eyebrows climbed. "So why lie to me? Why tell me that I bore you?"

"To keep you away from me, because I don't trust myself to resist you." *Fuck.* I leaned down, breathing in her scent. Her neck arched, inviting me. "The thing is, Rowan. I know how much you want me, too. It's part of being an incubus. I can practically taste your arousal. You drive me mad, but I know I do the same to you."

Her cheek brushed against mine, the soft feel of her skin driving me wild. I pulled back, staring into her eyes, drunk on her beauty.

Moonlight gleamed off her dark irises. "Even if that were the case, incubus, what are you going to do about it?"

"I plan to ruin you with a kiss."

The little smile on her lips was a dare, an invitation. I sensed her need, desire rippling from her body. Her allure was a command I had to obey.

She dropped her backpack on the floor. "What exactly does that mean, *ruin me with a kiss*?"

I trailed a finger over her throat, watching her body react. "I'm the last incubus in the world. After me, no one else could ever compare. You'll be ruined forever, love."

❧ 18 ❧

CHAPTER 18—ROWAN

*D*amn it.

    I moved nearer, inviting his touch.

    He knew exactly how to turn me on, with a look, with that intense expression, with a murmur of his deep, caressing voice. Sliding his hands around me, he pulled me closer.

I had a sudden impulse to be at his level and stepped onto the low bench, putting myself at his height. He gave me a knowing smile, a lock of silver hair falling before his eyes.

"Ruin me?" I tried to play it cool, but my voice sounded husky. I pushed him, which was childish, but this forest had made me irrational. "The arrogance is truly breathtaking. I really should have listened the first time you told me what a terrible person you are."

The sultry look in his eyes made my pulse race as his gaze swept slowly down my body. Every inch of my skin heated with desire, aching for his touch.

I needed to put an end to this. Of *course* nothing could happen between us. After all, I needed to take the crown from him. He was my rival. And maybe he really *would* ruin me.

"I think you're a terrible person," I said.

"We have that in common," he murmured.

"You don't deserve to be king." I reached for the collar of his coat, pulling it down over his shoulders with a rough tug. The garment dropped to the bearskin rug. "And you don't deserve these luxurious clothes."

"Are you trying to strip me, love? Go on, then. You're right. I don't deserve to be king." A sensual curve tugged at the corner of his lips. His mouth was an inch from mine now, his expression smoldering. "And yet, I'm going to be king anyway, and there's fuck all you can do about it."

Under his coat, he wore a buttoned shirt—ripped a little by the knife blade. I started popping the buttons open, one at a time. "You don't deserve the crown. You should still be living in filth in your dungeon." I pulled his shirt off and stared at perfection. His golden body practically glowed in the firelight. My gaze slid over his thickly corded arms, his divine abs.

"I hate you," I whispered. I didn't hate him, but I wanted to make it even, since he'd said the same to me several times.

This place had intensified my emotions beyond all reason. Annoyance became hatred. And attraction? That became uncontrollable sexual need.

"You think I should be in the dungeon still?" His voice was a seductive murmur, mouth hovering near mine. "I think you should be stripped naked and begging me to let you come. I think I'm going to make you call me your king, whether you want to or not."

"Absolutely not."

For a moment, I thought he was going to kiss me. Instead, with a low growl, he grabbed the front of my dress at the collar and ripped it, pulling it down to my waist. He kept tearing at it until I was clad in nothing but a pair of small midnight blue underwear.

I caught my breath, and my nipples went rock hard. Torn between lust and anger, I reached out and stroked the side of his face. "If you ask me, you should still be in the dungeon."

His expression darkened. "Is that right? Perhaps it's time I taught you a lesson. Is that what you're asking for?"

In a graceful movement, he sat down on the bench and pulled me into his lap. The next thing I knew, I was facedown, bent over his knees. Quite undignified.

"What are you doing?" I sounded irritated, but the truth was, I could have moved if I'd wanted to.

"Teaching you a lesson, love." His hand moved slowly down my spine, and he stroked the back of my underwear, his fingers grazing between my thighs. "After all those years of you torturing me, I think it's time we switched roles. And do you know what?" His voice was thick with seduction, and he cupped me between my legs. "As king, I really should claim what I want to be mine."

Searing need pulsed through my body, between my thighs. I could have reminded him that wasn't me, but—again—I didn't want to.

When he pulled down my underwear sharply, my breath hitched. I was practically shaking with need, my body begging to be touched by him. His left hand gripped me by the hair, holding me in place. As he slid my panties down my thighs, I became turned on beyond all reason. My lust was spiraling out of control. All I could think about was how badly I needed him inside me.

He brought his hand down hard on my ass, a momentary sting that was soon replaced by a wave of pleasure. I shifted my hips against him, wanting *more*, and he delivered as I arched my hips to meet his hand. Another stinging smack on my ass—and another—sent shivers of insatiable need through my body until I could no longer stand it.

"You know," he purred, still gripping my hair, "I have always wanted to see you completely helpless before me." He traced his fingertips over me, touching me where I was wet. He slid one finger inside me, and I clenched around him with a moan.

"I can feel how much you want me," he whispered. "But I'm going to need to hear you say it. Say that I'm your king."

I was going to lose my mind. I was getting close to orgasm. With the ache rising in my core, I was ready to do anything he wanted, say anything he wanted—

He pulled his fingers away from me again, and I gasped.

I had no response, just a wild desperation for more contact, more friction. Because he was right, I was completely at his mercy right now.

I wasn't going to let him drag out this torture any longer. Pushing myself out of his lap, I let my underwear drop to the floor.

He stared at me in awe as I stepped between his legs, unbuttoned his pants, and tugged them down.

"Come here," he said.

I climbed onto his lap, straddling him. He leaned into me, kissing me. His tongue swept in, and he stroked a hand down my body, over my ribs, my waist.

He froze and pulled away from the kiss, his gaze sliding down my naked body. Gently, he traced the scar on my side. "What happened?"

I had no interest in talking about the scar right now. It seemed an unfortunate distraction. "The demon hunters."

A quiet, possessive growl rose from his chest. "If you weren't within the city walls when it happened, you weren't able to heal completely. They tried to kill you when you were most vulnerable."

The warmth of the fire heated my back. "Forget it. That's the last thing I want to think about."

Orion rose and scooped me up, then lay me down on the rug. The fur tickled my skin.

Grabbing my wrists with one hand, he pinned them above my head on the bearskin. Usually so controlled, his dark expression was now wild. In fact, he looked like he was about to fuck me senseless, which was exactly what I wanted.

"Orion," I whispered, "I want you to know that I still think you're the absolute worst."

"That's one thing we agree on." He moved between my thighs and lowered his head to my breast, taking one nipple in his mouth. I moaned, my hips thrusting forward against him. A raw groan escaped his lips, and he worked his mouth over my peaked breast. The ache in my core had become insatiable.

"Open your eyes and look at me, love," he purred. "I want to see how much you want me."

I did as he asked. There was always something instantly hot about the way he stared at me. "Does it make you feel powerful?" My lips curled into a little smile. "In control?"

A soft laugh. "Yes."

But from the wild look in his eyes, I could see he was ready to lose control, too. As well-endowed as he was, it was impossible to ignore how turned on he was.

With a sudden burst of strength, I ripped my wrists from his grasp and reached for his underwear, pulling it down.

I stared for a moment at his intimidating length, wondering if this was an incubus trait. I reached down to touch it, to stroke it. He groaned, the air heating around him, and uttered a demonic curse. He gripped my wrists again, pinning me down to the floor. Possessive.

For a moment, he was pressed against my wet heat, his mouth hovering above mine. Desire coiled tightly in me, and I shifted my hips, moving against him.

"Are you going to admit I'm your queen?"

"No, love, because you're my worst enemy," he whispered, "but this I will admit. I can't stop thinking about you, and I never will."

Slowly, he slid into me, one inch at a time, his size nearly overwhelming me. "Tell me how much you want me," he said, and I could hear the strain in his voice. He was using everything in himself to maintain control.

"I think you know, Orion."

He slid inside me as far as he could go. He paused, searching my eyes to see how I felt, and I wanted him to stop holding back.

He pressed his lips against mine, delivering a kiss that would surely ruin me, as promised. His tongue slid against mine in a sensual caress. Slowly, he moved his hips back, then he thrust into me again.

Never in my life had I imagined anything could feel this amazing. I tightened my thighs around him.

He pulled away from the kiss, his gaze searching mine again. "You don't know how many times I have thought of this." His voice sounded raw, ragged, and his mouth lowered near my throat.

He was moving a little faster now, and he kissed me again—harder, more desperately, his tongue sweeping against mine as he fucked me.

As he thrust into me, intense pleasure made me moan into his mouth, my body coiling tighter with a need for release. He was moving faster now, with an animalistic ferocity, as if he were claiming me.

I moaned his name, throwing my head back against the rug, my breasts sliding against his chest.

I would have said anything in that moment, but I couldn't remember what it was he'd wanted me to say. My entire world had narrowed to the feel of him inside me, giving me the intense pleasure I'd craved for so long.

As my climax built, I breathed his name, over and over.. My climax ripped out of me, my body tightening around him.

"Rowan." He said my name with reverence, and then, with a shudder, he groaned against my neck as his fingers clenched under my ass. Orion wrapped his arm around me, his head resting against my neck. By the slump of his shoulders, he looked defeated. I touched his cheek.

Shuddering with the aftershocks, I caught my breath. His muscles had relaxed, and he held my gaze.

I stroked his muscled back. "I may have just ruined my life, but it was worth it."

I wanted him to kiss me again, but this wasn't love, was it? He'd made that perfectly clear.

He had the posture of a man who'd lost a battle. So who had actually been ruined here? I wasn't so sure it was me.

He pushed himself up on his elbows, staring into my eyes again. For the first time, he looked strangely innocent. Vulnerable, maybe.

"Orion?" I said, remembering my ripped dress. "I'm going to need your coat for the rest of the trip."

❦ 19 ❦
CHAPTER 19—ROWAN

We walked on snow-covered paths, the forest's magic still pulsing through the air. It swirled around inside my skull like a potion. I shivered in Orion's coat, nearly naked under the scratchy wool.

I hoped we found this Dying God before I got frostbite in very unfortunate places. The coat didn't fit me at all, and the pressure of the backpack kept popping a button open. As the bottom of the coat dragged over the forest floor, snow accumulated on the hem.

I tried to picture myself in the oversized wool garment and was pretty sure I looked like a nineteenth-century Russian clown.

Orion walked by my side, his hands in the pockets of his cloak. Now he looked completely relaxed, and he gave me a mischievous glance. "Sorry about the dress."

"Was tearing it really necessary?"

"Absolutely."

Did I regret what we'd just done? Given the way my body still felt, humming and electrified, I couldn't say that I did. Besides, there was no point in regretting something you couldn't control. Might as well bemoan the need to breathe. What was the point? Once he'd said he was going to ruin me with a kiss, I'd needed him like I needed oxygen.

There was no choice—my desire for him was like a command from a god.

I did regret the loss of the dress, though, because the biting wintry air sneaked into the gaps in the coat, stinging my bare skin, and the bottom of the coat had grown damp with the snow.

When an unnatural, silvery glow illuminated the trees, my mood improved. We were close, surely. The moonlight gleamed upward, beaming from the forest floor to the skies.

I tugged the coat tighter around me, wondering how much weirder things could get. I was about to meet a demon god wearing a wool tent with buttons and my tits ready to pop out.

"He's here," Orion said with a quiet reverence. He'd never seemed sure if the gods were real, and I wondered if he actually believed deep down.

From the corners of my eyes, lights flickered. I turned my head and caught glimpses of letters—not an alphabet I recognized. Cuneiform, maybe. Around me, writing formed, bright, vicious lines of light that looked like a knife had hacked through the darkness, revealing starlight behind it.

I touched Orion's arm. "What's all this?"

"Sumerian," he whispered. "Once, demons were worshipped as gods in the ancient world. Tammuz is one of the oldest among us. He lived as a god."

Whispers fluttered around me, but I couldn't make out the words at first. Then, I heard it—*Chaos. Chaos. Chaos.*

Goosebumps rose on my arms. Lord of Chaos—I thought that was Orion's thing...

"Do you hear that?" I whispered.

He lifted his finger to his lips. The light around us silvered his face.

He'd gone completely still, and after another minute, he finally spoke. "I'm going to summon him now."

Orion began speaking quietly in a rhythmic, percussive language. The dark and beautiful phonemes seemed to send me into a trance.

The glowing cuneiform symbols flickered away, and shadows stole the light in the forest. A low rumbling sound trembled over the forest floor, as if the earth were pregnant with thunder. Fear slid through my bones.

Stars glittered between naked boughs, illuminating the demon god.

Ice and snow encrusted the trees in the grove, gleaming with cold light like wintry chandeliers.

Chaos. Chaos. Chaos. The words bloomed in my mind.

I saw him and caught my breath. He was the size of Orion, but he didn't look nearly as tangible. He seemed to be made of smoke, and shadows swept around him. Dark tendrils cloaked him in a wispy toga.

Through the smoky strands, I made out two silver horns gleaming from the top of his head. They curved like a crescent moon, and thorny tattoos curled over his bronze skin. I looked closer. White flowers were threaded in his hair.

"Dying God," said Orion.

"You come into my forest once more." Shadows slid over him, and his voice rang inside my head.

He turned to look at me, his eyes bottomless darkness. I stared into them and felt madness, terror. Uncertainty filled me, and I was no longer sure where I stood. Was there earth beneath my feet? Was this a dream or a nightmare?

"Do you know who you really are yet?" His voice seemed to come from behind me this time, though his lips never moved.

"I'm my mom's daughter." The words came out of my mouth on their own, and I heard them from a distance. My breath puffed around me. "I don't need to know anything else."

Glittering shadows swirled around him. He glided closer now, the movements too smooth to be natural. I stared at his sharp, high cheekbones as he solidified before us, no longer transparent. A dark serpent slid from the darkness behind him and curled around his arm.

He reminded me a little of Orion—terrifying, beautiful.

This solved one mystery. I knew now why these Puritan women risked their necks to sneak into the woods.

Orion stepped forward, looking a lot more relaxed than I felt. "Will you sever a blood oath I made?" he asked.

"In the old days, people knew how to ask a question of the gods." Tammuz's voice boomed across the forest, a deep growl that shook snowflakes from the boughs. "When people made requests of the gods, they sacrificed something valuable. A lamb, a goat, a cow. A first-born child, delivered into the fiery jaws of Moloch."

A sliver of dread ran through my veins. His dark eyes made me feel unmoored.

Orion raised an eyebrow. "You want me to sacrifice a goat?"

The Dying God seemed to grow larger before us. "No. A goat has no value to you." He looked between the two of us. "I need what you hold most dear. Secrets." He held his arms out to either side. "Confessions. That is what you can give to me."

I hugged myself, shivering. "Confess what?"

Tammuz's eyes locked on me, and he took a step closer, moving with a catlike grace that reminded me of Orion. Behind him, bone-white mushrooms sprouted from the snow where he'd trod.

"You need to admit what you've been running from," his voice boomed. "Confess. Tell me what happened the night your mother died."

I shrank from him like I'd been burned. "I can't confess that because I don't remember."

"Perhaps you didn't see everything." His gaze had turned predatory. "Let me show you what *really* happened."

No. I didn't want to remember. I wanted to turn and run into the shadows instead of facing that night.

Tammuz reached out and touched my collarbone. As his finger grazed my skin, coldness spilled through me.

Out of the corner of my eye, I saw Orion step forward and felt the heat rippling off him. "Don't touch her. What are you doing?"

The god's eyes sparkled. "Taking what's mine."

I glimpsed Orion moving for him, but a vault of star-flecked night swept over me, and they disappeared.

❧ 20 ❧

CHAPTER 20—ROWAN

Lightning cracked the sky, and for a moment, I glimpsed another figure standing behind him—a horned man with a five-pointed star. My heart skipped a beat.

Lucifer?

But he vanished into the shadows with Orion and Tammuz, leaving me alone in the forest.

Snow swirled around me in wild vortices, then melted. Icicles turned to water, and the earthy smell of spring filled the air. The elms around me turned into pines.

I stared at the landscape, recognition dawning. The gentle roll of the hill and the rocky overhang to my right—this was where it had happened. The same exact place, in a different time.

I felt split in two. Half of me wanted to run from the buried memories of that night, while the other half needed to know what had happened. I needed to know who had killed my mother.

Time slowed. The wind caught in the pines, and the boughs strained. Raindrops slid slowly from the sky.

Fear stole my breath as a figure moved through the shadows. She moved closer, and I saw myself. I was running, red hair frizzy and sweat gleaming on my cheeks.

But where was Mom, and why weren't we together?

I watched myself running, moving in slow motion now. My arms pumped through the air. I ran alone with the precise form of a varsity athlete.

Storm clouds darkened the night sky, and lightning cracked the shadows. A loud clap of thunder rumbled over the forest. Rain hammered me as I ran, and rivulets streamed over the earthy forest floor.

Had I realized how far ahead of Mom I was? Had I even known what I was running from?

Mom couldn't keep up with me. She was a demon without her powers, and I was a trained athlete.

I wanted to close my eyes, but I couldn't. Tammuz wanted me to see this.

What if, when something so devastating happened, it left an imprint on the world? What if horror lingered forever—like Pompeii's victims, eternally contorted in their final moments, tormented tragedies perpetually encased in stone?

At last, Mom ran from the shadows. She looked younger than I remembered, her skin gleaming. Rain drenched her dark hair.

She wore a large backpack, too, and it looked heavy on her shoulders. I remembered now—she'd always kept it by the door, filled with food, water, and a knife. She had a gun at home as well, locked in a safe, for all the good it did when someone came for us. I remembered it all now—there hadn't been time to get the gun.

The forest thinned around me, and a new scene emerged—one with warm light and a familiar blue sofa. My heart ached. We were back now in our house, the bottom-floor rental in Witchcraft Point. With the sound of rain gently pattering the windows, a cozy scene emerged. Fairy lights were strung above the windows. I saw myself on the sofa, surrounded by books, trying to cram for a math test. I sat cross-legged and relaxed. One of Mom's crocheted afghans in light blue lay draped on the sofa behind me, just as it always had been. From the next room, the radio was playing Mozart on a low volume.

This teenage version of me had no idea of what was coming next.

I glanced at the clock on the wall—ten-sixteen at night. The second hand ticked loudly in the room, each strike seeming louder.

This had been my last minute of peace before the world changed completely.

Mom came into the room with a bowl of popcorn. Lightning lit up the sky outside, and she froze, staring out the window, her blue eyes wide. I'd seen those eyes recently—

She dropped the bowl of popcorn. "Run," she screamed. "Get out! Get your shoes on and run for the car."

I leapt up, trying to see what she'd seen, but nothing was out there except the dark, crooked street in front of our house. Back then, Mom always seemed to be freaking out over nothing, convinced that people were out to get us. In my high school psychology class, I'd learned about paranoid schizophrenia, and I'd wondered if that was what she had. The self-defense classes, the bug out bag, the constant fears that people were watching or following us. And here she was again, screaming that something evil was coming for us. I thought she was imagining it.

I'd argued with her, saying that I wasn't going to leave the house because she *thought* she saw something outside, not when I had more important things to do. I wasn't going to let her paranoia ruin high school for me. As I looked back on myself now, I wanted to scream, *Listen to her, you fucking idiot!*

A math test? *That's* what I'd been worried about?

I felt sick as I watched the argument unfold. Finally, I'd gotten my shoes on, a furious look on my face. We'd left the house through the basement, running into the rainy night. But the argument had flustered her, and she'd forgotten her car keys.

"He's coming!" she'd screamed. "Run into the woods. I'll be right behind you."

My younger self had stared into the shadows, peering from behind a tree. My face paled, jaw dropping open when I glimpsed someone who scared me. I ran, then, sprinting down trails I knew like the back of my hand—every turn, every crook of the path memorized.

Mom started behind me, but she didn't know the way, and she wasn't in shape. She bumped into trees in the dark, her arms grasping at shadows. She couldn't keep up with me, and I'd cost her precious time arguing. On top of that, she'd forgotten the keys, and that was my fault.

And there I was, my younger self, blithely leaving Mom behind to save my own ass. I'd assumed she was right behind me as I ran, but I hadn't stopped to check. Nor had I considered that fact that she couldn't run a five-minute mile like I could, or that she didn't run trails.

I sprinted into the heart of the forest, and the night swallowed me whole.

The murderer was there now, running fast behind Mom.

Hot rage seared me. His mark glowed—a false king. A twisted king, his pale hair streaming behind him as he ran, eyes pure black.

His mark wasn't a five-pointed star like mine or Orion's. He was never destined to rule, never blessed by Lucifer. And this he had to keep hidden.

King Cambriel—my half brother—raced behind Mom, and his forehead glowed with the mark of a golden eye in a triangle.

Mom veered to the right, off the path. Had that been an accident? She was taking herself off the trail, making it harder to run through the brush and brambles.

I had a horrible feeling that her actions were intentional, that she was trying to lure him away from me. She didn't want him to realize I was there, didn't want him to follow me.

Horror slammed into me as I watched him close the distance between them. Flame erupted from his fingertips, touching Mom's hair, which ignited an instant before her clothing went up in flames.

Her screams tore through the quiet forest as her body blazed like a torch. *Mom.* I wish I'd never seen this. Why had the Dying God made me watch this?

King Cambriel shouted a single word, one that punctured the night like a gunshot: "*Bitch!*"

Bitch. *Bitch*. That's what he'd shouted as my mother had burned. I wanted to rip his fucking throat out.

And someday, I would.

The false king—my twisted half brother—fled the way he'd come, scuttling off like a little rat.

The younger me had heard the screams, had seen the blaze of fire in the woods. Even in the driving rain, Mom had burned in flames too hot to be extinguished. I didn't want to hear her wails of pain.

As I watched, my teenaged self ran back to her, my hair as red as the flames. My demon mark glowed on my forehead, a five-pointed star. I was sobbing, the strangled sound nearly inaudible over her agonized screams. I ran closer. Taking my sweatshirt off, I tried to cover her with it. I wanted to stop the burning, but it was too late. She'd fallen silent. Mom lay on the ground, her limbs contorted, the jacket burning along with her. Only my screams filled the air now, and Cambriel probably never realized the difference—we sounded the same, just as anguished.

I watched my younger self stagger away from her body and run. Splashing through a puddle of muddy water, I'd glanced down and seen the demon mark glowing on my forehead. That's when my mind had broken, I think, and I'd lost my memory. It had been too much, the onslaught of horror and dark magic that I didn't understand.

Covered in ash, my younger self had stumbled through the woods like someone already dead, a zombie going through the motions of life.

All that had remained of the memories of that night was the golden star—not who it belonged to or where I'd seen it, but the image of the star. Deep down inside, I'd known that the person with the golden star was responsible for killing Mom. And it was true, wasn't it? My unconscious had put it all together. Somewhere in the hollows of my mind, I realized I was to blame. I'd argued with her. I'd made her forget her keys, and then I'd run away without her. She'd sacrificed herself.

And all along, I'd known I was to blame.

If I hadn't been there, she'd still be alive.

But Cambriel was more guilty than I, and nothing would stop me from seeking the revenge I craved.

I didn't care what Orion wanted. King Cambriel's death would be at my hands.

THE VISION DISAPPEARED, AND I FOUND MYSELF IN THE underworld once more, now on all fours. The icy forest floor stung my hands.

My entire body was shaking. Nausea overwhelmed me, and I retched. The buttons had popped open on Orion's coat, and the frigid winter air rushed in, chilling my chest. I didn't care. I was too overwhelmed by the horror of what I'd just seen.

Mom. She'd always been the one I'd called for when I was scared.

Someone placed a hand on my back, a gesture that was almost protective. Orion.

Lifting my head, I found the demon god staring down at me like I was an alien species. Some of the nausea passed, and I rocked back onto my heels. Grasping me by the waist, Orion helped me to my feet.

I pulled the edges of the coat together. My mouth still felt watery and sick, and I swallowed hard. I desperately wanted to be out of this place now, curled up in a warm room under a blanket. No—I wanted my mom, but that was stupid because I was an adult, and she was gone.

Shadows writhed and danced around the Dying God, and he smiled at me. "Tell me what you saw."

I took a deep breath. "Here is your confession. The secret you wanted. I remember what happened with my mom. I ruined everything. I argued instead of running when her killer was outside. I didn't believe her, and I made her forget her keys. I ran too fast, and she couldn't keep up. I left her behind." I was speaking in hardly a whisper, but the forest seemed eerily silent. Somehow, my words echoed off the ice. My gaze slid to Orion. "But I wasn't the one who killed her. It was Cambriel. He hated her deeply for some reason. I don't think he had any idea I was there that night."

"Cambriel," Orion repeated, eyes dark. "He wanted to destroy the last Lilu. I'm surprised he let you live, but maybe he thought you could form an alliance."

I wasn't going to say the rest out loud. No reason to let Orion know we would be competing to kill the same person.

Orion folded his arms on his chest, seemingly impervious to the cold. "What secret would you like me to confess?"

The Dying God gave him a knowing smile. "Why don't you tell us what you did in the dungeon?"

Orion went as still as the tree trunks, and shadows breathed around him. "Not *that*."

Not *what*?

Tammuz's green eyes sparkled with delight. "It's hardly a sacrifice if you are willing to give it up."

Why was Orion arguing when I'd relived the worst moment of my life?

Orion slid his hands into his pockets. His expression looked bored, but something about the heat coming off him told me he was raging beneath the surface. "I have plenty of secrets for you to choose from. That one is off limits."

Tammuz shrugged. "You will sacrifice that secret someday. I am in no rush. Time has no meaning here."

Goosebumps rose on my skin, and I had the disturbing feeling we were being watched.

I looked at the woods behind us. Nothing but darkness.

"Relinquish another secret, then." Tammuz's tattoos shifted and slithered over his skin. "I know. Tell me what you plan to do when you are king."

"I plan to get revenge."

"Everyone knows that." Tammuz's voice boomed, and I could tell he was losing patience. "What *exactly* will you do?"

The silence between us felt sharp and spiked.

"I plan to break the curse," said Orion. "The one that strips us of power when we leave the City of Thorns. I plan to free the demons from their gilded prison. We will roam among the mortals as we like."

"And then?" asked the Dying God.

For a heartbeat, Orion met my gaze, then he turned back to Tammuz again, his eyes darkening. Distant shouts rang through the forest, and Orion whirled around, his fingers twitching. The hair rose on the back of my neck, and I turned to look.

Torches flickered in the trees. "Thou foul witch!" someone shouted in the distance. "Come to make the wicked covenant with the devil, to let him poke his cock in your pole hole!"

I grimaced. *Poke his cock in your pole hole?*

"Osborne's best and brightest have arrived," muttered Orion. "This must be Malleus Daemoniorum, here at last."

I glanced down. I was naked except for the enormous coat. I didn't exactly look innocent of the *pole hole* charges. We needed to get out of here before we found ourselves hanged in the underworld.

Glancing up, I saw to my dismay that Tammuz, the Dying God, had disappeared into the dark forest.

The hunters were coming for us, and here in the underworld, we had no weapons or demonic strength to fight back.

21

CHAPTER 21—ROWAN

My mind swam with visions of Puritan prisons flooded with water and rats, infested with lice and dysentery. On the other hand, their old guns couldn't aim for shit. So that at least was a blessing.

The silvery light of the Dying God must have alerted them, or maybe his impatient shouting at Orion. Now that Tammuz was gone, our best bet was to quietly blend into the forest's shadows.

"Orion," I whispered, "we need to get out of here."

But he didn't look ready to run. He looked like he was waiting for them.

"Orion!" Desperation tightened my gut.

"You should run," he said quietly. "I have plans for Malleus Daemoniorum, and I'm really looking forward to them."

Ah. Were these the hunters who'd come for his family all those centuries ago?

"Yeah, we both should run." I grabbed at his arm, but he was as immobile as stone. "You can't even actually kill them. They're already dead. They'll just come back again. But me? I don't want to die. We could be stuck in this shithole forever."

He quirked an eyebrow, looking irritated. "Has anyone ever told you that you're a buzzkill? Killing Puritans is my idea of a good time. Stop ruining it. They will come back, yes. But I can make them feel terror and indescribable pain. Please don't ruin my good time with all the downsides you keep pointing out." He sighed. "But you should run. It doesn't have anything to do with you, and I don't need your help. We're all on our own here, love. Go on."

I wanted to scream. Instead, I muttered, "Idiot," and took off through the darkness. Maybe he was obsessed with revenge against people who'd died centuries ago, but I wasn't here to get shot and hanged.

I had a strong feeling Orion had forgotten what it was like to fight as a mortal instead of with the godlike strength he possessed in the world of the living.

Gripping my coat tightly, I started running over the frozen ground, snapping twigs.

The winter air bit at my skin, and I had no idea where I was going in the pitch black. Should I head back to town if I could find it?

Sharp regret pierced my chest. What would happen to Orion? What if he couldn't manage the fight on his own? I was leaving someone behind to die again, wasn't I? Just as that thought struck me like an arrow, a scream chilled my blood—an agonized male scream. I felt the air leaving my lungs. *Please, don't let it be Orion.*

I looked back, my heart stuttering at the sight of a body blazing in the distance. I wasn't sure who I was angrier at right now—Orion for refusing to run, or me for leaving him there.

I started sprinting toward him, a bony hand of fear gripping my heart. I had a terrible feeling I'd find him there, half-alive and burning. I could smell it now—the searing flesh, the ashes floating on the wind. *Please*, not Orion...

Despite our twisted relationship and everything he'd said to me, some part of me cared about the dickhead.

Flames bloomed from the forest floor, and as I drew closer, I saw three people illuminated in the light of a burning body. I exhaled when I spied Orion standing with his hands raised, facing me. Blood poured down his forehead.

I lingered in the shadows for a moment, trying to assess the scene.

One of the men had a gun pressed against Orion's head. Another pulled out a rope and pulled Orion's hands behind his back. The third hunter had his back to me.

"Thou wicked, fornicating devil with thy black book!" the man shouted. "Thou shalt be stripped to the waist and whipped through town at the back of a cart."

"Don't threaten me with a good time."

Orion must have used the torch to burn one of them, but he'd been outnumbered. I needed to act now before they bound Orion's hands behind him. For a moment, Orion caught my eyes. He raised an eyebrow nearly imperceptibly.

"We will have thy confession!" shouted the other, trying to bind his arms behind him.

I needed to take down the gunman first.

I looked down and picked up a large rock, jagged and frozen in my fingertips. With the crude weapon in my hands, I darted out of the shadows and brought the rock down hard on the back of the gunman's head. He staggered and whirled, slamming me in the temple with his flintlock. Pain flared through my skull.

But I was still holding my weapon. As panic ignited in my veins, I hit him again with the rock, harder this time.

I heard the crack of bone, and he wavered where he stood, dazed and bleeding. Something caught my eye that made my heart skip a beat. There, on his chest, was the same silver pin that the Corwins wore: a hammer. The hammer of the demons—Malleus Daemoniorum.

The man crumpled to the ground, blood pouring from his head onto the ice. I staggered back, staring at him.

When I looked up again, Orion had freed himself. Wrapping his hands around the throat of one of the mortals, he slammed the man's head into a tree trunk repeatedly, cratering the back of the man's skull.

I gaped at the horror around me: the man engulfed in flames, still twitching, the injured man crawling at my feet, the person Orion was battering to death. The last hunter standing scrambled for the fallen gun. Orion whirled and punched him in the skull with an animal ferocity. He hit him again and again.

Without the magical powers of a demon, killing wasn't quite as clean and tidy as it could be. All this could have been avoided if Orion had run with me, but these messy deaths were his goal.

In a daze, I walked away from the carnage, bile rising in my throat. Vaguely, I wondered if the Dying God would return now and break the oath so that we could get out of here and never come back.

I looked down at myself. Blood streaked my bare skin where my coat had opened, but I wasn't sure if it was mine or the man's I'd just killed.

Since I'd entered the world of demons, I was starting to realize there were only two options in some situations: you could kill or die. And with that in mind, I turned back to the men who lay dying on the forest floor and scanned their bodies for weapons.

The flintlock was large and unwieldy, so I'd leave that behind. The man I'd hit with a rock was still crawling over the ice, although he was half dead. He had another weapon strapped around his waist, a knife, and I pulled it from its sheath. As I did, I felt as if my soul was freezing over.

Goody Putnam had been right. These woods turned people into animals, naked, covered in blood. Stealing weapons from people as they died. Orion was drawing out the death of the man in his hands. I dropped my new weapon into my bag and started walking, not wanting to see any more violence.

A moment later, I heard footfalls behind me and turned to see Orion's silhouette.

His eyes shone brightly in the darkness. "Why did you come back for me?"

My head throbbed, and I wasn't sure I could feel the cold anymore. "I didn't want to leave someone else behind," I said, swallowing hard.

"Wait. Rowan—wait." He stood in front of me, peering down at me. He touched my temple, and his forehead furrowed. "You have a head injury."

"You should see the other guy." My head was pounding, and I wanted to throw up. "He hit me with that flintlock."

"This isn't good. You might be even less fun than you were before." He pulled his hand away. "I can't heal you here."

"Did you forget your lack of magical powers when you decided to take on those armed men?"

He stroked the side of my face again, just below where I'd been struck. Even if he didn't have magic at his fingertips, there was something soothing about his touch. "There is some method to my madness. If they reported back to town and gathered a larger group to hunt us down, we might not leave here alive. We'd be hanged in the town square before we could get back to the turnpike."

"Maybe."

He held my gaze for a moment, then let out a long breath. "I want to get you somewhere warm. Your eyes look unfocused. We'll look for the Dying God again tomorrow." He took my hands between his and chafed them, staring down at my fingertips. "You're starting to get frostbite."

My thoughts were going dim, like someone had covered them in a dark, fuzzy blanket, and I felt myself falter.

Orion scooped me up in his arms, and I wrapped my arms around his neck, warming myself against his body. As he carried me, I rested my head against his chest, listening to his heartbeat. "Why don't you feel the cold?" I mumbled.

"It was always cold in the dungeon," he whispered, picking up his pace.

I half wondered how he was going to explain the state of us, but with his warmth enveloping me, I was starting to drift off. I listened to the sound of Orion's heart, feeling strangely safe wrapped in the arms of my enemy.

❧ 22 ❧

CHAPTER 22—ROWAN

I woke naked in Orion's arms.

He gave me a crooked half smile. "There you are."

Frowning, I surveyed the candlelit room around me. Thick wooden beams crossed the ceiling above Orion's head, and the walls were plain white. A four-poster bed stood in the center of the room, and a copper tub steamed beneath a shuttered window. A fire burned in a hearth, filling the room with the scent of burning cedar.

My head was still bleary. "Why am I naked, Orion?"

In here, the ceilings were so short, he had to hunch. "Because I'm going to get the blood off you and thaw you out."

Carefully, he lowered me into the warm bathwater. At first, the shock of the heat on my frozen fingers and toes made my breath catch, and it almost stung. It felt like my fingers were swelling, but within moments, the warmth was pure bliss. I sank deeper into the water and rubbed my fingers together. "Where are we?" I asked.

"The Putnam Tavern."

"Ah, you charmed her again, did you? How did you explain that I was naked and covered in blood?"

"I told her that we and the other Malleus Daemoniorum members found the evil in the forest, and that a terrible fight ensued. But she really wanted to know about your wicked thoughts. She suggested that tomorrow, you should make a public penance for your unnatural desires."

I stared at him. "I believe you had some of your own unnatural desires."

"Always." He leaned down next to the tub, a cloth in his hand. Gently, he washed my face, dabbing the cloth into the water.

But that was all it was, wasn't it? We'd jumped all over each other because we were Lilu, out of control in the magic of the woods. I sank deeper into the water. "Are you going to fill me in about your revenge plan? Why was Tammuz asking about that?"

I stared at his achingly beautiful face, at the silvery hair that skimmed his sharp cheekbones. His eyebrows were thick and dark, a sharp contrast to the paleness of his haunted eyes. "I don't like to discuss nightmares directly before bed."

He washed the blood from my skin, then pulled the cloth away, his gaze shuttered. "I'm going to see if Goody Putnam has some clothes you can borrow."

When he left the room, the ache in my chest increased. No matter what happened between us, he would never completely trust me. And he'd never apologized for the things he'd said.

When the bathwater started to cool, I rose. I didn't see a towel—in fact, I wasn't sure they had them in the old days. Crossing to the roaring fire, I dried my naked body by the flames. I won't lie, I loved the heat of the fire, but it was hard not to think of this inn as a *slight* death trap without fire magic to protect me. This place was lit by hearths and candles and had zero fire alarms. When my body had dried off, I put my underwear back on, the only item of clothing I still had.

Normally, before I went to sleep, I'd scan through my phone looking at Instagram or text messages, or something with a connection to the outside world. Something to make me feel less lonely. But I didn't have that here, so I grabbed my father's note out of my backpack and slid under the sheets.

I unfolded it, staring at my father's neat, blocky handwriting.

Long live King Nergal. Long live King Nergal. Long live King Nergal.

I traced my fingertips over his words. It wasn't exactly easing my loneliness, but it was sparking my curiosity.

Why the hell would someone write this and save it?

As I touched the letter, I felt something in the paper—the tiniest of ridges. I frowned and held the note up to the firelight. My breath caught. There, tiny pinpricks of orange light streamed through the paper—little holes that formed delicate letters.

My heart sped up. This was a primitive system for encoding a message.

Pulse racing, I deciphered the contents of a letter addressed to my mom.

Aria,

I fear my time here is running out. The false prince, my disloyal son, is impervious to my threats to allow us to return. He does not know of our beloved creation, Rowan. I have spoken with the Dying God. He confirmed our fears. If the Lord of Chaos succeeds, the mortal realm will burn. Only Mortana's ka can reign. Only the third Lightbringer can restore us. I will return to you as soon as I can.

—Moloch

I read the letter again and again, trying to make sense of the words. I was shocked to see the Lord of Chaos mentioned, and the Dying God too, And my name! For the first time, my suspicions had been confirmed—Aria and Moloch were my true parents.

My thoughts spun, and I glanced at the door. How much time did I have until Orion returned?

Some of this was simple. The false prince, his disloyal son. That was King Cambriel, my half brother.

My heart was slamming against my ribs.

Three golden Lightbringer stars—the marks of Lucifer. Me, Orion, and—Mortana? They'd referred to us like we were two different people.

If the Lord of Chaos succeeds, the mortal realm will burn.

That...did not sound great.

Here it was at last, some proof that I was not who Orion thought I was. My heart stuttered to life as I read the words again.

Only Mortana's ka can reign...

I was the third Lightbringer.

But I had no idea what a ka was. An identical daughter? And why did he call me a "beloved creation"? That wasn't really a normal way to refer to a family member. It sounded like Frankenstein's monster.

I closed my eyes, and the vision of Cambriel played in my mind again. According to this letter, my parents had been threatening him. And if I had to guess, they had the same leverage as Orion. They were threatening to let the world know he wasn't the true king. And unlike Orion, they were easier to kill to get rid of the evidence.

Footfalls creaked outside, and I folded the note up again, shoving it into my little leather bag. The door opened, and Orion crossed into the room, a dress slung over his arm—and a shawl this time. *Nice.*

I watched him, an idea blooming in my mind. I had to take the crown from him. There were only two people I'd ever truly trusted in this world: my mom and Shai. Mom believed I should be queen. And you know what? I'd make a better ruler than he would. He was completely unhinged.

I watched Orion as he pulled off his shirt, and the firelight wavered over his powerful body.

I wanted to tell him—at last, I had proof that I wasn't Mortana. My parents thought we were two different people, like I'd been trying to tell him all along. Every childhood memory I treasured was real, not a fabrication. The Christmas mornings with just me and Mom—all of that was real.

But given what else this letter included, I knew I had to keep it a secret. No reason to let him know I was coming for his throne.

I pulled the blankets over my shoulders and rolled over, staring into the flames. Flickering in the dancing tongues of fire, I thought I saw forms moving. Writhing.

Orion and my parents had been blackmailing the king in their own ways—Orion for money, my parents for their own goals. But unlike Orion, they hadn't been strong enough to fight him off.

Just like my mom had sacrificed herself in the woods, I wondered if my father had died to save me. Maybe they wanted *me* back in the City of Thorns with them. As demons, we were safest there.

With the blankets tucked around me, I closed my eyes. Images were burned into my mind—Cambriel, with his glowing sigil, had ripped out my father's heart in front of his house, then burned his body to hide the evidence. Cambriel wasn't going to allow them to blackmail him.

If the Lord of Chaos succeeds, the mortal realm will burn.

Maybe, now that I was a demon, I hungered for power, too. Not because I wanted to burn the world down, like Orion. It seemed the only way to stay safe. When you had no power at all, the world chewed you up and spit you out.

I felt the mattress sag as Orion got in and his body warmed the bed. I stole a quick look at him. Firelight danced back and forth over his enormous muscles.

"I don't suppose Goody Putnam had pajamas for me?" I asked.

He slowly turned his sultry gaze on me, and I felt my core grow tight. "I'm afraid not, love. In any case, Goody Putnam argued that you won't need clothes for your public penance tomorrow. I'm quite looking forward to it. It will be a delightful event for Osborne."

"She's really into this." I stared at him. "She's the kinkiest person in this place."

A knowing smile. "Not sure about that. I was locked in a dungeon most of my life. I've hardly had the chance to explore yet."

He was flirting with me, but I wasn't going to give him the chance to hurt me again.

I narrowed my eyes at him. "As I recall, you said you felt nothing for me and that your attraction to me was the desperation of a Lilu to feed, nothing more. I thought we both understood that's all this was. That what happened in the forest was *just* the effect of magic. We don't like one another, right?"

He looked at me, and for a moment, I thought I saw a flash of hurt in his eyes. Then a bland smile appeared on his face, his eyes half-lidded with indifference. "Right. Like I said before, we are all alone in this world."

That was a very Orion outlook.

Using the blankets, I formed a barrier between us. He looked on with amusement as I tucked a pillow between our bodies.

"Have you ever heard of something called a ka?" I asked carefully.

A line formed between his eyebrows. "Like an automobile?"

Damn. "No, not a car—ka. I thought it was a demon thing."

"Never heard of it. Why are you asking?"

"It was something I saw in the vision," I lied. "The vision said I was Mortana's ka. It said there are three of us with the star of Lucifer."

He stared at me like he was trying to read me, his eyes strangely sorrowful in the firelight. Shadows danced over his high cheekbones. "An interesting theory, but one of two things are true. Either this is real and you are not Mortana—"

"Yeah. That."

"—or you could be Mortana, and this is another one of your many, *many* seductive lies." He reached for my face and brushed his thumb over my lower lip—a slow, sensual stroke. "I'm inclined to think the latter, love."

Inside, I felt something snap, like a twig cracking in a fire. "That was my last attempt to convince you."

He leaned in even closer and whispered next to my ear. "Good. It's the hope that kills you, isn't it?"

I pushed him away from me. "Stay on your side of the barrier. Now, if we both have the mark of Lucifer, aren't you worried I might beat you to the throne?"

He quirked a smile. "I'm not worried about you," he purred. "You don't have it in you. Not anymore."

Well, that sounded like a fucking challenge, didn't it?

I slid further under the covers, rolling away from him on my side of the barrier.

Orion made me thankful for one thing. His patronizing attitude was going to make it that much easier to ruin his dreams and take what he thought belonged to him.

And make it mine.

❦ 23 ❦
CHAPTER 23—ROWAN

I woke with a strange tingling in my body and an icy chill in the room. With chattering teeth, I rubbed my arms, trying to get warmer. The fire must have gone out, and frost had settled over the chamber, encasing the bed.

But it wasn't just the cold, was it? Powerful magic wrapped around me, vibrating on my skin under the blankets. There it was again—that feeling that someone was watching me.

I hugged myself and slowly opened my eyes. A feeling of dread slid through me, and I sat up straight, the breath leaving my lungs.

The Dying God sat in a chair in the corner of the room, darkness curling around him. From the fireplace, the embers cast a warm glow that tinged the smoke with red. The Dying God's dark eyes were locked on me, gleaming and forest green.

Not creepy at all.

"What the *fuck*?" I blurted, holding the blankets over my chest.

Orion shot upright in the bed next to me, then saw the Dying God and relaxed. "Ah. Tammuz." He yawned. "If you are hoping for a threesome, I'm afraid it won't happen." He nodded at me. "She's a bit annoyed with me."

"I'm here for your confession," said Tammuz. "And then I will destroy your blood oath. Tell me, now, what do you plan to do as king?" The sound of his deep, growling voice boomed off the walls. Surely Goody Putnam would wake? Not that she'd be disappointed to find him here.

Orion went very still. "Revenge."

From the darkness, the Dying God appeared again, closer this time, at the foot of the bed. "More."

Orion sighed. "I've already killed King Nergal, and I plan to kill the other demons who participated long ago. I will find them all. I will reclaim everything they stole."

The Dying God faded into darkness again, but his voice whispered next to my head. "More."

I practically jumped out of the bed.

How did he know that it didn't end there? I was starting to get the impression he already knew the answers to the questions he asked.

"The massacre began with the mortals," said Orion, his voice cold and quiet. "And now they keep us trapped within the city gates. We cannot leave the City of Thorns without losing our power. They have dominion over us. They fear what we are because we are better than they are. We are stronger, smarter, more beautiful. When I am king, I will find the spell that keeps us trapped and break it. Demons will be free to roam the world once more. Lucifer urbem spinarum libarabit. The Lightbringer will set the City of Thorns free. That is me. I will liberate my kind. And I will make sure that no one capitulates to the mortals again, sacrificing our own."

A cold shiver ran down my spine at his words. I'd seen them carved in the dungeon the first night we'd met. Liberation should be joyful— so why did he make it sound so terrifying?

"The mortals were the reason King Nergal slaughtered us," Orion's voice was glacial. "King Nergal, who sired me—"

"Did he?" For the first time, Tammuz sounded angry, and his guttural rage sent electric fear through my veins. I still couldn't see him, which only made him more terrifying. A growl trembled over the room, making the bed shake, and the sound of creaking wood grew louder.

"Yes. It is why I was marked as the true heir. It's why I could kill him. But he was a slave to the mortals. A coward. And one day, I will open the gates to Hell. I will unleash my demon brothers and sisters on the world of the mortals, and we will live like we did in the old days. Once, the mortals worshipped us. Now, they celebrate our demise. I will make them feel true terror. I will sever their heads and stick them on pikes. I will make them feel what I felt, such horror that they're not even sure if the world around them is real. I will burn the world for seven days, and demons will rise from the ashes anew."

Nausea rose in my gut. "Holy shit, Orion. The people responsible died centuries ago. They're not the same as the Puritans you hate. You can't just cut random people's heads off."

He shrugged, looking completely unperturbed by this particular detail. "I will begin with the demon hunters, then. They are the same."

"You'll start with the demon hunters," I replied. "But where will you end?"

A line formed between his eyebrows. "Wherever I want it to end. When I am satiated."

With his charm and his easy grace, I'd never realized how fucked up he was. Bloodlust ran through his veins, and he would never be appeased. I couldn't say he hadn't warned me. He'd told me since day one that he was terrible.

Of *course* he was a head case. No one could spend their entire life in a dungeon and turn out normal.

I stared at him. "So you would murder thousands of people who had nothing to do with what you're angry about."

His eyes grew shadowed. "Yes. You're not going to tell me that mortals are better than they once were, are you? Do you think they've suddenly become *nice*? The past hundred years of history tells me otherwise." He turned back to the end of the bed, where Tammuz had been. "Will you break the blood oath now? You had my confession."

I couldn't help but wonder why Tammuz demanded this confession if he already knew the truth. In fact, the note said that he'd told my parents exactly this—if the Lord of Chaos reigns, the mortal realm will burn.

There was only one reason for these confessions, then. Tammuz wanted me to hear it. He wanted me to stop Orion.

The Dying God crossed over to Orion and touched the center of his forehead. Silver light slid over Orion's body like water, streaming from the top of his head down his powerful shoulders, biceps, and back. Orion closed his eyes, his muscles tensing.

I looked down and saw the same thing—silver light sliding over me. An overwhelming sense of calm washed over me. The Dying God's magic was like the caress of a gentle wind, and I was caught in the crossfire, imbued with the same magic.

In the hollows of my mind, I heard him speak to me. "You are free of your blood oath, Rowan," he said.

Tammuz disappeared, leaving us alone again. Holy shit. Why had he broken *my* oath as well? A sense of freedom and calm washed over me, and I couldn't keep my eyes open any longer.

I sank into the mattress, the soft pillow. The bed felt glorious to my tired muscles, and my body melted into it.

❧❦❧

WHEN I WOKE AGAIN, THE BARRIER BETWEEN US HAD DISAPPEARED, and Orion was curled around me, his length pressed against my backside. He held me close to him protectively.

Don't get too used to this, Rowan. It's not real, even if it feels real.

I nudged him with my elbow, moving him away. "Orion. The barrier."

I turned to look at him, and he propped his head on his hand, staring at me with sleepy eyes. "We did it." His smile was satisfied. "We broke the oath."

A shard of rosy light pierced the gloom, and I turned to see the sun rising outside. Dawn was breaking already.

"Now," said Orion, "it's time for you to fulfill your promise. Don't think I forgot."

I glanced at the shadowy space where the Dying God had been standing. I'd heard him tell me that he'd broken mine, too. Now it was time to test it out.

I met Orion's gaze. "There's a book in his room," I lied. "During the day, one of his guards carries it around, but they're always switching guards, so it's hard to know which one might have it. But at night, Cambriel sleeps with it under his pillow. Get it from him when he's fast asleep. Destroy the book, and you can kill him that way."

"And your parents wrote all this down?"

"They wanted someone to kill him." I shrugged. "I guess it'll be you."

24

CHAPTER 24—ROWAN

Clad in Goody Putnam's scratchy wool dress, I crossed the icy fields with Orion, striding past the hanging women once more. The milky morning light shone brightly on the frosted grass and sparkled on ice-encased trees.

In the distance, the row of wooden pikes protruded from the frozen gray earth like rotten teeth. And beyond those pikes, the caves of Purgatory loomed. Orion nodded. "As soon as we cross this turnpike, we are back. We don't have to go through Purgatory this time."

I let Orion take the lead as we got closer to the pikes. Sliding the backpack off my shoulders, I reached inside for the knife.

Just at the turnpike itself—the barrier to the veil, Orion turned to look at me, one foot over the edge.

I pressed the tip of the knife against his heart and stared up into his eyes. "I'm sorry, Lord of Chaos. But this is where we part."

He glanced down at the knife. When he looked back at me, a faint smile dimpled his cheek. "Well, this is certainly unexpected."

"Take one step back, Orion. Like I said, I need more time here."

The wind ruffled his silver hair, and his eyes pierced me. "Why?"

I smiled back. "Just some things I need to take care of. I'd ask you to help, but I really don't think you have it in you. Now why don't you take a step back and leave the important stuff to me? I am, after all, the Lightbringer."

He arched a quizzical eyebrow. "Is this what it feels like to be patronized?"

"It's actually very enjoyable, you know. I can see why you do it. Now fuck off, love." I pressed the knife a little harder against him. It was, according to my guess, just above his heart. I didn't want to kill him, of course. I wanted him trapped on the other side of Purgatory. "Please don't make me end your life."

He sighed and leaned down, his face close to mine. "Well, I guess it's a good thing you're not capable of it, then. But why, exactly, would you want to stay *here* without me? You really don't think you can—"

He reached for my wrist, but I headbutted him—hard, slamming my forehead into his nose. He stumbled back and disappeared in a flash of light.

I stared at the space where he'd been and rubbed the ache in my forehead.

"Thanks, Mom," I whispered, "for making me take those self-defense classes."

IN GOODY PUTNAM'S INN, I SIPPED A PEWTER FLAGON OF HOT BEER. I'd been here all day. On the one hand, she kept asking me to make a public penance. On the other, it was nice and warm inside, with a cozy fire, hot beer, and soup.

Sharp-eyed, Goody Putnam approached me with an expression of concern. She leaned over the table, eyes darting in either direction. "Goodman Ashur told me what happened to the hunters last night. But why would a woman be among them? It isn't natural."

Without Orion here to charm her, she made me pay double for food and drink. Good thing I was the one carrying the coins.

I put my finger to my lips. She knew I'd taken a vow of silence, and it saved me from having to fake an accent—and also from trying to figure out the old-fashioned grammar. From what I could tell, they said "you" when they were being polite and "thou" when they wanted to scream that you were a devil-shagging whore. But I didn't quite have the intricacies down, so it was better to keep my mouth shut.

She narrowed her eyes and pressed her palms on the table as she leaned closer. "Were you with the Malleus Daemoniorum, Goody Ashur, or did you separate yourselves from them for your own safety? Maybe you saw the devil?"

There it was again—that strange name. I simply put my finger to my lips again piously.

She nodded slowly. "Aye, the devil murdered our demon-finders. Burned them. Hacked them. Feasted on their bones. True evil." She bowed her head. "You are blessed to have survived."

Not exactly, Goody Putnam.

❧

THE FLAGON WARMED MY HANDS AS I ENTERED THE DARK WOODS. I'd spent all day at the inn, filling my stomach and warming myself by the fire.

As I'd walked through the forest, the setting sun had tinted the clouds with shades of periwinkle and cherry. With night falling, I wound my way between elms and yews, searching for the Dying God again.

Once the daylight disappeared completely, silver light streamed through the tree branches, casting glittering flecks of silver on the mossy earth.

The deeper I walked, the colder I felt, and my breath clouded around me. But the shawl was a huge improvement, warm wool that covered my back and shoulders.

The forest grew darker as I searched, and a chorus of whispers echoed off the trees—my own name repeated over and over until it started to sound meaningless and bizarre.

At last, I sensed the charged magic of the Dying God. A low, guttural growl trembled through the boughs, making my hair stand on end.

The symbols of Tammuz carved through the darkness, bright

slashes of light from the shadows. Dread turned my blood to ice, and my heart started to race.

"Tammuz..." I whispered his name, waiting for him to appear. Then, a little louder, "Tammuz."

Cold wind rushed between the trees, stinging my cheeks and fingers, and darkness streamed around me, blocking out the moonlight. A rush of primordial power skittered up my spine, making my back arch, and I nearly dropped the shawl.

It took me a moment to recall the words of the strange spell Orion had uttered last night. Even if I didn't know what the words meant, they'd been branded in my mind.

I spoke the words, power surging through my veins and lighting me up like the symbols around me.

From the dark earth, a ring of ivory mushrooms sprouted, and from a glittering swirl of snow, the Dying God slowly appeared in the center of the ring. Smoky shadows twined with the snowflakes.

"You summon me again, Lightbringer." His deep, growling voice trembled over the forest.

My breath shallowed. "Did you want me to hear what Orion will do if he becomes king?"

Tammuz faded into the darkness, reappearing behind my shoulder. "Yes," he whispered in my ear.

I jumped at the unexpected closeness and turned to look at him. His eyes were deep wells of darkness and pain.

My heart slammed against my ribs.

He flickered away into darkness, but his voice rumbled out of the shadows. "You must fight for the crown."

My fingers tightened on my flagon. Right now, I felt unsteady on my feet, unsure if this was all a strange dream. "Can you tell me what I am? And why there's more than one Lightbringer?"

"You are Mortana's ka." His voice came from inside my own mind.

"What is a ka?"

A dark, throbbing sound pounded from the ground beneath my feet. "An essence. A spirit. A ka lives in a person's body, then separates at death. The ka is a double, and it travels to the double world." He was standing behind me again, coldness radiating over me. "A ka lives on forever. You were here, once. Mortana's double in the world of death."

Fear slid around me, ice-cold. My teeth chattered uncontrollably. "Orion said he didn't think demons had souls."

"That's because he feels like he died a long time ago."

"So I'm Mortana?"

"No. Mortana once knew a spell for forgetting. She came here to these woods to conduct it." His voice echoed off the rocks and trees. "She removed her ren—her true name. It's the part of the soul that contained her memories. But in the process, she removed her ka, her life spirit, and her akh, her intelligence. She became an empty vessel, wandering through the forest mindlessly until the mortals captured her and killed her. After they hanged her, they soon forgot she existed at all."

That was what I'd seen in the vision, then. Mortana's death—here. "And where do I come from?"

"Her ka remained—her double. With my help, your parents brought you into the world of the living as a new person, with a new akh and ren. As Mortana's double, you are destined to rule as well."

I sucked in a deep breath. "If I have her essential spirit, wouldn't I be evil, too?"

He appeared before me, the shadows lapping at the air around him. "No one is born evil. Your mother raised you with love. Mortana was raised in the court of the mad King Azriel, separated from your parents. She grew up in a poisoned garden, twisted and sadistic."

I felt the air leave my lungs as I tried to wrap my head around it.

The world seemed to tilt beneath my feet. "Why? Why are you doing all of this?"

"Chaos." The words echoed around the grove, and I heard the flutter of wings and rustling leaves as birds took flight from the trees. "Lucifer, my twin, marked one to rule—Mortana. But Lucifer is a god of order and light. I am the god of chaos and shadows, the Night Bringer." He shimmered in and out of view. "The universe was made from chaos, and to chaos it will return. Order is as ephemeral as ashes scattered on the wind. It is not the natural state."

I breathed in deeply. "So you wanted a competition for the throne to make things interesting? And you want me to have a fighting chance against Orion."

"Yes." He was standing before me once more, shining in the dark grove. His body was enormous, towering over me. His coppery skin looked as solid as marble.

"Orion is the Lord of Chaos." I thought of Tammuz's reaction when Orion mentioned his father. "Orion's mother knew you. Any chance Orion is your son?"

"Yes," he hissed, "and the name he gave you is not his real one. He hardly remembers who he is."

My breath caught. "Why is he so convinced he was Nergal's son?"

"Because of the star he bears, marking him as heir to the throne. But Nergal had no children, no natural heir. Orion is a Lightbringer because I chose him as one." Runes of light slashed the air around him. "Rowan," he boomed, "ask what you came here to ask."

My throat tightened. "If you want me to have a fighting chance at the throne, I need your help. Orion is right—I can't fight like he can. I don't connect to my demon side, and I still feel like a mortal. Can you help me?"

A subtle smile played about his lips. "Welcome home, ka."

❧ 25 ❧

CHAPTER 25—ROWAN

Tammuz turned and started walking away from me into the dark. "You fear death. That is your weakness."

I stared at him. "Everyone is afraid of death. It's a basic part of human evolu—" I stopped myself. "Right. I'm not human. Surely demons fear death, too. It seems like an important part of staying alive."

He turned to face me again. "The Lord of Chaos does not. If anything, he envies the dead. But you are soft, Rowan. You are weak. You will fail."

Rude. My throat tightened. "Okay. I need to be less afraid of death." I closed my eyes. "But there's the fear of pain—"

"Why fear something that is over so quickly?"

"And then there's the fear of what comes after. Do I end up here? Do I just stop existing?"

"Why fear nonexistence?" he asked. "Do you feel afraid when you think of the past, before you existed?"

"No."

"Your body will feed the earth, as mine does once a year. Mushrooms grow from my flesh, and their mycelium spread beneath the forest floor, wrapping around the roots of trees that drink the light of the sun. Death gives birth to life, Rowan, darkness to light, and the spirit lives on in the cycle of life and death."

I heard distant shouts in the woods.

I knew things repeated here, that the dead came back to life. But were the Malleus Daemoniorum already back? I turned, catching sight of torches that pierced the dark.

The shouts were growing louder now, and I recognized Goody Putnam's voice. I froze, my heart rate speeding up as I stared between the tree trunks. I couldn't let them catch me here with the Dying God himself. So many torches, like moving fireflies. This wasn't just the Malleus Daemoniorum. This was an angry mob. How many mortals had come into the forest?

I turned back to the Dying God, but he was gone. Darkness had enveloped the woods completely, clouds covering the moon and stars.

Either Tammuz had ditched me again or he knew I couldn't be seen with him. But all of this was deeply inconvenient when I needed his help.

I turned and started hurrying away from the oncoming mob. If they managed to find me, I would explain that this was part of my penance—wandering in the cold woods. I turned to look over my shoulder. Why were they running so fast?

"Witch!" I heard the shout echo through the forest—Goody Putnam again. "She was consorting with the devil when the Malleus Daemoniorum were murdered!"

My chest went tight. What the hell, Goody Putnam?

"Where are you?" I whispered frantically to the Dying God.

At least these people had torches, which meant I should be able to keep away from them in the shadows. I hurried over the knotted tree roots, over the icy rocks. They seemed to be homing in on me with a surprising amount of accuracy, considering it was pitch black here.

"The spirit leads me to her," shouted a man's voice.

What the hell? I reached into my backpack, feeling around for the hilt of the knife. This would be a fantastic time to have my magic.

With a racing heart, I looked around for a place to hide, but I could hardly see in the darkness. Gripping my knife, I sneaked behind a large oak and peered around the trunk, watching the torches growing larger. The shouts were growing closer now, the mob hurling insults at me. "Thou foul witch. Thou demoness. Thou hast returned!"

They were coming at me with the *thous* again. Rude.

Someone was calling me a whore. I wasn't quite sure how that fit into the scenario, but it seemed to be a classic go-to insult whenever men were angry at women.

My only defense was the darkness, but it wasn't slowing them down a bit. As they started to close in again, I realized I had to move. I took one step. Two steps. My foot snapped a twig. I froze. Gunshots rang out behind me.

What had suddenly sent them after me? Had Goody Putnam suspected me?

"Kill her!" A male voice, full of primal rage. "She murdered the Malleus Daemoniorum!"

Bone-deep fear charged my body, and I tried to run through the trees, but the ground was uneven.

There were too many of them, their shouts growing louder, closer—

Another gunshot, and pain exploded through the back of my left shoulder. I grunted, reaching for it. Agony electrified my body, and I fell to my knees. I had to fight now.

A primal desperation for survival took over, forcing me to my feet. I turned, wildly flailing with my knife as the torches and bodies surrounded me. I stabbed someone, but a blade cut through my side. Another blow on the back of my head, and I lost my footing. They were all around me, these men in dark coats and tall hats.

One more crack to my skull, and my world went silent.

❧❧❧

I WOKE WITH THE EARLY MORNING SUNLIGHT STREAMING OVER ME, startled to find that I was still alive.

It took a moment for the pain to register. And when it did, I felt as if a knife were splitting my skull open from the back to the front. I tried to raise my hand to my head, but my arms had been tied tightly behind my back. My shoulder muscles burned. I was lying flat on something hard, like a bench.

Above me, red and gold leaves trembled on a tree branch. A gust of wind swept over me, catching the leaves and rolling them in the air. I breathed in deeply, my stomach turning. It smelled like death here.

And then I noticed something moving in the corner of my vision. Dread sank into my lungs. A noose dangled from the branch, swaying forlornly overhead.

I'd been warned. *Do you want to see how you'll die?* Maybe that wasn't Mortana's death I'd seen. *Fuck.*

Above me, the bough groaned in the wind, a haunting sound. I shifted, trying to sit up to get a better view.

"The demon wakes!" The deep male voice sent shockwaves of fear through my nerves.

I scrambled to get up, but with my arms tied, I was unsteady. On my knees now, I took in the horrifying scene around me. I was kneeling in a rickety cart that was rambling up Gallows Hill.

Where hundreds of years later a Dunkin' would stand—and my old powder-blue home—a grim crowd gathered. Men, women, and children glared at me, and Goody Putnam stood in the front row.

She pointed at me. "I saw her! I saw Goody Ashur signing the devil's book!" She continued to point at me, her expression furious. "I saw a goat sucking on her witch's teat!"

Four hundred years ago, the mortals hunted down others of their kind based on hearsay, paranoia, and the ravings of attention-seekers. Right now, an actual demon stood before them, and they were still spouting bullshit because there was no devil's book or teat-sucking goat. This would be hilarious if it weren't so terrifying.

Behind them, in the distance, I could see the road I'd walked in on, and the old Osborne Woods. A black house stood before the forest, and smoke rose from a chimney.

When I turned to look behind me, I saw the four women's corpses rotting at the ends of ropes, their bodies gray and purple. Like me, their hands had been bound behind their backs before they'd died. The stench of death was overpowering.

To my left, two horses were hitched to the cart. A man stood near them, dressed in black with a wide white collar and a dark tapered hat.

I tried to stand again, but the pain shot through my head, so sharp that nausea started to take over. I doubled over, vomiting onto the wooden cart. My hands involuntarily tried to jerk forward as I was sick, but the ropes kept them bound. I nearly lost my balance. When I'd stopped vomiting, I wiped my mouth off on my shoulder.

I straightened again, staring out at the crowd. Goody Putnam took a step forward, pointing at me. "She bewitched the chowder. She made me feel lustful things."

The sharp forms of this particular terror were starting to take shape. I understood what was about to happen, and I could hardly breathe. I *had* been warned. Why hadn't Tammuz stepped in if he'd wanted me to have a chance against Orion?

"I didn't bewitch anything!" I shouted. "Don't I get a trial? A trial!"

"Listen to her strange manner of speech!" someone shouted.

The man in black nodded at two men in the crowd—a ruddy-cheeked man with a dark beard and a broad-shouldered man with piercing eyes. The two of them marched closer to the cart, then climbed inside.

"I haven't bewitched anyone or touched a goat. I swear to you," I said. "A trial! Even the Puritans had trials."

One of the men grabbed me hard, and the other slid the noose around my neck. I struggled against them, but without my arms, there wasn't much I could do. Once they'd secured the noose around my neck, the two men jumped from the cart.

With a hammering heart, I glanced at the horses. Once someone whipped them, the cart would disappear beneath me. My neck would break if I was lucky. I'd strangle to death if I was not. That could take twenty minutes.

At executions in the old days, loved ones would tug on the condemned person's feet to make it go faster if the victim's neck didn't break. What a terrible task that would be. Maybe it was a mercy no one I knew was here, a grim sort of blessing not to have family around to watch you die.

I wasn't really going to die, though, was I? This couldn't happen.

I surveyed the angry crowd in front of me.

"Demon, demon," they were shouting. "Wicked temptress!"

I struggled against my bound wrists, the ropes chafing my skin. I glanced down, my heart hammering, as I spotted the frozen, rocky earth beneath the cart. In the vision, I'd seen my own feet dangling above that very ground.

"Judge Corwin!" Goody Putnam's voice rose above the din. "Make her confess!"

The man in black stepped in front of me, wearing a black coat and a silver hammer pin. He clutched a black book to his chest. His eyes were a cold, flinty gray. The family resemblance was unmistakable. *Corwin.*

He looked every bit as nice as his descendant, Jack Corwin.

My heart skipped a beat. I looked out over the angry crowd as if I were expecting someone to ride up and save me, but I saw only the forest.

Tammuz, you chaotic bastard. Was this all you'd wanted from me? To die here surrounded by fucking morons?

The judge held up a hand, and the crowd went silent. He grinned, exposing long, yellowed teeth. "Confess, thou witch, and we might free thee."

That was a trick, wasn't it? If I told them I was a demon, they wouldn't let me go. They'd kill me. "I'm not a demon," I said desperately. That was a lie, of course. "I don't have any magical power." That part was true, at least at the moment.

"Didst thou kill four men last night?" the judge bellowed, steam rising from his lips.

"No!" I shouted.

True. I'd only killed one of them.

His eyes narrowed. "And didst thou kill thine own kin? Because thou wert afraid?"

The temperature plummeted, and I started to shake. The cart was rattling beneath me, and the sky started to darken. Charcoal gray clouds were rolling in strangely fast. Thunder rumbled overhead.

I stared at him, too stunned to speak. How did he know that? Did he know I'd left Mom behind in these woods?

"Didst thou kill thine own kin?" asked the judge. "Thou hast chosen thine own life! Thy soul art corrupted with evil. Woe be unto thee with wickedness in thy blood!"

How the fuck would he know that? I thought the underworld had been frozen in time. He was talking about things from a few years ago.

"Confess!" he roared. "And we will set thee free. We ask only that thou tellest the truth. Tell us all the wicked ways thou hast saved thyself, demon. How thou hast sacrificed thy kin."

What the *hell?*

The crowd started jeering again.

I shouted at them, "I should get a trial. Everyone had trials. We are English subjects. It's in the Magna Carta, for fuck's sake!" My voice echoed. My panic had me swearing at a group of bloodthirsty Puritans.

The judge's hammer pin gleamed in the winter sun. His grin widened, lupine. "Thou hath pleasure in thy wickedness."

"The keys," I said quietly. "Do you want to hear about the keys?"

The judge's smile faded completely. "Speak not in thy demon tongue! Thou shalt not suffer a demon to live!"

He lifted the whip and cracked it against the horses. They started to run, taking the cart with them and ripping it out from underneath me.

If you were lucky, your neck snapped, but mine didn't. The rough rope crushed my throat, and my legs kicked helplessly in the air. All the blood rushed into my head, and my body commanded me to live, even though I was dying.

My lungs were going to explode.

Never in my life had I understood how precious it was to breathe, how glorious it was to take oxygen deep inside your chest. Never had I felt so desperate to live, to savor every moment. Maybe they would still let me out of this. Maybe they were trying to scare me before the trial.

I wanted to dial back the clock, to relish each second from my past.

Ten-sixteen at night. I wanted to go back before that moment.

Memories exploded in my mind, and I felt myself tugged into the past—lying in the grass in summer and watching the clouds sliding overhead, my fingers sticky with melted popsicles. One day, I'd tried on my mom's bra and stuffed it with socks. The boy next door told me the big kids called them *tits*.

The summer sky melted away, and I was jumping into the town pool, making as big a splash as possible. The lifeguard blew the whistle. I'd nearly hit someone.

"Murderess!" The word ripped the memories from my mind again.

I'd been so sure the Dying God had wanted me for something, that he'd had a plan. I'd been *certain*.

Another memory: graduation from elementary school, when Mom took me to my favorite burger place and let me order whatever I wanted, and I had a chocolate milkshake. I thought it was the best day of my life, and I remembered how Mom laughed when I'd told her that, and I didn't understand why.

My mom used to sing me a lullaby...

I could feel her here now, with me. She was on the other side, waiting for me.

But my vision was going dark, and pure panic took over my mind until there were no words left. Until I hardly had a mind anymore to think with.

Death reached for me, but along with it came something warm and familiar. I could feel Mom. If this was death, I didn't have to be so scared anymore. I had no mind left, no body. Just the feeling of love on the other side.

And the darkness swallowed me whole.

26

CHAPTER 26—ORION

I knew I was dreaming, but I still felt as if she were right here before me. I could smell her in my dream, intoxicating.

She was standing on the coffee table in my living room, no longer in the thick woolen dress. Now, she wore a short black dress with long sleeves that puffed at the shoulders. A line of buttons ran down the front, and her red hair cascaded over the dark silk. She wore black stilettos.

My arms had been bound behind me with thick rope that chafed at my wrists...

Why was I dreaming about having my arms bound?

For a moment, I felt a strange sense of urgency, a desperation to rip free of them.

I was here now, with Rowan—or Mortana. If I could move, I could touch her. Taste her. She was only two feet away from me. If I could move my arms, I could pull her into my lap. I wanted to fuck her again, more than I'd ever wanted anything.

But that was a betrayal of Ashur and all the rest. I *owed* him revenge. There had to be, after all, a reason I'd survived when none of the others had. Why me, when I was the worst among them?

Because I could kill so easily—a brutal skill that I'd been born with.

It was my one purpose. I must speak for the dead, to exact revenge when they no longer could. I was their voice and their sword. I would make the mortals pay.

I couldn't trust Rowan. And even if she'd changed—even if she was a new person completely—I was sure she would betray me.

But all those ideas were flying out of my head right now because Rowan was standing on the table in high heels, and I could not keep my eyes off her thighs.

I pulled my gaze up to stare at her lush red lips. How was it that her face looked innocent and sinful all at once? Her beauty overwhelmed me. It always had.

She took a step closer to me, heels clacking on the mahogany. "You know, Orion, I still remember your real name. From the old days. You were always so desperate to please me back then. I loved it when you begged."

She started to unbutton the top of her dress, and my blood pounded. Under the dress, she wore a red silk bra.

"What are you doing?" My voice came out husky and desperate.

She bit her lip coquettishly. "What I've always done. Tormenting you. I like the feeling of power I've got over you, Orion." Her dress was unbuttoned to her navel now, and I stood entranced as she opened it further, revealing sheer red underwear.

She let the dress drop to the floor. I swallowed hard as she stepped down off the coffee table, posing before me with a tantalizing bounce of her breasts.

She pulled down one strap of her bra. "Orion, I want you to tell me that I'm your queen. Don't you think I would make a better ruler than you?"

Her nipple was exposed—pink and hard—and I could no longer think straight. Queen...? I wanted her mouth wrapped around me.

She pulled down the other strap, and I desperately wanted her to untie me. My cock was now painfully hard.

Between us, the air felt charged with sexual desire. I fed from hers, just as she fed from mine. "I don't even want you, Rowan. Haven't I already told you that? I find you tedious."

Her gaze moved to my crotch, where the evidence of my mendacity was obvious. "Is that so?"

"Why don't you start by untying me?" I rasped. "And then we will negotiate what I will and will not agree to."

She stepped between my knees and straddled me, pressing her breasts against my chest. Her bare thighs were wrapped around my waist.

I was going to lose my mind. Perhaps it was already gone. Every muscle in my body was tense, coiled tight.

I exhaled a long, shuddering breath. *Stay in control, Orion.* She was, of course, the same Mortana she'd always been.

Clenching her thighs around mine, she leaned back a little and started unbuttoning my shirt. "So much hate in you, Orion. Don't you think you would make a terrible king? Don't you think the world would be better off with you as my subject, seeing to my needs?" She pulled open the last button and stroked her hand down my chest. "Think about how much you'd truly love to submit to me..."

"Fuck, no." Right now, I wanted nothing more than to lie back and let her ride me. I ached to caress her, but for the sake of Ashur, I was denying myself what I wanted.

She unbuttoned my pants, fingers grazing against me.

I gasped, and she gave me a wicked smile. "Liar. I know what you want. I can feel it in the air, you know." Her fingers brushed against me again, and I gritted my teeth.

I will give almost anything if you use my body—

She looked down, then gave me a half smile. Leaning forward, she nestled her head into the crook of my neck. Her breasts pressed against my bare chest, and she trailed hot kisses over my skin. She moved her hips against me, and I groaned, no longer able to control myself. "Why don't you untie me, love?" I murmured. "And I'll give you what you need."

She brushed her lips against mine. "I think about you, Orion. Do you know, when I was near death, I thought of you? When the Malleus Daemoniorum nearly killed me, I hungered for you. Because you know, Orion, for Lilu like us, sex isn't just sex. It's life."

She stood up again, giving me a full view of her sexy body, and tension coiled tight within me.

Sliding her hands into the sides of her underwear, she pulled them down slowly. *Fuck.* She was pure perfection, and my tongue ached to caress every inch of her skin, to lick her between her thighs...

When she straddled me again, I could tell she was as turned on as I was. Her hand slid between her legs, grazing my shaft as she moved it. I couldn't take my eyes off her, and my hips jerked against her. "Rowan," I moaned in desperation.

This was *agony*.

"I think about you when I'm turned on," she said breathlessly. "I always have."

It was, I realized, what I'd always wanted to hear, and my breath caught. I was the dead coming to life with electric currents—a painful process, but the only thing that would get my blood pumping once more. I needed to be inside her.

As my lust mingled with hers, I'd been feeding, gaining in strength, in the power of an incubus. The ropes strained against my wrists, and I pulled with all my might, ripping the strands and fibers of the bindings apart. Rowan leapt up, but I captured her in my arms.

I threw her down on my sofa and spread her thighs wide. She had a victorious sort of smile as I pinned her wrists above her head. At last, I slid into her, the pleasure overwhelming. She reached for my hair, threading her fingers into it. This wasn't just sex though, was it? We were connected. She was a part of me, the music of my life, and I needed her. Flames ignited in my heart.

"Rowan," I said huskily, "tell me you will never betray me."

"Orion," she whispered, "I thought about you when I died."

The embers in my chest snuffed out. My blood ran cold, and I stopped moving. "What did you just say?"

She touched the side of my face. "I thought about you when I died in the underworld. You know I'm not really here, right?"

I WOKE, MY HEART SLAMMING AGAINST MY RIBS, AND LOOKED around my dark room. Loneliness pierced me, and my body felt cold. I tried to shake off the feeling of horror.

That was a dream though, wasn't it? She hadn't *actually* died.

Catching my breath, I touched my chest. My heartbeat felt sluggish and dull.

For the first time in ages, the embers in my heart lay dead.

Did I miss her that much?

I'd lived for one reason, and one reason alone: to act as the sword of the dead. To give them the revenge they wanted.

But something felt *wrong*, and I desperately wanted to see Rowan again.

✣ 27 ✣

CHAPTER 27—ORION

I sat on my balcony, sipping Syrah and trying to shake off the horror of my bad dream. Moonlight dappled the ocean with silver, and a warm, salty breeze rolled off the water. It was always magically warm here in the City of Thorns, a perfect temperature for my future kingdom.

Three in the morning was an absurd time to drink wine, but I hadn't been able to get back to sleep since I'd woken with my heart thundering. Something still felt *off* in the world. Unbalanced. Dread threaded through my veins.

Maybe the dream meant nothing, and it was just nerves for the impending regicide I had planned in a few hours. By dawn, I should be standing before the Tower of Baal's gates, holding the severed head of Cambriel, his blood dripping just below Nergal's head. The whole city would see the mark of Lucifer beaming from my forehead. They would all know their true king had arrived at last.

It wouldn't be long until my demon subjects would be ripping the mortals to shreds when I unleashed hell on Earth. I'd dreamed of this for centuries, ever since they'd marched me by my family's severed heads on the way to the prison.

So why the fuck did I feel such an overwhelming sense of dread?

I shifted in my chair, disturbed by the late-night quiet.

I lifted my glass of wine, watching the moonlight reflect off its dark surface. I suppose what bothered me was that I had no idea what Rowan was doing. But why would she delay her return here?

Maybe I needed to understand what she was.

I set the glass of wine on a table and went back into my library. Ka...a word from the ancient days, something buried deep under centuries of mundane memories.

From my bookshelf, I pulled out an old tome called *Book of the Dead*, its binding brown leather etched with gold letters. I dropped into a velvet armchair and flipped through the yellowed handwritten pages.

From a sconce behind me, candlelight wavered over the old book. It was written in an ancient demonic language that I could read, albeit slowly. I found a page with a strange drawing of a horned demon. Not quite horns, I supposed, but rather arms and hands jutting from his head.

My blood pounded harder as I read through the text. According to this book, demons had souls like mortals did. And a soul wasn't just a spirit but comprised of several different aspects: the life-force (ka), the personality (ba), and the memories (ren).

When someone died, their ka left the body and became a double. The ka lived on—a sort of demonic doppelgänger in the world of the dead. Rowan, then, had somehow come from the doubleworld.

My heart leapt at the implication. If all this was true, then the original Mortana was dead.

And the real question at the heart of this was whether this made Rowan the same person as Mortana.

Fucked if I knew. I wasn't a philosopher.

On the one hand, she was clearly different. She had different memories, different experiences to shape her life, a very different personality...all those aspects of her soul had changed. Rowan had chosen to save my life twice—once in Purgatory, and again in the forest. Letting me die would have solved all her problems, and all she'd have had to do was fail to act. Mortana would have left me to die, without a doubt.

Guilt clenched my chest. If she wasn't Mortana, I'd been cruel to her for no reason.

Then again, I had to find a way to keep myself away from her, no matter what. This new Rowan would try to pull me off my path. She'd never accept the revenge I craved.

I slammed the book shut and traced my fingers over its surface. Already, she was distracting me. I had a king to kill, and I needed to clear my head.

I prowled across the room for my collection of knives. This was all I would need to kill the king—daggers to slaughter the guards.

I strapped them to my waist, my thighs, loading myself up with blades.

Fully armed, I crossed out to the balcony. For a moment, I stood there, looking out over the dark sea. If things went according to plan, this would all be over soon. After everything that had happened to us, an incubus would be on the throne.

My wings shot out from my shoulder blades, kissed by the balmy ocean breeze. As they pounded the air, I took off into the dark night sky.

Now, I no longer cared if the whole city knew I was Lilu. Let them stare. They'd be kneeling before me soon.

Every one of them who'd stood by while the Lilu were slaughtered would be on their knees.

❈

AT THE TOP OF THE TOWER OF BAAL, THE AIR THINNED. I LANDED quietly on the balcony, the wind howling around me. No one bothered to lock a balcony door when it was over five thousand cubits high, piercing the night sky.

No one knew I could fly.

I pulled one of the knives from its sheath and slowly slid the balcony door open.

Silently, I moved over the black and white mosaic floor. With the moonlight streaming in, I could make out the contour of Cambriel sleeping next to someone in a bed with sea-blue blankets.

The enormous room was made of sharply peaked arches and columns of pale stone. Engravings of beautiful winged goddesses jutted from the tops of some of the columns, and the arches had been painted with constellations. Maybe the monarchs had killed my kind, but they still liked to use us as inspiration for art.

The air smelled faintly as if they'd just been having sex, which I didn't want to think about. Briny air rushed into the room, toying with the gauzy curtains.

Neither of them stirred as I quietly approached. The woman's presence was annoying, but I should be able to silence her easily enough. I pulled another knife from a sheath and threw it into the air. The blade found its mark, and the hilt jutted from the woman's throat. I'd severed her voice box, so she couldn't scream, and I rushed over to the bed before she could wake the king with her flailing. Up close now, I slit the king's throat. Blood sprayed over the bed.

This was how I had known that I was destined to rule: no one else could spend hundreds of years in a dungeon and emerge knowing exactly how to murder people with the precision and efficiency of a trained warrior. When Lucifer had marked me, he'd endowed me with unnatural gifts.

I pulled another knife out and crawled between the two demons as they bled onto their pillows. My claws elongated, and with a feral snarl, I ripped the king's heart from his chest.

I shoved his limp body out of the bed and lifted his blood-stained pillow.

Nothing lay beneath it.

What the *fuck*, Rowan?

The king started making a gurgling sound, already healing. This was the magic of the book, of course, because otherwise, he'd be dead without a heart. Had she lied?

I shoved the bleeding woman off the bed, and she dropped onto the tile floor with a thud. No book under her pillow, either.

My heart pounded like a war drum, and the king let out a strangled scream as he healed.

In the next heartbeat, two guards burst into the room, swords drawn. But a sword wasn't much use from across the room, which was

would be possible for her to lie to me about the book. Nor had I expected her to pull a knife on me and kick me out of the underworld without her.

Alarms started ringing across the city, but they sounded dull to my ears. I soared over the ancient city of stone.

Right now, the only thing that seemed real to me was that horrible dream—Rowan telling me that she'd died. But if it wasn't real, why did I feel her absence like a tangible thing, like it was cold soil burying me?

Why did the world seem so silent, so frozen? This beautiful city had become a tomb—an enormous dungeon.

She was dead.

Ice settled in my veins. As much as I wanted to scrape up the king's remains, my mind was on Rowan.

An unfamiliar feeling—*fear*—crept over my skin.

What if Rowan *had* died beyond the veil? Maybe if I hadn't been so hellbent on pushing her away, she'd be with me now.

You can't hate someone you don't respect.

Dread chilled my blood. I'd been an asshole.

I soared over the city gates and started to head for the world beyond the veil. It would take me days to get back to her, to get through Purgatory and find out what had happened, but I wasn't going to wait any longer.

CHAPTER 28—ROWAN

I opened my eyes, allowing them to adjust to the darkness. I lay on frozen earth. A grave, perhaps? A few rays of silver moonlight shone on the icicles hanging from the trees around me. Not buried underground, then.

It felt as though someone had ripped out my skeleton and shoved it back in my body.

My breath came out in icy puffs. The cold air stung my cheeks and hands, and my teeth chattered. I rolled over onto my side and pushed myself up. Would I see Mom here? My vision sharpened. I was still in the underworld, which I suppose made sense. After all, I *was* dead.

"Rowan." I jumped at the sound of my name and turned to see Tammuz, the Dying God. Star-flecked shadows slithered over his bronze skin. He took a few steps closer to me. "You've returned."

"Thanks for the help."

"I drew the mob here." He towered over me, unnaturally tall. "I thought you needed to die."

I was still on the ground, but I was too exhausted to stand. "Some might consider that insulting, you know."

"You needed to die," he said again, "so that I could bring you back to life again. It's the only way to stop you from fearing death."

I rose on unsteady feet. "You brought me back to life? So...I'm not dead? I can leave the underworld?"

I looked down. The dress was gone, and I was wearing leather pants, a shirt, and a warm coat with a black fur collar.

"You were right, Rowan," he said. "I want you to have a chance at the crown. It's no fun if Orion takes it without any competition, is it?"

He faded into the shadows and reappeared a few inches from me in a gust of cold wind. Reaching up, he touched my cheek. He had the same high cheekbones as Orion, the same sharp jaw. Thick black eyebrows. He was a god, tens of thousands of years old, but he looked no older than thirty.

"How did it feel?" he asked, his dark eyes gleaming with curiosity.

"Not great, Tammuz," I said. "Strangling to death is *not* my idea of a good time." I swallowed. "But at the end, I felt like I was heading to my mom." I waved a hand at my new duds. "How did I wind up in these clothes?"

"They grew with you from the earth." He held my gaze and nodded. "You were with your mother for thirteen hours."

My jaw dropped, and I felt a wild sort of excitement. "What? Why don't I remember it?"

"I can't allow you to remember it."

"Why not?"

"Because it's not a memory for the living," he said with finality.

"For the living..." I repeated, my thoughts slow and sluggish. But I'd recently died, so I wouldn't be too hard on myself.

His eyebrow arched. "Do you know, that's exactly how Mortana died? Your death played out the same way. You and she experienced the same death."

I rubbed my throat. "They kept yelling at me, saying that I'd sacrificed my kin to save myself. It was like they knew what had happened with my mom." I frowned. "I guess the same goes for Mortana. She sacrificed all the Lilu to save her own ass."

"In the double world," he said in a faraway voice, "people play out the same tragedies, again and again."

He stepped back on the frosted earth and lifted his right hand.

Silver claws grew from his fingertips. Shimmering, he vanished and reappeared a few feet away. "Orion has almost no fear."

"Because he believes his soul died in the dungeon." I looked down at Tammuz's claws, and my heart clenched. "You're...uh...not going to kill me again, are you?"

"No. I am going to teach you to fight like a demon. You may die in the process, if you are not careful, but you will return again."

I raised my eyebrows. "That'll take a long time, I'm afraid. How long do we have?"

"Time passes differently in the doubleworld. We will take as long as we need. As my son, Orion inherited my ability to kill, but you will have to learn it."

I was going to fight with the Dying God in a frozen underworld. I waited for terror or a feeling of dread, but I'd already died and had nothing to fear anymore.

I lunged forward. Claws sprang from my fingertips, and I struck at Tammuz's chest, but I'd been too slow, hesitating at the last moment.

His claws ripped through me before I could take another breath.

USING A TREE BRANCH, I PULLED MYSELF UP, FEELING THE ACHE IN my muscles. The ice stung my fingers, and the cold air burned my lungs. I sucked in a deep breath and exhaled, sending billows of frosty mist floating among the crystalline branches.

I'd died four times so far, and I was starting to get used to it. Tammuz had a thing for killing me and bringing me back...when he wasn't finding ways to torture me with exercise and endless sparring. But truth be told, I was enjoying the physicality of our encounters. It helped me shut off my mind and forget the visions he'd given me.

But it also made me wildly hungry, and I was surviving on acorns and berries, not the most satisfying of diets.

Tammuz materialized in the dark grove. "Enough. It's time for you to run."

I dropped out of the tree onto the snowy earth and did as the god commanded.

WITH MY WINGS OUT, I SOARED BEHIND HIM OVER SNOW-FROSTED trees. His deep gold wings glowed, making him easy to follow through the night sky. The speed of our chase exhilarated me. We pitched and rolled though the marine winds.

The icy sea air tore through my hair, and I raced after Tammuz over the waves. I angled my wings like he did, curving back over the rocky shore.

A WINTER WIND WHISPERED THROUGH THE TREES. THE DYING GOD stood behind me. Placing his hands on my hips, he shifted my stance slightly.

"Bend your legs more," he said. "Swing your torso, twist your hips, and use your whole body."

I obeyed, punching the air slowly, trying to perfect my form.

"Good. Faster."

My fist shot out, lightning-quick.

He disappeared, materializing again in front of me. I aimed for his jaw, but he blocked it.

FINALLY, I LANDED A PUNCH TO HIS TEMPLE, MY KNUCKLES STINGING with the force of the blow.

His response was swift and brutal. Pressing his right forearm against my throat, Tammuz crushed me against a tree trunk. I stared into his dark, forest-green eyes. Pain pierced me, a momentary shock, and then his claws ripped my ribs apart, and darkness fell.

FROM THE GROUND, TAMMUZ SWEPT AT MY FEET, SCISSORING HIS legs. I spread my wings and rose into the air. Snapping my wings shut, I dropped, landing on his ribs, and slammed my fist into his face.

Something caught my eye—a dark rock covered in snow. It reminded me of chocolate cake. Hunger was driving me mad.

He flung me aside, sending me crashing into a tree. Leaping to his feet, he darted into the woods. I followed close at his heels, dodging tree branches.

☙❧

AFTER MONTHS OF TRAINING WITH TAMMUZ, I'D GROWN INFINITELY stronger, but also hungry as fuck. There was no pizza here in the underworld, no ice cream.

Each day, I slept in the cottage with the warm fire and the bearskin rug. Tammuz had given me a gift—my demonic magic had returned. But he didn't seem to eat, so I was on my own in that regard. The thought of clam chowder from the inn was tempting, but if I left the forest, I'd be hanged before I had time to enjoy the first bite.

My stomach ached as I wandered back to the cabin, looking for anything I could forage along the way. Sometimes, I gathered mushrooms, juniper berries, acorns, cranberries, and wintergreen for tea.

The sun was up, and tangerine light spread over the snow. It *looked* good enough to eat, sweet and fruity, like Italian ice.

In the morning light, a splash of ivory caught my eye. My stomach rumbled. A large cluster of oyster mushrooms sprouted from a log across a snowy clearing. Ravenous, I hurried over and ripped them from the log, shoving them into my little leather bag. I knew from experience that they tasted better cooked. As much as I wanted to gobble them raw, I'd wait and fry them in an iron pan back at the cabin.

Unfortunately, mushrooms had almost no calories. Kneeling on the icy ground, I foraged every bit of the fungus, soaking the knees of my pants in the wet snow.

The forest was my guide and the key to my survival, telling me what to eat and where to find it. I knew, for instance, that the white mushrooms that sprang up behind Tammuz were toxic and would make me vomit for days.

Goosebumps rose on my skin. The forest was speaking to me. I looked up from the log, the faint sound of moving water catching my attention. A stream I hadn't yet discovered.

Lured by the promise of food, I started running, kicking up snow behind me. The forest didn't disappoint. Water swirled between rocks, and rainbow trout slowly swam in a pool.

My claws came out, my mouth already watering. Ignoring the freezing cold, I waded in to catch my dinner.

⚜

A HEAVY SNOW FELL AROUND US. FOR THE FIRST TIME, I WAS training with a full belly, and I felt strong. Tammuz swiped at me, claws out, and I dodged him. Momentum brought his head down, and I punched him twice, exactly like he'd taught me.

As he recovered, I thought I saw a faint smile.

⚜

WRAPPED IN A BLANKET BEFORE THE HEARTH, I SOAKED MY FEET IN warm water, muscles burning, and slowly ate a piece of venison jerky. Months of endless winter had passed. Maybe a year.

After the great trout discovery, I'd grown strong and fast enough to hunt deer with a knife. For the past two months, meat had been on the menu.

Chewing, I leaned back and let my calves soak in the warm water. Outside, the sun was starting to set.

The passage of time here confused me, and it didn't help that I'd died so many times. After the initial hanging, at least all the deaths Tammuz delivered had been mercifully quick. Each time he'd ripped my heart out, death had come too soon for me to register the pain. So far, I hadn't managed to return the favor, not once.

Each time he killed me, I awakened surrounded by snow and bone-white mushrooms and the vague impression that I'd seen Mom again.

Each time, I was wearing a brand-new warrior's outfit.

All night, I ran and sparred. I built my muscles. I learned to hit and kick and bring out my claws. I died, again and again. I learned to summon fire, to unleash my wings. Over and over, I practiced, using my demonic strength and sense of balance in ways that mortals could not. I leapt high, swinging from branches. I learned how to inflict damage with my elbows and how to hover in the air to kick.

Sometimes, when the Dying God had a blade to my throat and the shadows whipped around him, I'd feel the familiar sting of fear, but it wasn't the same, not like it once had been.

I'd learned. I knew now that it would all be over, and fast.

I returned from being dead again and again. The old terror no longer clung to me, sliding away like pasta coated in oil.

I finished the jerky and picked up my mug of hot pine needle tea. The steam swirled around me. Soon, I'd be asleep on the floor. Every time I curled up on the bear skin rug, I'd think of Orion and the first time we'd come here. And that was how I drifted off to sleep each morning.

A lonely sort of peace had found me in this cabin and quiet isolation.

Only one thing troubled me now: did I have it in me to take Orion down?

What if the only way to stop him was to kill him, but I couldn't bring myself to do it?

✣ 29 ✣

CHAPTER 29—ROWAN

The months stretched on, and my patience with the Dying God wore thin. I stood across from him in the clearing, ice daggers glittering from the tree branches around us. I felt infinitely stronger now than I once had, ready to take on anything, but he still didn't think I was ready.

Snowflakes drifted around us, sparkling in the moonlight. Dark, smoky magic twined around him, a tunic of shadows against his bronzed skin.

Tammuz moved in a blur of speed, but I was ready for him this time. I'd learned through painful trial and error that you couldn't simply lunge for a demon's heart—he'd find a way to protect it, pivoting away on instinct. I'd felt the same impulse every time Tammuz had darted toward me, and I'd turn, taking his claws in my shoulder or back. Anything but the heart, and a demon would be fine, recovering almost instantly. So when Tammuz wanted to kill me, he'd beat the shit out of me first, raining blows and punches to my head, until my reflexes slowed and I staggered, forgetting to shield.

While I wasn't so scared of death anymore, I was done with getting hit in the head. And the loneliness cut me down to my bones.

"Tammuz," I said, "you've got to let me go at some point."

Snow fell on his bare shoulders and arms and melted into glistening droplets. "No."

I sighed. "Are you lonely? Is that it?" I knew why he was keeping me here. It was no fun for the god of chaos if I didn't stand a chance in the fight for the throne, but I was tired of being controlled.

He faded into the shadows and appeared behind me. "You don't fight like you want to kill yet, Rowan. You fight like it's your hobby. You need to connect with your rage."

I didn't want to kill Orion, but maybe that wasn't who I needed to think about when I fought.

I closed my eyes, envisioning my half brother, Cambriel, hunting Mom through the woods. I pictured him unleashing an arc of fire on her. She'd burned to death trying to protect me.

Ice-cold rage slid through my veins. I turned to face the Dying God, but Tammuz had changed. He'd transformed into the false king, his dark hair lightened to pale blond. A golden crown rested on his head.

Cambriel. I hated that arrogant prick.

This was what I'd dedicated my life to—revenge. And finally, I was strong enough to make it mine.

He'd killed my whole family, all because he was desperate to stay on a throne he never deserved.

Fury cracked through my body like lightning. As he moved forward, swinging a punch at me, I grabbed his arm, blocking the blow, and slammed my other hand into his trapped arm. A bone cracked, and Cambriel grunted in pain.

Kill. The word blazed through my mind. *Kill.*

I leapt into the air, gripped a tree branch, and kicked him hard in the jaw. He flew backward into a trunk.

By the time I descended, he'd already recovered. He lashed out at my head, but I ducked. I straightened and sent another hard blow to his jaw, then a fast left hook. His head snapped back, but he landed the next punch. The blow dizzied me for a moment. I regained my footing and flew into the air, wings spreading out behind me. As I plummeted, I brought my heel down hard onto his head. The force of the kick slammed him into the frozen earth. Angling my wings, I dove for him, claws gleaming.

I came down on his chest, and Cambriel's dark eyes opened wide in surprise. Hungry for vengeance, I carved his heart from his chest with my claws. I caught my breath. Blood dripped from my hands onto the snow. Never in my life had I felt so much like a wild beast.

As I stared at the body, it transformed back into Tammuz—his skin and hair darker now, his arms bare. He was completely naked.

I held the heart of a god in my hands and watched him die, the life fading from his dark eyes. Panic gripped me, but then I remembered that Tammuz did this all the time.

My claws retracted, and I dropped his heart on the ground. Smoke swept around him, and his body disappeared, leaving bloodstains behind in the snow. I sat to catch my breath, trying not to think about what had happened.

I'd just been sitting on Orion's naked dad.

My body raced with adrenaline. So *that* was what it felt like to be a hunter—to be a demon. I stared down at my bloody palms, then wiped them clean on the snow, washing the god's blood from my hands as best I could.

Leaning back against a tree trunk, I waited for Tammuz to return. The loneliness of the quiet forest pierced me. For what had felt like ages, I'd been nothing but a warrior. Tammuz wasn't the best company.

Slowly, a circle of ivory mushrooms pushed through the snow—Destroying Angels, they were called. Maybe that was what I'd become.

Then the Dying God sprouted from the earth like a plant. He was lying on his back, his hair spread out around him. Smoke snaked around his powerful body, and his dark tattoos slid into place.

Fully formed, he opened his eyes and sat up, breathing in deeply. He rose to his full height, his expression bemused. He glanced to the east, toward the ocean where the morning sun was starting to rise.

I got to my feet, brushing the snow off my clothes. Exhaustion pulled at me. "Glad to see you back, Tammuz."

"No, you're not." His voice echoed around me in a deep chorus. "Go to sleep, Rowan. Rest. At nightfall, you will leave." He met my gaze. "It's time for you to kill the false king."

Joy leapt in my heart.

Finally, I was ready. I would take down the monster who'd killed my mom.

And I hoped Orion didn't get in my way.

◌◌

I AWOKE IN THE EARLY EVENING, MY NORMAL CIRCADIAN RHYTHM now fully backward, and prepared to leave the forest for what seemed like the first time in a year. Readying for my departure, I dressed in one of the outfits Tammuz had given me, tight black leather pants and a shirt, and a dark cape around my shoulders.

As I walked through the forest, the sun was starting to set, spreading across the sky in lurid shades of pumpkin and honey. Night had fully descended by the time I reached the old Walcott Street.

Since I had no interest in hanging again or getting attacked by a mob, I quickly headed for the coastline, reminding myself that only a few hours had passed in the rest of the underworld. If anyone caught sight of me, they'd realize I was no longer hanging at the end of a rope where I should be.

Dark waves churned and crashed against the rocky shoreline. Under the ebony sky, the sea frothed and foamed on slick rocks. Hiding my face in the hood of the cloak, I hurried along the coast, the briny wind whipping at me, following a salty tributary toward Salem Village. Heron stood along the edge of the river, and I wondered what they'd done to end up here. A strange little hut of twigs and dried mud had been built by the riverside. *Wattle and daub*, I thought. It had a thatched roof with a rough clay chimney, and smoke curled into the darkening sky. A strange, witchy little place.

I kept my face covered as I hurried along, but just as I scurried past the door, I heard someone call my name and went still.

"Rowan?" The voice was familiar. Familiar and loved...

My heart sped up as a woman poked her head out of the hut.

Shai's hair hung in beautiful black ringlets around her head. She was dressed in a gray dress with a wide white collar. I stared at her, stunned.

"Shai?"

She hurried over to me and grabbed me by the arms. "Are you really here? Oh, my God. Rowan?"

"Are *you* really here?" I was too shocked to say anything else.

"How long have we been stuck here?" she asked. "It feels like a week."

I shook my head. "I think time flows differently for you and me. I've been here a year."

Her eyes widened, and she gripped my arm more tightly. "*What?*"

"I don't understand," I said. "How did you end up here? I thought only demons could go beyond the veil, and mortals who—" I froze. "Mortals who died."

Her smile faltered, and she let go of my arm. "I don't think I'm dead. I'd know if I was dead, right?"

No one else here seemed to realize they were dead. With a lump in my throat, I asked, "What do you remember about how you got here?"

"The car disappeared as we were driving. Then I landed hard by a frozen forest. Oh, and there were caves...Rowan, I don't think I'm dead."

I swallowed hard. "It sounds like how I got here." I took her by the hand. "Let's see if we can get you out of here. Maybe you're part demon. Do you think you could be?"

She held out her hand, wiggling her fingers. "My mom said we were part Luciferian on her father's side, but I never knew if it was true. Maybe that's why I'm so good at animal healing magic, don't you think? I've always been at the top of my class. Magic comes naturally to me."

I glanced at the hut. "But how have you survived here?"

She heaved a deep sigh. "I've been healing sick cows. Someone let me use their old hut in exchange for helping their herd. They really value cows here. And goats. I need to get the fuck out of here before they realize what I am and hang me."

I took her hand and dragged her along the shore. "I can show you how to get back."

"Rowan, I cannot begin to tell you how happy I am that you found me. These people freak me the fuck out."

"Trust me," I said, "I know. I've already been hanged once."

"*What?*"

"Oh, it's okay. I got better. Think of it as a training exercise. The Dying God has taught me how to kill a king."

"Did you go insane here?"

"Come on, Shai. I'll explain along the way."

❆ 30 ❆

CHAPTER 30—ORION

I slid my hands into the pockets of my coat as I stalked the streets of Salem. Night had fallen by the time I reached the town center, and the dark sea battered the shore nearby. My lips tasted of salt. Orange lights punctuated the wooden buildings around me, and inside, people were dining by roaring fires. The air smelled of roasting meat. Apart from the people, the underworld wasn't really that bad.

If I breathed deeply, I could almost smell her floral scent here. Back in the City of Thorns, I'd been certain that Rowan was dead. Now, in the world of the dead, hope smoldered in my chest, and I felt myself coming to life again.

The sea wind stung my face, sharpening my senses—and I reminded myself how dangerous it was to hope. Was Rowan near?

Mortana had just been harping on that in Purgatory. Every time I came through that bloody cave, it was worse than the time before.

As I walked past the House of Seven Gables, with its flickering orange windows inset into black wood, the memory of Purgatory still haunted my thoughts.

I'd seen Mortana holding my mother's heart in her hand. In the vision, she'd laughed at me, a wild sound that had echoed off the dungeon walls. My mother's corpse hung behind her on a rope from the dungeon ceiling, and Ashur's emaciated body lay at her feet. Behind her, heads on pikes cast shadows on the walls.

"You had a single purpose—to avenge those you loved. You *promised* Ashur you would take revenge on the mortals. You said you would kill me," Mortana had exulted. "But what did you do instead? You fell for me again. And I have deceived you, of course. Haven't you learned how stupid it is to hope? You were an idiot to trust me. I thought I'd taught you that lesson well. Looks like I need to try harder. I lied to you, and I'm coming for your throne now, Orion."

I shook my head, banishing her from my thoughts, and glanced at the stocks. A different woman hung in them today, her hair filthy with mud. She looked at me with piteous eyes. For a moment, I thought of breaking the wood to set her free, but if I did that, she'd likely be hanged as a witch.

To the left, Goody Putnam's tavern glowed with warmth and light. I peered inside, hoping to see Rowan's beautiful shock of red hair.

My heart fell when I spied Goody Putnam through the window-pane, her cheeks flushed. I turned away and started for the Osborne Woods.

I'd taken but a few steps when Goody Putnam called after me. "Goodman Ashur," she shouted.

I turned to see her, pale hands clasped together, eyes gleaming with insane light. "Goodman Ashur, I am so very aggrieved to hear what happened to your wife."

I felt as if she'd shoved a blade into my chest.

"My wife," I repeated, hoping she'd fucking elaborate.

"Such an evil affair," she said, stepping closer to me. "She seemed familiar the first time I saw her. A creature from a nightmare. A most foul creature. She was caught in the woods with the devil last night."

I swallowed hard, torn between my need to hear more and the overwhelming desire to bash Goody Putnam's head against a wall. "Where is she now?"

The corner of her mouth twitched, and she licked her lips. "I have told everyone here that you must not have known—that you are a good man. But your wife was a witch. A demon. Judge Corwin hanged her on Gallows Hill as dawn broke."

The world shifted beneath my feet, and darkness swallowed me. This was my fault for pushing her away.

I gripped the woman by her shoulders. "Is she still there?"

"My husband died years ago, Goodman, and I have often hoped—"

I shoved her away from me and started for Gallows Hill, certain that my heart was breaking.

⚜

I DIDN'T FIND HER HANGING FROM THE TREE—JUST FOUR ROTTING strangers. And that most dangerous thing, hope, returned. Maybe Goody Putnam was mad. I wandered into the darkening forest, hoping to find Rowan, or at least Tammuz.

Tammuz might have a clue what was going on.

As I trudged over the snowy earth, clouds slid across the moon. We had been together here recently, but somehow, it felt like ages past.

I glimpsed the little cabin in the forest, webs of frost icing the glass. Pushing open the door, I stepped inside.

Without a doubt, I could smell her here, and the place looked different than it had two nights ago. Strips of meat dried by the fire, and baskets of berries sat on the hearth. Women's clothes, clothes that were *her* size, had been folded and set aside. Candles had burned halfway down.

The cottage looked lived in.

I crossed to the sofa and lifted a blanket to my nose. Rowan. *Recently*.

My heart slamming against my ribs, I left the cabin and walked back into the forest. No summons was needed this time. Tammuz stood in the moonlight, his face illuminated with silver and his body cloaked in darkness.

"Where is she?" I rasped.

"Mortana? Dead."

"No, Rowan. She's different." I heard the wild desperation in my voice. "Where is she?" Snow swirled in wild vortices around us, and the night felt sharp with danger.

He shifted closer, the edges of his form blurring. "Ah, but you see, she lied to you. She didn't tell you how to kill the False King. She is after your crown, Orion. She aims to rule, to take what is yours." His eyes glittered. "Orion, don't you know that you should never let yourself hope?"

I stared at him, my heart twisting. Without the crown, everything I'd ever planned would be doomed. I was alive for one reason: to fulfill my oath to the dead and feed the earth with the blood of their enemies.

Tammuz blended into the night again.

I waited for the familiar anger to sizzle in my veins, rage at the knowledge that Rowan had lied to me.

But the anger did not come. We were doing as our destinies commanded, and nothing more. She had her fate, and I had mine. Like the sea crashing against the rocks, we could not escape the forces pulling at us. We were all alone, weren't we?

She would try to take the crown from me.

And I would make sure she failed.

❧ 31 ❧

CHAPTER 31—ROWAN

I crouched on the outer wall of the City of Thorns, gazing up at the Tower of Baal disappearing into the clouds.

I'd left my cloak with Shai so it wouldn't trip me up when I tried to kill the king. To our great mutual relief, Shai wasn't dead. She was in an Osborne hotel room, asleep.

If the rest of this night went the way I hoped, she'd be back here for my coronation when the sun was up.

Did I want to be queen?

Hell, yes.

I breathed in the perfumed, humid air of the City of Thorns. I belonged here. Outside the gates of this city, I was nothing. Broke, lonely, hunted by the mortal police. Vulnerable.

Out there, I'd end up in jail, eating cold macaroni off a tray and trying not to get the shit kicked out of me by people who thought I was a weirdo.

What would it be like to have some fucking respect for once? What would it feel like to have other people listen to me?

Hell, yes, I wanted all that. I'd never hungered for power before. I'd never dared to. It had seemed out of my reach.

But I hungered for it now. If that was the only way to keep myself safe, I wanted it.

Excitement fluttered through my heart as I pictured myself wearing a crown, stalking through the city. Deep down in my id, maybe a part of me admired Mortana. Not her sadism, but her willingness to take what she wanted. She wasn't afraid to be strong.

I didn't have many weapons—just two daggers strapped to my thighs—but my magic would do most of the work.

From here, I could see what appeared to be the entire demonic army stationed outside the tower—a legion of armed demons, horns and weapons glinting under the moonlight. Demons had never adapted well to guns, which they considered a vulgar mortal invention. They had too much pride to rely on weapons that powerful. Unfortunately, they did have arrows.

Still, no wonder they'd wanted the Lilu dead. Our wings gave us an extreme advantage over the rest of them. And when you added fire to the equation, I was a dangerous weapon.

As soon as I launched off this wall, they'd be sounding the alarms, the army rushing upstairs to protect the king. They'd be looking for a Lilu, then, soaring through the skies.

Four guards stood outside a balcony window in the Tower of Baal. If I had to guess, that was where the king was sleeping. And if he was paranoid enough to station guards out there, he'd probably have powerful locks, alarms, reinforced glass…the hallways and stairwells outside his room would be packed with soldiers as well.

Were they well versed in fire safety? I doubted it.

My throat tightened. This was going to be messy and painful for everyone involved.

But if I was going to be queen, I couldn't alienate my future army by killing their friends. Whatever happened, I had to make sure the only person who died tonight was the fucker who'd killed my parents. Luckily, it was incredibly hard to kill a demon, so there shouldn't be any accidental deaths.

I hoped.

I cocked my head, staring from my perch on the windy tower wall at the army amassed at the base of the tower. They were everywhere. They hadn't swarmed the place like this when I'd been here before, so what had changed?

Orion.

I pieced it together. Of course. He'd entered the king's chambers, searching for the book I'd lied about. Guilt coiled in my chest. I hoped he hadn't been captured. But he'd made it *very* clear that I was on my own.

I glanced behind me, searching the skies for signs of him, as if he might swoop in at the last moment and ruin my plans. Only the constellations gleamed above me.

At my best guess, it was around five-thirty a.m. Apart from the army, the whole city was asleep, windows darkened in stone buildings but for a sprinkle of lights. The sun would be rising soon, and with any luck, people would wake to the sight of me ripping out Cambriel's heart. Proof I was destined to lead.

With that glorious thought in mind, I took off from the parapet, soaring under the stars. The night wind rushed over me, skimming through my hair and feathers. Around the Tower of Baal, the soldiers shouted and stirred in alarm. A great bell tolled, echoing off the stones.

On the one hand, that was unfortunate. If Orion was anywhere nearby, the noise would alert him to my attack. What's more, the king would have time to prepare. On the other hand, I wanted the city awake. I needed an audience when I eviscerated their king.

Arrows flew through the air, and I picked up speed, climbing higher and out of their reach.

My gaze locked on a spot a few stories down from where the king slept, a balcony open to the air, an arch of stones overlooking the sea. I angled my wings and swept to a landing. Leaving the balcony, I crossed into a ballroom painted with murals of beautiful, winged Lilu. A golden light glowed in the deep blue marble floor. My five-pointed star had appeared.

Roughly a dozen soldiers in royal blue rushed at me, swords drawn. I folded my wings and lifted my hands, summoning the heat. It crackled in my chest, surging down my shoulders, arms, and wrists, and

I unleashed a stream of fire in a protective arc around me. No one could walk through those flames without burning.

What would Mortana say at a time like this?

"Do you see my mark?" I shouted, my voice ringing in the marble hall. "I was made to rule. If you defy me, you will burn. And you should know that the king who sleeps in his room is a false king."

The soldiers stumbled back to avoid the fire. Regrouping, they pelted me with arrows. I ducked, but an arrow hit me in the shoulder, ripping through my muscle. I fell to my knees.

Just as Tammuz had taught me, I blocked out the pain and stayed on the offensive. From my knees, I let out another stream of fire. In the ensuing confusion, no one could aim properly. Gritting my teeth, I broke the arrow in half and ripped it out of my shoulder, grimacing as it tore my muscle. As soon as it was out, the wound began to heal.

I got to my feet and pressed on, fire streaming from my hands. Bright orange flames lit the darkness, warm light that danced over beautifully carved statues. Screams echoed from the tower's interior, and chaos reigned. People were alight, uniforms burning. They tumbled from the balcony, screaming on the way down. In the tower, balconies overlooked a fire pit far below, and curving stairways led between the floors. Shouting, the soldiers rushed to get away from me, fleeing the heat.

As I opened my wings to take flight to the top floor, another arrow pierced my bicep, hitting bone. Pain sent a shockwave through me. *Block it out, Rowan.*

Glancing up, I saw the archer above me. He was protecting the king's door. I blocked out the noise and confusion, and summoned the calm of the forest.

Taking aim, I unleashed a stream of fire at the upper story. The blazing archer screamed and dropped his weapon. Behind him, the closely packed group of soldiers caught fire and leapt off the balcony to douse the flames, like breath blowing out a birthday candle.

I yanked the arrow out, blood spilling onto the floor. I'd better make this quick before they riddled me with arrows. I'd been focusing on the archer, and the protective ring of fire around me had dwindled. A swordsman lunged at me, and I sidestepped. Grabbing his wrist as

I'd practiced so many times with Tammuz, I slammed his hands hard into the stone balcony, and he dropped his weapon.

My wings unfurled, and I took to the air, soaring to the top of the tower. Cool starlight streamed in through an oculus. Soldiers gathered outside the king's door, swords ready. The alarms were maddeningly loud, making it hard to think.

My heart was pounding hard, my body buzzing with adrenaline. Why wasn't Orion here, trying to stop me?

A soldier loosed an arrow at me, but his hands were shaking, and it went wide.

"Go!" My voice boomed over the tower. "You can see by the mark I bear that I am your queen."

"Not while the king still lives!" another shouted. "Only his heir can kill him. And he has no heir."

Two more arrows skimmed past my head.

I held up my hands. Fire crackled along my arms and danced from my fingertips. "Cambriel is not the true king. You will understand when you see his heartless corpse lying in your streets."

They were good soldiers, and they weren't moving from his door.

One of the archers took aim, and the arrow he fired struck me in the ribs. Agony slammed into me. I was fairly certain he'd punctured one of my lungs.

I sucked in a ragged breath and launched a stream of fire above their heads. Not close enough to burn them, but enough to make them panic. With the heat pressing down on them, the soldiers fled, a mad press of terrified men pushing and shoving their way down the stairs. In their haste, a few tumbled over the edge, plummeting to the lobby far below.

Clenching my jaws, I ripped the arrow out of my chest. The pain was exquisite. It would subside quickly, but for the moment, it was blinding, and I rasped for breath.

At last, I had a clear shot at the king's door—thick wood, reinforced with iron crosses and locked with an iron bar. My wings beat rhythmically behind me, pounding like my heart. I raised my hands and pointed at the door.

Hot magic sizzled through me, an inferno of heat that poured out of me. In my mind's eye, I saw my mother's death, her last agonized moments.

I was an angel of destruction.

Cambriel had put me through hell. I would do the same to him.

CHAPTER 32—ROWAN

T he door to the king's chamber caught fire, and the iron bars started to melt. The air smelled of seared wood and flesh.

The Tower was a pandemonium of shouting and fleeing, but I focused my attention on that burning door and the melting iron. Finally, the bar warped and slid to the stone floor in a puddle.

I swept through the fiery goo and into a great arched room. Three soldiers charged forward, surrounding me. One threw a punch, but I blocked it with my forearm. The force of his punch was crushing, and I heard the crack of bone.

The next one aimed for my head. Grabbing his wrist, I twisted it behind his back and spun him around to act like a shield.

I pivoted, placing his two companions between me and the door. The man I held captive elbowed me in the ribs with his free arm. His aim was either good or lucky, because he hit me in the *exact* spot where I'd just been pierced by an arrow. Pain shot through me, and fire exploded from my body. The man in my grip burst into flame, and the remaining two soldiers ran for the door. The fire spread, igniting the furniture and a tapestry on the wall.

I tossed the burned man aside and touched my ribs, wincing a little.

Cambriel stood alone in the center of the room, his face illuminated by the flames around him. His pale hair glowed orange in the
light.

The wind rushed in through the open balcony, fanning the flames
and tossing fiery sparks up to the high ceiling.

When I was queen, I would install fire sprinklers, because this
place was absolutely *not* up to code.

Cambriel seemed unfazed, but he had no reason to fear fire. I
turned quickly, unleashing another blast of fire at the door and locking
us in together with a barrier of flames.

I took a step closer to him. "Cambriel. I saw what you did to my
mother." I could hardly hide the fury in my voice.

He let out a short laugh. "How did you see *that*?"

"What happened between you two?" I demanded.

He placed a finger over his lips. "Do you know, Mortana, I don't
really feel compelled to tell you. You can burn my army, if you want,
but you cannot kill me. You're not my heir."

Hot anger churned in the depths of my chest. "You're not the true
king. You didn't kill Nergal. Tell me how you ended up lighting my
mother on fire."

In a blur of speed, he rushed forward and clamped his hand around
my throat, lifting me into the air. "Are you pretending that you care
what happened to your mother? You left her for dead, Mortana, along
with all the other Lilu. You don't give a fuck what happened to any of
them. But I was willing to overlook your ruthlessness. We could have
joined forces if you weren't so insane."

I kicked him hard in the chest, and he dropped me.

I just wanted the answer to one question before I ripped out his
heart. "What did my parents want from you?"

"What difference does it make? Obviously, you have designs on the
throne. That's why you're here, isn't it? I could have given it to you
through marriage. Together, we could have been powerful."

I clenched my fists. "You are my half brother, *and* you murdered my
parents."

He took a swing for me, but I blocked it, landing a hard punch in
his stomach.

He doubled over, clutching his gut. "I don't know why you sound so put out. You ripped out my mother's heart and left her carcass in a vat of wine." He straightened. "But why all the questions about your parents? Are you lonely, Mortana, after you murdered the rest of your kind and left them to rot in the dungeons? I thought you wanted to be the only one left with your power. That's why you did it, isn't it? To gain power and save your own skin. You sacrificed your kin."

My fingers twitched. There was that phrase again—Mortana's original sin, and mine.

As soon as the fires died down behind me, more soldiers would swarm in. My wings shot out from my shoulder blades, lifting me into the air. I kicked Cambriel in the head, and he fell backward onto the floor.

He leapt up and exploded with flames. A fireball engulfed me. Orange and red danced around me, scented of ash and burning cloth. This was how Mom died. Cambriel relied on fire in a fight, a tactic that would work on almost anyone.

Except me. I didn't burn.

When the fireball receded, I angled my wings and slammed down on top of him, knocking him back to the floor. His head cracked against the stone. I straddled his waist, my long, silver claws extended. Bringing them down, I slashed his right wrist, severing his hand with the ring.

He shrieked in terror and grabbed my hair with his good hand. I could have ended his life right then and there by ripping out his heart, but I wanted an audience.

I raked my claws over his heart, threatening to pierce it, and drew a dagger from its sheath.

"My parents were blackmailing you," I snarled. "Why? What did they want?"

His eyes wide with fear, he shook his head wordlessly.

I poked his chest with my claws, drawing blood. "I watched her burn to death, Cambriel. Tell me what she wanted from you."

"Something I couldn't give. They wanted to come back. I don't know why they suddenly had a sense of urgency after all those years."

Because I'd been born. This was my home, and they were trying to keep me safe.

"And why didn't you let them?" I roared. "He was your father, too."

His forehead glowed with his mark—a golden eye in a triangle. "And what if there were more? There was a reason the Lilu had to go. Nergal agreed to the mortals' demands because he wanted you gone, all of you. How can a wingless king rule over those who can fly? It was fine if you were the last one. You and I could marry. Our claims to the throne would be stronger than any others."

The fire had spread across the room, engulfing his bed.

His severed hand was already starting to heal, and I was out of time. I had the answer I needed.

I plunged the dagger into his heart. He froze, eyes wide. He'd be incapacitated until I got him out in a public square.

His words still rang in the hollows of my mind. *But what if there were more?*

I slid off his unconscious body and crouched to pick him up. I'd carry him through the window and—

A figure loomed in the burning doorway, someone impervious to the flames around him.

Orion. Coppery light and shadows danced over his features. Embers and smoke swirled around him, and his ice-cold eyes pierced the gloom. The scent of burning mahogany and heated stone filled the air, and ashes rained around the room.

The promise of violence hung thick in the air. "Well, Rowan. It would seem you found a way to break the blood oath and lie to me." He smiled. "But maybe I need to thank you. You've already done the hard work for me."

I wasn't here to have a dialogue with Orion, nor would I allow him to steal this chance from me. I wouldn't let him get in my head.

With the king in my arms, I raced for the open balcony door. Outside, the first blush of dawn spread over the demon sky, staining it a pearly coral.

When I reached the balcony, I would let my wings out—

A force like a train crashed into me from behind, knocking the wind from me before I could escape. I dropped the king, and we tumbled to the mosaic floor. I pushed onto my elbow and round kicked Orion in the knee.

He staggered, and I leapt to my feet, delighted by his surprised expression.

He wanted to fight? Fine. This is what I'd trained for. I widened my stance and cleared my head, calming my thoughts as the Dying God had taught me. Watching for signs of what my enemy would do next without emotion or fear.

I expected Orion to look furious, but he seemed amused instead. "Well, well," he said, the corners of his lips curling. "You *do* remember how to fight after all."

Smoke filled the air as the flames engulfed the furniture. "I learned a few things in the underworld."

"You want power for yourself."

I returned his faint smile. "When was the last time a queen ruled here instead of a king? And look at what angry men do when they have power. We saw it in the underworld. Men run that city. Women are hanged, put in stocks, and whipped, all because men can't bear the thought of women having the tiniest bit of control."

He arched an eyebrow. "So it's not for your own sake? You're doing this for all of womankind?"

"Forgive me for thinking it's a little unethical to slaughter all the mortals because someone pissed *you* off four hundred years ago."

His smile faded, and his eyes turned to ice. "Someone pissed me off? That's how you're describing it?"

"And yes, I do want to rule," I shouted. "So what? Maybe I'm sick of being pushed around by broken people on power trips."

He gave me a knowing smile. "And that's exactly what you would be, isn't it, a broken woman with half a soul on a power trip? I saw what you did to those soldiers burning outside—"

"They'll recover."

"The moment you learn how to use your magic, you start lighting people on fire and throwing them off balconies. Tell me how you're different from Mortana, again? You're already fighting just like her."

A sharp coil of doubt started to wind through my thoughts. What was I doing? I was letting him get in my head.

Tammuz hadn't trained me for that, and if I listened to this too long, I would lose.

I needed to end this conversation before he completely got the upper hand. I shifted forward, ready to land a punch, but he swung for me first. Lightning fast, I ducked, then came up again with my claws aimed at his throat. He grabbed my wrists, pushing them out of the way, and slamming me onto the floor. I rolled, looking up at him from the ground.

Smoke billowed around me from a flaming chair at my side. Alarm bells clanged loudly in the city, a cacophony of noise and chaos.

Of course—Tammuz would be delighted with this anarchy.

"What's different between me and Mortana? Unlike her, I'm loyal." I turned, grabbed the flaming chair, and hurled it at him. He blocked it, but his dark clothes caught fire. Flames rose around him, gilding his features. He patted out the flames, trying to salvage what was left of his clothes.

"You're loyal? Doesn't look that way to me." His shirt had burned almost completely away, leaving black rags draped over his thickly muscled chest.

Another distraction Tammuz hadn't prepared me for.

"Not loyal to you," I said. "You've been telling me quite consistently how much you hate me. No, sorry. You don't respect me enough to hate me because I'm *boring* and talentless. Why would you expect me to be loyal to you?"

My temper soared.

I was done being pushed around, and I didn't have to take it anymore. I lunged at him, punching him hard in the jaw with a loud crack of bone. The force of the blow dazed him for a moment, and I kicked him in the chest. He slammed back into a hot stone wall, and it cracked behind him. Before he could recover, I shifted, aiming my next kick at his head, but his hand shot out and he grabbed my right ankle with shocking speed.

His dark eyes glinted, and the mark of Lucifer shone from his head. Was it just me, or was he enjoying himself a little, holding my ankle in his steely grip at his shoulder?

I let my wings burst open, lifting me into the air, and slammed my other foot into his head. His skull shot back into the wall, but as I retracted my wings and landed, he charged me, knocking me flat on my back. He moved to leap on top of me, but I lifted my legs, trapping his throat between my thighs. I squeezed hard, but he lifted me up from under my ass.

Spinning around, he slammed me down again on the burning bed. Fire engulfed us. I didn't feel a thing apart from Orion's waist between my thighs.

He tried to pin me down by the wrists, but before he got a good grip, I smashed my left elbow into his temple, then smacked him on the other side with my right, knocking him off me and onto the burning floor.

I landed on top of him, straddling his waist. Now was the time to act. I drew out my claws—

He trapped my wrists, and we strained against each other, his fierce, shadowy gaze locked on mine. "Am I about to die, just as I started to live again?" he asked.

I had no idea what that meant. Getting in my head again.

And what would happen if I got my hands free? Could I really end Orion's life?

I was pretty sure he could have ended mine on the bed if he'd simply swiped for my heart instead of grabbing me by the wrists.

That gave me pause.

Sweat rolled down my temples.

I brought my forehead down, breaking his nose. He dropped my wrists, and I brought out my long silver claws.

I slashed for him.

✣ 33 ✣
CHAPTER 33—ROWAN

When it came down to it, I couldn't kill Orion, so I settled for slashing his throat with my claws instead. His blood pumped over the black and white mosaic, and I leapt off him. I didn't know how long it would take for him to recover, but I wasn't going to wait around to find out.

With a pounding heart, I crossed over to the unconscious king. The smoke from the fires had started to fill my lungs and sting my eyes. Coughing, I bent down and scooped up Cambriel. The knife still jutted from his heart, and his mouth gaped open, blood streaking down his chest.

Holding his limp body in my arms, I ran out on the balcony, blinking in the bright morning sun. In the sweet, fresh air, I inhaled deeply, clearing my eyes of smoke and sweat.

My wings shot out of my shoulders, and the wind rushed over them. Beneath me, the army swarmed, tiny as ants.

I flew off the balcony and into the honey-rose sky, soaring above the dawn-kissed demon city. Beneath me, soldiers were scrambling, still bound by their oaths to protect their living king. But soon, they would pledge their loyalty to me. I wanted them to see what was about to happen to their false king, the charlatan on the throne.

I *really* wanted to kill him in front of my parents' house. Poetic, but not the best strategy. It was too far, and I'd have to wait for the army to catch up. I wasn't going to waste another moment.

I streaked toward the sandy stones of the Luciferian ward, not far from the tower, unleashing a stream of fire as I raced toward the earth. Total chaos ensued, disrupting the arrows that might come for me. As I drew closer, I cleared a space on the amber stones with tongues of fire.

I landed hard on the stones but managed to steady myself. The Acheron River flowed behind me. In real time, it wasn't that long ago that I'd been sitting at a nearby restaurant eating pasta, convinced I was mortal. Not long ago, I'd passed the initiation in the wilderness, using fox piss, deodorant, and lighters to save my own life.

Firmly on solid earth once more, I looked up to see the demon army charging me, stones rumbling at the horde's approach. I had to protect myself before they ripped me to pieces.

I surrounded the prostrate king and myself with a circle of flames, watching the army halt on the other side. This was it. I didn't have long.

"Only the true heir can slaughter a king," I shouted. "I am here to prove to you that I am your queen."

Silence reigned. The hairs on the back of my neck stood up, a sixth sense that danger lurked behind me. Lifting my gaze, I saw Orion hurtling through the sky, wings outstretched, headed straight for me. I dropped the king and rose to meet him. We collided in midair, wings thrashing, and grappled with one another. He grabbed me by the waist and tossed me aside, and I veered clumsily toward the earth, arms wheeling.

I righted myself again, and horror unfurled beneath me. Orion was on top of the king. Landing on his back, I tried to pull him off, but it was over in an instant.

Orion ripped the king's chest open, clawing out his heart in a single stroke. He lifted it into the air, brandishing it above his head. Seething with bitter disappointment, I saw the five-pointed star beaming from his head.

I'd done that. I'd figured out how to kill the king. How to get past his army. How to kill him in public. And Orion had swept in at the last moment to steal my victory. I shook with anger.

I wanted to shout that it was mine, that Orion had stolen the king's heart from me. This was *my* revenge. Cambriel had killed *my* mom, not his. Orion had taken that from me, and the crown with it, but there was no way to say it without sounding petulant and insane. But it wasn't just about me, was it? Orion was going to fucking murder everyone.

The flames were dying down around us, and the army of soldiers in midnight blue knelt for their new king. Red-hot jealousy burned through me.

Yes, I wanted power. Who didn't? When you had power, you could stop the crazy people from burning the world down.

The placid smile on Orion's beautiful face sent molten rage through my veins.

He lifted the king's heart again, blood dripping down his arm. The rising sun washed him in gold—a beautiful god of wrath. "Cambriel was not your true king. It was I who slaughtered Nergal, and *I* who will right the wrongs of your former kings. No longer will we live in a jail of mortal making. No longer will I allow them to control us. Together, we will find a way to break the bonds that trap us here and once again become gods!"

The crowd roared, and ice slid through my veins. They were eating this up.

Orion turned to look at me, his expression glacial, and I gritted my teeth.

"Escort this woman out of my realm," he boomed. "She tried to burn down the Tower of Baal. She is not allowed within our city walls."

"What are you doing?" I demanded.

"What I promised from the beginning. I told you that I would banish you from the city. I can't be around you, Rowan."

I glanced at the soldiers marching for me, then back to him. "The mortal police will arrest me. Immediately."

His eyes danced with cold amusement. "You're resourceful. I can see that now. I'm sure you'll think of something."

The crowd was shouting his name, ecstatic. Bare-chested, Orion glowed with amber light, looking every bit a king. I inhaled deeply, breathing in the scent of smoke and blood. Red sun rays beamed down on us through soot and cinders.

If the Lord of Chaos succeeds, the mortal realm will burn.

My gaze flicked to the oncoming soldiers, and I wanted to scream.

Why wait to be escorted out? Unfurling my wings, I rose into the ashen sky.

I would see myself out—but I'd be back.

Of that, I had no doubt.

❧ 34 ❧

CHAPTER 34—ROWAN

From Shai's hotel room at the top of the Glover Inn, I had a perfect view of the historic district of Osborne. The climates were different in the underworld and the City of Thorns, and it was strange to see that it was still autumn here, the trees bursting with fiery colors under the glow of the streetlights.

This was the nice part of Wallcott Street, with colorfully painted shops, brick sidewalks, and gold signs. Warmth shone from the windows of brick buildings, and people walked around with steaming cups of coffee and hot chocolate. A narrow, cobbled road sloped down toward shadowy Witchcraft Point. Even that looked nice from here—orange dots in the darkness.

How was Mr. Esposito doing tonight? I would absolutely have checked on him if it didn't involve returning to the scene of a crime.

And from here, I could see all the way up the opposite hill. In the distance, the City of Thorns glowed with pale light the color of butter. I pressed my palms against the glass, fogging the window a little.

How long before Orion arrived and started killing people?

The door opened, and I turned to see Shai wearing a black turtleneck and a short tweed skirt. She was carrying two wine glasses. "I got these from the bar downstairs. Cheaper than room service."

I sighed, taking in the cozy hotel room. Walnut bookshelves lined the walls on either side of the fireplace. Shai slid the wine glasses onto a desk by the window. "They're both for you."

"You're not having any?"

"I got permission to go back into the City of Thorns. I don't think Orion trusts me because of my connection to you, but the oath he made to me included a promise to keep me safe. He can't really keep me safe if I'm not in the kingdom, can he?"

I let out a long sigh. "Why wasn't I clever enough to demand an oath like that?"

"I was raised by two parents who were constantly learning how to one-up each other. It's an art form." She crossed to the wardrobe and pulled it open. "You should stay here for a while, though. I can pay for it. Isn't this room amazing?"

My gaze wandered around the space. In a weird way, it reminded me of the coziness of the underworld cabin—lots of dark wood and candles for ambiance. Except here, there was unmistakable luxury: a red velvet comforter, bookshelves crammed with beautiful old volumes, and an antique mahogany desk by the window.

Rain started to fall against the glass.

In her elegant skirt and black sweater, Shai looked like she belonged here.

"Thank you, Shai. It's beautiful. But I'm not sure it's a great idea to stay in a room with your name or credit card info. Jack and the mortal police have already connected us." I sighed. "It's only a matter of time before they find me here."

She pulled out her suitcase. "Okay. Where will you go, then?"

"Into hiding, I guess." I didn't really have a plan yet, but I knew I could live through winter with almost nothing. "I'll forage for acorns and berries in a forest."

She pulled on her wool coat. "I'm serious. Why can't you try to convince Orion to at least let you back in the city?"

"Because I'm his rival, and even if I weren't, he doesn't like me." Oddly, after everything I'd been through, the words stung worse than an arrow through my ribs.

"You can't charm him?"

I handed her one of the glasses of wine. "You're going to want a sip of this, Shai. Sit down for a second."

In her coat, she perched on the end of the bed and took a sip of wine. "Okay. You're scaring me. What's happening?"

I twirled my wineglass. "I haven't been sure how to tell you this, but Orion is going to kill everyone."

Her brown eyes widened. "Sorry, what?"

"Not in the City of Thorns, although I'm sure he'll kill a fair number there, too. But mostly out here. He wants to murder all the mortals. He thinks he can find a way to break the spell that keeps demons bound to the city, and he wants to set them free. To feed. To get revenge."

Her mouth opened and closed. "I always knew he was unhinged. Is that really possible, though?"

"Orion will probably find a way to do it. This is a man who dug himself out of a dungeon over a century, and the whole time, he was dreaming of murdering mortals. For all his other flaws, he gets shit done in the most impossible circumstances. And he's all fucked up."

She tilted her head back and drained her glass. When she'd finished, she wiped her mouth. "Okay. We need to tell everyone. We need to *evacuate* everyone."

"To where? He's not going to stop at Osborne."

She set the empty wine glass on the desk. "Please tell me you have an idea of what to do. What about that forest god?"

I took a deep breath. "I've been thinking of going to see him, but I don't get the sense he cares if mortals die. He's actually really into death. I think he helped me because he wanted to make the fight for the throne a little more interesting."

"But it's over, right?" she asked. "Orion is king now. There's no changing that."

A lump rose in my throat, and I swallowed hard. "If I want to stop him, I'll have to kill him."

"You? You can't kill him!" She stared at me. "I'm sorry, Rowan, I'm having a hard time adjusting to your killer demon abilities. I still think of you as the person who got nervous and puked at graduation."

"Yeah, me, too." I watched the rain pelt the glass. "Look, Shai, you should go to the City of Thorns. We know it's safe there. And I'm going to figure something out. I'll come up with a plan, I promise. I'll stay here a little longer to clear my head."

Her phone buzzed, and she pulled it out of her pocket. "Shit. My Uber is here."

"Go. We'll be in touch over text."

Her gaze flicked to the window. "What are you going to do if the police show up?"

"At the rate my magic is draining, I should be able to fly for a few more days. I'll be fine. And after that, they'll never find me." Insanely, I was even considering hiding out in the underworld cabin.

She hurried toward the door. "Okay. Text me, if you can. I'm leaving you the hotel keys. You can stay here for a week if you don't think you'll get caught."

When she shut the door, I dimmed the lights a little, preferring the candlelight. I sipped the wine and stared out the window. I'd failed, yes. But that couldn't be it. My parents had given their lives trying to keep me safe, believing Orion must not rule. I couldn't bear to think of how disappointed they'd be right now, knowing that he'd won. My chest ached.

A clanking sound made my ears perk up.

I looked to the right and caught a glimpse of someone shuffling along the sidewalk on a walker. It was Mr. Esposito, getting drenched in the rain. Why was he always out in this weather? He really needed looking after.

As he walked past the hotel, I saw him drop something—a brown paper bag.

Damn it. It was lying there in a puddle now, and he hadn't even realized. I tapped the window a few times, trying to get his attention, but he shambled on down the hill.

I grabbed a key, left the room, and hurried down all four flights of creaking stairs. Rushing past the receptionist, I went out the front door.

Mr. Esposito was gone. The hotel sat on the peak of the hill. Streetlights gleamed off puddles, and rivulets of rain streamed down the deserted cobbled streets. Everyone had scrambled inside to get away from the storm.

The old man had vanished. I wasn't sure how he'd been able to move that quickly, but maybe he'd taken cover indoors, too.

His little brown paper bag still lay on the sidewalk in the rain. I jogged over and snatched it off the ground, planning to drop it by his house later. Tucking it under my arm, I pushed the buzzer to get back into the hotel.

What was in the bag—a book, maybe? While I waited for the receptionist, I turned the sack over and found the letter *R* written on it.

R for Rowan?

Curiosity sparked, and I opened the bag and peered inside. It *was* a book, one that looked far too old and precious to be left in a puddle. But someone had carefully wrapped it in plastic to protect it. A velvety midnight blue cover was embossed with gold text, filigrees, and little symbols of stars. The title jumped out at me.

Trial by Combat in the Demon World.

I stared at the book, my mind ticking back to something Mr. Esposito had said the night I'd killed the congressman: "Get to the City of Thorns."

He knew, didn't he?

What if there were more...

Cambriel had feared that if he let my parents in the city, he'd have to allow more Lilu entry. Maybe he'd known something.

I was so stunned that I nearly missed the buzz of the door. Pushing inside, I ran up the stairs and back into Shai's room. I hurried to the desk, then sat down and carefully pulled the book from the plastic.

As I cracked it open, my pulse raced. This felt like a message to me. Long ago, King Nergal had taken the crown from my grandfather Azriel in trial by combat.

I sipped the wine Shai had left for me and started to read. As the rain pattered against the window, I learned more about the demonic beliefs concerning monarchy. Demons believe that when a crown is contested, the gods will choose the winner. A series of trials determines who is suited to rule. When a demon with a legitimate claim wants to challenge a ruler, they make a public declaration.

I looked up from the book, gazing but unseeing, into the darkness outside the window.

This was what Tammuz had prepared me for.

I was going back to the City of Thorns.

ALSO BY C.N. CRAWFORD

For a full list of our books, please check out our website, cncrawford.com. You can find a free book there.

Amazon and goodreads also have a full listing of our books. Reviews are appreciated!

Read on for a sample of a completed series—the Shadow Fae series—to see if that is what you want to read next!

GARDEN OF SERPENTS

✻ I ✻
ROWAN

Sunlight streamed through autumn leaves, lighting them like tongues of flames against the sky. I stared out a third-story window, watching a little boy stuff his mouth with cotton candy on the brick sidewalk across the street. Just next to him, his mom chatted with a friend, her hair the same bright red as the autumn leaves above her.

The little boy reached out to grab his mom's pinkie finger—one hand on mom, the other on his treat. Crystalized pink sugar smeared across his cheek, striking against his pale skin. From the oak tree above him, a bright orange leaf drifted onto his tufted auburn hair, then slid off to the bricks. His green eyes followed the leaf's motion.

My chest felt tight.

Any day now, Orion could be ripping through this town to murder everyone. This sugar-covered toddler with Band-Aids on both knees wasn't responsible for anything that happened four hundred years ago. He just wanted his mom and dessert.

I watched the peaceful scene, my breath fogging the glass.

This could be the last moment of peace in a while.

By midnight tonight, my head would either be resting on a silken pillow or hanging from the gates before the Tower of Baal. After the first night of the trial, those two paths lay before me. Nothing else.

But if Tammuz—the dying god—thought I had a chance at winning the crown, who was I to argue?

When I took a step back from the window, a ray of light caught on the word *love*, etched in the glass with a diamond long ago. I could almost see a version of this world where an unbroken Orion would welcome me into the city. A world where we could rule together. But that wasn't this reality, was it? Because he'd thrown me out on my ass to fend for myself against demon hunters as my magic faded.

In reality, Orion's soul had never left the dungeon. Even if his body made it out, he was trapped there still.

With a tight throat, I turned, taking in the eighteenth-century mansion. Shai's aunt's house was one of the most beautiful places I'd ever seen, the floors delightfully crooked and creaking with age, the walls carved mahogany. One half of the living room opened into a kitchen with marble countertops. On the other side of the room, diamond-pane windows looked out over the churning, sun-kissed Atlantic.

Amber sunlight streamed through the old glass, falling on the portrait of one of Shai's relatives, a New England merchant sea captain with brown skin, a white cravat, and a brass-button navy coat. Impossible to tell if he was part demon, like Shai.

I absolutely adored this place, and it had become my hiding spot while Shai's aunt was away in Paris. I had the whole house to myself.

Breathing in deeply, I closed my eyes for a moment, relishing the calm before the storm. I'd been awake all night, my mind whirling. The mortal police were still after me for killing a congressman, and I knew what horrors Orion had planned.

I crossed to the antique sofa, and I pulled out my phone to check the time. Nearly noon. Shai should be here any minute with something I desperately needed.

When I looked up again, a chill rippled over my skin. Shadows had spread through the room, and an electric crackle of magic skimmed up my spine.

I jumped up again and crossed to the window. Unnatural iron-gray storm clouds had claimed the sky.

The little boy still held his mom's hand, but now worry creased his brow. He stared up at the darkening clouds, wiping his sticky hand on his shirt, leaving behind smears of pink.

A gust of wind swept through the trees, tearing leaves off the oak's boughs. All at once, clouds opened above, unleashing a wild rain storm that hammered against the window.

My heart started to race as I craned my neck to peer down the hill through the old glass.

It's starting. I couldn't breathe. Already, they were coming—the demon horde, their silver claws extended, eyes black as pitch. The earth seemed to rumble with their approach. This was it—the vengeance that obsessed Orion, his lust for mortal blood.

I banged on the glass, screaming to get the mom's attention. Why wasn't she running? She needed to get that little boy the fuck out of here. My voice seemed trapped in the room, and I bitterly regretted that I'd let my magic run out.

At last, the boy's mother turned to see the horde, and her face went white. She grabbed him by the wrist at first, then under his armpits, and started to run. But she was slow and human, no match for the demons. I couldn't watch this.

I pivoted and raced for the stairs. They creaked as I thundered down, my body shaking with adrenaline. By the time I flung open the front door at the bottom of the stairs, the mom's screams had gone quiet, and the little boy's, too—

My heart stopped as I turned to look in the direction of the City of Thorns.

Dressed in a cloak, Orion stalked closer, his face half shrouded. He was death incarnate. Blood dripped from his claws, and my heart twisted in my chest.

The question was, what made me so fucked up that I was drawn to him?

2

ROWAN

I woke, gasping, my face pressed against embroidered chartreuse silk. My heart lurched. Slowly, I sat up on the sofa and clutched my chest.

Holy hell, that had seemed so real.

There's still time.

I was still in Shai's aunt's house. The sun still shone outside.

As my gaze slid around the room, I took in the calm swirls of mahogany, the portrait on the wall, still washed in gold light. Slowly, the nightmare began to fade.

A book lay on the coffee table before me. Gilded stars and letters were engraved in the deep blue surface: *Trial by Combat in the Demon World*.

I opened the cover to the first page, staring again at the strange text inscribed within.

I will always help you when I can.
-Sabazios

This was my gift from the elderly Mr. Esposito—and also the only way to stop the nightmare I'd just seen. In the past few weeks, I'd learned everything I could about how to dethrone Orion.

With a heavy sense of dread, I padded barefoot to the window. The sun shone through leaves the color of pumpkins and honey. A woman with pink hair walked with a ginger cat in her arms, a flat-faced and sleepy creature, its eyes blinking slowly.

No demons, no blood, no cotton candy–covered little boy. No oncoming demon horde rumbling over the street. Just a beautiful October day in New England.

Outside, the pink-haired woman pivoted, and her gaze slid to my window as she stroked her orange cat. Unease flickered through me. I'd seen her before, hadn't I? I had the disturbing sense that she was spying on me, and I wondered if the demon hunters were finally catching up.

I slipped back out of her eyesight and dropped onto the sofa again. After another minute, I heard the sound of someone climbing the old, creaking stairs. Relief flooded me as the living room door swung open, and Shai stood in the doorway.

Her hair was a halo of brown curls, and a little leather bag rested against the houndstooth fabric of her skirt. "Hey girl. Are you just waking up?"

"Is it that obvious?" When I looked down at myself, I saw my tangled red hair hanging over wrinkled pajamas. I rubbed my eyes. "I couldn't sleep last night. I passed out here sometime after the sun came up, I think. I just had the worst fucking nightmare about Orion."

She crossed the living room to the kitchen. "I'm making us cappuccino."

"I love you," I called out.

"You'll love me even more when you see what I brought back for you."

Excitement lit me up. "Is it the iron gauntlet, by any chance?"

"Sure is," she called out from the kitchen over the sound of frothing milk. "And I already started spreading the word that you're not Mortana. The whole city is abuzz with the gossip."

A few minutes later, she crossed back into the living room, holding two white coffee cups on saucers, and slid them onto the table.

I picked up my cup, delighted to see that she'd powdered the frothy milk with a dusting of cocoa. Gods, it was really nice to be taken care of. "How did you get your hands on the gauntlet?"

She sat in the armchair across from me but made no move to open her bag. "Are you sure you want to do this *tonight?*" she asked, ignoring my question. "It seems so soon to take on the son of a demon god."

Any moment, that glorious buzz of caffeine would hit my veins, jolting me awake. "It's never going to feel like a good time to challenge a demon king, and I don't have a ton of time. There's a woman with a cat who keeps walking past the apartment like she's spying on me."

"Okay..." Her voice trailed off, and then she said, "I know you're the Lightbringer." She didn't sound convinced, though.

"Shai. Tonight's the night." I stared at the velvet book. "It's the moonlight festival. It's perfect. Everyone will see the trial by combat. If I win, there will be thousands of witnesses."

She tapped the side of her cup. "Well, if you're going to go ahead with it, let's not say *if* you win. Let's say *when* you win. Anything else is unacceptable and simply cannot come to pass. Do you understand?"

I had the sense that Shai was annoyed at me for putting my life at risk, but I didn't have much choice.

"It'll be fine." I still had that little boy's pink-sugared face in my mind. "I'm a Lightbringer, remember?"

She took a deep breath, her expression relaxing. "If you say you can do it, then I believe you."

At last, she reached into her bag and pulled out an ancient-looking iron glove, a piece of carefully crafted armor. She gently placed it on the table next to the book. I stared at the hinges and delicate metal plates that had once allowed a warrior's fingers to move, to grip the hilt of a sword. In a ray of honeyed sunlight, Lucifer's star gleamed from the back of the gauntlet—a bright spark of gold on the iron. I reached out and traced my fingertips over it, surprised by the jolt of ancient magic that shot into my fingertips when I touched it. A smile curled my lips. That felt like a sign from the demon god himself.

"Shai, how, exactly, did you get the gauntlet? I thought it was hidden in a secret temple."

"Legion helped me."

His image flickered in my mind—the black-haired demon with golden skin and tattoos that twisted over his muscular forearms. "So the leader of the Sathanas Ward knows I'm coming in for the trials."

"*Everyone* knows. The rumors already spread. They know Mortana is dead and that you're her sister. Or whatever. They know you're a Lightbringer." She sipped her coffee, then licked the froth off her upper lip. "Everyone saw your mark when you were about to kill Cambriel. You have a claim to the throne. Any demon would try it." She leaned back in her chair, peering at me over her coffee cup. Steam curled before her face. "Even if they don't know you're coming tonight, they think you're either going to challenge Orion or marry him. Either way, if you live, you'll be queen."

"Marry him." I snorted. "Did they miss the part where he kicked me out of the city?"

"No, but you're a succubus. Hard to resist. And everyone knows he's an incubus." She slid her coffee onto the table. "And since he didn't kill you, people still think there's a chance it all ends in marriage."

"Yeah, that's not happening. Orion is fundamentally broken. I don't think he actually has the capacity to love anyone. All he cares about is murdering people. Revenge. That's it."

She peered at me over her coffee cup. "Yeah, I think people are pretty terrified of him. You know, some of them were around during the Lilu massacre, and they didn't stop it. No one knows if he's going to rip their heads off like he did with King Nergal." She smiled faintly. "That's why Legion helped me find the gauntlet."

"I'm surprised Orion hasn't started the bloodbath already."

She took a sip of her coffee. "No one really knows what he's been up to. Tonight will be one of his first public events." She gave me a measuring look. "And you're going to show up and...what, exactly?"

I took a deep breath. "It's very simple. We fight, and the first person thrown to the ground loses. All I have to do is throw Orion to the earth, and then I become shadow scion. His official challenger."

She sank back into her chair, considering this. "Alternately, the first person to be killed loses."

A bit of fear danced up my spine. "Well, that *is* one way of falling to the ground."

"That's the point I'm stuck on," she said. "I mean, you literally just said he's broken and bloodthirsty, so it doesn't fill me with a great deal of confidence about his level of restraint. He's going to try to murder you, right?"

"Shai! I'm trying not to think about the worst-case scenario. I'm trying to envision success. If I win tonight, I'm in charge of the second trial. I'll have an advantage." Nodding at the book, I said, "There are a whole bunch to choose from in there." I dropped my coffee onto a coaster and cracked open the soft blue volume, flipping through the ancient pages. "It could be a quest. An endurance test. A battle of magic. Jousting. I've read through every option. But they all require magical spells in Demonic, so I'll need your help with that part."

She smirked. "Please tell me you're going to joust."

"Yeah, I'm gonna pass on that one. But I'm not committing to anything yet. I want to see what it's like to fight Orion first."

"I *do* want to be besties with a queen." Shai took the old book from me and began paging through it. "I can totally lend a hand with the spells. But I also have two friends who can help. Legion and his friend Kas have been teaching me magic. They're, like, the best professors in the history of the demon world."

I narrowed my eyes. "I've only been gone two weeks, and you have a whole new friend group. Do I need to be jealous?"

"Absolutely not, because you're going to love them, too. They're very easy on the eyes. And they helped me discover my hidden demon powers."

I arched an eyebrow. "Okay. Can I get a demonstration?"

She stood and crossed the creaking floor to one of the windows overlooking the sea, then turned to face me, her brown eyes glinting. "Watch and be amazed." She faced the window again and lifted her hands toward the glass, then started to mutter under her breath.

At first, nothing happened, and I just drank my coffee, waiting. But after a few minutes, an electrical rush rippled through the room, raising the hair on the back of my arms. Magic hummed along my arms and legs. Around her body, the air glowed silver, and her curls rose higher off her shoulders.

A chill ran up my spine. Outside, shadows began to creep across the clouds. The air thinned and grew darker.

Outside, the ocean waves churned against the rocky shore. Just like in my nightmare, storm clouds unleashed fat drops of rain. Within moments, they were hammering against the window, sliding down in rivulets.

Stunned, I held my breath.

Slowly, Shai lowered her hands. When she turned to look at me, her eyes shone with a certain wildness.

"Holy shit, Shai."

"I've been trying to summon lightning, but it's not happening for me yet." She dropped into the velvet armchair once more. "Cool, though, right? I'm not just an ordinary mortal student anymore."

"You were never ordinary."

She leaned over to pick up her coffee. "I wish I could help you in the trials. I could just hit Orion with lightning." Rays of sunlight peeked through the clouds, gilding Shai's brown skin and rose-gold cheekbones. "Exactly how broken and bloodthirsty is he?"

My breath quickened. "I mean, he spent centuries in prison thinking of nothing but avenging the Lilu. He feels like he died in that dungeon. Where his soul used to be, there's now only lust for revenge."

"Shit."

"And that's where you have to keep me on track, Shai. Because if I win this trial, he's going to use every trick in the incubus playbook to throw me off. An incubus is seductive and charming, and he's going to use all that to try to get me to quit. Not because he cares, or because he likes me. An incubus uses his beauty and magic as a weapon to control other people, and that's exactly what he'll do with me. An unrelenting, seductive charm offensive of sensual magic and pretty words."

Shai arched an eyebrow. "Unsettling. But also weirdly hot at the same time?"

"The Lord of Chaos is all about mind games, but I absolutely cannot fall for it. If I seem like I'm going soft on him, please remind me that he shoved me out of the City as soon as he no longer needed me. He killed the man I'd been hunting, even though he knew it was my life's goal. Remind me that he said I'm boring and that he doesn't respect me."

She narrowed her eyes. "Okay, he might be broken, but he doesn't think *you're* boring. Like, it's obvious—he's kind of obsessed with you, I think. Otherwise a king wouldn't let his rival live. But yes, he's all messed up, or he wouldn't have said something so insane in the first place."

He'd sort of taken it back in a moment of passion, but that wasn't exactly trustworthy, was it? "That's because we're both Lilu. We feed off lust, and we're the only two left. Our feelings aren't real, just the deceit of magic."

"Absolutely. Forget about Orion, because I really think you'll like Kas. He's got these huge muscles and these tattoos—"

"I'm all done with men, Shai," I said, interrupting. "You know Queen Elizabeth I, the redheaded queen who never married? That's going to be me. She was the best monarch England ever had because she didn't have a man around getting in her head and trying to take over. She was married to her kingdom. That's gonna be me."

"Cool, but get back to me after you hear Kas's voice. It's deep and rough. You can't have Legion, though. Legion is mine."

"*Really*? You have something with the duke?"

Her lips curved. "I will. And if you go out with Kas, he might help you melt away this whole 'bitter, sad woman' vibe."

"I'm not bitter," I protested. "I just think most romance is bullshit. It's cotton candy. It looks nice, and it tastes kind of good at first, but ultimately, it just makes you want to puke."

"That's a lot of rage you have for cotton candy."

Our feelings for each other were an illusion, the product of Lilu lust magic. They were spun sugar that dissolved at the first sign of a storm.

She nodded. "No more Orion. I'm just saying there are better, less genocidal options who are also hot as fuck. You know, once you win the trials. Get yourself in a positive headspace before you come into the City of Thorns. Find a new man, one less murdery."

Every inch of my body was tightening with resolve. "I'm perfectly happy. But what matters now is stopping a tyrant before he slaughters all the humans." I lifted my coffee in salute. "And that all starts tonight."

She heaved a deep breath. "Okay. But you should probably know that the demon hunters are completely staked out by the entrance, waiting for you to walk up to that gate."

Anticipation crackled over me. "Good thing Orion showed me the tunnel system, then."

❧ 3 ❧

ROWAN

Beneath the City of Thorns, the world was quiet as death. I stalked through the shadows in borrowed clothes, all black. A bag bounced against my hip as I walked, heavy with the weight of the gauntlet.

From under the city, I could hear vibrations through the stones—the sounds of dancing and singing.

In the initial trial by combat, no weapons were allowed. Fortunately, Tammuz had trained me to fight like a demon: unarmed, but using my claws as a weapon.

Just beneath the demon city, the promise of magic beckoned me closer. Once I was in their world—*my* world—power and grace would flow through my body. Images flared in my thoughts: Orion's eyes darkening to black, his lip pulled back from his fangs as he lunged for me...

Hard not to hear his words replaying in my mind. *You don't have it in you, love.*

My fingertips curled, and ice-cold anger rushed through my body, chilling me to the marrow. My fury was a hurricane wind that drowned out all the thoughts in my mind.

As I reached the place where a few cracks of light pierced the darkness, I no longer had words with which to think.

Fingers and toes gripping the spaces between the rocks, I climbed up the tunnel wall. With one hand, I pushed the metal covering aside. The star-dappled night arched over me, and I breathed in the fragrant, humid air of the City of Thorns.

When I pulled myself out onto the dark riverside, my magic slammed into me, spreading outward from my lungs. Power skimmed down my thighs, my calves—hot and delicious, a buzzing warmth. Faintly, I was glowing, overcome by the urge to run and fly and tear through the air, singing to the stars. The return of my power was like taking the first breath of air after being held underwater—*glorious*.

Forcing myself to focus, I crouched down and slid the cover back over the opening, then straightened to take in my surroundings. The Acheron River rushed past me to the left, and the dark Elysian Wilderness spread out behind it, its shadows strangely inviting. My mouth started watering; I hungered to sprint through that primal darkness—to hunt like I had in the underworld.

I'd fought there once, but I was no longer the Rowan who needed makeshift flame throwers to survive a battle. I'd journeyed to the underworld. I'd died at the hands of a raving mob. I'd come back to life. I'd learned lessons at the hands of a god.

I wasn't stupid enough to think this would be easy, but I had a *chance*.

I turned, eyeing the apartment I'd stayed in—the one with a view of the pool. A little blade pierced my chest when I recalled the alliance Orion and I once had when he was teaching me to *act* like a succubus. Didn't really need those lessons, as it turned out.

I started to hurry toward the festival, my nerves sparking. I moved quickly past the Asmodean Ward and into the ward of Abaddon. As I turned away from the river, golden stone buildings towered over me. When I drew closer to the Tower of Baal on the eastern edge of the city, the sound of the festival floated on the wind, rhythmic and intoxicating.

My skin tingled with anticipation as I stalked through an alleyway, and I felt my hips swaying with the confidence of a succubus. Through an archway, I crossed into the broad square before the Tower of Baal. A glittering, bejeweled crowd spread out before me.

I had to hand it to Orion. Seemed like he knew how to put on a party, even after all those years in isolation. In the air, glowing lights hung suspended by magic, some shaped like crescents and some like full moons. On the other side of the square, rays of silver light projected the moon's cycles onto the walls outside the tower.

Demons whirled and danced to a mesmerizing beat, with the sound of vocal harmonies layered over it. Most of the guests wore white and silver, and their flutes of champagne seemed to shimmer, opalescent. A tree stood in the center of the square—one that hadn't been there weeks ago. It towered above the revelers, and pearly lanterns hung from its gnarled boughs like plump jewels.

Tonight, the stars seemed brighter than ever, and the vibrance of the full moon almost made it seem like it had shown up to party along with its worshippers.

No one had noticed me yet, lurking in the shadows. Unseen, I reached into the bag at my hip and pulled out the gauntlet.

From the corner of the square, I scanned the crowd, searching for the king. Most new monarchs would relish the limelight and take center stage. But apparently, that wasn't Orion's style. A festival honoring night was perfect for him, when he kept as much as possible cloaked in darkness—including the truth about himself.

I dropped the empty bag at my feet.

Gripping the iron gauntlet, I took a few steps into the square. Slowly, the eyes started to turn to me, and one or two people yelped, smacking the arms of their dancing partners. A hush spread over the festival as whispers began to spread. The music faded to silence, and the crowd parted around me. Tension thickened the air.

At last, the only noise remaining was a quiet murmuring in the crowd, and the slamming of my heart against my ribs. How would Orion handle this?

"Rowan." The king's voice from behind me was a stroke of velvet up my spine, and a hot shiver ran through every inch of me.

I turned to see him standing behind me, a lock of hair falling in his eyes. He didn't wear a crown, and he looked perfectly relaxed, his hands in his pockets. He wore a simple dark blue button-down shirt that stretched across his muscled arms and shoulders, and dark gray trousers.

Shadows wrapped around him, but his eyes glowed with icy light. If it weren't for his shockingly beautiful face and silver hair, he'd have blended with the darkness behind him.

I tossed the gauntlet down, and it clanged at his feet. Nevertheless, he kept his eyes locked on me.

With a practiced tongue, I invoked the archaic Demonic challenge to the king. "*Parzilu Sarrum Tahuzu*."

"You've come for the crown," he said, a faint smile curling his lips.

"You don't seem surprised."

He shrugged slowly. "Maybe I was starting to miss you."

Ah. There it was—the incubus charm. The façade. It was a trick that Tammuz had taught me: confuse your opponent until they can't figure out how to respond, get them to let down their guard.

Orion had no choice now, though. The trial was starting either way.

He cocked his head. "You don't seem scared, considering what you're about to undertake."

My fingers twitched. "Of course I am," I said quietly, so only he and I could hear. "But I'm gonna kick your ass anyway."

His response was what looked like a truly dazzling and genuine smile. Disarming. Throwing me off guard.

He arched an eyebrow, taking a few graceful steps forward. "You don't think we should join forces, love? Everyone else seems to think so, including Lucifer himself. After all, he did mark both of us."

Was that a hint of mockery in his tone? Hard to tell with him.

According to the ancient courtly customs of demonic fighting, I was supposed to wait until he was ready to begin the fight—when he picked up the gauntlet, formally accepting the trial. But that part wasn't a *law*, per se, just a convention. And the longer I waited, the greater the opportunity I'd give him to flirt with me until I no longer knew what was happening.

I lunged forward. Lightning-fast, I slammed my fist into the side of his head.

❧ 4 ❧
ROWAN

The force of the blow echoed off the stones, and he nearly lost his balance. He regained his composure well enough to retaliate with a punch, but I blocked it with my right forearm. I brought down my left fist hard, into his shoulder.

My feet landed on the ground, and my claws shot out from my fingertips. In a fraction of a heartbeat, I made a move for Orion's throat, but he arched his back, his head dodging out of the way. As he did, he grabbed my wrist, *hard*. For just a moment, the world seemed to slow as we stared at each other, and a briny wind toyed with my hair. Why did he look so fucking exhilarated by this? Like he was enjoying himself?

"I wanted revenge," I whispered. "You took it from me."

His pale eyes had a sorrowful expression that *nearly* made me feel bad for him...that is, until he twisted my arm behind my back, spinning me away from him.

Pain shot up my arm, and he leaned down to whisper in my ear, "I'm sorry."

My jaw clenched. *Fucking incubus mind games.*

I brought my left arm back into his ribs with enough ferocity that he dropped his grip on my arm. I spun, then slashed my claws through his gut. But something stopped me from going deeper, pushing harder—even though he'd live. It was an instinct I couldn't overcome.

Orion still hadn't brought out his claws, and he punched me again —but I blocked it. The force of his wrist against my forearm was like a sledgehammer falling from a thousand feet, and I was pretty sure my bones fractured for a moment. But as a demon in the City of Thorns, I healed quickly.

As my wings burst from my back, I lifted off the ground. Orion was up in the air faster than I'd expected, his wings pounding the night.

If I'd expected him to look fearful or enraged, I'd have been disappointed.

In the air, he was giving me a look of pure mischief, pale eyes glistening. We might as well have been dancing. "Did you miss me as much as I missed you?"

"Only if you didn't miss me at all." My claws glinted in the moonlight—but before I could strike, he soared past me, blending into the darkness itself. Had he just...disappeared?

I'd never seen him do that before. How many hidden powers did this cocky fucker have? And how was I supposed to win if I couldn't even see him?

I inhaled, trusting my demonic instincts to help find him. Soon enough, his exotic magic thrummed faintly along my skin, and I detected his scent. *Cedar.* He'd moved closer to the tower walls. Soaring through the air, I followed his seductive, fragrant trail, but I still couldn't see him.

I turned, scanning the night air, the crowd below. That was when he appeared again—a powerful warrior's body materialized out of moonlight. He rushed forward, and I started to fly to meet him, to strike first.

But his velocity was so intense that he slammed me hard into the tower wall. I flinched, anticipating the shock of pain that would splinter my back. But the pain didn't register. Orion had deftly managed to cushion the blow—one hand around my waist, holding me closer to his rock-hard chest, and the other pressed against the stone wall itself to stop me from making contact.

His warm magic swept around me, singing over my skin. The night wind whipped over us. I'd never felt so alive.

"I shouldn't have kicked you out," he said softly. Up here, the silver light washed over his perfect cheekbones and sparked in his eyes. For the first time, I noticed that the pale blue in his eyes was shot through with silver flecks like moonlight. "I'm sorry I took the revenge that should have been yours."

"Here it is," I hissed, pressed against him. "The incubus's most confounding weapon. Charm."

His fingers were tight around my waist. "Do you know what I like about you, Rowan? This city is full of powerful demons, and not a single one of them has the balls to admit that they're scared of anything." His eyes seemed to be searching mine. "And that's a lie we're living. Because we're all terrified of something."

"What scares you?" I breathed.

His mouth was an inch from mine now, and he was staring at my lips as if he were going to kiss me. "You." His eyes flicked up to meet mine again. "Among other things."

"What other things?"

His breath warmed the crook of my neck. "Someday, I'll tell you."

Throwing me off guard. I slid my palms up his chest, then pushed him away from me with all the force I could muster. He flew back into the air, but he managed to stay suspended, looking startled.

I rushed forward, angling my wings for speed. I brought out my claws, ready to strike again. But Orion rushed forward, caught me around the waist, and pulled me in against him again. Our wings pounding behind us, and we hung suspended in the air like the moon itself.

I wrapped my arms over his shoulders.

Staring deep into my eyes, he murmured, "Why not join me, love?" His breath warmed the crook of my neck.

"Because, *love*," I said, "you want to fucking murder everyone."

No denial from him. Instead, he cupped the side of my face, and he stroked his thumb gently over my cheek. "Don't you want to be free?" he purred. "Demons were never meant to be caged. Cambriel might have been the one to murder your parents, but the mortals are the reason they were in hiding in the first place, vulnerable without the power that belonged to them."

The little boy from my nightmare flashed in my mind, and a surge of protectiveness lit me up. A long-buried animal instinct sent aggression snapping through my nerves.

I wasn't mortal anymore.

Demons hunt.

I wanted to devour the beautiful thing before me, to feed off his essence.

My fangs lengthened, and I sank them deep into Orion's throat. His blood surged into my mouth—deliciously sweet and with a metallic tinge, a dark sort of ambrosia. This was life. This was power. I dominated him.

No *wonder* demons liked drinking blood.

With a snarl, he pushed me away.

He held his hand against the puncture marks, his brow furrowed. "No one's ever bitten me before."

Remember when you said I didn't have it in me? That you didn't respect me enough to hate me?

I wiped the back of my hand across my mouth. "Fair's fair. You drank my blood the first night we met."

I'd learned something from this fight—Orion was still stronger than me, still faster. But he was vulnerable to the element of surprise.

The corner of his mouth quirked. "You've changed, Rowan."

Force your enemy to let down his guard.

I flew a little closer, eyebrows rising. "Of course I've changed. I trained with the Dying God. The *Chaos* God. Bit of a dysfunctional family you've got, isn't it? He's your father, and he taught me how to kill you."

His faint smile faltered with uncertainty.

Now.

The night wind swept over me, and I swiped for his throat with my claws. Blood arced through the air, and I used my wings to give me the speed of a hurricane. I slammed into Orion, and we hurtled toward the ground together. We hit the stone with a force that cracked the rock beneath him. It sent shockwaves across the square as the ground fractured. Orion's wings were still out, spread beneath him in dark arches of feathers. I was straddling him, legs wrapped around his waist. He stared up at me, catching his breath.

I'd won.

Around us, the crowd of onlookers gasped.

It must have hurt like a bitch when his wings met the rock, but the pain didn't even register on his perfect features. "Tammuz," he said, his voice rasping.

It was glowing now—the star of Lucifer on his forehead. I reached down to touch it.

"Your real father," I said. "He's the one who gave us these marks. To cause chaos."

He grazed his fingertip over my forearm, and I realized it was the spot where the tattoo of the skeleton key marked my skin. "Is it true?"

Orion's blood had spilled down his front and started to dry on his neck, but the gash in his throat was healing already.

I shrugged. "It's what he said. But I don't trust either of you to tell the truth, so who knows?"

"He told me you were after my crown."

I leaned down, so mesmerized by the thrill of victory that I nearly forgot the silent crowd around us. "He was right."

He cupped my jaw and whispered, "This was a painful way to get your legs wrapped around me again. But maybe it was worth it."

I slid off him and rose to my full height, surveying the hushed crowd around us. Orion got to his feet by my side.

The crowd of onlookers stared at us silently, as if they were still waiting for more bloodshed. I almost had the sense that this trial had been a disappointment for them, that they'd craved a fresh, beating demon heart pumping on the stones, and all they'd gotten were some broken wings.

I caught Shai's attention as she stood near the front of the crowd, her eyes wide. She beamed at me, grinning. Legion stood by her side. The leader of the Sathanas Ward wore a crisp white shirt, his sleeves rolled up to show off his tattoos. His long black hair was tied up. On the other side of her was a blond demon with piercing amber eyes and thorny tattoos coiling over his forearms, spiky swirls that wound all the way up to his neck. With a faint smile, he nodded to me—almost a bow. Shai's new friend, I assumed.

By my side, Orion's body faintly glowed with silver like the moon we were celebrating.

I raised a hand. "City of Thorns! You have two leaders now, a king and a shadow scion. And when the trials are completed, I hope to be your queen."

"Do not try to win my favor by hurting her." Orion's voice boomed. "The ancient laws of the demon trials protect her, and I will personally tear out the heart of anyone who lays a finger on her." He held my gaze for a moment before turning back to his subjects. "The woman you see before you is not the monster who murdered the Lilu. Don't make the same mistake I did. This is Rowan Morgenstern, not Mortana, and the two of them could not be more different." He cast a sidelong glance at me. "Rowan is welcome here, and as king, I will be giving her the best I have to offer until the trial has ended." His smile was truly dazzling.

The incubus charm offensive.

And with his gracious speech concluded, darkness swept around him. He slipped into the crowd again, enveloped in the shadows.

Lucifer was the original Lightbringer. His twin, Tammuz, reigned in darkness. And here was Tammuz's son, a creature of chaos and night.

Was there anything else I didn't know about him? Another godlike power I hadn't yet seen?

As ever, Orion was always keeping the truth about himself hidden in the darkness.

5

ROWAN

Orion had disappeared without explaining what I was supposed to do, so I figured I might as well enjoy myself. This was, after all, a festival. Long ago, a Lilu like me would have been to plenty of these. The music swelled in the air again, and mortal servers rushed around with trays of pastries and champagne.

Even if I was only a shadow scion, I was being treated like a queen already. A small crowd had formed around me, and someone handed me a champagne flute. Another person handed me a small crescent-shaped cake with silvery frosting. I bit into it, delighted to find that someone had decided the moon should taste like chocolate and raspberry.

Shai stood by my side, and given the way she was swaying, I guessed she was on at least her third glass of bubbly. "I swear to the gods, Rowan. My heart was in my throat the whole time. I really can't handle this shit."

Next to me, a woman with platinum hair and a silver dress leaned in closer. "What was he saying to you when you were fighting? Was he proposing a truce?"

Orion was predictable, even to them. He'd been fine with exiling me weeks ago, but now that I'd returned to challenge his power, he'd decided that teamwork was the way to go, and maybe I could drop the whole idea about taking his crown from him.

I shrugged. "Oh, you know. He was just being his usual charming self. Trying to distract me from winning."

Around me, the other demons craned their necks, listening to every word I said.

"You look radiant!" said another woman from the back.

A male demon with bronze horns lifted his champagne flute. "Truly regal, Shadow Scion."

I cast a quick look at Shai, who just shrugged. I wasn't used to being showered in compliments, and I had no idea how to respond. Of course, they were only hedging their bets, hoping to be on good terms with the next ruler. As soon as I walked away, they'd be doing the same to Orion.

"Do you need anything, Lady Morgenstern?" someone asked from behind.

What I really needed right now after that exhausting fight was not to be the center of attention.

I lifted my empty glass, and before I could say another word, someone snatched it away to refill it. But I'd been in a dark underworld for what felt like a year, and then in a quiet apartment by myself. I wasn't quite used to all these people yet. Even the moon seemed too bright, somehow. Why did I feel like I could hear everyone's breathing?

I held up my hand. "Thank you, I've had enough champagne. I'm going to get some rest and think about the next trial."

I forced my way out of the crowd, desperate for space. Once I reached the edges of the festival, my gaze flicked toward the river. Following the Acheron was always the easiest way around the City of Thorns, and walking west along the bank would take me back to my apartment that overlooked the pool. Towering stone buildings loomed over me on one side. On the other, the forest seemed to beckon. When I'd first arrived here, the wilderness had struck me as sinister. Now, it looked like heaven. The sight of it made my fangs lengthen and my heart beat faster. I ran my tongue over my teeth, dizzy for a moment with hunger.

What was I hungry for? Something I couldn't name, a power I'd once possessed.

I glanced down at the tattoo on my arm and traced my fingertips over the dark contours of the skeleton key. In the underworld with Tammuz, I'd lived like a real demon. With just the two of us there, I'd trained in a primal world, becoming a predator. A memory flashed in my mind: I'd taken down a stag with my bare hands, sinking my teeth into its neck to feast on it.

I swallowed hard, shocked to remember I'd eaten it raw.

I started toward the stone river walk, breathing in the humid air. For now, the ball was in my court. As the shadow scion, I would choose the next trial. The time, the location, the task...

What I'd learned from tonight was that anything involving physical strength was a risk. Maybe I'd win, maybe not.

As I crossed onto the river walk, I heard Shai calling my name, and the sound echoed off the stones. I turned to see her walking between Legion and the blond demon. They really did make a gorgeous trio.

"I wanted to introduce you to my friends," said Shai breathlessly as she drew closer.

The blond held out his hand, and I shook it, my gaze trailing over the tattoos that snaked around his arms. His eyes were the color of whiskey. "I'm Kasyade. But almost everyone calls me Kas. And I am absolutely delighted to meet a real succubus." With his messed-up hair, he had an almost boyish look—which made his deep, gravelly voice unexpected. "I was already intrigued by Mortana, but I didn't want to get anywhere near her, given her reputation."

This close, I got a better look at him. He was styled much more casually than most of the demons I'd seen, in dark jeans and a T-shirt that gave him a kind of tattooed, muscular, James Dean look.

I glanced at Legion, who was clean shaven and dressed more formally. "We've met before," I said, "but I suppose I was Mortana then."

Moonlight glinted in his angular brown eyes. "It took a long time for Shai to convince me that you were someone different. But then I suppose if you were the real Mortana, a Lilu king would have ripped out your heart by now. And he still might, of course, since you're trying to take the crown from him."

Kas sighed. "Please excuse my blunt friend." He glanced over his shoulder. "But he's right. You're not safe here, no matter what the king said."

I shook my head. "I'm sure Orion knows the rules are very strict. He's not allowed to hurt me outside the trials."

Shai hooked her arm into mine. "We'll escort you home anyway."

Kas quirked a lopsided smile, his cheek dimpling on one side. "I didn't want to miss the chance to meet our city's first queen."

"I like your confidence in me, Kas," I said.

As we started walking, the music from the festival faded into the distance.

Legion's black eyebrows knitted together as he looked at me. "The Asmodean quarter...don't you find it a bit..."

"Haunted?" asked Kas.

I glanced between them. "Do you two always finish each other's sentences?"

"We've known each other since we were little boys," said Kas. "Since before the city was founded."

"So you're older than Orion?"

"Old and wise," said Shai. "Exactly why they'd be perfect to help you prepare for the next trial."

My gaze flicked between the two male demons. "What if I lose? And what if Orion takes out his rage on you two?"

"We survived the mad king Azriel," said Legion. "We can survive the mad king Orion."

"All things being equal," said Kas, "we'd prefer someone sane. That's why we'll help you."

The wind rushed off the river, giving me goosebumps. On our right, we passed a stone building with turrets and windows lit up with warm light.

"What do you think of Orion, then?" I asked.

"They know he wants to murder all the mortals," said Shai. "Because I told them."

Legion's dark eyes slid to me. "I remember what it was like back then, when the mortals invaded our City after the war. First, they weakened our magic. Then they cut off the heads of the Lilu who resisted and stuck them on pikes. Anyone who survived was marched past the remains of their families. We thought the Lilu were being led to their deaths. None of us ever imagined some of them survived. We never spoke of them. We all felt guilty. We had no clue Orion was still down there. The idea that someone was locked up by himself in a dungeon after all that—there's no way he could be sane."

Kas ran a hand through his messy hair. "Honestly, the thought of someone enduring that is unbearable."

"Stop," I said. "You're going to make me feel bad for him, and then I'll lose."

"Just remember," said Shai, "he said you were boring. It's really the worst thing a person could say, even if he didn't mean it."

Kas's brow furrowed. "King Nergal told us that the mortals' revenge on the Lilu was the price we had to pay for losing the war. It was a sacrifice. But the truth was, he wanted the Lilu gone, too. They were a threat to him. They were too powerful, and he had no conscience whatsoever. And that is why, sometimes, I wonder if the mortals have it right. Maybe we should, I don't know, *vote* for a leader instead of letting people decide it by ripping someone's heart out of their chest." He smiled at me. "But if I have to support someone's brute strength, let it be yours. You've at least lived among the mortals. You know how they think. They modernize. We don't. You have that advantage, don't you?"

I narrowed my eyes. "And why should I trust you two ancient demons?"

"Because I said so," said Shai.

"Well, that's your first lesson." Kas's expression had turned serious. "You shouldn't trust us. In the City of Thorns, you shouldn't trust anyone or anything except your own senses."

"And sometimes," added Legion, "don't even trust those."

"True," said Kas. "You can hide things from yourself. Like, you didn't know you were a demon, right?"

"When did you first feel your magic?" asked Legion.

I bit my lip. "I guess the night my mom died was the first time. I saw the reflection of my demon mark in a puddle. But I lost that memory for years, so yeah, you can't always trust your senses or your memories."

"Ah," said Kas quietly. "*Gaze no more in the bitter glass.*

The demons, with their subtle guile

Lift up before us when they pass,

Or only gaze a little while;

For there a fatal image grows

That the stormy night receives."

His words made my skin tingle, and a hush fell over us for a moment.

"No quoting Yeats," said Legion, breaking the silence. "I've had enough of random poetry from you."

Kas leaned in close, his voice low. "The thing about demons is that we keep most of our powers hidden until we really need them. It's part of our culture. We all do it." Kas crossed in front of me, walking backward to keep his twinkling amber eyes on me. "Everyone keeps secrets here. I'm sure you have some of your own." The wind caught his hair as he walked, his movements graceful as a dancer. "So don't trust anyone. Not even me."

My gaze slid over his tattoos, the wild swirls and patterns covering his muscular forearms.

A mournful thought nagged at the back of my mind. I never did find out what Orion's serpent tattoo was about, and at this point, I doubted I ever would.

In front of me, Kas stopped walking abruptly, and I nearly bumped into him. His gaze was on something over my head, and shadows slid through his golden eyes. I looked up, and in the next heartbeat, I knew exactly why.

Orion's tantalizing magic sang over my skin, and I spun around.

Here was the king, draped in shadows, the wind toying with his silver hair. "Thank you for escorting our shadow scion home, but I will take it from here." Underneath his smooth, velvety voice, I heard a distinctly sharp edge. He prowled closer and rested his hand on my waist.

To my surprise, I heard the sound of Kas and Legion growling behind me, and tension crackled the air.

❦ 6 ❦

ROWAN

I stared up at Orion, who was looking over my head at the two other demons. The entire time I'd been fighting him, his eyes had remained pale blue. Only now, when we were standing by the side of a river without a single hint of a threat, did they darken to black.

Orion's gaze slid from Kas to Legion like he was about to murder them both. "As king," he said quietly, "it is my job to keep the shadow scion safe."

"From *whom*, exactly?" asked Kas.

Orion's hand tightened on my waist. Maybe it was time for me to stop this macho display of possessiveness before my new friends ended up as piles of ash on the stones.

"Okay, everyone—" I began.

A flash of hot magic interrupted me, searing the air. Heat slid through my blood, and I stumbled back from the force of Orion's magic.

For one horrible moment, I was certain that Orion had just incinerated everyone around us until I realized I'd been thrust back into Kas's powerful chest.

When I turned to look at the others, I found them staring, dazed and open-mouthed. Shai swayed, a little smile playing on her lips.

I touched her arm. "Shai?"

Ignoring me, she stepped closer to Orion, fluttering her eyelashes. She reached out, touching his chest. "Your Majesty! Do you work out?"

With a low growl, Legion's hand snapped out, and he grabbed Shai's bicep, then spun her around to face him. "Why don't you forget him and show me your room?"

She bit her lip, staring dreamily into Legion's face.

My jaw dropped in disbelief as I realized what he'd done. Orion had slammed them with his incubus magic, and now they were all lust drunk. Somewhere deep down, I had this power, too. I'd just never learned to use it—nor would I ever use it on my friends, because *what the hell?*

When I caught Kas's gaze, the look he was giving me was searing, carnal, his eyes dark as jet. His gaze shamelessly swept down to take in every inch of me. "Rowan." His voice came out as a deep, husky rumble.

In a rush of shadows, Orion swept in front of me and gently wrapped his fingers around Kas's throat. "I *suggest* you find someone else for your attention."

Kas swayed on his feet for a moment, staring into Orion's eyes in a stupor. He sighed deeply, then repeated, "Find someone else."

"Orion. Stop fucking with them," I snapped. "This is why everyone hates the Lilu."

I could feel the effects of his lust magic, too—a warmth that coiled tight in my core, the sensitivity of my skin—but as a succubus, I had more control over myself.

Kas turned away from him, stalking back to the festival. I felt a twinge of disappointment. It would actually be nice to have a group of friends for once.

I cut Orion a sharp look. "This is a little stalkerish, don't you think? Following me and chasing off my new friends?"

He cocked his head. "Everyone hates our kind. We are the last two left, and I'm not letting anything happen to you. Besides, I need to show you to your new room."

"You're not letting anything happen to me?" I started walking quickly, even though I had no idea where my new room was. "Not long ago, you kicked me out of the city and left me to fend for myself, with no magic, surrounded by demon hunters who want me dead. And I'm supposed to suddenly believe you care about my safety?"

"I didn't leave you," he said smoothly. "I had guards watching over you. First in the hotel, then in Shai's aunt's house."

I swallowed hard. "Guards?"

"Anna, with the pink hair. And her cat, Taffy. I thought you would have noticed them."

"Hmm." *Don't trust him, Rowan.* I'd come prepared for his charm, and my iron defenses would withstand it. "So nice of you to look out for me. And yet, you killed my half brother Cambriel, knowing that all I wanted was to avenge my mom."

When he met my gaze, his large blue eyes gleamed. "I made a promise, too, Rowan. A vow to *all* the Lilu dead that I would avenge them. It's why I must be king. And I knew you'd try to stop me, but I made an oath of vengeance to Ashur before I watched him dragged to his death. I promised it to the memory of my mother. To each of them."

I inhaled deeply. "But that's not what's best for the demons who live. Starting a war with the mortals."

Silence stretched out between us, and I listened to the sound of the Acheron rushing past. "I went to find you, Rowan," he said at last. "When you were still in the underworld, and I finally realized you weren't Mortana. I woke one night with this terrible realization that you'd died. Not Mortana, but Rowan. And I felt like my heart had been ripped out." He touched my elbow, leading me away from the river and under a dark archway.

A shiver of pleasure rippled through me from the point of contact, where his fingers were brushing against the back of my arm. Clearly, his incubus magic was still affecting me, because desire swept down into my belly and settled there, making it hard to concentrate. "Okay," was all I could muster.

"Why would I feel your death, Rowan, unless we were connected? We are the twin stars. Our fates are entwined."

My heels clacked over the stones and echoed off the narrow alley. *Iron defenses.* "I'm not giving up the trials, Orion, if that's where you're going with this. Where are you taking me, by the way?"

"To your new palace."

"Palace?" I repeated.

"In the Luciferian Ward, near me." He turned to look at me, his eyes piercing the dark. "Listen, when I thought you were dead, I traveled to the underworld. I was desperate to find you again if I could. And I really didn't know I could feel like that anymore."

"Like what?"

With a sharp intake of breath, he looked away. "Anything," he said vaguely. "I didn't know I could feel anything for the living. And after I passed through Purgatory and found Tammuz, he knew exactly how to get inside my head. He knew exactly what to say, because it had been my mantra for centuries. He knew all along exactly what I'd experienced with Mortana. Tammuz didn't lift a finger to stop it because the chaos delighted him. He played us both, don't you think? He just wanted to be entertained."

"What did he say to you?" I asked.

Orion stopped walking and turned to me. "He said, 'Orion, don't you know that you should never let yourself hope?' He knew that was the lesson I'd learned from Mortana. Letting myself hope was what killed me slowly in the dungeon. Mortana used to promise me I would be released, only to laugh in my face every time I believed her. But maybe it's time I stopped taking my lessons from her."

"Does that mean you no longer want revenge?" As soon as the question was out of my mouth, I was already wondering if I was simply falling into Orion's seductive trap again.

Instead of answering, he led me into an alleyway that opened into a rounded courtyard where myrtle trees bloomed. Their crimson petals scattered over the stones like drops of blood. Here, the air smelled of salt and lemons. It smelled like home to me.

On one side of the courtyard was what I could only assume was the palace—three stories, with turrets and narrow, glowing windows. A few chimneys rose from the roofs, and the star of Lucifer was engraved above enormous oak doors. Buildings ringed the courtyard—stone with steep peaked roofs, some with balconies. Cute place.

Orion turned to me. "I made a promise to Ashur that I would get revenge. I didn't specify what it would be. But I believe the demons must be free, or it could happen again."

"Setting the demons free would start a war."

He studied me. "You mean the mortals would start a war. But we would win. And it's my responsibility to protect demons, not mortals. If mortals want to engage in a suicide mission just because we're no longer trapped in here, then that sounds like their problem."

I shook my head. "I feel like you're repackaging your revenge as 'freedom.'"

He arched an eyebrow. "The demons in the City of Thorns must be set free. It's what a Lightbringer is supposed to do. *Lucifer urbem spinarum libarabit*—the Lightbringer will set free the City of Thorns. It is our destiny, whether you realize it or not."

"Free so they can feed on mortals again?" I asked. "Like you once did."

"Yes, I like the idea of restoring the world to the way it once was. You know something is missing, don't you? We're creatures of the forest, of the wild. We're not meant for cities of stone." He reached for my cheek, then pulled his hand away, his fingers tightening. "We are supposed to hunt—and yes, sometimes that means hunting mortals. That is our nature, love. And we are meant to terrify."

My eyes narrowed, and I took a step closer. "Demons seem happy here. This place is fucking amazing."

A lock of his silver hair grazed his cheekbones. "But it's not enough, is it? This place is a prison of *civilization*." Disdain laced his tone. He leaned down, and his breath warmed the side of my face as he whispered, "Why not give in to what you desire? I know that you feel it, too." The warmth rolling off his muscled body made my breath catch.

Maybe it was the leftover lust magic, but my pulse was out of control.

"I don't want people to die." I was reminding myself, wasn't I?

"And yet, I could hear your heart racing at the thought of freedom."

I pulled myself away from him, heading for the wooden doors.

Of course I couldn't expect Orion to change—he'd been like this for centuries.

Don't you know that you should never let yourself hope?

From the stairs, I turned to face him. "I'm going to sleep, Orion. I'll let you know when I've decided on the next trial."

"Don't trust those demons you were with," he called out.

"I don't trust anyone." I gave him a wry smile. "Least of all you."

7

ORION

By my library window, I sipped a scotch. Books and candles littered my desk. From here, I had a view of the Abraxas courtyard, dappled with red petals, and Rowan's palace just on the other side. Inside, the windows of her new home glowed with warm light.

I'd watched as she'd stepped inside the heavy oak doors and they'd closed behind her.

I rose and ran a hand through my hair as I crossed through the library. Three weeks ago, when I'd become king, I'd moved into this house.

I always hated the ostentatiousness of the Tower of Baal, and I had no intention of living there. Ever. I didn't want to be the center of attention—that was for people like Cambriel and Nergal. And now that I was no longer pretending to be a duke, I didn't need the swanky seaside apartment. I just wanted a little cottage in the shadows.

But I wasn't exactly deprived here. I had a library, a balcony, bedroom walls lined with books. Everything was tidy, in exactly the right place.

In the evenings, I ate dinner with my cook at the dining room table with a roaring fire. Amon had been my family's cook before the Lilu massacre. He'd returned to me as soon as he'd learned who I really was. He was the only person here who seemed willing to talk to me about the Lilu, and the only one who talked to me like I was a normal person.

Every night, his two black Labs would curl up under our feet as we ate, hoping for scraps. Castor and Pollux, they were called.

I stepped into my bedroom. This was an old home, built around the time when I was born. The walls were dark wood, with two carved mahogany columns in the center. A little fire burned in the fireplace. In my room, the balcony doors were open, making the flames dance. A single painting hung on the walls: the succubus Lilith, with a snake climbing up her bare leg. Her hair was bright red.

Whisky in hand, I stepped out onto the balcony and glanced up at the stars. I settled into a wooden chair that overlooked the Abraxas courtyard.

With my free hand, I traced my finger over my throat. Even though I'd healed, I could still feel where she'd ripped it open with her claws. When she'd done that, I'd had the distinct impression she'd enjoyed it. The viciousness suited her.

The problem was, she wasn't going to let herself give in to her true nature.

I heard the little clicks of Labrador claws on the tile floor, and I turned to see Castor ambling over to me, a silvery sheen on his black fur. Moonlight glinted in his dark eyes, and he looked up at me with a distinctly guilty expression. When I noticed the smears of butter on his face, I understood why.

"Castor," I said. "You absolute glutton."

He lowered his head and crossed to my feet, where he made himself at home, curling up with a sigh. A salty wind swept over us, rustling his dark fur.

Behind me, the sound of footfalls echoed off the wooden walls.

I turned to see Amon crossing toward me, a glass of whisky in his own hand. His dark brown hair hung over broad shoulders.

Drinks on the balcony—our nightly ritual in these past few weeks.

As he sat down in the chair next to me, my gaze snagged on the jagged scar that ran down his face, from his scalp, across his nose, to his bristled jawline. When the mortals had come for us, he'd tried to protect my mom. I remembered when they'd split his head in half, and I'd assumed he'd died.

He took a sip of his whisky. "You could have won that fight tonight."

I glanced at him out of the corner of my eye. "I'll convince her to come around to my side."

His eyebrows rose. "You still think you can charm her after everything you said and did?"

As soon as I'd kicked her out of the city, I'd started to regret it. Rival or not, I'd *missed* her.

I sucked in a deep breath. "The problem is, she objects to the idea of freeing the demons."

Amon flashed me a sly smile. "Is that maybe because you told her you were after a bloodthirsty revenge crusade against the mortals, and that you wanted to slaughter all of them, even though they had nothing to do with events four hundred years ago? Can't imagine why she'd take issue with that plan. Seems perfectly reasonable."

I grunted, irritated that Amon agreed with her. "It might have something to do with it." I sipped my whiskey. "Fine. Maybe she has a point. But we still need to break the spell trapping us here. The mortals are after her, and they won't relent until I hand her over. As long as we're stuck, they could keep escalating."

"Is it actually possible to break the spell, Your Majesty?"

"Stop calling me that, Amon."

"Fine. Orion, if that's what you want to be called. But why that name? It's not your real one."

I stared at the night sky, so bright here in the City of Thorns. "I was comforted by thinking of the stars in the dungeon. It was the one spark of brightness—thinking of constellations like Orion. I tried to carve them so I could look at them."

My gaze slid over to the constellation of Gemini, the twin stars that beamed near Orion, seeming to reach across the darkness for each other.

I didn't remember my old name, nor did I want to. Whoever I was before had died in the dungeon. When I made the memorial for the Lilu dead, I'd include a nameless silver-haired boy.

Amon breathed in deeply, staring at the sky. "The twin stars. The two Lightbringers. Rowan and Orion."

"I used to dream of them at night when I wasn't dreaming of food. The twin stars. I never knew what it meant."

"Ah," he said quietly. "And is that why you are sitting out on a balcony staring at your ex-lover's house like a heartbroken lunatic? You are quite literally written in the stars."

I cleared my throat. "It's better if she stays close to me. There are many people here who fear the return of the Lilu."

When I'd thought she was dead in the underworld, it had nearly broken me. I couldn't handle the thought of her dying when she was under my protection here.

Rowan terrified me every bit as much as Mortana did. Mortana had been a sadist with my life in her hands. Rowan, on the other hand, has my heart in her hands.

When I'd first met her, she'd been fragile, easily scared. Innocent. Now, she looked like she wanted to rip my head from my body. But it wasn't death that terrified me. It was the look in her eyes, her anger with me that made me so scared, I could hardly breathe.

In the dungeon, revenge was the promise that had kept me sane. Without a purpose to it all, I would have gone completely mad. That blood oath had been the only way to make meaning out of the horror —a single pinprick of light in the darkness.

Vengeance was the righting of a wrong.

"Orion," said Amon, his voice gravelly, "when are you going to tell me what happened to you?"

Unlike me, Rowan wasn't afraid to tell the truth about herself. My secret would die with me, but Rowan wasn't like the rest of us demons. She was better.

"What happened to me?" I said. "Nothing. Just a lot of boredom and starvation. I ate more than a few rats." Another sip of scotch. "What do you know about Legion and his friend Kas?"

When I'd seen her walking with the two demon males, I'd felt an overwhelming urge to vaporize both of them.

Amon stared at me. "You really don't remember them, either?"

A hazy, distant memory danced in my mind—a dark-haired boy

with brown eyes, leading me into the Elysian Wilderness. Older kids I'd once looked up to.

"Oh. A little." But I didn't want to remember that time.

"So many secrets," Amon muttered. "Even keeping secrets from yourself."

I had one other secret: I would love Rowan until I died.

And that was why I deeply regretted what I had to do next.

❦ 8 ❦

ROWAN

I didn't need to follow Orion's orders here. As a shadow scion, I could make my own decision about where to stay. But as much as possible, I wanted Orion to think of me as the clumsy mortal he'd first encountered. I wanted him to let down his guard and completely fail to prepare for the next trial. Which he probably would, because his ego would get in the way.

The palace's lower floor had looked positively medieval. In the entryway, I'd found soldiers lined up on either side of a stone, each one wearing the blue uniform of a soldier, and the royal insignia of the king on their lapels—a crown with a star above it.

All the king's men...

As I'd entered, the king's men stared at me silently, still as statues on a floor of black and white tiles. Without a word, one of them had marched me up to my room.

When he'd shut the door behind me, I'd felt relieved.

My room faced the sea. In here, oak bookshelves lined two of the pale stone walls, and a few candle flames cast warm, dancing light over the room. A bed stood by the open balcony doors, covered in a cream duvet and enormous pillows. A wood table stood next to it, and a brass lamp for reading.

When I surveyed the whole room, my heart squeezed *hard* in my chest. On one of the walls hung two portraits of my parents, taken from their mansion in the Asmodean quarter.

In a daze, I walked closer to them, staring. Before me was the father I'd never known, Duke Moloch—the same red hair as mine, fading to blond around his chin, plus high cheekbones and dark brown eyes like mine. Next to him, my mother looked out over my head, her dark hair piled high—elegant in a way I'd never known her.

The gilded frames looked brand new.

Why, exactly, would Orion reframe these and bring them here? He hadn't known I was coming tonight, I thought. He must have left the festival after the trial and rushed around to get this room set up.

I stared up at Mom. Of course Orion was trying to make me comfortable. He would do whatever he could to get me to let down my guard.

When I glanced at the bedside table, I saw a pen resting beside a small pad of paper, which seemed like an odd touch. But when I moved closer to it, I realized it wasn't just *any* pen. In a daze, I traced my fingertips over the little glittery rainbow symbol on the side, slightly worn with time. Here it was—my lucky pen. I'd been carrying it the night I'd met Orion. Which meant, of course, that it hadn't been very lucky at all.

Still stunned, I turned it around in my fingertips. He'd *kept* it all this time? I'd even asked him for it in the prison cell, and he hadn't given it back.

All these charming attempts to win me over...

I dropped it on the table and turned to eye the rest of the setup.

On the wall overlooking the sea, light streamed through a glass door. When I looked outside, I had a view of a balcony made of sand-colored stone. Beyond a low stone wall, the dark silver-flecked sea stretched out forever, blending into the night. Gorgeous.

I opened the door and stepped out into the salt-tinged air. As a demon, my vision was so much better, and I could even see stony islands far out to sea, silvered in the moonlight. The waves pounded against the rocks below me. Tucked in one corner of the balcony, a small, heated pool released curls of steam into the dark sky.

When I peered over the balcony, I found soldiers lining the shore-line. Who did they expect to be coming out of the water? If I had to guess, Orion had probably told them to report to him if I flew off this balcony.

With a sigh, I crossed back into my new room and shut the balcony door, then ripped a piece of paper off the pad. I scribbled a note to Orion:

I don't need this anymore.

WITH THE NOTE FINISHED, I PULLED THE DOOR OPEN. IN THE DARK palace hall, two guards stood across from me. I walked up to one of them and thrust the note and pen into his hands. "Please give my regards to the king when you return this pen to him."

❧

THE MORNING SUN WASHED OVER ME AS I WALKED THROUGH THE meandering streets of the Luciferian Quarter, looking for somewhere to get breakfast. A servant had knocked on my door this morning, offering to bring me food, but I wanted to get out and stroll around in the daylight.

On one side of me, a canal ran between stone walls, sparkling with gold morning light. On the other side, vine-covered stone homes lined the cobbled road, their roofs sharply peaked. I paused to look in the window of a shop selling curiosities and magical items for witches—a human skull, vials of blood, and large books of magic, their spines etched with silver writing.

Mortal witches learned magic from demons at Belial University and at universities in other demon cities. If a mortal became very, very good at magic, he or she could become a witch.

And for the next trial I had in mind, we would be summoning a powerful dead witch from the underworld. Thus, I had nine days to master necromancy.

I pulled the door open, listening to the tinkling of bells as I stepped inside. The walls in here were painted black, and bell jars lined crooked shelves—stuffed birds, a brass hand with contorted fingers, and jars of herbs and potions.

A mortal man with a long beard sat behind the counter, staring at me. "Shadow scion..." he muttered.

When the bells chimed behind me, I turned to see Kas in the doorway, leaning against the frame. His sleeves were rolled up, revealing tattoos of stars on his forearms. His chin was tilted down, and a smile ghosted over his lips. A lock of his messy blond hair fell before his eyes. "Shadow scion," his deep, rough voice rumbled over the room. "We've been looking for you."

My eyebrows rose. "*We?*"

He turned to step outside and held the door open for me. "Shai and Legion. Breakfast awaits you."

I followed behind him, squinting in the bright sunlight. "Do we have plans?"

He turned back to me with a little smile. "We do. I'm making us pancakes and coffee, and then we're going to figure out how to make you queen."

Intrigued, I walked beside him. "You told me not to trust you."

"Absolutely do not." His eyebrow quirked. "But I'm going to help you anyway."

9

ORION

It felt haunted in here, in the old brick mansion where my family had once lived. My footfalls echoed off the dusty tile floors. I could have this place cleaned, but something stopped me from bringing it back to life. It was a mausoleum now, the air musty and stale. This home was a grave.

So why the fuck was I in here?

I supposed this was the only place where I could douse the fire of my lust for Rowan. Because when she was around, I couldn't think. I couldn't breathe when her image came into my mind. Every time I thought of her, my heart stopped. Her deep brown eyes, with the faint ring of gold at the edges. Her full lips painted red, the tiny smattering of freckles on her nose, the curve of her hips. The way she'd moaned when I'd fucked her—

Anyway, what sort of king would I be if I couldn't get my mind off her?

This was the only place I could find respite from thinking of her. Sadness twined through this place like a heavy mist.

From the tile floor, I eyed the old busts in the hallway alcoves, their faces smashed, some shattered on the floor.

I felt the world tilting beneath me as my gaze roamed over the deep red stain on the floor. That was where my brother, Molor, had been murdered while I watched.

My breath sped up, and I couldn't quite get enough air in here.

He'd tried to stand in front of our mother because he was so strong—

At least, my older brother had *seemed* so large and powerful to me then. I was shocked that the soldiers had knocked him down. Back then, I'd thought of him as a god. A titan. Someone who would always protect me. And maybe that was why I hadn't unleashed the fire I had in me, because if only I'd been thinking clearly, I could have burned the mortals to ash. They'd weakened our power before invading, but I'd still had some.

But surely Molor would stop them.

Molor had been the one to teach me curses, and he'd tried to teach me to land a punch. Every time he'd left the house, I'd screamed that I wanted to go with him.

In a daze, I walked through the hallway to his old room. He'd always been tidy, and it was neat even now, despite the dust and cobwebs. His was a simple, elegant room with white walls and dark wooden beams across the ceiling, an old flagstone floor and a thread-bare rug. Stags' antlers jutted from the wall above the mantel. His bed was a four-poster, the mahogany posts etched with thorns. Pale light streamed in through mullioned windows onto a desk stacked with old books.

I opened his wardrobe, stunned to see how small his clothes were. Had he really been that *small*?

And the children's toys in here—a doll in a white dress with black beads for eyes, and a wooden top with black numbers on it. I picked the top up, turning it over between my fingers. If the mortals hadn't come, Molor would have taught me how to play this game. As it was, I had no idea what it was for.

When my gaze flicked up at the clothes, I felt my breath leave my lungs. How could he have been so tiny? So delicate?

I pulled out one of his old suits, one with black velvety fabric trimmed with gold. I remembered this one...Molor had been so proud of it. He'd planned to wear it at his fourteenth birthday. Fourteen was a big deal for demons, and my parents had been planning the party a year in advance.

I laid it on the bed, staring at it. He hadn't quite grown into it by the time he was killed, and he never would.

With a lump in my throat, I crossed to the window and stared out at the Asmodean clocktower. At some point, it had stopped working, the hands frozen at six p.m. I couldn't help but wonder if time had frozen there when the mortals had arrived at dusk, because that was when the world had stopped. Or maybe it stopped with Molor's death—

When the Puritans cut out Molor's heart on the living room floor, it had really felt like they were taking mine with it. The pain had been blinding.

Clouds crept across the sun, casting the abandoned town square in shadow.

I stared through the old glass at the clock tower, a beautiful work of art for its time—a stone structure with gold-painted discs that had once moved. It had not only told the time, but also the position of the sun and moon and the astrological signs. A stunning feat of technology, learned from the mortals. A faint memory flickered at the recesses of my mind—mechanical statues that had once appeared from doors on either side of those gleaming discs: a figure of the king, and one of the god Lucifer, appearing to hand him a crown.

Long ago, everyone in the town had set their pocket watches by those gold hands. I remembered staring at it, waiting for the king to slide out from the door. Captivated by the magic.

I couldn't breathe in here anymore.

When the mortals came, my world had stopped, the sky had gone dark, and the air had turned to ash.

I could never let myself feel loss like that again. And what if I caused *her* to feel that pain because I let her love me? Because there really was nothing worse.

I turned, desperate to be out of this tomb.

I'd tried to create prison walls around me to keep myself safe, but Rowan was breaking them down. This was a problem.

I pulled her pen from my pocket, staring at the absurd chipped rainbow symbol on the side. A ridiculous thing. It shocked me how much it had hurt when she'd returned this to me. What the *hell*, Orion?

Furious at myself, I threw the front door open and stepped into the stone square.

One of my soldiers stood by the door, always protecting me—as if *I* needed protecting. With his pale skin and long, black hair, he looked like a spirit from the underworld. "Jasper," I said, "I have a very important task I need you to undertake."

Because I would do whatever I could to avoid feeling that agony of loss again.

❧ 10 ❧

ROWAN

Kas lived in a home on a crowded street, a house with a white Tudor-style front and crisscrossing wooden beams that overlooked the busy lane. Unlike Orion's pristine apartment, this place was littered with trinkets and oddities: a desk strewn with books before a mullioned window, a telescope, an old globe.

Kas stood at an iron stove before the kitchen window, making us pancakes, and the scent of butter filled the air. It all seemed almost... human. Normal.

Shai and Legion sat across from me, sipping coffee at a table littered with handwritten notes, plates, and a little pile of cutlery. A window to my right overlooked a narrow city street and shops covered with climbing ivy.

Shai picked up one of the papers, frowning at it. "What's this?"

"Oh, gods." Standing above the frying pan, Kas glanced over his shoulder. "That's my art. Don't look."

Of course we looked. I saw beautiful pencil drawings of the natural world—birds, trees, butterflies. A self-portrait lay among them, perfectly rendered. His skill was truly remarkable, almost photorealistic.

Legion sipped his coffee and picked up a sketch of two toadstools. "Are you ever going to do anything with your art?"

"More tattoos, maybe," Kas grumbled. He carried a heaping platter of pancakes in one hand, and he forked two onto my plate. "But we're not here to discuss my hobbies, are we?"

The corner of Shai's mouth quirked. "Legion's hobbies, then? Because he looks like a giant, tattooed badass, but he's been painting little pewter figurines of soldiers."

Legion pinned her with his gaze. "I wouldn't expect someone from the mortal realm to understand the fine art of miniature battle recreation."

"Just admit you're a dork." Kas dropped pancakes onto his plate.

My mouth watered, and I poured out a thin stream of maple syrup onto my pancakes. "What's on today's agenda?"

"We're planning for your trial," said Shai. "Have we decided what we're doing yet?"

"*We?*" I bit into the pancakes—thin and buttery, just the way I liked them. "Well, I've decided. I'll be announcing it later today. The trial requires summoning a witch from the underworld and stealing his magical talisman. In this case, a crown of blackthorn that enhances his magical powers."

"Spellcraft," said Shai. "Invocations in Demonic. You've never been to school for that."

"Neither has Orion. I heard him use a Demonic spell once, in the underworld, but he never had any formal education." I picked up my coffee cup, warming my hands. "In any case, *all* the trials involve demonic invocations. They're supposed to test not only physical strength and strategy, but the ancient art of Demonic spellcraft, too. And tonight is my deadline to announce it."

"How do you win?" asked Shai. "You just steal the crown?"

"The person who is successful at the summoning will have an advantage. I'd be linked to the witch, and that would make it easier to find him. But it doesn't guarantee a win."

"Summoning the dead requires extremely powerful magic," said Legion. "Can you compete with Orion in how much power you have?"

Shai caught my eye. "She's a Lightbringer, just like him. She has as much power as he does, and she has the advantage of not being insane."

"True," said Legion. "But none of us really know what Lightbringer power does. We've never seen it or experienced it."

"Magic is new to me," I admitted. "But there's no way around it. All the trials involve some sort of invocations, magic summoning. And since this one doesn't involve direct combat between Orion and me, it's one of the least dangerous options."

"Okay." Kas watched me over his steaming coffee. "Summoning requires precision. How good is your pronunciation of Demonic spells?"

I winced. "Maybe the three of you could help me practice."

"Who is this witch you'll be bringing back from the dead?" asked Shai. "Is he dangerous?"

"He was a king sixteen hundred years ago, Alaric of the Visigoths. Powerful enough to sack Rome. So here's how it works. First, Orion and I mark our foreheads with the blood of a dead witch. That will help break down the barrier to the dead people. Then we do the creepy demonic chanting. Whoever summons the dead witch first will have a bond with him, and the bond will help us locate him. So hopefully, I summon him, use the bond to find him, bind him up with magic, and snag the crown. And rule over a golden age, as your unmarried ginger queen."

Legion stared at me over his coffee. "We maybe have to go over some of the magical terms."

"Sure," I said.

"Taking a crown from a mortal isn't hard," he added. "It's the necromancy you'll struggle with."

"Not hard?" Kas's eyebrows rose. "He's a witch, not an ordinary mortal. Do you have any idea how dangerous the most powerful witches are? Those from the greatest generations long ago?"

Outside, the sky was growing darker, shadows sliding across the sun.

Legion frowned. "Are you scared of mortals?"

"I am." Shai's eyes flashed. "And if you're not, you're underestimating them. Have you heard of *la sorcière de Brocéliande*?"

"Who was she?" I asked.

A cold tingle of magic shivered over my skin as I sipped my coffee. Outside, a light rain started pattering the windows and sliding down the glass in rivulets.

Shai leaned forward, her mahogany eyes gleaming. "She was the most terrifying witch who ever lived. In the fifteenth century, she singlehandedly killed an entire army of demons in Rennes-le-Château. She blamed them for murdering her family, and she had them ripped to pieces by ravens, and their flesh crushed under stones." Lightning split the darkness outside, and rain started to hammer the windowpanes. "She absolutely loathed demons."

Thunder boomed, and Kas startled. "Is that you, Shai?"

She shrugged and picked up her coffee. "I wanted to add a bit of atmosphere."

Legion shrugged. "Well, she's dead now. That's what mortals do. They die."

Kas met my gaze. "Until they're raised again by a Lightbringer."

"I'm not raising *la sorcière* de whatever," I said. "Alaric is wily and powerful, but not insane and murderous. The demons who compiled the trials didn't want the whole city slaughtered. We're supposed to find the best leader, not end the demonic species."

The rain still pattered against the windows, a gentle sound.

"And you think you can win this?" asked Legion.

"It's possible," I said. "I've heard Orion use invocation spells before, but I don't think he's spent much time actually practicing magic. Magic didn't work in the dungeon, and he had no one to learn from once he'd freed himself. And I have you all to help me. Orion doesn't understand the concept of asking others for help, or even preparing for anything."

"Raising the dead always works best in the wilderness, where magic is most powerful," said Shai. "Learned that freshman year."

I nodded. "So I'll go there to practice."

Kas rubbed a hand over the back of his neck, looking worried. "Before you practice raising the dead, let's just go over some of the basics, shall we?"

~

FOG WOUND BETWEEN THE LARGE, SINUOUS OAK TREES IN THE Elysian Wilderness.

To start, I'd been practicing the name *Alaric* with the correct pronunciation. "Alaric," I said for the twentieth time.

"More emphasis on the *Ala*," said Legion. "Pronounce it like German."

It was adorable that he thought I knew German.

In a black buttoned coat, Shai stood with her arms folded, leaning against the trunk of a gnarled oak. "She's almost there." She flashed me a wicked smile and walked closer, crunching over the leaves. "Can't we try out some real spell magic? I want to see what she can do."

"What do you have in mind?" I asked.

The breeze washed over us, lifting curls of Kas's blond hair. "There are three types of magic that we practice," he said.

Shai cleared her throat. "Excuse me, Kas. I was about to show off." She lifted a finger. "So, we've got medicine—when we use natural materials in magic, like the blood you'll be putting on your forehead. Then there's thaumaturgy. Only demons can use that, not mortals. That's the innate, elemental power that you have, like when you explode with fire. And then finally, invocations. Using language to draw on the magic of the gods and channel it to your will."

I wasn't entirely sure I'd taken all that in. "So can I try raising something from the dead?"

Shai stood directly in front of me. "Magic is connected to emotions," she went on. "If you're dead inside or apathetic, you won't be able to use your elemental fire magic. When I want to control the weather, I think of something that pisses me off, like how my mom forgot to mention that I might be a demon because she's deeply committed to conformity among the mortals." She smiled brightly.

I nodded. "Okay. I've got plenty of intense emotions to choose from."

With his hands in his pockets, Kas took another step closer, crunching over the leaves. "Everyone's magic has a different feel to it. Mine is smooth and silky," he said, "like ribbons gliding over my skin."

Legion held up his hand, and I watched as dark silvery magic played about his fingertips. "Mine feels ice cold."

"And mine vibrates." Shai held up her hands to the side of her mouth to stage whisper. "Now you know why I've been practicing so much."

I cracked a smile. I already knew how my elemental magic felt—hot and bright, just like Orion's.

Legion gripped a thick book of spells, the spine etched with gold letters. "As a demon, your spellcraft is all about trying that innate power you have and using language to create something new. The pronunciation and syntax are key, but you have to have a clear intention, too. You're taking a raw force—your innate power—and shaping it to your will."

"Go ahead." Shai waved a hand at me. "Put it in psychology terms. I know you want to."

I exhaled. "It's like how creativity works," I said. "There are the dreamlike states in your occipital cortex. That's like the gods' power, the raw, unshaped creativity. And your prefrontal cortex at the front of your brain needs to organize them into something meaningful."

Legion stared at me, then blew a strand of black hair out of his eyes. "Sure. Whatever. Maybe just try the spell."

He handed me the book, opened to a page with a short spell, and I took it from him.

I scanned the text, inhaling deeply. The Demonic alphabet was different than ours, and I had no magical ability to read it, sadly. Luckily, there was a phonetic translation on the right side of the pages.

"What does this do?" I asked.

"It's a simple spell," said Legion. "Just bringing clouds into the sky. Anyone should be able to do it."

Shai glared at him. "It's not that simple."

Legion smiled at her. "In the future, I'll remember that you have all the sensitivity of a mortal, and I will phrase my thoughts more carefully."

"It's okay." She smirked at him. "Someday, I'll learn to be condescending and emotionless like the rest of you."

"But emotions and passion are our source of strength," he

murmured. "We just save them for the most important occasions. Like magic, and...other things."

They stared at each other, holding eye contact for so long, it was starting to get uncomfortable.

"Right." Kas sighed and pointed at the book. "Ignore them, and channel your emotions. As you read the spell, keep your intention in mind. Envision the clouds. You're directing the magic of the gods. There are two fundamental pillars of magic, power and control. Understood?"

First, the power. That came from emotions, so I held the book open in my hands and envisioned Orion's face. Always good for stirring up some feelings. Anger mixed with regret when I conjured the perfect contours of his face. My blood started to warm up, and I felt the air grow more humid around me. A faint glow beamed from my fingertips.

With my magic summoned, I started to chant the spell as it was written out, careful with my pronunciation.

But when I glanced up at the sky, I was frustrated to find that sunlight still streamed through the leaves.

"That was good," said Shai. "Maybe just a bit more emotion."

I stared at the book, summoning more magic. This time, I thought of Orion swooping down to murder Cambriel. Kicking me out of the city. My mind was aflame with a sense of loss.

Fire sparked in my chest, and it began coursing through my blood as I read the spell. Around me, the wind began to pick up, rushing past. My gaze flicked up again, still seeing blue.

I chanted the spell again and again, and in the hollows of my mind, I heard Orion speaking, his voice cold and emotionless: *Escort this woman out of my realm.*

As I read the spell, light started beaming from my body, illuminating the book's pages. They began to flutter and flip in the wind. Magic crackled around me, and my chest beamed with power. The wind whipped at my hair, and iron-gray storm clouds spilled like ink across the sky. Lightning cracked the clouds, searing the air. As it touched down at the top of a nearby oak tree, an electrical charge sparked from the soil up into my feet.

"Rowan," shouted Shai above the wind. "Too much! Too much!"

Above, the sky opened up, unleashing torrents of ice-cold rain and pelting us with hail. As the wind lashed the trees, leaves caught in the currents and tumbled through the air. The lightning strike had lit the oak on fire, and it blazed like an enormous torch under the dark sky.

"Fuck." Kas pushed his dripping hair off his forehead. "We're going to need to work on that control part."

❧ II ❧

ROWAN

S oaking wet, gripping hot cups of tea, the four of us sat around
the roaring fireplace in Kas's home. He'd given each of us soft
blankets with which to warm up. None of us had managed to
stop the rain and hail, and it still hammered the windows, threatening
to crack the glass. On the plus side, the ice storm had managed to
extinguish the blazing oak tree very nicely.

The two men sat shirtless, showing off their muscles in the dancing
firelight. Shai and I weren't complaining.

"Why don't we start next time with something less dangerous?"
asked Shai.

"The floating paper," said Legion. "It's one of the first things
students learn in magic school. A simple spell, and no trees will catch
on fire."

Kas slid me a devious look. "I wouldn't rule it out."

"We have time," I said. "There are still nine more days."

"You'll be fine." He nodded. "Only those blessed by the gods can
get this far. At least, that's how the story goes."

"The story?" asked Shai. "You're not a true believer?"

Kas shrugged. "The gods seem a little insane to me. Any being as old as time must be demented. I sometimes wonder what it would be like if we just *voted* for a leader instead of leaving it up to trinkets and the whims of the gods."

"Don't be ridiculous," said Legion.

"You're right," said Kas. "It makes much more sense to see who can hunt down the magic crown from a dead witch first."

"Hey." I shrugged. "I didn't make the rules."

Just as I finished my sentence, something caught my eye in the rain.

I let out a long breath, annoyed to see a demon in a navy blue uniform lurking outside. With his milky white skin and long black hair —wet in the rain—he looked like *he'd* been raised by the dead. "One of Orion's soldiers is spying on us."

"Not a very good spy," said Legion, "if he's hovering right there in the window like a Peeping Tom."

The creepy man disappeared, and a moment later, a knock sounded at the door.

Bare-chested, Kas pulled open the door and lifted his chin. "Can I help you?"

The man's dark eyes slid to me, and he nodded curtly. "The king requests the shadow scion's presence this evening at a memorial service for the Lilu dead. It begins in the Asmodean Ward by the clock tower."

Of course Orion had sent someone to follow me here, no doubt trying to learn what I was doing, in order to gain an advantage.

Kas leaned against his door frame, and his blanket slid off him. "Sorry, who are you?"

"Jasper. Loyal servant to the king." He cut me a sharp look. "May the true king reign until the sun consumes the earth with its flames."

"Okay," said Kas. "Thanks for...that." He shifted from the doorframe and slammed the door. "Weirdo," he muttered.

I met Shai's gaze. Did Orion really want me there to remember the dead, or did he have something up his sleeve?

AT MY SEASIDE PALACE, I'D SELECTED A LONG BLACK DRESS WITH capped sleeves.

As I'd arrived in the square just before six, some of Orion's servants had handed out little silver model ships with a candle in the hull. Each one had a handle so we could carry them along. I didn't know what the ships were for, but I held mine now in the hushed silence as a crowd gathered around the old clock tower. Overhead, the setting sun stained the sky with crimson.

This must be the first time the Asmodean square had been filled in hundreds of years.

As I looked around me, I felt like Orion was as remote as a star. An adoring crowd gathered around him. Jasper was right by Orion's side, looking tense, his jaw clenched. He reminded me of a guard dog. Orion, on the other hand, looked perfectly at ease, his beautiful face gilded by the dying sun. Taller than most of the other demons, he leaned down to speak to anyone who approached. All around him, a sea of candles flickered and bobbed in the silver ships.

I was quickly starting to get the impression that apart from my little crew, everyone favored Orion.

I held up my model ship, studying it. For something that looked metallic, it was surprisingly light, and its surface was etched with Demonic words. "These things are beautiful."

Kas leaned closer to me, whispering, "Once, this was how the Lilu mourned. They were creatures of the night and sea. The memorials were called *challariu*. It meant..." His eyebrows drew together. "To be called home. The gods called them home when they died." Kas held my gaze for longer than seemed normal, his amber eyes studying me. He reached up and brushed a flyaway strand of my red hair from my face. "The candles are supposed to light their way to the underworld. It's a path from this world to the next."

I pulled my gaze away from him to find that King Orion was no longer paying attention to the other people in his orbit. Now, his eyes were drilling into Kas, his jaw tensing. The look he was giving Kas sent a chill through my blood.

Orion stalked closer, his eyes locked on my new friend. "I will be escorting the shadow scion. You may find someone else to amuse you."

Rude. I thought I caught a hint of an eye roll from Kas before he stalked away.

"Let's walk to the river," Orion said gruffly. "I know a shortcut. We need to talk. Away from everyone."

He led me toward a narrow street carved between two stone buildings. I should feel nervous that my bloodthirsty rival was leading me into an isolated alley, but I just never felt scared around Orion. This close to him, I breathed in the scent of burnt cedar, heady and masculine. Fuck. I'd forgotten how good he smelled, and I was very much trying not to stare at the broadness of his shoulders or think of the dark shirt stretching over his ridiculously large muscles.

As we walked, I glanced behind us. "Are we going to talk about the spies you have following me?"

"Spies? Think of them as protectors."

I arched an eyebrow. "Right. War is freedom, and spies are my protectors. You have an amazing skill for making words mean different things."

A line formed between his eyebrows. "As long as I am king, Rowan, it's my responsibility to make sure you are safe. And speaking of which, do you really trust two ancient demons you've only just met? You know they were around when the rest of our kind were slaughtered."

Of course he knew they were training me. "Except for Shai, I don't trust anyone. And that includes you, so forgive me if I don't take everything you say at face value."

"Will you at least come to me if you're in danger? When I thought you were dead, Rowan—" A muscle flickered in his jaw, and his eyes darkened. "As I said, it's my job to keep you safe here. That's why I've sealed up the tunnel so no one can get in—the demon hunters have become obsessed with you, and someone has told them that you're in here."

I let out a long breath. "But there's an agreement, right? If a mortal enters without permission, he can be killed."

"And yet, they're willing to risk death just so they can drag you out and kill you. But in the meantime, they're lobbying politicians to put in emergency measures to attack us."

A shudder ran through me. "Attack the whole city? Just because of me?"

"Not just because of you." Orion stopped walking and turned to look at me. Across the river, the shadows from the forest's trees crept over the grass. Clear, crystalline water rushed past us. I tilted up my head to meet his cool gaze. "My spies followed you and the demon hunters in Osborne. I didn't let them get anywhere near you. But unfortunately, that has created new problems. Some of their agents learned of your location. We had to deal with them before they could relay the message."

I sucked in a sharp breath. "You killed more demon hunters."

"It's usually how I deal with things, yes, but it also happened to be the only way to stop them from murdering you in Shai's aunt's apartment. It was only two days ago. I was about to bring you back here when you decided to show up on your own." His expression darkened. "If you win the trial against me, if you become queen, you need to know what you're up against. If they're successful in convincing mortal politicians that we're a threat, they could wipe out this entire city. And all I can do for now is try to head off an attack using our magical wards to keep us safe."

I closed my eyes. "This all started with me killing the congressman."

"You had to, Rowan. He was going to slaughter you like an animal. And the fact is, it was always going to come to this—us against them. This was always going to happen."

And there he went, sowing doubt in my mind.

I turned away from him, staring at the river as it rushed past. "But they haven't waged war against us yet. You don't need to start one."

"For now, I'll be asking my strongest spell casters to protect us from the mortal missiles that could rain on us at any moment. But as long as demon power fades without these city walls, we will always be at risk. It wasn't the case centuries ago, but now they have weapons that could take down all the walls at once. So, Rowan." He touched my arm, and I turned to face him. "If I die in the trial, you need to carry on that work of protecting the city."

His words took my breath away, and I stared at him. "Don't be ridiculous. You're not going to *die*."

"Why not?"

Good question. I mean, that was usually a primary component of these trials. And yet...I grabbed his arm. "We don't need to kill each other to win the trials. The trial I'm choosing involves summoning a dead sorcerer and stealing his crown. I'm not going to kill you, I just plan to win. Nine days from now. This is your official notice. We're raising Alaric." I did the math in my head. "October thirty-first."

The fact that the trial would fall on Halloween was either a fantastic omen that I was destined for success or a terrible idea. I couldn't yet decide which.

He cocked his head, his pale eyes glinting in the darkness. "You would let your rival live? You don't worry that this would cause problems?"

"I'll deal with those problems later," I said, and let out a long breath. "I don't want you to get hurt."

His expression was serious, transfixed on me. "I don't want to hurt you, either."

"But that doesn't mean we're on the same side. We both know that freeing the demons is an act of war. The streets will run with blood, and innocent people will die. And I know that's what you want."

He turned away from me, shrugging. "If mortals decide our freedom is a pretext for their aggression, that moral failure is on them, not us. And Rowan, the tensions have already begun. You and I were the tinderboxes that lit the spark. The revelation of your presence scared the shit out of them. A demon embedded in the mortal world, one who spent years around a demon hunter, no less—they're feeling extremely vulnerable right now. They no longer know who's mortal and who's a demon, and panic is running through their world like wildfire. They're terrified that there are more of us out there. They're not going to let us live."

I swallowed hard. "Do you have any evidence, or am I supposed to take everything the Lord of Chaos says as truth?"

"You'll have to trust me."

Nope. "Sure. But how about we let the gods decide who should rule? Through the trials, like we agreed. And as for whatever happens next —we'll just cross that bridge when we come to it."

"Fine." The corner of his mouth twitched in something like a smile. "The gods will decide. Since they're always so fucking rational."

12

ROWAN

Distantly, I heard the sounds of mournful singing echoing off the city's stones, beautiful and eerie at the same time. My heart felt heavy.

"It's starting," said Orion quietly.

He reached into his pocket and pulled out two objects, a pale white clay pipe and a pearl necklace. "On the night of *challariu*, this is one way to honor the dead. The Lilu used to believe that rivers and the sea connected us to the underworld. Before we began singing, we would give the river something that belonged to the departed so that the ones we mourned would have some of their favorite things in the afterlife. Then we'd walk along the water and sing the songs of the dead. We believed it would help them have an easy journey to the underworld."

"Did those belong to your parents?" I asked, staring at the pipe and the necklace.

He shook his head. "No. These belong to yours. I found them in your parents' house. You can keep them, of course, if you want, or you can give them to the river. It's your choice."

I found my eyes stinging as I took the necklace and pipe from him.

My mom never had anything this beautiful in Osborne. "Thanks," I said quietly.

This seemed...oddly thoughtful of him?

Tears brimmed in my eyes as I took a few steps to the river's edge, and I thumbed the smooth pearls on the necklace, imagining how it would have looked on Mom. Maybe she'd look beautiful wearing this in the underworld...

I dropped it in the river, watching as the dark waters claimed it. Then I turned the pipe over in my fingertips—a man I'd never known, but one who'd been looking out for me when he died. I let that go, too, watching it tumble in the waters. Now that the sky had grown dark, moonlight shimmered over the river's surface.

On the river bank, Orion knelt beside me. Warmth radiated from him. "The silver ship goes in, too," he murmured. "It's supposed to light the way."

I dropped the model ship into the river and watched it float along the surface, swirling a little in the eddies.

"One for each soul," said Orion. He let his go in the water, too, and our twin sparks of light moved toward the ocean.

I glanced at him through blurred eyes. Had he known I wouldn't want to do this in front of the crowd?

I couldn't read his expression as he held out a hand to help me up.

When I felt a tear slide down my cheek, I wiped a hand across my face. "What did you bring for your family?"

His mouth opened and closed, and he took a moment to respond. "I already let them go in the river earlier today. For my mother, I brought her favorite book. My stepfather, I gave him back his pocket watch. My big brother, Molor, had a suit I returned—" His voice broke, and he looked away into the alley from which we'd come. He cleared his throat. "The others should be here soon."

Without entirely realizing what I was doing, I found myself putting my hand on his chest. He turned to look at me, his lips parted in surprise. I started to lift my hand, but he covered it with his. He breathed in deeply as the crowd grew nearer.

An ocean of candles floated toward us, like stars in the night, the sound of singing floating on the wind.

"We will lead them now to the yew grove in the Elysian Wilderness," said Orion. "I've made the memorial there."

When I'd first heard the news that we'd be spending the night at a memorial, it felt like a distraction from my preparations, or maybe a trick of some sort. But now that we were walking under the starlight, with the sorrowful music filling the air, it seemed necessary...and right. As we passed, some of the demons dropped their model ships into the river, and the waters carried them away.

"Are you all right?" Orion asked.

"Yeah. You?"

He held my gaze for a long time, his expression unreadable. "Same as always."

I had no idea what that meant. "Full of quiet rage and loud confidence?"

"Not quite."

We crossed the bridge. Illuminated silver ships were streaming down the river now, bobbing over the water. Just across the river, lanterns hung from tree boughs, swinging a little in the breeze. Orion led me into a yew grove, where the dots of warm light illuminated tree trunks. Around the grove, large, rough stones had been carved with Demonic letters, the shapes serpentine and elegant. A fitting resting place for a culture that belonged in the wild.

I stepped through the mossy forest, wishing I could read the names. The stones seemed to go on endlessly, which in itself was heartbreaking.

"It's a beautiful memorial," I said.

"Spell casters worked on the lanterns. The candles will never go out." He touched my lower back lightly. "Here." He nodded at a couple of large stones by one of the river's tributaries.

I crossed to look at the stones, and my eyes stung when I saw the names. These were the only ones here carved in both Demonic and English. I crouched down and ran my fingertips over Mom's name: *Aria Morgenstern, Duchess of Asmodeus.*

How strange that I'd never known her full name, nor my father's name at all. *Baal de Moloch, Duke of Asmodeus,* next to her. Gold and shadows danced over the stones from the lanterns, making the carvings come to life.

My throat felt tight. "Why are these in English?"

"They're for you. They're your family."

But there was a third stone here, too, tucked off to the side, hidden in shadows.

Lady Mortana de Moloch.

"You made a memorial for Mortana," I whispered. "Unexpected."

"I made one for every dead Lilu."

I turned to look up at him. "Why her?"

Again, a line formed between his eyebrows. "Once I learned that she'd died in the underworld after losing her mind...I don't know. The threat is gone. Maybe she helped Nergal because it was the only way to survive. Or maybe she was truly evil." Shadows danced back and forth over his features. "I don't really know what she was thinking, and I no longer care. She's dead, and I'm not. Every dead Lilu gets a marker."

I rose, staring out at the forest of glittering lights and the stones beneath them. "How did you dig up all their names?"

"I remembered them. There wasn't much else to do in the dungeon except think of their names, engrave them on my heart, and promise to avenge them."

I swallowed hard. "You were only five."

He slid his hands into his pockets, his expression serious. "I had Ashur to help me remember every name."

My heart felt like it was cracking. Orion would never break his promise to Ashur. And I wasn't even sure I could blame him, but I'd try to stop him anyway.

Closer to the river, demons were filling the forest. He turned away from me, and his face fell into shadow. "We should join the others for the memorial songs."

Mom must have known all the words to these songs once, but she'd never taught me.

"I don't know the Lilu songs," I whispered.

"You'll learn them," he said quietly.

Those didn't sound like the words of a man who intended to get rid of me. Then again, how could anyone ever really know what someone as unpredictable as Orion was really thinking?

❧ 13 ❧

ROWAN

I stood on the balcony outside my room, staring at the sea. After the *challariu*, I felt emotionally drained. I think I was exhausted from the mental puzzle of trying to figure out what was real and what was a lie. So I'd eaten by myself on the balcony, under the stars. Orion's servants had brought me a bottle of Malbec and grilled salmon with delicately spiced rice.

Now, my head was swimming, my mind racing with worries about the upcoming trial. On the one hand, I'd demonstrated a bit of control today. Just before the memorial, I'd managed to make a piece of paper float across the room to Shai without lighting anything on fire.

On the other hand, Orion was such a wild card, I couldn't predict him as well as I'd thought.

As the sea wind skimmed over me, I poured myself another glass of wine. Sipping, I glanced up to the sky. Clouds were creeping over the moon now, and the wind started to pick up. A sudden gust of wind knocked over the wine bottle, spilling a little stream right onto my dress.

Yikes. Had I already finished most of that bottle? On my own? Let's hope demons didn't get hangovers like mortals did.

As I hurried to clean it up, lightning speared the sky. Clouds had blotted out the stars, and a heavy rain started to fall. I grabbed my glass of Malbec.

I needed to get my shit together and clear my mind. I *could* win this and become queen.

Except at this point, I was certain of only one thing: despite all my warnings to myself, Orion was deeply, firmly messing with my head.

When I thought you were dead—

Something was making my cheeks heat, and that was bad news, indeed.

❧

DAMP FROM THE RAIN, I LAY IN BED WITH THE SHEETS PULLED tightly around me. A storm was raging outside, and the sea sounded violent and angry. Thunder boomed across the ocean, making the walls rattle. Every time I started to drift off, a flash of lightning ignited the sky, waking me again.

I rolled over, imagining the gentle bobbing of the silver boats down the river. I closed my eyes, listening to the rain hammering against the windows and the stone walls.

At last, I started to drift off, and I almost thought I could hear the funeral song of the Lilu washing in from the sea...

❧

MY HEART SKIPPED A BEAT AS AN UNNAMED PANIC STOLE MY BREATH. The room felt unnaturally cold.

My eyes snapped open, but shadows had consumed all the light. I started to sit up in bed, but when I was only halfway up, my airway constricted sharply. What the *fuck?* Someone or something was crushing my neck, and I started to thrash wildly, unable to see my attacker. Fear snapped through my nerve endings. Already, my lungs were burning from the lack of air.

Panic summoned my magic, and golden light flared from my body —enough of it that I could see the person choking me. Pale skin, long black hair, and eyes to match. *Jasper.* The king's right-hand man. How was he so fucking *strong?*

With one hand around my throat, he raised the other above me. Long ivory claws shot out, aiming for my heart. Frantic, I blocked the strike, and his claws carved into my forearm, slicing against the bone.

Pain electrified my arm, igniting my survival instincts. I kicked at Jasper as hard as I could, knocking him off the bed. When I summoned my fire, it raced down my arm to my fingertips. But as I did, the room went cold, dark...and the flames snuffed out on my fingertips. Shadows enveloped me.

Shit. I could no longer see Jasper. Glacial air stung my lungs as I inhaled.

When lightning flashed again outside, I caught a glimpse of him.

Flames burst into life in my palm, and I hurled a fireball at the corner of the room where I'd just seen him. But before the fire met its target, the flames sputtered and died in the icy darkness. Arctic air stung my lungs and skin, making my limbs shake.

My heart was a wild beast. "Why are you trying to kill me, Jasper?" Somehow, the cold air seemed to swallow up the sound of my voice.

"Because I follow King Orion's orders," he hissed.

"The king?" Heat started to erupt inside me. Cracks of light were splintering my skin. Once I let go, I could burn the world to ash. Flames rose and guttered to life on my fingertips—

The door burst open, and a muscular frame stood silhouetted against the hallway light.

"What the fuck do you think you're doing?" Orion's voice came low and controlled from the doorway, and his eyes were on Jasper.

Jasper's eyes glowed from the shadows. "I will not relent until your orders are complete. As you said, Your Majesty."

Orion's muscled body looked coiled with tension—a snake about to strike. "I commanded you to keep her *safe.*" He turned to look at me, glowing with golden light. "Did he hurt you?"

Furious magic still crackled through my body. Whatever was going on here, it only reaffirmed one thing: in the City of Thorns, things were never quite as they seemed. "Nothing that will last."

Jasper's dark eyes were intent on me. "Even if you tried to stop me, Your Majesty, you said I must—"

The air went icy, and Jasper lunged for me, his ivory claws drawn. But in one swift move, Orion swung for him, using his claws to slash Jasper's heart out of his chest. With a snarl, he threw the heart onto the floor, and Jasper's pale body crumpled to the tiles.

Blood covered Orion's arm and chest, and he turned to look at me, his body beaming with light. "What happened to all the soldiers I stationed around the palace? Why did none of them intervene?"

I stared at him. "You're asking *me*? They're under your command. I was asleep."

"Come with me," he said abruptly. "You can't stay here, obviously. It's not safe."

"He just said that you ordered this." I followed after him anyway, eager to get away from Jasper's corpse.

In the hallway outside, a single soldier stood in the marble hall. Orion stalked over to him and gripped him by the neck, lifting him high into the air. "Why did you let someone in here? You were tasked with keeping the shadow scion safe."

The demon's green eyes were open wide, his mouth moving wordlessly. Orion was crushing his throat.

"I don't think he can answer you like that," I said.

Orion dropped the soldier, and the force of his body hitting the floor cracked the tile. The demon's face turned white as milk as he stared up at Orion. "Your Majesty? You asked us to let him in. You ordered all the other soldiers to leave, and you asked me not to intervene, no matter what."

Orion stared down at him, and he took a step back like he'd been hit. "When did this supposedly happen?"

"Thirty minutes ago..." the soldier stammered, looking baffled.

Orion stared at the soldier, then at me, as if he was expecting me to answer this conundrum for him.

I folded my arms. "Did you stage all this, all by any chance, so you could swoop in and save me?"

A flurry of emotions crossed his features. "And what purpose would that serve, exactly?"

"To get me to trust you."

His withering look drilled into me. "If I wanted to create an opportunity to save you, do you really think I would have done such a terrible job? If I'd set this up, do you think I'd leave all these loose ends of people telling you about it?"

He had a point... I shrugged. "I don't know. Maybe you're preoccupied with panicking about how I'm going to steal your crown."

He narrowed his eyes. "Clearly, someone enchanted my soldiers. This is obvious mind control—spellcraft. Someone is trying to put us at odds with one another. Someone is trying to make you think I'm a threat."

My nose wrinkled. "That would be a waste of time, considering we already are at odds with one another."

Orion's eyes dipped down for just a fraction of a moment, his jaw clenching. Only then did I realize I was braless, in a tank top and underwear that were still wet from the rain. Ah, but that was power. I stepped closer to him. "Tell me, how did you know I was in trouble at that exact moment?"

He pinned me with his intense gaze. "The same way I knew you were in trouble in the underworld. I felt my heart racing, and for a long time, I didn't remember what that sensation was. But then you reminded me. It was fear. And I feel it when you're in danger. We are connected. We are the twin Lightbringers, and I know when you're not safe."

"Hmm. I've never felt *you* in danger."

"I'm never in any danger," he said impatiently, like it was a ridiculous concept. "Not since I got out of the dungeon." He stalked down the stairwell. "You'll be staying with me now. I can't trust anyone but myself."

"But can you even trust yourself, Orion?" My voice echoed. "Because maybe you're losing your mind."

He pivoted and marched up the stairs again toward me. With a stony expression, he scooped me up in his powerful arms, like a groom carrying a bride, and carried me down the stairs.

Warmth from his skin slid over me, and I felt acutely aware of all the points of our bodies that made contact. Orion wore a thin black sweater, underneath which I could feel his muscles moving as he carried me. Outside, the air was a cool salt mist—and Orion's body was all steel and heat wrapping around me.

"I'm perfectly capable of walking," I said. "And I was also about to kill Jasper on my own."

Orion's pale eyes stared straight ahead as he carried me out of the palace. "You were moving too slowly."

Maybe he was just trying to keep his enemy close. But that worked both ways, didn't it?

Living in his house, I'd get a firsthand look at what my rival was up to. I wrapped my arms around his broad shoulders.

"I hope you realize," I said, "that I'll need my own room. You can't be around me when I'm planning for the next trial. And I don't want your spies watching me, either."

"Rowan." He looked at me evenly and pulled me in close to whisper in my ear. "I promise to play fair," he said in a velvety tone that I didn't trust at all.

14

ROWAN

Orion's house was surprisingly small—and surprisingly close by. A two-story stone cottage, it looked more like a gatehouse than a palace. He had no soldiers protecting the exterior, but as we crossed through a wrought iron gate, the sizzle of magic over my skin told me that it had been protected with charms.

Inside, two black dogs followed us up dark wooden stairs.

As he carried me up to the second story, my gaze flicked up to meet Orion's eyes. I felt a strange flutter in my belly. I shouldn't be here, of course, and yet, I felt safe with him. My insane animal instincts trusted him and told me he'd protect me, even if the rational side of me knew better.

"I didn't order that to happen." His silver hair was rustled and sticking up, and he seemed unusually rattled.

"I don't really know what I believe anymore," I admitted.

"Rowan." His voice sounded rougher than usual. "I was here with Amon. He can tell you that. I'll find out who was behind that attack."

Upstairs, he carried me into a tidy bedroom, then into a second bedroom that connected to it, one in the corner of the cottage. Dark beams scored the ceiling. Like Orion's apartment, this place was neat and tidy, and sparsely decorated—just white walls and elegant mahogany furniture. A cream-colored cashmere blanket covered the bed. The only color in the place came from the spines of books on a large bookshelf, and a few stacked on a desk by the window. Another door was open to a small bathroom with a shower.

Orion set me down on the hardwood floors and pointed back to the first bedroom—just slightly larger than this one, with a four-poster bed and darker walls. "If you need anything, I'll be in there."

"Cozy." I crossed to a large mullioned window and peered out at the moonlit garden below. "So if I'm going in and out of the house, I'll be walking past you?"

"More importantly, if anyone tries to come *in* the house, they'll be going past me."

For a moment, I indulged in a fantasy—one where Orion and I were two normal people in a cottage like this, with two black dogs. We had no marks of Lucifer, no murdered moms, no horrific memories, or centuries of imprisonment. In this phantom world, we were two normal people who could wake up tangled in each other's limbs and wander out to have morning coffee in the garden. We could live surrounded by books and quiet...

But it was stupid to let myself indulge in that fantasy.

I turned to find Orion watching me. Studying me closely, he crossed to me. "He left a bruise on your throat, and it's not even healing properly." He cocked his head. "That makes me wish I'd killed him more slowly."

"I don't even feel it anymore."

His eyes had darkened to black. "Rowan, I returned to the dungeon today. Do you remember that cell I kept you in the first night we met?"

"Being imprisoned by the Lord of Chaos isn't the type of thing a person forgets, Orion."

"That cell was the exact cell where my mother and I were first kept. Right before she was killed, the guards moved me to a different cell by myself. But when I looked in the first cell, I saw that she'd carved something in the wall."

"*Lucifer urbem spinarum libarabit,*" I said, finishing his thought. "The Lightbringer will set free the City of Thorns."

His dark eyebrows drew together. "That's what I'd thought, too, when I first saw it. But some of the lines were worn, and ivy was covering part of it. When I was mulling everything over, trying to understand my destiny, I went back to read her carving. I pulled the vines away. It says *Luciferi urbem spinarum liberabunt*."

I swallowed. "It's plural. The *Lightbringers* will set us free."

"We're meant to do this together. It just took me a long time to see it."

I ran through my promise to myself, all the reasons that I wouldn't let him sway me. "You told me you didn't even respect me enough to hate me. You called me neurotic, dull, and unskilled at everything. 'Apart from our one little tryst,'" I said, mimicking his British accent, "'I find you tedious and pathetic.' And then I died, and I learned I'm a lot stronger than I ever realized. I should be ruling here, not you, Orion."

His jaw flexed. "None of those things I said were true. I was trying to keep you away from me. I didn't think I had the strength to resist you, so I was trying to keep you at arm's length, because I'm terrified of what could happen..."

My fingers tightened. "*What*, exactly?"

"That it could happen again!"

I stared at him, not understanding. "That *what* could happen again? What are you talking about? There are no more Lilu left to murder."

"There's us." He seemed uncharacteristically at a loss for words, and he raked a hand through his hair. "Rowan—of course I respect you. Of course I—" His mouth closed, and his gaze slid down my goosebump-covered arms. The next thing I knew, he was wrapping me in the soft cream blanket from the bed. "We can turn the heat up in here."

The cashmere felt amazing against my skin, but my thrill also came from his warm, smoky scent curling around me. This blanket was my armor. I could resist his charms. Unwilling to let him off so easily, I glared at him. "Okay, so let's talk about avenging the Lilu. I want you to understand something about mortals and your theory about how they're the root of all evil."

He sighed and leaned against one of the bookcases, folding his arms. Annoyingly, that only served to show off his biceps, which seemed to strain the fabric of his white shirt. "I'm listening."

My eyebrows rose in surprise. He was actually willing to hear me out? "Demons and mortals are alike. It's not that complicated. Some of us are evil, some are good, and some are fanatics who want to destroy anyone different."

"Are you calling me a fanatic?" he asked dryly.

"Yeah, I am. You're the demon equivalent of Jack Corwin."

His muscles tensed. "I'm *what*? That is, I think, the worst thing you could have said to me."

I shook my head. "I meant only in fanaticism. Not your charm or intelligence or whatever else. His demon hunters want to kill all of us, and you want to kill all of them. You're both extremists."

He seemed to relax a little. "Go on."

"And yes, I know you've catalogued every instance in history of mortals committing atrocities, and there are plenty to choose from. The same goes for demons. But what about the good things mortals have done?"

He cocked his head. "Do you have a single example?"

I bit my lip, wishing I'd prepared a little better for this conversation—maybe I could have used a PowerPoint and academic references. "Keanu Reeves," I blurted. "He's amazing. He donates money to cancer research, to children's hospitals. He gives up his subway seat on trains! What kind of maniac wants to kill Keanu Reeves?"

"I have no idea who you're talking about."

My eyes widened. "Right. Of course you don't! The world *stopped* for you four hundred years ago. For you, time froze, and you came out wanting to murder the people who hurt you. And you know what? The mortals you encountered back then fucking *sucked*. No one likes Puritans. No one. But they're gone, and the world kept moving on for everyone else. You missed several centuries of human existence. So maybe you should learn more about the people you want to murder, you know? I have more examples." I lifted a finger. "Steve Buscemi."

"These are friends of yours?"

"Ha! I wish. No, but he was a firefighter, and then he became an actor. And when some fanatic mortals flew airplanes into skyscrapers in New York City, he got on his old firefighting gear, and he put his life at risk to help save people. Not just him, but lots of firefighters made a huge sacrifice trying to get people out of a burning and collapsing building. Tons of them gave their lives to help people they didn't even know." I was on a roll now. "And in Fukushima, a nuclear reactor was melting down after an earthquake, and people actually volunteered to help clean it up, even though they would die of cancer. These were mortals saving other people. Saving strangers."

His eyes shone brightly as he listened to me. "I haven't read about these things."

"It's all pretty new. It wouldn't have been in your ancient dungeon books, and it's not like you use the internet." Now that I'd started thinking about heroic mortals, I couldn't stop. "John Robert Fox! A lieutenant in World War Two, he intentionally gave his own coordinates to the Nazis to give the rest of his unit a chance to escape. He died in enemy fire to save his crew. These were all mortals, Orion. As a whole, they're not any better or worse than us. Some of them are fucking terrible, and some are heroic. The only difference I can see between mortals and demons is that mortals kill with weapons, and demons use magic. And the mortals out there now are not the ones who killed your family. Killing them isn't vengeance. It's insanity."

His gaze slid to the window, and I had no idea if I was actually getting through to him. "You and Amon both," he said quietly.

"What do you mean?"

"He's on your side." He let out a long sigh. "But the fact is, Rowan, the mortals have too much control over us in the modern world. One bomb could take out our walls, and then we're done. That's what the curse means. And what sort of king would I be if I didn't prioritize the safety of my own subjects over outsiders?"

He was almost sounding reasonable, which was making it hard for me to keep my resolve. So reasonable that I *nearly* forgot that several people were claiming he'd sent someone in to try to kill me tonight.

And here was the real question: what did I have to lose by taking the crown from him?

The simple fact was, if I were in control, I wouldn't have to worry about who to trust.

I straightened and lifted my chin. "Listen, Orion. There are only two options for this trial. If I win, I decide what happens. Or you win, and that's when you can prove to me that you do really want me to rule with you. Because right now, you have all the power. Of course you want me to give up. Let's see you offer me an alliance when it actually counts."

His eyes sparkled, and he took a step closer. He gave me a slow, dazzling smile that made my heart skip a beat. "I'll be happy to prove it to you when I win the trial. And do you know what?" His voice was low and silky. "I like being challenged by you."

The vulnerable side of Orion was gone, and he'd turned on the charm again. So I can't say I was shocked when he left the door open between our rooms. He crossed into his own room, pretending to ignore me as he unbuttoned his shirt. When he pulled it off, I told myself not to stare at the absolute masculine perfection that was his body—the thickly corded muscles, the visible V in his abs just over the top of his pants.

But telling myself not to stare was just about as useful as telling the moon to stop shining.

When he turned to me, his lips curled in a beautiful half-smile, I was momentarily mortified to realize my mouth had been hanging open.

He crossed to the door frame and leaned against it. My gaze roamed over his snake tattoo, then down to his chiseled abs again. "Something the matter, Rowan?" And here was Orion's cocky attitude, replacing that brief glimpse of his vulnerable side.

I took a deep breath, trying hard to ignore the heat sliding through my belly. "Are you trying to seduce me? Because I don't care how pretty you are—I'm still going through with the trial." I'd somehow lost control of my voice, and it had come out louder than necessary. One of the dogs poked his head in the door, looking between us to make sure everything was all right.

Orion's eyebrows rose. "I simply took my shirt off because I'm getting ready for bed." The look he was giving me was positively smoldering. "Love, surely you know by now that if an incubus were seducing you, you'd be writhing beneath me and begging for more right now."

I felt my cheeks flush, and my mind clouded with a haze of lust. I wasn't exactly sure what was happening, only that Orion was getting the upper hand. Throwing me off my game, getting me flustered.

But I was a succubus, and two could play at this game.

I let the blanket drop from my body, knowing that my wet tank top was falling off one of my shoulders and that my underwear hardly covered a thing. As soon as I did, I felt the atmosphere in the room change—a flash of heat and light that seemed to pulse from the demon king himself.

✿ 15 ✿

ORION

As soon as she dropped the blanket, I knew I was in trouble. All the blood seemed to rush from my head, making my cock harden until I could no longer think straight.

I stared down at her—big brown eyes, her full lips, nipples straining at the wet fabric...

In the salt breeze off the coast, I knew that if I kissed her, she would taste of the sea. I loved kissing her, and the way she looked at me. I loved...

Stop it.

Only a thin sheath of fabric covered her naked body, and I could see her perfect contours beneath it.

As a succubus, she could feel me drinking in her beauty, and her chest was faintly flushed.

"Not trying to seduce," I managed, forgetting the basics of language.

I was repeating myself, though, wasn't I?

And yet, it was the truth. I couldn't seduce her—not when I risked everything.

I'd simply wanted her to realize that little blond pretty boy Kas had nothing on me. Quite simply, jealousy was making me act like a fucking idiot.

She sat on the bed and leaned back. The damp tank top stretched over her breasts. She was quite obviously not wearing a bra, and her nipples were hard against the fabric. What I wanted to do, more than anything, was to throw her down and rip that cotton off her body. I wanted to kiss and lick her between her thighs until she screamed my name loudly enough for him to hear...

"Of course you weren't trying to seduce me. My mistake." She looked up at me from under her long eyelashes and rolled over, giving me a view of her ass. I was desperate to run my fingers over that fabric, to feel her heat.

Her cheeks were lightly flushed. "Something the matter, Orion? You look...dazed."

She was using my exact phrase against me. *Smart-ass.*

I didn't feel entirely in control of myself as I found myself moving closer, back into her room. A moth to a flame. I sat next to her on the bed, but my eye was drawn back to that fucking bruise on her neck.

I reached out to brush my fingertips over it. At the contact of my fingertips against her skin, she gasped slightly.

My heart was ready to explode.

"Just making sure you're healing properly." My voice sounded husky, and I pulled my hand away from her.

Her lips appeared full, slightly pouted. There was something about how she looked right now—seductive and adorable all at once—that was robbing me of rational thought. I wanted to taste her so much, it hurt.

She bit her lip and brushed her fingertips over my wrist. "I'm fine. I'm a demon now, Orion. You don't have to worry about me breaking."

She was right, of course, and yet, I'd never felt more compelled to keep someone safe. All I could do was thank the gods she trusted me enough to come with me here, into my home. I stood, trying to force myself to move away from her, to douse the fire in my thoughts.

"I want to kiss you, just once." The truth tumbled out of my mouth before I could stop myself. "But that's all, Rowan. Just one kiss tonight."

One kiss was fucking dangerous enough.

"Just one?" She cocked her head. "What are you so afraid of?"

One more heartbreak, and it will be the end of me. My sanity already hung by a thread. "You," I said softly. "I already told you that."

With her big brown eyes locked on me, she rose from the bed and wrapped her arms around my neck. Under the thin cotton, her breasts brushed against my bare chest, making me stiffen even more.

I cupped the side of her face. Fire swept through me as I leaned down to press my mouth against hers.

When our lips made contact, I immediately knew this was a mistake. If she rejected the real me, I'd lose my mind. If I fell in love completely and lost her, I'd also lose my mind. But around Rowan, I made fucking terrible decisions, and my tongue swept in to taste her. My whole body had come alive for her. I savored the way her tongue welcomed mine, and her muscles became soft and pliable in my arms. Oh, *gods*.

For the first time, I felt her succubus magic entwined around me, an inviting caress that stroked my back. I slid my hand up her spine, gripping her hair to tilt her head. I was overwhelmed by the urge to strip her naked and make her scream.

She would ruin me.

Arching into me, she moaned lightly, and that sound nearly made me lose the little control I had. I needed to fuck her hard against the wall. I wanted her to remember how perfectly we fit together—

I hardly knew what I was doing as I lifted her higher off the ground and she slipped her legs around me. One of her hands gripped my hair. With her back against the bedpost, I pressed my hard length against her. Had I ever been this desperate for anything before? Not even after centuries in prison.

The sound of one of the dogs barking interrupted us. Rowan broke from the spell first, pulling away from the kiss. Her lips were swollen, her cheeks pink. She'd never looked more beautiful.

"Don't really know what I'm doing here." She caught her breath. "You're my rival."

I pressed my forehead against hers, trying again to remember how to form a sentence. What had she said?

Ah...the rival thing. She thought I was dangerous.

As it happened, I thought the same about her.

Rowan had shown up in my life and thrown everything wildly off course, and when I was around her, I felt as if the world were tilting beneath my feet.

My plans for vengeance had always been the light that shone a path through madness, like the little illuminated ships floating along the river. Without vengeance guiding my way, I was in the dark again. Chaos. She brought that into my life.

"You're the Lady of Chaos," I breathed.

She touched the side of my face. "What?"

"Lady of Chaos. Ever since I first ran into you in that bar, you've lit every one of my plans on fire. You've destroyed everything I thought I understood."

"Sounds dangerous. Maybe you should put me down, then."

By the racing of her heart and the hot pulse of the magic around the room, I knew she wanted me as much as I wanted her. But how much of her desire for me was real? She was a succubus, responding to my lust magic. Lilu power thickened the air. That didn't mean she *cared* for me one bit—it just meant she was high on desire.

Meanwhile, I cared about her far more than I should. And that was why I was burning my centuries-old plans to the ground.

It wasn't her descriptions of John Robert Fox or the other mortals that had planted seeds of doubt in my mind—it was the fact that the mortal world had created Rowan. Could mortals be that terrible if they'd produced the perfect mix of terrifying and adorable, sweet and ferocious, that was Rowan Morgenstern?

"Right. I'm putting you down." My whisper sounded choked, and it took a shocking amount of effort to release my grip on her.

She narrowed her eyes at me as she slid down my body, and my stomach turned in knots. "If you were trying to get into my head, it's not working. The trial is still on," she said coldly.

She moved away from me, climbing over the bed, and I felt a sharp sting at the loss of contact.

"I just wanted you to think of me and not Kas when you're going to sleep." Sweet Lucifer, why had I admitted that out loud? *Idiot.*

She shifted back under her covers, staring at me in disbelief. But I caught a hint of a smile, and then it deepened into something truly dazzling. "Hang on. Is the incubus king *jealous?*"

"Don't be ridiculous. Why would *I* get jealous?" Gods below, exactly how often did I lie to everyone?

"Sure, you don't."

She saw right through me, of course. Which was strangely refreshing.

I leaned against her bedpost, unwilling to let the night end just yet. "Rowan. You saved my life in the underworld..." The rest of my thought died on my tongue before I could bring myself to say it out loud: *Do you really think I was worth saving? And more importantly, would you still think that if you knew the truth about me?*

She stared at me for a long moment, and a little line formed between her dark eyebrows. "Yeah, of course I did. And I'd do it again. I don't trust you to run a kingdom without murdering everyone, but I want you alive."

I could still taste her on my lips, sweet and salty. "What if you were wrong about me?"

"Oh." Her expression shifted, eyes glistening. She looked sad enough that I wanted to climb over the bed and gather her in my arms again.

I was holding my breath as I waited for her reply, until her expression shifted again. Becoming more guarded.

"I can tell you want to say something, and you're holding back," I said.

"How can you tell that?"

"Your nostrils flare when you're frustrated."

"I can't tell if you're saying all the right things to try to get me to let down my guard, or if you're genuine. But assuming you're being real here...Orion, did you try to make me hate you on purpose? Because you wanted to beat me to the punch before I realized what you were like?"

The accuracy of her words was like a fist to my throat, and all I could do was swallow hard.

She bit her lip. "Because you *do* love to tell strangers that you're terrible as soon as you meet them. It's like you're constantly trying to warn people."

My chest tightened. She really could see right through every one of my defenses, and it left me feeling confused, completely without my armor. "I don't have a lot of experience with people."

She gave me a sad smile. "I think you're crushed by the guilt of what happened to you. I still have hope for you. But I'm still going to kick your ass in the trial and become your queen." She arched an imperious eyebrow. "*Then* we'll figure out how to fix you."

"We'll see about that, love," I said, almost to myself.

And maybe—now—it was here before me. The light in the darkness, the new plan.

At some point, I would take the greatest risk of my life: finding out if she still cared for me when she really knew me.

But I was getting ahead of myself. I wouldn't play too much with the dangerous fire of hope, or I risked letting my last shreds of sanity go up in flames. Letting myself hope that Rowan could love me when she knew what I'd done—that was just about the scariest thing I could imagine. If she truly cared about me, then maybe I was meant for something other than avenging the dead. Maybe I had actual fucking worth.

My heart was about to beat right out of my chest with fear.

"I'll see you in the morning, Rowan." I brushed my fingertips over my lips as I crossed back to my room, still replaying the memory of that mind-blowing kiss. I knew I'd be thinking of it until the sun rose over the sea at dawn.

Maybe that last little thread of sanity had already gone up in smoke.

✣ 16 ✣

ROWAN

Eight days until the trial.

    Last night's conversation had left me so deeply confused that instead of sleeping, I'd simply replayed his words over and over in my mind.

And not just the conversation, of course. That *kiss*. The way he'd kissed me had been as intense and hot as fucking, and I couldn't stop thinking about it. Something had changed in the way he kissed me—a sort of reverence that wasn't there before.

In the morning, I'd woken early, sneaking out past a sleeping Orion. On my way out, I'd stolen a glance at his muscular back, and I'd briefly met his sweet friend. Amon had sent me off with coffee and scones. I peered out the door cautiously before leaving, surveying the square for any errant assassins. I found nothing amiss, but I kept scanning the streets as I walked.

As long as I was around Orion, I risked getting so distracted that I'd fail the trial. And the depressing truth was, I was still struggling to push him to the back of my mind.

What are you so afraid of?

You.

I sipped my coffee and replayed it for the millionth time. Was he trying to tell me that he was scared I would reject him? That I'd break his heart?

Someone—Mortana, I supposed—had well and truly convinced him that hope was the most dangerous thing of all.

Unless...

Unless, of course, that was all an act.

I blew out a long breath, trying to center myself by focusing on the world around me. My gaze skimmed over the flowers gently blowing in the salty breeze—pink peonies, violet foxglove, lavender...

As I walked through the garden, a fountain burbled gently. I breathed in the humid scent of wildflowers, and my mind cleared at last. Sunlight warmed my cheeks. Another sip of coffee sent a jolt of caffeinated life into my veins.

I pulled my phone from my pocket, relieved to see a text from Kas. Our magical lessons were beginning soon. I really had lucked out with teachers who were so willing to help me.

I crossed the bridge toward the forest, glancing at the sun sparkling off the river. As I approached the wilderness, the humid scent of moss and soil filled my nostrils.

I found Kas and Legion in the oak grove.

Legion stood with a large spell book in his hands, while Kas sat on the mossy forest floor, leaning against a tree trunk. He wore a crown of ivy and blue primroses that rested—crooked—over his delightfully messy blond hair.

I smiled at him. "Looking regal."

His cheeks dimpled when he smiled. "Not all of us are born royal. Some of us have to make the crowns ourselves from Mother Nature."

"Where is Shai?" I asked.

"Uh..." Legion's gaze moved from me to the spell book. His hair was pulled back, but a few strands of black caught in the breeze. "She's on her way."

I raised an eyebrow. "Everything okay, Legion?"

Kas rose, and he dusted off the back of his jeans. "Everything is fine. But we have a long day ahead of us because Legion decided to give you the most tedious possible task, and we're all going to be sitting through it for hours."

I took a deep breath. "As long as it helps me win the trial, I'm fine with tedium."

"Good." Legion flashed me a faint smile. "First, you will practice control of your magic. Then you can practice summoning more power. But first comes mastery. Understood?"

"Otherwise, we could all die in a fiery hell-world of your exploding magic," said Kas.

"Of course." I held out my hand for the spell book. "What spell?"

"Sifting soil," said Legion.

I frowned. "What is that, exactly?"

"Really, just what it sounds like."

Kas crossed his arms, his caramel eyes gleaming with amusement. "Legion has decided that you will spend the entire day making small piles of twigs using magical spells, and maybe trying to build tiny structures with them."

Good thing I'd brought the coffee.

BY THE TIME SHAI SHOWED UP, I'D MADE TWO TINY TWIG HOUSES, and I was ready for an afternoon nap. On my twentieth recitation of the spell, I was yawning uncontrollably.

Shai was rubbing her eyes as she crossed into the grove in wrinkled clothes.

"Late night?" I asked.

She exchanged a quick look with Legion, then shook her head. "The storm kept me up."

It was so brief that I nearly missed it, but the look she'd given Legion made me think they'd been together.

"What's your excuse?" she asked.

I let out a long breath. "Now that you're all here, there's something I should maybe mention...don't freak out, though." I touched my throat, right where Jasper had tried to crush it last night. "Orion moved me into his home."

Shai glared at me. "*What?* You can't stay with your rival."

"Did he give you a choice?" asked Kas, anger lacing his voice.

I shrugged. "Well, I didn't say *no*. He saved me from an assassin." Why was I feeling so defensive on Orion's behalf?

Shai raised a hand. "Hang on—"

"An *assassin?*" Legion finished her thought.

"Do you know who it was?" asked Kas.

I felt that unwelcome sense of protectiveness again for the demon king. "It was Jasper. The king's right-hand man. But Orion killed him." I let out a long sigh. "The weird thing was, Jasper thought Orion had ordered him to do it. And some of his other guards said the same thing. Orion thought that maybe they'd been enchanted. Mind control magic."

Shai's nose wrinkled. "Only Lilu have mind control power, and even then, it's rare."

"A spell, maybe?" I offered.

"Rowan," she said sharply. "You said that if he started to seduce you, I was supposed to remind you about Queen Elizabeth and the cotton candy."

Kas pulled off his flower crown and dropped it on the ground. "Seems like a brilliant ploy to get you to trust him. Maybe he even hoped you'd call off the trials."

Of course that was the most likely explanation. And yet...if Orion were going to stage some kind of ruse, he wouldn't be dumb enough to leave all these people telling on him. "At this point, I know one thing and one thing only for certain: I need to win the trial, and nothing else matters."

Kas stared at me. "Nothing else matters except that you're now living with a psychotic king who probably wants you dead."

"I'll be fine," I said sharply. "I really don't think he wants me dead." What would they think if they knew I'd kissed him last night? If *kiss* was really sufficient to describe what that had been.

Legion pinched the bridge of his nose. "You don't think your rival for the throne wants you dead? What, do you think the mad demon king is...*too nice?*"

He managed to make the entire concept sound insane.

"Look, I have eight days left," I said. "So am I going back to the twigs, or what? We're wasting time."

Legion glanced at the mounds of soil. "I think you've mastered those. I have something new for you."

I smiled. "Exciting. Are we going to raise the dead?"

"You're going to summon ants."

I took a deep breath. "You remember that I only have eight days left until I need to summon a dead witch, right?"

Legion nodded. "We're getting there. No shortcuts in magic."

"I mean, they exist," added Kas, "but if you take them, sometimes, a whole lot of people die."

I held out my hand for the book. "Ants it is, then."

❧

I WAS ALMOST DELIRIOUS WITH FATIGUE BY THE TIME KAS OFFERED to walk me home. After the initial twig successes, my magic had grown unfocused, flames bursting out in trees around me. I'd accidentally summoned red ants instead of black, and Shai had shrieked at me every time she was bitten.

And yet, tired as I was, I still didn't want to go back to my new room. The problem with Orion's cottage was that Orion lived in it, and I desperately needed to avoid him.

So as we walked, I slowed the pace, rambling to Kas about my favorite morbid facts. "Mary Tudor burned several hundred people at the stake. Did you know how long it took them to burn on average?"

"I think I'd rather not."

"Forty-five minutes," I answered anyway.

Kas smirked at me. "Aren't you just a ray of sunshine?"

I grinned. "Well, I *am* a Lightbringer, so I've got to have some sunlight deep down. Somewhere. Buried under lots of horrific trivia and obsessive fears."

"They say you get the leaders you deserve. Our two Lightbringers are a genocidal maniac and an absolute neurotic downer who tends to light things on fire when practicing magic—"

"*Excuse* me, I'm not always a downer." I racked my brain to think of something fun, though I'm not sure I fully understood the concept. "Tomorrow, when we practice, I'm going to bring cupcakes. With sprinkles. Like, rainbow...flower cupcakes. Very fucking *fun*."

His cheek dimpled. "As we eat them, will you tell us how many small children choked to death on cake last year?"

"If you don't think that's useful knowledge, I don't know what to tell you."

His eyes twinkled. "I'd gladly take you over a genocidal maniac. A ruler's job is to keep everyone safe, and I have no doubt that you will keep us all from harm with your wealth of knowledge about ways to die."

"I'm glad someone understands my true value."

He slid his hands into his pockets and scowled at Orion's cottage as we approached. "Did the king *order* you to stay in his house? Is he allowed to make demands of the shadow scion?"

"There's no protocol for that in the books." I sighed. "But there *is* a protocol for attacking each other. If one of us murders the other between trials, we get executed by the Council."

A pulse of warm electrical magic washed over me, and goosebumps rose on my skin.

I turned to see Orion stalking from the shadows, his pale blue eyes sparkling in the moonlight. "Ah, Rowan. Are you and your pretty friend weighing the consequences of murdering me?"

I narrowed my eyes at the king. "No. But *Your Majesty*, out of curiosity, are you ordering me to stay with you, or do I have the option of leaving?"

He pinned me with a heated stare. "I'll keep you safe, Rowan, whatever it takes."

"That's not really an answer, is it?" said Kas.

The air thinned, and Orion cut him a sharp look. "I don't owe you an answer, Kasyade." Darkness slid through his eyes, and he took a step closer. "Lest you forget, I am still your king. Rowan is a Lightbringer. You are not."

Kas held his gaze, and thorns grew in the silence.

Menace rippled off Orion. I was starting to get worried that he was going to rip Kas's heart out—his usual method of dealing with inconveniences—and I sucked in a sharp breath. "Kas wasn't questioning your authority. He just pointed out that it wasn't a real answer."

Orion's violent gaze was still locked on Kas, and the air around him heated. "You were around then, during the purge of the Lilu."

Oh, here we go.

The low, quiet tenor of his voice sent a shiver up my spine. An unspoken threat laced the air.

Kas lifted his chin. "I was a child then, same as you."

"Not *exactly* the same as me." Venom under that velvety voice. "I remember you, Kasyade. You were older than me. So lucky not to be a Lilu, weren't you?"

Gently, I touched Orion's arm. "Many of your subjects were around then. You can't threaten them all."

Orion had to realize he couldn't fight a war on two fronts. If he was truly expecting a confrontation with the mortals, he'd need every demon on his side, whether or not they'd stood by during the purge of the Lilu.

Orion tilted his head. "Then don't consider it a threat, but I do have a warning. You, Kasyade, are not qualified to help a Lightbringer learn to practice her magic. You have no idea the kind of danger you're playing with."

And with that, he stalked off into his house.

I stared after him. "Any idea what he's talking about, Kas?"

"If I had to guess," Kas replied dryly, "he's going to try to tell you that your magic is too dangerous to use, and that you should probably just let him win the trials so no one gets hurt. And that it's all too complicated for you to understand."

I snorted. "Right." So why did I feel this sharp tendril of unease at Orion's warning? "Don't worry, Kas. I'm ignoring everything he says."

Liar, liar.

That *should* be the truth, but it wasn't.

"See you at dawn," Kas said, and then he leaned in and lowered his voice. "Keep ignoring him. You've got this, Sunshine."

I ignored the nickname, and my chest unclenched a little at his reassurance.

When I crossed inside, I found Amon sitting with his dogs by the fireplace, a book in his lap. Over a steaming cup of tea, he raised an eyebrow at me. "The king is in...a *mood*."

Delightful.

✣ 17 ✣

ROWAN

I climbed the stairs and crossed into my cozy little room, surprised to find he wasn't in his. So I shut the connecting door and flicked on the lights.

Exhausted, I closed the wooden shutters, in case any rogue assassins were watching me. My clothes smelled faintly of woodsmoke from the accidental fires I'd lit in the forest today.

A buried worry snagged at my thoughts as I slipped into a pair of shorts and a tank top for sleep. Orion had never had the chance to learn magic, either, but like everything else, it came naturally to him, easy as breathing.

My ears perked at the sound of the door opening in his room. I crossed to the door, pressing my ear against the wood to listen.

And I nearly fell into his room when he pulled the door open. He arched one of his dramatic black eyebrows. "Yes? I heard you breathing against the door."

You'd think I'd be used to it by now, but the sight of him shirtless took the breath from my lungs. His skin looked bronzed in the warm light, his silver hair lit up from behind like a halo. I forced my gaze from his muscled chest to his devastatingly perfect face. His skin was so *golden.*

I leaned against the doorframe, trying to look casual.

He opened the door wider, motioning for me to enter. Of course, it was extremely stupid to step into his room when he was shirtless, but here I was, walking in anyway.

"Cotton candy," I whispered to myself. "Queen Elizabeth."

He turned, his glacial eyes striking in the warm light. "Did you just whisper *cotton candy* and *Queen Elizabeth* to yourself? I remember recently you suggested that I was losing my mind, but I now wonder if you were *projecting*. That's the word, isn't it?"

"Have you been reading psychology books?"

He shrugged. "I read everything I can."

"How did you hear me breathing on the other side of the door?"

"Demons have incredibly good hearing."

He sat on the edge of his bed, leaning back. His posture, unfortunately, highlighted his perfect body, gilded in the candlelight. I thought of that kiss—deep and sensual, like he was fucking me with his tongue.

"Rowan?"

"Yeah. Here." I dragged my eyes up again and tried to put my thoughts together. "My hearing isn't that amazing."

"You've lived your whole life as a mortal. It would probably be overwhelming for you. Maybe you just need time to get used to it...like you need time to learn how to manage your Lightbringer power."

I sat as far away from him as the room would allow and found myself perched awkwardly on the edge of a chair. Why did I find it so hard to relax around him, as if we hadn't already had sex and traveled to the underworld together? As if I didn't—at this point—know him better than probably any other living person? As if we hadn't *just* kissed passionately last night?

"What did you mean about the Lightbringer power being dangerous?" I asked. "And how have you learned to manage it? You've hardly had much more time than I have with your magic."

"No. But I'm naturally good at things, and you're...not."

"Oh, my *God*," I muttered.

"Really, Rowan, you needn't address me that way, although I suppose I am technically divine. Thanks for telling me about that, by the way. But *Your Majesty* is perfectly fine for me."

I stared at him, uncertain if he was joking. But what difference did it make? I was here for one reason alone: information. "Tell me how you know the Lightbringer power is so dangerous if you don't actually have firsthand experience of this danger, since—according to your theory—you just naturally do everything perfectly."

"Oh, I didn't say I do everything *perfectly*. I make plenty of bad decisions. I'm just good at things. Like you said, I'm basically a god—"

"I didn't say that."

"But to answer your question, I've felt it happening. The power of starlight streaming from my body. And the things it touched...it was like all the matter around me was falling apart. Turning into dust that could be swept away with the breeze. It was like the world crumbled around me."

I sucked in a sharp breath at this horrifying image. "So how did you control it?"

He rose. "Stand up, love. I'll show you."

At what point did I stop hating that he called me "love"? As I stood, I caught a glimpse of his eyes brushing down my body.

Heat rippled off him. "I think magic is different for us than it is for other demons." He spoke quietly, and his deep voice was making my pulse quicken. "Most demons are simply trying to call on their magic and make it as powerful as possible. For us, I think we have to temper it. Some emotions are hot and full of energy. Anger, passion, love. Even fear. Others are dark and cold, like sorrow and loss. And it's the cold emotions that temper it."

Just hearing Orion speak the words *passion* and *love* made my blood pump harder.

"When you want to summon magic," he said, "you draw on the hot emotions. That's why you were able to call up enough magic to kill the congressman. Try it now. Think of something that fills you with an intense emotion." He reached out, gently touching me just above my belly button. "This is where you feel it first, right? Between your ribs?"

Heat radiated from the point where his finger contacted my white cotton tank top, and my gaze flicked down to the V just above his trousers.

"Yes."

"Try it. I want you to summon your magic but try to focus on an intense emotion as you do so."

My pulse raced as I stared up at him, meeting his gaze. He must *know* the effect he had on me because his incubus powers would tune in to that. But could I hear *his* heart racing, too?

Better to think of something else. I closed my eyes and replayed the worst things he'd ever said to me.

I don't respect you enough to hate you... I find you tedious and pathetic... You don't have it in you...

Anger simmered in my blood, boiling away the desire. And the coup de grâce for any positive feelings, the memory of him saying *Escort this woman out of my realm.*

Power swirled between my ribs, just at the point where Orion was touching me. After all that, how dare he try to seduce me again? Molten wrath swept through me.

"Rowan," he barked.

My eyes snapped open, and I found Orion gilded in light that was emanating from my own body.

When I looked down at myself, I *glowed*, the light nearly blinding. I gasped at the sight. I'd seen this happen to Orion before, but never to myself. He was still touching me, and the heat from his fingertips helped to center the magic in my body. Tracing his fingers up a little bit, I felt the electrical buzz of magic move with them. Now, it spilled into my chest.

"Rowan," he whispered. "You are *shockingly* powerful. You need to draw on one of the colder emotions before you destroy my house. Think of something sad."

Ah, but there was so much to choose from there. And the first thing that popped into my mind was an argument I'd had with Mom the week before she died, when I'd told her that she was always annoying me with her paranoia. I'd told her if she kept it up, she'd make me as crazy as she was.

I still vividly remembered the look of hurt on her face...

God, I was an asshole. Guilt and sorrow slid through me, and I watched the golden light fade from Orion's features. Tears stung my eyes, and I tried to blink them away.

Reaching out, Orion brushed a strand of my hair out of my face—a gesture so natural I nearly forgot I was supposed to be keeping my guard up.

"For Lightbringers," he said softly, "our power is different. Overwhelming. If it feels too intense, you could shut it down. Or it could explode out of you and incinerate everything around you, which is what would have happened just now if I hadn't been helping you center it."

He seemed sincere, but I could already hear Kas's response in my mind. Kas would tell me he was trying to convince me to lose.

I sighed, still trying to shake off the devastating image of Mom. "Okay. Well, if it seems like I'm losing control, I know what to think about."

His pale eyes searched mine. "What is it?"

"Guilt."

"Ah," he said softly. "I know that one well. It's with me always. And maybe that's why I will never lose control of my magic completely."

"Thanks for the help." I swallowed. "I guess." I blinked. I was having a hard time putting coherent thoughts together, which wasn't wildly unusual around Orion.

But right now, I was particularly confused.

The world seemed to be dimming. Each word, each phrase, was floating by like a puff of dandelion seeds blowing on the wind. I almost wanted to fall right into his powerful chest and let him wrap his arms around me. "Something doesn't feel right."

He put his hands on my shoulders. One of his thumbs moved back and forth slowly, giving me clarity again. "It's not just the risk of the damage you can do to the world around you. Powerful magic like that has a cost. When you release your light magic, you leave a vacuum. And chaos magic slips in to fill the void."

With his touch, my mind started clearing again. I reached up and pulled his hands off my shoulders. "Why would you help me steal your crown?"

"Because we're on the same side."

Exhaustion washed over me, and I wanted desperately to curl up into his bed. But my own was just a few feet away. "I should go to sleep." I turned, my muscles like lead. "Good night."

"Rowan?"

When I turned to look at him, I thought I saw a flicker of sadness pass across his perfect features—but it was so fast.

"Yeah?"

"*Sunshine.*" Disdain laced his voice. "What is that?"

I rolled my eyes. "It's sarcastic. Because...you know..." Suddenly, I found myself desperate to know what he thought of me. "Because I'm a downer."

He studied me closely, and I expected him to say something mildly insulting. Instead, he said, "A downer?"

Given Orion's history, I probably *was* a veritable ray of sunshine. "You know, I have a lot of stored facts about death and general fears."

A line formed between his brows. "But of course you'd need that. Mortals die so easily. And you seemed particularly accident-prone."

"Thanks for the vote of confidence."

"You're not a downer. You are one of the most entertaining people I've ever known."

"You only know, like, four people, and one of them had his head split open with an axe."

A smile played about his lips. "See?"

I swallowed, then turned to walk back into my room, distinctly disturbed by the warm glow his words had given me.

I was, after all, ignoring him completely.

❧ 18 ❧

ROWAN

Five days until the trial.

After Orion helped me learn about my magic, I'd been rigidly controlled about avoiding him. Leaving the house at dawn before he woke, returning home when he was out. For the past three days, I'd managed to stay perfectly focused, envisioning a crown on my head and a peaceful demon city spread out before me.

With my teachers, I'd worked my way through one magical task after another.

At last, Legion allowed me to raise a monarch butterfly from the dead. Now it fluttered around my head, ignited with apricot light in the setting sun.

"Pretty zombie butterfly," cooed Shai.

"Brilliant." Kas beamed at me. "What do you think? Head home for the night, or do you want to go for gold and try summoning a witch?"

"I'm ready for the witch."

"Let's get the blood," said Shai, looking perfectly witchy in a long black gown with lacy sleeves.

"I think she's ready," said Legion. "We have four days left. If there are problems with the witch summoning, we'll need all that time to fine-tune it."

"Oh, thank the gods." Kas grinned. "I was getting incredibly bored."

I inhaled deeply. "I'm going to need to recite the spell quickly, too. Belial University's head witch will signal us to start, and then we'll be racing to get to the end of the spell first."

"Hmm." Legion pulled a small crimson-filled vial from his pocket. He turned it over between his fingertips, then met my gaze. "So, you're ready for this?"

I shrugged. "Might as well try it. But can you do me a favor and back up? Behind the trees, at least. In case I lose control of my magic."

Legion arched a dark eyebrow. "You haven't set anything on fire in days."

"Right," I said. "But none of us have much experience with Light-bringer power. Who knows what will happen?"

He shrugged. "Okay. Well, when you get to the summoning spell, let's try with a witch we know. Someone gentle and forgiving. Someone who won't mind being summoned from the dead."

I took the blood from him and opened the vial. "Do you have anyone in mind?"

"Goody Pendleton," said Legion. "Also known as Chemosh. I knew her long ago. She studied here in the eighteenth century."

"Ah, good choice." Kas's deep voice seemed to hum off the tree trunks. He wore a dandelion behind his ears. The combination of a flower with his tattoos was very fetching on him. "Chemosh is lovely. She used to make me hot cross buns every Sunday. I think she had a thing for me."

Legion sighed. "You say that about every woman."

"Her Demonic name is Chemosh," said Kas, ignoring him. "You'll need to call her at the end of the spell."

"Chemosh," I repeated, with a sound like a hard H.

"You've got the pronunciation down." Shai was flipping through one of the spell books. "Hang on, I'm finding the summoning spell."

I pulled open the cork on the vial of blood. "Just so you know, once you begin the summoning spell, you could see a few visions of the dead."

A little dread flickered in my chest. I'd seen enough visions of my dead mom to last a lifetime.

Legion took a deep breath and glanced at Shai. "I suppose we should hide."

She handed the book to Kas, and he held it open to the right page.

I raised my eyebrows when he didn't leave the grove. "You're not staying, are you? What if I explode with fireball magic?"

"You don't need to be worried about me. It's the benefit of being a demon, isn't it? Even if I burn to ash, I'll recover—it'll just take a few days. I only ask that you refrain from cutting out my heart, Sunshine, and I'll be fine."

I dipped my pinkie into the blood and carefully drew a five-pointed star on my forehead. The coppery scent of mortal blood filled my nostrils. As soon as the liquid was on my skin, I could feel my body reacting to it, my magic heating in my veins. I closed up the little vial and tucked it in my pocket, then wiped my fingers on my jeans and took the book from him.

Kas's amber eyes glowed.

With the blood on my skin, the world seemed to grow brighter, even though twilight was upon us. Light beamed through the oak leaves, and little motes of dust floated in the rays. All around me, sunlight heated the air. I felt *high*.

Kas himself seemed to glow with light, beautiful as an angel. "How does it feel?" he asked.

I sighed, my breath shaking. "Euphoric."

He let out a low chuckle. "Good. Connect to the earth, and see if you can intensify it."

I blinked in the golden rays of sunlight. "What?"

He stepped around me, and now his lovely gravelly voice was coming from just behind my back. "Take off your shoes."

Shai was right about his voice. It really *was* nice.

"Take them off," he said, "and feel the earth beneath your feet. It can help to intensify the power."

I slipped off my little brown flats and stood on the soil. An earthy forest breeze rushed over me, raising goosebumps. From the ground up, I started to call my magic, heat spreading through my body. "Okay. Here I go."

I started reciting the spell as I'd learned it in Demonic, and power thrummed up my nape.

I closed my eyes, thinking of a *hot* emotion. And as much as I tried to focus on bringing to mind the masculine sound of Kas's voice, Orion's sensual whisper kept intruding...

I wanted you to think of me and not Kas when you're going to sleep...

Warmth simmered between my ribs. I repeated the spell again, thinking of how it felt when Orion had kissed me, pressing me against the bedpost. The way his eyes had looked when I'd dropped the blanket...

A surge of magic kindled in my belly, and I could feel the light heating up my skin—

"Shit," I whispered. "Wait, it's too much." I let the sorrow of loss curl around me, dampening the force of my Lightbringer magic.

When I opened my eyes, I glanced at Kas, catching his worried expression.

He shook his head. "No, you have to use powerful magic for this," he said. "Try summoning everything you have, because I know Orion will."

I frowned, taking a step back from him. "Have you heard anything about a Lightbringer's power being dangerous? Like, if I use all my power, I could make everything around me dissolve, and also lose my mind?"

His forehead wrinkled. "Dissolve?"

"Hang on." Shai stepped out from behind an oak. "Who told you that? Orion?"

I realized how it sounded. "He didn't just tell me. He showed me. When I used a burst of my Lightbringer magic, it left me feeling confused. He said that for a Lightbringer, we can create a vacuum, and chaos replaces the light."

Shai grimaced. "*Rowan.* You can't really believe he's trying to help you, right? You're *rivals*. He tried to assassinate you. He wants to keep his throne."

The sun had slid down below the tree line now, and shadows spilled throughout the forest.

"He *is* the Lord of Chaos," said Kas. "I'm sure he could use chaos magic to make you feel...chaotic."

"Rowan," said Legion, "what do your instincts say?"

My instincts said Orion was right—but who the fuck knew if that was actual instinct or the influence of his mind-blowing kiss?

Shai walked closer to me and cupped both sides of my face. She lowered her chin, our foreheads practically touching. "You wanted me to remind you not to fall for his charm and manipulation, yeah? I'm doing that now."

"Right." I pulled her hands from my face. "Okay, well, just humor me and get further back than you were before."

"Really?"

"There's a small chance that Orion is correct, isn't there? And if I lose control of my magic, not only could I lose my mind, but I could dissolve everything around me."

"Dissolve," said Shai.

"I'm serious," I said. "I don't care if you don't believe it. I felt the Lightbringer power about to explode, and I don't want you near it. I'm talking, like, get on the other side of the Acheron River. I don't care if you'll all recover because you're demons—I don't need more horror burned into my memories." I pinned Kas with a serious stare. "I mean *all* of you. I'll come find you if the spell works."

Shai took a deep breath. "Fine, but we should FaceTime it."

Legion frowned. "Is that a spell?"

She pulled her cell phone out of her pocket and waggled it. "We can watch her through video, and if anyone tries to assassinate her, or on the off chance she loses her mind, we can save her."

"Fine." I pulled my cell phone from my jeans and propped it up against an oak. "Call me when you're on the other side of the river. And if my phone suddenly goes dead, it's either poor reception, or I exploded."

Shai's forehead wrinkled. "Right. Okay."

Night had fallen in the City of Thorns, and my friends quickly disappeared into the darkness, leaving me alone like I'd asked. As the sounds of their footfalls faded, the air seemed to grow colder.

On my forehead, the witch blood tingled.

It seemed like ages before my phone rang, the little screen lighting up with Shai's picture. I crossed to the oak tree and flicked it on to answer.

Shai's face popped up on the screen. "We're here. Hanging out by the river."

I waved at Shai. "I'm ready."

"Go for it, Sunshine!" Kas said from behind her.

Rolling my eyes, I stepped back into the grove. Barefoot, I took a deep, shuddering breath.

As I did, I called up a memory certain to instill fury in me—Orion standing over King Cambriel and slaughtering the man I'd vowed to kill. Taking my revenge from me...

In my mind's eye, I saw the hot splatter of blood on the stone. Anger started to rise, tightening my muscles. Just the right amount of power...

I opened my eyes to see the wind whipping through the trees. A faint golden glow emanated from my body, and I started to recite the spell, reading from the book. As I read, goosebumps rose on the back of my skin. From the corner of my eye, ghostly images flickered past. Between the trunks, shadows seemed to twine with wisps of light.

I glanced down at the page once more, but it took me a moment to find my place again on the page. I started again, pronouncing each word carefully. The hair rose on my nape as I felt I was opening the door to an ancient, powerful world. In the corner of my vision, silvery lights twinkled. From the soil upward, power rushed through me.

Glowing, I felt a primal connection to the world around me—to the generations of mortals and demons who'd come before me, who'd grown from the forest soil, then fed it with their bodies. The night spread its shadowy mantle, and I breathed in the humid, ancient air of the woods. This was where the Lilu belonged—in the wild.

Magic slid around me as I neared the end of the spell. But unwelcome memories started to intrude along with it: Orion's fingers tightening around me as he hoisted me up against the bedpost to kiss me hard. That deep, sensual kiss was too powerful for me to think of—

I tried to push the lust to the back of my skull.

"*Chemosh*," I said, completing the spell once again.

Light poured from me, and I tried to dampen the ardor of my emotions by thinking of the worst day of my life. But I felt like I could smell him now, the scent of burnt cedar wrapping around me. His skin tinged with gold.

Orion's eyes were on me as I leaned back on the bed, darkening because he liked what he saw. He was about to lose control of himself...

What are you so afraid of?

You.

Distantly, I heard Shai calling my name. But I wasn't in her world anymore. My body grew hotter, brighter. Shaking with the power of the stars, until my mind no longer formed words. I lived in a world of light now.

But I no longer knew where my feet met the earth, or if I had a body at all.

❦

I WOKE IN ORION'S ARMS, TO THE SOUND OF HIM SWEARING. WHEN I opened my mouth to say something to him, I couldn't remember how to speak, or how I got here. I only knew that I needed to heal, and that I craved his body on mine.

Delirious, I kept my eyes on his square jaw until I could no longer remember his name.

19

ORION

I held Rowan in my arms, carrying her into my room. As soon as I'd seen the searing burst of light from the wilderness, panic had begun to claw at my mind. I'd raced through the skies, only to find her in a clearing of dust and ashes. The air still shimmered with gold around her.

Her magic had consumed a large circle of trees, and she lay in the center of it all, her clothing destroyed by the force of chaos. For a moment, I'd been so stunned by the sight of her lying naked on the earth that I could hardly think straight. But once I'd realized how badly she needed me, my thoughts became crystal clear.

I couldn't sense her soul.

She was clearly here—I could see her, feel her weight in my arms, smell her scent of ripe cherries with the mossy scent of the forest still clinging to her skin. Her chest rose and fell with each breath. But I couldn't sense her life. Normally, I could feel her energy, but like the music of the spheres—or an air conditioner that suddenly switched off—it was hard to notice a constant presence until it went silent.

Rowan's energy had been like that, I think since even before I'd met her. Maybe since she'd been born—my twin star, a vibrating, humming power just at the outer edges of my consciousness.

When the mob had hanged her in the underworld, I'd felt the same dreadful quiet. Fear had stilled my heart.

Now, I laid her gently on my bed, and her arms flopped over her head. Her hair fanned out above her, billowing like a mermaid's. Or like Ophelia in the paintings after she drowned herself with a kingdom at stake. With the mad, murderous prince Hamlet driving her insane...

Regret tightened my throat.

Fuck. I was the mad, murderous prince. And this is what I'd wrought. I should have been there for her always instead of throwing her out of the city walls.

Rowan had been so ferocious when she'd tossed down the gauntlet, and now she looked so delicate—alabaster skin, narrow wrists. Her calves and back were smeared with dirt.

Rowan had used all her Lightbringer power at once, holding nothing back.

Kasyade and Legion weren't proper teachers. They were reckless arseholes so convinced of their own righteousness.

But it wasn't their fault Rowan didn't believe me. The sad truth was *I* was the one who'd convinced her not to trust me. I was the one who'd pushed her away because I was so afraid of losing someone again.

She knew that someone like me would cheat and steal to get the vengeance I'd promised to Ashur.

What she didn't know was that I prized something else above the throne right now. It wasn't revenge, either.

I just wanted her to open her fucking eyes and look at me.

She consumed me, and right now, nothing else meant anything anymore.

Raw fear replaced my anger, and fear was the one thing I couldn't really deal with. This was exactly what I'd hoped to avoid with Rowan, why I'd pushed her away—the dizzying terror of losing someone you cared about. I wanted to avoid that particular horror again, the one that had devoured me so completely, the one that had broken me until I no longer really knew who I was.

I touched her chest, just between her breasts. Whatever light remained inside her was now just a guttering lick of flame. Darkness and chaos swirled around it. That light would be gone for good unless I could heal her soon.

If I fucked this up, she'd be lost to me for eternity to the chaos inside.

A wave of my hand brought the candles in my room blazing to life —I still preferred them to electric lights. And I needed to stoke those flames inside her now, just like that. The Lilu healed by feeding off lust, but it had to be done properly.

Slowly.

Too much lust too quickly would overwhelm her. I'd have to take her to the brink and keep her there for as long as I could. A slow, erotic build-up was the best way to restore a Lilu depleted of power. A simmering heat. And with my hand on her chest, I could already hear her moaning quietly. Even if she couldn't think clearly yet, her body's primitive instincts knew what she needed.

I extended her arms toward the corners of the bed and followed suit with her ankles. I spun my index finger in the air, and tendrils of my magic coiled around Rowan's limbs, holding them fast. If anything went wrong—if I overwhelmed her with power—I needed her under control.

Her heart started to race, her chest flushing. Something in her body liked being bound, which was a detail I'd have to think about later when her life wasn't on the line.

Already, her warm succubus magic stroked over my skin. It invited me in, making my breath quicken. There was still a chance to bring her back.

My gaze raked down her naked body, and I fought for restraint.

I remembered reading about a glutton demon named Shedim who used famine and starvation as torture devices, but with a kicker. He kept mortals on the brink of death, within a heartbeat of the end, for weeks or longer. He'd provide just enough sustenance to keep the mortals breathing. Just strong enough to move and stand, but no more. The twist was that he'd then present the poor fools with a sumptuous feast—a long table filled with all manner of rich meats and cheeses, fruits and desserts, breads and wines. The starving people would inevitably gorge themselves like wild animals, trying to stuff everything into their mouth at once.

Shedim fed off their gluttony.

They'd become violently ill. And some would go so far as to eat until their stomachs burst, much to Shedim's delight.

And as I stared at Rowan now, tied to my bed, I had some inkling what had driven those starving mortals, because she looked like a feast before me. That same madness threatened to overwhelm me.

But really, this wasn't Rowan at all. Her mind wasn't functioning.

And I'd promised not to kiss her until she trusted me. I *hated* breaking promises, and she had no way to tell me she trusted me in the state she was in.

I threw one of my blankets over her, covering her from her breasts down to her thighs, and she sighed at the contact. Every muscle in my body went taut at the sound, my blood pounding. Already, she was feeding off my raw desire, healing from it. All I had to do was be in the same room with her, and she could drink from my erotic charge. But with the right technique, I could heal her sooner.

I reached down to touch her bare legs, slowly letting my fingertips trace the swell of her calves up to the backs of her knees.

When I reached her thighs, my palms flattened, and her muscles tensed and relaxed involuntarily as I pressed on them more forcefully. She made a tiny, whimpering sound, her mouth opening as she breathed more deeply. There it was—a little more light in her eyes, and her gaze was locked on me. She tugged at the bindings. Already, she was healing—feeding off me. Her body was calling to mine like a siren.

I traced slow, gentle strokes over her thighs. Hungry for me, she breathed faster, and her heart raced.

My nostrils flared as my own arousal stampeded through my body. My incubus magic slid over her as I caressed my way back down her legs to her feet, massaging them one after the other, my thumbs applying pressure up and down her soles and down to the balls of her feet. I took my time returning to her upper thighs, which made her groan as she moved her body against the restraints. The blanket slipped down a little, revealing a nipple that seemed painfully peaked, aching to be touched.

She whispered my name so quietly, I could hardly hear it.

And it took everything inside me not to have her right then and there, to act as one of Shedim's tortured mortals and surrender to my basest desires. I growled, a low, guttural sound, and I moved my hands to the hollows of her hips, pulling the blanket aside just enough that I could stroke her skin. Holy hell, I wanted to rip the blanket aside and see all of her, but this wasn't the time.

Sparks danced where I touched her, as if she were made of steel and my hands were welder's torches. I watched it, entranced. The Lilu were truly amazing creatures.

Light flared in her eyes, and she whispered my name. Relief flooded me as I realized it was working, and I traced my fingertips down her ribcage.

"Rowan?" I whispered back. "Are you returning to me?"

She gasped as I slid them up again, just below her breasts. "Yes," she breathed.

Her hips rose, rocking, as her body sought the sexual release that was the lifeblood of a succubus. When she said my name again, I started stroking her thighs again, stoking her lust.

Every part of me burned for her, and each beat of my heart sent blood pumping to the only place I needed it.

Fuck.

Nothing mattered at that moment except her.

❧ 20 ❧

ROWAN

Hot, velvety, erotic magic charged the room, making my body swell with need.

I *needed* Orion.

I'd never ached for something like this before. Not just one Orion —I wanted two of him. Three? Mouths on my nipples, one between my legs—

I could imagine a whole bunch of them surrounding me, kissing me everywhere, giving me the sex I craved. The silky blanket was a light, torturous friction on my naked skin. Had he done that on purpose?

He'd brought me into this wild state of sexual arousal, but he wasn't finishing the job. Fuck, I'd say whatever he wanted if he just gave me what I needed. If I could remember how to make words...

What I really wanted was to leap on him, straddle him, satiate myself on his body. But I couldn't move—I was held in place, bound at my wrists and ankles with shimmering bands of energy. Gods *damn* it, Orion.

His thumb traced circles over my hipbones just under the blanket, and my body shook, my breath catching. That wasn't where I really needed him.

"Orion," I managed in a hoarse whisper. Light from candles danced on the walls as I tried to put together the wheres and whys and hows of my predicament. I only vaguely remembered how I'd ended up here.

I wanted to ask him to remove the restraints and the fabric off my body, but my thoughts were still a jumble of confusion.

He leaned over me, elbows on either side, his eyes searching mine. He looked golden in this light, and I thought I read relief in his eyes, and a faint smile. "There you are, Rowan."

The way he said my name sounded reverent.

Gods, he smelled amazing. *Kiss me, you hot bastard.*

He stroked his thumb over my cheek. "You drained yourself completely. I guess you had to learn the hard way." A seductive smile curled his lips. "Lucky for you, I'm prepared to bring you back the hard way."

He leaned down, brushing kisses over my jaw, then moved lower to my throat. My body arched into him, my hips moving upward. Every touch of his lips against my skin sent heat sliding through my body, pulsing between my thighs. My breasts ached for him, and the light movement of this silky blanket against my nipples was pure torture. I was on *fire*.

He stopped kissing the tops of my breasts, glancing up at me from under his black eyelashes. His cheeks looked flushed, and the dark look in his eyes said he wanted to devour me. So why wasn't he doing more? Untying me so I could participate? Holy hell, this was excruciating.

"Orion," I said again, louder this time, like a desperate prayer for salvation. It seemed the only thing I could remember how to say was his name...though another word was rolling around in my mind, the word *fuck*, because that was what I needed.

The ache between my thighs was overwhelming. Slick with desire, thighs spread open with these bindings, I desperately needed him to fill me.

"I said I wouldn't kiss you until you said you trusted me," he murmured into my neck. "But it doesn't count if it's not on your mouth." Another flick of his beautiful, silver-flecked eyes at me. "And this is, after all, an emergency."

"More," I groaned, finally managing a new word.

"Not yet." He kissed my breasts, and I tried to wrap my thighs around him. I *needed* satiation. "Too much is dangerous, love. But you're feeding from me because I'm desperate to fuck you."

That made me shake again, trying to press my thighs together so I could clench them, but they were pulled too far apart.

Gasping, I tugged on my restraints, struggling against my bindings. I could find nothing to provide me with the pleasure I craved. I let my head fall back into the pillows, aroused beyond all reason. I could think only of how much I needed pressure between my thighs that would give me my release.

I felt nearly as empty as I had when my magic left me, just in a very different way.

If he just gave me what I needed, this could all be over. Instead, he pushed himself up so he was sitting on the bed next to me, then slid the blanket up a little higher on my thighs, his eyes burning with dark heat as he stared at my body. I was sure he could see how turned on I was. His jaw was rigid with tension, and he looked as if he was about to snap.

He traced circles between my thighs—too light, not high enough. Teasing me. Making my hips buck as I shamelessly tried to move against him. Higher now, moving over my sex, but too light—

Writhing in my bonds, I hissed, "Please, Orion." Lilu magic charged the room, warm threads of our magic entwining, humming over my skin. And as I moved, the blanket slid off my breasts. His gaze shot to my hardened nipples, and he cursed under his breath. His muscles tensed, and he pulled his gaze away from me.

Then the bastard yanked his hand from me, too. I gasped audibly, certain he was doing this to mess with me. This was torture, wasn't it?

He turned, shoulders tense, fists tightened like he was about to fight. "No more for now, love. Your magic must return slowly, and I'm about to snap."

I gritted my teeth. "You're just doing this to torment me."

His gaze slid back to me, his eyes filled with shadows. "You've already regained enough strength to speak in complete sentences. This was the right way to heal you. Your body can heal itself with our lust magic. But if it goes too far, it will drain you, and then we're back to square one. Trust me," he murmured. "I'm not enjoying this any more than you are."

But did I actually trust him? Now there was a question. And I absolutely could not remember the answer.

I pulled at the restraints as he crossed through a doorway into another room, feeling vulnerable and exposed—and thoroughly unsatisfied.

From where I lay, I heard the sound of a bath filling. Slowly, with Orion out of the room, my heart slowed, and I sucked in deep breaths. I hadn't fully recovered, but my strength was returning.

I hoped my sanity would follow soon after. Begging for sex wasn't my style, especially from a rival I'd been intent on hating.

Orion returned to the bedroom clad only in a pair of black boxers, his tan, muscular physique on display. My gaze swept down to his abs— then lower. From the looks of it, maybe he was as painfully aroused as I was.

"I'm going to release you and carry you to the bath," he said.

"I can walk," I protested weakly.

"Suit yourself."

With a flick of his wrist, the coils holding me captive dissolved into thin air. I curled into a ball before stretching like a cat, twisting my back in every direction it could twist. If he wasn't going to give me what I needed, then what I really wanted was some alone time. But he had warned me that too much sexual pleasure was dangerous. And clearly, it was time for me to start heeding his warnings.

"Promise me you'll be more careful with your magic," he said quietly.

"Oh, I promise." I swung my legs off the bed, then stood to walk to the bathroom adjoining his room. I made it about two steps before I promptly collapsed.

Orion was close enough to catch me before I hit the floor, flinging an arm around my lower back. He scooped me up and carried me to the bubbling, lavender-scented water.

"Not there yet," he said as he gently slipped me into the tub.

The water was divine, and it helped to take my mind off my sexual torment. I surveyed his bathroom, which was as neat and clean as everything else he inhabited. The white tiles and the marble sink gleamed, and sunlight spilled through the diamond-shaped window-panes. Neat piles of white towels were folded on a mahogany table, and a mirror hung on the wall above it. In the reflection, I watched Orion behind me.

He dipped a white ceramic mug into the bath. "Tilt your head back."

I did as he instructed, and he poured water over my head, careful not to let it splash into my eyes. On the forest floor, I'd been covered in dirt. Now, Orion washed my hair, massaging my scalp to clean me off. In the hot water, my skin started to go pink.

If you've never had your hair washed by somebody while you luxuriate in a hot bath, I highly recommend it, even if you can't find a sexy incubus to do the job.

I relaxed under his expert hands and let the scalp massage become a shoulder massage, then a foot massage, and before I knew it, his face so close to mine that I could feel his breath warming the side of my cheeks. Whenever he touched me, his fingers played my body like a concertmaster on a Stradivarius.

But the more I healed—and the more that clarity returned—the more a disturbing thought started to worry at the back of my mind.

I'd fucking exploded, hadn't I?

"Orion, what happened? How much did I destroy?" I asked.

"It's fine, love. You just took out a whole bunch of old oak trees."

"Shit," I muttered under my breath. "But everyone was okay?"

"No one was caught in the blast."

"Thank the gods." My body relaxed, eyes drifting closed as steam curled around my body.

Gods, it was comfortable in here.

My eyes started to drift closed, my muscles turning to jelly. Orion must have noticed, because the next thing I knew, he was wrapping me in the towel and scooping me up. He carried me back into his room and laid me on his bed. He didn't seem to mind that I was making his sheets all damp, and I was too tired to worry about it. I curled up in his covers, delighted to have the smell of burnt cedar—his smell—all over me.

My breath slowed, and I pulled his covers up over my shoulders. The last thing I felt before I drifted off was his arm wrapping protectively around my waist.

But in a surprisingly gentlemanly move, Orion was sleeping on top of the covers, and I was below.

ॐ

I WOKE UP TO THE SOUND OF A WOMAN'S VOICE FILLING THE ROOM. I blinked at the sight of the setting sun outside, and I tried to make sense of my surroundings. When I looked down at myself, I saw that someone had dressed me in a white nightgown and underwear.

Bleary-eyed, I blinked at the window—a sunset streaked with periwinkle and rose. I thought I'd slept a full day, and I sat up to drink the water someone had left on the bedside table.

I was in Orion's bedroom, where everything was in its right place. Slowly, the memories started to return to me—the blast of magic, the sexual torture of healing.

But who the fuck was this woman talking?

The fog of sleep cleared more, and I tuned into her words.

"...but Lenore was always an anxious raven..."

I startled, looking back at the bedside table. An old-fashioned cassette played a very familiar book.

How did he remember? We'd talked about this in the underworld. This was what my mother would read to me when I was home sick from school, or she'd play the audiobook for me when I couldn't sleep.

Lenore the anxious raven, who had to learn to slow her breathing before she could sleep.

My mind shot back to a conversation I'd had with him, the things our parents had done to soothe us. It shocked me that he remembered.

My heart swelled when I thought of him finding this for me.

Then it constricted again as I realized I was running out of time to prepare for the trial. And that Orion would be doing whatever he could to throw me off.

If I didn't get my shit together—fast—I'd lose everything.

✣ 21 ✣

ROWAN

Evening of the trial.

Rosy sun rays spilled through the trees, and the forest's shadows grew long. As nerves tightened my muscles, I wished I had something to do with my hands.

Twilight was the most powerful time to lower the veil between the worlds.

After I'd recovered my sanity, I'd had three full days to practice. And that was about how long it had taken to summon Goody Pendleton, and to successfully bind her with magic. Just as Kas had promised, she'd been very good-natured about the whole thing, so I'd summoned her and bound her again and again, until my throat was hoarse and Legion yelled at me to get some rest before I lost my mind all over again.

I closed my eyes.

I'm ready.

I'd memorized the spells, and I could rattle them off fluently. I knew the exact memory to conjure up to summon just the right amount of magic.

I doubted that Orion had practiced at all, which had been my hope. He leaned against a tree, his arms folded, hair falling in his eyes.

Insouciant as ever. His gaze slid to me, but his expression was unreadable.

Focus on the trial, Rowan. Not on him.

If I let his pretty face distract me—and the memory of his abs flexing under my fingertips—I'd lose. No question about that.

I scanned the grove of mossy oaks, my heart beating a little faster. When I'd practiced, I hadn't had an audience. But today, half the city was out here in the forest to watch the start of the trial. There was no way to know where this competition would lead us today, but seemingly everyone in town had left their homes and lined up in the woods and city like they were waiting for a parade, hoping to get a glimpse of the moment that might fell a king or crown a queen.

Mist snaked around the ancient boughs and trunks.

I closed my eyes again, mentally reviewing the spells. I didn't *need* to review them at this point, but it kept me from looking at Orion's eyes, and from remembering the feel of his strong hands on me—

Focus.

My jaw clenched. Practicing, I mouthed the words like I was murmuring a prayer for salvation.

The sound of footfalls crunching over twigs pulled my attention from the spell. The dean of Belial crossed into the grove. Mistress Blacknettle, a stunning mortal woman, wore a crown of bluebells and white bloodroot flowers over her long silver curls.

Standing ramrod straight, she lifted her chin. "It has been centuries since a shadow scion has challenged a king. Two Lightbringers, each blessed by Lucifer, vie for the crown tonight, according to the ancient rules of the trials. At dusk, in the boundary between the world of the living and the dead, we will begin. And as night falls over the ancient city, the gods shall decide who will rule the City of Thorns."

A shiver skittered up my spine. Did the gods really have anything to do with this beyond Tammuz's fervent desire to create chaos?

Mistress Blacknettle pulled out two small vials of blood, one for each of us. Inhaling deeply, I pulled the cork open, then dipped my pinkie into the blood and leaned over to draw the star on my forehead.

"Whoever is able to first summon Alaric will have a bond with him, and the other competitor will not," the dean declared. "But the bond does not guarantee a win, only an advantage. The trial will not be concluded until the crown is in someone's hand. Understood?"

As I painted the star onto myself, the shadows thickened around us, and the sultry breeze picked up, catching leaves in the air. Distant thunder rolled across the forest.

The dean took the vials from us and stepped away, her gray eyes flitting between Orion and me.

I inhaled the forest air as I started to summon my magic. Over the past few days, I'd discovered the perfect memory for invoking just the right amount. In my mind's eye, I thought of a happy memory—one filled with love but tinged with just a bit of sadness to keep me from destroying everyone.

I remembered being sick one night with a fever, and Mom lay next to me in bed. The moonlight streamed in the window, and Mom made a shadow puppet in its light. There were two she could make, a dog and a rabbit. She told a little story with them, and it didn't make a lot of sense. But the important thing was that she'd been lying next to me. Thinking of how she looked after me, love bloomed in my chest, and magic glowed faintly from my body.

And as soon as the dean spoke the single Demonic word that heralded the start of the trial, a sense of calm spread over me.

I launched into the spell I'd memorized, desperate to form the bond with Alaric.

As I spoke, the air chilled, mist rising from the frozen underworld. Around us, spirits began moving between the trunks, their forms silvery and transparent. I was pronouncing each word with precision, the words flowing as quickly and fluidly as the Acheron River. It was as if the gods were inhabiting my body...

Shadows pooled in the grove, and a warm fog slid between the gnarled, mossy trees. I no longer worried that Orion would distract me. In fact, I had the power to throw *him* off course. As I recited the spell, I looked up at Orion and gave him a sultry wink.

His eyes widened just a touch. I heard him trip over a single syllable.

With a half-smile, I finished the last word of the spell—*Alaric*.

I'd done it. With that final word, magic crackled over my skin, heralding the arrival of the Visigoth somewhere in the city.

An invisible thread formed, connecting me to him, tugging me north.

My wings burst from my back, and I shot upward, ripping through the oak leaves on my way.

My bond with Alaric compelled me northwest toward the Sathanas Ward, where the gates marked the boundary with Osborne.

Orion raced behind me. Even as I flew, I could feel his hot magic floating on the night air, skimming around me. Beneath us, torches dotted the dark landscape, pricks of orange light that moved toward the bridge. Beneath us, a crowd of onlookers was trying to follow our path.

One way or another, I had to slow Orion down, or he'd just follow me to Alaric. He could steal victory from me at the last moment —again.

So when I reached the outer boundaries of the Sathanas Ward, I angled my wings to touch down a quarter mile from him. I landed fast and hard on a crooked little lane in the old part of the city, my feet slamming onto the cobbles. My wings retracted, and I whirled to see Orion land just behind me. His enormous body was silhouetted against the amber windows of a restaurant.

"You never quite do what I expect, Rowan."

Under my breath, I began chanting the words for the binding spell.

Only Orion's pale, icy eyes pierced the darkness. "You—"

With the final word of the spell, ribbons of darkness spun around Orion, binding him in place. It wouldn't last forever, but it would give me enough of a head start.

With a smile, I turned to stalk through the darkened streets. The invisible thread felt a little weaker now—moving? I took off on foot, sprinting through the sinuous alleys, past a bakery, past a magic shop crammed with skulls and stuffed birds.

The thread pulled me around the corner to an old, abandoned temple.

And there he was, Alaric himself, a giant of a mortal. He shouted something that sounded like *zookooboos*, which I was guessing was the old Gothic word for "succubus."

Alaric wore a brilliant red cape and gold-plated armor, and he towered high over the cobblestone road. But most importantly, the crown of blackthorns rested on his head.

I summoned my magic again from between my ribs.

As the Gothic king turned to run, I started to rattle off the words of the binding spell. But before I could get to the final word, a flash of vibrating magic burst from the king's enormous body.

From the skies, a horde of ravens swooped down, aiming for me. Some of their beaks dug into the flesh of my forearms, and I gritted my teeth. Their pecking was vicious, down to the bone.

As I shielded myself with my arms, I managed to finish the last words of the spell. I fell to my knees, and the ravens seemed to lose focus. Their wings beat at me, and they started to career away, veering wildly down the narrow stone lanes. My ravaged arms were healing already.

I glanced at Alaric, finding him frozen in place. Ropes of my golden magic snaked around him. I rushed closer, whispering the only German phrase I knew, *"Tut mir leid,"* hoping the apology bore some similarity to ancient Gothic.

I just needed a little help reaching that crown on top of his towering body.

As my wings burst from my back, I lifted off the stones and reached for it. My fingers grazed the thorns. But as they did, a powerful hand wrapped around my forearm, wrenching my hand away.

22

ROWAN

O rion gripped my arm, his pale eyes gleaming. "You *have* been practicing."

Fast as lightning, I shifted my arm out of his grip and grabbed his wrist. Snarling, I started to twist his arm behind his back—

Behind me, the sound of snapping bindings echoed off the stone as the Gothic king broke free.

Orion twisted out of my grasp, and I grunted with frustration. When I whirled to look for Alaric, the king was already gone.

Without another word or wasted breath, Orion and I lifted into the air, searching for the king. But clever Alaric had cloaked himself in darkness for now.

I turned my attention to the feel of the bond again as I soared over stone spires, over steep-peaked buildings that glowed with warm light. The sea-kissed breeze rushed over me, exhilarating. Gods, I loved flying.

At last, I felt it again—a strong tug between my ribs. The bond was luring me east, toward the sea. I glanced behind me, but I couldn't see Orion. Either he'd cloaked himself as well or he was finding his own way to the Visigoth king.

No matter. Without the bond, all Orion could do was follow. I angled my wings to soar toward the water.

Alaric was hurtling through the streets like a meteor, using magic to give himself speed. At least he wasn't sending the birds after me anymore.

With the marine wind whipping at my head, I soared after him— past the Abaddon Ward, the Luciferian Ward, the Tower of Baal. If he made it into the sea itself, I'd never catch him. A skilled witch like him would know spells for breathing underwater, and I didn't have the first clue there.

Licking the salt off my lips, I angled my wings to land, hoping to head him off before he made it to the ocean. Here, on the city's eastern shore, a few narrow alleys led to the sea. Once Alaric reached them, he could race down the ancient stone stairs, hiding in the depths.

My heart slammed against my chest as I glided downward.

I touched down hard in a little lane crowded with Tudor-style buildings, and I felt his momentum stop.

I turned to scan the little street, but I couldn't pick him out. I could *feel* him nearby, though, and I stared at the space before me as I caught my breath.

In my chest, I felt the pull of my connection to him, urging me forward just a little. Warm light beamed from behind leaded glass windows, illuminating old books and displays of sugared cakes. But in the center of the alley, the shadows looked unnaturally dark, sucking up the light from the shop windows. *There.*

Quietly, I began to chant the binding spell. I kept very still, whispering under my breath, trying not to spook him.

But unfortunately for me, I could hear someone else whispering a spell—and the disturbing sound of slithering behind me made goosebumps rise on my skin. A loud *hiss* turned my head, and my heart stuttered.

A serpent as large as an ancient oak bough snaked up the stone stairwell, scales gleaming with iridescent light. The monstrous thing opened its mouth, showing off fangs longer than my hand.

I exhaled sharply and called up my flames at my fingertips, but the serpent darted for me, its teeth sinking into the flesh at my side.

"Rowan!" From a distance, Orion's voice called to me.

With the excruciating pain racing through my body, flames burst out of me—a white-hot instinct I hadn't quite thought about. The serpent didn't quite catch fire, but the heat must have hurt it, because the creature unlocked its jaw. The air smelled of burning flesh, and the snake's head swerved from side to side, mouth gaping. My blood dripped from its fangs.

From above, Orion landed on the serpent's back while it reared its head. Orion's silver claws shot out, and he plunged them into the back of the monster's neck, starting to sever the head.

I gripped my side, doing my best to block out the pain. I didn't think I could breathe correctly. Dizzy, I started swaying, staggering back.

Focus on the crown, Rowan. I whirled to scan the narrow road for the shadows again, but my vision seemed blurred.

I was pretty sure Alaric was gone already. Vaguely, I could feel him moving down the sea-slick stairwell. My wings burst out of my back, and I lifted into the air, above the serpent in its death throes.

With my thoughts on the crown, I soared above the stairs just in time to see Alaric waist-deep in the waves. I flew out after him, but I couldn't quite summon my magic. It sputtered and died in my chest.

In the ocean, Alaric's body shifted, turning sleek and dark, the blackthorn crown still resting on his head. As a seal, he dove under the dark surface.

A shock of pain rocked through my body where the serpent had bitten me, and I found myself losing control of my flight, careening down toward the water. My wings weren't working now, either.

Salty spray misted over me, and then I crashed hard into the sea, the agony blinding. Injured as I was, I hadn't managed to retract my wings in time before I hit the surface. The force of the fall plunged me under the waves, and pain splintered my bones.

I'd become so used to healing quickly, but that wasn't working out for me right now. In fact, I felt distinctly mortal. I felt like I wanted to vomit. Where the fuck was *up*? Where was down? My wings slowly slid back into my shoulder blades.

At last, my feet struck rough stone, helping to orient me. I pushed forward toward the shore until my head popped above the waves, and then I sucked in a furious breath.

I dragged myself from the sea, rasping for air. *Holy hell*, that serpent's venom had wrecked me, and the saltwater in the puncture wounds didn't feel amazing.

I trudged through the waves, my whole body shaking.

Orion stood on the rocky shore, knee deep in the water. His sleeves had been rolled up, and the sea spray had dampened his white shirt, making it translucent and leaving it clinging to his abs. "You okay?" he called.

I managed a smile as I trudged closer to him through the crashing waves. "I'll live, right?" I didn't want to puke in front of my rival but avoiding that wasn't the easiest thing right now.

As I moved nearer, he stepped forward, just in time to catch my arm as I started to fall. "I need to get the venom out of you."

I clutched my side, staring at up him. "We're competing."

He slid his arm around my waist, helping me to walk. "All we can do now is wait until old Alaric comes out of the sea, and I don't need you to be in pain that entire time. Alaric won't be able to stay transformed forever, but we might have a long night ahead of us."

I leaned into him, too agonized to refuse his help. Was his body shaking a little? I felt like his muscles were vibrating. "What *was* that creature?"

"A monster called a Ladon, with venom toxic even to demons." Even in the darkness, I could tell that Orion's face was drained of color. "Alaric must have called him from the sea. The venom won't kill you, but it'll hurt like hell and interfere with your magic."

I gritted my teeth as I sat on the stairs. "Legion thought taking a crown from a mortal would be easy."

"Legion has no idea what he's talking about." Orion knelt between my knees and lifted the soaking hem of my shirt. I grimaced at the sight of two deep puncture wounds. Dark poison flowed through my veins beneath my pale skin.

"How do you get it out?" At this point, I could hardly get the *words* out, and they mumbled forth as more of an incoherent moan than a question.

Without answering, he lowered his mouth to my skin just above my hip bone. He swirled his tongue once, and then he began to suck. The relief of pain was almost instantaneous, replaced by the warmth of Orion's magic—the fucking glorious healing power of an incubus. Heat spread from my hip bone outward, making my muscles go supple and relaxed. The feeling of relief quickly slid into something pleasurable that had me threading my fingers into his hair. Molten heat slid through my body.

Gods, I loved the way he healed me. Might as well admit it. His mouth moved above the hollow on my hips, and desire hummed through me, a hot vibration that made me want to pull him up over me. Except at any minute now, we'd probably have a whole crowd of onlookers, and I didn't want them to see their future queen in a compromising situation. I tried to keep my eyes on the sea as Orion worked his mouth over my skin, occasionally spitting venom onto the stones.

He really didn't *feel* like a rival right now. But of course he didn't— he was Orion, the last incubus. His sexual appeal burned with all the heat of a star.

My thighs clenched around him, and he looked up at me with a half-smile playing around his lips. "Seems like you'll be fine now."

I felt breathless as I released my grip from his hair, forcing my gaze from him to the dark sea. "You could have left the poison in me and won easily."

He shifted away and sat next to me on the stairs. When he turned to face me, his eyes were burning bright blue. "And you could have killed me instead of binding me. But the thought of you in pain makes me want to die. Or massacre people. And I'm doing my best to avoid both at the moment."

My chest flushed at that, but I tried not to dwell on it too long.

When I glanced at the seaside wall above us, I saw the first onlookers appear, bearing torches. "I'm afraid they might be in for a boring few hours."

Orion didn't answer. His shoulders looked rigid, his skin ghostly pale. His hands were tightened into fists.

"Did the serpent get you, too?" I asked. "You look a little ill."

He stared straight ahead, and silence filled the air between us. "I don't like snakes."

"I used to, but that fucker may have changed my mind."

He cast a quick glance up at the onlookers above us. "No, I mean I *really* don't like snakes," he whispered. "You asked what I was afraid of beside you. It's snakes. And that one scared the shit out of me." The moonlight sculpted the beautiful planes of his face.

"Why get a snake tattoo, then?"

"Just a reminder of things." His fists flexed again. Clearly, he was done with this conversation.

"But...all snakes? Even little garter snakes?"

His slid me a cool look, and his gaze bored into me. "I really didn't mean for this conversation to go on this long."

"Okay." I swallowed hard. "How long do you think we have until he changes back?"

"Could be hours. Maybe all night."

I rose from the stone, crossing back to the shoreline. My bond with Alaric was gone for now.

"I missed you when you were in Osborne," Orion said quietly.

My heart fluttered, and I turned back to look at him. "You knew where I was if you wanted to talk to me."

"I needed time. For centuries, Rowan, I teetered on the edge of sanity. And the single constant thread that kept me from descending into madness was my oath to Ashur. It's not something I could abandon overnight."

Cautiously, I slid my gaze to him. "And it's still the only thing keeping you from madness?"

From the steps, his eyes met mine. "You were the only person in centuries who cared for me. And when you were gone, I couldn't sleep. I felt like I'd returned to the prison cell. I needed you near me, Rowan. I needed time to I realize that we were twin stars. And that I'd always dreamt of you."

I stared at him, feeling like my heart was breaking and healing at the same time. But we were *mid*-trial right now. And how was I to know what was real? The entire kingdom was on the line. "Orion, we can't do this right now. I'm not going to speak to you during the trial. I'm concentrating."

I turned away from him, staring at the dark sea again. My gaze flicked up at the sky, my pulse racing as I caught sight of the spot where Gemini would rise.

❧ 23 ❧

ROWAN

B y the time the first pale blush of dawn tinged the sky, Alaric
still hadn't returned. Even so, the crowd of eager onlookers
had waited up all night, watching us from the streets and
buildings above. For the most part, I managed to keep my eyes locked
on the sea.

I'd spent the night right here, watching, waiting. Orion lounged on
the stairs just behind me.

A slight tug in my ribs had my muscles tensing. Faintly, the bond
with Alaric was moving again, rushing toward the shore.

My fingers twitched with anticipation.

Orion must have sensed me tensing because he moved closer along
the shoreline, quietly whispering a spell to himself.

After a night of standing vigil here, my legs ached, and my stomach
felt like it was eating itself alive.

I glanced at Orion. "Hello, my shadow. What was that spell you
were just chanting?"

He leaned in and whispered, "I thought we weren't speaking."

"Just wondering what you're up to."

"Not a spell, love. I was merely reciting the names of the Lilu dead.
That is how I pray."

A ripple of cold magic spread over me from behind, like an arctic wind. A distraction, maybe. Orion playing a trick, getting me to take my eyes off the sea so he could steal the crown.

When a low growl rose from behind me, I glanced over my shoulder. A woman stood at the top of the stairs, her pale blonde curls radiating from her head. She wore a crown of spiked silver woven with ivy.

"Reciting the names of the Lilu dead or calling up a distraction?" I snapped.

But something about the glacial magic radiating from her body told me this was more than just a trick. The woman was eerily beautiful, with gray eyes and a wicked smile. She wore a blue velvet cape around her shoulders. Underneath, blood stained her white gown in great streaks of crimson.

My jaw tightened. This really wasn't the time for...whatever the hell this was.

Tightening my fingers into fists, I turned back to the sea once more. I had the sense that Alaric was barreling toward us under the waves, homing in.

Orion turned to face the newcomer, nodding at her. "Who the fuck are you?" Irritation laced his tone.

I rolled my eyes. Maybe he wasn't *always* charming. Maybe he saved that for special occasions, like trying to convince me we should murder everyone in Osborne.

From behind me, I heard her speak in a faintly French accent: "But, Your Majesty."

I glanced back again. Her breath frosted the air with a cold mist, and the sound of her wintry voice sent a chill down my spine.

"Your Majesty, you summoned me yourself. And here, in the City of Thorns, I will feast on demon blood." She turned her cold gaze to me, her smile vulpine. "And I will start with the *succube* who would be *la reine*. It is as we discussed."

"*La sorcière de Brocéliande*," Orion murmured.

"You *summoned* her?" I hissed.

Turning back to the sea, I glimpsed Alaric rising from the waves—human once more, the sea pouring off him. And there was the blackthorn crown. My wings burst from my back. Just as my feet left the rocks, a clawed hand gripped my wings and threw me down hard to the rocky shoreline with shocking force.

Pain screamed through my wings, and I stared up at *la sorcière* as she leapt on top of me. She gripped me by the hair and smashed the back of my head into a sharp rock—once, twice—oh, *gods*, she was breaking my skull open.

I had to think...I had to think...

My head was broken, and I had no words to think with.

I moaned on the rocks.

Fangs bared above me. "*Les démons* murdered my family, and I have come to feast on your kind."

I stared dumbly as the witch drew a long, sharp silver blade. "Your lover and I share one thing—a lust for *la vengeance*."

She raised her blade above my heart, and the world seemed to tilt beneath me.

As she started to bring it down, a blast of fire rolled across the horizon from the place where Orion had been standing. Searing flames engulfed me, but the fire didn't burn me. It gave me life, healing my broken skull like a salve of flames.

La sorcière de Brocéliande blazed above me, screeching with pain in the inferno. Her cries withered in the blaze as the fire consumed her.

But there was another figure here, burning in the inferno. Screaming to the heavens. Through the fire, I caught sight of the writhing figure of Alaric, his crown blazing like a torch.

No.

I pushed myself up, trying to reach for it. But the Visigoth king burned to cinders before me, and the crown crumbled in my fingertips.

A cloud of smoke and ash wafted above me, mixing with the sea spray. The flames started to die down, sputtering in the crashing waves.

I stood, stunned, on the hot rocks. Shaking, I tried to dust the ashes off myself, but I was so wet, they formed a sort of gray paste.

I swallowed hard. A gray paste composed of two witches...

My gaze flicked up to where the crowd had been, but they'd all fled. I could still hear them screaming in the distance. The stones around us had been blackened with the force of the blast.

I stared at Orion. "That was you, wasn't it? That was your fire."

"She nearly killed you," said Orion, sounding shocked. "I was waiting for you to fight her."

I touched the back of my head. It felt disturbingly *dented*, but there was definitely no longer a gaping wound. "I was having a hard time remembering how to summon magic with my head cracked open." I glanced at the rocks, sickened to see gore glistening on the stones. If I weren't a demon, I'd be dead. "She said you asked her to kill me. Is it just me, or is this a recurring theme, Orion?"

He'd gone completely pale again. "I didn't summon her. Of course I didn't. She loathes demons. She was lying."

"So everyone is lying but you?" I said sharply. "All your soldiers and *la sorcière de Brocéliande?*"

His expression darkened. "I just saved your life, Rowan. Again."

I clenched my jaw. True, he had. Several times. Right now, I couldn't figure out what was real and what was a lie.

I sighed. "You crisped Alaric."

Orion inhaled a deep breath. "Well, I didn't hold back."

I glanced out at the waves, which were stained claret under the rising sun. Disappointment coiled through me. "Okay. We need to raise him again, I guess, to start the trial over. Though I imagine he'll be a bit furious about being burned to death. And I need some Advil."

"Ah, Rowan." Orion's eyes twinkled as he crossed to me over the rocks, graceful as ever. "You don't remember what happens if the first trial is a draw?"

My throat tightened, and I narrowed my eyes at him. "You get to choose the next trial."

A lock of silver hair fell before his eyes, and he nodded. He leaned down, speaking quietly enough that only I could hear. "But when I win, love, you could be my queen. And we will protect the demons together."

I felt my cheeks heat again. Seductive bastard that he was, he made it sound so damned appealing, even as we stood here among the blood and the windblown ashes of two powerful witches.

24

ROWAN

When the trial ended, I'd returned to Orion's house. I'd changed into leggings and a T-shirt, then turned off my phone and closed the shutters.

In the darkness, I'd let a deep sleep wash over me. I'd dreamt of the green-eyed boy, crouching to watch ants on a sidewalk with his hands on his knees. I'd dreamt of him making cookies and eating the sugar off the table. I'd dreamt of him drawing a picture with vigorous scribbles and burbling narration about a battle between the demons and the mortals, blood staining the streets—speaking of things a child should never have seen...

By the time I woke, the sun was already setting, and rosy light slanted at an angle through the wooden slats. Disappointing, yes.

But I wasn't done yet. One more trial. I hoped.

As soon as Orion announced what it would be, I'd start preparing.

Sitting up in bed, I surveyed the darkened room, my stomach rumbling sharply. I had no doubt my phone would be blowing up with text messages from Shai, but I didn't want to look at them. I didn't want to face the disappointment of my little team who'd been helping me all this time. And what could I say that they didn't already know?

The news must have spilled through the streets as soon as the trial had ended.

I rose from the bed and opened the shutters.

The sun had dipped low and the sky darkened to indigo. The night's subtlety was much prettier than the garish daylight.

As much as I wanted to stay in here, hunger was compelling me out of my room. But to my delight, when I opened my door, I found that Amon had left a tray outside for me—slices of chicken breast, roasted baby carrots, and buttered cauliflower. A small flagon of wine and a glass stood on the tray next to the food.

Perfect.

I ate by the desk, staring out onto the dark garden. I had no idea what to make of everything—the fact that assassins kept reporting Orion wanted me dead, and then Orion would swoop in to save me. But if he were going to have me killed, surely, he'd make damn sure the assassins didn't keep telling me about it. Leaving a bunch of stupid loose ends wasn't his style.

I sipped my wine and drummed my fingertips on the desk. If you'd asked me a few weeks ago, I would have said that clearly, his incubus charm had scrambled my brain, that I was ignoring the obvious. That Occam's razor would say it was just Orion trying to take me down.

As I stared outside, I saw him cross into the garden and sit on a stone bench, his shoulders slumped. The boughs of an apple tree arched over him. I watched him as he pulled out a handkerchief and started wiping blood off his hands, staining the white cloth red.

Cool. Yeah, not suspicious at all.

With dread crawling up my spine, I turned to head downstairs and into the salty night air. I'd drunk the wine quickly, but the buzz had worn off with the sight of blood. When I crossed into the garden, his head snapped up, the masculine beauty of his face cast in silver.

"Have you been...murdering people all day?" I asked.

He tossed down the bloodied rag on the bench next to him. "Have you been sleeping all day, Shadow Scion?"

"Hell, yes." I sat down on the bench next to him. "Whose blood is that?"

"Someone from our great city has been passing along information to the *Malleus Daemoniorum*, which is how the demon hunters know you're in here. I caught some hunters probing for weaknesses in our defenses, trying to find a way inside. Someone gave them a clue where to start. Someone with information about our magical signature."

"And if the demon hunters broke down our wards and walls?" I asked. "We could kill them before our magic faded."

"The mortals have missiles. If they obliterate our city walls and vaporize us with their weapons, we'd never have time to recover. We'd simply *die*."

A shudder rippled over me. "The demon hunters are very influential, unfortunately. They've been donating to politicians for ages, buying power."

He glanced at me, something sparking in his eyes. "Maybe not as influential as they once were. I've been working on weakening them." He looked down at his hands. "The blood is from two demon hunters. I wanted answers about who's trying to frame me, and who's working with the mortals."

I sucked in a deep breath. "Did you get any?"

"Not about those questions. But I learned something much more important." His pale eyes met mine. "I learned the location of something I want very much. The *Grimorium Verum*." A small smile curled his lips. "Finding that book will be our next trial."

A dark, unsettled feeling snaked up my neck. "Why is this book so important?"

He held my gaze for a long time. "According to the book of Demonic Trials, I'm not required to tell you anything about it, but I will because the book is more important to me than the crown. Because if I lose these trials, it will be your job to protect our city, and you will need this, Rowan. The grimoire is the very thing that keeps us locked in here. It contains the spell that makes our magic fade after a few days out of the city walls or trapped in the dungeons. The spell that sends us into the underworld if we stray too far. The *Grimorium Verum* will set us free. And it's locked in the demon hunters' headquarters in Sudbury."

Whoever controlled that grimoire would hold the fate of the mortal world in their hands.

Clearly, it would be safer in mine. "Why open the city gates when we know where to find the demon hunters now? They're the ones we need to kill, not the rest of the mortals. If we can take out the demon hunters, maybe we avert the war." I breathed in deeply. "You're reducing their influence. Maybe we could make them disappear."

"I need to unlock the curse with which the mortals saddled us."

"And without the curse, the demons could feed on mortals indiscriminately. Isn't that how it was in the old days? I think you were the person who told me that. Hunting them. Drinking their blood. Feeding off lust or sadness or gluttony."

He heaved a sigh. "I can't say I ever experienced that myself. But as king, I could order the demons not to hunt if it would keep the peace."

I swallowed hard. "But you're singularly dedicated to your revenge oath."

"Maybe, as you said, I could satisfy myself with killing the demon hunters. They were the mortals in charge when the Lilu were slaughtered." He cocked his head. "But we need the control in our hands, and not the mortals'. With the grimoire, we can turn back the clock to before it all happened." Sorrow shone in his blue eyes. "We could be safe again. And we could destroy the dungeons."

I got the sense that all this was his way of trying to find his way back to his family. "Turn back the clock," I repeated. "That sounds nice."

Silence spread between us, broken only by the rustling of the wind through the trees.

"What was life like for you before the mortals came?" I asked after a few moments.

He flashed me a sad smile. "When I was a boy? I just wanted to be Molor, my older brother. He looked like me, but bigger. He was brilliant with a sword. Indestructible." A line formed between his eyebrows. "Or so I thought. He was only thirteen. But he seemed so much older. He could play the lute, and he could draw monsters. He once shot a stag out in the Elysian Wilderness. He was a real man. So I wanted to be him because he could do anything. And I also wanted to run a bakery with bread pudding because I could never get enough of it, so I thought I might as well control the whole supply."

I smiled at him. "Molor." I could imagine two beautiful silver-haired boys, one a tiny version of the other.

"It's hard to imagine, but after a while in the dungeon, I envied him. I felt like my brother died quickly, and I'd died so slowly. I was a Lightbringer, so I was hard to kill. But Molor died a hero, and I didn't. Not at all." He stared down at his hands again. "I always think of him as fully grown, but when I went home again, I saw how much I was mistaken." When he looked up at me, his eyes were shining. "And I don't feel as jealous anymore. Because I'm here with you now, and he's not." A sad smile played over his lips.

I felt my cheeks flushing, and I brushed a silver strand from his eyes.

"What were you like as a child?" he asked.

"Dreamy. Always in a book, lost in thought. And as soon as I learned what a psychologist was, that was what I wanted to be. In my psychology classes, at the start of the year, we would always go around the room and say why we wanted to study it. Everyone, one after the other, said it was because they wanted to help people. If I were a better person, I'm sure I would have thought the same. But I think I was just fucking nosy." I smiled. "I wanted to hear everyone's stories, and that's what psychologists do. You sit and listen to them talk about their lives. And my life always seemed so stifling at home. I wanted to know about everyone else's. Mom was..." I trailed off, my chest tight.

"What?"

"Chaotic. Unpredictable. I thought she was paranoid. She was always checking the windows, the locks, setting up traps, and she just seemed so unstable. I didn't realize there were actually people after her. She panicked a lot when I wasn't home, and sometimes, I caught her spying on me at school. None of it seemed normal. And she had no sense of what modern kids were like, or what they wore or did for fun, and we were these two strange outsiders in weird clothes...it seemed important at the time to fit in, to have a stable home. So I just became fascinated by other people's lives. I wanted to know what went on behind their doors, in their pretty houses." My breath had gone shallow. "I can see now she wasn't crazy. She was trying to keep me safe from my half brother. I just wish she'd told me what was happening."

"Why do you think she kept it from you?"

I looked at the beauty around me, the white flowers that bloomed in the night against the stone cottage. "Maybe she thought I would have wanted to come back here. This place feels like home. Especially at night." I found tears welling up in my eyes, and I didn't want to look at Orion. "It would have been hard to resist, even if it was dangerous."

"It is your home," he said softly, "and so is the wilderness. And the night. We are creatures of darkness—the incubi and succubi. In the old days, we were awake all night. We had festivals of starlight and shadows. We celebrated in the night sky, and we fed from mortal lust. Before the mortals caged us, we were free to race through the night, tearing over the forests and drinking from their dirtiest dreams." He leaned on his knees with his forearms, his gaze intent on me. "I think you can feel it. You're drawn to the dark, to the wilderness. You want to hunt like we once did. You feel that wildness trapped inside you, and you want to set it free. We may be Lightbringers, but we were born in the dark."

I hated how he could read me so easily. He could tell me things about myself I hadn't even put into words yet. Yes, I wanted to hunt and tear through the wilderness. "Lightbringers born in the dark. I'm not sure I understand."

He glanced at the sky, and I followed his gaze to Venus. "They say everything began with chaos. Then a light sprang from the darkness, and he was the god Astaroth. Every night, he would return to the shadows, and from the chaos, he'd rise again. They say Astaroth was a fallen god, beautiful as the dawn. His sons were Lucifer and Noctifer—the Lightbringer and the Nightbringer, order and chaos. And Noctifer's other name is Tammuz. My father."

"Beautiful as the dawn," I repeated. "A long day of beating the shit out of people brings out your poetic side."

"I should probably torture people more often so I'm in top form for the spoken word poetry night I'm starting on Tuesdays."

"It scares me that I can't tell if you're serious."

The corner of his lips curled. "Scares you, or excites you?"

"Oddly enough, I'm not turned on by brutal violence. Though I have maybe spent more time than I should have looking at the Wikipedia page about medieval torture devices."

"Of course you have," he murmured.

"Did you know there was something called the Pear of Anguish?"

"Rowan," he purred, "are you flirting with me?"

"Orion." I leaned closer, so our lips were almost touching. "Surely you know that if a succubus were flirting with you, you'd be on your knees between my thighs by now." The words just seemed to slip out of my mouth before I had the chance to consider them. My heart started to pick up its pace.

His eyes darkened, and his gaze slid slowly down my body, resting at the apex of my thighs. "Well, my Lightbringer, that is quite the image you've put in my mind." He met my eyes again, his gaze molten.

Tension charged the air between us, and I wanted to crawl into his lap so badly, I had to grip the bench to stop myself.

"What?" I asked at last.

"You're beautiful, that's all." His midnight voice wrapped around me.

"Beautiful." My stomach flipped. "I'm identical to your worst enemy."

"No, you're not. You look nothing like her now. The way you hold yourself, your expressions—you're completely different. The flush on your cheeks when something excites you or angers you. The way you look at me like you actually want to understand me, like you're trying to see into my soul. How you pull your gaze away every time your heart starts to race. The way you look like you're overwhelmed sometimes with the responsibility of trying to keep everyone safe, and you retreat into your own thoughts. You are nothing alike."

I let out a long, slow breath. "I wish you could have realized sooner."

He winced ever so slightly. "Somewhere, there's another world where you and I met before my soul died in the dungeon."

I turned to him, draping my elbow over the side of the bench. "This is going to blow your mind, Orion, but you're not actually dead."

His mouth ticked up at the corner. "It's a metaphor. Soulless. Dead."

"Hmm. But maybe you're not soulless. You've saved me over and over again, and you created a beautiful memorial, and so far, you only seem marginally psychotic. And that's mostly because I just saw you wiping blood off your hands."

He nodded sagely. "I always wondered what regal moniker would stick through the ages. 'King Orion the Only Marginally Psychotic' has a certain ring to it." His eyes sparkled with life, and he reached up, grazing the back of his knuckles lightly along my jawbone. "And what would tell you that I'm salvageable?"

The touch sent a hot thrill over my skin, and I desperately wanted to lean into his hand and close my eyes. "I need to see if you have a merciful side. If you can forgive the mortals."

He pulled his hand away. "Ah. But if they're trying to hurt you, love, I will never show mercy. I will make them suffer."

A sharp coil twisted in my chest. If what he was saying was true and the mortals were trying to break into the city to murder me, this had all become much more complicated.

All of this was starting to feel like a secret I was keeping from Shai, these late-night conversations with Orion. I'd been so certain coming in here that I understood him—that he was all charm and artifice, that I couldn't trust a word he said. But now, even though everyone kept saying he was trying to kill me, I wasn't sure of anything at all, except that Orion and I were trying to find our way back to the past.

❧ 25 ❧

ROWAN

No matter how much we had in common, I still needed to win the trial.

I rose from the bench. "Thanks for telling me about the grimoire. I'm going for a little walk since I won't be sleeping for a while."

He stood and peered down at me, then reached into his pocket and pulled out a strange little misshapen piece of wood. "Wait, I have a gift for you."

My first instinct was to make some kind of a joke—maybe *Got wood for me?*—but then I realized it was such a strange gesture from him that I should keep my mouth shut until he explained. When I took it from his hand, I saw that it had been whittled roughly in the shape of a woman in a dress with a spiky head. "What is it?"

"She's a queen. It was a birthday present for my mother. Somehow, I thought she hadn't noticed me whittling it in the same cell. But her birthday didn't come in time. Or maybe she lied, because she knew I was excited about the birthday, so she wanted to keep giving me something to look forward to. Anyway, it's a Lilu queen, and I never got to give it to her. So it's yours. Because you are the last succubus, and you are queen of the Lilu." He met my gaze. "And as queen, you will need the grimoire. Learn everything you can about the Noyes Mansion in Sudbury. That's where we'll find it."

"Thanks, Orion." I was still staring at the little queen, my eyes going blurry. It really did break my heart to think of a tiny Orion looking forward to giving this to his mom, then never getting the chance. "Well, she would have loved it. But I'll love it instead." I turned away from him, because for some reason, I didn't want him to see the tears that were about to start rolling down my cheeks.

As I walked away, I clutched the wooden queen, thinking of his mom and little Molor.

Was it insane to think that Orion and I could actually work together? We were the last of our kind, trying to find our places in the world again after we'd lost everything.

Everything hinged on what form he wanted his revenge to take.

As I crossed out of the garden gate, I already knew Orion would order guards to follow me—that is, if he wasn't going to follow me himself.

Until I found myself heading toward the river, I wasn't entirely sure where I was going,

I was heading for the dungeons.

Maybe I wanted to see the cells for myself, the place where Orion had been for all that time.

As I reached the tunnel's riverside opening, I slid the little wooden queen into my pocket. The Acheron flowed past, glittering under the moon. Carefully, I lowered myself into the tunnel, and my feet dropped hard on the wet stone. As soon as I was in its depths, I felt a subtle weakening of my magic.

Because of the grimoire's spell that depleted our magic outside the city walls, Orion's magic had no longer worked in the dungeons. If it had, he'd have blown the entire fucking place apart and ripped off the king's head centuries ago.

Down here, I was in the liminal space between the world of the mortals and that of the demons—a place where magic would fade after a few days. In the dungeons, Orion had been as vulnerable as a mortal but deprived of the mercy of death. If he got his fingers on the grimoire to reverse the spell, he'd never have to fear that kind of help-lessness again.

It took me about twenty minutes of wandering aimlessly with a little fire burning in my palm before I found the dungeon itself. It was the scent of burnt flesh that eventually led me to the right place, a miasma of death pulling me forward.

The iron gate was open to the row of cells. When I stepped inside, the orange light from my hand wavered back and forth over rows of cells lining either side of a dark stone corridor. I hadn't seen most of this dungeon when I'd first come into the City of Thorns.

But as I walked further, I saw a large hall jutting off from the central corridor. Firelight wavered over, blackened with time and glis-tening with moisture. Here in the hall, an old, threadbare noose hung from a gallows. It swung gently back and forth—which was very eerie, considering there was no wind in here. The sight of it made my heart clench. I could almost feel the sadness emanating from it.

This was the execution room. The Puritans loved a good public execution, but no one knew the Lilu were kept alive down here, so they were killed in secret.

It didn't take me long to find the fresh bodies whose scent had drawn me here—or rather, the two piles of ash on the floor. The smell of blood faintly lingered in the air, too.

In the light of my flames, something metallic flashed on one of the piles of ash. I leaned down to brush some of the cinders away. When I did, I found a silver pin shaped like a hammer. The symbol of the *Malleus Daemoniorum*.

Orion had incinerated them, but I'd done the same when the congressman threatened my life. We all did what we had to in order to protect those we loved. Sometimes, it meant killing. And sometimes—in my mom's case—it meant dying.

With the light wavering over dark stone walls, I found my way back to the cell at the end of the row. This was the place where I'd first woken up in the City of Thorns, where I'd stood when Orion had tasted my blood.

The cell's walls crawled with ivy, and my throat tightened with emotion as I thought of Orion in here as a little silver-haired, blue-eyed boy. Holding up my palm of light, I found the carving in the wall. I leaned down, brushing aside the vines. Before, I'd only had my fingertips to feel the contours, but now, I could very faintly see the full text.

Luciferi— The *i was* faded and worn at the end. I ripped aside the rest of the vines to reveal the rest: —*urbem spinarum liberabunt.*

Just like Orion had said: *The Lightbringers will set free the City of Thorns*.

My chest warmed as I thought of his mom carving this. I felt an overwhelming urge to protect the boy who'd once been in here, carving the little queen in my pocket, but he was long gone.

A heavy sense of sadness hung in the air, a chilled mist that clung to the stones.

Right before she was killed, the guards moved me to a different cell by myself.

I crossed into the corridor again, sorrow twining with curiosity. From cell to cell, I scanned the stones, looking for something that would show me where he'd lived for all that time. On a few of the other walls, I found carvings, but nothing that could clearly be connected to him. Disturbingly, some of the carvings looked like claw marks.

About halfway down the row of cells, I went still. Through a tiny crack in the stone wall, a pinprick of light shone near the ceiling. It looked familiar somehow, the exact image of it seared on my heart. I'd seen that little crack before.

Under it, the warm light of my fire illuminated elaborate carvings in the dark stone walls.

My breath went still when I saw what he'd marked in the stone— three queens with spiked heads like crowns. He'd carved them three times, the markings violent and desperate, like the little Orion was trying to bring her back to life through the rock.

After the three queens, some of the carvings became more sophisticated. He'd rendered the Asmodean clocktower, frozen in time at six, the way it looked now. He'd carved a snake that seemed to writhe back and forth in the guttering light of my fire. Odd, given his terror of snakes.

There was the word *Vindicta*—revenge—carved with what looked like thorns jutting from the letters' curls. And next to that, the carvings reminded me of the old Puritan gravestones—the skulls and crossbones, the words *Memento Mori—Fugit Hora.*

Remember death—time flies. I was sure that down here, time didn't exactly fly, especially for an immortal. But that phrase wasn't about Orion, was it? Even as he was trapped in here, he was reminding himself that the mortals who'd crushed the Lilu would be dying in Osborne. A comfort to him, maybe.

And above it all, he'd carved stars—the shape of Orion's constellation. Beyond the tiny pinprick, he had no real light in here, so the stone stars were all he had.

I didn't want to stay in here a moment longer. But as I turned to leave, the real horror of this place hit me. His cell stood directly across from the execution room, where the noose still hung from the ceiling.

Right before she was killed...

Orion had been locked in here with a perfect view of his mother's death. And that was where he'd stayed, trapped for centuries right across from the gallows. No wonder he felt like his soul had died. They'd wanted to crush his spirit completely.

As I took another step, a vision slammed into my mind—the same one I'd seen when Orion and I had first agreed to a blood oath, and we'd pressed our bleeding palms together.

In my mind's eye, I saw a crystal-clear vision: stone walls, cracked to expose a bit of the stars. Then a shadow swinging over the stone—the bloodied, swaying feet of a hanged body. Wood creaked above, and a pain pierced my heart to the core.

The vision cleared again, and I pressed my hand to the stone, steadying myself as I caught my breath. My heart pounded against my ribs.

Holy hell, how had he managed to stay sane at all in here?

I rushed out of the corridor, sick to my stomach. Desperate to be free, I hurried out of the dungeon, back into the tunnel.

And there, I discovered I wasn't alone.

One of the shadow figures cleared his throat, and I summoned a burst of fire to get a better look.

The flame in my hand illuminated the smiling face of Amon, his hands raised to placate me.

"Sorry," he said. "The king wished me to ensure your safety." If I had to guess, Amon was just about one of the only people Orion trusted now.

"I'm fine, Amon, thanks." Physically, I was. Emotionally? Not really. But Amon didn't need to know that. "I was just heading back."

But what I really wanted to do was find Orion and help him forget everything that had happened down here.

My throat constricted.

So much for my determination to keep him at arm's length.

❧ 26 ❧

ROWAN

By about three a.m., I gave up on lying in bed, because every time I rolled over and closed my eyes, I saw that noose swinging. And those three carved queens...

Maybe it was because I was a Lilu, or maybe it was the nightmarish visions I'd seen in the dungeon, but trying to sleep tonight was like trying to catch fog in my hands.

Orion was just on the other side of the door, fast asleep, and I couldn't keep my mind off him.

From my window, I stared out at the garden, watching the wind rustle the apple blossoms. My eyes locked on the bench where Orion had given me the wooden queen—the birthday present that never made it to the birthday. I plucked the figurine off the desk and ran my fingertips over it. My heart gave a sharp flutter.

Tomorrow, I'd be meeting with my team of teachers, and I needed them to help me stay focused on the trial. I had nothing to lose by having the crown on my head, the decisions in my hands.

But I glanced at the door, feeling claustrophobic, like part of me was still trapped in the cell. Restless, I opened the window, then climbed back into bed, curling up under the sheets and breathing the scent of the sea.

With the sultry night wind floating in my room, I managed to sleep, dreaming of the stars.

⚜

I WOKE TO THE ROOM ON FIRE. FLAMES SURROUNDED ME, ENGULFING everything.

Oh, *fuck,* I was going to burn alive...

From the confused haze of sleep, fear had a tight grip on my heart. It took me several terrified moments to remember that fire could no longer burn me, and by the time I'd recalled that very important fact, my brain was still lagging behind.

So when a cloaked man jumped from the fire onto my bed, I reacted more slowly than I should have.

I stared at him, stunned to catch a glimpse of silver hair and pale blue eyes. The beautiful face of the king. "Orion? What the hell—"

He raised his hand, and ivory claws shot out.

Panic stole my breath. Had he lost his mind?

I reached out and grabbed his wrist, twisting it to the side so he lost his balance. I shot up and headbutted him, his bone cracking as my forehead slammed into his nose. My claws extended, and I swiped wildly, slashing across his face. He let out a strangled growl as he staggered away from me.

I jumped from the bed, my body glowing with golden light. Heat simmered through my blood. As I lunged for him again, he leapt out the window into the garden below. Fleeing on foot, he trampled through the garden and disappeared into the shadows.

"What the *fuck?*" I shouted.

A second later, the door to Orion's room burst open. Shirtless, he stood on the threshold, raking a hand through his hair. "What's wrong?"

"You're just waking up now?" I asked. "Your house is literally on fire. Why don't you have alarms?"

Orion's gaze slid across the room, a line between his eyebrows. "What are you talking about?"

I started to gesture at the burning room, but not only was the fire gone, it had left no signs of damage whatsoever. No smoke, no ashes or char.

I glanced back at the window, confusion whirling in my mind. Everything looked just as it had been—still and dark under the night sky, white flowers blooming in the shadows.

I turned, staring at the unburnt room. "Maybe it was a nightmare."

"We *are* the nightmares, love." He nodded at the window. "But was the window open? The protection wards depend on having the gates and windows locked. Was someone in here, Rowan?"

Outside, the sky was just starting to turn pink and gold. I searched my bedsheets, and when I spotted the crimson streak of blood on them, I felt a strange sort of relief.

I wasn't losing my mind.

"Yeah, someone was in here. I raked my claws across his face, and his blood is on my sheets. I thought he had silver hair. I thought it was you for a minute. He *really* looked like you."

Orion crossed to the window and slammed it shut, then scooped me up and carried me into his perfectly tidy bedroom.

"What are you doing?" I asked.

"Not letting you out of my sight," he whispered against my ear. "We have two more hours before it's reasonable to wake, and I still have no idea who wants you dead. But I do know that two Lightbringers are stronger than one."

He dropped me down on his bed, and I slid between his sheets, which smelled so beautifully of him. He lay down next to me and wrapped me in his powerful arms. I nestled my head into the crook of his neck, feeling far more comfortable than I should have.

As he relaxed, I listened to the slowing of his breath, and I felt the gentle rise and fall of his chest.

I loved the sound of his heart beating.

Fuck.

Why not just admit that I loved being near him?

❧ 27 ❧
ROWAN

In Kas's kitchen, I sat before a bowl of freshly made *spaghetti aglio e olio* as he filled our glasses with Syrah. My mouth watered as I twisted the pasta around my fork. Night had fallen, and a lantern swung outside his little house, casting swaying shadows on the Tudor buildings.

Shai held her wineglass in her right hand, not touching her food. "You two first, Rowan. Did you and Legion check out the Noyes Mansion?"

"Yep," I said. "We spent the day in Sudbury. The mansion is completely cloaked with magic, but it was easy to find. There was a group of demon hunters patrolling the woods, giving the game away. So Legion turned invisible and moved close enough to learn the magical signatures of the protection spells." I took a big bite of the spicy, garlicky pasta, hoping no one was going to ask me to elaborate, because right now, I really needed to eat this.

Legion nodded. "There's the spell that cloaks, and another that will kill any demons who pass by the wards. I'll be able to disable the demon-killing spell on the day of the trial without them even realizing. We'll leave it cloaked so as not to alert them. They don't need to know that Rowan is going in."

Shai looked even more exhausted than I was, and she rubbed her eyes. "Only problem is that this all benefits Orion, too."

I sipped my wine. "Well, Orion, unlike me, won't have a whole team to help him. He won't know where the book is in the headquarters."

Kas was already refilling my wine glasses. "Why do you two lovely women look so exhausted?"

I picked up my glass, feeling a sharp pang of protectiveness for Orion. If I told them about the assassination attempt—a silver-haired, blue-eyed assassin who looked a lot like the king—I could only imagine how they'd respond: *That's because Orion is trying to kill you.*

"Just insomnia," I said.

"Same." Shai's eyes darted away from me as she spoke, and I had the feeling she wasn't giving the whole story, either.

Interesting. If I had to guess, she and Legion were keeping each other company late into the night.

"Okay," Legion said. "Kas, what did you learn today?"

He stood, pushing back his chair. "Hang on." A minute later, he returned to the room with a large, rolled-up piece of paper. He spread it out between glasses and plates, and I found myself staring at the blueprint of a building.

"Blueprints for the Noyes Mansion," Kas declared. "Now owned by the Corwin family."

"It was built in secret by a creepy religious fanatic named Reverend Nicholas Noyes in 1690," Shai said. "He used to operate a grist mill nearby. The demon hunters built their headquarters near the site of a battle the English lost to the Wampanoag. It's a sacred place to them. Something about the blood of the righteous feeding the soil."

My ears perked up. "Reverend Nicholas Noyes from the Salem Witch Trials? He's the guy one of the victims cursed with, 'God will give you blood to drink.'" A shudder rippled over me. "I'm pretty sure he hanged me in the underworld."

Silence fell over the room, as no one knew exactly how to respond to that.

I waved a hand. "Okay. Never mind. Back to the blueprints."

"Our American demon hunters come from a long tradition of English witchfinders," said Kas.

"The *Malleus Maleficarum*," added Shai. "Hammer of the Witches. They published their manual by the same name in the late fifteenth century. And the demon-specific sect is *the Malleus Daemoniorum*."

"Of course, what they never admitted in their texts," Kas went on, "was that they also used magic. They realized they were no match for demons or witches without the use of spellcraft."

I stared at the mansion's blueprint before us. "Where did you get this?"

Kas's cheeks dimpled as he smiled. "Mortal librarians are truly amazing. I just had to flirt with a young woman at the library in Lexington. She showed me to a locked room where they'd collected historical documents about the *Malleus Daemoniorum*. As soon as she left us alone, we hunted through every document until we found a locked safe."

My eyebrows crept up. "You stole it from a locked safe. Any chance the demon hunters are aware we're coming?"

Kas glanced at Shai. "Shai helped with that."

"I learned a spell for erasing memories," she said.

My jaw dropped open. "Holy shit. You can do that?"

"I can now." Her smile faded, and her dark eyes bored into me. "But don't you think it's weird that Orion would tell you where the book is held if the trial rules don't require it? Is there any chance this is a trap?"

I shook my head. "I believe him. I can't really explain why, but I just do." I breathed in deeply. "I think he's more invested in finding the grimoire than he is in being king. He views it as crucial to keeping the demons safe. That's always been his main goal: protecting demons in some ongoing war with the mortals."

Legion scrubbed a hand over his jaw. "And he's not wrong. Mortal warfare isn't the same as it was centuries ago."

I stared at the blueprint—a stately building with three separate wings, forming a sort of angular U shape.

Legion pointed at a room labelled *chancery*. "In old buildings, this is where official documents would be kept and handwritten. I already identified this as the most likely location for the grimoire."

I leaned back in my chair, narrowing my eyes at Legion. "What if..." I lifted a finger to my lips. "What if you did a trial run? Tomorrow? Go invisible, sneak past the magical defenses. Get into the building and search the chancery. You can find out if the book is actually in that safe before I go in. Do you know a spell for unlocking safes?"

Shai pointed at the map. "That's how we got this blueprint. Which, by the way, is like three hundred years old, so maybe we shouldn't be getting garlic pasta all over it?"

Legion nodded. "I can do that. But you should all be there, hiding, in case I need your help. I'll find a spell that will allow me to communicate with you, even when we're separated."

I stared at him. "Sweetie, that's what cell phones are for."

He glanced at Shai. "*Right.*"

"Shai can teach you how to text," I said. "Like, this is a really important skill."

No matter how emphatically Kas had said not to trust anyone, trust was an element of nearly everything I was doing here. It was quite simply part of working with other people.

❦ 28 ❦

ROWAN

Day of the second trial.

I awoke in Orion's arms again, my legs wrapped tightly around him. I could tell I'd been moving against him in my sleep and that he'd liked it.

For the past three nights, I'd been fighting the sexual torment of being in bed with him but unable to kiss him.

But wrapping my arms around his abs—that was allowed.

We hadn't spoken about the trial, even if it hung over us like a shadow. This morning, however, there was no way to ignore it.

He turned to me and brushed the hair from my eyes. "Today's the day we set the city free."

"We'll see about that." My heart kicked up a notch. Over the past few days, I'd done an amazing job of staying focused and compartmentalizing, but now that we were out of time, a million new worries spiraled through my brain. After all, I was Rowan Morgenstern, and whether I was mortal or demon, my brain would offer up the worstcase scenarios on a platter. Without fail.

I looked up at him. "Orion, what if somehow, we fuck this up and lose our chance to get the grimoire? Or what if the demon hunters report us to the federal government, and the feds just bomb the City of Thorns before we get a chance to unlock the spell?" I swallowed hard. "What if our actions kill all the demons? And aren't you worried I'm going to fuck it all up, and you'll miss your chance at getting the book?"

He stroked his hand down my spine, slowly. Heat shivered in the wake of his fingertips, making my muscles melt into him all over again. "First of all, I have complete faith in you not fucking it up." His face was close to mine, our cheeks nearly brushing. "Second of all, the protection spells will hold the City for now. And I don't think the hunters have enough influence to attack us."

"Why?"

"Since I took the throne, I've been working on isolating the demon hunters from powerful figures. Human politicians are remarkably susceptible to blackmail and various forms of bribery. Money rules the world of mortal power brokers. Campaign donations, threats to fund their opponents. Managing them is honestly much easier than I expected. For now, at least, the demon hunters are on their own. They have no political capital whatsoever."

My eyes widened. "For an ancient, marginally psychotic demon, you're surprisingly savvy about the modern world."

"I love it when you say sweet things about me." His hand slid up and cupped the back of my neck, and he pressed his forehead against mine. "If you ever decide you trust me, I'm going to fuck you until you beg for mercy. Until you forget your name."

My core coiled tight, and I fought the urge to kiss him. "Only in you, Orion, is that kind of confidence not misplaced."

The corner of his mouth twitched—not with a smile, but with something like uncertainty. He was looking at me with an expression I'd hardly seen on him before: vulnerability. His chest rose and fell faster, his heartbeat racing. Orion—the big bad Lord of Chaos—was nervous. "But you're going to need to know what I did. You're going to need to know the real me."

I stared at him and the dark sweep of lashes framing his blue eyes. My chest ached. "What do you mean? What did you do?" It came out a bit sharper than I'd meant it to. I just wasn't sure I could handle any more horrific surprises from him.

His gaze shuttered, and he rolled away from me. He rose from the bed, and I found myself staring at his muscular back. "The trial is today, but I will tell you later."

As I stared at him, I felt like ice was spreading between us, chilling the air.

And something else was bothering me. Something I'd avoided talking about in the past few days. "He really looked like you, you know. The person who came in through the window."

He turned back to me, one eyebrow raised. "You were half asleep, weren't you?"

I swallowed hard. "I had a doppelgänger. Sort of. What if someone else looks like you?"

"Doppelgängers are mortal. They don't have claws." He turned to me with a frown. "And you exist because Mortana died. I'm not actually dead, as you pointed out."

I didn't want to say it, but I had to ask. "It's just...everyone thought my parents were dead. And they weren't. You said your brother looked exactly like you—"

"Rowan," he said sharply. The temperature plummeted. "I saw him die. I will never forget it."

I let out a long breath. *And I saw you attack me.*

A new set of worries had now taken root in my brain, thorny vines that pierced every other thought. But I didn't say a word as I found my way to the shower in my room. I turned on the water and stripped, letting the steam fill the bathroom. His words from a month ago echoed in my mind.

Consider it an accident if it makes you feel better. My hands slipped, and I accidentally ripped off Carl's head and shoved his remains under the desk.

Orion felt guilty for some terrible secret. What would someone like him feel guilty about?

As I stepped into the shower, I closed my eyes, trying to visualize that conversation—the entire mental image of his room—boxed up and locked away. Everything hinged on how today went, and I needed my mind to be one hundred percent focused. In the next half hour, my goal was to stop thinking about Orion's promise to fuck me until I forgot my name and everything else he'd just said to me.

Mentally, I started reviewing the plan I'd made with my team. Chant the invisibility spell as I flew, and race to Sudbury. I'd touch down near the mansion. Kas and Legion would be sheltering nearby to disrupt the mansion's wards and protective spells. I knew how to find the entrance by a little stone marker, even when the house remained cloaked.

With a spell for invisibility, I'd slip past the three or four guards—or their dead bodies if Orion got there first. I'd use a spell to open the front door and the safe. I could waltz right in. Unnoticed.

I'd head straight for the chancery.

If the hunters detected us, the mansion's automatic locks would trap us inside, with great iron bars that would slide across the doors. The mansion would become a sort of prison for us, with hunters hell-bent on killing us.

But the doors could be opened from the outside, so Shai would be waiting for me by the southern exit with an unlocking spell. I'd knock four times, letting her know she needed to open the iron bars.

I could be back here by sunset, grimoire in hand, ready to be crowned.

In theory.

❦

Orion and I stood across from each other beneath a cloudy sky. Although my muscles were rigid with tension, he was simply relaxing against the stone wall, his hands in his pockets. He wore a dark gray T-shirt that stretched over his large shoulders, and my gaze slid down to his serpentine tattoo. My mind flicked back to the feel of his fingertips stroking down my spine this morning...

I ripped my gaze away from him. I was keeping that mental lock on my thoughts.

The rules of the Demon Trials required that we start in the City of Thorns itself. From here, we'd be racing to Sudbury.

Turning from the wall, I glanced at the crowd around us. I recognized Lydia, the duchess who'd once tried to murder me. Apart from Amon, I didn't know most of the other demons yet.

To spare us from any leaks that could alert the demon hunters, no one in the crowd had any idea exactly where Orion and I were going today, only that I could be queen by tonight.

Mistress Blacknettle pushed her way from the crowd, draped in silver robes that matched her hair. "Today, you leave from the City of Thorns. The first of you to return with the grimoire wins the trial and the crown. While none of us know where you are headed, we eagerly await your return from this journey. May the gods bless you both."

I nodded at her. My blood pounded in my veins, a steady war drum of nerves. As soon as the clock struck with the ringing of bells, we'd be racing through the skies.

I stole another quick look at Orion. A sly smile curled his lips as he looked back at me, like we shared some kind of secret.

I took a deep breath, and my body jolted as the bells began to peal, signaling the start of the trial.

My wings burst from my shoulder blades, and I shot into the air, soaring beneath the cloudy sky. The sea wind tore through my hair as I headed southwest toward Sudbury. As I flew, I chanted the cloaking spell, and magic hummed over my body as it took effect. Adrenaline raced through me.

When I reached my hand out before my face and saw nothing, I had a dizzying sense of madness. It took me a few minutes to get comfortable with not being able to see myself.

Scanning the skies, I searched for Orion, but all I could see was a faint twisting of shadows under the clouds. Good—the *Malleus Daemoniorum* wouldn't see either of us coming.

Orion had been right. I'd been craving this kind of wild flight, spiraling free through the air above the earth, the way a succubus was meant to be. His intoxicating scent floated on the wind, wrapping around me like a caress.

But as I flew, my phone buzzed in my pocket, jolting me out of my exhilaration. *Really?* Now?

Immediately, my pulse started to race. Only Kas, Legion, and Shai had this number. I'd been very clear that they were only supposed to text me if something had gone very wrong.

I pulled my phone from my pocket and stared in horror at—nothing. The fucking phone was invisible, too.

With frustration mounting, I pushed the side button and yelled at Siri to call Shai.

I pressed it to my ear, and my blood pounded when it went straight to voicemail.

Fortunately, Legion picked up immediately, barking, "This is Legion," into the phone.

Breathless, I shouted at him. "What's happening? I can't read the text. I'm falling behind, Legion."

"Something is wrong, Rowan. I think the hunters knew you were coming."

My blood turned to ice. "The demon hunters? How? No one except us knows where we're headed."

"I have no idea. Someone tipped them off. Because it's not just the three or four guards—there's a whole army out there."

I scanned the clouds, but I saw no trace of Orion's shadowy presence. "Where's Shai? She didn't pick up."

"She's fine. She told me she'd be waiting for you at the southern wing if you need help getting out. I just can't see her because she's invisible."

"Legion, it's too late for me to stop this. I've lost Orion, and I won't get the chance to tell him before we arrive. This is happening, no matter what. All we can do is fight our way in and out."

I shoved the phone back into my pocket and focused on my flight, trying to pick up speed.

My heart pounded hard as I raced further west and the land beneath me grew greener. Drawing closer to Sudbury, I swept closer to the ground, my eyes sharp on the earth beneath me. If I overshot the mark, I'd find myself in the underworld again, and the last thing I needed was another angry Puritan mob...though I supposed I was heading for an angry Puritan mob either way.

And there it was—the outer edges of the Great Meadows conservation land stretched beneath me. In the cool autumn air, the trees had turned the color of flames.

As I homed in on the Noyes Mansion, the metallic scent of blood hung heavy in the air.

29

ROWAN

My stomach turned at the sight of the slain mortals—some of them decapitated, others burned. Blood pooled over the earth, staining the grass. Feeding the soil, just as the Puritans had done.

And for a moment there, I'd almost been worried for Orion's safety.

I swallowed hard, ignoring the shaking in my legs as I found the stone slab that marked the entrance to the invisible mansion. I pressed my hand against the spot where the door should be for the unlocking spell, but Orion had left it open for me.

Inside the mansion, distant shouts rang across the building. This place was far grander than I'd ever imagined, with towering arched windows that let the forest's light spill onto an old stone floor. Oil paintings of demon hunters festooned white walls above mahogany wainscoting. At either side of the hall, sweeping stone stairwells led upstairs.

But the chancery was on this lower floor.

Demon hunters were racing around the large halls, shouting orders at each other. They passed by me, completely unaware of my presence.

One of them slammed the door shut behind me, and the sound echoed off the stone.

Quietly as I could, I raced toward the chancery. I sprinted through the eastern wing, counting four doors on my right. Then I slipped into a stone room with stained glass windows that let in flecks of colored light. A wooden cabinet stood in one corner. Legion had found the safe —and the grimoire—in there.

But as I approached the cabinet, a loud bell started ringing.

"Lockdown procedures in place," a voice boomed over the intercom. "Demons have been identified in the building. We are initiating lockdown procedures."

Breathing hard, I knelt before the safe to whisper the unlocking spell. A thrill rippled through me as the lock spun and the door clicked open. Relief loosened my breath as I pulled out the leather-bound grimoire—though it was much smaller than I'd expected. And much *newer,* too.

When I cracked it open, I found that it was not a grimoire at all, but a list of ordinary names and addresses.

My stomach clenched. *Fuck.* Had Orion already found the grimoire, then? Or had the demon hunters known to move it?

My gaze snagged on one of the names in the book, my heart hammering.

Giuseppe Esposito, 8 Gallows Hill Road, Osborne MA. Missing since September. Believed to use glamour to appear older. Likely dangerous. Missing.

I flipped to the start of the book, my hand shaking as I read the handwritten inscription: *Suspected Lilu Fugitives.*

The book had about a dozen names and addresses spread all over the world. Holy shit.

There were more of us out there. Suddenly, this felt like a bigger find than the grimoire. Maybe Orion and I weren't the last Lilu after all.

My heart hammered. I stood and sniffed the air. Faintly, I smelled cedar, the scent that had become like home to me. I was now starting to understand what Orion had meant about demon senses being heightened—and overwhelming. Because along with Orion's smell, there was a whole lot of blood and burnt hair and skin, pungent human sweat, and other things I absolutely did not need to think about.

I tried to tune out the clanging of alarm bells, just focusing on Orion's smell to lead me to him. Still completely invisible, I crept down the hall. In the wide corridor, mortals rushed past, armed with long rifles. Did they think they could stop us with bullets?

And only now did I listen to catch some of what the mortals were saying to each other.

"One of those Lilu fucks is leaving a trail of bodies behind."

"The grimoire is gone," someone bellowed.

"How are we supposed to find them if they're invisible?"

My blood roared. How did they know we were *Lilu,* specifically? The only people who knew exactly what was happening today were Orion and my three friends—and yet, the mortals had known *exactly* who to expect today. So who the fuck had passed along this information?

I had no idea where to look now, so I simply followed Orion's scent —until an arm shot out and pulled me into a small library. The door slammed behind me, and I whirled to see the shadows unwrapping from Orion.

Despite my perfectly laid plans, someone had fucked this up. I felt more stunned than angry, unable to accept that one of my friends could have been so careless with this secret.

A smile played about his lips as he lifted the grimoire—a faded, deep green book with chipped gold text. "Looking for this?"

A sharp tendril of disappointment coiled through me. "Do you *want* me to fight you for that? Because I will." I glanced behind me at the closed door. "But why are you still here? Why didn't you leave with it?"

His expression grew serious as he held out the book to me. "I want you to trust me." He wasn't quite meeting my eyes, because I was still invisible, but he was looking in my general direction. "It's yours, Rowan. The book. The crown. You can have them."

I felt like my heart was about to burst. I didn't know what to say, so I just took the book from him, and I watched as my cloaking spell made it disappear. "I can't believe you're giving it to me."

"I trust you to make the right decision."

I inhaled a shaky breath, hardly believing this was real. "How did you know where to get it?"

"The same way I always learn things. I found a demon hunter and started breaking his bones until he gave me the answers I wanted."

Maybe it would've been better if I hadn't asked. "I have something for you, too, Orion." I handed him the book of Lilu names, watching it materialize as I handed it to him. "I think there are more of us out there. The demon hunters have been tracking some of the Lilu."

He flipped through the pages, his body glowing. "Holy hells, Rowan. Do you think this is real?"

"I recognized one of the names, Mr. Esposito. And yeah, I think he could be a demon. He's the one who told me about the trials. He was friends with my mom."

He stared at me with a kind of awe. "Maybe revenge doesn't have to be a massacre. Maybe it can be the return of the Lilu that these fuckers tried to exterminate." His forehead furrowed, and a wicked smile curled the corners of his lips. "But I'm still going to kill the demon hunters, and I'm going to enjoy it."

"Can we at least get the books out of here before you incinerate everyone? We can get out quickly at the southern exit. Shai's waiting for us there to unbolt the door in case of a lockdown."

I watched his perfect features disappear as shadows enveloped him.

"Let's go, love," he whispered. "I'll come back for the demon hunters later."

✵ 30 ✵

ROWAN

We pulled open the door, finding the hall mostly empty.
Hand in hand, we walked unseen through the corridor, and I used my mental map of the building to lead him. The southern exit was just ahead of us—a great wooden door, crisscrossed and studded with iron. I glanced behind me, making sure no one was around. Holding my breath, I leaned forward to knock —*One. Two. Three. Four.*

I waited for the door to open.

"Shai's not there," a deep male voice said from behind me.

My muscles froze at the sound of a voice I recognized.

"Seems like your friend didn't really want you to leave," the voice added.

I turned to see two men holding rifles. And one of them was Jack Corwin.

Now, *here* was a question—how the fuck did they know I was standing there when they couldn't see me? Seems my friend had told them that, too.

Pain ripped through my stomach. When I looked down, I saw that I hadn't been hit with bullets, but rather darts. One had slammed into my ribs; the other caught me in the gut. I plucked them out, but as the poison from the darts spread through my veins, it seemed to be eating away at the magic protecting me. My body was becoming *visible*.

I fell to my knees, turning to look at Orion. He'd been hit too, but he was still standing. He rushed the hunters like a wild animal, flinging one of them against the wall. Jack turned to run, screaming for help.

Blocking out the pain, I scrambled to pull my phone from my pocket. I pressed the button on the side, frantically screaming into it. "Siri. Call Legion!"

The phone started ringing, but I could tell by its crackle that we didn't have a good connection. I glanced up to see Orion trying to chase down Jack, but he was stumbling now with the poison in his body.

"Legion here!" My friend's staticky voice came through the phone.

"We're trapped! Can you get to the south exit?"

I couldn't hear his reply, but my skin was growing hot from behind, and smoke billowed through the air. Tears stung my eyes.

I whirled to see flames consuming part of the door behind me, climbing up and blacking the wood and iron. This should be a good thing. Fire could burn us out of here. But the heat was making me feel sick, the heated air searing my face. And when I swiped my hand across the flame, pain screamed through my fingertips.

Fire *hurt*. The poison was fucking up our magic.

"Orion," I shouted.

I turned to see him staggering back to me. Jack must have sensed Orion's growing weakness, because he turned to walk after us—cautiously this time. I wondered if we could die out here without our magic. Ordinary demons, yes. Lightbringers? I had no idea.

Mentally, I reviewed the map of the place. There was a stairwell just to our left, and two more floors upstairs that would probably have fewer hunters.

I shouted at Orion to follow me and tried to ignore the searing pain of the poison moving through my body. In the stairwell, I glanced behind me, relieved to see Orion was on my heels. Pain etched his features, and I wondered how much extra energy he'd expended trying to chase down Jack.

I didn't love the idea of running *up* into a burning building, but we were low on options. And as we climbed the stairs, a sprinkler system started going off, and cold water rained down on us. I shoved the grimoire under my shirt to keep it dry.

Orion pushed ahead of me, opening the door for me on the top floor. When I caught a view of an empty hall, I exhaled with relief. The sprinklers hadn't set off in here, and I pulled the book from my damp shirt.

"We can't rest, Rowan," said Orion. "We have to find a way out."

"I know." My body burned with the toxins. I dragged myself through the hall, still clutching the grimoire.

I just no longer had any idea how we were going to get out.

I pulled out my phone again, ordering Siri to call Legion. This time, the ringtone was clear, and he picked up immediately.

"Where are you?" he shouted into the phone.

I didn't have time to waste on elaborate explanations. "We need you to open the front door for us. Not yet! I'll knock. Just wait for me there, okay?"

We'd nearly reached the end of the corridor, so I pushed myself as hard as I could, and Orion ran at the same speed.

We finally made it to the wooden stairwell at the front of the building and staggered down as fast as our broken bodies would take us.

As we reached the lowest level, my heart thundered.

Jack Corwin stood there, aiming his gun at us.

If I'd had the ability to summon my magic, I'd have turned the mansion to ash to keep Orion safe.

Jack's face was red, and sweat dripped down his forehead. "Did you just think you could kill my dad and get away with it?" His shouts sounded ragged, crazed.

Orion turned and started to pull me back up the stairs, his arm around my back like he was shielding me. But I felt the sharp sting of pain as the darts ripped through my skin from behind.

"Hawthorn berries and Ladon venom," shouted Jack. "Doesn't feel so good, does it, my friends?"

Orion whirled. "You stay the fuck away from her." His voice

boomed off the walls, like the knelling of a dark god. "If you harm her again, I'll make you wish you'd never been born. I am a nightmare the likes of which you cannot even comprehend. I will burn this place to the ground and make you choke on the smoke, and then I'll rip out your lungs, Jack."

"Not with the venom in you," he shot back. I could tell he was attempting mockery, but his voice was shaking, ruining the effect.

I fell to my knees, horrified to hear the sound of footfalls upstairs. We were about to be trapped in here between Jack and the rest of the demon hunters.

With a wild snarl, Orion barreled toward Jack and pushed him against the wall. He pressed his forearm against Jack's throat, pinning him hard. Jack's face turned as red as the leaves outside.

"Stay away from my queen," Orion growled.

Jack dropped the gun, and his legs kicked at the air.

I had no idea how Orion had found the strength for that, as the Ladon venom felt like it was corroding me from the inside out.

"Go, Rowan!" Orion was shouting, but it sounded hazy to me. "I'm right behind you. Get it out of here!"

I staggered past the two of them, my mind whirling as I reached for the door.

Orion had trusted me with this grimoire, and I was going to get it to safety. Distantly, I heard Orion and Jack shouting at each other, but my senses seemed muddled, like the poison was eating at my brain. I narrowed my focus to getting the book outside. I leaned against the door, then knocked four times until it gave way.

I fell to the ground outside in the blinding sunlight, where the air smelled of death. I clung to the book as I felt a pair of strong arms scoop me up, and then the wind rushed over me.

I leaned into Orion's chest, and every bone in my body sang with agony.

Now, there was only the feel of my nerves splitting open, and the rest of the world faded away.

MALE VOICES PIERCED THE AIR AROUND ME. I WAS GOING TO BE SICK. I rolled onto my hands and knees, and vomited onto the dirt.

"Rowan!"

I looked up to see Legion's face before me, blurred like the world was smeared with Vaseline.

"Rowan," he shouted again, crouching beside me. "I need to know what they poisoned you with."

I fought the urge to throw up a second time and tried to cast my mind back. Jack had told us what it was...

"Ladon," I muttered, leaning back on my heels. Gripping my stomach, I lay on my side. But no position was relieving the pain, no matter how much I shifted around. "Ladon venom. And hawthorn." I fell onto my back in the dirt. "Where's Orion?"

❧

AN ARM CURLED UNDER MY NECK, AND I LOOKED UP INTO LEGION'S face looming above me. He was holding a cup to my lips, one that smelled of pine needles and berries.

"Open, Rowan," he said gently, cupping the back of my head. "This will help."

The scent of it nauseated me, and I wanted to puke again. My mouth felt dry, fiery.

"Open, Rowan," said Kas. "It's medicine. It will make you feel better."

He reminded me so much of my mom right then that I only wanted to please him, so I took a sip of the viscous, earthy liquid, and drank it down. It tasted like dirt and leaves—but the effect was almost immediate.

Whatever it was, it washed away the corrosive pain, soothing my muscles. Slowly, my vision started to clear, and the nausea settled in my stomach. My limbs shook, but they didn't hurt.

I looked up into the concerned faces of Legion and Kas. At last, I was strong enough to sit up, and I wiped the back of my hand across my mouth.

But something still felt wrong, and my heart thumped wildly with panic. Fear still gripped every muscle in my body.

I looked around me as I realized the source of the fear. "Where's Orion?"

Legion shot a confused glance at Kas. "I don't know. We were trying to get you to safety as quickly as possible."

"We weren't waiting around for him," said Kas.

"You got the book, Rowan!" Legion passed the grimoire to me. "You won."

"Wait." I was scrambling to keep up with their conversation. "Orion's still there?"

"When you said you were trapped," Kas went on, "I thought it would help to light a fire, because the two of you would survive it, but—"

"Kas," I shouted. "I need to go back for Orion!"

Kas looked startled, then frowned. "Of course. But shouldn't you bring the grimoire back to the City of Thorns first? He'll be fine. He's Orion."

"He's survived worse than a few mortals," added Legion.

I gripped the book tight against me. "No. Our magic wasn't working with that poison. I won't let the mortals break him again."

I was already rushing to my feet when Legion touched my arm. "Wait. Shouldn't you leave the book with us?"

My gaze slid between the two of them, and the thought still nagged at the back of my thoughts—someone had tipped off the demon hunters. "Shai never showed up at the south entrance. Where is she?"

Legion shook his head. "She's not answering her phone. We couldn't find her. But you don't think she would..." His sentence trailed off. "She wouldn't have left you there on purpose, Rowan."

Kas scrubbed his hands over his mouth. "Sadly, no one is above mistrust. Not even our dearest friends."

"And that's exactly why I'll be keeping the book with me." I pulled the glass from Legion, the one filled with the antidote. "Thank you both for getting me to safety. I'll see you in the City of Thorns."

They were shouting after me to leave the book with them for safety. As long as I brought it back to Orion, he could still win.

But the fact was, at this point, I trusted Orion more than I trusted them.

⚶ 31 ⚶

ROWAN

I felt it for the first time—the unrestrained panic of knowing Orion was in danger. My twin star. Even if he didn't realize his soul was calling to me, it was. He *needed* me now, and nothing would stop me from getting to him.

Our separation was a sharp physical pain in my chest.

What if he thought I'd abandoned him on purpose?

The thought made my heart slam against my ribs. He'd sacrificed himself to the demon hunters so I'd have a chance to escape, giving up the book, the crown, his life—

I wouldn't let them break him again.

Racing west, I soared over autumn leaves the color of hellfire under a cool blue sky.

I'd rip Jack's head from his body if he killed Orion. I'd leave nothing behind of that mansion but a dusty miasma of blood and bone. Darkness unfurled inside me—shadows that I'd always kept wrapped up tightly. The demon in me that craved blood, vengeance.

I swooped down on the clearing where the mansion stood, and the scent of mortal blood filled the air around me.

I crossed to the stone marking the door and kicked it open. The door slammed off its hinges, and I stepped inside. I tucked the book under one arm and gripped the antidote with the same hand. If any mortals showed up with dart guns again, I'd be ready to unleash flames from my fingertips.

Apart from the portraits of demon hunters above the wainscoting, I found the hall empty.

I sniffed the air, inhaling blood, burnt wood, and the scent of fear.

I wasn't just Rowan now, but a demon who hunted by scent. And when I heard footfalls behind me, I reacted immediately. I had no time for coherent thoughts, just my hands gripping a mortal throat and slamming his head against the wall. I hit him hard enough to make him panic, not enough to knock him out. His eyes snapped wide open so I could see the whites, like a frightened horse.

"Where is your prisoner?" I hissed. "The incubus."

His mouth opened and closed soundlessly, so I drew out my claws against his neck. He let out a whimper as I drew blood.

"If you scream," I whispered, "I'll kill you. Now tell me, is there a dungeon? A jail?"

I'd be killing him either way. Were these Orion's methods? Yes. But I was a demon now, and it seemed I needed the ruthless efficiency of violence to protect those I loved. I'd keep him safe, and I knew he'd do the same for me.

"Where is he?" I demanded.

"O-on this floor." he stammered. "The northern wing. We don't have a dungeon or anything like that. We're not the monsters. He's chained to a chair in the drawing room."

"He's just in an open room?"

He shook his head. "There are bars, like a prison cell."

"Tell me exactly how I get in, mortal, or when I come back to find you, I'll slowly drag your entrails from your body."

"The code is...it's 1486," he stammered.

The year the *Malleus Maleficarum* was written.

For an instant, I released my hold, and then I slashed my silver claws against his throat. His blood arced from his neck as he fell to the floor. I couldn't risk him pulling the alarms as soon as I left.

With the air rushing over me, I raced to the northern wing,

tracking Orion by his scent. Shouts echoed through the corridor as Jack barked questions at him.

Fury snapped through me, so sharp and hot I had to take care to temper it with cooler emotions. If I gave in to my rage, this place would turn to dust, and the grimoire along with it.

I was closing in on the drawing room, where iron bars blocked off a stately chamber. Pressing my back against the wall, I had a glimpse only of an antique rug and a stone fireplace, but I could smell Orion here. I desperately wanted to curl around him and keep him safe.

I could easily melt the iron if I had to, but I didn't want to give them advanced warning. If they had their dart guns ready, this wouldn't go well.

"Tell us how to get into the City of Thorns!" It was Jack's voice, teetering on the edge of hysteria.

"I think we need to stop." An unfamiliar voice. "If he dies, we won't learn anything from him. A demon corpse is no good to us."

I tried to block out the particular horror of that comment. Hidden from view, I clutched the book and the antidote tight, and I punched in the code: 1-4-8-6.

The iron gate slid up, and I shifted into the room. For a fraction of a breath, my brain registered what was happening.

Everything in the space looked expensive and luxurious—the antique furniture, the Persian carpet. Everything except the chains and the rickety wooden chair they kept Orion in.

To my left—my Orion, shirtless. Jack had carved his body with symbols all over, and Orion's blood streamed to the floor, pooling red.

Three hunters stood to my right, blood covering all of them.

A fraction of a breath later, I loosed a stream of fire that engulfed those three men, setting them ablaze.

Jack was too close to Orion to risk the flames, and he started running as soon as he caught sight of my fire. The pungent stench of Jack's fear filled the air.

I'd be going after him, but I'd be healing Orion first. What was better than one ferocious Lilu hell-bent on vengeance?

Two Lilu hell-bent on vengeance.

But when I looked back at Orion, sadness welled in me, along with panic. They'd ripped him apart.

Was he even breathing? I rushed over to him, shaking with horror. They'd carved the word *matricide* into his chest in vicious slashes. What the *fuck?*

And it was a merciful thing that my sorrow for him dampened my fury at Jack, or everything around me would be tiny flecks of ash.

They'd carved swirls that looked like snakes...

I cupped the back of his head, and when his eyes fluttered open, relief swelled in my chest. Oh, thank the *gods*.

"Rowan," he murmured. "You need to go."

"Fuck, no." I lifted the antidote to his lips. "Drink this."

He'd lost so much blood, he was struggling to keep his head up, and he looked like he was going to be sick. But he managed to close his lips on the edge of the cup. I tipped it, and the earthy liquid slid onto his tongue.

At first, he nearly choked on it. He was barely swallowing, but then he closed his mouth, and I watched his Adam's apple bob.

"Open, love," I whispered. "It will make you feel better." Mirroring Mom's words, and Kas's.

One tiny sip at a time, I let the potion slide into his open mouth. And when his eyes started widening to that ethereal blue—almost focused on me—joy lit me up.

"Orion," I whispered. "Come back to me."

I tilted the rest of the antidote into his mouth, and he swallowed it, stronger now. His eyes closed as he drank it down, and my gaze swept over his skin. As he finished the potion, his body was already starting to heal. The brutal carvings were disappearing as his demon strength and magic returned to him.

His head tilted down, and he stared at me, a fierce look in his eyes. "You came back for me."

"Of course I did. I always will." I slipped behind him. Gritting my teeth, I ripped through the chains that bound him. He slumped forward a little, resting his forearms on his knees. Blood still dripped from his arms onto the floor.

I knelt in front of him, peering up at his face. I'd never seen him look so exhausted. "Orion, I need to know this now." I gripped his thighs. "If we can bring the Lilu back into the City of Thorns, do you promise that will be enough for you? Or at least that you won't launch any preemptive attacks on the mortals to satisfy a centuries-old blood oath?"

He looked up at me, weary, a smile flickering over his lips. "I think I like your interrogation better than theirs, although you're somehow more terrifying."

"Do you promise?" I pressed.

"Yes, Rowan. I can restrain myself from launching preemptive attacks. I never promised Ashur specifics about how I'd get revenge. And the return of the Lilu is certainly revenge." He cocked his head, raising an eyebrow. "If we can't find them, we could always *make* more Lilu."

I ignored the flush of heat in my cheeks at his comment, trying to stay focused before I lost my chance to hunt down Jack.

I shoved the grimoire at him. "Good. Take this home."

He rose, handing it back to me. "You take it home. You return and take the crown."

I gripped him by the elbow, and helped him to his feet. "I'm going after Jack to see what he knows about Shai. She never showed up where she was supposed to be, and I don't know if she was the leak, or if she's locked in here, or what the fuck happened. And I want the book of names back."

I breathed in deeply, smelling the air for sweat, listening for heart-beats. My heightened senses told me the whole place was empty. Jack —and every other hunter—had fled.

I touched the side of Orion's face. "I need to go. Take the grimoire. Bring it back to the City of Thorns."

He leaned down, resting his forehead on mine. "I think this means you trust me now."

"I do. And when I get back, you and I will figure out how to rule together." I turned to run for Jack, but Orion grabbed my bicep.

When I turned to him, his eyes were burning with a strange intensity. "Wait, *wait*. You need to know what I did before you decide that you trust me."

I cupped his face. "Tell me now, then. Quickly."

His face was so close to mine, and he pulled my hands from his cheeks. Pain etched his face, and his shoulders slumped.

"I condemned my mother to death," he said quietly.

That wasn't what I'd expected, and my gaze slid down to the words carved on his chest, now healed over into angry scars. *Matricide.*

"I don't understand," I said. "How is that possible?"

"Molor died defending her, Rowan. Molor was a hero. But only a few months after they locked me in prison with her, I was brought to another cell. She was highborn, and they wanted a crime on the record books. So they asked me to say she wanted to kill the king, and I did. All they had to do was scare me, and I told them whatever they wanted to hear."

His sorrow seemed to fill me, a well of pain so deep, I'd never reach the bottom.

He met my gaze again, his expression ravaged with pain. "I did that because that is what I am deep down. I'm someone who will always save himself. I'm not Molor. He died because he was better than me. I always thought the ones who live are the worst ones. There is something twisted inside me, Rowan."

Something in his words struck a chord in me because we were the same—the ones who lived. But he was wrong.

I wrapped my arms around his neck, pulling him close to me so I could hear his beating heart. "You didn't condemn your mom because you're an abomination, my love. You condemned her because you were five—or six? You were a young child, and any other young child would do the same." I stood on my tiptoes to nestle into his neck.

Tentatively, his arm slid around my lower back. "A hero should protect people," he said, and the sentiment was strangely childish, like that part of him had stopped at five.

I kissed his neck. "But a little boy shouldn't be a hero. And the abominations were the people who tried to break you, because that wasn't just about getting a confession on the books. They were trying to break the Lightbringer. Orion, I know your mom would have wanted to go to her death instead of you. My mom ran into actual fire for me, and I know yours loved you just as much. How could she not?

You weren't born broken. You were just a boy who loved his family, and they used it against you. You have some scars, inside and out, but we all do." I stared up into his eyes. "How many times have you saved my life? You went through torture today to keep me safe. You're protecting me."

His hand slid up, and he cupped the back of my head.

I traced my fingers over his scarred skin, finding it already more healed, the ridges nearly gone. "You're my Lightbringer—the shining one who fell into the shadows."

Ferocity gleamed in his pale eyes. He leaned down and kissed me deeply, pulling me up by my lower back so my heels lifted off the floor. I felt all my anger melting away, and my fears too, as his warm magic vibrated around me.

He withdrew from the kiss, looking at me from under his dark eyelashes. "Rowan Morgenstern, Queen of the City of Thorns."

I pressed the grimoire to him again. "Bring it home, Orion."

❧ 32 ❧

ROWAN

I t was a good thing that I'd left Orion when I did, because I was pretty sure Jack was getting close to the boundary—the magical turnpike that kept demons trapped.

I found him by an old stone grist mill. The trees around it burst with crimson, the colors enflamed with scarlet, marigold, and ochre. But since blood covered Jack's clothes, it was easy to hunt him by scent. And by the time I reached him, he'd run out of energy. Jack was limping along below me, red-faced. Orion's blood soaked him, and another hot rush of rage burst through me. I landed before him, my wings spread out.

I savored the look of fear seizing Jack's body as he took me in and stumbled back. "Rowan. Just remember, we were friends once."

I took a step closer. "Except we were never friends, Jack."

"You're not like these demons. I *know* you, Rowan. We grew up together." He lifted his hands. "Remember the talent show? You did a magic show! In high school." A wild laugh escaped him. "It was...it was...it wasn't even *good*, Rowan. *You fell off the stage.* And now you can fly? You can incinerate people? This isn't the Rowan I knew growing up."

My lip curled. "Even when you're begging for your life, you can't stop yourself from reminding me what an asshole you are. You took a video of me falling off the stage, and you uploaded it to Instagram. Remember that?"

He looked like he was about to cry. "But you're not like them. That's my point. You're just...you know. Rowan. You're harmless."

My hand shot out, and I lifted him by the throat, squeezing. "You hurt someone I loved. And it turns out, when that happens, I am *very* much like a demon. I'm not harmless anymore."

I dropped him on the ground. He started scrambling to get away from me, and I reached for him again. This time, I let my claws out a little, piercing his skin when I lifted him above me. "I have a few questions for you. First, I want to know where the book is. The one with the Lilu names. When I release you again, I'm going to find a way to make you tell me."

I dropped him a second time, then slammed my heel into his knee. He screamed, grabbing the broken bone. I had to wait until his cries subsided, and then he managed to choke out, "Burned."

My teeth clenched. "You burned it?"

I brought my heel down hard into the same knee. His screams ripped through the air.

"We didn't need it." He rolled over, looking like he was about to be sick. "It's digitized now."

Such a banal statement in the midst of all the carnage, but it was useful.

"Where is Shai?" I demanded. "Was she the one who turned me in?"

Even as he was shaking, he managed to smile at me. "She's not exactly who you think she is. Even now, you don't have any real friends, Rowan. The demons don't care about you. I could be your friend if you let me live."

"Where is she?"

"Back in Osborne." He cradled his knee, tears running down his face, his features contorted. "You killed my father. You killed my brothers. And now you're going to end me. This is why we hunt you," he shouted. "Because you're monsters!"

I knelt next to him. "You and me both. You nearly tortured Orion to death. What's Shai doing in Osborne?"

"Orion isn't who you think he is, either. He's forever stained by his sins. Did you know he killed his mom?" Streaked with dirt and blood, Jack looked up at me from the ground. "All they had to do was put snakes in his cell, let them slide all over him until he shrieked for mercy, and he sent his mom to her own death." A wild laugh escaped him. "Your big bad demon was scared of snakes."

"He was *five*, you fucking maniac."

"Only the blood of demons will cleanse the world of all your sins. It's the sacred duty of the Hunters to spill it."

I gritted my teeth. "Except you'll all be dead soon, Jack. We'll hunt down and wipe out every last one of you. And when that's done, we'll have peace between mortals and demons. Too bad you won't be here to enjoy it."

Jack was shaking. "You grew up among us, Rowan. What if you joined us again? No one needs to know. Your friends betrayed you. And Orion will, too. Demons aren't loyal. They only look after themselves, like animals." He was desperate now, white as milk. "You can't trust the Lord of Chaos. The man is *insane*, Rowan. Of course he is. He condemned his own mom, and then he spent the rest of his life staring at the scene of his crime, staring at the noose that killed her. Dwelling on his sins, on how rotten he is underneath, because that's what demons are. Abominations." He yelled at me. "And when we carved his chest, we marked him for his sins, we spilled his blood to force him to atone, the way Cain was marked as a murderer!"

As he was speaking, my body had been growing hotter, brighter. They'd done this to him—tried to break him. They'd branded him with the guilt of condemning his mom when he was no more than a little boy. Jack was both a physical and mental sadist.

I heard myself say, "You're wrong, Jack. I'm not like you. Maybe I'm an abomination, but I'm a demon, not mortal. And I'm loyal down to my bones. I'll keep those I love safe."

"Then show some loyalty to the mortals you grew up with!"

Fire raged in my mind, and my voice echoed off the stone of the grist mill. "I'll keep the *innocent* mortals safe. But that's not you."

Starlight spilled around me as my wrath lit up the world. It was a strange sort of ecstasy to let myself go.

I was the light descending into darkness. Lady Lucifer, the fallen.

Jack's screams spiraled into the air, and traces of blood and bone, earth and rock drifted upward, swirling around me as I took him apart, a maelstrom of destruction. I was the nightmare, and I would take the wicked down with me. I let the light flow out of me, and I opened myself to the darkness.

Empty inside, I devoured the world. "I am Chaos, the eater of worlds," I heard myself whisper. "I was the first to exist, and I will be the last."

33

ROWAN

Shadowy nightmares flooded my mind. Now I lived in a palace of ice, of crushing solitude.

I am the nightmare.

Thoughts spiraled in the darkness of my mind, tiny whirling galaxies in darkness. Heat did not exist here.

I wasn't sure if *I* existed...

I died, I think...my body consumed itself in its fury, and my soul along with it.

Order and chaos...a light falling into the underworld.

Shadows consumed my light.

I am infinite. The alpha and omega.

I ached for warmth again. For him. A beautiful, fallen god—so perfect that the shadows desired him for their own. I among them wanted to devour his beauty.

A craving split me open, and I was grasping for him.

I could feel again. I needed to consume that light...

If I could feel, I was alive.

Someone I loved kissed my throat and jaw. What was his name?

My nostrils flared as I smelled him on me. And along with his scent, the faint perfume of lavender soap was bringing me back into my body.

I *craved*. I hungered. The chaos inside me demanded to be fed.

My muscles were warm, slick, and limp, and water dripped down my body. I wanted to be naked, to feel the fallen god's bare skin against mine.

He wasn't giving me what I wanted.

Cotton covered me, damp with warm water. Muscled arms wrapped around me, then laid me down in a bed of cool, clean sheets. The sensation of the sheets against my skin, that smooth and light friction, was an erotic torment that made me feel as if I were swelling with need.

He tried to pull away from me, but I wrapped my arms around him. My fingernails were in the bare skin of his back, pulling him closer. Distantly, I heard myself moaning for him. The fallen god was what I needed, and I knew he was the one who could fill me with light again. I licked his neck, tasting him. My skin felt sensitive, desperate for his touch. I couldn't decide if I wanted to bite him or fuck him. Both? I needed to devour.

"Rowan?"

I opened my eyes, looking up at perfection. Blue eyes, golden skin, angular jaw—a god of masculine beauty.

His darkening eyes burned with ferocity. "You're coming back to me." He kissed me lightly on my lips, but it wasn't enough.

Strength poured into me. I pushed him onto his back, delighted to find that I wasn't wearing underwear. Because I wanted to feel myself right on his bare skin, and I wrapped my thighs around him.

I ran my hands over pure, sun-kissed muscle. When I looked into his obsidian eyes, he seemed on the edge of losing control, his expression fierce. His fingers were on my thighs, clenching tight. I ached for him.

"Rowan, careful," he said. "We can't have too much."

I wanted too much.

And I knew if I took off these damp clothes, he would give me what I needed. So I tugged at the hem and lifted it off in one smooth motion. I watched his eyes slide down to my breasts and the apex of my thighs, naked on his body. This is where I should be—on top of my fallen god.

Conquering him.

His hot, silky magic twined around us, making my skin glow.

I watched his throat bob, and I moved down to his pants to unbutton them.

"Rowan, no!"

And then something happened that I didn't like at all. It was those magical bindings, snaking around my wrists and ankles, pulling me off him. Completely naked, I was bound to the bed, unable to get what I needed.

And worst of all, the fallen god threw a blanket over me again. I ached for him, and the faint friction of the sheet was nothing but torture.

He lay next to me, his head slumped against my shoulder "A little at a time, love."

Love.

With that word, his name dropped through the darkness in my mind like a falling star. "Orion." The memory of the word filled me with a little light.

A faint smile curled his lips. His eyes were still that coal black, telling me that he wanted to fuck me.

Under the blanket, he traced his fingertips over the curve of my hips. "I didn't want to leave you alone, Rowan. Even though you told me to. I flew back, following you. And I saw the flash of light, and I've never felt more terrified."

His hand traced down my thighs, making me shudder at the contact.

⚜

I DREAMED CARNAL, FEVERED DREAMS…THAT WE WERE IN THE Temple of Ishtar, the night after my initiation. I was sitting in his lap, and he toyed with me, touching me where I was wet. Hunger ripped through me, and my thighs opened wider, shamelessly demanding more. I didn't care that everyone was watching as long as I could come...

I dreamed that he bent me over a desk and ran his finger down my spine. He slid his hand into my hair and forced my skirt up, my underwear down to my thighs. Gripping my hair, he took me hard and fast, filling me while I screamed his name.

When I woke, the restraints were gone, but he was still next to me. Darkness filled the room. I was clothed again, which was annoying, but I twined my body around his. He stirred in his sleep, moving his arms around me. I could feel his hard length through my nightgown. Turning toward him, I searched for his lips, and when I found them, I kissed him deeply.

He moaned into my mouth, hips moving against me. But he pulled away with an agonized sigh, his eyes dark with shadows. "Not yet, love."

I needed more contact. *More.* "Orion."

There was something important I needed to tell him, and it was just at the edge of my consciousness. Where my mind had been whirling with chaos before, clear images started to flit through my thoughts...

A silver-haired boy covered in snakes.

"You didn't mention the snakes." The words startled me, and I wasn't yet sure what I was talking about. Then the memories began to flood me, flickering in my thoughts like an old film reel. "They covered you in snakes in the dungeon until you broke down. You didn't tell me."

He pulled away from me, staring at the ceiling. Another, worse memory burned in my thoughts—I'd made *fun* of him for his fear of snakes. I touched the side of his face and angled it toward me. Exhaustion shaded his sensual features, his eyes half-closed. He stroked his thumb over my cheek, and I felt myself lighting up from the inside out.

"Do you know what happened to the book?" he asked quietly. "The Lilu names?"

That's what it was—the thing I needed to tell him. I closed my eyes, trying to remember the specifics. "He burned it, but they're still there."

"Still where?"

What was the word he'd used? "In the Puritan building."

"The Puritan building," he repeated, brushing his thumb over my skin.

The darkness inside me wanted him to lick me and kiss me, for us to be a tangle of limbs and tongues, but I knew this was important, so I tried to focus and picture the face of the demon hunter...the one I'd destroyed. Images burst in my mind like fireworks. His sneering, freckled face. A maroon sweatshirt with Greek letters. A silver hammer pin, a knife dripping with blood. *Matricide.* He'd been my tormentor for years, and tears ran down his cheeks, streaking through the dirt on his face—

He'd carved words into my fallen god.

I inhaled sharply. "Digitized. That's what he said. It's in their files."

A smile creased his face. "Nice work, love." He traced his thumb over my lower lip.

With the important task completed, I felt I deserved a reward. And the way he was looking at me with that intense heat, that love—it was almost enough of a reward. But not quite.

My hunger for him would never be satiated. When I ran my hands down his hard, muscled body, the look in his eyes told me he was at war with himself, too.

I kissed him, taking his lower lip between mine. His fingers slid down, tightening on my ass. He pushed my hips against his length and groaned, a desperate sound that made my nipples tight. I needed my clothes off, our bodies sliding against each other.

I'd become a monster, turned the world into ashes around me. I'd made people burn. And I needed primal, animalistic sex to forget it all.

Agonizingly, he pulled away, his muscles tense as he lay flat on his back.

"You're not ready, my queen. Slow and steady, love. Almost there."

Orion kept denying me what I needed. I was about to rip off my clothes again, but I felt him curling into me, his hand cupping my face.

My eyes were growing heavy, my body limp. He was using magic on me —a different kind of Lilu magic. We were creatures of the night, of sex —and sleep.

Erotic dreams filled my mind before I could say another word.

Soon, I knew, I'd be getting everything I wanted from him.

✣ 34 ✣

ROWAN

I woke by myself, to a room streaming with light. Orion's room.

For the first time in days, my muscles felt imbued with energy, my thoughts clear. I jumped out of bed and looked down at myself. Orion had dressed me fully in sweatpants and a long-sleeved shirt, which made me smile. This outfit was for him, not for me—so he could restrain himself.

I crossed to the window and opened the shutters to look out at the garden. Immediately, sharp hunger gripped my stomach. I was starving. When I sniffed the air, my mouth watered. Was that baking bread? And something with cream? Potatoes? Butter?

Gods, I needed to eat, or I'd lose my mind.

I pushed the door open and raced downstairs. Before I reached the bottom, Orion swung around the corner from the kitchen into the stairwell. He grinned up at me. "You've returned to us."

"I've never been this hungry," I said, salivating at the scent of food.

I glanced hopefully at Amon, who was cooking something in front of an expansive stone hearth. He nodded at the table. "Clam chowder?" he asked.

"Oh, God, yes." I sat at the wood table, and Orion slid bread and butter across to me, then filled a glass of water.

My throat was dry as sand, and I drank it down. As Amon ladled chowder into a bowl for me, I attacked the fresh bread, slathering it in butter. Curls of steam rose from the bread, and the butter melted immediately. Salt and fat melted on my tongue...

Orion sat across from me at the table, his eyes glinting with amusement. "Take it easy, Rowan. You haven't eaten in almost a week."

The bread was gone.

The chowder—thick with cream, potatoes. Heavenly. More bread.

Orion touched my hand. "If you eat too much too quickly, you'll make yourself sick." It felt very much like something he'd been saying, something that had annoyed me *very* much over the past week.

"Always with the restraint," I muttered.

Sunlight streamed in through the kitchen windows, over clean white walls and a terracotta tiled floor. Slowly, the memories from Sudbury started trickling back to me.

I leaned back in my chair. "I was out for a week?"

A smile ghosted over Orion's lips. "We've been waiting for you to recover. I have something planned for the moment you're better."

I shook my head, my brain scrambling to keep up. "Wait. How did the trial end?"

He inhaled deeply. "I returned with the grimoire and you in my arms. The crowd was waiting for us, and they saw us return with the grimoire at the same time."

So he was still king.

As if hearing my thoughts, he added, "I announced that we would rule together. A king and queen in the City of Thorns. And if you're feeling well enough, tonight, you can address your subjects at the festival."

"What festival?"

He beamed at me from across the table. "A Lilu celebration to commemorate the triumphant return of our people."

My eyes widened. "You found them? Already?"

"It only took a few days," said Amon.

"Traditionally," said Orion, "the Lilu celebrations involve a human sacrifice, usually a prisoner dressed up as a mock king, and we tear him to pieces with our hands and consume his flesh."

I gaped at him. "Can we just do, like...a taco truck, maybe?"

"But since we've already killed all the demon hunters," he added quickly, "we can consider the spilling of mortal blood already completed."

I had a feeling he was trying to placate me, and that if I weren't here, he'd just go with the original plan. "Sounds like a fun festival."

The afternoon light gilded his beautiful face, bathing him in warmth. "Also, traditionally, the king publicly mates with his lover during the celebration," he murmured. "It symbolizes the primordial coupling of light and dark."

This was all a far cry from the two college parties I'd been invited to, with keg stands and red Solo cups.

Wait a minute—*was* I more like the mortals than the Lilu? My mind was churning, roiling, trying to keep up with everything. The world seemed to be moving in fast motion suddenly, and there was still so much I didn't know about Lilu culture.

"Yeah, we're not doing that in public," I said. "Though if you'd asked me a few days ago, when I was writhing in the depths of chaos and lust, I'd have been up for any kind of fucking with any kind of crowd. As it is, the Lilu will have to be happy with light and dark coupling away from their prying eyes."

Orion nodded. "The rest is fairly normal for a festival. Dancing, eating, a reenactment of Astaroth's descent into chaos, and the ritual slaughter of a bull so the Lilu leaders can bathe in its blood."

I cleared my throat. "I might skip that part?" He looked so freaking happy, though, I almost wanted to do the bull blood.

If it weren't for Orion, I would absolutely stay inside and read a book for a few weeks. But after all this time, he had his people back, and he wanted to celebrate—so I'd try out things the Lilu way for tonight.

"The Lilu are already in the Asmodean Ward." His unguarded smile was a thing of beauty. "We've been repairing the windows, cleaning out the dust. And at night, they've been swooping through the air, circling the city." Orion stood. "Come with me. I have a dress for you."

Gods, I loved seeing him like this. He took me by the hand, leading me back upstairs and into the room that I'd first stayed in. There, he'd laid out a dress for me—one both stunning and daring at the same time. It was a sheer material of midnight blue, beaded with tiny pearls in the shape of a constellation. A little slip under the dress would hit me below the hips, and it would just about cover my breasts and tummy, but the rest of me would pretty much be on display through the transparent material.

Still—I was a Lilu, and this was normal for them.

Not to mention, I was fairly certain that everyone had already seen me completely naked when Orion had returned with me in his arms from Sudbury.

"It's gorgeous," I said honestly. And alongside the dress was a necklace—silver that curled and twisted like delicate vines—and a crown to match, the silver vines dappled with pearls. "All of it is gorgeous."

The idea of Orion picking these things out for me, thinking of what he'd like to see me in, was beyond delightful. I slid my hands around his waist, pressing my head against his chest. I loved listening to his heart beating.

But a worry still nagged at the back of my mind.

I pulled away from Orion and looked up into his face. "Did you hear anything about Shai?"

He shook his head. "I don't know what she was thinking, Rowan."

I slumped down on the bed next to my dress. "But you killed all the demon hunters. And she wasn't with them?"

"She's just gone, love. She ran away. But we'll find her eventually."

I was ruining his joy over the festival and the return of the Lilu after all this time, so I smiled at him as I sat on the bed. We would find her.

Kas had told me not to trust anyone—not even him. Not even Shai. But I *knew* her, and she'd never disappear on me without a very good reason.

Hadn't I just discovered that people would do terrible things when survival depended on it?

I'd turned into a chaos god to keep Orion safe.

If Shai had turned on me, she must have been desperate.

WHEN I CROSSED INTO THE ASMODEAN WARD FOR THE FESTIVAL, I felt like a goddess in the dress. The sheer material caressed my legs, and the silk covering my breasts and hips was heaven on my skin. But even if I felt like a goddess, I was perfectly happy to stand on the edges of it all, watching the festival unfold.

Music from stringed instruments filled the air, melodies that were both new and familiar at the same time. I had the unnerving sense that I'd carried these melodies in a part of my soul. A drum beat steadily, and a lilting song rose above it all—a man with a beautiful countertenor voice. Tonight, the air was perfumed with jasmine, and incubi and succubi swooped through the air overhead, wings spread under the moonlight. The joy here was palpable, infectious. I found myself laughing for no reason.

After hundreds of years, the Lilu had their magic back, and the gift of flight. Once dark, the Lilu quarter had come to life again, and it thrummed with happiness. A star rising from the darkness.

Demons of all kinds danced wildly around the clock tower, and the golden hands moved once more, marking the time now as seven past nine at night. By Orion's side, I sipped an exotic Lilu beer, spiced with orange peel and safflower, and sweetened with honey.

Orion's face shone with joy as he looked out onto the festival, the dancers who moved in graceful arcs like the whorls of a solar system. He leaned down to kiss me on the lips.

When we pulled away from the kiss, the crowd was chanting for us both. *Long live Queen Rowan! Long Live King Orion!*

Technically, I wasn't queen yet. But they seemed to accept me as one already, and Orion slid his arm around my waist and leaned down to kiss me on my temple. Warmth flickered through me, and I wanted nothing more than to get him away into the Elysian Wilderness so we could reenact the primordial coupling of light and dark. Just—in private.

As if hearing my thoughts, Orion warmed the shell of my ear as he whispered, "I'm dying to get you alone, my queen." Heat flared across my chest, and I wanted to wrap myself around my demon king and drag him into the wilderness before anyone made us bathe in bull blood.

"Rowan!" A drunken, familiar voice rose above the music, and I turned to see Legion and Kas staggering toward me, shirts opened at the collar, buttons undone.

Kas lifted his beer. "Queen! Queen Rowan. Teamwork!" He held out a hand for a high-five, and I slapped his palm.

I smiled at them, but my throat tightened at the painful absence of the fourth member of our team. No wonder they were already trashed to forget that missing piece of the puzzle. And I had to wonder if they were a little disappointed that Orion was still on the throne, since they'd worked so hard to get rid of him.

Kas's beer sloshed out of his glass as he leaned over in a deep bow. "Your Majesty," he slurred. "My queen. May I have this dance?"

Already, I could hear the low, possessive growl emanating from Orion's chest. I was perfectly fine ignoring that, but another demon male was approaching, smiling at me like he knew me.

"Rowan!" The beautiful stranger beamed at me, opening his arms. He was nearly as tall as Orion, but with bright red hair that hung around his chin, his eyes deep brown. Abstract, curling tattoos curved over his thickly corded forearms. He was Lilu, his dark wings stretched proudly behind him.

I stared at his grinning face, unwilling to go in for a hug. "Have we met?"

His smile fell. "Of course. Yes." He looked down at himself and straightened his deep green shirt. "But I didn't look like this when you knew me." He met my gaze, waiting for me to catch on. "Your mother did fine without magic, but my body didn't do as well. It withered and aged outside of the city walls."

Understanding started to dawn. "Hang on..."

"I was the weak and doddering old man you played chess with every week." He ran a hand through his hair. "I brought you the book, and then I ran. Or at least tottered away as fast as my walker could take me. The fucking hunters found me."

I could hardly contain my shock. "*Mr. Esposito?*"

"That was not my real name." His wings spread out behind him, resplendent in the moonlight. "Your first cousin, Sabazios, on your father's side. I was at your house all the time when you were a baby, helping your mom."

"Sabazios!" I beamed at him. "You wrote the inscription in the demon trials book."

"I did!" He looked around at the dancers. "God, it feels good to be back. When are we bringing out the bull? I've been desperate to scent bull blood. One of the things you really miss, you know?"

I laughed at the absurdity of it all, then threw myself against Orion's muscled chest, wrapping my arms around his waist.

He looked down at me with a wicked glint in his eye, a sensual curl of his lips. "We have another ceremony to enact now, but that one will be out of view."

Heat slid through me, and everyone around me seemed to fall away, so it was just Orion and me. "Come with me, *now*."

We were heading for the place that demons belonged—the wilderness.

35

ORION

I *could* walk by Rowan's side into the Elysian Wilderness, but I preferred to watch her walk. I was entranced by the sway of her hips through the forest before me. The material of her dress was so thin, I could see her legs from the thigh down. It would be hard not to rip through that beautiful dress and take her like an animal.

For the first time since I'd thrown Rowan out of the kingdom, my body actually started to relax. I was comfortable in my own skin again, apart from the increasing tightness in my trousers as I watched Rowan walk.

I'd been holding back for so long now, driven out of my mind by temptation. Tonight, our lust magic would entwine, and I felt like the power of it would shake the earth and harrow the hells.

Rowan turned to face me, a curl of red hair falling before her face. A sly smile crossed her lips. "We're alone, finally."

My gaze slid down her body, and I breathed in her scent. I pulled her close to me, purring, "Rowan, you perfect creature. You brought the Lilu back."

She looked up into my eyes and responded with her own dazzling smile. "We both did."

I locked eyes with her and let the back of my hand slide down her cheek. Energy crackled where I touched her. "You're not going to bite me again, are you?"

"I might." Her voice held a seductive promise, and I can't say I hated the idea of it.

This cocky, succubus version of Rowan was nothing like the Rowan I'd first met—and I loved them both.

"I swore I wouldn't kiss you until you trusted me," I said. Our mouths were inches apart.

"And you understand that I trust you now?" Rowan's lips looked plump and red, ready for mine.

"You gave me the book," I said, my index finger on her chin, tilting her face to meet my kiss.

Instead of her sweet mouth, however, my lips found the first two fingers of her left hand, raised to block me.

My brow furrowed with an unspoken question. Who refused a kiss to an incubus?

I wanted her. She wanted me. But she intended to toy with me tonight—and I can't say I minded that, either.

With unexpected force, she shoved me flat on my back and leapt onto me like a wild creature—which she was. In the moonlight, I could see the flush of her cheeks, the untamed light in her eyes.

She straddled me, the hem of her dress riding up, and leaned closer. "Remember when you told me I didn't have it in me to take you down?"

I smoothed my palms over her thighs. "You haven't entirely forgiven some of the things I've said, have you?"

She unbuttoned the top of my shirt and pressed her palms on my skin. A wicked smile curled her red lips. Her fingernails raked over the top of my chest, ripping the shirt open more. "I may exact my revenge little by little. You belong to me now."

Desire flared in me, and sparks ignited in the darkness at every point where our bodies made contact. "I do."

But even with Rowan, it was nearly impossible to suppress my instinct to dominate. A demonic impulse snapped through me, and in the next moment, I'd shifted her off me until she was facedown on the mossy earth, her dress hitched up from behind. Her gasp made me stir with lust.

I pinned her wrists to the ground, then pressed over her, drinking in her delicious scent—ripe fruit. I wanted to mark Rowan's body and soul as mine. I fought the urge to rip through her underwear and take her right now. I *had* to savor this.

I lowered my face to hers. "I want you to never again think of another man like you think of me."

She turned to look at me and licked her lips. I hardened even more as I watched the movement of her tongue sliding over her lower lip. "Still jealous, are you? I thought you were supposed to be a god or something."

I yanked her dress up higher, exposing her arse in tiny lace underwear that nearly made me forget how to speak. "The gods are all jealous," I snarled. "It's why they get so angry when you worship other ones."

"I never should have told you about Tammuz."

"Let's not talk about my dad right now." With one hand pinning her wrists, I used the other to trace over the dark silk between her thighs. She moaned, shifting her hips upward with my touch. Just under the silk, I could already feel how much she wanted me. I fought the urge to pull the silk aside and dive in because I delighted in tormenting her.

"Orion," she moaned my name. And I could hardly take it anymore.

I found myself covering her with my body, my erection pressing against her through my trousers. "Yes, love?"

Unexpectedly, she shifted her hips upward and elbowed me in the chest. This was more strength than I could possibly imagine from someone so small, and I was flat on my back again, the wind knocked out of me.

Holy hells.

One of her perfect thighs slid over me once more, and her hair was a wild tangle around her head, embedded with a few leaves from the forest floor. She looked like a gorgeous wood nymph with her thighs spread over my hips. Her dress had hitched up, and I had a view of that little triangle of silky underwear again, where I'd just been stroking her. I already knew how much she needed me, but she was determined to be in control—for now.

This time, I let her pin my wrists down—welcomed it, even. And when she leaned over to lick my neck, the heat shuddering through me told me I'd made the right choice. Gods, she was divine.

"Do you remember me begging you to fuck me when you healed me?" she murmured into my neck. "Let's see how you like it."

My muscles coiled tightly, and all the blood had rushed from my head. "An incubus never begs, love."

"Just pray to Lucifer that you beg well enough that I give you what you need."

With that, she let go of my wrists and ripped the rest of the buttons off my shirt. Then she moved further down, stripping off my trousers. With the fingernail of her index finger, she traced my length from the tip to the base. Every muscle in my body tensed, and I throbbed at her touch.

I was at her mercy.

There was nowhere I'd rather be.

36

ROWAN

Already, I wanted him inside me. Like an animal in heat, my body had immediately responded to the way he'd pushed me down and yanked up my dress. To the way he'd dominated me and pinned me. What I really wanted was for him to take me hard right now.

But I was going to draw this out anyway. I wanted him to feel a little of the erotic torment he'd blessed me with so many times.

I kissed his neck, tasting the faintest hint of salt—from the sea, or the heat. With my thighs spread over his hips, I rocked against him and heard him catch his breath. He reached up, threading his fingers into my hair, gripping it hard and pulled me in for a kiss, his tongue sweeping against mine. This was it—the kiss he'd withheld from me. With this kiss, I claimed him as mine, and he claimed me as his. A kiss of such overpowering sexual pleasure, it could *almost* be enough to kiss all night...but not quite, because the rising ache between my thighs demanded more. More friction, more fullness between my legs.

I moaned into his mouth as he gripped my hair, holding me in place. One of his hands was on my hips, pinning me over his length. He nipped my lower lip, pulling away from me to look into my eyes. Desire hummed through every inch of my body.

His thumb stroked my cheek, then brushed my lower lip. "I loved you the first time I saw you, but I refused to let myself believe it. Not just because you looked like her, but because I never wanted to feel the maddening grief of loss again."

My lips hovered above his, and I breathed in the perfect scent of Orion. "What made you change your mind?"

His unwavering gaze locked on me. "Because being without you was the same maddening grief of loss. I realized that in the weeks after I kicked you out. I need you. I wasn't really free of the dungeon until you brought me out. You set me free. And I had to take the risk to see if you'd still accept me, all of me."

"And I do."

He pulled me in for another sensual kiss, and I felt my magic twining with his, vibrating over our bodies. My body was shaking with need for him. But I'd promised to draw this out, hadn't I? Like he'd done with me so many times...

I moved down to his chin, brushing kisses over his jaw, down his throat. I felt each of his muscles tense as I moved down over his abs, then lower as he moaned my name like a prayer. I ran my hands over his glorious body, kissing, licking, nipping. His skin was a soft gold, his body gloriously muscled. A perfect warrior.

My mouth hovered over his shaft. His length stood tall and proud, an obelisk below his carved abs. I licked him once, twice. I kissed him, swirling my tongue.

His inhale was sharp and loud, fingers tightening in my hair. "Are you trying to make me snap?"

I pulled back, staring at him. "What were you saying about being an incubus?"

Orion was all done playing, and with a wild growl, he sat up, his hand cupped around the back of my neck. "I was saying that I need you naked now, succubus."

I was straddling him, moving my hips against him. "But a succubus needs to be worshipped, love."

"And worship you is exactly what I'm about to do." He leaned in, his midnight voice heating my skin. "With my mouth, my hands, my cock."

The king—my king—reached up and pulled my dress from my shoulders, exposing my breasts. Savoring the view, his gaze caressed me. "I know you want to be in control, love, but my instincts drive me to dominate you."

My nipples were already painfully hard, and when Orion palmed them, his control seemed to fracture. My beautiful, delicately beaded dress was gone with it—ripped off, tossed onto the soil and rocks. A cool breeze slid over my naked skin.

But demons were creatures of the wild, and the dress was a thing of civilization. It had no place here between two Lilu. Our bed was the moss, and the king wanted me naked and spread out before him.

Orion's hungry gaze slid over my body, wild with his desire. The forest air began to shift, growing heated now as the lust magic crackled between us.

The corners of his lips curled. "I must see all of my queen." He slowly slid my underwear down my thighs, my calves. The cool forest air whispered over me, and wild need coiled tightly within me.

He was kissing me now, his mouth on my shoulders, my breasts. His lips closed over my nipples, making my back arch. His tongue swirled, his kiss devotional. With every brush of his lips and tongue, he claimed me. His mouth moved down to the hollow of my hips, and my body was on fire for him. A moan threatened to escape my lips.

When Orion spread my thighs, my body flushed. I was ready to cry out for him, my body ripe with desire.

I gripped his hair and lowered his mouth. Not a kiss this time. He raked his fangs across my inner thigh, the touch making my breath hitch. Teasing me. I wanted his mouth on me so desperately, his tongue inside me. I nearly crushed his head between my thighs.

"*Now,* Orion." Not a plea this time. An order.

🕸 37 🕸

ORION

I dipped my tongue into the warmth between her perfect legs.

Locked in prison as I'd been for all those years, the number of women I'd actually seduced could be counted on one hand. I'd desperately needed to feed from their lust when I escaped, but those experiences had been nothing like this. That was merely feeding, satiating a need.

This was an act of devotion, and the woman lying before me was a goddess.

I greedily inhaled the perfume of her arousal, and it enflamed me. Wisps of heated magic rose from her body, stroking me as I kissed her. Holy hells, the hellfire within threatened to consume me. Rowan's hips circled slowly once she made contact with my face, seeking the key to unlock her climax. But I wanted to keep her on the edge for just a little while because the air was aflame, and her power surged through my veins. I pulled back for a moment, and she barked another order for more, sounding more desperate this time.

She was mine, exactly as I needed her to be.

I pulled her tighter against me, allowing me even deeper access. My tongue swirled, licked, explored while her fingers ran through my hair.

Her hips bucked as she moved against me, but I held on to the top of her thighs.

"You'll be doing this..." she hissed, "every day." She gasped, her hips moving up and down.

If I could have spoken, I would have agreed. Magic shimmered around her, lavender and gold, hot to the touch. She was right on the brink of release...

She tilted forward so I could reach her exactly where she needed me. I slid one finger into her heat, and she clenched around it, her muscles tight. A second finger glided in. As I moved my fingers in and out, I heard her shuddering cry. The orgasm ripped through her, and I felt as if the earth were shaking beneath us, and the air sparked with heat.

Her thighs tightened around me so hard that if I'd required breathing the way mortals do, I'd have been in real trouble. Rowan held me in place, undulating in her afterglow as I kissed and kissed.

But of course, I wasn't yet done with my queen.

✤ 38 ✤

ROWAN

The reverent strokes of his tongue had left me dizzy, limp-limbed. Every one of my muscles had gone supple.

But he'd kept kissing at the apex of my thighs, and that molten need had built again. Orion, naked and glorious, moved up my body, his mouth on my skin. My hips, my breasts. Worshipful, indeed.

With each brush of his lips, liquid heat slid through me, and an ache coiled more tightly in me all over. Gentle and reverent though he was, I could feel the tension vibrating through him. His careful control could snap at any moment. My gaze slid down over his strong arms, the shadows carving his muscles. I gripped him by the shoulders and pulled him up higher over me. "More."

"More," he repeated.

My body was slick from lust and the humid air, ready for him.

His coal black eyes bored into me, letting me know he'd taken control. I raked my hands over his back, urging him into me. I brought my thighs up on either side of him and slid my hands toward his hips to move him closer. He paused at my entrance, teasing me, and my arousal unfurled in me. "I need you now, Orion."

This time, he wasn't making me beg. Rock hard, he slowly pushed into me, filling me. He stretched me just to the edge of discomfort. Oh, *gods*...

My head tilted back as the erotic charge hummed through my core. I whispered his name, raking my fingernails deeper into his flesh.

"Look into my eyes, love," he murmured.

I met his gaze, my breath catching at his unreal beauty as I adjusted to his size. My thighs wrapped around him.

The temperature in the forest had climbed so high that some of the leaves had begun to burn like candle flames—but that was a problem for later.

With his enormous body, he pinned me to the moss. Slowly, he started to move in and out of me, taking me, stoking my arousal. Not Rowan anymore...just a succubus, a creature of the wild.

Ecstasy spiraled through me, primal and overwhelming.

He thrust in again, slowly, his eyes locked on mine. "You're mine, Rowan," he breathed. "I love you."

I felt I should return the sentiment, but a plea for *more* was all I could manage as his powerful strokes had me coiling with sexual pleasure.

He covered my mouth with his, moving faster in me. Making the ground shake beneath us and the air glow with the gold of the sun. The world was on fire, and we were creatures of the light.

I shuddered as my orgasm tore through me. My cries must have reached the forest's canopy, the city across the river—a scream only a banshee could appreciate.

Orion growled as my clenching muscles gripped him.

Just when I thought it was over, everything started again, the dip only the marker to begin another climb. I rocked my hips at a blinding speed, and before I knew it, my mind was fracturing again, my body shuddering.

With Orion's release, his mouth opened wide enough that I could see golden flames licking at the back of his throat from deep within his core.

In that moment, I had no words anymore, only the heat and the light, and the perfect ecstasy of a wild beast set free.

❦

I CURLED UP INTO HIS ARMS, LISTENING TO HIM BREATHE, AS RAIN slid down our naked bodies. Once my mind had cleared again from the mist of arousal, I'd managed to remember the words for the storm spell and doused the flames.

Orion stroked his hand down my damp hair and nestled me further into him. Goosebumps had risen on my skin in the cool air.

"Rowan," he said softly, "I ripped your dress. Again."

"Either you're going to need to take up sewing, or I need to start wearing things that are much easier to take off around you."

He kissed the top of my head. "You could just stay naked. Around me," he clarified. "Not around anyone else. I don't need Kas and Legion getting an eyeful."

"I'm genuinely not at risk of becoming a nudist."

"Rowan." He propped up on his elbow. The shockingly pale blue of his eyes gleamed in the darkness. "When are we getting married?"

I stared at him. "Is this...a proposal?"

He traced a fingertip over my collarbone. "A proposal?"

I fought the urge to smile. After seeing Orion uncharacteristically vulnerable so many times recently, I found myself relieved that his wild confidence had returned. Also, he really had no idea whatsoever how normal social conventions worked.

"Usually, it's a question," I said. "You ask someone if they want to marry you before assuming. And there's kneeling and a ring."

"Ah." He nodded slowly. "Shall I get a ring?"

"Yes." I ran my fingers through his hair. "Orion, do you think we have everything we need now? We have the grimoire and the Lilu."

We'd both rule the City of Thorns. But what I was really asking was, *You're not hell-bent on revenge anymore, right?*

His fingers stilled on my collarbone, and he took a breath before answering.

My nerves fluttered with dread at his silence until at last, he said, "Yes. We have everything."

I lay flat on my back on the damp earth, staring up at the star-flecked sky through the boughs. I was perfectly satiated and happy, and his hand trailed down my body, following the curve of my waist, my hips.

But as I stared up at the heavens, a vision bloomed in my mind:

Stone walls, cracked to expose a bit of the stars. Then a shadow swinging over the stone—the bloodied, swaying feet of a hanged body. Wood creaking above, and pain piercing my heart to the core.

Why did I have a nagging feeling that I was still missing a piece of the puzzle, that even Orion didn't yet fully understand himself?

※ 39 ※

ROWAN

T he morning after the festival, I woke alone in Orion's bed. I stretched like a cat until I had the energy to get dressed and search for coffee.

As I was pulling on a pair of jeans, my gaze caught on a handwritten note left on top of the bed: *Meet me by the clocktower, love.*

I cocked my head, staring at it.

What did my incubus king have in store for me today?

I smiled to myself. The ring. He'd probably found a ring.

❧

I CROSSED INTO THE ASMODEAN WARD WITH A COFFEE IN MY HAND, shocked to find that the entire city had turned out, thronging the square like they had last night. This time, however, there was no music, no dancing—just a silent crowd, and Orion standing in the glaring sunlight on top of a stone pedestal by the clocktower. All eyes were on him, waiting.

Oh, gods. Was he about to propose in public?

But that was so unlike him, and so unlike me. I didn't want that happening in front of a crowd.

And then dread started to slither up my nape when I caught a glimpse of something tucked under his arm. The grimoire.

What was he doing with the grimoire out here in public? In the wrong hands, that thing was dangerous as hell.

A horde of Orion's soldiers stood around the dais, protecting him. I couldn't even get to him.

Orion's blue eyes locked on me. His expression was cold as ice, sending a flutter of unease through my veins. "Our former shadow scion." His voice boomed across the courtyard, dripping with disdain. "Is a traitor. And when I called her queen last night, I was merely under the spell of a succubus."

Icy dread danced up my spine. What the *fuck?*

The crowd parted around me as everyone stepped back. Where was he going with this?

Yes, technically, I was a former shadow scion. Someone who'd tried and failed to take the crown from the king. *Technically,* I was someone who'd committed treason, and that usually came with a death penalty.

But Orion and I loved each other, so none of that mattered right now.

Right?

My throat went dry as I stared at him, waiting to see if this was leading to something less terrifying. But if it was, I wasn't a fan of this kind of surprise.

"I cannot in good conscience rule over you and keep you caged," Orion's voice echoed off the clocktower, his eyes locked on me. He lifted the grimoire above his head.

Darkness started to rise in me.

"But I have the key to unlocking my people." His eyes held the crazed light of a fanatic as he held up the book. "Here. The grimoire. I am the one who can set you free once more. I am the Lightbringer prophesied to set you free. We must not live in fear of mortals any longer. We cannot allow another massacre to happen in our city walls. And we cannot allow traitors among us to keep us living in danger. Traitors like the disgraced shadow scion."

Everyone edged away from me—keeping their distance, like I was suddenly emitting a toxin that could bring them all down.

Frantically, I searched the crowd. Was anyone else baffled by this sharp change of personality?

I saw only Mr. Esposito—newly hot—catching my eye. He looked like he was panicking as much as I was, sweat running down his furrowed brow.

Orion had lost his fucking mind, and I needed to speak to him alone before he made this any worse. "Orion," I shouted. "You—"

My words were cut off by a hand gripping me by the throat, then a sharp needle piercing my neck. The effect was instant, a corrosive poison flooding me. I knew the feel of it anywhere—Ladon venom mixed with hawthorn. The poison screamed through my veins, weakening me.

My heart started to pound out of control as I realized I was all out of magic now. The only person here moving toward me was Legion, who was fighting his way through the crowd to get to me.

The world seemed to be tilting beneath me.

This was a nightmare come to life.

Orion's eyes were on me as he held the book over his head. "Three days from now, I will open the City gates. We will feast again. We will hunt again. We will drink mortal blood once more. Never again will we make a contract with the faithless mortals that will put us at risk. And what do we do with traitors?"

A soldier gripped my arm, ready to drag me up to the dais along with Orion. For one moment, my heart went still.

He couldn't possibly...

My heart shattered. I should have seen this coming.

I'd missed something. I'd been too trusting.

A powerful arm gripped me by the bicep, and I felt the air go arctic around me. Frozen wind rolled through the square, powerful as a hurricane. Legion's magic ripped through the crowd as he scooped me up, and I did my best to wrap my arms around his neck. He was moving with me. Racing. Getting me away from the danger.

I looked up into his face as he carried me swiftly through the streets of the City of Thorns. I dug my nails into him as he ran, trying to manage the blinding pain.

Three days from now.

I closed my eyes against the brutal heartbreak and leaned into Legion's icy chest. Shai was gone. Orion had lost his fucking mind...

They all said he was too crazy to trust. The snakes had ended him...

I swallowed hard, tears stinging my eyes. It couldn't be, though. He'd saved me too many times. He'd sacrificed himself for me at the headquarters.

Hadn't he?

Maybe he'd just snapped. The shadows had consumed him, the chaos taken over.

In the City of Thorns, things aren't always what they seem.

I was vibrating from rage and confusion, unable to put it all together. But all I knew was that right now, Legion was the one taking care of me.

Fleeing with me from the man I'd thought loved me to the ends of the earth.

❧ 40 ❧

ROWAN

I was on my hands and knees in an abandoned garage, my body shaking with the exquisite agony of the poison. When I looked up through blurred eyes, I saw three forms. One of them was Kas, rushing over to me with a glass of that sludgy antidote, which was exactly what I fucking needed.

He knelt by my side and helped me shift back off my knees. I leaned into the curve of his arm, and he tilted the cup to my lips. "That's it, Rowan."

I sniffled, covered in snot and tears—hardly regal. But as the antidote filled my throat, some of my shaking subsided, and the pain seeped out of my bones. I collapsed against Kas and let him wrap an arm around me.

My vision was filmed from tears when I looked up at the other two. With a twinge of disappointment, I realized I'd been hoping for Shai and Legion, but the third figure was Mr. Esposito, also known as Sabazios. Ginger and hot as fuck, but also very much related to me, so I needed to stop thinking of him as *hot as fuck*.

"Are you okay, Rowan?" Sabazios asked.

I nodded. "Physically, I'm recovering." I shifted away from Kas and sat cross-legged on a concrete floor. "Do you all realize you're commit-ting treason with me right now?"

"Yes," they answered, all at once.

Sabazios lifted a leather bag. "But at least this time, before fleeing, I was able to get my things."

"And we're not leaving you," said Kas. "This was why we wanted you to rule in the first place."

"Of course I'm not leaving you," said Sabazios. "You and your mom were literally the only friends I've had in the past several centuries."

I couldn't stop my tears. "We have to warn the mortals. We need to evacuate…"

"Rowan," said Legion, "you're still the only one who can stop Ashur."

I stared at him with the strange disorientation of feeling like the world was tilting beneath me. "Ashur?"

"Or whatever he calls himself now." Kas scrubbed a hand over his jaw. "Orion."

I shook my head, trying to understand what he was saying. "Ashur was someone else." My heart started beating faster. "That was who he made a blood oath to. Ashur."

Sabazios shook his head, "His parents named him Ashur. I remember him. They were part of our social set, and the little silver-haired boys were Molor and Ashur." His eyes took on a haunted look. "I had no idea he'd survived. We didn't know that anyone lived in the dungeon, or that it existed at all."

I staggered to my feet, my blood roaring in my ears. My mouth had gone dry, and I tried to swallow. "Maybe Ashur is his dark side, then. The part that wants blood."

Kas stood and rested his large hands on my shoulders. "It's okay if you love him, Rowan. But we always knew he wasn't coming back from what happened to him. And you're the only one who can stop him from starting an apocalyptic war."

I shook my head. "I'm not going to kill him."

Kas breathed in deeply, his amber eyes gleaming. "Only an heir to the throne can kill a king."

I threaded my fingers into my hair, and memories of Orion's midnight voice whispered through my thoughts.

Because being without you was the same maddening grief of loss...I wasn't really free of the dungeon until you brought me out.

My breath was coming too quickly, my heart beating out of control. I couldn't explain what was happening, only that deep in my soul, I felt he didn't need killing. He needed saving.

And in the meantime, I needed the mortals to evacuate every town around here.

"I have to go to the police," I muttered.

I didn't wait to hear the others' response because I knew what they wanted from me. Something I wasn't ready to give them—the death of a king.

I knew this town like the back of my hand, and I started sprinting for the police station, a one-woman rampage along Gallows Hill Road. My powers hadn't quite returned to me yet after that poison, but they were slowly trickling back. With the wind in my hair, I picked up speed, hurtling up the hill. It was cold out here, the November chill biting at my skin.

But by the time I realized my destination, I was out of steam and breathless, my legs burning. I'd used up most of my energy.

I slammed through the door into the police station anyway, finding a guard working at the desk. She rose, alarmed, and put up her hands, asking me to stop. "Can I help you with something?"

I rested my hands on my knees, trying to catch my breath. "We need to evacuate the city." I pointed toward the City of Thorns. "They're coming. In three days, the demons are coming to feast. To hunt. They're going to try to kill everyone."

"Okay, ma'am? I'm going to need you to calm down. Have you ingested any substances today that could be affecting your mental state? Any alcohol? Drugs?"

I was shaking, vaguely aware that my hair was wild and that it might have vomit in it. "No, but I *have* been poisoned." Some part of me was aware that I wasn't communicating in a way that suggested I was sane. "I'm a demon. I'm supposed to be the queen."

"Ma'am, you appear to be under the effect of a substance of some kind. If you have a care coordinator—"

"I'm not on drugs," I shouted. "I'm telling you about a real threat." I pointed back at the City of Thorns. "I'm a demon. I know the king personally..." *Fuck.* "Look, demons from the City of Thorns are planning an attack on Osborne. It's revenge for something that happened several hundred years ago. I need you to get me in touch with someone who can help."

She nodded at me slowly, then drummed her fingers on the desk. She stood before a locked door, and I wasn't getting through it without her permission. Or violence, which I was trying to avoid. "We haven't had any reports of threats from the City of Thorns' leadership." She narrowed her eyes. "Are you with the demon hunters?"

Of course. Orion had already bought as much influence as he needed.

"Is there someone else I can speak to?" I asked desperately. "A detective? The police chief?"

"Ma'am, I'm going to ask you to step outside now, okay?" She started moving from behind the desk.

A little strength was crackling back into my body, and I raised my hand, summoning enough magic that fire flickered from my fingertips. "See? I'm trying to let you know about a credible threat—"

The officer drew her gun, and my stomach dropped as she started barking for backup. I turned and fled out the door again.

❧

I HUDDLED ON THE SOFA OF SHAI'S AUNT'S HOUSE WITH MY NEW mobile phone. With shaking hands, I called one person after another to report the need for an immediate evacuation. A senator's office. Homeland Security hotlines. The FBI.

I opened the window, screaming at the mortals to leave.

But demons and mortals hadn't been at war in centuries, and most people had forgotten it was a possibility. None of them knew anything about a grimoire, or that the magical boundaries placed on demons could be dissolved.

And every one of them thought I was insane.

My phone buzzed—a message from Kas.

Where are you? I'm going to help you, Sunshine. I promise xo

I shoved the phone back in my pocket, choking down my ragged sense of loss. I wasn't giving up on Orion this easily.

I lay flat on the sofa, trying to clear my head. Everyone in the City of Thorns had been telling me all along that things weren't always what they seemed. That I couldn't trust anyone, not even my own senses.

So what did I believe deep down? What did my instincts say? I covered my eyes with my arm, and my mind looped back to the night I'd been attacked in Orion's house. Someone fled out the window, and Orion came out of his room.

My instincts told me my assailant hadn't been Orion. Someone, somehow, had been impersonating the king, convincing others that he was trying to kill me.

Deep down in my soul, I knew he wasn't responsible for this. We were the twin stars, and I knew him as well as he knew himself. His fear of snakes. His crushing guilt. The lacerating loneliness of all those years, so indescribable that he'd imagined a friend in the next cell. And the way all that pain had finally started to heal when someone finally showed him he was worth saving.

I didn't have a doubt in my mind. The person who'd stood before the clocktower and declared me a traitor—that wasn't Orion.

An incessant ringing was interrupting my thoughts, and I bolted upright on the sofa, irritated.

Was that...a landline?

The phone kept ringing as the call came in again, and I followed the sound into the kitchen. When I peered down at the phone, I read the caller ID displayed on the back.

A 508 area code—all the way down near the countryside of Sudbury. My heart sped up.

Were there some remaining hunters trying to get in touch with Shai?

I picked up the phone, staying silent.

"You have a collect call from"—a robotic voice cut off, and I heard my old friend's voice say, "*Shai Morton,*" before the recording continued

—"at the Massachusetts Correctional Institution in Concord. Do you accept the charges?"

My heart hammered as I cleared my throat. "Yes."

The phone line clicked. "Hello? Camille?" I'd recognize my friend's voice anywhere.

"*Shai?*"

A long pause. "Wait. Rowan? Oh, thank the gods. What happened? Fuck. Did Orion win? I haven't been able to get any demon news in here."

My mind whirled at her barrage of questions. "Shai. Why are you *in prison?*"

"I was arrested in Sudbury when I was waiting for you by the southern entrance. Even though I was invisible. I can't really go into the specifics here on the phone. But is there any chance you can bail me out? I've been desperately calling my aunt and my mom to get me out of here so I could get to you. There are things I need to explain. Someone screwed us over, Rowan. We just...can't talk about it on the phone. But I *really* need to warn you."

Yeah, I supposed we couldn't mention murdering an entire cadre of demon hunters on the jail phone. "Why didn't you call me?" I practically shouted.

"They took my phone when they arrested me. These are the only numbers I have memorized."

"It wouldn't have mattered anyway, I guess," I muttered. "My other phone evaporated."

"What?"

"Never mind." I gripped the phone tightly. "So...that's why you disappeared? You've been in jail this whole time? How much is the bail?"

She cleared her throat. "Can you get a hundred thousand dollars? I know it's a lot."

Fuck.

Orion could easily get a hundred thousand, but it's not like I could hit him up for that right now. Or really anyone I could think of. "I've been kicked out of the City of Thorns. That's why I'm hiding here. Something's happened to Orion. I'll try to get the money, though—"

"So he won the trial and just kicked you out?" Anger laced her voice.

I closed my eyes, trying to understand how to explain this to her without sounding like an absolute fucking moron. "That's what it looks like on the surface," I said carefully. "But like you said, we need to talk in person."

"Hang on." I heard the sound of her muffling the phone and talking to someone behind her. "Shit. Rowan, I've got to go. I'm going to try to call back soon."

Shouting echoed in the background, and then she hung up. I needed to talk to her *now*, though.

I crossed to the window, staring at the exact spot where I'd seen the boy with his cotton-candy fingers in my dream.

Now, where the boy had once been, my disturbingly hot cousin was casually sitting on a bench outside, sipping a coffee.

Sabazios—Mr. Esposito—had a habit of turning up when I needed him. I remembered him. He'd come to our house for tea and biscuits and bring my mom books he liked. He'd given me warnings when the hunters were coming for me. Sabazios was the one who'd given me the demon trials book. He'd been there on the fringes, helping me the whole time, without ever being intrusive or pushy.

I turned and ran down the stairs to find him.

❧ 41 ❧
ROWAN

T he wind whipped at Sabazios's red hair as he drove away
from the Concord prison, the windows down in his new
convertible. Chilly October air stung my cheeks.

The setting sun tinged the sky with honey and lavender, warming
our faces as we drove toward Osborne.

From the back seat, Shai leaned forward. "How did you get the
money?" she shouted over the wind. "And the Porsche?"

"The first thing I did when I got back into the City of Thorns was
find my family's buried gold," Sabazios replied. "So if I'm stuck in
Osborne again, at least I can do it in style." He coughed. "Or as much
style as an old man can have. My magic is already fading. I hate it. But
at least I'll be rich, and I can buy a fancier walker."

"We're going to get you home," said Shai. "This is just a temporary
setback. But Rowan, here's what I need you to know. Someone fucked
us over. Someone told the state police where I was the day we went to
the demon hunters' headquarters. They were waiting for me right at
the southern entrance, and even though I was completely invisible,
they were able to find me."

"But why were you arrested, Shai?" I asked.

She let out a long sigh. "Either Legion or Kas screwed us. Or both of them."

I swallowed hard and turned around to face her. "Explain."

"Okay, so...a few weeks ago, Legion and Kas were helping me learn a spell to control the weather. It was just the three of us. That's it. And I lost control of the spell. I have no idea how it happened, but it was too much all at once, and I caused a storm in the Atlantic. Or someone I was *with* caused it, because I didn't feel like I was losing control at all."

My mind flicked back to the night of thunder booms and a churning sea, when Jasper had attacked me. "Yeah, I remember the storm."

"I didn't tell you about it because you had so much stress already. But either Kas or Legion reported to the mortal police that it was my fault. No one was killed, but it wrecked a ship and caused a bunch of property damage. Then the cops knew exactly where to find me. I've been freaking out this entire time because I had no idea what happened to you."

My veins buzzed with anger. "Do you think it was both of them?"

She stared at me for a long time before answering. "I think it was Kas. I don't have a rational explanation, but I just don't think Legion would do that to me. I think he actually cares about me. Like, I *know* him. Does that sound stupid?"

I shook my head. "That's how I feel about Orion, even when I watched him call me a traitor and kick me out of the City of Thorns. I know him, and that wasn't him. Orion technically won the trial, but he *gave* me the book in Sudbury. He left himself behind just to save me. He sacrificed himself to torture, and he only won because I went back for him and exploded with magic. *That* was the real Orion. I know the real Orion. And the person who kicked me out? That wasn't him."

"Okay," she said tentatively. "Magic can create so many illusions, Rowan."

"Kas told me not to trust anyone, not even him. He said a demon never lets you know all the kinds of magic they've mastered because it's an advantage to keep their weapons hidden."

She swallowed hard. "Yeah, well, he was right about not trusting him. But what do we do now?"

My phone buzzed again, and my hands shook as I read another message from Kas.

"What is it?" The wind whipped at Shai's dark curls.

I took a deep breath, staring at the text. "Kas says he managed to trap Orion in the dungeon, and he can break the wards to let me in there. He says I can't trust anyone, and I shouldn't speak to anyone, and it's time for me to take matters into my own hands."

"He's desperate to end Orion's life," said Shai. "This isn't even subtle."

I swallowed hard. "He's panicking."

As the Porsche hurled northeast on Route 128, I felt sick.

"What, exactly, are we doing?" asked Sabazios. "For your mother's sake and yours, I'll do anything in my power to protect you, but please just clue me in."

"Thank you, Sabazios." I pulled out my phone and flicked to Legion's number. "Before we get too close to the city walls, let's start by trying to find out whether Legion is working with Kas. As subtly as we can."

"He isn't," said Shai from the back seat.

"Okay, but let me prove it, Shai." I dialed Legion's number, and he picked up after just one ring.

"Rowan?" he asked in a loud whisper. "What's happening?"

"Legion, have you been back into the City of Thorns, by any chance?"

"Yeah," he said, sounding surprised. "I'm here now. Invisible, of course. I wanted to see what Orion was doing. He's been making speeches throughout the day at the Tower of Baal. He has a crowd there thoroughly worked up. Seems completely unhinged."

I closed my eyes. "When was the last time you saw him?"

"I just left one of his rants fifteen minutes ago. He's talking about enslaving mortals and seeking revenge on them. He's lost his mind."

I took a deep breath. "I'm a bit confused because Kas sent me a text saying Orion was locked in the dungeons right now."

"*What?* No. Kas told you that?" he asked, baffled. "I haven't been able to find him since you ran off. Are you sure it was him?"

It would appear Kas hadn't filled in Legion on his latest lies. "What do you know about Kas's magical abilities?"

A long pause met me on the other line. "Why don't you ask him?"

"Why don't I ask him?" I replied. "Because I'm trying to figure out who the fuck to trust, and—"

Shai grabbed the phone from my hand and turned on the speaker. "Legion, it's Shai. Someone turned me in to the mortal police in Sudbury. Now that someone was either you or Kas. We all know someone from our team gave advanced warning to the hunters, the cops. So if you have any knowledge of Kas's abilities, now is the time to tell us. How good is he at creating illusions? Can he glamour himself to look like another person?"

Legion waited so long to answer, I almost thought he'd hung up. "Shai," he said softly, at last. "Are you all right?"

"Yeah, it's me. Straight from the Massachusetts Correctional Institution in Concord. Can you answer my question?"

"Kas is extremely powerful, yes," he said at last. "He's an artist. You've seen his work. His illusions are as skilled as his drawings. Yes. He can appear as another person. He really loathes the entire concept of the monarchy. But I have a hard time believing—"

"Legion," she interrupted, cutting him off. "Sorry, but that's all we needed to know."

"It's not Orion," I shouted. "It's *Kas*, Legion! Pretending to be him. He created the illusion. I'm going to guess you haven't seen the two of them in the same place at the same time today."

"I haven't," he admitted.

"Meet us outside the City of Thorns," said Shai. "Where the secret entrance leads underground. Stay away from Kas and King Orion. We're going to need to work together."

"And Legion?" I shouted. "I'm going to need more of that antidote."

❈ 42 ❈

ORION

I lay on the cold stone floor of my own cell, my hands bound behind my back. The caustic poison slid through my veins. In a few days, the poison wouldn't matter. In the dungeons, outside the city walls, my magic would ebb from me.

I'd be locked in here once more—my old home.

Kas had bound my wrists behind my back and gagged my mouth. I'd left my cottage before dawn because I'd wanted to bring Rowan back my favorite fresh bread. I didn't need guards—at least, that's what I'd thought.

But all it had taken was a few darts fired from a distance, and I'd fallen to my knees.

I remembered Kasyade, all those years ago. When the mortals had taken me from my home and marched me past Molor's severed head on my way out, Kasyade had been standing there, watching it all. An older boy, a friend of Molor's, he'd watched it unfold. I'd screamed at him for help, and he'd done nothing. Hadn't even looked upset. He'd just watched.

He'd always been competitive with Molor, resentful of his aristo-cratic background. I remember thinking that Kasyade was delighted to see his friend's head ripped off.

Kasyade must think I was going to end his life at some point for that.

And he was probably right.

The cloth in my mouth smelled of some kind of oil, and I wanted to vomit, but that would make the situation considerably worse. The effect of the Ladon venom and hawthorn was only getting more painful, and I wasn't sure how much longer I'd be conscious here, or if I'd ever wake again.

The worst fucking thing was that Kas had probably learned about this particular poison from the demon hunters after Rowan had been captured.

A tiny light burned in my chest. Would Rowan know the truth?

Kas said she wouldn't. He said she'd come to rip out my heart, that she didn't really trust me anymore.

From the damp floor, my gaze slid over the carvings in the walls. It had always been so quiet in here during the decades when they didn't even bring us food.

It had just been Ashur and me, starving together in cells side by side.

My gaze flicked to the noose hanging across from my cell, where I'd last seen my mother. They'd left her there so long...

Ashur had shown up right after she'd died, I think. Mom and I had been the last ones, then Ashur. My thoughts were growing foggy, and I couldn't remember where he'd been before she'd died.

And his face—I couldn't remember that, either. He'd been strong, and then he'd grown weak. He'd lost his mind. But every time I tried to remember his expression as he was dragged away to his death, I only saw my own—an agonized, ravaged visage. My own.

The poison must be confusing me.

On the stone floor, my body shook. I loathed feeling weak. My gaze slid over those carvings of the queen with her spiky crowns. Even as a little boy, I'd hated feeling weak, so the slashes in the stone had been vicious, brutal.

My eyes started to drift closed, and I could hear my mom saying my name in her soothing voice, like she was right there.

"Ashur."

A jolt of recognition ripped through me.

The crack of stone, the noose swinging in the gallows. The heartbreak that tore me in two.

Ashur had arrived. Someone older, stronger.

Someone who'd taught me to be angry instead of scared, to stay sane by marinating in wrath instead of sorrow. Someone I'd promised to avenge.

Someone who'd never existed at all.

Ashur.

The name Kasyade had called me when he'd dumped my limp body here in the dark, because he remembered me better than I remembered myself.

But all those thoughts drifted away from me as the venom started to seep into my brain, and all that was left was her—

Rowan.

My light in the darkness.

43
ROWAN

Shadows thickened around Osborne as night fell, and an autumn chill nipped at our skin.

In an alley around the corner from the gates to the City of Thorns, I stood in the shadows. Here was my new team—Shai, Legion, and Sabazios. Fallen autumn leaves spread out beneath us.

Every time you put trust in someone, it was a risk. But all the same, I didn't think I could do this without them.

"Okay," I said, "let's lay our cards on the table. I know it's not part of demon culture, but we have to be honest right now."

Sabazios's green eyes locked on me. "I always have been. Especially after you gave me those elasticated pants to protect my dignity. And do you know that I gave you that bear you always had with the red sweater you chewed on until it ripped..."

My eyes misted. "Mr. Huggins?"

He nodded.

Legion stood with his arms folded, eyes averted from me.

"Legion!" I grabbed his arm. "I need to know if you're with us or not."

His eyes slid to me. "I've known Kas for centuries. Since before the City of Thorns was built." He glanced at Shai, his features softening.

"But he's always kept secrets. He's always had an angry side that he hid from the rest of the world. Without the Lightbringers, he'd be the most powerful demon in the city. He's never told me he had anything planned, or that he was going to call the police on Shai. It was all behind my back, using me for information. I knew there was something about that storm that night...I didn't think Shai lost control of it. Someone was causing it." His eyes were still locked on Shai. "And you are where my heart lies now, Shai. So yes, I'm on your side."

She beamed at him, her eyes twinkling. "Good."

He turned to me again. "And yours. Kas wants Orion off the throne for good, and I did, too. I wanted to replace him. But unlike Kas, I have limits to what I'll do to stop him. It's no good getting rid of an unstable maniac if we just replace him with another one."

I nodded. "Okay. Not the most ringing endorsement of Orion, but I'll take it. Now we lay our cards on the table about what powers we actually have."

"Fuck knows anymore," said Sabazios. "But I can tell you what I used to be able to do."

"And Legion?" Shai brushed her hand over his bicep, and that was all it took to make his eyes darken. "We're gonna need to know exactly what Kas can do."

⁂

MY MUSCLES HAD GONE TENSE, AND A QUIET RAGE COURSED through my blood.

The last time I'd trod this path, it had been on a mission to beat Orion in the first trial. Now my body hummed with fury at the thought that Kas had laid a finger on him.

So as I approached the old stone overpass—the one that shielded a secret door into the city—I focused on masking my true emotions.

I stood before the vine-covered door under the bridge and knocked on it four times. Our signal.

A little flicker of magic crackled over the door, and Kas pushed it open. He looked exhausted, his eyes shadowed. His blond hair was wild.

I swallowed hard as I stared at him, schooling my features. "Kas. I'm so glad you're here to help me." The words tasted like acid on my tongue.

He ran a hand through his hair, feigning anxiety as we walked through the dark tunnel. We were both wearing masks here.

"He wanted to execute you as a traitor, Rowan. I had to do something. Even if it was dangerous. Orion would destroy our city, and he'd hunt you down. I couldn't accept either."

Acting cool when my mind was racing at a million miles a minute has never been my thing. Months before, I could barely handle the pressure of giving a psychology presentation. And now here I was, strolling next to a powerful enemy, on the way to break a demon king out of jail.

Even if *I* wasn't good at acting cool, Mortana was. My sister, my dark shadow. I let my hips sway a little, pure composure, as Kas led me into the dungeons.

"I feel stupid for letting him fool me again," I said, my voice steady. "I actually thought he'd changed. But he's just the same Orion who threw me out before. How did you capture him?"

"It wasn't easy, but I used the venom. The demon hunters taught me that, I guess. I imagine this is an old secret of theirs, the way they stopped the Lilu from fighting back all those years ago."

Underneath my placid smile lurked a deep well of fury. "Thank you for looking out for me, Kas."

We crossed into the dungeons themselves. In here, a haunted sense of pain thickened the air. It slid into my lungs and settled in my bones as Kas led me to Orion's cell and pulled out an old iron skeleton key to unlock the door.

My heart was ready to shatter as I looked at Orion, who lay unconscious on the floor. Kas had locked him up in his old cell with his arms bound. His dark eyelashes swept over his cheeks, still beautiful as ever, even now.

Legion's warnings played in the back of my mind: *The moment Kas realizes something is wrong, his claws will be in your chest, ripping out your heart.*

"I know this will be hard for you, Rowan," said Kas, his voice dripping with feigned sympathy. "But I also know you're a survivor. And a protector. You won't let him destroy you or our kingdom."

I stepped into the cell and glanced back at Kas. Behind him, the noose swayed in a phantom breeze.

"Could you give me a minute alone with him?" I asked.

A muscle twitched in his square jaw, but then the bland smile returned. "Of course."

He stepped back into the shadows, and I crossed into the cell.

I reached into my pocket, and my fingers tightened around the syringe filled with the antidote. But as soon as I started to pull it out, I could already feel the burst of Kas's smooth magic wrapping around me, tendrils of silk that slid around my neck, cutting off my air.

That was when I understood exactly how powerful Kas could be—even down here, where magic started to fade.

❧ 44 ❧

ORION

I t was her scent that made my eyes flutter open, and the warmth
of skin bathed in light.

For a moment, I wondered if I'd died. Of course *she'd* be the
first person I'd think about in the afterworld—her presence. And it
was as if I could feel, that deliciously warm magic like the glow of
summer. The scent of ripe fruit...

My heart went still. I couldn't feel her now. A dreadful silence hung
over me.

I opened my eyes, and my blurry gaze swept over my cell walls.
With a hazy sense of dread, I wondered if this would be my afterworld.
Just—here. Forever.

Rowan.

I felt her soul calling to mine. My fingers flexed behind my back.

Maybe I wasn't dead, then.

My heart still beat. And tiny rivulets of strength were flowing
through me once more, from my thigh upward.

I glanced down to see an emptied syringe jutting from my upper
thigh, and from that syringe, strength was coursing through my body.
The antidote.

Where was Rowan, then?

Fear snapped through my nerves, making my muscles go rigid.

Someone was screaming nearby. A male voice I hated...

"You think you're the hero?" he was bellowing. "A leader chosen by finding a magic crown? Or a book? Fucking trinkets and games? A twenty-two-year-old with no magical knowledge. What the fuck do you think you deserve?"

I strained my gaze upward again. And that was when I saw her—

She swiped her claws across Kas's face, drawing blood. But his retaliation was swift and brutal. Spidery tendrils of his magic bound her arms. He lifted her by the throat, his claws springing from his fingertips—

My blood roared.

I would end him. I would tear him apart, piece by piece. I would feed these old stones with his blood.

I hardly had any strength in my body. But for her, it was enough to rip through the ropes binding my wrists.

My world went silent apart from the sound of my heart beating, a war drum in my chest. As I rushed to my feet, I tore the gag from my mouth, and my fangs lengthened.

Rowan was just breaking out of the bindings, her claws ready. She struck Kas across the chest, and blood arced through the air. When he spun, facing me, I drew my own claws, ready to eviscerate him.

But where I'd just been staring at Kas, Rowan now stood before me, looking terrified.

Two Rowans, both soaked in blood. I staggered back, trying to work out what the fuck was real here.

And while I was making that calculation, one of the Rowans disappeared into shadows.

The other stumbled forward, clutching her neck. Blood poured from her throat, and I caught her around the waist. By her scent and the way she folded into me, I knew it was her.

I pulled her in close to me. "You're still losing blood. We need to get you out of the tunnels."

"He can shapeshift," she rasped.

"I just about put that together."

She turned to me, one hand around her bleeding neck. "Get to safety. I've got this under control."

She must be fucking joking. As if I'd leave her to fight an ancient demon alone.

Rowan was already off, racing after Kas, blood trailing behind her. I ignored the ache in my muscles as I ran after her, trying to keep up. She was a blur of speed through the tunnels, like smoke disappearing between my fingers. But as soon as we burst into the City of Thorns, my magic would be restored.

I watched her shimmy up the side of the tunnel and disappear through the opening. Fatigue corroded my bones as I forced myself forward and up the tunnel wall.

At last, under the canopy of the stars, my magic surged through me. First, Rowan brought my soul out of the dungeon, then my body.

I roared as my wings burst from my back, and I followed my love into the clear night sky.

☙ 45 ❧

ROWAN

A s soon as I'd hoisted myself into the City of Thorns, my magic
had slammed into me with the force of the ocean. I took to
the skies, swooping under the stars to search for Kas.

Orion's warm magic beamed over my body as I felt him soaring
near me. The wind rushed over my wings, whipping at my hair as I
raced above the trees. This was the old Lilu way—washed in silvery
moonlight, hungry for blood. Hunting from the skies while our prey
scuttled around on foot.

My heart slammed against my ribs at the strange thrill, and I
turned to catch Orion's gaze. His pale eyes gleamed at me, and his
demon mark, the star of Lucifer, beamed from his forehead. Divine.

We were Lightbringers. And when the shadows consumed us, we'd
rise again.

I just hoped Orion wasn't going to unleash his power until the right
time, because I wanted to leave this city standing.

I breathed deeply, catching Kas's perfumed scent. He'd cloaked
himself, of course, so I couldn't see him. But it didn't matter. In the old
days, we hadn't used vision to hunt, and I could sense him moving
toward the Tower of Baal—which was exactly what I'd feared. Kas was

calculating that as long as he was around enough other demons, we wouldn't use our Lightbringer powers. We wouldn't want to destroy the whole city, after all, and everyone in it. Who wants to rule a city of dust?

But unlike the Lilu of the old days, I had a cell phone to coordinate. So as I swooped through the air, I pulled it from my pocket and called Legion.

"Yes," Legion whispered. "What's happening?"

"Can you clear the area before the Tower of Baal? I'm closing in on Kas, but we can't have anyone around. And make sure you get to safety when you need to, got it?"

I shoved the phone back in my pocket and circled above the esplanade. A throng of demons stood before the tower.

Storm clouds churned above, and an icy wind began sweeping across the stones. The temperature in the air plummeted so quickly, my teeth started chattering, and my breath misted around me in the dark.

Lightning speared the sky, and a maelstrom of ice spun from the center of the square, forcing the crowd away. Screams rose as people started to flee. A crack of Shai's lightning touched down on the stones —and another, scorching the rocks beneath us. The glacial storm lashed at us, and I fought to keep control as I flew. Snow and hail whipped at me. Legion's magical storm sent a chill right down to my marrow, and the gale battered at my wings, my feathers. Shivering, I touched down in the cleared space.

Orion landed by my side, his coal-dark eyes scanning for signs of our prey. Legion seemed to have cleared a space for us, an eye in the storm. My muscles started to soften again, and my breathing slowed.

We could hunt for Kas, or we could get him to come to us. A man like him might be powerful, but his ego would get in the way. That's really what all this was about, wasn't it? His mortally offended ego.

A twenty-two-year-old with no magical knowledge. What the fuck do you think you deserve?

Kas might hate Orion, but that wasn't what really lit the fire beneath him. He thought *he* should be on the throne.

An icy squall swept the air around me, but I rooted my feet to the ground and stood in the center of the stones to address the crowd. "Kasyade has deceived you," I shouted above the winds, hoping the crowds could hear. "He used his magical glamor to take the form of your king. But he's a poor substitute, a shadow of your true king. Kas was not blessed by the gods as we were. He's an illusion, a commoner, and nothing more than a charlatan."

"Blessed by the gods?" Kas's voice boomed, but I couldn't see him yet. "The gods are insane. Let the people choose! Let the demons see who deserves to rule! Let he who possesses the most skill take the throne!"

"You want the people to choose—the same people you're willfully deceiving?" Orion snarled. "The same people you've been lying to?"

"I was protecting them," came Kas's voice. "Neither of you are fit to rule. I studied magic for centuries. While you were locked in a prison losing your mind, Ashur, I was dedicated to the craft. To our history. To understanding what a demon truly is. And Rowan, long before you were born, I'd memorized every spell book in the city's libraries. Suddenly, you stumble in, ignorant of our world, and think you deserve the crown? Because of an accident of birth?"

"Why don't you show yourself?" shouted Orion. "Since you're so confident of your skills. Let's see who survives, shall we?"

They burst into silvery light before us—six versions of Kas. All tattooed, muscular, and glowing with pale light. A demon mark shaped like a crescent moon glowed on their foreheads, and their eyes were dark as pitch. Orion's claws shot from his fingertips, and he slashed at one of them, then another. He was moving at the speed of lightning, but every time he struck one, a new one appeared.

Silky threads whipped around me, ripping me from the earth, high into the sky. They slammed me back down again, breaking me hard on the stones. The agony splintered me, and for a moment, I felt each of my bones shatter before they started to heal again.

From the ground, I looked up at the sky, where inky shadows spread above us all—a shield of ice and shadow, trapping us inside.

There it was—Sabazios and Legion, working together. Exactly as planned.

Good.

Darkness wrapped over us.

The tendrils of silky magic spiraled around me again, lifting me high into the crushing darkness—

But it didn't matter anymore because I was summoning my light.

ORION

✤ 46 ✤

ORION

Do not mistake me for a hero. I'd destroy the entire world to save the person I loved the most.

Shadows slid over us, and I could no longer see Rowan.

The terror of losing her unmoored me until I hardly knew which way was up and which was down. If I lost Rowan now, the world would stop again—a frozen clocktower, a stilled heart. A world of silence.

Once, I'd failed to protect those I loved. This time, I'd burn my enemies to cinders, even if I had to take the rest of the city down with them.

Because I only loved her—Rowan. She was the beginning and the end for me. And when someone was hurting her, I'd tear the stars from the skies and hurtle them like spears.

Rowan and I would be the last ones standing, and that would have to be enough.

Ice and shadows enveloped me, and my thoughts began to spin wildly into little pinpricks of light. A queen with a spiked crown. Molor teaching me to play chess. My mother telling me her birthday would be next week—always next week. A beautiful woman with red hair sleeping in my arms, someone who meant the world to me now. A soft hand against my face bringing me to life again. Leading me from the dungeons to the world beneath the stars.

Order and chaos...a light falling into the underworld.

Shadows consumed my light.

I am Chaos. I am the beginning and the end.

I will consume.

✷ 47 ✷

ROWAN

T he light bloomed in the darkness, pale gold and blinding. It swelled to fill the shadows under the shield, burning away each illusion of Kas until all I could see was light. I hadn't even finished summoning my own before Orion's exploded under the shield like a dying star.

Hot magic rushed over me, into my blood and bones, healing my broken body. Orion's infernal light was a baptism of pure flame, and it gave me strength.

Kas was now nothing more than particles drifting around in a glittering mist.

Slowly, the light started to fade, leaving behind a world of shimmering dust—and only one other person remained.

Orion lay naked on the ground, surrounded by glittering motes of light and the darkness sweeping over us. Warmth flooded my chest as I looked at him.

I pushed myself up from where I'd landed and hurried over to him, resting his head in the crook of my arm. His dark eyelashes fluttered, and he opened his eyes. Pale blue eyes, flecked with silver, stared back at me. He was in there, but dazed, unfocused.

A faint smile curled his lips, and he reached up to touch my cheek. "You're here."

I smiled down at him, brushing his hair from his eyes. "You saw the shield."

His brow furrowed. "Shield?"

My eyebrows rose.

So maybe Orion was fine with destroying the entire city with his Lightbringer power. I supposed it was a good thing he'd have me to rein him in, because I wasn't leaving him.

I glanced up at the haze of light and shadow until the stars began to appear in the sky again and the shield slid away. The shimmering mist around us drifted into the night, whirls of gold that floated toward the moon. Orion still looked delirious from the burst of his light, but I slid my arm around his back and lifted him to his feet. He leaned into me, nuzzling me, as I surveyed the damage.

A large circle surrounded us, and the stones beneath us had been destroyed. On the edges of that circle, where the shield had been protecting us, a crowd stood gaping. The Tower of Baal loomed behind them, nearly obscured by the haze of dust.

I caught Legion's eye, finding him standing by Shai and Sabazios.

It was at this point I thought about the fact that Orion and I were completely naked, because the blast had destroyed our clothes.

I stood tall anyway. We were Lilu, and we weren't ashamed of our bodies.

"This is your king, Orion," I shouted. "And I am your queen! We will protect you, but we will not start a war with the mortals to do it. And we will never sacrifice you like Nergal once did. We will not bend to unreasonable demands. Our city will be a beacon of light in the darkness."

I heard them chanting my name and Orion's as I supported his waist. I was taking him home.

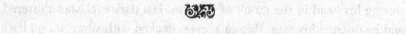

I STRADDLED ORION AND BRUSHED MY THUMB OVER HIS LOWER LIP. He nipped at it, then tugged at his magical restraints.

I leaned down and kissed his throat, feeling the muscles in his shoulder jump.

"Rowan," he growled, "it's been a week. You can let me free now. I'm fully healed."

I kissed his chest. "I can't be sure."

When I looked up, I caught an indulgent smile on his lips. "I already presided over your coronation. I've proven myself healed."

I pressed a finger over his lips. "That's too much talking from you. You'll wear yourself out."

I nibbled at his lower lip. As I did, the sound of voices rose up through the stone floor.

"I think Amon has company," I said. My ears perked at the sound of a female voice. "Is that Shai?"

"Perhaps some clothes are in order, then," said Orion.

I frowned and released the magical restraints. "What day is it?"

"I have absolutely no idea."

We'd hardly left Orion's room in the past week, and dates no longer had meaning.

I jumped off him and pulled open a drawer, yanking out underwear and a long black dress. "I think Shai's birthday is this week."

"Ah! I'll get the sacrificial altar ready. Perhaps there's a criminal we could slaughter in her honor..."

I turned to him as I slipped into my underwear. "You know, Orion, I still can't quite tell when you're joking, but I think drinks and music will be sufficient for Shai."

I pulled a dress over my head, and it hung to my ankles.

When I went downstairs, I found a little crew sitting around the table, sipping wine with Amon.

Shai was sitting on Legion's lap. Sabazios was extravagantly dressed in a maroon velvet suit with a black shirt underneath. "Rowan!" He beamed. "Your Majesty."

"Let's go with Rowan."

"Come on," said Shai, lifting her glass. "It's my birthday. And it's two-for-one cocktail night at *Cirque de la Mer*."

My eyes widened. "Ooh, I need a flatbread. And mojitos. And now that I'm queen, I'm buying."

Barefoot and shirtless, Orion entered the kitchen wearing only a dark pair of jeans. He ruffled his hair. "You're going to spend the night among mortals?"

I blinked at him. "And you're coming. I've never seen you dance to Daft Punk."

"And you never will, my queen. But I'll join you anyway."

"Good," said Shai. "Because I want to help plan the wedding. And I guess you might have some thoughts about it, but, like, what if the ceremony was in the old disused temple of Asmodeus? Ceremonies are usually so boring, so maybe there could also be a cocktail bar for that part. Then we could have the party in the wilderness, but we'd turn part of it into a garden. Total 'whimsical enchanted forest' vibe, with the food on wooden discs like tree trunks, and—"

"Shai?" Orion interrupted. He pulled on a shirt and started buttoning it. "I'm not sure about whimsy. There are the ancient Lilu wedding customs: the oils and perfumes, the consummation before the guests, the augury with the entrails of a slaughtered pigeon—"

I cleared my throat. "Let's just go out for drinks, maybe?"

"Fine." Orion slipped into his shoes. "If I'm going to hang out with mortals, I will be flying there." He turned back to Shai. "What do you want for your birthday?"

"For you to have a whimsical themed wedding?" she said.

Orion turned away, heading out into the night. Sabazios followed after him—no doubt lured by the inexorable tug of an incubus to the skies.

I turned to Amon. "Come with us! When was the last time you went out in Osborne?"

He frowned, his scar deepening. "I've literally never gone out in Osborne. Mortals and demons don't mix."

I looped my arm through his as I walked to the door. "That changes tonight, Amon."

The more time demons and mortals spent around each other, the more they'd realize that apart from lifespan, they had plenty in common.

Outside, I unhooked my arm from Amon's. I glanced up at the

starry sky, where Orion and Sabazios were already circling overhead, their outlines lit with silvery moonlight. Breathtaking.

I turned to see Shai and Legion stepping outside, hand in hand. "Meet you guys there in twenty."

My wings burst from my back, and I raced into the sky, tasting the salty air. Exhilaration lit me from inside as I arced higher with the two incubi. It was so thrilling, all I could do was laugh wildly, and I could hear Sabazios and Orion doing the same. We'd all been missing this from our lives, and now that it was back, the thrill gave me life.

High up, I peered down at the City of Thorns, and it seemed to glow with gold in the night. The Lilu were free once more.

Maybe there'd come a time when we really did need to open the grimoire and free the demons completely. But for now, we had everything we needed here—and our little city was a light rising from the darkness again.

❧ 48 ❧

THIRTEEN YEARS LATER

I sensed him in the room, and when I opened my eyes, I saw him there—my little green-eyed boy, his eyes wide. I should be annoyed that he was waking me from the dead of sleep, but he was so ridiculously cute that it was hard to resent him here, even at this hour. Moonlight washed over him, and his auburn hair stuck up in all directions.

I glanced at Orion, who slept as still and immobile as a statue, not waking for any of this.

My little boy held one arm up. The other clutched his stuffed wolf, imaginatively named Wolfie. "I want snuggles," he said in his small voice, waiting to be picked up.

He was wearing his pajamas with the cartoon octopus that said, "More arms for hugs."

As I stared at him blearily, he reached out for the sheets and gripped them hard as he tried to pull himself up. Already, his bum was in the air, and he grunted with the effort.

I scooped under his bum to help him onto the bed. "Come on up here, sweet boy."

He nestled in tightly, trying to get the covers over himself. He was getting as close as he possibly could, like he wanted to crawl back into the space in which he'd once lived.

I wrapped him in a hug and pulled him close against my enormous, round stomach. "Be careful, baby. Remember, Mommy has a baby in here."

"Sorry, Mama," Nico said as he nuzzled into me. "And sorry, baby," he added as he reached down to pat my belly.

Nicodemus shoved the collar of his shirt in his mouth to chew on it, his favorite habit since we got rid of his pacifiers.

"The baby is fine," I assured him, rubbing his head. "Just too big."

"Hey, Nico." Orion reached over me, touching Nico's hair with sleepy fingers.

"Hi, Daddy," Nico replied. "I need to be in the middle." He climbed over me, carefully trying to avoid my stomach and stepping on my boobs instead. He settled in the gap, delighted to be between his two favorite people. "I'm the middle of the sandwich," he declared in a voice too loud for the hour.

Given the size of my belly, rolling over wasn't easy. But I flopped onto my back first until the lack of air from the baby made me shift again, and then I hoisted my large stomach over the other way. You'd *think* being a pregnant demon would be easier than being a pregnant mortal, but while I'd never experienced pregnancy as a mortal, I had a sneaking suspicion that this wasn't really a better deal. When the gods had cursed women with this discomfort, it had applied to us all, demon and mortal alike.

My body finally relaxed when I was facing Nico and Orion, and I could breathe a little easier again. I slid my arm over Nico's toddler belly. "Go back to sleep, sweetie."

He furrowed his brow in deep thought before producing the question we'd come to expect on a nightly basis: "Are ghosts real?"

No need to ask what the bad dream was about. It was always the same.

And even though Orion and I knew firsthand that ghosts *were* real, and that they haunted the Asmodean Ward, I didn't see any reason to fill Nico in just yet. If we did, we'd be sharing our bed with him until he was at least a teenager.

"I don't believe they are," said Orion. "And even if they were, so what? They can't do anything. They're just like fog. Maybe the fog is a little sad sometimes, but the fog can't hurt us."

Nico nodded.

"And let's pretend," Orion added, "just for fun, since none of this is real anyway, that a ghost managed to get past the magical wards and then somehow got into our palace. What do you suppose would happen to that ghost when Mommy got a hold of it?"

"No more ghost?" Nico asked.

"That's right." My eyes started to drift shut. "No more ghost."

Of all the scary things in the world, especially in *our* world, my baby had, for some reason, glommed on to ghosts as being the worst kind of nightmare fuel. While I was no fan of hauntings, they posed no threat to any of us. Ghosts were as insubstantial as smoke.

In any case, when it came to threats, our little Nico didn't have much to worry about.

Not once we learned what the gods had bestowed upon him.

❧

WITH A SMILE, I CRACKED ANOTHER ANZU EGG INTO THE BOWL AND whipped it. The scent of coffee filled the air, and sunlight streamed into our kitchen. Amon still came over for dinner in the evenings, but the mornings we had all to ourselves. At some point in the night, Orion had carried little Nico back to his room after he'd kicked us too many times in our sleep. Now Nico was slumbering away upstairs after an exhausting night of thinking about ghosts.

We'd moved into a new palace—larger than Orion's cottage, but smaller than the Tower of Baal. A palace of golden stone, filled from top to bottom with libraries, right across from the clock tower in the Asmodean Ward.

While we had several cooks, I liked making breakfast for my two boys, Orion and Nico. Granted, I also liked it when I slept in and Orion woke me with hot coffee and fruit.

I pulled out a loaf of fresh bread and started cutting slices to toast in the oven. I'd be slathering them in butter before piling them with the anzu eggs. We hadn't had any anzu eggs since before Nico was born, but now our son had developed a taste for scrambled eggs. An anzu was like nothing else, so I was already smiling at the thought of him tasting it for the first time.

There were only about three anzu in the Elysian Wilderness, demonic birds three times the size of condors, each one with the head of a lion. When they were hungry, they thought nothing of taking a horse or a cow for lunch. They loved to eat pigs. Demons weren't generally on the menu, but if the anzu were hungry enough, mortals would be advised to take cover.

Anzu eggs fetched a premium when they came to market, as harvesting them was a nasty, bloody business. If a group of hunters found a nest with a clutch of eggs inside and managed to spirit them away before the mother tore them all to pieces, they could live for a year or more on the profits.

As I was popping the bread in the oven, warm magic slid over me. I turned to see Orion crossing into the kitchen, shirtless, his silver hair ruffled. Even now, every time I looked at him, my breath caught.

His gaze swept down my body, and I heard his appreciative growl. "You're wearing my favorite silky green robe. Are you trying to tempt me?"

I rested a hand on my bump and felt the *thump thump* of little hands as the baby made his presence known. "I can barely move. I'm not trying to tempt anyone."

He quirked an eyebrow at the bright red eggshells. "Where did you get the anzu egg?"

"A gift from the Duchess of the Luciferian Ward herself, also known as Lydia."

Orion ran a hand through his hair. "Which means she wants something from us for the next meeting of the Council."

I arched an eyebrow. "Apart from extra financing for Shalem Square, she's always wanted you."

"Of course." He slipped the green robe off my shoulder and started covering my bared skin in kisses. Heat tingled along every point of contact. "But she can't have me. Not for all the anzu eggs in the world."

I cupped my hand around the back of his neck. "Let me make breakfast, love, before Nico wakes up starving." The little guy didn't handle hunger well.

Orion checked his watch and frowned. "He's never slept until nine."

My heart started to beat faster. Was it nine already? Nico was normally up at seven or earlier. I supposed I shouldn't look a gift horse in the mouth.

I heard the distant sound of Orion's weight creaking on the stairs as I cracked another egg and added a dollop of cream to the mixture.

"Rowan!" Orion's voice pierced the silence, booming through the palace and echoing off the stone stairwell. "Where is Nico?"

I froze, and my heart slammed into my ribs.

As fast as my pregnant body would take me, I ran up the sweeping stone stairs into Nico's room. Orion stood in the center, clutching our boy's crimson blanket.

But Nico wasn't in the room.

All the air left my lungs. This shouldn't be a big deal. He was four and probably hiding somewhere. But Orion and I felt the same thing—the terrifying absence of Nico. We couldn't feel his magic now or hear his little heartbeat.

"Nico?" I shouted, my eyes scanning Nico's bed, bookshelf, and pile of toys.

Blue-uniformed soldiers began rushing in to hall, their bodies tense, awaiting orders.

Orion's eyes darkened to night. "I can't sense him anywhere."

This palace exterior was protected with the most powerful wards and a horde of demon soldiers. We had layers of magical protection as well as the old-fashioned brute force of hellhounds patrolling the thorny gardens around it. If an intruder had come in, the hellhounds would have let us know.

I closed my eyes and concentrated. Orion and I shared a bond with Nicodemus that allowed us to always monitor his whereabouts psychically, no matter where he was.

I gasped for air. Right now, I felt nothing.

Orion raked a hand thorough his hair. "Search the house," he barked at the soldiers. Then, more quietly, he said, "He's probably in a closet or something."

Like all parents, we had been eager for our son to start walking. And like all parents, once he did, we wished he would stop. He wanted to climb everything, to know what was behind every locked door, in every cabinet and drawer. His curiosity and energy were boundless.

And now he was missing.

"I'm going to check the grounds outside," Orion said.

I went from room to room carrying Nico's blanket, calling his name, then quietly listening for a reply. Our soldiers were searching now, too, tearing the place apart piece by piece.

Silence met our calls, but I couldn't believe he was gone—it just wasn't possible. I was furious at someone, but I couldn't quite pinpoint who it was. The soldiers who should be patrolling this place? Nico?

Myself, I thought.

In his bedroom, decorated with octopus imagery (his favorite), I started ripping the place apart with a growing sense of urgency—flinging blankets, pulling open the closet. The windows were closed, so he hadn't jumped out or been abducted. How could no one have seen him?

Exhausted, I sat down on his little bed.

What we needed was some magical help. I grabbed my phone and called the City of Thorns' best mortal oracle, Isabeau. There were magical ways to contact her, but she preferred text.

I wasn't waiting for a text now, though. I was calling her.

Midway through the first ring, she answered. "Good morning, Your Majesty," she greeted me. "Nico, is it? Missing?"

"Yes, thank you." Already, I was reassured that she knew what was happening. "We can't find him. I haven't seen him."

"Curious," the oracle replied. "Your sigils and glyphs are all in place. The wards continue to function."

"Yes, I believe so…"

"That wasn't a question." Her abilities allowed her some leeway when it came to snark, but I wasn't in the mood for her games.

"If they're in place, then where is Nico?" I demanded. "How could the spells have been bypassed? Who took him, and how are they shielding him from us?"

"So many questions," she answered slowly. "But no answers. If he were on this plane, I would know. If he'd left this plane, I would know that as well, even if I couldn't follow. He'd have left a trace behind."

Panic snapped through my body. "Is he in Osborne? With mortals?"

As I listened to her reply, Orion rushed into the room, all color drained from his face. He shrugged and turned both palms up in resignation.

"There are those with the talent to hide things from you," Isabeau observed. "And a very small number with the ability to conceal things from me. But none of them would have reason to harm your son. The person you need...the person who can help you...a duchess from the House of Shalem."

Orion motioned for me to hand him the phone.

"Lydia delivered anzu eggs to our cottage this morning," Orion informed the oracle. "I don't believe in coincidences." I watched him nod as he listened to Isabeau. "Find him. Do you understand?" He handed the phone back to me.

I nodded and stared at Nico's blanket in my hands. I considered a thought too awful to contemplate, and nausea rose in my gut. "Orion, if neither of us can sense him, and neither can the oracle, can it mean he's...he couldn't be..."

I had to keep a distance from that terrible thought, and Orion only shook his head. When he glanced over my shoulder at the soldiers, his eyes had turned the color of ink.

"Bring the Luciferian Duchess to me," he said, a deathly chill in his voice.

※

WE SAT ON THRONES. I DIDN'T WANT TO SIT ON A THRONE—I wanted to be running around, tearing the city apart for Nico. But apparently, the thrones were a show of power that could strike fear into someone and convince them to tell the truth. I gripped the edge of the throne, staring at her.

Lydia of the House of Shalem crossed into the marble hall before us with a grace that made it seem as if she were floating rather than walking. In her long red dress, her fiery tattoos were on display. It was hard to believe that she'd do something so rash. Years ago, when I was still mortal, she'd tried to kill me. But that was part of the initiation trials to enter the city, and since then, we'd been on good terms.

"Welcome back, Lydia," I said.

"I trust you enjoyed the eggs?"

"We're not here to talk about the eggs," said Orion evenly. "We're looking for our son. You were here this morning. Our oracle thought you might have an idea where he is."

"Me?" She put a finger to her lips. "Ah. My son used to go missing all the time. It was really very easy to find him."

I leaned forward over my belly. "How?"

She cupped her hands around her mouth and bellowed into the air, "Fig pudding!" Her voice echoed off the stones.

I stared at her, stunned. I'd never seen her do anything undignified before. But then, I supposed, I'd never seen her as a mom.

She turned to me, frowning. "That was a long time ago. Fig pudding was his favorite back then. What does your son like most in the world to eat?"

"Cotton candy," I said.

She cupped her hands to her mouth again. "The cotton candy will all be gone! Poor Nico won't have any left. Will everyone spread the word that the cotton candy is almost gone?"

He seemed to materialize from the shadows in the corners of the hall.

His face was tear-streaked, and his nose was runny. He'd obviously been crying. "I'm hungry, Daddy!"

Orion lifted Nico into the air and wrapped his arms around him. Nico was red-faced, already searching for the promised cotton candy. He was about to burst into hungry tears when he realized there was none here, but he was back with us all the same, and I couldn't be more relieved.

I actually hugged Lydia before she left, pressing her against my giant stomach.

And I turned to look at Nico, crying for the sugar he'd been expecting. Where the hells had he been?

☙❧

THAT AFTERNOON, WE VISITED ISABEAU. IF ANYBODY COULD GET TO the bottom of what had happened to Nico, our mortal oracle friend was the one. We found her in her little cottage, her white hair threaded with flowers and seashells. She welcomed us all with tea.

For a few minutes, Isabeau sat with him and held his hands, letting her consciousness join with his to see the world through his eyes. At last, she nodded, leaning back a little in her chair. "Oh, yes, that's it," she exclaimed. "That's exactly it!" She released Nico's hands and beamed at him. "A very special young man."

I swallowed. "What, exactly, happened?"

"Let's show them," the old woman suggested, and she stood and offered a hand to our son. He took it, and they walked across her cluttered room together, a strange place full of animal skulls and dried flowers. When they reached the far wall, Nico turned and waved goodbye to us with a cheery smile—and the two of them proceeded to walk directly through the wall, out into the cobblestone street.

My stomach dropped, but in the next moment, they crossed back through the wall in the same way.

"How did you..." I began, but I was too astounded to finish. I crouched down over my stomach, pulling him close to me.

"I'm a ghost," he shouted with glee. "A big, big, *big*, huge ghost!" He stomped his feet for emphasis.

I looked up at Isabeau.

She shrugged. "I can't explain the magic behind it, exactly, but Nicodemus can walk through walls. Or, evidently, drop through floors. Into places like dungeons."

"Fuck," I muttered.

"Fuck," Nico repeated.

"Shh, no, baby." I placed a finger over his lips. "*Duck*. I said duck."

"He can *fall* through the floors?" asked Orion coolly.

"A strong emotion can trigger it," said Isabeau.

"A big duck ghost," a delighted Nico shouted to remind me.

I rose slowly. "So what do we do to keep him safe?"

Isabeau rubbed her hands together. "There are some great witches here at Belial to help him harness his gifts. But in the meantime..." She pulled out a tiny cloth bag tied to a piece of yarn. "Put this around his ankle. Yew leaves. They'll keep his magic subdued enough that it won't get out of control."

"Yes. Thank you," Orion agreed.

We left with a list of instructions from Isabeau and an entirely fresh set of worries to accompany those that concern every other set of new parents. How the fuck did you baby-proof a house for a child who could go through the walls?

YEARS AGO, I WAS PLAGUED BY A TERRIBLE NIGHTMARE INVOLVING A little green-eyed, auburn-haired boy. About a horde of demons racing across the world, across *his* world, slaughtering everyone in sight. A demonic host led by my husband, Orion.

The dream was so vivid, it had struck fear into my heart.

Sometimes, the dream came back to me. But now, it was Kas unleashing horror on the mortal world. When the dreams were at their very worst, I'd picture that little boy as the sole survivor, see the terror in his eyes as everyone around him was killed and he had no one to turn to. I'd wake crying, reaching for Orion. I'd seek out Nico as he slept to make sure he was okay. Sometimes, I checked on him twice a night.

I'd love to say that as a parent, I lived in a world of bliss, where my anxiety went away and everything was contentment.

But I would never stop worrying about Nico, or the baby in my tummy who constantly had the hiccups.

There was no love without terror. The fear of loss.

But these three demons were my world, and I would gladly carry that fear to live in their warmth.

THANK YOU FOR READING THE DEMON QUEEN TRIALS. IF YOU WANT to stay updated, you can sign up to my newsletter.

Or, join the reader group to talk to other readers about Garden of Serpents.

Our newest release is an enemies-to-lovers fae romance described as "Hunger Games meets The Selection." You can download it now, or read on for a sample of the opening.

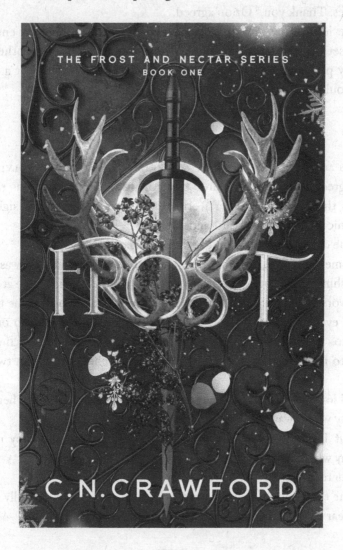